Bronwyn Parry grew up surrounded by books, with a fascination for places, people and their stories. Bronwyn's first novel, *As Darkness Falls*, won a prestigious Romance Writers of America Golden Heart Award for best romantic suspense manuscript in 2007. Her second and third novels, *Dark Country* and *Dead Heat*, were voted the Favourite Romantic Suspense Novel by the Australian Romance Readers Association (ARRA) in 2010 and 2013, and were both finalists in the Romance Writers of America RITA Awards – the Oscars of romance writing – and the Daphne du Maurier Award for Romantic Suspense. Her fourth and fifth novels, *Darkening Skies* and *Storm Clouds*, were finalists in the ARRA Awards and *Storm Clouds* was shortlisted in the Davitt Awards for Best Crime Novel 2016. An occasional academic, Bronwyn's active interest in fiction and its readership is reflected in her PhD research and she is passionate about the richness, diversity and value of popular fiction. She lives in the New England tablelands in New South Wales and loves to travel in Australia's wild places.

www.bronwynparry.com

Also by Bronwyn Parry

As Darkness Falls
Dark Country
Darkening Skies
Sunset Shadows

Dead Heat
and
Storm Clouds

BRONWYN PARRY

THE GOODABRI SUSPENSE NOVELS

hachette
AUSTRALIA

hachette
AUSTRALIA

Dead Heat first published in Australia and New Zealand in 2012
Storm Clouds first published in Australia and New Zealand in 2015
by Hachette Australia
(an imprint of Hachette Australia Pty Limited)
Level 17, 207 Kent Street, Sydney NSW 2000
www.hachette.com.au

10 9 8 7 6 5 4 3 2 1

This compilation published in 2016

National Library of Australia
Cataloguing-in-Publication data:

Parry, Bronwyn, 1962– author.

The Goodabri suspense novels: 2 romantic thrillers for the price of 1/Bronwyn Parry.

978 0 7336 3672 1 (paperback)

Murder investigation – Fiction.

Deception – Fiction.

Suspense fiction, Australian.

Romance fiction, Australian.

Parry, Bronwyn, 1962– Dead heat.

Parry, Bronwyn, 1962– Storm clouds.

A823.4

Cover design by Christabella Designs
Front cover photograph courtesy of Getty Images
Text design by Bookhouse, Sydney
Typeset in 12.75 pt Adobe Garamond pro by Bookhouse, Sydney
Printed and bound in Australia by McPherson's Printing Group

Dead Heat

ONE

Vermin.

They had to be the worst thing about her job. The feral dogs, pigs, cats, goats and horses did enough damage, but the vermin Jo really disliked – the ones responsible for the vandalised camping ground in front of her – were the two-legged, hoon variety.

Five days since the State Minister and her entourage of hangers-on and media had, at this very spot, declared the new National Park open, and already the vermin had left their mark. Not only had they hauled down the information board – the one she'd dug the post-holes for herself because they couldn't get the mechanical digger repaired in time for the Minister's media event – they'd cut the posts into pieces with a chainsaw.

The door to the loo hung crookedly on a single hinge, the watertank beside the covered cooking area was riddled with bullet holes, and, judging by the copious amounts of broken glass around the campfire remains, they'd also smashed – or perhaps shot – a fair number of beer bottles. Presumably after drinking the contents.

They sure hadn't come out here to appreciate the natural environment.

But they weren't here now. She could see the whole camping area – no cars, no tents, no people.

She reached into the cab of the vehicle for the radio mike and rattled off her boss's call sign. 'Are you there, Mal?'

'Yeah, Jo.'

'Can you give the police a call? A mob of *Homo idiota* has been rampaging. The tank's full of bullet holes, the loo door is cactus and the info board's down – they took to it with a chainsaw.'

'Damn it. Are you all right? How many of them are there?'

'I'm fine, Mal. They're gone.'

'Are you sure?'

'Yes. Brazen louts aren't likely to be skulking in the bush, afraid of a lone woman.' Being out in the wilderness by herself was a normal part of her job, and if she spooked easily she wouldn't have lasted a week, let alone ten years.

'Okay. Can you wait until either the cops or I get there? I might be an hour. And even if there are police available, they'll probably be at least that long.'

Jo stifled a sigh. She would just have to hang around and wait for the police to take whatever evidence they needed before she would be able to start clearing up the mess.

'No worries. I'll photograph and document the wreckage.'

Photograph and document – a standard procedure she'd completed too many times, although she'd hoped such deliberate vandalism would be less frequent out here in the north-west of New South Wales than in the parks she'd worked in further east, closer to cities and city hoons.

It would take all of thirty minutes, if that. Then maybe she could map the track to the lookout while she waited, so the morning wouldn't be a total waste. Checking and updating the maps they'd inherited from State Forests was only one task on the long list of jobs to be done now that the area had officially become a National Park.

The sun's heat already warm on her back, she retrieved her camera from her day pack in the rear of the vehicle. Taking a moment to scan the large camping area, she watched, listened, alert for anything that didn't belong. The typical morning birdlife filled the air with sound. A flock of corellas, white on the dark branches of a eucalypt near the river, squabbled among themselves. A young magpie, fatter than its parents, squawked on the grass, demanding more food, and a treecreeper hopped up the bark of an iron gum, foraging for insects. At one end of the car park some of the local mob of kangaroos sprawled lazily in the shade, their morning grazing completed.

Nothing out of the ordinary, nothing disturbing the peace. Other than the wildlife, she was alone out here. Exactly the way she liked it: peaceful, without distractions, just her and the natural beauty of the wilderness. A different beauty from the parks she'd worked in for most of her career, on the eastern fall of the Great Dividing Range, but this dry, scrubby landscape of the western slopes and plains brought her almost full circle, back to the kind of landscape where she'd grown up.

She drew in a deep breath of warm, dust-dry air. A good decision, moving here, away from the constant reminders of loss and grief, as well as an enjoyable professional challenge, establishing the new park. Definitely plenty to keep her busy.

This vandalism added a few more tasks to her list for the day. Nate Harrison, the lone constable based in Goodabri, might come the twenty or more kilometres out if he was in the area, but the chance of any other police driving the fifty-plus kilometres from Strathnairn, let alone bringing a crime-scene officer, was close to zilch. Yet, just in case, she took care to disturb as little as possible as she photographed the destruction and recorded the details in a notebook.

On the edge of the camping ground, among the undergrowth, a family of fairy wrens flittered in the bushes. Two young males, just coming into their adult plumage, chased each other, the half-grown tufts of blue feathers on their heads punk-like.

'At least *you* don't go around wrecking camp sites, boys,' she murmured, zooming the camera on them.

From this distance her voice didn't disturb them, but as she snapped a few shots they flew off, startled. She turned the camera to the dingo emerging from the low bushes, breakfast in its mouth. She caught its face close-up in the frame, the eyes watching her warily, ears upright, jaws clenched tightly around . . .

The image in the viewfinder began to shake violently but she snapped the photo, and another. Five fingers. A tattoo winding past the knuckles, up to the stump of the wrist, blood dark against the pale skin.

4

The dingo turned away and she yelled at it, desperate for it to drop its find, but it disappeared back into the undergrowth.

'Shit, shit, shit, shit.' Indecision held her motionless while she ran through her options, her heart racing as quickly as her thoughts. Follow it and see what she could find, or radio Mal to report it? She flicked the camera back to the two images she'd taken. No, it wasn't a joke artificial limb left over from a Halloween prank. Real flesh, mostly whole, so it had not been lying on the ground for days. Whatever had happened, it had to be recent. Not a minor injury. So where, and in what condition, was the person the hand belonged to?

She jogged back to her vehicle. With insufficient mobile phone reception for a call, she radioed her boss again. First things first: find out if there was still reason to worry. 'Mal, have you heard anything about someone being injured out here? Calling an ambulance, yesterday or overnight?'

'Nothing I know of, Jo. Why?'

She hesitated. No, not information she wanted to broadcast on an open radio channel, with farmers, truckies and others potentially listening in. 'There's some signs of a major injury,' she explained briefly. 'I haven't heard anything about an ambulance call-out last night, but maybe they left here by car. If you hear anything, let me know.'

Still on edge, she surveyed the camping area and surrounds, the key questions ringing in her mind: How the hell had someone lost a hand out here? Where were they now, and in what state?

The hoons had felled the posts with a chainsaw, but it would be pretty damned hard to accidentally cut off your own hand with one. Likewise with an axe or a hunting knife. Fingers, easily enough, or a chunk out of a leg or foot, but not your own hand.

That meant a much higher probability of foul play than of accident.

If the injured man was out here, the sooner she found him, the better. Aware of the isolation, kilometres from anywhere and anyone, while she checked her backpack for first-aid kit, satellite phone and portable radio she listened again for any indication of company.

Nothing but bird calls, insects and the breeze stirring the leaves.

Not far from where the dingo had trotted back into the scrub, she found drag marks, half a metre or so wide, and a few ants still gathered, here and there, around dark smears in the gravel. Pairs of footprints flanked the drag marks.

Boot prints, not wild pig or dog tracks.

She stared at them, the skin on her arms prickling despite the heat of the sun. No, there couldn't be any sort of innocent explanation for this.

Wary, making herself breathe slowly and evenly, she followed the drag marks and tracks over the rough, rocky ground among the trees.

Less than forty metres in, she found a pile of broken branches under a tree, glimpses of denim visible through the thin, dry foliage.

She'd done her share of search and rescue over the years, and dealt with more than her share of injury and death. And she could do it again.

She steeled herself and pulled aside one of the branches to check what lay beneath . . . and then jerked away, gagging, her mind reeling in horror. Not an accident. No way an accident. The man whose body lay semi-hidden had been coldly, brutally, tortured and murdered.

☙

The cow stood in the middle of the narrow dirt road and stared at him. Nick stared back and inched the car forward. The cow didn't budge.

A second blast from the horn finally had it ambling to the verge, and he pressed down on the accelerator as soon as he was past.

'Turn left in one hundred metres,' the female voice of the sat nav intoned.

Down a rough track with a locked gate across it, and an 'Authorised Vehicles Only' sign?

'That'd be another "no", honey,' he muttered and turned off the useless system.

An hour since the call had come in and he still had to travel at least ten kilometres to get there. Assuming his constable's directions for the 'shortcut' route between Strathnairn and the National Park were correct. Assuming he hadn't taken the wrong road. Both the map and the sat nav had proved useless – the scale of the map not large enough to show the minor roads, the sat nav thinking every farm track and fire trail was a public road.

He mentally added *decent maps* to the list of resources he would request. Only three days into the job and his list was already long. His predecessor in the senior detective position at Strathnairn might have been content to work without adequate resources, but Nick wasn't. Although, given the large number of open cases Nick had inherited, he wondered if the word *work* had been in the man's vocabulary. That made his own posting to the almost-outback command not just a banishment but a poisoned chalice as well. Detective Garry Coulter, killed in a car accident over a month ago, had apparently been held in high regard by the locals, so raising questions about the man's competence or integrity would not make Nick popular with his new colleagues.

He would worry about that later. Right now, he had a murder to investigate – once he reached the crime scene. At least the body that had been reported wouldn't get any deader. Just – he flicked the airconditioning up a notch – just riper, in this heat.

The road joined another at a T-junction, and a National Parks sign helpfully pointed to Ghost Gums Camping Ground. After another ten minutes of winding road through dry, rocky bush he descended to the camping ground on the river flats, the parking area already busy with three police cars, an ambulance and two National Parks utilities.

The two paramedics stood beside their ambulance, idly talking, but as Nick got out of his unmarked car, one strolled across.

'Are you the new detective?'

'Yes. Nick Matheson.' He shook hands, unblinkingly meeting the man's frankly curious and not entirely trusting gaze. So, the gossip had gone beyond his new colleagues in the Local Area Command to other emergency services. So be it. He had a job to do, and he'd do it.

'Where's the victim?'

The paramedic nodded towards the police cars at the other end of the camping ground. 'In the bush over there. He definitely doesn't need us.'

'But you're hanging around anyway?'

The guy shrugged. 'It's pretty gruesome. Someone might faint or suffer from shock.'

'Who found him?'

'Jo did.' He waved a hand towards two people in khaki shirts and trousers, leaning against the bonnet of a National Parks vehicle. 'Jo Lockwood. She's a bit shook up but she doesn't need us, either. Jo's tougher than she looks.'

Jo would be the slim one with the light brown hair held back in a ponytail. Nick couldn't see the woman's face, but from her hands-in-pockets, straight-backed stance, Jo Lockwood clearly wasn't falling apart in hysterics. That would make his job of interviewing her a hell of a lot easier.

'Thanks. I'll talk to her after I've seen what she found.'

What she'd found, he discovered when he followed the local constable through the scrub to the scene, was enough to give most people nightmares for months.

The smells of death – piss, shit and blood – turned Nick's stomach, but he quelled the response automatically. *Never show weakness*. That had been life's first lesson growing up on the docks of Newcastle, and kids who didn't learn it early suffered constant beatings and degradation.

The constable stayed to one side, staring intently at the body. 'Must be a sick bloody psycho, to have done that,' he said.

Nick crouched and, without touching a thing, surveyed the body. Facts. Evidence. That's what he needed to focus on. A rope tied tightly as a ligature above the amputated hand; another above a mangled and bloody foot. A major wound to the other knee, covered in blood, dirt and grit. The gunshot to the head probably the final of many other cuts and injuries.

The sustained violence and torture of this death – the patterns of blood flow suggested that the injuries were ante-mortem – were among the worst of the innumerable violent crimes he'd seen.

'No,' he mused, as much to himself as to the constable. 'Not *a* psycho. This guy's big, and he fought. It would have taken more than one man to restrain him.'

'From the looks of the camping-ground damage there were a few crims here last night,' the constable said. 'And he's got some unusual tattoos. Haven't seen anything like them before. Must be some sort of gang thing. You'd know about that, wouldn't you, Sarge?'

Another one who'd heard the rumours. The question might have been asked out of curiosity, but the sly grin suggested insolence.

Nick kept his expression carefully neutral and muttered a noncommittal 'Hmm.' Yes, he knew about gangs. Street gangs, bikie gangs, criminal mobs. The possibility of a gang connection in this youth's death was on his rapidly growing list but, far more than most cops, he knew there was no such simplistic crime as a 'gang thing'. He knew the complexities, the constantly shifting dynamics of power and personalities, of opportunity and risk, of adrenaline and testosterone and fear.

No, tattoos on the man's arms – which weren't any gang tattoos he was familiar with – didn't amount to evidence of an organised gang. If there were even any such thing out here in the north-west of New South Wales.

He stood and glanced at the constable's name tag. Harrison. A senior constable. Young, confident to the point of cocksure; the know-it-all type who probably didn't like taking orders. Too bad, because Nick would be giving plenty of them.

'This area needs to be taped off, Harrison. From the grassed area to past here. I called Forensic Services when you first reported in and the Crime Scene Officers are on their way from Inverell. They're contacting the forensic pathologist.'

'Don't expect one to come in person, Sarge. We're too far from Newcastle.'

Eight or more hours' drive, Nick knew. Too far from city resources . . . but not far enough from his memories. Not that Newcastle had a monopoly on bad memories. He'd collected more than enough of them from all over the map during his career. The poor dead bastard in front of him was just another drop in the ocean. Just one more crime that might, or might not, be solved.

'Have you got an ID on him? Or found his car?' he asked Harrison.

'No. None of us know him. He's not local. CSOs will search his pockets for ID.'

Nick nodded but he doubted they'd find anything useful. And judging by the burns on the remaining hand, identifiable fingerprints might be almost impossible to obtain.

He also doubted they'd find a car. If the guy had driven his own car, the assailants had probably taken it, could be a few hundred kilometres away by now.

He couldn't learn much more from the victim until after the crime-scene officers arrived, so he would have to start with the nearest thing he had to a witness.

'The National Parks officer who found him – do you know her?' he asked.

'Jo? She's a newcomer to Goodabri. Setting up things for the new park. She's the quiet type, doesn't socialise much. Seems to work hard enough though.'

Nick had taken a detour through Goodabri on his way to Strathnairn on Sunday, scoping a fraction of the large region covered by the police command. The town was thirty kilometres off the main road and consisted of fifty or so scattered houses, a police cottage, a small primary school, a row of empty shop buildings in the main street and a run-down pub. Not a thriving community, and presumably reliant on the larger Strathnairn, seventy kilometres away.

A woman who kept to herself in a small community . . . He mentally filed that piece of information. Jo Lockwood turned as he walked towards her across the grass, assessing him in the same kind of way he instinctively assessed her during those few moments.

She's the quiet type . . . Her emotions tightly leashed behind her pale face and closed expression, she shook his hand with a firm grasp when he introduced himself, and the constable's description underwent a swift revision in Nick's mind. Quiet perhaps, but from reserve, not shyness.

The calloused hand briefly in his, her lean, fit frame and her lightly tanned skin confirmed the 'seems to work hard' part of Harrison's description.

Despite her control, the haunting determination in her hazel eyes held his attention. Shock, yes – she still fought to keep it from overwhelming her. But she knew she could. He'd seen that same determination in the eyes of too many colleagues over the years – people who'd seen incomprehensible death, and survived it.

He guessed she'd be in her early thirties, but those eyes were older. No makeup, no artifice, nothing *pretty* in her face, only a stunning, stark beauty he found compelling.

Her colleague stepped forward and extended his hand. 'I'm Malcolm Stewart, senior ranger for the Strathnairn National Parks division. Do you really need to interview Jo now? She's had a tough morning.'

Before Nick could answer, Jo threw her boss a glance that mixed affection with slight exasperation. 'I don't need mollycoddling, Mal. The sooner we get this done, the sooner we can all get on with our jobs. I presume you'll want this part of the park closed, at least for today, Detective?'

'Yes. Perhaps you could liaise with the uniformed police, Mr Stewart, while I ask Ms Lockwood a few questions?'

'It's Doctor Lockwood,' Stewart corrected him. 'Doctor Joanna Lockwood. She has a PhD.'

With a gentle hand on Stewart's arm, Jo said, 'It's just a piece of paper, Mal. The title is irrelevant.'

Irrelevant? Not in Nick's estimation. He added intelligence and perseverance to his impressions of capability and control.

For all the cool calmness of her manner, the late morning was already hot, and she'd been standing around waiting for a couple of hours. Nick dragged his gaze away from a trickle of sweat running down her neck and disappearing below her open collar.

'Can we find somewhere in the shade to talk?' he asked her.

She nodded. 'There's a table down by the river. I don't think we'd be disturbing any evidence there.'

She slung a small backpack over her shoulder and led the way, skirting around the edge of the camping ground, along a thick line of trees and rough undergrowth that obscured the river from view. He could hear it – water running over rocks – but only caught glimpses now and then. So he looked, instead, at the open area of the camping ground. He would go over it closely later, but for now he concentrated on getting the general layout, the context in which the crimes had occurred. Even from this distance, the damage was obvious.

'They sure made a mess. I don't suppose you collect names, addresses or car registrations from visitors?'

'Names and postcodes sometimes – when they fill in a form. But that's hit and miss.' She turned on to a path through a break in the trees, into a clearing beside the water's edge. 'However, I can tell you that there were at least two vehicles here. And two dogs.'

Hope sparked in him. 'You saw them?'

'No. I was only here yesterday morning, and it was after that. The tyre tracks are there, though, and dog tracks and faeces beside where they were parked.' She rested her backpack on the wooden picnic table and drew out a camera. 'I have photos. I was compiling evidence for a long list of offences – criminal damage, bringing dogs and chainsaws into a National Park, lighting a campfire during a total fire ban – but I guess . . .'

She sat down abruptly on the bench seat, her bitter, somewhat shaky laugh a small crack in her control. 'Murder pretty much trumps all of those.'

'It would. *If* the people who did the vandalism committed the murder.' Avoiding a lump of bird shit on the seat, he sat opposite her, taking the camera she offered and flicking through the images while keeping half his attention on her. It was incongruous, sitting in such a cool, restful spot under the trees, the river winding its way over rocks less than ten metres away, when thirty metres behind him havoc had reigned in the night.

She stared at the table, circling a knot in the timber with her fingertip. Short, unpainted fingernails, he noticed. And tanned wrists and hands that, although small, were corded with lean muscle.

After a few moments of silence, she looked up at him and said, 'If it wasn't them, then the timing would have had to be close.'

'Why do you say that?'

'When I arrived this morning, the dog faeces were still moist. Only a few hours old. And the . . .' she steadied her voice and continued, 'the victim – there was no sign of rigor. And few insects.'

She had all his attention now. He considered her argument, and explored possible holes in it. 'The dogs might belong to the murderer.'

'The vehicle the dogs were tied up beside is the same one that rammed down the information board. There's a distinctive tyre track.'

'You're very observant.'

'I'm a scientist.'

She said it simply, as though it explained everything. Which, he supposed, it did. Scientists relied on logical processes and evidence – just as he did.

But he also relied on gut, on the sense of what fitted and what didn't fit, on his experience of patterns of behaviours that might not seem rational but could all too easily be the caustic results of mixing personalities, power and passions.

With the niggling certainty that the elements of this crime scene didn't fit neatly together, he flicked through the images on the camera one more time. She had taken some broader context shots as well as detailed close-ups, and despite the small screen, from her photos and the general view of the destruction he'd seen he could construct a fair picture of some of the night's events.

He handed the camera back to her. 'Can I get copies of those images, today?'

'Of course.' She opened the side of the camera, slid out the memory card and passed it to him. 'Take the card. I've got spares.'

'Thank you.' He waved a hand at the camping ground behind them. 'This kind of vandalism – does it happen often?'

'It happens sometimes. A mob of louts, full of beer and testosterone, with no respect for others' property, having what they'd call "fun". There's something about the isolation and the wilderness that can bring out the Neanderthal. But—'

She stopped and, curious about her thought processes, he prompted her, 'But?'

'It's just . . . Look, I'm no detective or psychologist, but I've been going over it these past couple of hours and it seems to me that the murder doesn't fit the same behavioural pattern. The vandalism is . . . well, if we were talking about animal behaviour,

I'd call it marking a territory. I suppose it's the hoon version of it – refuting authority and order and claiming the space.'

'But you think the murder is different.'

'Yes. Possibly. It's intense, over a period of time. Focused on a person, not property. And I know that cruelty can be about power – it usually is – and vandalism also is, but vandalism is general, and cruelty . . . well, this seems more personal, more emotional. Anger or hatred or punishment.'

He stared out over the water, flowing along the path it had carved out over millennia, and considered her thoughts. She'd put her finger on what was unsettling him: the two crimes didn't naturally evolve from one into the other. If they had been perpetrated by the same people, then something must have happened to shift the mood. Something or someone.

His instinct guessed *someone*. Someone who'd manipulated the restless mob's energy and adrenaline, turned it, focused it on a target and let it loose.

He'd seen it happen before, countless times. And he knew exactly how it was done, because he'd been that kind of ruthless, manipulative bastard himself, more than once.

TWO

Jo took a gulp from her water bottle, despite her still-queasy stomach. The heat and her fatigue from a late night and early morning had dampened her appetite even before she'd made her gruesome discovery, but in this weather dehydration was too real a risk to ignore.

She studied the detective as she made herself drink another couple of mouthfuls. The new detective, mentioned in last week's Strathnairn newspaper. Much easier to consider him than to let her mind recall the sight of the victim.

Nick, she remembered from his brisk introduction. Detective Senior Sergeant Nick . . . Morrison? Matheson? Something with an M. All business, focus. Nothing boyish or soft in his face. Attractive, in a hard-edged way. Compelling, with dark eyes and equally dark hair.

When he turned his attention to her and their eyes met, she caught a glimpse of power before the mask of cool detachment slid into place. The kind of power that marked him as predator, not prey.

Her instincts told her his steadiness, his self-possessed strength, would make him a formidable opponent. Just as well they were both on the same side of the law.

'You may be right about the murder,' he commented evenly, 'but it's too early in the investigation to rule anything in or out.'

'Of course.' The victim's image appeared again in her mind, and she fought to diminish its effect, black humour the only weapon her brain could find. 'Except, I presume, natural causes.'

His sharp glance seemed to assess her mood before he let a thin, wry grin crack the inscrutable demeanour for just a moment. 'A machete-wielding dingo is low on my list of possible causes, I admit,' he said dryly, as if he knew that belittling a horror with absurdity could almost, for a short while, make it manageable.

He was a cop, a detective – he'd probably seen far more than she'd ever have to deal with. She didn't envy him.

'You said you were here yesterday morning. Was there anyone else here then?' he asked.

Good, something easy to answer, to focus her thoughts on. 'Yes. A retired couple in their van – grey nomads. They were here for a few days and were just packing up to leave. As I was talking with them, there was a guy on a motorbike on his way in. He told me he wasn't staying, just visiting the lookout.'

'Did any of the other staff come by later in the day?'

'No. We're a small division, based in Strathnairn, and we're responsible for four parks and three conservation areas. Yesterday afternoon there was a grass fire at Campbell Creek, so we were all out there.' Would he understand the size and range of the areas they managed? Perhaps. The Strathnairn Police district covered much of the same area, and presumably he'd done some research on his new posting. 'I'm currently living in the old Riverbank homestead on the edge of this park, which we use as a depot and staff quarters, so I usually do the camp fee collection, toilet paper and loo-cleaning rounds here. Officially this park is new, but we took over management from State Forests a few months ago.'

'You mentioned camping fees. What happens when you're not here when people arrive?'

'There's a lock box on the info board. People are supposed to fill out an envelope and put the money in it, in the box. The box is still there, among the debris. I didn't touch it, just in case they left fingerprints, or their names. I assumed your people would check it.'

'I doubt vandals are the kind to do paperwork and pay fees, but yes, we'll check it. The average crim can be pretty stupid.'

She could agree on that. Trashing a public campground was hardly an intellectual exercise.

'Are there other camping grounds nearby?' he asked. 'Other people who might have heard or seen something last night?'

'There's a picnic area at Casuarina Falls, a few kilometres up the river. I've already been there this morning, and there was no sign of anyone having spent the night. We should probably check the path up to the lookout.' She nodded across at the hill behind the camping area. 'People aren't supposed to camp there, but sometimes they do. There's no unattended cars parked nearby today, though.'

'Any farmhouses or other residences in the area?'

There had been gunshots and a chainsaw . . . perhaps somebody had heard. But, thinking about the land around, she shook her head. 'Riverbank, where I live, is probably the nearest residence, but that's a good ten kilometres as the crow flies, and well off the main road. I didn't hear anything last night. McCulloch Downs is the next property to the west, about ten kilometres from Riverbank, but Jack McCulloch moved into town last year and there's no-one living there now.'

He fell silent again, a frown narrowing his eyes. She hadn't been able to give him much to go on.

She couldn't keep her mind from straying back to the victim, and she gave up trying. Far better to think about the practicalities, the process from here, than to succumb to emotion and become useless. Not here. She would not be a burden to anyone.

'What happens now?' she asked, straightening her spine. 'Will you be able to take him away soon?'

'The deputy coroner and crime-scene officers are on their way. It may be a couple of hours before they've finished.'

Unsure she wanted to hear the answer, she asked, 'Do you need me to stay?'

Candid dark eyes studied her for a long moment, making her even more determined not to fall apart. He must have seen that in her face because he answered, 'If you can stay, and are willing to, the CSOs will probably want to talk with you, and I'd like you to show them the tracks you noticed.'

'Of course. I'll do whatever I can to help, but I'd rather keep busy instead of just hanging around. I was going to walk up to the lookout, map the track with the GPS. Would that be okay? It won't take long – it's less than a kilometre.'

'You said that the guy on the motorbike yesterday was going up there?'

'So he said. Most people who come here do. It was in the morning, though, so I doubt he stayed overnight.'

The detective's face remained impassive while he considered. 'Okay. But give me five minutes to make a couple of phone calls first. I'm coming with you.'

Delivered politely enough but a statement of fact, not a request. She didn't argue. His crime scene, his decisions.

'You'll be lucky to get much phone reception out here. A text might get through.'

They returned to the car park and as soon as he'd left her by her vehicle he had his phone out, texting as he walked across the grass to where Mal was deep in conversation with Nate Harrison and another police officer, presumably trying to agree on which park roads to close and where.

She refilled her water bottle from the cooler she kept in the back of the ute and filled a second one, tucking them into the pockets of her backpack; anything to keep busy. Taking a map from the front seat, she walked across to join the men.

'I was just telling your colleagues that there's a group of fifteen year-eleven students and a couple of teachers camping in the park,' Mal was explaining to Nick, 'I'm wondering if we should evacuate them. Do you know exactly where they are, Jo?'

Jo unfolded the map on the bonnet of one of the police cars and the men gathered around.

Beside her, the detective reached out to catch a corner of the sheet and hold it down, restraining it from flapping in the breeze. Momentarily so close to her that she caught the faint tang of aftershave and the undeniable awareness of powerful *male*.

Pheromones. Just damn pheromones, and of no relevance to her responsibilities here – the park, the students and any other visitors. No relevance to her at all.

'I've already radioed to check on that group,' she assured Mal and the others. 'They're fine, and they've seen no-one else around. They're over here on the north-west side of the park.' She saw Nick glance from the place she pointed at on the map, to the scale. 'It's about fifty kilometres from here as the crow flies, but there aren't many access roads into the park and no roads directly through it. It'd be about a hundred-and-twenty-kilometre loop around to get to where they are.'

'This lot had vehicles and resources,' Nick said decisively. 'There's no reason I can see for them to stay within the confines of the park. Assuming they left a few hours ago, they could be hundreds of kilometres away by now.

'We need to isolate this area around the crime scene until forensics have examined it thoroughly,' he continued. 'But there's no need to restrict access to the whole park. If the access road is closed there, at the intersection, are we shutting off any sites other than this one?'

'No, it's fine,' Jo answered. 'Visitors can still reach the waterfall viewing area by that other road, and it has toilets and barbecue facilities. There's basically nothing down this road except for what you can see here.'

'Good,' he said, turning to his uniformed colleagues. 'Harrison, get a team to put a road block in place there. I don't want anyone else down here except police and the deputy coroner. We'll also need an operations base closer to here than Strathnairn, for at least a few days. Does your station at Goodabri have suitable space?'

'No,' replied Nate. 'It's just a century-old police cottage, designed for one or two officers. Three people in the station makes it feel crowded.'

Having been to a couple of meetings with Nate and others, Jo could agree with that. 'We're leasing a double-front shop building and only using half,' she offered. 'There shouldn't be any problems with you guys using the other half, should there, Mal?'

'No worries at all,' Mal agreed. 'We've used the second shop space to coordinate joint emergency exercises a few times. There's power, water and basic furniture. Your people could set it up with mobile comms and such in no time.'

They could, and they would. With the old Mechanics' Institute hall closed for repairs, there was no other suitable empty space in town. So, for the next few days at least, the peace of her office environment was going to be disturbed.

❦

Nick checked finding an ops base off his mental list. While not police, Jo and Malcolm must know the kind of requirements for a critical incident operation centre, so he would trust their judgement. On to dealing with the other practicalities. 'Is there suitable accommodation in Goodabri? A couple of specialist homicide detectives are on their way from Sydney.'

'The hotel is okay,' Jo assured him. 'I stayed there when I first arrived. It's clean and the rooms are a good size. The food's standard pub food, but quite reasonable.'

Luxury, compared to some of the places he had stayed over the years. 'Good. Sounds like that's the best plan. Assuming we can get the arrangements made quickly.'

Malcolm already had his satellite phone out. 'I'll contact the Strathnairn commander and make the offer, and get over to Goodabri to liaise with your people. And I'll take Jo back home on the way, if you don't need us any more.'

'I'm not going yet, Mal.'

Definitely a woman accustomed to speaking for herself. Nick nodded at both of them. 'I'll leave you to discuss it.'

As he walked away towards his car he heard Malcolm say, 'Jo, you know we have to follow all the incident procedures. I should be making sure you see a counsellor or a doctor.'

'I don't need a counsellor, Mal,' she retorted. 'I'm perfectly capable of over-analysing my own emotions.'

Nick almost grinned. Along with her independence, the scientific Dr Lockwood had a wry sense of humour.

His phone vibrated in his pocket and any trace of amusement evaporated when he read the text message from Aaron Georgiou, his detective constable: *Dalton & Brock ETA Goodabri noon.*

Dalton? It was standard procedure for the Homicide unit in Sydney to be involved in murder cases, but why the hell were they pulling Hugh Dalton off Strike Force Dragon and sending him up here? Unless Hugh knew something he didn't, at this stage Nick could see nothing to suggest a connection between the murders of a prominent Chinese–Australian couple in Sydney, and a dead, non-Chinese man in the scrub nine hundred kilometres away.

He would ask Hugh soon enough.

He disregarded the twinge of tension in his neck. He *could* work beside Hugh, despite the competitiveness that characterised their personal history, from long before they'd joined the police force. They had done it before. Hugh would strive hard for success, strive to show himself as good as, or better than Nick, so the case could only benefit. Not the most comfortable of working relationships, but then when, in the past ten years, had he ever been *comfortable* in his work?

Nick didn't know Brock – quite likely a detective constable like his own offsider, Aaron Georgiou. Nick had already arranged for Aaron to collect the Homicide detectives from Goodabri's landing strip and bring them out to the park.

He'd have to wait for the CSOs, for Hugh, for the deputy coroner, liaise with the forensic pathologist, and make sure the area was searched thoroughly before he'd be finished here. It was shaping up to be one hell of a long day.

He keyed a message back to Aaron: *Bring lunch.*

He tossed his phone and keys on the roof of his car and pulled out the bag from the back containing his search-and-rescue uniform. Far more practical for the tasks ahead than the business shirt and trousers he wore.

Jo Lockwood was the only woman around, and he doubted that she'd be offended by the sight of a man's skin, so for the sake of expediency he changed beside the car. The sun's heat prickled on the scar on his side as he swapped shirt for police T-shirt, but his bad leg held his weight without harsh pain while he changed into the dark blue overalls and heavier boots.

Never show weakness. He'd had plenty of practice at that through weeks in hospital and recovery. The bullets had narrowly missed arteries and vital organs, but the nerve and muscle damage would take months to properly heal, particularly in his leg. Determined *not* to spend months on restricted duties or sick leave, and accustomed to full body-contact street-fighting and martial arts, concealing pain from the doctor who'd assessed his fitness for duty had been no challenge.

He transferred his Glock from the light holster he'd worn with his street clothes to the one on the full equipment belt, and was buckling that around his waist when a shadow fell on the ground nearby.

'Now you look like a copper.'

Jo. The broad brim of her hat shaded her face, and he couldn't tell from her dry tone if she thought it was a good or a bad thing.

The ambiguity of her comment heightened the mixed emotions of pulling on even this informal uniform. After so long in plain clothes and undercover, the sense of pride and rightness in wearing a police uniform was dulled by the knowledge that a good many of his colleagues believed he no longer belonged to the tight-knit police community, and should be in prison overalls instead.

⌘

Jo silently willed the heat rising to her cheeks to pass as an overdose of sunshine. Definitely not the most intelligent comment she'd ever made. Probably the damn pheromones again, taking advantage of her emotional shakiness, making sure she didn't miss, after several years of celibacy, the prime example of male before her.

She'd classed him in animal terms earlier as predator rather than prey, but in human terms he fitted the warrior archetype.

His close-fitting T-shirt emphasised muscular strength that his shirt had camouflaged, and the darker colour and military lines of the uniform gave his appearance a harder, rougher edge.

But so what if she found him sexually attractive? He was an unknown quantity, and she was much more than the sum of social conditioning and biochemistry.

He was a police officer doing his job, she was doing hers, the day was getting hotter the higher the sun rose, and professional friendliness was all that was called for.

She took the spare water bottle out of her pack and held it out to him.

'Have you got room on that serious-looking belt for this? It's going to be a scorcher, and there's not much shade on the way up to the lookout. You might need it.'

His hesitation in taking the bottle was so slight she might have imagined it. But years of working in a predominantly masculine environment had ingrained the habit of humouring her way around macho behaviour. 'Don't worry. There shouldn't be any girl germs. I washed that bottle this morning.'

'Oh, I think I've developed a pretty good immunity to girl germs. They won't kill me.' His grin softened the hard lines of his face, and the playboy look might have been convincing if it had made it as far as his eyes.

He'd probably returned her light teasing to put her at ease, a courtesy to a possibly traumatised witness. But she recognised a performance when she saw one; despite his undoubted physical attractiveness, those eyes belonged not to a playboy, but to a man who hunted murderers.

His focus on that task had him noticing, before she did, the tyre marks around the bollards at the start of the walking track to the lookout.

Another motorcyclist who couldn't understand the plain-English sign, 'Pedestrian Access Only'.

'Did you happen to notice what kind of tyres the motorbike you saw yesterday had?' he asked her.

'No. It was a BMW bike, though. I figured him for a corporate-type, out for a road trip. We see a few of them.' She cast a sideways glance at him. 'It seems to be a fashionable male ritual.'

This time, his grin seemed to come naturally. 'A man, a bike and a long, straight road? I can see the appeal.'

She understood the appeal. Not so much the powerful, status-symbol bike, but the escape, the freedom to choose what she did next and when, being alone and unfettered. She'd done it herself, many times. On horseback, as a kid, exploring beyond the large family grazing property. Later, in a ute or a car, taking to the roads during uni vacations.

A comfortable silence between them, they walked side-by-side up the track. Jo scanned the way ahead continually, keeping an eye out for snakes, and noting out of habit the animal tracks crisscrossing the dusty path. Wallabies, lizards, a dog – perhaps the dingo she'd seen, perhaps a feral dog – and here and there a few shoe prints, all interspersed with traces left by the motorbike.

In a sandy area, sheltered from the winds by a large boulder, she paused to take a better look. 'The bike tracks may have been the man I saw,' she said. 'Looks like they're from yesterday.'

He stopped beside her. 'How can you tell?'

With years of experience educating park visitors with limited knowledge of non-suburban environments, she explained simply, outlining the facts. 'The tracks are blurred in many places, blown by the wind, and quite a few animals have crossed the tyre marks.'

He knelt down, studying the ground with interest, and she crouched beside him. 'Those marks are a wallaby or a young kangaroo – you can see the imprint of the long hind legs and the tail.' She picked up a twig to indicate a much smaller line of indentations in the sand. 'That's a lizard – see the drag line of the tail and the footprints either side? And that one there – see those brush lines? That's a snake.'

'Impressive. I guess most people – including me – never think to look properly. And don't have the knowledge or skills to know what we see.'

She rose to her feet again and shrugged. 'It's no special skill. I'm familiar enough with some of the wildlife to recognise a few animal tracks. The rest is just logic.'

He studied the dust in front of him for a few more moments, as if committing the marks to memory. 'Logic requires knowledge to interpret the evidence. You're a useful person to have around, Doctor Lockwood.'

The compliment sounded genuine, a statement of fact rather than an attempt at flattery.

'Drop the "Doctor" stuff,' she said. 'I'd rather be called Jo.'

'Then call me Nick. I didn't have to work as hard for the detective title as you did for your doctorate.'

She wasn't so sure about that. A person didn't get to the rank of detective senior sergeant without considerable experience, and she'd far rather tackle a mountain of research papers and analyse gigabytes of data than face the kinds of things he must deal with on a regular basis. Like a murdered man, and the twisted humans capable of such a brutal killing. And whereas she could walk away once she'd given her statement and answered any questions, he'd be living with the investigation and whatever it turned up for days, weeks, maybe longer.

No wonder his smile rarely touched his eyes.

❧

If the hoons who'd vandalised the camping ground had come up to the lookout, Nick saw no evidence of it. The granite boulders on the summit held only pockets of sand and their surface retained few identifiable tracks, human or animal, to indicate who'd been there before them. He'd wondered, the whole way up, what they'd find, but the wooden benches, viewing platforms and information boards were all undamaged, and the wind, though hot and dry, carried no trace of the death stench.

They hadn't climbed a great distance, but the lookout was the highest point in the area and had a good view over the river gorge and across the undulating hills to the south and west.

They stood on the first platform, overlooking the camping ground and the gorge. The cleared camping area was dwarfed by the bush as far as the eye could see; dry scrub, eucalypts, cypress pines and plenty of trees and bushes he didn't know, thick on the river flats, a little sparser on the rocky slopes of the lines of hills beyond.

'There's a hell of a lot of bushland out there to dump a body in,' he mused aloud. 'So, why so close to the camping ground?'

Jo leaned on the wooden rail beside him. 'Most people don't venture very far away from the roads and walking tracks. And carrying a body across rough ground, through scrubby undergrowth, is hard work. I've done a few rescues. Even with a stretcher, in that kind of ground, fifty metres might as well be a mile. If I hadn't seen the dingo this morning, chances are no-one would have discovered the body for weeks or months. It happens, often enough. Usually suicides, or accidents.'

Yes, he'd worked a case like that – where the victim had lain, undiscovered for a couple of weeks, in a reserve backing onto suburban housing.

He had to hope that if the killers had assumed their victim wouldn't be quickly found, they might have been careless and left evidence.

Jo crossed to the other viewing platform, GPS in hand, comparing the reading to the landscape around.

Doctor Lockwood. It hadn't surprised him. The way she'd defined herself as a scientist, the seriousness and focus beneath the easy manner and humour, all added up to an intelligent professional. A stark contrast to many of the women he'd been surrounded by in the past few years: drug addicts, prostitutes, gang girlfriends and victims . . . women trapped in poverty, violence, addiction, and crime.

He dealt with female police officers often enough, and lawyers, but rarely professional women outside law enforcement. Twice this morning he'd caught himself wondering how to play his role with her, only to remember as soon as the thought occurred that he no longer had to perform, or be anyone else but himself. A detective senior sergeant with a cooperative and observant witness, and no reason for the uneasiness working its way through his muscles, at least as far as she was concerned.

She tucked the GPS into her backpack as he joined her.

'I just saw a couple of cars on the road in,' she said. 'So we'd better go back.'

'They can wait a few minutes, if you need to finish anything.'

'No, I'm all done. Except I just want to duck down to that tree stump. Someone's stuffed some plastic in it.'

In the direction she pointed, sunlight glinted on the plastic in the hollow of a small stump, poking up among the rocks in the rough ground, twenty metres beyond the platform.

'You'd think it would have been easier to take their rubbish home,' he commented.

'You'd be surprised how many people have an aversion to carrying rubbish in their cars.' With the agility of a gymnast, she climbed easily over the railing and readied herself for the drop to the smooth boulder below. 'You head back. I'll catch up with you in a minute.'

He took a few mouthfuls of water from the bottle she'd given him and waited while she strode through the low-growing scrub among the rocks. Perfectly at home and capable in this environment, she didn't need protecting, but he waited nonetheless.

She reached the tree stump, picked up the plastic – and then stopped, her hand holding it mid-air. A spider on it, maybe? Or some other bug? From this distance, in the sun's glare, it didn't seem large enough to hold anything grim.

She turned and called out to him, 'You'd better come here. This isn't rubbish.'

Plastic bag, not rubbish . . . not good, whatever it was. Normally he'd have followed her over the railing, but with his leg less reliable than usual, and no urgency requiring the risk, he took the conventional route around the side of the platform.

In the sand around the cement supporting one of the platform's legs, he saw the bike track again. Not far away, in the shade of a small tree, the smudged marks and a single indentation suggested the bike had been parked there. A boot print pointed towards Jo.

Nick swore under his breath. His suspicions hardened when he reached her and saw the bag she held by its corner. A zip-lock bag the size of his hand, containing a dozen smaller plastic bags, each half-filled with white powder.

He pulled an evidence bag from his belt and held it open as she dropped it in.

'Is it what I think it is?' she asked.

'If you're thinking cocaine, then yes, probably.' He'd look at it more closely when they were back in the camping ground. 'There's bike tracks just up there, so it's possible the man you saw yesterday might be involved.' His voice sounded harsher than he intended, his thoughts racing, too crowded with possibilities and implications for courtesies. Because if they were connected – a biker, a violent death and a stash of cocaine – it signalled a dangerous combination.

THREE

Questions, questions, and more questions . . . By the time they'd reached the camping ground again after a grim, silent descent, the crime-scene officers were waiting for her with their questions: where she'd walked that morning, what she'd seen, what she'd touched or moved. She went over the scene with them, patiently answering each of the queries.

As she finished, a car arrived with Aaron Georgiou and the two detectives from the Homicide unit in Sydney: a man, probably in his thirties, tall, blond and well-muscled under the suit; and a slim woman in her twenties, short blonde hair sharply bobbed, neat in navy trousers and a fitted white shirt.

Drinking some more water, Jo watched Nick meet them, and her idle observation sharpened to curiosity as his subtle body language contrasted with the male detective's lively greeting – a vigorous handshake and the slap on the back of an old mate. Nick returned the handshake with equal strength and direct eye contact, not giving an inch of ground. Not rejection, not unfriendliness, but although he smiled and exchanged a quip with the man, Jo saw a practised and finely enforced dominance.

They knew each other, these two, and despite the ease of familiarity and friendship between them, she didn't read a relaxed affection.

Not that it was any of her business how two men chose to relate to each other. It was only the lack of anything else to do that had prompted her observations.

Okay, that and the fact that Nick had caught her intellectual interest. Cool and calm on the surface, like the waterhole beyond the trees he probably needed a sign warning of hazards and dangers in the depths. Not a man who could be neatly categorised.

After a brief conversation, the four detectives crossed the ground towards the place she had found the victim, and disappeared from sight into the bush.

With her head starting to throb from the heat and tension, and probably from lack of food, she returned to her utility and sat on the tailgate in the shade to eat some dried apples from the cooler.

The fruit giving her system a little sustenance, she washed down a couple of headache tablets with another swig of water and struggled not to retch them back up as the last of the adrenaline faded and a wave of reaction hit her.

She closed her eyes, shutting out the sight of the vandalised camping ground, trying to still the jumble of ugliness in her head. Drugs and murder in the area she'd worked hard to make safe and welcoming. A camping ground that should have families and kids and grey nomads enjoying the environment, instead of police cars and crime-scene officers and a mortuary van making its way down the road to collect a young man's remains.

&

'You said the ranger discovered him?' Hugh asked, kneeling near the victim. 'Did she disturb anything?'

Nowhere near as much as a parade of police and crime-scene officers had. Nick surveyed the trampled ground, the pile of branches moved away from the victim.

'She knows to preserve a crime scene, Hugh. CSOs have been over it all with her. She pulled aside a branch to see him, that's all.'

The sun beat down on Nick's head, heightening the ever-present, low-level irritation of dealing with Hugh. He had long acknowledged the truth to himself; he was never entirely easy with Hugh because Hugh was here and Patrick wasn't, and his brother's ghost hovered silently between them.

Hugh beckoned his constable, waiting nearby with Aaron. 'Shelley, come and look over this unlucky bastard, take some notes on what you see. Another fine example for you of humanity's barbarism.'

Typical of Hugh, that cynicism, but darker, more biting these past few years, the lighter humour he'd used as armour during his youth left far behind. Not unusual for cops. Given they'd both started their careers with more experience of violence and crime than most cadets, and their respective paths had taken them deep into criminal underworlds, Hugh's black cynicism came as no surprise to Nick.

From the struggle for composure evident in both Aaron's and Shelley's ashen expressions, they hadn't – yet – witnessed as much violent death as he and Hugh.

They'd have to get used to it, learn to channel revulsion and anger into analytical investigation that could ultimately bring killers to justice.

Nick indicated the victim's wrist, drawing their attention to observable facts. 'The tourniquet stopped him bleeding out. But you can see that blood flowed from the other wounds there . . . and there . . . and there. The autopsy will confirm that the injuries were inflicted when he was still alive.'

'Yep,' Hugh added dryly. 'Not much point going to all that effort if he was dead.'

'Bastards,' Aaron said, through clenched teeth.

Shelley gasped in a breath, trying to swallow a sob, and she turned away, fumbling for a handkerchief. Not hardened to it yet, for all she worked in Homicide.

Nick saw Hugh watch her for a moment, his face wooden, before he turned in the other direction, abruptly leaving the scene and heading back through the scrub.

'Aaron,' Nick instructed in a low tone. 'Bring Brock when she's ready. And tell the CSOs we've finished here, so they can bag him whenever they're ready.'

'The ranger – did you say her name's Lockwood?' Hugh asked when Nick caught up. 'Was she around Gloucester, Barrington Tops, five years or so back?'

Was she one of Hugh's many former girlfriends? Not a comfortable thought, but he refused to let it linger. He held aside a low branch for Hugh and answered impersonally, 'She's been in the district a few months. There was no reason to ask from where. Why?'

'Just curious. Might have come across her on a case. Anyway, I'd like to ask her a few questions.'

Nick briefly considered objecting, but held his tongue. Technically, in murder cases such as this, Homicide had charge, although collaboration was the norm, and he and Hugh held the same rank. Nick had no intention of giving over control, but nor would he push Hugh into claiming it. And in Hugh's shoes, he'd want to speak to the key witness himself.

As they emerged from the scrub, he scanned the area, looking for Jo. She rested on the tailgate of her ute, head against the canopy frame, not stirring while they crossed the camping ground towards her, opening her eyes only as they came close. Nick saw no recognition of Hugh register, but he could see shadows of a headache or tension in her eyes, and her skin had paled despite the heat.

'Jo, this is Detective Senior Sergeant Hugh Dalton, a specialist from the Homicide unit in Sydney. It can be useful to have several perspectives in an investigation, so he'd like to ask you a few more questions, if you're okay for that.'

She nodded, despite her evident strain. 'I'm fine. What do you need to know, Detective Dalton?'

If Hugh recognised her, he gave no sign nor made mention of it, but Nick caught the quick, challenging grin he tossed at him before addressing Jo with cool, distant professionalism.

Nick would have stayed, ensured Hugh kept the conversation brief, but Harrison had more questions about the search area.

As he walked across the dry grass, away from Jo and Hugh, he resisted the urge to look back. A respected senior detective and a competent professional ranger – neither needed him to monitor their discussion.

⁓

The high-spirited friendliness Hugh Dalton had shown in greeting Nick was nowhere in evidence in his manner towards her.

After ten minutes of detailed questions, Jo reminded him, 'I've already told Nick all of this. And your forensic people.'

'I know. Sorry. But I have to note it all down for the case records.'

And in case you're lying. The man didn't say the words but the suspicion was there, in his coolness and the insincere apology.

She'd met the type before, run the gauntlet of the questions and insinuations and suspicions even while she grieved. She mentally braced herself for the ordeal.

'Can you tell me where you were last night, Doctor Lockwood?'

Yep, here we go again. With nothing to hide, she gave the honest answer. 'We were fighting a grass fire sixty k's west of here well into the evening. I must have left there about eight-thirty and drove home. I'm staying in the old Riverbank homestead that's now part of the National Park. It's about ten kilometres this side of Goodabri.'

'Do you have a partner or housemate who can verify the time you came home?'

'No. We use the homestead as staff quarters, so there's sometimes others there when we have major projects on, but I'm currently there alone.'

That would be another black mark against her in his notebook – no alibi at all.

'So, let me get this right, Doctor Lockwood: you saw no-one between around eight-thirty last night until the police arrived here this morning?'

'That's correct.' She looked him straight in the eye, determined not to be cowed or to lose her temper in frustration. Keep cool, keep calm, keep repeating the truth until he believed it. 'And I was nowhere near here between ten a.m. yesterday and eight this morning. Now, as I have told you and your colleagues everything I know – multiple times – I am going to get back to my job.'

'I'd prefer you to remain here a little longer, Doctor Lockwood. We may have some more questions for you.'

Not just routine enquiries, then. He seriously thought her a suspect. Either that or he was being annoyingly methodical and painstaking in his investigation and suspected everyone unless they could prove otherwise.

'I didn't murder the man, Detective Dalton. It would be very stupid to commit a murder and then draw attention to the body, instead of leaving it hidden.'

He smiled, as if he was enjoying this. 'Oh, you'd be surprised how often killers who think they're being smart try that tactic. Don't go too far away, Doctor Lockwood.'

The spring in his step as he returned to the others was almost joyous, and he clapped Nick heartily on the back as he joined them. Nick looked around, as if to check on her, and he made some brief comment to Dalton – chilling, if she read the expression on his face correctly – before he turned back to speaking to Nate Harrison.

She waited in the back seat of the ute, the doors open to catch the breeze. She'd been just as innocent last time as now, but there'd been more justification for the questions in that case. She'd coped by reminding herself that an investigation should be a logical process, devoid of emotion, open to all possibilities until excluded by rational evidence. She could, at one level at least, understand that approach, even if being in the spotlight made her uncomfortable.

She'd give them ten more minutes. After that, unless they arrested her, she'd go into the office and try to get some work done. And maybe try to shake off some of the horror of the day.

But sitting in silence with her eyes closed only allowed the gruesome images she'd seen to resurface in her mind. The old grief of Leon's death, mixed with the irritation of the detective's inquisition put her in a poor frame of mind to still her thoughts and memories.

The crunching of footsteps on the gravel made her open her eyes. She braced to confront Dalton again but it was Nick Matheson standing before her, with more concern in his expression than suspicion. Still the reserve, though. Tight. In control.

'How are you holding up, Jo?'

She stepped out of the ute. 'Other than tiredness, caffeine withdrawal and fatigue from not eating much today, I'm fine.'

He nodded slowly. 'I'm sorry we've kept you so long. I really appreciate your help. But I have one more favour to ask you.'

A favour, not an order. Obviously she wasn't on top of *his* list of suspects. Or else they were playing bad cop, good cop with her. If they were, then Nick, despite all the potential power she'd glimpsed beyond his cool, courteous exterior, was doing a damned good impersonation of a good cop.

'The deputy coroner has given permission for the victim to be transported. Jo, I need to know if he is the motorcyclist you saw yesterday morning. You can say no to this if you wish – I know it's not an easy thing I'm asking. But if you could look at his face, and tell me if it's the same man, it would be a huge help.'

'The motorcyclist? But why do you think—' The answer hit before she finished the question: because some bike gangs dealt drugs.

'With the bike tracks near where you found the drugs, we have to consider him possibly involved,' Nick explained. 'He may simply have been admiring the view or taking a leak, but the coincidence raises questions.'

She recalled her encounter the previous day, tried to remember any detail about the man that might be relevant. 'He looked more like a tourist than a gang member. Neat haircut, no tattoos or insignia that I saw. And it would have been a good ten hours before dark that he was here.'

'You saw his haircut? He had his helmet off?'

'Yes. Not while we spoke – he was on the bike then, just slid the visor up – but he parked a short distance away while I was talking to the caravan couple, and he took off his helmet then.'

Could he be the victim? She hadn't clearly seen the victim's face under the branches he'd been covered with. The prospect of seeing the dead man's face shouldn't have unsettled her, but it did. He was dead, there was nothing left but a physical shell and the need for justice. Justice she might be able to help to find.

She thrust her hands into her pockets and squared her shoulders. 'I'll do it. I doubt it's the same man, but you're right – we need to be sure.'

He stayed close beside her as they walked across the grass to the mortuary van, and he remained beside her in silent support when the attendant unzipped the body bag on the trolley just far enough to expose a face.

A young face, round and soft with easy living, framed with tousled dark hair, the skin marked by blotches where blood had settled after death. Green eyes stared blankly; lifeless, bloodshot, empty of emotion.

Tears stung her own eyes and she turned away.

'It's not him. Not the motorcyclist. He's too young. He's . . .' Her voice clogged in her throat, and she hugged her arms around herself, as if that could stop the cracks in her control from becoming crevices.

'Take your time, Jo.' She was grateful he didn't touch her, but the unspoken understanding in his voice steadied her.

'Sorry. It's stupid. I should be able . . . I don't even know him.'

'It's never easy, whether you know them or not. It's a natural reaction, Jo. Sit down over here for a minute, if you want to.'

The crime-scene officers had finished at the nearby sheltered picnic table, and she sat on the bench, facing the river. Behind her, the trolley rattled, sliding into the van, and someone closed the door on it as the engine started.

Whoever the young man was, they were taking him away.

Jo dug in her pocket for a handkerchief, blew her nose to clear the remnants of her tears, and kept her reddened eyes averted from the man who sat beside her. She had to pull herself together, to focus on facts and do what she could to help, instead of recalling the way the body bag had framed the young man's face, and the painful memory of Leon's face, framed in similar plastic.

Focus, describe and let the police do the analysis. Nick sat beside her, silent, undemanding; leaning forward comfortably, forearms on his knees, hands loosely clasped, as though he had all day to admire the view. She turned her head towards him, and immediately he shifted his gaze to meet hers, as if he'd been aware of her every movement while he waited.

'The man yesterday seemed older than the victim,' she began. 'Maybe in his thirties. His hair was just as dark, but more closely cut. What I saw of his face was thinner. Higher cheekbones, and his skin . . . well, not quite an olive complexion, but he wasn't fair. His eyes were darker. They were—' She stopped, catching the thought before she vocalised it.

'They were what?' he prompted.

She shook her head. 'It was just an impression I remembered, not a fact.'

'Impressions can be useful.'

'They can also be biased,' she argued, her own experiences after Leon's death clear in her mind. 'They can be based on nothing but the observer's assumptions, beliefs and culture.'

'Or,' he countered evenly, 'they can be the result of the subconscious mind instinctively recognising and interpreting small signals from body language and voice tone. You're observant, Jo, which is why I'm interested in your impressions.'

He had a point, yet still she hesitated, seeking among her memories of the short encounter for evidence she could trust.

'We only talked for a couple of minutes. I said hello, asked a few polite questions. On the surface he seemed relaxed, but he was . . . watchful, I guess would be the right term. He made plenty of eye contact, but he didn't smile and he didn't volunteer much or ask any questions himself. Some people are very open and friendly, and are ready for a long yarn as soon as you say hello. Others are curious, they want to know about the park, where to go, what to see. He wasn't like that. But maybe . . .' She had to be fair to him, non-judgemental. 'Look, maybe that was just a cultural thing. His English was fluent, but he had a slight accent. I'm not sure what it was. Some American pronunciations, perhaps, but I don't think he was American.'

'You said he was watchful.'

'Yes. But then, so are you.'

He threw her a rueful smile. 'It's a habit that comes with the badge.'

'No. It's more than that.' She rose to her feet and strolled a couple of metres away, stretching her arms back to loosen the tension in her shoulders. While she worked her muscles, her mind avoided emotions by tackling the intellectual challenge he'd handed her. 'Your colleague, Detective Dalton, was watching me only to find what he wanted – evidence of my guilt. He was pleased that I have no alibi for the time that the man was killed.'

She thought she saw his eyes narrow slightly, and an almost imperceptible firming along his jaw line. But the instant passed

46

and she could no longer discern any change. She took the risk of prodding that control.

'In contrast, while you may be playing the good cop right now, you're constantly observing. Not so much looking for threats, not looking for guilt, but a continual scanning, gathering data, analysing it. The motorcyclist was like that, too, but he gave no indication of warmth or emotion. Just that detached study. Like a predator.' She tilted her head to one side and watched for his response. 'Like you.'

She'd surprised him, and he allowed himself to show it, raising an eyebrow as wry amusement curved his mouth. 'I'm a predator?'

She shrugged. 'Classifying things is a habit that comes with my type of work. I don't mean it with the nasty human connotations. In animal terms, a predator has strength, skills and intelligence to hunt prey when it needs to eat. On the basis of our few hours' acquaintance, I think you're a person who knows your own power and exactly how and when to wield it. On the basis of only a few minutes with the motorcyclist, I'd lean towards a similar category for him.'

Rather than arguing, taking offence or making light of her comments, he leaned back against the table, considering them.

'Do you think you could describe him to a police artist?' he asked eventually.

'I could try.'

'Good.' He stood and reached for his phone, and as simply as that their discussion was done, bar the practical arrangements from here. 'I'd like to get your fingerprints, too,' he said, 'so we can exclude them from the drug package and the fee box.'

'One of the crime-scene officers has already taken them. Do you want me to see the police artist this afternoon?'

'No. I have to go back to Strathnairn now, then down to Newcastle for the autopsy, so I won't be able to arrange it today. And you've done more than enough for one day. Perhaps you should head home, take the rest of the day off. I'll be in touch tomorrow sometime, but here's my card, in case you think of anything or see anything that might be relevant.'

His phone beeped, and with a faint smile of apology he checked it, walking away from her as he read, keying a response with nimble thumbs, all focus and work.

A small group of police officers emerged from the bush, their search completed, and milled around one of their vehicles. The forensic team packed the last of their equipment into their car.

She stood alone by the picnic table, where the activities should have been light and happy instead of shadowed by violent death.

Home. She'd planned to go into the office, but she needed the peace and silence of her own space more than she needed to keep busy, and Mal wouldn't object if she took the last few hours of the day off, in the circumstances.

She slid Nick's card into her pocket. She'd done all she could, and they no longer needed her here.

And she hoped she'd never have another day like this one.

❧

During the trip back to the temporary operations centre in Goodabri, Jo's assessment of him echoed again and again in Nick's mind.

I think you're a person who knows your own power and exactly how and when to wield it.

Yes, she'd pinned him, probably more accurately than she realised. That was who he was, who he'd been, what he did. And that's what he'd taught Hugh. Survival in the world they'd grown up in, and then worked in, required more than martial arts skills and fighting strength. Power mattered. Personal power, intellectual power, psychological power. Power and control.

As for the predator definition, if one counted criminal dealers, killers, traffickers and extortionists as prey, then yes, in a way that fitted him too. A predator of predators. But while Hugh's temperament matched that of a jaguar or a tiger, Nick couldn't see himself in that light. More of a hunter, camouflaged in the same criminal stench, behaving in the same criminal ways – to all observation, exactly like his targets – until he'd found enough evidence to draw the web tightly around them.

Dangerous tactics for dangerous work. Three days into his return to normal duties after ten years, and he doubted he'd adjust to 'normal' again. Not that a brutal murder of this kind equated to normal, even for Homicide.

He made it to Goodabri five minutes before the first scheduled briefing, to find the old shop building buzzing with activity, the basics already in place. As well as a mobile ops van, a van with the logo of the regional television station was parked out the front, beside a car from the three-times-a-week Strathnairn newspaper. Avoiding them, he parked around the back of the building and entered through the rear door, passing an office, storerooms and a small kitchen to reach the main room, already looking like an incident room. Blinds on the front windows kept curious eyes from peering in, several tables already had computers set up, and screens divided the room into sections. In the larger space, photos of the victim and the scene were up on a board; the second board, headed 'suspects', was empty.

At the urn set up in a corner, Hugh was helping himself to coffee.

He'd known Hugh long enough to dispense with courtesies and get straight to the point. 'What's happened with Phoenix that they sent you up here?'

'A dead end. All the signs point to a hit from China – some old family feud – but the Chinese government isn't much interested. This came up, I'd heard you were here, so I volunteered. Change of scene, catch up with an old mate, catch a villain or two.'

Catch up with an old mate . . . Nick poured himself a glass of water. An easy term for a complex relationship. Perhaps the complexities were as much in himself as in their relationship. Whatever the case, he didn't feel entirely *matey* towards Hugh just now.

'Why did you press Jo Lockwood for an alibi?'

Hugh casually stirred sugar into his mug, seemingly unperturbed. 'She knows this area, she had the opportunity, she's got no alibi, and she very conveniently discovered the body without any witnesses.'

Classic Hugh thinking: regard everyone with suspicion, consider everyone capable of murder. Everyone *was* capable of murder, Nick knew, but not everyone was capable of every murder. 'So what about the minor details of means and motive?' he challenged, low and direct. 'I grant you she's a fit and strong woman, but even you or I would have had difficulty committing that murder alone.'

Hugh tried to cover his hesitation by taking a sip of coffee, but couldn't disguise the way he watched Nick for a reaction, despite the pretence of nonchalance. 'She could have had help. Look, mate, fact is, I've come across her before. It's not the first time she's been involved in a death. She obviously doesn't remember me – I didn't interview her then – but I recognised her name from that case in the Barrington Tops four, maybe five years back.'

Five years ago Nick had been working an undercover drug case in Queensland, out of touch with his colleagues. Few family connections or close friends were among the prerequisites for the specialist work he'd spent the past decade doing.

'What case?' he asked.

'Her fiancé – he was a park ranger too – fell off a cliff in the Barrington Tops during a search-and-rescue one night. She was the only one with him. Turns out he was about to head off for a job overseas without her, but he carked it and she inherited a tidy sum. Coroner ended up ruling it an accident, but there were a few of us not sure about that.'

Others were coming into the room now, gathering for the briefing, so Nick dropped his voice. 'You seriously think she pushed her fiancé off a cliff?'

Hugh shrugged, gathering up a file in one hand while balancing his mug in the other. 'Means, motive and opportunity, mate. She certainly had all three. And experienced abseilers don't usually walk off cliffs without ropes.'

Nick couldn't leave it there. Not enough information. Not enough facts. And he wouldn't allow Hugh – or anyone – to get away with sloppy investigation. 'Was there *any* evidence that suggested foul play?'

'Couldn't find anything definitive. He was pretty banged up, died of his injuries before they could get a chopper in to him. But if you'd seen her afterwards – she was too controlled. Not like a normal woman would be. My gut says she could have done it. And we have to explore every possibility.'

As he walked to the front of the room with Hugh to lead the briefing, Nick's gut insisted she didn't commit either crime. But how could he know for sure, without going over both cases, finding evidence? He'd spent hours with her today, gained a strong impression of an intelligent, dedicated professional. Yet she'd argued herself that impressions could be biased.

He liked her, dammit, respected her – but was he creating a false image of her, based on his own assumptions, and on what he wanted to believe?

ॐ

She had to concentrate hard on the drive home along the narrow dirt road. The current affairs program on the radio did little to distract her thoughts, and the image of the victim's face, framed by the body bag, kept floating into her mind, blurring with her memories and becoming Leon's.

By the time she parked beside the homestead, fatigue and reaction had set in and her whole body shook, cold despite the heat. She stumbled through her back door, dropped the keys on the kitchen table and went straight to the bedroom. Stripping off her uniform, she crawled under the blanket, clutching the pillow to her, letting the tears flow as she hadn't let them since the night, years ago, she'd huddled on a narrow rock ledge cradling Leon in her arms, crying in the driving rain while the storm raged around them and his life ebbed away.

FOUR

The reality of remote policing hit home as Nick surveyed the officers assembled for the briefing. Hugh and the detective constable from Homicide, Shelley Brock, would likely only be here for a couple of days, to lend expertise and support to the critical early stages of the investigation. If they didn't close the case in forty-eight hours, he'd only have the officers available in the local region, and most of them were in front of him: a dozen uniformed police from Strathnairn and outlying stations pulled off general duties, and Aaron Georgiou, a keen young detective with good instincts but inexperienced in crimes other than domestic violence, assault and stock theft.

With his new colleagues still to trust him, Nick let Hugh take the lead in the briefing, using the opportunity to observe the reactions of the team, assess their contributions, get a solid feel for the people he'd be working with.

Those who hadn't seen the victim at the scene paled as Hugh flicked through the graphic photos projected on the large screen, and there were more than a few muttered swear words. But when Hugh finally showed an image of the victim's face – for some Hugh-logic reason, he'd left that until last – one of the constables swore more loudly and rose to his feet.

'I think I know who he is,' he said. 'Picked him up a year or so back for DUI and marijuana possession, when I worked at Tamworth. Mitchell, I think his name was. Travis Mitchell. He'd been DUI before, so he got a six-month sentence. Nice enough young bloke, but a bit wild, and not too bright with it.'

Nick went to the whiteboard and wrote the name, the first real lead. Before Hugh could pass responsibility for looking into it to Brock, Nick forestalled him. 'Can you follow that up – it's Carruthers, isn't it? I think the CSOs got a partial print from the vic's burned hand. See if it matches Mitchell's prints from his records. And since he's in the system, there should be a next-of-kin record and, if we're lucky, a current address for him.'

He scrawled the constable's name as the action officer beside Mitchell's name on the whiteboard and set down the pen, returning to where he'd propped on the edge of the table. Hugh threw him a decidedly unamused look, but didn't object out loud. To object would be to acknowledge a threat to his leadership, and they both knew it. It had been one of the first lessons Nick had taught him, almost twenty years ago.

He'd given Hugh the lead on this one, but only because he chose to do so, for the benefit of the investigation, and he'd simply take it back the moment he needed to.

Hugh steered the briefing through the key issues and allocated tasks – mostly standard general enquiries, fishing expeditions, since they had so little to go on. He didn't make the mistake of naming Jo as a person of interest. Scarcely mentioned her at all, in fact. Either a wise decision in a small, possibly partisan community, or because he planned to keep his suspicions to himself until he had some evidence.

When it came to the point of identifying local drug dealers to question, Hugh received blank stares from most in the room.

Aaron shot Nick a glance before he volunteered an explanation. 'There's not much in the way of drugs out here,' he said. 'Not illegal ones, anyway. Alcohol is a much bigger problem. There's a bit of dope, but it's mostly low key. There's occasional methamphetamines and party drugs, but young people tend to bring their own back from the city. Some heroin along the truck routes, but that's pretty much it. I haven't heard anything about coke in the district.'

Nick doodled some figures on his notepad. Strathnairn, the largest town in the district, had a population of barely seven thousand. Add in a couple of other towns like Goodabri, a handful of small communities and a thinly spread agricultural population, and it still made fewer than fifteen thousand people in an area of thousands of square kilometres. Not a large or potentially profitable market for drug dealing. Not to mention the difficulties of running an illegal operation where secrecy would be hard for a local to maintain, when every second person in the street probably knew their name and at least half their history.

The cocaine they'd found was a small quantity, less than five grams in each of the twelve packs. Not a significant drop, just enough for a small private party, or for a minnow dealer.

Nick figured that if the biker had left it there for the vandals' party, something had to have gone wrong with the deal. And something had definitely gone very wrong for a young man, perhaps Travis Mitchell, who'd dabbled in drugs and served time in prison.

But they were still no nearer to finding out the identity of the biker, or of the vandals who'd smashed up the camping ground. Until they had some more leads, he was working blind.

ॐ

Curled up on her bed, Jo woke abruptly from a deep sleep. Evening light slanted across the room, with the apricot tinge of sunset.

The soft creak of something treading on the timber back veranda sounded again – the noise that had woken her.

Still groggy from sleep, rattled by the emotional exhaustion of her breakdown, she delved for the security of logic and tried to concentrate on the noise. It could be a possum or a roo, or a dog. A wallaby had polished off the potted herbs she'd had out there, just last week.

But they'd have tripped the rear security light, and there was only the fading sunlight shining into the room. No light coming from her bedside clock, either, or from the computer desk in the corner, where the printer, wireless router and external hard-drive usually glowed like a Christmas tree.

Pushing aside the pillow she'd been hugging in her sleep,

she slid off the bed to the floor and dragged her discarded clothes closer.

Creak.

If it was someone, rather than something, then she'd rather they believed she wasn't alone. If whoever was out there expected the house to be empty, the sound of voices might frighten them off.

Despite the constriction in her throat, she forced a laugh into her voice and said, 'No, I'm *not* coming back to bed.' Clothes in hand, she rose to her feet, slipped out the door and into the corridor, mumbling a protest in a passably low tone.

'Yes, the power's off again,' she called back to her imaginary lover. 'And I'm starving, so it looks like you're on barbecue duty again tonight.'

In the bathroom, she fumbled as she pulled on her rumpled uniform shirt and trousers, checking the pockets for her phone and keys.

Phone, but no keys. Kitchen table – maybe that's where she'd left them. *Damn.* Kitchen, with the curtains wide open at the large window, looking out over the back veranda.

Creak.

Okay, so the sound of voices hadn't discouraged her visitor. What next?

Normally, she'd simply go out and confront someone poking around. That was part of her job, and she'd dealt with all types – lost hikers, itinerants looking for a place to sleep, roo shooters scouting the landscape, young louts on the lookout for mischief – time and again, even alone and at night.

But tonight, with a man in the morgue and his murderers still on the loose, she'd be cautious.

With mobile phone reception more reliable at the front of the house than at the back, she walked as quietly as she could down the corridor to the room the National Parks staff used as a storeroom and general office. French doors leading on to the front veranda and spare keys for the service truck in the desk drawer gave her an exit strategy if she needed one. A heavy metal torch from the storage shelves could serve as both a light and a weapon.

Trying to breathe evenly to steady her heartbeat, she stood to the side of the window, watching out through the gap between the light curtain and the glass. The sunset glow had faded away, but nothing moved in the twilight shadows in the front yard, and she could hear no sounds other than the frogs croaking down at the river and the low, pulsing *oom-oom* of the frogmouth that lived in the grove of eucalypts over the fence.

She flicked through the contact list on her phone for the Goodabri police station. Not usually staffed twenty-four hours, but with the ops centre nearby maybe someone would be there, or the phone forwarded through.

Catching sight of headlights through the trees, she paused with her finger on the dial button. Definitely coming this way; the vehicle turned in at the driveway entrance and slowed to cross the cattle grid at the fence line.

In the glare of the headlights she couldn't identify the vehicle until it pulled around to park in front of the house.

She breathed easier. A service ute, and fellow ranger Erin Taylor driving it. Jo pushed open the French door and crossed the veranda to meet her.

'Mal sent me,' Erin announced cheerily as she opened the driver's door. 'I'm under orders to ensure you're okay, make sure you're fed and stay overnight if you want me to.'

She'd half-expected Mal to phone or call in this evening, and blessed his sense in sending Erin instead. Practical, down-to-earth Erin would not fuss over her, or panic in the current situation.

'Your timing is great. Not only am I starving, but the power's out and I think there's someone wandering around the backyard.'

'Shit. Have you phoned the cops?'

'I was just about to.' She rapidly reconsidered options. 'But now you're here, I think I'll phone Mal and tell him we're going to take a look, and if we don't phone back in ten minutes, to call the police station. It could just be that the fuse tripped and the wallaby came back for more herbs.'

'Good plan.' Erin grabbed a torch from behind the front seat and started unhooking the tonneau cover on the back of the ute. 'But phone Simon rather than Mal – if one of our colleagues is going to come charging out here in a white ute to save us, I'd prefer it was Simon.' She lifted out a crowbar, gave it an experimental swing and grinned. 'Not, of course, that we actually need saving. Let's go and scare off your rampaging wallaby.'

Her apprehension lightened, Jo tossed the phone to her.

'You phone Simon. I know you want to.'

But as Erin made the call to the third ranger in their team, Jo focused beyond her voice, on the sounds around, listening for anything that didn't belong.

With Simon duly alerted, and determined to ride to their rescue whether they needed it or not, they walked through the house, making noise and chatting as they went, flashing the torches around the rapidly darkening rooms. Jo much preferred to scare away an intruder than to confront one.

Nothing moved on the back veranda or in the yard beyond it, except for a possum, scrambling up one of the ancient fruit trees near the dilapidated chook shed.

'Maybe that's your culprit,' Erin said.

Jo gave a slight nod, but didn't for a moment believe it. She'd grown up in the country, knew the difference between a human footstep and a possum's. And she'd become familiar with that possum since she'd moved in here; it regularly climbed up veranda posts, scrabbled along the roof, breathed its rattling possum breathing outside the windows, but it had never made the timber boards of the veranda creak.

She waved her light towards the corner of the house. 'I'll check the fuse box.'

The hard ground under the fuse box grew little in the way of grass, and there was too little dust to see any discernible marks. But she covered her fingers with a handkerchief, just in case, when she lifted the lid and ran the light across the switches inside. All three power circuits sat just below 'on'.

Tripped by a power surge? All three of them? It might be possible; power supplies out here could be erratic. But she kept the handkerchief covering her fingers as she flicked each switch properly off, then back to 'on', to protect any fingerprints that might be there.

In the distance, above the croaking of the frogs and the possum's hissing, she heard an engine kick to life and she looked across the paddock beyond the homestead in time to see a single headlight swing away and speed off down the road.

FIVE

He drove to Newcastle through the night, music blasting from the speakers to keep him awake, stopping for strong black coffee at the few twenty-four-hour truck stops on the way.

At five in the morning he pulled into a motel on the edge of town, aiming to grab three hours' sleep before the scheduled nine o'clock autopsy. But sleep didn't come easily, and he stared at the ceiling, too many unsettling thoughts circling in his brain to switch off. The bitterness of his partner's betrayal, and the whispered rumours about his own loyalty from his new colleagues . . . a brutal murder, with no leads . . . Hugh, never easy to deal with . . . and a woman whose eyes he couldn't get out of his mind . . .

He rolled over, pummelled his pillow into softness, and buried his head in it.

When his alarm jerked him out of a dream at eight, he'd been back in that brothel in Melbourne, pain ripping through his body, a bloodied gun in his hand, and two bodies beside him. But in this dream the bodies weren't those of Terry Costello and the mistress of his mob target; they wore the faces of Hugh and Jo.

A cold shower made him alert but did little to improve his mood.

While he dressed he checked his emails. One from Malcolm Stewart with the names of the couple in the caravan he flicked on to Aaron, with instructions to follow up and find them. A brief message from Hugh confirmed that the partial fingerprint from the victim was a match with Travis Mitchell, twenty-two years old, three months out of prison, no fixed address.

Running out of time, he shut down the laptop and headed out the door. At least he had a confirmed name to take to the coroner's office.

Being able to refer to the victim by name did not make the autopsy any easier. Nick had attended many, knew the process, the smells and the sights, but they'd never, ever become easy to watch. In this one, the violence that had been disturbing when the victim was clothed became harrowing when the full extent was laid naked.

But he fulfilled his responsibility to observe as the forensic pathologist and her assistant did what had to be done efficiently and with respect, and he answered questions as to the crime scene and the sequence of events following the body's discovery to aid the doctor's analysis. She confirmed that the majority of injuries were inflicted prior to death, their nature clearly amounting to torture, before the final, fatal gunshot wound to the head. Nick found himself hoping that the toxicology reports would reveal ingestion of significant amounts of alcohol or other numbing drugs.

By the time it was finished, they were all grim. The doctor stripped off her mask and hat at the edge of the room, and leaned back against the wall, ashen-faced.

'I have a son around his age,' she said. 'That was as bad as—' She broke off, stood up straight. 'Let me check the records. I'll meet you in the conference room in ten minutes.'

The furnishings and warm timber tones of the conference room made for more pleasant surroundings than the sterilised stainless steel of the autopsy lab, but the scent of death clung in his nose, and the sunshine and chirping of birds outside the window grated against the harsh reality of death he had been witness to and the anger growing inside him.

The doctor returned in a little over ten minutes, handing him a file with photos and documents.

'That's the original file, but I can email you a copy. He's a John Doe, found in bushland near Coffs Harbour four weeks ago. Estimated date of death around three weeks before that. A difficult examination, because of the decomposition, but you may want to follow up with the investigating officer. There are similarities, including an amputation and the manner of it. Although this victim lost a foot, not a hand.'

Nick flicked through the pages, stopping at the list of those present at the autopsy when a name leapt off the page: Detective Senior Sergeant Hugh Dalton.

Hugh, who'd shown the images of their victim on the screen at the briefing last night and neglected to mention a similar case. Who'd labelled Jo Lockwood a likely suspect.

Just what was Hugh's game?

'Thanks, I will need a copy of this report,' he told the doctor. 'And there's another one, coronial findings from a few years back, that I need to get hold of, too.'

Not unusual for Hugh to run his own agenda; he'd never been a strong team player. But since they had scarcely seen each other in the past few years – hadn't worked directly together for even longer – Nick was determined to keep on top of every facet of this case. And as Hugh had suggested Jo's involvement, that included finding out about the death of her fiancé.

'I don't know the name, but perhaps you might remember it – he was a National Parks ranger, involved in a search in the Barrington Tops.'

'Yes, I remember that one. Rossetti. Leon Rossetti. I examined the scene and performed the autopsy. He was struck by a falling tree limb during a storm and fell thirty metres down the face of a bluff. What's your interest in that case?'

Unwilling to voice Hugh's intimations, Nick carefully kept to the bare, factual minimum. 'The ranger who found Mitchell yesterday was also with Rossetti when he died.'

The pathologist raised an eyebrow. 'His fiancée? If you're implying a possible involvement in Rossetti's death, as I reported to the coroner, Rossetti's injuries were consistent with her statement and the scene I observed. Rescue services were not available, due to the storm, so she climbed down to him alone, with only a basic rope fastened to a tree. I saw it there – one hell of a scary climb, even in sunshine.'

'Could Rossetti have survived, if he'd been airlifted to hospital immediately?'

'He survived the initial fall, but even if he'd been in an intensive care unit within the hour, he might not have lived. As you'd expect from such a fall, there were skull, spinal, thoracic and limb fractures and significant internal bleeding. It's a wonder that he lasted some hours, but there was nothing his fiancée could have done, in the circumstances.' She paused, steepling her fingers in contemplation. 'I doubt he was aware of it, but I hope it was some comfort to her that he didn't die alone.'

His top priority had to be returning to Goodabri, so he packed the report she printed for him in with his laptop, to read later. Nothing she'd said suggested any basis for Hugh's suspicions. Which left three possibilities: that Hugh knew something the pathologist and Coroner didn't; that his cynicism had skewed his judgement; or that he was playing some kind of game.

Nick suspected the latter. He just wished Hugh hadn't dragged Jo into it.

⁂

Describing a face she had only seen partially obscured by a motorbike helmet, and from a distance without the helmet, challenged Jo's memory for detail. In the small office off the main incident room, the artist patiently manipulated graphics on the computer screen, prompted her with questions and options, and at the end of an hour they had an image that resembled Jo's memory of the face she'd seen two days ago, and in her dreams last night. The physical shape, skin tone, dark-brown eye colour and cropped black hair were as close as she could recall; what she couldn't adequately describe for a static image was the unemotional, shuttered expression, the lack of warmth or response in his eyes.

The memory of that cool, unchanging gaze had woken her numerous times in the night, and a cheerful breakfast with Erin and Simon in another dry, hot morning had not erased the chill in her spine or the prickling sense of being watched.

In the tiny bathroom at the rear of the makeshift ops centre, she splashed cold water on her face.

'Get a grip,' she told her reflection in the mirror. 'Plenty of people ride bikes in the park.'

The power *did* go out occasionally, a wallaby would forage where it had found tasty green food before, and the biker she'd spoken with the other day might simply rate high on the autism spectrum, with a brain not wired for instant empathy.

And she had paperwork piling up in the office next door, deadlines to meet and no desire to lose another day of work.

Glancing back into the main room, she could not see Hugh Dalton. Probably still outside, giving a media statement to the small crowd of television and newspaper reporters.

The annoyance at seeing her own face on the evening news still rankled. Dalton hadn't mentioned her by name in his carefully worded statement yesterday afternoon, but with little solid information to go on, a local reporter had filled in a few seconds' airtime with an image of her taken at the park opening last week. She'd had to field anxious phone calls from her mother and her brother after they'd seen the news. This morning's *Strathnairn Standard* had also carried the story, but now that the name of the victim had been released, there was only passing mention of her.

The 'Closed' sign on the front door of the National Parks office hadn't dissuaded a number of people from knocking and rattling the handle this morning. She'd have to keep a low profile today, using the rear entrance, skulking in the back office, out of sight and hearing from a media mob hungry for any morsel of information to fill out a so-far thin story.

Slipping out the back door of the police building, she encountered Aaron Georgiou coming in. As with many of the regional police officers, she'd met him a few times, through liaison meetings between the services, a bushfire preparedness exercise last month and the occasional social gathering. She liked Aaron; he reminded her of her younger brother, although Aaron was more serious and showed her far more deference than Todd ever did.

'Have you got another minute, Jo? I have a quick question for you.'

'Sure. If you don't mind coming in.' She unlocked the door of her building and ushered him inside, locking the door behind them. Despite the rough-and-ready nature of this temporary office, at least it was her territory.

He accepted her offer of a chair in her sparsely furnished work room and took out his notebook. 'That couple you saw on Tuesday – the Baxters, according to the camping permit Mal gave us – did they happen to mention which way they were headed? The sarge wants me to track them down.'

'They said they were planning to stop in the Bunya Mountains on their way to Noosa.' They'd been a friendly, pleasant couple, obviously devoted to each other, so the brief conversation she'd had with them stood out in her memory. 'Their names are

Tom and Shirley. They were driving a newish-model white LandCruiser and towing a large caravan – a Jayco, I think.'

'That's a fantastic help. Now at least I've got a general direction.'

'Try the Bunya National Park office.' She did a quick search on her computer. 'If they're in the park, the office should be able to find them. Here's the phone number.' She read the number from the screen and he noted it in his notebook.

'Thanks, Jo. I'll call them.'

Her chair squeaked as she leaned back. 'He really suspects the motorcyclist is involved somehow, doesn't he? Detective Matheson, I mean.'

Aaron tucked his notebook away in his shirt pocket, his young face sombre.

'I guess so. That's why he wants to talk to the Baxters. He's worked a stack of investigations involving drug rings and violent crime, including undercover jobs. He's familiar with how they're organised, how they operate, how they think. So I trust his instincts.'

Undercover jobs – that explained Nick's control, the power she'd sensed in him, his ability to switch from serious to friendly, to wear different faces. And that left her wondering who the real Nick was, under the careful control.

A detective who suspected the motorcyclist of involvement in one or both crimes carried out in the park, and was allocating resources to investigate that lead; that much she knew for certain.

'Aaron, you should know . . . it may be nothing at all, but I might have had an uninvited visitor yesterday evening. On a motorbike.'

'Shit, Jo. Why didn't you report it?'

'Nothing definitive to report. Some strange sounds, a power failure, and the sound of a bike in the distance. Erin Taylor arrived and we had a look around together, but there was no-one there.'

He dragged a hand through his hair, clearly worried. 'I'll tell the sarge when he gets back from Newcastle.'

So, he would tell Nick, not Hugh Dalton. The Sydney detective must have higher-priority suspects than a biker seen twelve hours or more before the crime. Like her. But Aaron at least didn't seem to share those suspicions.

'If you see or hear anything else unusual, Jo, call us straightaway. I don't like thinking of you out there alone.' He paused in the doorway, cleared his throat. 'Look, I know you might not feel you know any of us here yet, but believe me, people respect you, and we'd rather a dozen false alarms than . . . well, than anything else.'

As she closed the door behind him, Aaron's friendly concern touched her, and his efforts to assure her of her acceptance in the community. Four months wasn't long to be in a rural area, especially since she wasn't much good at making connections outside work. Although the division's main office was in Strathnairn, she went there only a couple of times a week, in between her duties in the various parks, establishing the new park and setting up this building for its role as temporary visitor information centre until the new Goodabri centre was built. She worked with a great team in Erin, Simon, Mal and the field staff, but they all worked out of the Strathnairn office, and she sometimes went days without seeing them.

She liked people, but being alone much of the time suited her nature. More so since Leon's death.

Flicking the overhead fan up to its highest setting, she returned to her desk. She had plenty of work to bury herself in to distract her thoughts from yesterday's events, and a quiet office with no interruptions to allow her to focus on crossing items off her To Do list. A funding submission to double-check and submit before five p.m. Wildlife survey data to incorporate into a report for the Minister, due by the end of the week. A plan for upgrading the fire trails to be finalised for next week. The summer family activity program to proofread before it went to the printer. Determined to catch up, she concentrated solidly for hours.

By late afternoon she had reached the summer family program. She stared at the list of activities. In just over a week, schools would be finished for the year and the busy summer season underway. Camping grounds across the four National Parks they managed would be filled with families, daytrippers would drive out from nearby towns, and the rangers and field staff would be flat out from dawn past dusk until the new school year started in February.

She checked the date on her computer. Eight days until the first weekend of the school holidays. Eight days before she was scheduled to take a twilight spotlighting walk along the gorge track from Gumtree Flat. Always popular with families, and usually she loved taking them – excited kids watching for possums, sugar gliders and bats, and their parents, almost as wide-eyed.

But unless the police caught the murderers before then, she'd be on edge, worried about safety, apprehensive about what they might find.

Had Travis Mitchell been part of the group of vandals, or an innocent camper caught up in their violence? Twenty-two years old, according to the news reports – younger than her brother. Younger than Aaron Georgiou. A man who should have had a long life ahead of him, instead of a terrifying, agonising death.

Her chest tightened to a painful lump, sorrow and despair swirling murky shadows in her mind. *No.* No, she would *not* permit gloomy thoughts to take over, to take her back to the desolation of depression she had worked so hard to escape. She pushed her chair back, crossed the office to the kitchenette and filled a glass with water from the cooler.

No wallowing. She'd allowed herself a good cry last night, the release of tension. Getting stuck in negative patterns of thought wouldn't help herself or anyone.

The back door slammed, and footsteps sounded down the corridor. Jo glanced at her watch – quarter to five, almost the end of the work day.

'It's just me,' Erin's voice announced, seconds before she appeared in the doorway. 'Everything all right?'

Jo leaned against the windowsill, not quite able to paste a smile on her face.

'I'm okay.' She drank a couple of mouthfuls of water, pressed the cool glass against her cheek. 'Diversion therapy just failed there for a moment.'

'Sucks when that happens and you remember, doesn't it?'

Typical Erin: no tiptoeing around, just down-to-earth understanding.

'Yep.' Not a topic she wanted to dwell on right now, so she switched the subject. 'I thought you were at that tourism planning conference in Tenterfield today.'

'I was.' With a wry grin, Erin helped herself to juice from the fridge. 'I escaped.'

'That exciting?'

'Oh, if we'd played buzzword bingo, I'd have filled my card before morning tea.'

'I'm glad it was you and not me. So you're here because . . . ?' No real need to ask the question. To check on her, naturally. Erin knew about Leon's death, and although she didn't tiptoe around her, she cared enough to worry, assuming Jo's solitary life meant still-active grief. Maybe it did. Jo wasn't too sure anymore.

'Thought I'd pop in on the way back to 'Nairn,' Erin said breezily. 'It's Thommo's farewell tonight. Are you coming? You're welcome to stay at my place if you don't want to drive back home.'

A crowded pub, farewelling the popular captain of the Strathnairn volunteer emergency service? Her head throbbed just thinking about it.

'I think I'll pike out of that one tonight, Erin. I've got a rescued sugar glider to release, and after that I'm planning on an early night.'

Glass halfway to her lips, Erin frowned at her. 'Where are you releasing it? Can it wait until tomorrow and I'll go with you?'

'The wildlife carer dropped it off this afternoon. There's no sense giving it the trauma of carting it around for another day, when it's not far out of my way and I can just release it before I go home. It's no drama.'

It wasn't. Couldn't be a problem. She'd gone over it again and again since the wildlife carer had emailed this afternoon.

Erin gnawed on her lip, unconvinced. 'What if someone follows you?'

Jo drained her glass of water, rinsed it out at the sink. Sensible. They all just needed to be logical and sensible.

'It's not far off the road, Erin. If someone follows then I'll see them. I've got the radio and the phone. But honestly, I see no reason for anyone to target me. Just because some kid on a trail bike decided to poke around the homestead last night doesn't mean I should cower inside and not do my job.'

Even a mere seven hours in the office had her restless, longing to be outdoors again. She hated the idea that fear should force her into hiding behind locked doors. The mystery biker from the camping ground could well be in Tibooburra or Bourke or even Thargomindah by now, enjoying a cold beer in an outback pub, oblivious to any crimes that had occurred.

'Do you want Simon and me to come and stay at your place tonight?' Erin asked. 'The cops have finished with the crime scene, so Mal wants us to go out to do the clean-up first thing in the morning. It's just as easy to do that from your place.'

Your place. But not her place, in reality. Staff quarters and work depot, a base for major projects in the area, and only a temporary home for her.

Jo kept her face neutral as she dried her glass and put it away in the cupboard. 'Of course you're welcome anytime you want to come, for work reasons or not.' No lie there – Erin was easy company and a good friend, and observing the deepening friendship between her and Simon made Jo happy for them both, even if they hadn't quite worked it all out themselves.

Time for another gentle nudge, perhaps. With an air of pretended innocence, she said, 'But if you're going to be partying tonight, wouldn't you be better off staying at Simon's? You can walk to his place from the pub, so you could relax and have a few drinks, instead of staying sober to drive back here.'

Erin blushed an attractive shade of pink. 'But—'

'But nothing. You know what you want, and I'm betting he wants the same.' She paused to regard her friend, deciding how much to say, remembering the goals and dreams she'd waited too long to grasp, lost in Leon's unexpected death. 'Don't do nothing and maybe regret it later, Erin. Simon's a good bloke. You can trust him.'

'Yeah, I know that.' Erin paced towards the window, changed her mind and propped on the edge of the table instead. 'Speaking of trust, what did you think of the new detective?'

'Nick?' The change of subject – and the sudden shift in thought from Leon to Nick – took an unsettling moment for her brain to process. 'Highly competent, I'd say. Professional, tough. Not one to tolerate fools. Why?'

'I was at the pub Tuesday night after rescue-squad training. A few of the boys in blue joined our table, and there was some talk. Remember that police shooting, a couple of months back, in Melbourne? A copper was killed and some underworld thug's girlfriend. An undercover cop was the only survivor, and the only witness.'

A vague memory lurked in her mind, devoid of detail. 'I heard about it, but didn't pay much attention. Seems they're always shooting each other, down there.'

'Yep. Anyway, the undercover guy's name was suppressed, but apparently it was Matheson, seconded to the Victoria Police.' Erin dropped her voice, as if concerned they could hear her next door. 'And some of the local boys think the official enquiry that cleared him was a whitewash.'

That she hadn't expected. 'Funny that they'd talk about it in the pub,' she wondered aloud. 'Don't police usually stick together over that kind of thing?'

'Well, they weren't shouting it from the treetops. I just happened to be at the end of the table where the muttering was loudest. I was a bit surprised, too – the blokes are usually pretty tight-lipped – but the close-ranks-and-protect-the-brotherhood loyalty doesn't appear to apply to Matheson. And the words "corruption" and "murder" were thrown around.'

Aaron had mentioned the undercover work, and she could imagine Nick passing as a convincing criminal – not a thug, but a sharp, intelligent mastermind behind complex crimes, able to act any part required.

In his own role, he showed little softness, despite his unfailing courtesy towards her. Tough and uncompromising. If he chose to walk on the wrong side of the law, he'd be a dangerous man.

She pushed that image from her mind. He was a police officer, a detective; she'd have to trust in the system and her instincts, and he'd given her no reason to believe that trust misplaced.

There had to be more to the story. There always was. Police faced dangerous situations and had to make split-second decisions every day. The suspicions about him might be a sign of the occasional tensions between regional and newly arrived city cops, and possibly held as much substance as the whispered accusations against her, after Leon's death.

⁂

He reached Uralla around seven, and pulled in to a late-night service station and café on the edge of the town. Despite little in the way of appetite, he bought a couple of muesli bars and a Coke, his body needing the break from driving and the caffeine as much as the food. With a good two hours still to go, he didn't plan on blacking out at the wheel from fatigue and lack of sustenance, and there'd be few places open on the roads between Uralla and Goodabri.

He chose a corner table, his back to the wall, with a clear view of the other tables and the area outside through the windows. Old habits died hard.

He'd taken the back road from Newcastle, winding up through the mountains. A quicker route than the highway, but with little phone reception, so his phone had beeped with voicemail notifications as he'd approached Uralla and come in range of a phone tower.

Two messages. He cracked open the soft-drink bottle and drank some while he listened to them. Hugh's response to the voicemail he'd left earlier was typically casual and brief.

'We never turned up anything on that John Doe in Coffs, mate. No leads, no witnesses, nothing. The case is pretty much dead in

the water. Or the bush, so to speak. I'm following up on Mitchell's connections. I bet we'll get something from his prison mates.'

Aaron's message consisted of a brief but concise recap of the day's developments, the last on the list – the news about Jo Lockwood's possible intruder – making Nick grip the phone tighter.

An intruder, so soon after a murder – he didn't like those kinds of coincidences. Hugh had been bloody careless, letting slip to the media who had found the body, and although Nick couldn't see how it could result in a threat to Jo, it worried him nonetheless.

He deleted the message, took another mouthful of Coke and was about to check his emails when the phone buzzed. Aaron's number.

'Sarge, glad I've caught you.'

The relief in Aaron's voice set Nick's radar for bad news on alert. 'What's up?'

'I've just heard from the Queensland police.' There was a brief pause while he swallowed, but he continued, 'Going by the rego and the car description, they're pretty certain the vics found in a burned-out caravan this morning are the Baxters, the couple that Jo spoke with the other day.'

Nick set the bottle down slowly on the table. 'Two vics?'

'Yes. Both of them, in bed. Won't be certain until the autopsy, but the detective I spoke with reckons it's suspicious. Gas bottles don't usually explode these days.'

No, they don't. Not at night, with an elderly couple tucked up in bed.

He stuffed the muesli bars into his pocket, picked up his drink and headed for the door, the phone still at his ear. 'Any witnesses?'

'None. It was an isolated camping area. They were the only ones there.'

Not the only ones, Nick would have bet. Someone else had been there. Someone who had killed them. Money and thrills aside, there weren't a lot of reasons to kill an elderly couple. But they'd been in the National Park on the day Travis Mitchell was murdered. They'd spoken to a motorcyclist who might be linked to drugs. So had Jo – and she'd had an intruder last night, on a bike.

'Aaron, get on to Jo Lockwood. Send a couple of uniforms out to her place, or go yourself. Make sure she's not alone, anywhere.'

'I already tried to phone her, Sarge. There's no answer on her mobile or at home.'

'Keep trying. Keep trying until you find her and make sure she's safe. Then keep her that way. I'll be there in ninety minutes.'

SIX

The sun, close to setting, cast a red–gold glow across the landscape. Jo left her truck under a tree by the creek, taking only her backpack and the small covered cage holding the sugar glider.

She walked along the road a short distance, then up the ridge that formed the border of the park. To the east lay bush and rough granite hills, too rough to farm, small creeks cutting through rocky valleys.

To the west the hill sloped away more gently, and there the land had been cleared a century ago for grazing, leaving only small pockets of timber. The thousands of trees Jack McCulloch had planted in green corridors over the past forty years would not be fully grown, with the hollows necessary for many birds and mammals, for another twenty or thirty years. But the bush was slowly regenerating, the old forest and the new seeding young trees and gradually encroaching on the shearers' quarters and shearing shed, deserted since Jack switched from sheep to cattle many years ago.

The homestead itself lay a kilometre away, deserted, too, now that Jack was in the nursing home, with no-one to pass the property on to. He'd sold off his stock, leased some of the land, couldn't yet bring himself to sell the whole property and the homestead that had been in his family for four generations. Jo knew the heartache of that; a run of bad years and her father's terminal illness had seen her own family forced to make a similar decision when she was seventeen. She felt for Jack, hoped the property would see new owners who cared for the land and continued his family's stewardship.

But for now McCulloch Downs was empty, save for a few cattle on agistment, and with the park on one side and the quiet paddocks on the other, she walked along the fence line at the top of the ridge for half a kilometre, to where she'd found the dehydrated glider at the bottom of a tree a couple of weeks ago. After recuperating in the care of the local wildlife rescue service, his best chance of survival lay in release here, where he came from.

The sun had set, the cloudless western sky deepening to a deep mauve. A gold glow peeked over the ridges to the east. Although she knew the basic science of atmospheric effects and refracted light, the huge golden orb of a full moon rising never ceased to bring her pleasure. She took the few minutes to simply stand, watching it, the cage resting at her feet. Belatedly she remembered her camera in her backpack, and, setting the exposure for the dusky light, she framed a few shots of the moon silhouetting the trees on the next ridge.

When moonlight spilled around her, she knelt by the cage on the ground and slowly opened the small door. Using her knee as a makeshift tripod, she steadied the camera, capturing a couple of images of the sugar glider's striped head as it cautiously poked a nose out into the fresh air, but gave up trying to photograph it as the glider made a sudden dash for the nearest tree, and scampered up the trunk.

And there it was, done, a wild creature returned to its habitat, to the natural cycles of life among the trees. Always satisfying, one of the many pleasures of her job.

'I hope you find your family, little fella, and live a long life with lots of offspring,' she murmured.

Buoyed by the beauty of the evening, she began to make her way back to the truck, the rough track clear enough in the moonlight so that although she took a torch from her backpack, she didn't turn it on.

The sounds of nocturnal creatures stirring accompanied her; rustlings among the leaves, the swoop of a microbat in front of her, and the reverberating call of a tawny frogmouth, a short distance ahead. As she approached what appeared to be the stump of a limb on a branch it transformed into a bird, the frogmouth gliding away from her, down the ridge.

Being out alone in the dark, miles from anywhere, normally didn't spook her. She didn't believe in ghosts, the native animals posed little threat, and statistically she was far safer out here than on a city street.

But tonight she moved more quickly, wary, eyes and ears alert for anything that didn't belong. Only two hundred more metres to walk, then down the hill to the creek and her truck, and she could head home for a late meal, a shower and bed.

She heard the oncoming vehicle before she saw its headlights through the trees to the west. Her pulse rate lost its regular rhythm, pounded erratically. Only a handful of people lived along the dirt road between the tiny community of Derringvale and Goodabri, and it was hardly a short cut to anywhere. It could be a local, travelling back to the Goodabri area, although there was a quicker route from Strathnairn. Hoons out for a drive? Kangaroo shooters, perhaps?

Her truck would be obvious once they crested the rise and headed downhill again, but maybe they'd assume it had broken down or been deserted. Phone, wallet, keys, camera – yes, she had most things of value with her in her backpack.

She wouldn't let anyone know she was there unless she knew exactly who they were. Having to be so cautious sat uncomfortably with her, rubbing against the grain of a lifetime of country living. It was the Australian bush, dammit, not the back streets of some city.

But instead of coming up the hill, the car slowed, turning off the road near the derelict shearers' quarters, about a hundred metres from where she stood.

Now *that* didn't make sense. Why would anyone go there, especially at night? The place had been picked clean by antique hunters years ago.

The vehicle – a ute – pulled up in front of the shearing shed, leaving headlights blazing at the building while the driver climbed the old wooden steps and went inside.

Keeping in the shadows of the trees, Jo moved closer, about fifty metres from the shed, while the man was out of view. It technically wasn't National Parks property, but out here, with large properties covering thousands of hectares, neighbours kept an eye on things for each other.

While some of the blokes who wandered the bush might camp for a night or two in the many old shearers' quarters that dotted the countryside, Jo knew from yarning with them that the larger, draughtier, lanolin-soaked woolsheds weren't a preferred camping spot. So a ute swinging in to park so confidently by the shed in the dark didn't . . . well, it didn't *feel* right.

She tugged her camera out of her backpack and made sure the flash was turned off. Steadying it on a tree stump, kneeling behind it so she stayed out of view, she zoomed in on the illuminated area between the ute and the shed. When the man came out again and hurried down the steps, the headlights cast his face in good light, and she snapped several frames.

She cursed the flutter of nerves that made her hand shake but continued to photograph, despite the poorer light beside the ute, as he quickly undid the tonneau cover on the back and slid something long – about a metre, maybe wrapped in cloth – from the tray. He glanced several times to the west, as if keeping a watch out for another vehicle on the road.

Whatever he was doing, Jo doubted there could be an entirely innocent explanation. Maybe it was some sort of prank, or maybe he was hiding stolen goods, but with a man murdered just two days ago, and a stash of cocaine found, she kept clicking photos, and stayed out of sight.

He came out after a couple of minutes, taking the stairs two at a time, before getting in the ute and driving back the way he'd come, away from the ridge concealing her truck.

Jo breathed deeply again, and waited until his headlights had disappeared from view before she walked down to the shearing shed.

It was Jack McCulloch's private property, but she had a good relationship with him, had visited him a number of times in the nursing home to talk about the history of the area, and she doubted he'd mind her trespassing in the circumstances, to check things over.

The timber steps creaked as she walked up them, and the corrugated-iron door into the shed opened with a squeak, rubbing against the floorboards. Moonlight streamed into the shed through the door and through the propped-open corro vents along one wall.

The wool press and the skirting tables were long gone, but the pens waited, empty, where they'd once fed sheep to the shearers on the boards. She counted eight shearing stands, some of the old flywheels above still draped with electric cord. Behind where the shearers had stood, the chutes they'd pushed the shorn sheep down to the pens outside were draped with spiders' webs.

She shone her torch into the darker corners, where the moonlight did not reach. A stack of empty pallets leaned against one wall, some draped with old hessian wool sacks. The only signs of recent disturbance she could see in the shed were scuff marks in the dust around those pallets.

Whatever the guy had brought in had to be among the pallets. There was nowhere else to hide anything in the open shed. She pulled aside the wool sacks. The pallets were stacked haphazardly, some upright, some flat between them. But underneath the top flat one, the shine of metal glinted in the torchlight, and she shifted the pallet aside.

A large steel lockbox, the kind that most of the farmers and workers in the region had fitted on the back of their utes and trucks for tools and equipment. She had one herself, although this one was older, battered, and the latches had no padlocks.

Who would go to the trouble of stowing a large tool box in an empty woolshed, and hiding things in it?

Drugs, perhaps. Or reptiles or birds for smuggling. Or it could be . . . no, what he'd carried hadn't been big enough to be a body. Unless . . . She tried to veer her mind away from that thought.

Damned unlikely, but the possibility would haunt her if she didn't find out. And if it were reptiles or birds, then that was her responsibility, and the sooner they were freed the more chance they had of survival. The illegal wildlife trade was lucrative, increasing – and often deadly for the creatures. On other occasions she'd found animals stuffed in socks, sealed in cardboard tubes, and in boxes and tins, drugged, dehydrated, dying.

She doubted there'd be snakes loose in the box, but just in case – and to protect any fingerprints – she pulled on the leather work gloves she always carried in her backpack before she carefully lifted the lid.

A frayed poly feed bag covered the contents. She raised a corner of it, then more.

Nothing slithered or wriggled, and the torch light glinted on cold metal.

She exhaled a long, slow breath. Not reptiles, not birds, not drugs.

Weapons. At least two semi-automatic rifles, a pump-action rifle, and a couple of handguns visible in the top layers. She touched nothing, just shone the light around to get an estimate of the size of the box. Large enough to have more weapons beneath what she could see.

She swore under her breath. A cache this size, of this type, meant serious criminal business, not an amateur collection or a hiding place for someone's unlicensed guns.

She took her phone from her pocket – as she expected out here, no signal. And this wasn't something she was going to report on an open radio channel. Without moving anything, swapping her phone for her camera, she took a couple of shots, using the torch to provide light, then she replaced the feed bag and closed the lid of the box.

But as she slid the pallet back on top of it, she heard the rumble of an engine, and the glow from headlights shone in through the open door.

If the vehicle went straight past, it would be okay . . .

The engine changed down a gear or two, the vehicle slowing, the rumble sounding more like a large truck than a ute or a car as it turned on to the rough track to the shed.

Shit, shit, shit.

She huffed out a frustrated breath while she mentally raced through her options. She'd faced down illegal hunters in the past, confronted licensed shooters who'd strayed into the park, all just part of the job. But with murder, drugs and now weapons, she'd be stupid to take the risk without back-up.

She stuffed the torch into her pack, dragged the wool sacks back across the pallets, and crossed the floor quickly to the most distant shearing stand. Pushing her pack in front of her, she crawled into the sheep chute, dropping down out of sight under the woolshed, crouching in the darkness as the truck parked beside the shed. Doors slammed, and at least two pairs of heavy footsteps climbing the stairs sent vibrations through the timber building.

The moonlight didn't reach here, and she groped through the blackness and spider webs, easing her way past the old sheep pens, closer to the footsteps above. They'd gone straight to the stack of pallets, clearly not worrying about noise as they dragged them out of the way.

The thump of a pallet falling to the floor covered the gasp she couldn't quite stifle when something ripped into her upper arm with a sharp pain, cutting through her shirt and her skin. A nail, sticking out where one of the sheep pens had fallen apart. The wet warmth of blood trickled down her arm. She unhooked her shirt sleeve, pressed it against the wound, and stayed still, listening to the men's conversation.

'Is it there?'

'Yeah. They're all there. He found it in time.'

'Just as fucking well. Otherwise he'd have gone the same way as his stupid fucking mate.'

'Yeah.'

Jo crouched in the dark, fist against her mouth to stifle any sound. Travis Mitchell. Were they talking about him?

'Trying to rip off the boss. What a fucking fool.'

Metal scraped against the wooden floor. 'Yeah. Stop squawking and grab the other end. We ain't got all bloody night. Buyer'll be waiting and we don't want to fuck this up.'

Her heart pounded so sharply it almost hurt. She forcibly slowed her breathing, stayed entirely motionless, while they made their way back across the shed and down the stairs. She abandoned the brief idea of trying to photograph the truck's rego plates. Stay out of sight, stay safe, stay alive. If they didn't know she was here, they couldn't hurt her.

She didn't move until they'd loaded the box, reversed and swung back on to the track, headlights well away from her direction. Slipping to the edge of the shed, she stayed behind one of the thick support posts, noting what she could of the size and shape of the truck as it drove away in the moonlight.

When they were out of sight she emerged, her limbs shaking. She gulped in lungfuls of the night air, and then made her unsteady legs work well enough to run from the woolshed, back into the bush on the ridge.

SEVEN

The phone on the dashboard lit up, and seeing the number, he punched *answer* before it finished its first buzz.

'Jo! Where are you? Are you okay?' His headlights made ghostly shadows of the trees lining the dirt road ahead. With the few houses of Goodabri just behind him, it was still another ten minutes to the Riverbank homestead.

'I'm fine.' The breathless catch in her voice belied the words. 'Listen, there's an empty cattle truck heading west on the Derringvale Road with a stack of weapons.'

Derringvale – where was Derringvale? He tried to picture the map. North of Strathnairn. Maybe forty minutes west of Goodabri.

She hurried on. 'There are rifles, semi-autos, pump-action and handguns. It will probably be at the Derringvale Junction in less than fifteen minutes. If you can get a patrol up there you might be able to catch them. There are two men in the truck – and I think they're connected to the murder.'

He swore under his breath. 'Where the hell are you, Jo? You're not with them?' The thought of her huddling in the back of a truck with weapons and murderers made his mouth dry.

'No, they didn't see me. I'm near the McCulloch Downs woolshed, where the guns were hidden. It's off the Derringvale Road, about fifteen k's from Goodabri.'

He slammed down a couple of gears, veered to one side and spun the wheels as he did a U-turn on the dirt road, back towards the road he hoped led to Derringvale.

Fifteen kilometres from Goodabri. From his recollection of the map, there was nothing between the two towns, except grazing properties and the southern end of the National Park. And Jo was out there, probably alone.

'Stay on the line, Jo. I'll radio for any cars out that way. I'm on my way to you now.'

He put the call in on the radio, heard two cars respond from north of Derringvale. Depending on which way the truck turned at the junction, they might or might not catch it. Too far away himself to catch up with the truck, Jo's safety became his first priority.

'Jo, if I take the road that goes out past the Goodabri race course, is that the right road to get to where you are?'

'Yes.' She paused a moment, then asked, surprise in her tone, 'How come you're out there?'

'Looking for you.' His actions, his orders, would be the same for any witness potentially at risk – but not the worry eating at his control, and the frustration of the past hours, not knowing.

That was new, a level of anxiety he hadn't felt since his youth, looking out for his siblings. 'You haven't answered your phone for almost two hours.'

'Not much phone signal out this way. I've only just seen the messages.' Concern sharpened her voice. 'What's happened? Is everyone all right?'

'Yes.' Everyone but the Baxters, and she probably wasn't thinking of them just now. 'I'll fill you in when I get there. Are you somewhere safe?'

'Yes. Really. I'm up on a ridge in the one spot there's phone reception, perfectly safe, and I can see for miles around in the moonlight. If you put your emergency lights on as you approach, I'll know it's you. You're coming from Goodabri?'

'Yes. Just turning onto the Derringvale Road now. I'll be a few minutes yet.'

'You'll see my work truck when you get to Eight Mile Creek. Go past it, over the ridge, and the old woolshed is on your left. I'll meet you there. My battery's getting low, so I'm going to hang up now. I'll see you soon.'

The minutes, and the kilometres, seemed to go inexorably slowly, even though he took the dirt road as fast as he dared in the darkness. He turned on the unmarked car's police lights when he crossed Five Mile Creek, the strobing blue and red flashing from the grill casting eerie flickers on the road ahead.

At Eight Mile Creek her truck sat on the side of the road, dark and deserted. Over the rise and out of the park, the farmland spread before him, well lit under a full silver moon, the woolshed and its outbuildings easy to see among a small cluster of trees.

He'd forgotten how bright a full moon could be when there were no other lights competing with it. Bright enough to cast shadows, bright enough to see without a torch.

Bright enough that when he'd parked beside the woolshed and switched off the headlights, he could see her sitting on a fence post, waiting for him. She slipped off the post and walked towards him, the soft, pearly moonlight silhouetting her, slim and lithe, her head haloed by wisps of windblown hair that had escaped from her ponytail, almost ethereal.

Dammit, where had that thought come from? It wasn't like him. Fatigue, worry and relief must be scrambling his brain. He dealt in facts, not fairytales.

And she was no goddess or spirit, but an entirely down-to-earth woman, her uniform trousers grimy at the knees, a dark stain on one sleeve and blood trickling down her arm.

'You're hurt. What happened?'

She glanced at her arm and gave an unconcerned shrug. 'Just scraped my arm on a nail. I washed it, but if you have a first-aid kit, it could do with a little more disinfectant than the couple of wipes I had.'

'There's a kit in the car. While I clean it up, you can fill me in on events.'

She sat on the woolshed steps, and he switched the headlights back on to give more light.

'I warn you,' she said, as he joined her with the kit. 'Tonight's perfume is Eau de Woolshed, featuring base notes of well-rotted sheep manure, with subtle highlights of old lanolin. I'd take shallow breaths if I were you.'

Despite her attempt to make light of things, he could see the fine lines of strain around her eyes, the effort to smile, the weariness in her shoulders. She must have been worn out, because she let him examine the wound on the back of her upper arm instead of trying to do it herself. Her shirt sleeve had ripped, and the ragged cut, a couple of inches long, still seeped blood.

He sat on the step behind her, first-aid supplies in easy reach beside him. Beneath the whiffs of Eau de Woolshed he caught the scent of something lightly floral, and he had to drag his brain away from dwelling on the smooth skin under his fingers and the elegant curve of neck and shoulder to concentrate on crime and his responsibilities to investigate it. 'What the hell happened, Jo? Erin Taylor said you were going to release an animal and then head home. That was hours ago.'

'That plan worked fine until the "head home" part.'

He worked silently while she explained, briefly and concisely, what she'd witnessed. No drama in the telling, although her jaw tightened and the muscles in her neck tensed as she spoke of waiting for long minutes in the sheep pens under the woolshed while the two men were inside. She'd been scared, well aware of the danger.

'I'm sorry, I don't have a description or photos of the truck or the guys who took the guns. Hiding seemed the wisest course of action, in the circumstances.'

He carefully taped a dressing over the wound, making himself breathe in and out, slowly. If she had been discovered . . .

If she'd been discovered, she'd likely be dead by now. Whether or not the comments she'd overhead referred to Mitchell's murder, crims who dealt in quantities of illegal weapons did not leave witnesses alive to report the matter. It would have been easy – too easy – to commit murder here in this isolated place and to conceal a body where it might never be found.

The notion of Jo dead – or worse, tortured as Mitchell had been – tested Nick's control, and he averted his face, packing up the first-aid kit to avoid exposing the unaccustomed, inexplicable emotion.

Plan, act, protect. Emotion had no place in what he had to do.

'If you're able to drive,' he told her, as he carried the kit back to the car, 'I'll take you to your truck, and then I'll follow you back to your place. I'll organise a couple of officers to protect you there tonight.'

'Protect me?' She pushed herself up off the step. 'These guys don't know I was there. I'm in no danger from them.'

'That's not the main reason I'm worried.' He didn't beat around the bush. 'Jo, a couple were murdered last night in Queensland. Set up to look like a gas-bottle explosion in their caravan, but the detective I spoke with is fairly certain they were shot at close range first. They're still to be formally identified, but it's likely they're—'

Her face paled as she interrupted him. 'Tom and Shirley Baxter.'

'Yes. The car and the van are registered to Tom Baxter.'

Biting her lip, she turned away, her breathing ragged as if she were holding back tears. 'Their daughter's due to have a baby soon,' she said after a moment. 'They were thrilled about becoming grandparents.'

How many times had he heard something like that? A new baby, a new job, retirement – always a reason why the dead should not be dead. And yet they were.

'It's never fair, Jo,' he said, cursing himself for the empty platitude. Sixteen years of policing and he still had no useful words to offer.

She dragged the heel of her hand over her eyes and gave him an apologetic glance. 'Sorry. It's not as though I actually knew them. But they seemed a lovely couple, very happy together. The way it should be.'

The way it should be . . . He hadn't read her as a romantic, yet out of all that had happened, this was one of the few events to crumple her composure.

She blinked again, tight and slow to gain control. Within seconds she'd focused on the issues, the practical implications. 'You're worried that the motorcyclist is connected. The Baxters saw him, probably spoke with him, and now they're dead.'

'Yes. Aaron told me about your visitor last night. If the men you overheard tonight are connected with the murder – I think it's likely – then chances are "the boss" they spoke of has a number of people working for him.' A number of people killing for him, as they'd killed Mitchell. Nick's gut instinct shouted that the motorcyclist could well be the 'boss'. 'We can't take any risks, Jo. You saw him too. You can identify him and place him at the scene. I want you under protection at all times until we have some more answers.'

Her face set, she nodded without arguing, and when he held the passenger door of his car open for her she got in without hesitation. He drove her the short distance to her truck and then followed close behind her along the winding dirt roads until they reached the homestead.

And all the way, he turned the facts of the case over in his mind, searching for answers. Three murders, drugs, weapons, an unidentified motorcyclist and an identified, but dead, ex-con. An ex-con who'd stolen a rifle, tried to cheat his boss? That could add up – losing a hand was a traditional punishment for theft. But that was only one piece of a larger puzzle, and he still had to work out how to fit all of the pieces together.

⁓

The corrugated iron of the homestead roof shone in the moonlight as she approached, the house itself still and dark, a familiar haven. Not much prospect of the quiet, early night she'd hoped for, though, with all that had happened to distract her, and the likelihood of strangers guarding her.

A police car waited in the driveway, but it was Aaron, not a stranger, standing beside it.

'Hi, Jo,' he greeted her through the window. 'Nick radioed ahead that you were on the way, and asked me to meet you both here. I've checked the garage and around the house, and there's no sign of intruders.'

He'd left room for her to drive past his car to park in the garage. Dropping her head on the steering wheel for a moment after she'd switched off the engine, she tried to gather enough courage and mental energy to face the challenge ahead. If she'd discovered Travis Mitchell's body days or weeks after his death, there would have been no clear date of death, nothing to connect him with any visitors to the park. But she'd discovered him within hours, while recent events and visitors were still fresh in her mind, and potentially in the minds of others.

As much as she hated the thought of being under guard in her own home, she didn't need convincing that the risk was real. The Baxters were dead, murdered, and if she hadn't woken up yesterday afternoon, if Erin hadn't arrived, she might not be sitting here now.

And she shouldn't be sitting here, but getting out and going inside . . .

Nick waited for her just inside the garage, and when she took her backpack and the cooler box out of the back of the truck, he picked up the esky.

'I can carry it,' she protested.

'So can I,' he answered mildly.

Not much point insisting on her independence in the circumstances, especially over such a small thing.

She led the way along the back veranda to the kitchen door. As she unlocked it, Nick and Aaron both moved to enter before her, hands hovering near their guns. Both serious, both intent on their duty, working silently together as if they'd done this a thousand times before.

While they checked the house for intruders, she dumped her backpack on a chair, flicked the electric kettle on and grabbed mugs, tea and coffee from a shelf. Easy, practical tasks that almost kept her thoughts from the reality of having police officers with guns in her home.

'I don't know about you guys,' she said when they returned, 'but I'm hanging out for a cup of tea. And a shower.' *And five minutes' peace and quiet to get myself together.* 'You'll probably both be glad if I have one. Help yourselves to coffee and anything else you want. There are some bacon and cheese scrolls in the freezer if you're hungry. I'll be back by the time the tea's brewed.'

She fled to the privacy of her bedroom, the sound of voices following her as the two men began to patrol around outside the house. She should have joined them, showed them the layout and the sheds, instead of walking out on them and hiding. She just couldn't . . .

Yes, you can, she told herself. Shower, change and go back into the kitchen. Composed and ready to deal with the situation. In control.

Less than ten minutes later, out of the shower, she brushed the last of the spiders' webs out of her wet hair, and pulled on cargo pants and a T-shirt.

Ready to return to the others, she put a hand on the door knob. In control. Mostly. Scared and tired and worried and still grappling with shock about the Baxters, but composed enough that she wouldn't fall to pieces on anyone.

'I reckon the sheds are the danger spot, this one in particular,' Aaron was saying as she approached the kitchen. 'Anybody could sneak down the hillside at night – or even in daylight – and hide until they find an opportunity.'

Her bare feet made no sound on the timber floor. Nick was the first to see her come through the door, looking up from the hand-drawn diagram lying on the table, as if he'd caught her movement in his peripheral vision.

She thought she saw an instant of surprise widen his eyes, but maybe she'd imagined it, for he acknowledged her return with a bare nod before including her in the conversation.

'The sheds – can they be locked?'

'The large machinery shed, yes,' she answered. 'But the tool shed doesn't have much of a lock on it. We don't keep anything valuable in there.'

She pulled up one of the vacant chairs, looking quickly over the diagram of the homestead buildings as she reached for the teapot and the mug waiting for her. They'd got the layout of the place pretty right, even after only a few minutes' survey.

'If we park the tractor right in front of the tool-shed door, no-one would be able to get inside. The door opens outwards,' she explained.

But that only solved a small part of the problem. The diagram only reflected the buildings. The reality of the situation was more complex, with extensive wooded areas to the north and west, reaching up the hill behind the homestead.

'How would you do it, if you were a crim?' Aaron asked Nick, and then flushed. 'Sorry, Sarge, I didn't mean . . .'

The undercurrent in Aaron's flush and Nick's impassive expression brought the rumours Erin had mentioned to mind, but he answered the question with only a trace of dry coolness in his tone. 'A sniper shot from the hillside back here, assuming there's tree cover. And assuming a simple elimination of the target is the objective.'

And there was something in that stony face that said he could do it – wait motionless in the bush, watch for the target, take precise aim, pull the trigger.

A simple elimination of the target . . . The stark, emotionless words referred not to a kangaroo, or a wild dog or boar, but to her.

EIGHT

He'd scared her, and he'd meant to. He wanted Jo to understand just how easy – too easy – it would be for someone determined to kill her. Acting alone, the sniper shot would be the simplest. But if the killer didn't care about attracting attention and collateral damage, and had assistance and weaponry, then nowhere would be safe. A raid with several guys and semi-automatics blazing, and they could all be dead within minutes.

Although few groups would be brazen enough to run that kind of attack, signs pointed towards the possibility. The mob violence of Mitchell's death indicated that a group already bound by murder existed in the area; the weapons Jo had found, if connected, gave them firepower.

He shoved away the image of this peaceful country kitchen strafed by gunfire, the red pottery teapot shattering, Jo falling, blood-spattered and lifeless.

He couldn't let that happen, had to keep her safe.

'Are there still rooms at the hotel in Goodabri, Aaron?'

'No. The Goodabri Show is on this weekend. I booked the last two rooms for Dalton and Brock.'

How could he protect Jo with the few resources the district commander, Keith Murdoch, had given him? Overtime for just one officer to stay with her. Plus himself, because he'd be damned if he left her and something happened.

He didn't have many options. 'I'll call Hugh. You should be able to stay in Shelley Brock's room.'

Jo didn't object, but her nod lacked enthusiasm. As he scrolled for Hugh's number on his mobile, she said, 'Reception's scratchy out here. Use the landline.' She indicated the phone on the wall as she rose from the table. 'While you're doing that, I'll get my laptop and download tonight's photos.'

Aaron's chair scraped as he stood. 'I'll go round the house, check the doors and windows are secure.'

Nick nodded his approval. Thorough and dedicated, Aaron, with more experience, would make an excellent detective. Unlike some he'd worked with.

'You can't put her in with Shelley, mate,' Hugh said when Nick outlined his request. 'She's . . .' The hesitation gave him away. 'She's pretty buggered. Didn't get much sleep last night. And there's only one bed in her room.'

Which Hugh was sharing. The self-satisfied amusement and innuendo made that obvious. Leaning against the wall by the phone, Nick gritted his teeth in silence. Hugh had always had plenty of lovers, but a junior officer, on a job, broke both rules and ethics. With Jo returning to the room with her laptop, he couldn't respond in the blunt terms that immediately came to mind.

'That's . . . *unfortunate*,' he said, his coolness loading the word with censure.

Hugh merely laughed. 'Jealous? Oh, well, you can keep your Doctor Lockwood company tonight.'

He made an effort to restrain his anger. 'I didn't hear that, Hugh. I'll see you at the briefing in the morning.'

He cut the connection, swearing silently. Damn Hugh and his cowboy attitude. He'd always been a good cop, despite his propensity to skate around the edge of proper procedure. But now alarm bells were ringing, loud and clear, in Nick's mind. Sometime, in the past couple of years since he'd spent any time with him, Hugh's idiosyncrasies had become more pronounced. If that was affecting his professional judgement, Nick would have to act.

Jo glanced up from plugging the laptop into a socket. 'Is there a problem?'

Even without hearing Hugh's side, she couldn't have missed the tension in the phone conversation. Or Nick's abrupt end to it, jamming the handset into its cradle.

Too aware of her ability to read him, he returned to the table and his rapidly cooling mug of coffee. 'The plan to have you stay in Shelley Brock's hotel room isn't going to work. Is there other accommodation in Goodabri or nearby?'

'There are a couple of very basic cabins at the caravan park.' She flipped open the computer and booted it. 'But it's right next to the showground, and all the showies are already there, to set up for tomorrow. Showies are mostly fine, but I'd feel safer here.'

No argument from him on that. A showground full of itinerant sideshow workers that could at times attract a rough element didn't constitute 'safety' in his definition. He made a mental note to check if Travis Mitchell had any connections with the sideshow circuit.

Jo rested her chin on her palm, watching him over the screen. 'Nick, I know this homestead. I know the house, the outbuildings, the land around it – even in the dark. The home-ground advantage has to count for something, and your colleagues at Goodabri are only ten minutes away. It's as safe as any other place I can think of in this area.'

He could take her into Strathnairn – but to where? The motel he was staying in fronted the highway on the edge of town, with bushland behind it. No more secure than this. And he didn't know the town well enough yet to be familiar with the other motels.

Aaron's footsteps sounded along the corridor, and he stifled a yawn in the doorway. 'Everything's secure. There are decent locks on all the doors and windows, Sarge.'

Locks wouldn't stop bullets, but they'd slow down an assault, give at least a few seconds' warning. With two armed officers, and Jo's familiarity with the environs, it would have to be enough.

Running low on alternatives, he made up his mind and looked squarely at Jo. 'You can stay here, with police protection, for tonight, Jo. I'll remain on watch, and I'll see if I can call a female officer in as well.'

Relief in her eyes, she smiled slightly. 'It's the twenty-first century, Nick,' she said. 'I'm sure your female colleagues have more important things to do than play chaperone.'

'I'll take a watch, too,' Aaron offered. 'That way we can sleep in shifts.'

'Shouldn't you and Aaron be off-duty? It's getting late, and you've been on the go all day.'

He swallowed another mouthful of coffee, the coolness dulling the caffeine kick in his brain. Off-duty? The job took as long as it took. The rhythm of work and sleep underscored his life. After ten years living immersed in undercover roles, little else remained.

'Unless you have an objection, I'm staying,' Nick said.

Nothing in her body language or expression suggested discomfort. She'd relaxed as soon as he'd said she could stay at the homestead.

'I live way the other side of Strathnairn, Jo,' Aaron said. 'Not much point driving all that way when I'd only get a couple of hours' sleep before I have to come back. So it's actually easier to stay here.'

'You can use the bunks in the room opposite mine,' Jo said. 'Make yourselves at home. It's not much, but you should be comfortable enough. We could all do with some sleep. I'm planning to head to bed, just as soon as I download these photos for you.'

Sleep would be a long time coming, if at all. On the pretext of getting his own laptop from the car, Nick stepped out into the night, pausing on the veranda to survey the moonlit grounds, listening for movement. A possum scrambled over the fence, away from him, and some kind of owl hooted nearby. Otherwise it was quiet and still – a stark contrast to the constant city sounds he'd become used to.

In the car, he radioed in, requesting a patrol to cruise nearby roads, and relaying enough of his plans that anyone listening in would know that Jo was not unprotected and alone.

Alone. Other than colleagues, she'd made no mention of friends, or family, or a lover. She lived by herself out here in the bush, yet with her easy manner and occasional light teasing she didn't give the impression of a recluse or even an introvert.

She'd only lived a few months in the district, so perhaps close friendships were still to come. Or maybe she still grieved for Leonardo Rossetti.

He slid the report from the coroner's office into his laptop case before he picked up the overnight bag he'd taken to Newcastle. He would read the report tonight, find out if there was any evidence at all for Hugh's suspicions.

No point denying it, curiosity drove him more than doubt. Curiosity about Jo, and the man she'd loved, as much as the circumstances of his death. He needed to untangle the interests of the case and his attraction to Jo. Go back into the kitchen, set up his laptop and work.

Only a few more minutes, and she'd probably go to her room and close the door.

Only a few more minutes, and the hyper-awareness that tensed his body would ease, once he no longer had her in such close proximity. A witness, under his protection – that put her even further off limits than a colleague.

Intellectually, he knew it. But ever since she'd walked back into the homestead kitchen after her shower, her hair loose about her shoulders, the masculine khaki shirt replaced by the simple T-shirt that clung softly to her curves . . . ever since then, the low-level awareness of her had ratcheted up multiple notches, and his subconscious kept taunting him with how good it might feel to brush his fingers over her cheek, to touch the smoothness of her skin, and to simply put his arms around her and hold her body close to his.

CS

The curtains she'd never before drawn across the kitchen window deprived potential snipers from a line of sight, but they also deprived Jo of her customary view across the back yard. Bright, 1970s-style gold, orange and brown circles blurred in front of her eyes instead of the moonlit silhouettes of trees and sheds.

A wave of claustrophobia threatened, her pulse kicking up, her brain telling her to move. Stupid, stupid, that the room so familiar to her seemed so small, dark and stuffy with the windows covered.

She turned her back to the window. *Breathe.* She couldn't feed the fear and adrenaline. Calm thoughts, a mug of chamomile tea, and some distraction, and she would hopefully unwind enough to sleep. Nick and Aaron were here, and she would be safe.

With her focus firmly on the kettle, not the window, she refilled it and set it to re-boil.

Aaron's muted voice, out on the veranda phoning his housemate, altered tone as he exchanged a few comments with Nick, before Nick came back inside carrying a laptop and an overnight bag. The fluorescent lights cast harsh shadows on his face, accentuating the lines of worry around his eyes. Not a man who smiled a great deal, despite the seeming ease of yesterday's not-quite-playboy grin. Did the weight of duty ever lift enough for him to relax and put his own needs first? Did he have a partner, a wife, a friend to support him through the tough times?

She pushed that thought away. No business of hers what he did off-duty, how he dealt with the stresses of his job. But making his burden as light as possible by being positive and uncomplaining was well within her power.

'I've put pillows and bedding on the bunks in the spare room for you and Aaron. The bedding's basic camping stuff – we're not a luxury resort,' she added, keeping her tone cheerful. 'There is, however, decent coffee and tea.'

He relaxed enough for the side of his mouth to quirk. 'That ranks it several stars above many places I've stayed. Decent coffee is usually only a luxury.'

'Help yourself any time you want, it's in the cupboard.'

'Thank you, I will. I could do with another caffeine shot to keep me going.'

Always that quiet courtesy from him, respect for her in his understated good manners.

He rinsed the cold grounds from the plunger and tossed in several heaped scoops of fresh coffee. He wasn't intending to sleep anytime soon, apparently. Perhaps if she went to her room and he thought she was sleeping, he might relax his guard a little.

The photo download complete, she quickly clicked through the images. She'd almost forgotten the sugar glider – it seemed days, rather than hours, since she'd released it – but she'd lucked on a good shot of it escaping the cage.

The photos that followed didn't make her smile. Some of the images of the man going into the woolshed were blurred, or underexposed. A couple were clear, including one where she'd caught him with the zoom, almost face-on, his features lit by his car headlights.

The two she'd snapped of the weapons were reasonably well exposed, at least where the circle of torchlight fell on them. She made a copy of both images, adjusting the exposure and contrast settings to make the shapes of the guns beyond the central lit area clearer.

Aaron returned, calling out to identify himself before lightly rapping on the locked front door. Nick rose to let him in, and Jo watched him check through the blinds before opening the door.

Cautious, not taking any risks with their safety. Her safety.

Hopefully the images might help the case move forward.

'You'll want to see these, Nick,' she said, before he returned to his chair.

He stood behind her, looking over her shoulder, Aaron beside him.

'You can't see it so well in this image, but this one—' She indicated the area on the screen, 'It was definitely a pump-action, and you can see the two semi-autos.'

'Looks like a couple of handguns underneath. That could well be the magazine of another semi-auto.' Crowded as they were around the table, his arm inadvertently brushed her shoulder as he pointed, and she stared at the screen, drawing on all her willpower to ignore the wave of awareness and the jumbled mix of reactions to his nearness.

He moved away, pouring another mug of coffee as he asked, 'How big did you say the box was?'

'Over a metre long, a good half a metre wide and deep. You can see it's pretty full. There's at least a dozen, maybe more weapons in there.'

'Quite a haul,' Aaron commented. 'We've had a few reports of stolen rifles in the past four months or so, but not that many.'

'I saw the open files,' Nick said. 'No-one's going to report an illegal weapon missing, though, and I'm guessing some of these aren't legal. Jo, is there much hunting around the area? Do you know any of the professional shooters?'

'We had a feral-goat-control campaign in the new park not long after I came here, so I can give you names and contact details of some of the professionals. Mal will know more. I don't know much about the recreational hunters. They often come from outside the area. If you can find this guy, though, you'll find out where he got at least one of the guns.'

She flicked back a couple of images, so that the man she'd seen filled the screen. Young, maybe late teens or early twenties, he had a round, boyish face that should have been grinning. Instead, the tightness in his expression, the furtive, slightly sideways glance, suggested worry, or fear.

'Shit,' Aaron swore behind her. 'I think I know who he is. Can I . . . ?'

She made way for him, and he sat at the laptop, studying the image on the screen.

Nick drank a mouthful of coffee while he waited. Not exactly patiently – he fixed his attention on the screen, too – but without pushing Aaron for more information immediately.

Aaron dragged a hand through his hair as he faced his boss. 'Jesus, Sarge, I can't be a hundred per cent sure, but . . . the detective before you – Garry Coulter – I saw him at the pub not long before he died, with a guy he said was his nephew. Don't know his name, though, the sarge never introduced him. But I'm fairly certain it's this bloke. They weren't happy – looked like they'd been arguing. Come to think of it, Gazza was pretty stressed, all round that time. Something was worrying him.'

'He was stressed? How did he die?' Nick asked sharply.

'Car accident.' Aaron's face drained of colour. 'On the Derringvale Road, not far from McCulloch's woolshed. He must have fallen asleep at the wheel or something. Rammed into a tree on a straight section of the road. Car was burned out before he was found.'

Jo clasped her hands around her mug. Where the hell was that herbal calm?

'It could just be a coincidence.' Who was she trying to convince? Herself? Certainly, a moment of distraction, a nano-sleep, or a swerve to avoid an animal could all so easily result in a deadly accident on rural roads. She'd not met Coulter, but his nephew was involved with the stolen weapons, and Coulter had died close to the place they were hidden. She didn't like the chances of coincidence.

Beside her, Nick's stillness radiated tension.

'Aaron, we need to look for connections,' he said after a moment. 'We've got rifle thefts going back nine weeks or so, and Coulter died about six weeks ago. We'll review the accident investigation and his case notes, and we need to find the nephew.'

The draught from the overhead fan blew cold on her neck and shoulders, and she stepped away from the stream of air.

'Your safety is a top priority, Jo,' Nick said quietly, as though he'd seen her involuntary shiver and guessed her train of thought. 'I'll ensure that you're protected at all times until we've arrested the perpetrators.'

'Thank you.' He deserved the courtesy of her gratitude, even if the last thing she wanted was to go into hiding, denied her normal life, without her space and independence. But there were at least three deaths already – four, if Garry Coulter's death was suspicious – and she would do whatever she could to avoid adding to the tally.

NINE

The beeping of his phone alarm dragged Nick from a deep sleep. Groping for the phone, forcing his eyes open, recognition of his surroundings took his brain a sluggish half-second. Six-thirty. Sitting on a bunk, having attempted to stop himself from falling into a deep sleep, a couple of pillows cushioning the bars between his back and the wall. No sign of Aaron, only Jo passing the open door of the room, in a blue cotton robe, her hair loose over her shoulders.

A cramp shot through his bad thigh as he too-quickly swung his legs to the floor, so that he had to dig the heel of his hand again and again into the muscle to release it.

So much for being ready to defend Jo in an instant. So much for showing no weakness.

Jo was either tactfully giving him privacy as he woke, or she hadn't glanced through the door as she passed, so she didn't see his moment of near-helplessness.

The sound of running water from the bathroom down the corridor answered the question of Aaron's whereabouts.

Standing, he adjusted his weapon belt over the jeans and T-shirt he'd worn to sleep in, and went into the kitchen.

'Morning,' Jo greeted him with a smile, spooning tea into the ever-present red teapot. 'I won't ask if you slept well, because Aaron said you didn't wake him to take over until after three.'

'I had enough to keep me going.'

Not that he'd drifted off immediately, despite his exhaustion, his thoughts too preoccupied to easily silence. It hadn't just been the unanswered questions about the crimes. While on watch last night he'd read the coroner's report into Leonardo Rossetti's death.

Despite the coroner's careful, objective language, the events described were chilling, and had haunted his dreams when he'd finally slept. Two ten-year-old boys missing in rugged country. A desperate twelve-hour search by volunteer emergency services, police and National Parks staff before forecast wild storms arrived, and the hard decision to call off the search at dusk. Stranded by flash flooding and downed trees, Jo and her fiancé had hiked to higher ground, Rossetti going to the edge of the bluff to check for any sign of the kids in the valley below. In the gale-force winds, a falling tree branch had struck him hard, knocking him over the edge. With no chance of a rescue team until daylight, Jo had climbed down to him, stayed with him on a narrow ledge all night while his internal injuries slowly killed him.

Despite Hugh's proclaimed suspicions, it was *that* action that convinced Nick of her innocence. A murderer wouldn't put themselves at significant risk, climbing down a cliff face in a ferocious storm, to stay with an injured person for hours. That could only have been an act of dedication. Or of love.

He could scarcely imagine how harrowing it must have been for her. What Hugh interpreted as coldness Nick recognised as control, a personal armour protecting deep emotions. Even her humour served as protection, keeping those emotions private. Not unlike himself.

Her strength, intelligence and courage, both physical and emotional, impressed him. Attracted him, if he was honest. Invaded his thoughts and his dreams. Made him envious of a dead man.

Hell, he needed to get some mental distance. Sane, professional distance.

Oblivious to his wayward thoughts, at ease in her own environment, Jo reached for the container in the cupboard and asked over her shoulder, 'How would you like your morning coffee?'

'By the litre.' Okay, so friendly humour probably didn't count as professional distance – but with Jo, it came more naturally than detachment. He opened his laptop, in the vain hope that distraction might work better.

'Not a morning person, huh?'

'I cope.' Late nights, early mornings, lack of sleep – he coped with it all on a regular basis. Everything except sharing his waking moments with an interesting, beautiful, out-of-bounds woman. Definitely out of practice at that.

Emails. He'd check his emails, drink his coffee, wash, shave and dress, and arrange protection for her for the rest of the day.

'I presume I won't be working out in the field today?' she asked, bringing over his coffee.

'Not today.' He ran through some logistics in his head. 'As long as there are other staff around, either in your office or our operations room, you could work indoors.'

She gave an exaggerated grimace. 'Oh, good. I just love days filled with paperwork.' Her light-hearted tone made it more self-deprecating joke than complaint. 'Which would be why,' she added, 'even though I was stuck there all yesterday, there's still enough on my desk to keep me busy for a week.'

'You and me both. I'd far rather be out catching the bad guys than compiling statistical reports.'

Standing by the table, sipping her tea, the blue Japanese-style fabric of her robe shaping softly over her lithe, feminine curves, Jo seemed more at ease than he felt. With a small smile, she commented, 'Well, since I won't get my life back until you get this lot of bad guys, I'm all in favour of you ditching the reports for now.'

Since he wouldn't get his equilibrium and effortless detachment back until she was no longer in close proximity, ditching everything but the investigation worked for him.

None of them had eaten dinner the night before, but with Nick and Aaron due at an early briefing in Goodabri there was little time for a hearty breakfast. Jo grabbed some fruit bread out of the freezer and set Aaron to toasting it while she dressed in a clean uniform and brushed her hair.

An electric razor hummed in the bathroom, and the acrid

smell of burned toast wafted from the kitchen. Almost like an ordinary morning, when members of her team stayed overnight. Except these were police officers, not rangers, and while Aaron buttered toast his handgun sat securely in its holster on his hip.

When Nick returned to the kitchen, shaved and changed back into business trousers and white shirt, his grim expression held no hint of relaxation or the humour he had shown just minutes earlier.

'We'll need to get there early,' he said, shutting down his laptop. 'I'll have your building checked out before you go in, Jo, and I'll find a female officer to stay with you today.'

Despite the butter and marmalade, her toast tasted dry in her mouth. She hadn't objected to working in her office, with the police next door, but someone staying with her and cluttering up her space all day? She washed her mouthful down with luke-warm tea. 'Is that really necessary? When there are cops just next door?'

He watched her, as if assessing how much of a fight she would put up, and replied evenly, 'Most of them will be out on the job during the day. So, yes, I think it's important that there's at least one officer assigned specifically to you.'

Damn. She could understand the rationale, but she didn't look forward to it.

She pushed a plate of toast towards him. 'Eat some. You won't be much use to anyone if you collapse from lack of food.'

He ate on his feet, packing away his laptop, retrieving his overnight bag from the bunk room. He finished his second piece of toast as they walked to his car, while he gave instructions to Aaron to follow them in.

He was silent in the car, preoccupied with his thoughts, and she might have let him remain that way if it weren't for the restlessness of her own mind, and the need to focus on *something* other than that unease.

'You don't ever stop for long, do you? You know, for incidentals like food and sleep.'

He threw her a quick glance. 'Not when there are murderers, guns and drugs out there.'

'But aren't there always murderers, guns and drugs out there?'

He slowed for the turn into Goodabri, the indicator clicking loudly in the silence, his profile sharp and unsmiling. 'Yes,' he said after a moment. 'There always are. Too many.'

They drove without talking through the quiet, early-morning streets of Goodabri, with fifteen minutes to spare before the briefing.

He turned into the lane behind the shop buildings, and through the open gate into the shared yard. Surrounded by a less-than-sturdy timber paling fence, the yard had a derelict wooden shed, a gravelled area for five or six cars to park, and a patch of grass that had long ago ceased to be either lawn or green.

The small crowd of police officers on the grass set her pulse drumming, until she saw that they were cheering on a pair of fighters.

'What the . . . ?' Nick muttered, his attention half on them as he pulled in to park close to the door of her office.

She had a better view from her side of the car. 'It's Hugh Dalton. And Nate Harrison. But it's okay – they're grinning.'

Nick swore and slammed his car door, and Jo kept pace with him as he strode across to the group. The six officers watching the tussle made way for them, just as Nate threw Hugh to the ground and held him there.

Lying on the ground, Hugh laughed. 'Good one, Harrison.' With a quick jerk of his body and a punch, he dislodged Harrison, sent him crashing to the ground, and then rolled away and stood up, brushing dead grass off his shirt. 'Hiya, Nick. Thought we'd start the day with a short training session, get the metabolism going, since Harrison here was bragging at the pub last night that he's a black belt in Tae Kwon Do.'

Nick didn't smile, coolness in his hard face and his cross-armed stance. 'You must be losing your skills, Hugh, if he dropped you.'

'Nah, I was just letting him think he had me.'

A few of the watchers snickered, but Jo couldn't discern in that confident grin whether he spoke the truth or was simply saving face. A testosterone-fuelled performance, either way, with the competitive mood spreading – already infecting those watching, keen for excitement.

Still performing the alpha-male role, still grinning, Dalton turned to his opponent, already back on his feet. 'Hey, Harrison, I bet you a hundred bucks you can't drop Nick.'

Harrison's eyes lit up. 'You serious, Sarge?'

Nick's coolness dropped to arctic chill. 'I'm not playing games, Hugh. We've got work to do.'

'Are you getting past it, Nick? The body not what it used to be? Too old?' Hugh's mock concern had to be intended to taunt.

Nick didn't blink, didn't react at all. 'Too busy. Carruthers, you and I will check the Parks office is safe before Jo goes in.' He turned on his heel and walked away.

She saw Matt Carruthers' hesitation, heard Hugh's chuckle, but she followed Nick, only a couple of steps behind. Two quick footfalls on the dry ground, a catch of breath, and a flash of blue uniform passed her, lunging at Nick.

Her warning shout faded in her throat, already too late.

Nick's reactions, far quicker than hers, had Nate Harrison flipped onto his back on the ground in what seemed a single, smooth move.

Nate swore; Hugh and the others laughed. Nick silently held out a hand to Nate, helped him to his feet.

Hugh joined them, clapping Nate on the back, all masculine mateship. 'I may have neglected to mention, Harrison, that Nick has cupboards stuffed with black belts and dan scrolls, and is feared by street fighters from Cairns to Hobart. So I'll waive the hundred bucks you owe me. Okay, everyone, fun's over. Briefing starts in four minutes. Carruthers, Harrison, make sure Doctor Lockwood's office is clear, and do it quickly.'

Jo watched Hugh stride away. Interesting how he'd done that – switched effortlessly from one-of-the-guys to commander, from irresponsible larrikin to dedicated officer. How he'd managed the whole scene so that Nick's new colleagues had witnessed his skills, and strengths, in action, yet none of them – not even Harrison – came out of it looking a fool. Interesting, too, the tension between Hugh and Nick, Hugh's competitiveness, Nick's impassiveness.

Not quite impassive. As he took his laptop from the back of the car and locked the doors, the hard line of his mouth and jaw hinted at temper and displeasure.

'A cupboard full of black belts and dan scrolls?' she asked as he joined her again.

He shook his head. 'I only kept the few that matter.'

The few that matter . . . Matt and Nate swung out the door of her building, announcing it all clear, before she could find words to ask what mattered to him and why.

But as he held the door open for her, he added, his voice flat, 'I've been fighting since I was a kid, Jo. I had to be good at it. It's not something I'm proud of.'

He turned away abruptly and walked into the adjacent building, without waiting for her response or looking at her again.

She shut the door behind her, locked it and leaned against it, her thoughts whirling, trying to process all those new facets of Nick and piece them together with what she knew already.

A complex, layered man, practised at concealing his emotions – yep, that summed up Nick Matheson. But her initial instincts, days ago, hadn't been far wrong, and perhaps his physical fighting skills shouldn't have surprised her. He did, after all, have a superb body, lean and fit and muscled, even though she was doing her damnedest not to notice it. Or to think about it.

She pushed herself away from the door and went into her office. As she switched on her computer and waited for it to boot, the fight scene replayed in her mind, and two points stood out clearly: Nick had no taste for violence, and had bested Nate without hurting him at all; and Nick and Hugh had a long history, and not necessarily a happy one.

121

She shook her head in frustration as if that physical act might dislodge the stubborn thoughts. The relationship between Nick and Hugh was no business of hers. *Nick* was no business of hers. They might have been thrown together the past couple of days due to the investigation, but her involvement would be over, soon enough, and all she needed to do in the meantime was cooperate when requested, a professional, responsible citizen.

The very last thing she needed in her life was a complex, intense man who could disturb – shatter – the emotional balance she'd finally found.

༉

Hugh started the briefing as Nick walked in to the ops room and he propped on a table at the back and studied him while he gave the rundown of the previous day's developments and events.

On the surface Hugh seemed unchanged, with the same brash energy he'd had twenty years ago as a wily, smart-mouthed kid on Newcastle's toughest streets, only lightly smoothed after fifteen years of policing. The whole scene outside had been typically Hugh.

But under that confident surface Nick could discern cracks. Dark smudges under his eyes. Tiny hesitations in his speech. An edge of brittleness in his top-cop performance, and, most telling, his frequent micro-glances towards Nick.

The Hugh of old was skilled enough to avoid acknowledging a rival. Two years Hugh's senior, responsible for him, Nick had channelled the kid's naturally competitive streak by challenging him, fighting him, letting Hugh compete with him. A tradition of competition Hugh had continued into adulthood, into the police service, a constant in their relationship. Like this morning.

So Hugh's inability to conceal the hyper-awareness in a setting as familiar as a case briefing was a dead giveaway that something was up.

Nervousness? Lack of confidence? Complex though this case might be, Hugh had worked plenty of tough ones in the past.

Hiding something? Nick scanned the room. Shelley Brock sat in the middle, a couple of local cops on either side. Interesting that she'd placed herself there, and not at the front near Hugh. Even more interesting that she kept her face down, apparently concentrating on her notes, her shoulders rigid. When Hugh ran through the list, allocating tasks, he gave her a couple of things to follow up, but carefully avoided looking at her.

Whatever had happened between them in the night hadn't left them happy lovers.

'Which brings us,' Hugh was saying, 'to the matter of the weapons cache allegedly discovered last night by Jo Lockwood. According to her statement, she saw it loaded into a truck and driven away from a shearing shed on the Derringvale Road.' He tapped the location on the large map on the wall, and Nick gave him credit for his research. All part of being seen to be in control, of being on top of the details. 'Unfortunately, neither of the patrol cars in the general area was able to pick up the truck. I'll take Jo out to the woolshed again this morning, go through what happened and see if we can find anything else in daylight.'

Now he did look directly at Nick, the challenge clear, watching for a response. Nick didn't give him one. Objecting would play straight into Hugh's game, whatever it was. And logically he had no grounds to object. Instead, he smoothly took control again, strolling to the front of the room, plugging a USB drive into the laptop projecting onto the screen.

He clicked through the file folders as he spoke. 'Jo was able to take some photographs of a man who deposited what was likely a rifle into the cache shortly before two others arrived and removed it. Aaron saw the photos last night, and thinks the suspect might have local connections.'

He scanned the group for reaction as the image filled the screen. Most showed no signs of recognition. Nate Harrison stared pointedly out the window. Matthew Carruthers frowned, but said nothing.

'Carruthers?' Nick prompted.

'I might be wrong, Sarge.'

'And you might be right. Spill it, Carruthers.'

Reluctantly he shifted in his seat, glanced around at his colleagues. 'Thing is, Sarge, he looks like Garry Coulter's nephew. Garry was here before you. I saw the lad come in a few times. Bit on the wild side he was, and Gazza was worried. Not much of one to talk about private stuff, was Gazza, but I think the lad had been inside.'

Strike two. Aaron had been correct – identity confirmed. Almost. 'Do you know his name, where he lives?'

Carruthers cleared his throat. 'I think he might have stayed for a couple of weeks. I heard Gazza complaining a few times that he was a bloody layabout, bludging off him the whole time. He buggered off before the funeral. Took some of Garry's stuff, too, I reckon. Can't prove it, though. His name is Bradley. Bradley Coulter.'

Nick wrote the name up on the whiteboard, his thoughts racing to connect the few facts they had. Another ex-con, like Travis Mitchell. But it seemed prison hadn't reformed Bradley Coulter. Nick had seen a hundred similar stories – young men preferring a fast buck and an easy life to working a legal job.

Hugh took advantage of his momentary silence to move to the lead again. 'What about other family?' he asked. 'Did Coulter have a wife? Kids?'

Nate Harrison snorted. 'His missus ran off with another bloke six months ago. Didn't even bother coming for the funeral. She's selling the house, doesn't want anything of his, except his money.'

Nick brought the focus back to wrapping up the briefing. 'From the conversation Jo overhead last night, we have strong reason to believe that the people handling the weapons are connected to the murder of Travis Mitchell. So we'll follow all lines of enquiry. Carruthers, get hold of Bradley Coulter's record. Find out if he could have met Mitchell in prison.' Nick's gut said they had. If they could find the links, follow them, they'd get to the answers. 'If Coulter's on probation, get on to the probation officer and see if they have an address. Brock, track down Mrs Coulter. See if she knows anything about Bradley, where he might be.' He half-expected an objection from Hugh, but there was none.

'Harrison, you'd know some of the professional shooters around here?' A guess based on some knowledge of small-town culture, but confirmed by Harrison's nod. Good. He'd give him a task that implied trust, and no rancour from the incident this morning. 'They'll have an idea about activities in the nearby parks and forests. See if they've heard any rumours about missing weapons, rifles for sale, that kind of thing.'

He continued, assigning tasks, and the briefing finished within a few minutes.

Hugh held a media conference immediately afterwards, a task Nick left to him by choice, although it meant he had no opportunity to speak with him. He had nothing solid to confront Hugh with, only a growing, uneasy feeling that Hugh was no longer on top of his game. It happened to some cops. The pressures of the job created physical and emotional tensions that at times left scars. Some cops made it through the bad times and stayed good cops. Some didn't.

∝

With the low rumble of voices drifting through the wall from the operations centre next door, and a police constable sitting at the kitchen table, Jo battled to concentrate on statistical reports.

Squeak. Her old chair protested her restless movement, for the umpteenth time. *Squeak.* She pushed back from the desk, crossed the corridor to the kitchen.

'That chair is driving me crazy,' she said to Dee Edwards, her minder. 'Probably you as well.'

As she pulled open the door of the general storage cupboard and reached in to hunt for oil, a sharp knock sounded on the back door.

'Stay there,' Dee ordered, her hand already on her Glock.

Jo bit her lip. Crazy what her life had become, locked into her building, half-hiding in a cupboard, while a police officer answered the door for her. She closed her fingers around the small oil can. Not much of a weapon, household oil, and the chances of anyone attacking her so close to the police had to be minuscule, but the flight-or-fight response kicked in, and she had nowhere to run.

She relaxed her grip on the can at the sound of Nick's voice and Dee's cheery request for permission to duck back next door, now that he was there.

His gaze ran a quick sweep of the kitchen as he came in. Practised, as if he expected danger in every room he entered.

Dark eyes studied her. 'Everything all right?'

She fell back on her determination to remain professionally friendly, and her old standby for uneasiness – humour. 'Yes. Other than a terminal case of boredom. Dee's pretending an interest in microbats,' she nodded at the booklet on the table, 'but I don't think she'll make an enthusiast.'

He might have smiled, for all of a millisecond. 'Hugh Dalton wants you to accompany him to the woolshed, to go over the scene there again. But there's no requirement, Jo – you don't have to go if you don't want to.'

Getting out of the office appealed more than staying in. But spending time with Hugh Dalton would likely raise other issues – namely Hugh's suspicions about her past – and she didn't want them clouding this case. Better to get everything out in the open.

She took a breath. 'I didn't recognise him the other day, but it seems we've crossed paths before,' she said. She left that as an opening, wondering if he'd discussed it with Hugh.

Nick inclined his head slightly. 'He did mention it.'

She swallowed. Hugh had *mentioned it*. The very tactfulness suggested Hugh had *mentioned* a whole lot about the case. Just to Nick, or to all of them?

Cold anger stilled her body. She looked directly at Nick. No running, no fighting, just standing firm. 'He seems to believe I pushed my fiancé off a cliff. He also implied I was involved in Travis Mitchell's murder. So, am I on your list of suspects, too, or is he just naturally suspicious?'

He took a moment to consider his answer, but not for an instant did he avoid her gaze. Honesty – or at least a good semblance of it. But he'd worked undercover, had to be a good actor.

'Hugh's a good detective,' he said, evenly. 'He's suspicious of everyone, and that makes him look in places others might discount. Police work is adversarial by nature – it usually comes down to us trying to get crims to say what they don't want to say – and a lot of effective cops thrive on that. Hugh's one of them.'

Okay, so there wasn't anything defensive about the explanation, and it made logical sense. Adversarial by nature – yes, she'd seen that in Hugh. She could find a way to deal with him. Probably.

'As for my list of suspects for Mitchell's murder,' Nick continued, careful and deliberate, 'I keep an open mind because everything is possible, so yes, you're on it.'

Ouch. Not what she wanted to hear.

'Along with everyone else within a four-hundred kilometre radius,' he added. That almost, but never quite a smile softened his blunt honesty. 'But I do have you ranked somewhere down near the dingo.'

It took a moment for his meaning to sink in. She blew out a breath. 'I guess that's a relief. For me and the dingo. At least, based on what I saw, the autopsy should clear the dingo.'

She knew more than most people what a wild dog could do. There'd been nothing, even in the brief look she'd had, that suggested any carnivore had mutilated Mitchell's body.

Nick nodded. 'Final analysis and reports are still to come, but I was at the examination yesterday and the pathologist found no evidence of canine interference.'

'You were there?' Of course he'd been there – that's why he'd gone to Newcastle. She just hadn't considered what that involved. Observing while a pathologist investigated all of those injuries, seeking answers. She had to swallow again. 'It must have been rough.'

He looked away, briefly closed his eyes. 'They always are,' he said.

And there was something in that moment of unguardedness, the admission of vulnerability, that told her he spoke the truth.

TEN

Garry Coulter's house, in a quiet street in Strathnairn, stood out from its neighbours only because of the overgrown garden, the closed curtains and the For Sale sign on the front fence. Nick knocked on the door for form's sake, but no sound came from inside.

'What was Coulter like?' he asked Aaron, as they walked around to check the back.

'Quiet, mostly. A bit old-fashioned, you know, as a detective, but a decent enough bloke.'

Old-fashioned? Yes, that fitted with the records Coulter had left. Only the bare minimum online, but a fair few notes, in hard-to-decipher handwriting.

In the backyard, vegetable plants lay brown and dead in square, wood-bordered plots, under a shade-cloth covered frame to protect them from the worst of the sun. A corner of the shade-cloth, loosened from the frame, flapped in the breeze.

Near the back door, the lid of the garbage bin sat crookedly, sunlight glinting on the neck of a beer bottle, preventing it from closing. Through the open gap, Nick could see other bottles piled in haphazardly.

'Was Coulter a drinker?' he asked Aaron.

'Not much of one, at least that I saw. A social beer or two, that's all.'

Nick pulled on latex gloves, and raised the lid of the bin. There were dozens of beer bottles tossed inside. Beside the garbage bin, the rectangular box for recyclables was also full, but when he lifted the lid of that, the mix of soft drink bottles and household plastics were neatly packed for maximum space efficiency.

Everything he'd seen of Coulter, except that pile of beer bottles, suggested a desire for order. Handwritten file notes, all on the same size paper, in date sequence. Straight, regimented garden beds. Mineral water bottles on one side of a box, fruit juice on the other.

The beer bottles didn't simply not fit the garbage bin, they didn't fit the man.

He went up the three cement steps to the back entrance. The closed fly-screen door shadowed the main, wooden door, but when he looked closely he saw beyond the screen the split in the wood, around the lock. The door itself sat slightly ajar.

The hunch that had brought him here – the fact of an empty house, and a possibly homeless ex-con who knew it well – might just have proved worth following.

'There's been a break-in,' he told Aaron. 'Phone the real

estate agent. Find out the last time anyone was here, whether they know about it.'

'I know Mrs C had everything of value put into storage, not long after the funeral,' Aaron said, pulling his phone out. 'So there shouldn't be much to steal. The agent should have an inventory of what's here, though.'

With clear evidence of a crime having been committed, Nick could legally enter the house. He pushed the door open cautiously. The warm, slightly musty air of a closed-up building hit his nostrils, and he listened for any sound before he went into the laundry. The older-style washing machine mustn't have been of sufficient value for Mrs Coulter to want, but it was clean and undamaged.

His senses alert, Nick mentally catalogued all he saw. An unpretentious 1960s weatherboard house, on the inside as well as the outside. Lino floors in the laundry led into the kitchen, but a quick scan showed nothing obvious disturbed, only a couple of the chairs sitting at an angle to the simple wooden table. Unlikely that Coulter had left them that way.

The lino gave way to grey carpet in the empty living room. From the indentations in the carpet pile Nick could visualise the layout – coffee table and side tables, sofa and chairs facing a long cupboard, probably an entertainment unit, and bookshelves against a couple of the walls.

In the master bedroom, the furniture remained – Mrs Coulter obviously hadn't wanted the marital bed. The matching ensemble of timber bedhead, chests of drawers and wardrobes was not the most fashionable but was in good condition, the bed neatly made with a plain blue bedspread drawn over the pillows. The wardrobe still held Coulter's clothes – a collection of white shirts, navy trousers, jeans and moleskins – and a couple of shelves of linen and towels.

The screen door thwacked against the frame as Aaron entered, and Nick left the bedroom to meet him in the passageway.

'The agent says no-one's been here for more than a week,' Aaron reported. 'There was no sign of forced entry then. He's on his way over to inspect the damage.'

'There's not much I can see so far, but there's the other bedrooms still to check.'

One bedroom was empty, the marks of a desk and possibly filing cabinets pressed into the carpet pile. But in the last bedroom they found a different story. An unmade single bed, the covers strewn as though by a restless sleeper. A couple of pillows and a blanket on the floor suggested a second, makeshift bed. The mirror on a chest of drawers had been removed from its framework, and lay propped on the chest, along with several empty beer bottles.

The sickly smell of something rotting hit Nick's nostrils, and he walked into the room, around the far side of the bed. Half a dozen beer bottles lay on the floor, alongside two pizza boxes. He crouched down, lifted the lid on one of them. Two wedges of pizza remained, congealed cheese growing a green mould over stinking pepperoni and ham.

'It's only a few days old, by the looks of it,' he said to Aaron. 'We'll need to call the CSOs in here, see if they can pick up anything to ID Bradley Coulter, and whoever was with him.'

'You definitely think it's Bradley?'

'Yes.' Nick considered it almost a certainty. 'Other than the broken lock, there's no vandalism. He's used this room, presumably where he stayed before, not the others. Is the agent bringing the inventory? We'll need to see what, if anything, is missing.'

'Yes, he is. Apparently, the Salvos are booked to come and clear out the rest of the stuff on Monday.'

Nick studied the room, looking for hints to the young man who'd stayed there. No personal belongings, no clothes in the wardrobe. He'd moved out, even if he did return to camp occasionally. Had he left the district around the time of his uncle's death, only returning some days ago? Or had he just been staying elsewhere in the interim?

As Nick went to the door, his blurred reflection in the mirror propped on the chest of drawers caught his eye. Lines of fine dust marred the surface; fine *white* dust. He knew those types of dust patterns. Another quick scan of the room showed nothing more suspicious, but when he returned to the pizza boxes and raised the lid on the second one, he found the evidence: two small plastic bags, fine white powder clinging to them, and a couple of plastic straws.

He left Aaron at the house to wait for a uniformed officer to guard the scene until the forensic specialists arrived, and drove across town to the Strathnairn police station. He needed to get Coulter's files, go through those handwritten notes in detail. And he needed to update the district commander, inform him what they'd found at the house of the deceased officer.

Unanswered questions chased around in his mind on the drive. Would the drugs at the house match the drugs found at the lookout? Those still puzzled him; if they'd been for the mob at the camping ground, why had they still been there? If they'd been left for someone else, then who? Just how many criminals were using Jo's National Park for their activities?

Jo. Thoughts of her never seemed far away. As he'd left Goodabri earlier, he'd seen Hugh's car also leaving, Dee Edwards in the car as well as Jo. With another woman present, Hugh would surely behave professionally towards Jo, not aggressively. He had no doubts about Jo's ability to handle him if he stepped out of line; she was confident, assertive, and experienced at law enforcement within the National Parks context. More than a match for Hugh. Nick wouldn't have let the plan go ahead otherwise.

But still he wondered how she was going, where she was now.

In his office, he booted up his computer and added the recent events to his personal notes – the murder of the Baxters, the weapons cache, the drug evidence they'd just found at Coulter's house. Under the heading 'Suspects', he included the two images they had – the police artist's image from Jo's description and her photos of Bradley Coulter. He also added Garry Coulter's death to the event list, with a question mark: Accident? Murder? Suicide?

Then he printed out his notes, and went to report to the district commander, Inspector Keith Murdoch.

He'd met the Inspector on his first day, had a few short conversations with him since, was still forming his impression of the man. A busy man, certainly, with a district station and multiple small satellite stations under his command. On his way out to a meeting, Murdoch granted him five minutes.

'Tread carefully there, Matheson.' Murdoch tapped a finger against the name of Nick's predecessor on the notes, after Nick had provided a brief summary. 'Coulter was a well-respected officer here.'

Nick regarded him evenly, held his ground. 'I gathered that. But he left at least five unsolved gun thefts, and now there's evidence linking his nephew to possibly stolen weapons and perhaps even to murder. That raises questions I can't ignore.'

Murdoch nodded, unruffled by Nick's assertiveness. 'I'm not suggesting you ignore them. Simply that you understand that some of his colleagues may be resentful of any suggestion from you that questions his character.'

'I'm here to investigate crime, not to win a popularity contest.'

'Respect is part of effective teamwork, Matheson.' He handed back the notes. 'By all means, review his open cases, and the accident investigation. Keep me informed of progress. If Coulter made mistakes, or was compromised by his nephew's actions, I'd like to know first. I can't back you up if I don't have all the facts.'

As an indication of trust, it was strong enough, but Nick accepted the reminder; he needed the rest of the team on his side as far as possible. Tact in dealing with the questions surrounding Coulter had to be part of his strategy.

Back in his office, he checked his emails and skimmed through a couple of forensic reports that had arrived. The lab in Newcastle had found little on Travis Mitchell's clothing; a couple of partial prints on the belt tourniquet, but no matches in the database for them. The examination of the cocaine had found it was high-grade, not cut with other substances. They'd lifted a couple of prints, again not matched to anything on file. Not many answers there – yet.

He was about to click the file closed when a line caught his eye. *Ten small resealable plastic bags each containing approximately five grams . . .*

No. Not ten bags. He'd counted them himself, up on the hill where Jo had found them. There'd been twelve bags contained in the larger bag. Twelve, not ten, that he'd handed to one of the CSOs once he'd returned to the camping ground, to go into the locked evidence bag. With the forensic pathologist on the phone, they'd been too busy, then, to complete the drug evidence log. He knew Hugh had looked at it later; he'd seen him talking with a CSO, drugs in hand, and had assumed they'd logged it then.

So when had those two bags of coke gone missing? He'd have to follow the trail back – from the lab, to the officer who'd logged the evidence, to the forensic team on site, to Hugh.

Don't let it be Hugh. That he'd even formed the wish in his thoughts felt like a betrayal.

He'd have to report the missing drugs to Murdoch. Let Murdoch set the investigation up according to procedure. Official processes would determine at what point in the evidence chain they'd gone missing.

He had his hand on the desk phone to call Murdoch when Aaron swung into the office.

'The truck that took the weapons has been found. Dumped on a road east of Derringvale. At least some of the guns are still there. Dalton is on his way there now.'

Dalton. With Jo. Nick grabbed his car keys. 'So are we.'

⁂

Hugh Dalton played the cool, alpha cop confidently enough, and no longer treated her with outright suspicion, but once in a while as Jo showed him the woolshed and described the events she noticed a momentary lapse in concentration, a slow response, an abrupt transition between one question and the next, as though he'd lost his train of thought.

Granted, he had to have plenty on his mind, with a murder investigation and stolen weapons, but where Nick translated his concerns into focused, direct action, Hugh seemed to lack that focus.

In the car, travelling to the lane near Derringvale where the truck had been found, Hugh carried on a lightly flirtatious conversation with Dee Edwards.

Watching from the back seat, Jo didn't discern signs of genuine interest from either party. More likely the cheeky innuendos and easy manner were his habitual style in talking with women. Not unusual for a good-looking, fit, confident man in his thirties. She'd met plenty of the type.

Not that he tried any of that charm on her. He might flirt with his colleagues, but she apparently held no attraction for him. A mutual feeling.

When his phone rang, the relaxed charm evaporated. He slipped the earpiece on before answering and from where she sat, Jo saw his knuckles turn white on the steering wheel.

His brusque responses to his caller gave little clue of the topic of the call. 'Yes. No.' He glanced at her in the rear-vision mirror. 'Not possible.'

Not possible to discuss a police issue with a civilian in earshot? That would make sense. But it didn't explain the tension in his hands, the flare of his nostrils as he exhaled a pent-up breath, or the clipped words, delivered with barely restrained force.

'I'll sort it out.' He disconnected abruptly, and his eyes found hers again in the mirror. Rather than ignoring it to check the road behind, this time his direct, second-long consideration stayed on her, anger or some similar emotion narrowing his eyes.

She broke the eye contact, looked out the window at the passing landscape. The stresses of the past days were making her paranoid. He'd probably just been arguing with a wife or girlfriend over some domestic matter. That would fit the tone and content of the brief conversation.

In an hour or so they'd be back in Goodabri, and her involvement in the case would be mostly over, other than whatever actions Nick recommended for her safety. She could go to the office and concentrate on her job.

She tried to still her uneasiness by mentally listing the tasks she'd tackle this afternoon. Updating fire-management strategies could absorb some hours. Outside the car, the strong sunlight accentuated the summer dryness, the yellow–brown of shrivelled paddocks, the dust blowing in the wind. A few seasons of above-average rainfall had driven significant growth of grasses, undergrowth and trees throughout the region, but the wet cycle had finished months ago, and an early, hot summer had already transformed most of that growth into dry fuel. The fire trails in the new park needed more work, clearing overgrown areas, widening in some places, and signage.

Yes, she'd finish writing up those recommendations today. As soon as she was done with the police.

With that practical decision made, she paid attention again to the view outside the window.

'Church Lane is coming up on the right,' she told Hugh. 'Just around the bend.'

'Looks like a road to nowhere,' he muttered, slowing to make the turn.

'It only goes as far as the river. In the eighteen-hundreds there was a large sheep station down there that supported a small community. A huge flood in 1893 pretty much wiped it all out.'

Except for the deserted stone church, which sat on higher ground a hundred metres from the river, the cattle truck she'd seen last night on the grass behind it.

Hugh parked on the road a short distance behind a couple of other police cars. He paused briefly, staring at the scene before saying abruptly, 'Come with me, Doctor Lockwood, so you can identify the box and the weapons. Dee, find out if that lot have an ID on the truck rego yet.'

Outside the airconditioned car, the dry heat sucked at Jo's skin, and she jammed her hat well down on her head so the wind couldn't catch it.

At the faded sign in front of the church listing the monthly services, the detective stopped suddenly, a harsh, humourless laugh breaking from him.

'Saint Patrick's,' he muttered to himself. 'That'd be bloody right.' With no further comment he strode on, not looking to see if Jo followed. To add to his strange behaviour, in the short distance through the dry grass around to the back of the church, she saw his hand go to the holster on his belt, then jerk away, twice.

Unease slowed her steps. He was wired tight, tension radiating from him. Maybe this situation reminded him of some past trauma. An officer who'd served in Homicide for some years had probably been in tight corners at times. She knew too well how memories could haunt, how a small trigger could bring them flooding back, strong and real, even years after the event. But officers had already cleared this site, and with at least four other cops less than fifty metres away, they had to be safe. She had to be safe.

The tailgate of the truck was open, the loading ramp down, but other than the remnant odour of cow shit, it was empty.

'Is this the vehicle you saw?' Hugh asked.

'I'm pretty certain. Same type, same colour, same kind of trailer.'

Drag marks down the ramp and in the dust led around the other side of the truck, where the box lay open on the ground, its battered metal glinting in the bright sun.

But she paused before joining Hugh beside it, studying the tracks in the dust.

Tact might be the best option. 'You'll have seen the bike tracks here?' He hadn't of course, but he glanced back with a vague nod. 'Two motorbikes, is my guess,' she continued. 'Carrying their own getaway transport, I suppose. Or maybe they were stolen, too.'

He ignored her suggestion, kneeling by the box and staring into it. The guns absorbed his attention. 'You said there were semi-autos and a pump action in here?'

'Yes. Nick has copies of the photos I took.'

'Yeah, well, there's not now.' He regarded her for a long moment. She heard another car arrive, a door slam, and saw Hugh glance past her towards the road before he gave a weird grin and said, 'I don't suppose *you* took those rifles, did you, Doctor Lockwood?'

Irritation with him bloomed into full-on anger, pulsing in her head. 'Photos were all I took, Detective Dalton.' She struggled to keep her voice even, the words scraping in her throat. 'I suggest you concentrate on finding the felons out there who are now well armed.'

He rose to his feet, his gaze scanning along the tree-lined river below them. 'Yes,' he said, almost absently, without looking at her. 'Get someone to give you a lift back to Goodabri, Doctor Lockwood.'

No word of thanks for her cooperation, no attempt to delegate an officer to drive her.

Furious at his lack of common courtesy, she spun on her heel and strode away.

◆

Jo came around the front of the truck at such a pace that Nick caught her by the shoulders to cushion their impact. As he steadied her, he registered the warmth of her shirt fabric, the firm muscle beneath his hands, and the anger blazing in her eyes. She had a temper, and wasn't trying to hide it.

'Sorry.' She found her balance, and stepped back a pace. 'That man is a pain in the neck.'

'Hugh?'

'Yes. The semi-automatics aren't there, and he accused me of taking them.'

Damn Hugh and his games. And damn the need to show a united front and support him. 'You've been with me since last night,' he said. 'That's a pretty solid alibi.'

She hesitated, glanced back at the truck, and dropped her voice. 'Look, it's not my business, but Hugh's behaviour this morning . . . well, it's been erratic. Made me wonder if he's not coping well with some kind of recent trauma. If he was a colleague of mine, I'd be worried.'

Oh, Nick was worried, all right. More worried about Hugh than he'd been since the scrawny street kid had befriended Patrick and became another responsibility to protect. But memories couldn't help him now, and Hugh had long ago ceased needing his protection. If Hugh had taken the cocaine, if he was crooked, there's no way he could protect him.

'I'll keep an eye out.' A mild, even-toned response that betrayed none of his concern. Playing a role again, concealing his thoughts. He grasped at the small matter in which he could be more himself with Jo. 'I shouldn't be long here. If you want to wait, I'll give you a lift back to Goodabri.'

'Thanks. I'd appreciate it.' She nodded towards a scattering of old gravestones under a large tree behind the church. 'I'll wait in the shade over there. Might cool down my temper.'

Her wry, self-aware smile stayed in his mind as he turned away and walked around the side of the truck . . . and vanished when he found himself looking down the barrel of a rifle.

He stilled, focusing on Hugh's eyes, his awareness encompassing man, hand and rifle. 'What got into you, Hugh?'

Hugh laughed, the rifle dipping slightly lower as he relaxed the aim. 'Just testing your reflexes. I don't think you're quite the man you used to be, Nick. Your hand didn't move near your gun at all.'

'You used to be a better cop, Hugh.'

'So did you. Or so I thought. Until you murdered Terry Costello and that woman in Melbourne.'

That Hugh – *Hugh*, of all people – could accuse him twisted like a knife in his chest. But then, didn't he have his own doubts about Hugh?

He kept a carefully neutral face. 'Is that what you think? That I murdered them?'

Hugh shrugged, as casually as if they were discussing the weather. 'Your fingerprints were on her gun. The one that killed Costello. There's rumours you were screwing her. You visited her brothel often enough.'

Hugh had laughed naturally a few moments ago, but now his smirk came tardily, tacked on at the end. A performance, and not a smooth one, with the rifle still pointed loosely in Nick's direction. What the hell was going on in Hugh's head? He'd play it easy, neither defensive nor aggressive, until he could work it out. The truck screened them from the view of the other officers; he needed to resolve things before the situation exploded.

'You know how it is with undercover ops. My role was as a security contractor, providing bouncers, bodyguards and security systems for the brothel. Besides, the mistress of the head of an organised-crime syndicate is really not my type.'

'I'm not sure you have a "type", Nick. You've been living like a monk for years. Although you do seem taken with Jo. Noticed that the other day, at the camping ground. I don't blame you. Cute butt.'

Control. He needed to retain it, not hand it to Hugh by responding to his provocations. The sun shone hot on them both, and sweat glistened on Hugh's face. The hand he dashed under his nostrils wiped away a trickle of blood.

Nick held steady, but he subtly shifted his weight on to his good leg, ready to spring. 'Put the rifle down, Hugh. You're a better man than this.'

'No, I'm not. I never have been.' His bitter laugh ended with a crack.

Regret, conscience – whatever it was, that fracture in Hugh's bravado gave Nick a sliver of faith to hold on to. 'Is it just the drugs? Or are you in deeper than that?'

'Oh, I'm a good six feet in. I'm not as strong as you, Nick. I screwed up, and now they're jerking the strings. I've got no choices left. I hope you had fun with Jo last night, mate, 'cause I'm supposed to shoot her. Should I do it, Nick?' He raised his voice, injecting it with anger. 'Would that get you to show some fucking emotion for once?'

Nick launched himself as Hugh gripped the rifle tighter and swung it in Jo's direction.

He knocked the rifle out of Hugh's hands before they both hit the ground, hard, and pain almost paralysed him. The rifle fell wide, but instead of twisting towards it, Hugh took advantage of Nick's weakness to dislodge his weight.

'Took you bloody long enough,' Hugh said while they grappled on the ground, a wild, crazy grin distorting his features. 'Keep fighting. When there's enough witnesses, shoot me.'

Nick turned the moment of disadvantage – being flat on his back – into advantage, using the leverage of the ground and the strength in his limbs to throw Hugh sideways, twisting the opposite direction himself and springing to his feet.

I'm supposed to shoot her . . . Whatever Hugh was planning, whatever this performance was about, his comments were warnings, not threats.

The Hugh of old was still there, and Nick had to trust him enough to go with his plan for now, make the fight last long enough to keep them all alive.

They circled slowly, watching for any break, any signal of intent. Instincts on full alert, Nick pinned Hugh with his eyes, asserting his control.

'Just like old times in the dojo, isn't it?' Hugh mocked.

'More like on the street. Dojos have rules. I suspect you're not planning to follow any of them.'

Footsteps pounded, and his peripheral vision caught blurs of khaki and blue near the truck. Without taking his eyes from his prey, he called out, 'Stay back, all of you. That's an order.'

Hugh attacked, feinting a cutting chop with his right hand while his left foot kicked into Nick's thigh. Nick caught his arm, turning the energy of the thrust into leverage to unbalance Hugh and throw him to the ground.

Hugh rolled to his feet in an instant, came at him again, raining blows and kicks that he had to work fast to block, again and again and again. Full-body contact fighting, hard and rough and powerful, a dangerous mix of martial arts and raw street brawling. Not quite back to condition after his injuries, Nick caught a couple of punches to his head, but with a lifetime of experience he shook those off, not slowing down.

Spinning away to come at him once more, this time Hugh leapt in with a sharp kick that caught Nick's injured thigh, eroding his balance, weakening his defensive throw so that they locked together, each immoveable.

'Almost time to go for your gun, Nick,' Hugh murmured, before he threw himself into a somersault to the ground, as if Nick had thrown him, and rolled, drawing a blade from an ankle holster as he did.

'Sarge!' Aaron called. 'He's got a knife.'

Nick spared a quick glance away from Hugh. Aaron and four others were fanning out, surrounding them, weapons drawn. Apparently Hugh's intention, and exactly what Nick had hoped to avoid. Hadn't they seen that he'd made no attempt to draw his own gun? He'd have to, now, so that they wouldn't think him defenceless and fire to protect him.

'Don't anyone shoot. It's under control. Hugh, drop the knife. We'll sort this out.' With no intention of firing it he drew his own weapon, holding the gun by his side, pointing to the ground.

'Sorry, Nick. Can't be sorted any other way.' Hugh locked eyes with Nick, a tumult of emotions behind them. He raised his arm with the knife, began to move in with a wide, easy to read, swiping movement.

But even as Nick braced his left arm to deflect the strike, shots sounded in quick succession, Hugh's body jerked twice and crashed to the ground, while a flock of birds screeched and screeched in the distance.

ELEVEN

Aaron had pushed her behind the truck when they'd drawn their weapons, but in the seconds after those shots Jo cautiously emerged, taking in the scene quickly. Nick kneeling beside the fallen Hugh, yelling for an ambulance. Aaron running to him. The other officers, guns in their hands, casting questioning glances at their colleagues.

Down at the river, the corellas circled in a mass cloud of white noise but below them she caught a dark shadow moving, filtered sunlight through the trees glinting a reflection.

A bullet ricocheted off the steel truck frame, inches from her.

'Shooter by the river!' she yelled, ducking back behind the truck.

'Everyone down!' she heard Nick roar.

She hunkered behind the rear wheels of the truck, out of the line of sight of the sniper. But through the gap under the truck she could just see Nick, and part of Hugh's prone body, and she held her breath as Nick and Aaron rose to their feet, carrying Hugh between them.

Just metres from the truck, the church offered better cover, and the wooden door into the vestry was aged and cracking.

Calling for them to follow, she made a run for it across the open ground, ramming the door with her shoulder to break the old lock, pushing the splintered timber open with them only a step behind her.

The tiny vestry had too little space, but the door into the main church stood open, swallows flittering among the ceiling beams, the seats stacked at the side, unused for many years, covered in dust and bird droppings.

Blood soaked Hugh's stomach and chest, dripping into a pool on the floor even as Nick and Aaron gently lowered him. Critical wounds. Fear and worry rushed round her thoughts, memories overlaying them, threatening panic, and in the incoherent whirl she sent a silent wish to Saint Patrick for a miracle. She didn't believe in saints, but if there'd ever been a benevolent presence in this place, Hugh sure as heck needed it.

Nick immediately knelt beside Hugh, his already bloodied hands pressing against the two wounds. 'We need a rescue chopper, Aaron. Then call for back-up, and make sure no-one takes stupid risks. If you can get a fix on the snipers, good. Pursue if you can.'

Concentrating on action to quell her rising fear, she rapidly unbuttoned and slipped off the shirt she wore over her crop-top and folded it roughly into a pad. She dropped to her knees in Aaron's place, sliding the pad under Nick's hand onto the abdominal wound and applying pressure.

Hugh groaned, the sound gurgling in his throat, and Nick gripped his hand. 'I'm here, mate. The ambulance is coming.'

Jo knew better than both men that the ambulance was at least half an hour from Strathnairn, the rescue helicopter a similar time away in Tamworth. With her free hand she checked Hugh's pulse: uneven, barely there. His skin was pale, his abdomen distended beneath her hand, and his blood already soaked her folded shirt.

Internal bleeding, and quite likely damaged organs. Even if Saint Patrick lent a hand, the chances of paramedics and equipment arriving in time were slim.

She closed her eyes to steady the panic threatening again. Hugh, not Leon. *Not Leon.* No storms, no long, agonising wait for help that couldn't come. She *could* stay with Hugh, *could* comfort him. She *could* stay here with Nick, and be strong.

Nick. Despite the sounds of shouts and revving cars outside, he made no move to leave, his hand still gripping Hugh's, concern cracking his usual impassive mask. She'd thought them only colleagues, until that out-of-the-blue fight erupted. None of it made sense to her. The violence of the fight contrasted sharply with Nick's concern now, and that linked grip. Whatever the history between them, Hugh mattered to Nick. She closed her hand over both of theirs in silent support.

Hugh tried to move, moaning as pain twisted his face.

'Hold still, mate,' Nick urged, all his focus on the injured man. 'Won't be long and you'll have some pain killers.'

'No . . . have to . . . could have saved them, Nick . . . my fault . . . Christie was meeting *me* . . .'

150

'I've always known that, Hugh.' Nick spoke quietly, with a gentleness that belied his usual distance. 'It doesn't matter.'

Hugh's eyes flickered open, searching for Nick's, his breathing increasingly ragged. 'Grace . . . see her sometimes . . . but they know . . . they think . . . that's why . . . I *had* to. For Grace.'

Whatever Hugh's words meant, they were a shock to Nick, his face paling.

'Someone's threatening *Grace*? Who is it?'

'Files . . .' Hugh's breath came now in slow, shallow gasps. 'Pat's birthday . . . you have to . . .' The voice faded, eyes drifted closed, air expelling from his lungs. Seconds passed before he drew in another shallow breath. 'Failed . . . you . . . brother . . .'

'No, Hugh. You made good.' The steadiness of Nick's deep voice wavered again. 'More than made good.'

Jo felt for a pulse, found nothing, and there was no movement in Hugh's chest, no more breaths.

'Shit, no.' Nick yanked open Hugh's shirt, began compressions, and Jo moved to Hugh's head, training kicking in to administer mouth-to-mouth. *Don't think, just do. Breathe, count. Breathe, count.* They established a rhythm, cycled through it several times, but Hugh lay motionless and silent.

Beaten, her own breath uneven as she fought back tears and failed, Jo sat back on her heels. 'He's gone, Nick. I'm so sorry.'

'Yes.' It was a long moment before Nick closed Hugh's shirt over his bloodied skin, and he grasped his hand one last time before laying it on his chest and letting go.

☙

Thoughts raced and jumbled around in his head, defying any order or sense. He pushed himself to his feet, paced a few steps away, stared at the peeling white paint on the wall in front of him, his chest painfully tight.

Hugh was dead. He'd tried to *orchestrate* his own death, might well have succeeded in his plan, but someone else shot him first, silencing him. Someone out there, beyond the river.

Hugh's partially revealed secrets left too much unexplained. Nick needed to sort out his thoughts, take charge of the whirl of emotions muddying logic.

Anger with himself – he acknowledged that. He tried to still his shaking hands as he wiped the worst of the blood from them with his handkerchief, but the metaphorical blood remained. He'd failed Hugh. Should have paid more attention, made more of an effort to keep in touch. He would have for Pat, if his brother had still been alive. But he'd let Hugh flounder, unsupported, when Hugh had no-one else but him.

Christie . . . Yes, he'd always known about Hugh and his sister, known she'd come to meet him the day she died. It's why he'd sent Pat to gatecrash the date, worried about the intensity of their heady teenage attraction. *His* fault Pat had died with Christie in that hail of bullets, moments before Hugh arrived. Not Hugh's fault.

But Grace – what had Hugh meant, that he'd been seeing Grace? She was a doctor, in Queensland – Nick knew that much about his youngest sister, although he'd not contacted her since he was eighteen. For her sake. For her safety, he disappeared from her life, to protect the last of his shattered family.

The young Hugh had always had a strong core of loyalty, and a fondness for Grace, but they hadn't spoken of her in years.

Had Hugh sought her out, or had Grace found him? Either way, protecting Grace might go some way towards explaining Hugh's erratic actions. But who had threatened her, and held that over Hugh? Was she really in danger? And where was the connection with this case?

A feather-touch on his shoulder alerted him to Jo's presence beside him, compassion and questions in her eyes. Of course she had to be wondering, curious about Hugh's behaviour, the fight, his last words. Nick wished he had answers for her.

'He was a friend of my brother's.' Gravel in his throat made him stop. *Get a grip. Take control.*

'You don't have to explain to me, Nick.'

He did have to. Had to acknowledge aloud each of them, even if they could no longer hear it. 'He was a homeless kid who helped Pat in a street fight one day. They stuck together after that. Christie . . .' After all this time, he should be able to say her name naturally, without revealing the pain. 'Christiana was my sister. She and Pat were killed, murdered almost nineteen years ago.'

'I'm so sorry, Nick.' Not just customary words repeated by rote. She understood loss, her unwavering eyes holding the echo of her own grief.

Emotion an indulgence he couldn't afford, he dismissed her empathy, and his lingering sense of failure, with a brief shake of his head. 'It was a long time ago.'

He should explain about Grace, couldn't think of adequate words. 'Grace is my youngest sister. I haven't seen her since she was twelve. I don't know what Hugh meant about her.'

He couldn't see how Grace could be in danger, couldn't make sense of any of it. But, Grace in danger or not, he had to solve it – the whole complex case – before anyone else died. His job, his responsibility. Memories were irrelevant.

Movement outside the cobweb-draped window caught his eye – a probationary constable securing crime-scene tape to a fence post. A blowfly buzzed into the church, diving for Hugh, and Jo moved quickly to wave it away.

'I'll stay here with him,' she offered, with only a slight waver in her voice, 'if you need to go out there.'

Leave *her* alone with the body of the man they'd been unable to save? Despite her courage, her determined composure, he would not put her through that.

He pulled out his phone. The death of an officer required a formal investigation – especially when other officers had weapons drawn. He had procedures to follow, notifications to make.

And when that was done, he needed to find out who had fired the bullets from near the river. Three bullets. He'd heard all three, seen the last ricochet off the truck, just inches from Jo.

The bastard had murdered Hugh, and tried to murder Jo.

TWELVE

Nick turned his back to her, thumbing a couple of buttons on his phone, briskly asking for the Strathnairn commander when the call went through. Unemotional, in control, he reported the facts of Hugh's death.

Standing uselessly in the middle of the empty church beside the dead man, Jo had no idea what to do next. Nick didn't need her. Hugh didn't need her. Her hands too sticky with Hugh's blood, she couldn't thrust them in her pockets or tuck loose strands of her hair back from her face. Couldn't *do* anything, except concentrate on keeping it all together, resisting the urge to give in to an emotional and physical reaction to the situation. What use would that be to anyone? She had to support Nick, not be a burden.

She made herself stand by Hugh's side and look at him. In death, without the animation of his macho behaviour, Hugh appeared almost boyish. In his thirties, around her own age, maybe a year or two older. Too young to have died. Like Leon, who'd died at barely thirty, with so much achieved, and so much potential unrealised. Whereas Hugh had died believing himself a failure.

Dull, empty blue eyes stared, unmoving. Nothing remained of the street kid who'd gone to the defence of another youth, of the confident man who'd played the flirt. Nothing remained but memories, questions, and the grief Nick had been unable to completely hide.

Hugh's last words made little sense to her, despite Nick's explanation of the family connection. Files, coercion, a threat to Grace – even added to Hugh's erratic behaviour and the bizarre fight with Nick, all she came up with was confusion. Confusion, and apprehension.

'As soon as the situation's in hand here, I'll have Jo Lockwood escorted back to Strathnairn.' Nick faced her as he mentioned her name, dark eyes holding hers. 'We'll need to organise protection for her. Yes, it's warranted. There was a clear attempt on her life.'

Despite the baking heat in the building, she had to clench her hands to stop them shaking. That third shot from the sniper had almost hit her. She'd seen him, caught the reflection off his telescopic sight, because nobody else had been in the direct line between them. Either the sniper had misfired, or he'd been aiming at her and missed. She wanted to believe the first option – a wild shot, an attempt to drive them under cover to enable his escape – but Nick's certainty rammed reality home. The sniper had killed Hugh, then turned his sights on her.

'What's going on, Nick?' she demanded as soon as he finished his call. 'Did you understand what Hugh meant?'

'Not much of it. Yet. You said he was acting strangely this morning, Jo. Did he say or do anything in particular that made you think that?'

Just about everything he'd done was strange, but she zoomed in on specifics. 'There was a phone call that seemed to rattle him. He was very short with the caller. Just a few words. He said, "No, not possible." And then he said he'd "sort it". It's just an impression, but he looked at me in the rear-vision mirror and I had the feeling that I was what he'd "sort".'

Nick swore under his breath.

She recalled the start of the fight, the raised voices that had made her turn, the sight of Nick throwing himself at Hugh, and the rifle falling to the ground. The rifle that had been pointed towards her.

'He was going to kill me, wasn't he? He would have shot me.'

Nick gave a slow shake of his head. 'No. He warned me so that I'd stop him. He had no intention of pulling the trigger, Jo.'

The sweat trickling down the back of her neck tracked a chilling path, spreading along her spine. She shrugged her shoulders, rolled her head to dislodge the uneasy sensation.

'Will you be able to find out who made that last call?'

'I'll ask for his phone to be checked, although it was probably a blocked number. But this is a crime scene now, and since I'm involved, I won't touch anything more. There'll be an internal investigation team arriving within a couple of hours. They'll want statements and interviews. They'll want to speak with you, too.'

'They're not going to blame you, though? The evidence must be clear enough that he provoked the fight, and that the sniper shot him?'

Nick stilled, watching her, and weighing his words before answering. 'They'll know quickly enough that I didn't pull the trigger. However, as I was brawling with a fellow officer when he was shot, there's bound to be suspicion and questions, about my relationship with him, and our involvement in the case. I'm new here, and I've been an undercover specialist for almost ten years, the last job ending badly. That doesn't lead to a whole lot of trust between police officers. But you're under no obligation, Jo. You've had a stressful few days. You don't have to talk with them if you don't want to.'

No obligation? Her obligation, as he had put it, went deeper than simply telling the truth about the scene she had witnessed. Nick had torn the rifle from Hugh's hands. She owed Nick her life.

⌁

'You were behind the truck, you said. So you didn't actually see who fired the shots, did you, Doctor Lockwood?'

Jo sipped water from her glass and mentally counted to three to steady her temper before she answered. 'I also said that I heard rifle shots, fired from a distance, not a handgun less than five metres from me.' She eyed the detective senior constable from the Critical Incident team. 'Do you not understand that there's a distinct difference in sound?'

Raised eyebrows acknowledged his surprise, but then he smiled, with more of the condescension that had driven her mad half the afternoon. 'Not everybody knows enough about firearms to recognise the difference. Especially when the situation is tense.'

Did he think she spent her days hugging koalas? She clasped her hands around the glass and drew on her stretched patience to set about educating him. 'My job involves enforcing the laws banning firearms in the National Park, and also coordinating regular campaigns against feral animals. I'm more than familiar with firearms, and estimating direction and distance in a range of landscapes. The shots that killed Detective Dalton were fired from the river. I'm sure everyone present will tell you the same thing.'

'We have to be thorough, make sure nothing is missed. So, you know some of the local shooters? Have you seen anything out of the ordinary or suspicious lately?'

She raised an eyebrow. 'Apart from a vandalised camping ground, a dead body, cocaine and weapons stashes and a murdered detective? No, I can't say I have.' Not a particularly helpful response to the question, that burst of sarcasm, but in her overtired state it eased her annoyance more effectively than a polite answer.

Apparently not an entirely insensitive clod, he laid down his pen and started to gather his notes together. 'You've had a tough few days. Your information has been very helpful. Thank you.'

Her muscles stiff from over an hour in the uncomfortable plastic chair, she rose to her feet slowly, rubbing the ache in her neck, the sudden change in his approach leaving her uncertain how to respond. 'What happens from here? Do you need a formal statement from me?'

He held the door open for her. 'We've got more interviews to conduct. I'll contact you tomorrow if we need a statement.'

She would have asked about Nick, but before she found words the detective had ushered her down the short corridor to the reception area and left her there with no more than another brief word of thanks.

Where to now? The abrupt ending to the interview had denied her the chance to find out more about how this situation affected her from here, and she stared out the glass doors, trying to gather coherent thoughts as she watched the slanting sunlight glow on the low hills behind Strathnairn.

An afternoon in Strathnairn police station hadn't been part of her plan for the day. Being stranded in Strathnairn without her vehicle definitely wasn't in any plan. Pretty much any chances of planning anything had been shot to hell when she'd found Travis Mitchell's body the other day.

Should she try to organise a ride back to the homestead, or find a place to stay overnight in Strathnairn? Where would she be safe? The seriousness of the threat against her loomed in her mind, but she pushed it down while she focused on practical matters. No-one, other than Nick, had expressed concern about her safety, but she hadn't seen Nick since they'd arrived at the station hours ago, and she hadn't seen Aaron – who seemed to be the only officer *not* treating Nick like a leper – since leaving the old church.

Despite Nick's matter-of-fact explanation, she didn't comprehend enough about police culture to interpret the undercurrents, suspicions and tight-lipped attitudes of most of the cops this afternoon. Her observations and instincts about Nick couldn't be *that* far wrong, surely? On one level he frightened her, but not in a way that made her doubt his integrity; she had never once felt unsafe with him. Perhaps it was her response to him that frightened her.

The door behind her opened again, and she turned at the sound, the small hope it might be Nick or Aaron flickering out in an instant. Shelley Brock carried her overnight bag in one hand, a pair of dark glasses in the other.

'Jo.' Shelley stopped beside her, lowered her bag to the floor and slid the glasses into place on top of her head, making no attempt to mask her red-rimmed eyes. 'Have you got a moment?'

A tête-a-tête with Shelley Brock? They'd had hardly exchanged more than a couple of words until now. Off following some other lead this morning, Shelley had only arrived at the church just as Jo was leaving, and she'd barely spared Jo a glance in her distress for Hugh. But the woman had lost a colleague, a friend, perhaps more, and Jo well knew the agony and desolation that was just beginning.

'Sure, Shelley.'

'I wanted to thank you . . .' Shelley began, taking a moment to blink back tears. 'I heard you did CPR. Thank you for trying to save him.'

'Nick and I just did what anyone would do. I'm very sorry for your loss, Shelley.' Stupid words, useless words. Words she'd heard recited by too many people. 'You and Hugh were close?'

Shelley gave a bitter half-laugh, half-sob. 'If "close" is a euphemism for "lovers", well, it's not much of a secret that we sometimes were. I don't think he let anyone get close to him; not really. Certainly not me. He made that clear, last night. But he was so full of life, of energy . . .' She screwed her eyes shut for a moment, sniffed, on the edge of falling apart. 'I couldn't help falling for that.'

'Of course not,' replied Jo, at a loss for anything else to say. She'd fallen for a similar man herself. Lived with him, loved him, had planned to marry him. Until he'd died, just as suddenly as Hugh, leaving her adrift and alone.

Shelley straightened her shoulders, a mask of determination settling on her face. 'Yeah, and aren't I a bloody fool? Anyway, I've got to get out of here, but . . . well, thank you. I'm sorry you've been caught up in this mess. But you can trust Nick to get it sorted out. Hugh thought the world of him.'

If Hugh really thought the world of Nick, then what had the fight been about? More questions without answers.

'Do you know where Nick is?' Jo asked.

'In with the boss, apparently. Oh, and Jo, can I ask you a favour? For Hugh?' She looked directly into Jo's eyes. 'For Nick?' She tugged an envelope from a side pocket on her laptop bag.

A car horn tooted, and she glanced out anxiously, then back to Jo. 'That's my taxi. Look, I found this in my laptop bag this morning. Hugh's bag is the same as mine, so maybe he confused them. I think it's some notes about an old case he was writing up last night, but I think he would have wanted Nick to see them first. I've got to go. Can you see that he gets them safely? Thanks, Jo.'

She handed the envelope to Jo and whirled out. The squarish, masculine handwriting in heavy black pen, stark against the white paper read: *Nick Matheson. Personal and Confidential.*

Personal and confidential notes about an old case? In a handwritten envelope? Goodabri might be off the beaten track, but it had Next G internet, and the pub had free wireless, so why hadn't Hugh emailed the notes to Nick?

'Files . . .' Hugh had said, in his last breathless moments. For all Shelley's belief he'd simply mixed up their bags, she hadn't been privy to that final conversation between the two men.

Footsteps sounded along the linoleum floor, and Jo turned the envelope in her hands, making her decision. She wouldn't go anywhere until she'd seen Nick and handed it directly to him.

℅

After repeated interviews during the afternoon, Murdoch's directive to go home came as no great surprise, but Nick wasn't prepared to accept it without objection.

'Are you ordering me off-duty? Or suspending me?'

The challenge didn't ruffle his superior's easy manner. Murdoch played it relaxed, leaned back in his desk chair and gave him a straight answer. 'No, I'm not. But you've worked five days straight since you started on Monday, including a night drive to Newcastle and overnight protection duties. And you lost a long-time colleague today. You probably need some down time.'

'I need to investigate several linked murders. These first days are critical.'

A lesser man would have bridled at the disagreement, and at the deliberate avoidance of the customary 'sir' from a subordinate, but Murdoch showed no sign of annoyance or anger. An excellent actor, or a man comfortable enough with his command to treat a detective as an equal? Perhaps elements of both. Everything Nick had seen so far of his new boss suggested the man was no fool. Probably as sharp as a street knife, under that comfortable persona.

'The Critical Incident team will give me a preliminary report this evening. Brock is returning to Sydney this afternoon, on compassionate leave, but there are two more detectives on their way from Homicide. I expect the CI team to hand over to Homicide, and you'll cooperate fully with them on both Mitchell's and Dalton's murders, as the cases likely overlap.'

'I've told the CI team everything I know for a fact.' A careful truth, not a lie. But he wasn't prepared to have strangers dig into Hugh's life until he'd found a few answers himself. Hugh had said he was in trouble, and there was the missing cocaine – but accusations of corruption could sometimes see a dead cop carry the can for everything, and little investigation beyond that. He wouldn't let that happen to Hugh.

Murdoch strolled to the window and ran a perfunctory glance over the view outside before turning so that the sunlight silhouetted him, the sharp contrast casting his face into shadow, obscuring his expression. A textbook interrogation technique.

'Do those "facts" include the reasons why Dalton appeared to be deliberately provoking you?'

Not a fool at all. Either he'd been watching the interviews, or someone from the CI team had briefed him.

Still sitting in the chair in front of the desk, Nick purposely relaxed, lounged back, despite the upright, symbolically more powerful stance Murdoch had taken.

'I don't know –' Nick stressed the word slightly – 'the answer to that.'

'Then give me your educated guess.' An order, not a request. From his commanding officer, who had the power to suspend him, deny him access to the investigation and police resources.

The fact that he hadn't done it, yet, indicated that Nick could trust his judgement, to a degree.

He chose his words with care. 'It's possible that Hugh may have been acting under coercion. But I don't believe it was his intention to harm anyone.'

'Is that why you didn't fire when he came at you with a knife? Or has the incident in Melbourne affected your reactions?'

Of course he would ask that, as any responsible commander should. 'No, it hasn't. Hugh and I trained in various martial arts together for many years. I know how he fights, and today he wasn't really serious. He deliberately swung the knife in a move any twelve-year-old with a week's training could block.'

'I'd still like to know why a man of Dalton's experience would appear to threaten a fellow armed officer when surrounded by others with weapons drawn.'

A reasonable query, calmly made. Murdoch knew how to apply pressure.

Nick leaned forward, elbows on his knees, relying on honesty to build the tenuous sense of trust between him and Murdoch. 'I need some more time to think it through, sir. All I have so far are fragments, and I have to work out how they go together.'

Murdoch strolled back to his desk, reaching for a pen as he sat. 'We'll have a briefing with the additional detectives at Goodabri at eight this evening. Go home and get some rest after that, and report your progress to me tomorrow morning.'

A reprieve, of sorts. But he heard the unspoken message: he'd better come up with some answers by morning. He intended to – he had a case to solve, and Jo's safety to ensure.

'Thank you. About protection for Jo Lockwood, sir. Do you have a preference for which officers I allocate?'

Murdoch rolled the pen between his fingers, taking his time to respond, his gaze unwavering. 'Matheson, the reality is that with five officers pulled off the roster for CI debriefing, and a crime scene in the middle of nowhere to preserve, we simply don't have sufficient staff. I suggest you arrange for her to stay with a friend or colleague. The National Parks team here are reliable and practical. If she's somewhere in town, a patrol can check every hour or so.'

A patrol every hour or so? Nick didn't waste breath arguing. Facts couldn't be changed; Strathnairn had limited resources, and he'd just have to deal with it, find his own way to keep Jo safe.

But first he had to find her.

He came across Matt Carruthers in the corridor outside Murdoch's office.

'Jo?' Carruthers answered his query. 'I saw her in reception, a while back.'

He found her standing by the window, staring out. Tense, like some kind of caged animal, longing for escape. Who could blame her? They'd disrupted her day, her week, and even though she had kept it together today, the emotional strain had to be difficult for her.

She must have heard the door, or seen his reflection in the window. Without any haste she turned to face him, studying him as he approached, lightly tapping a white envelope against her fingers.

Since he'd last seen her she'd changed out of her blood-stained crop-top into a T-shirt. A simple one, but the low neck, fitted shape and pastel colour brought back to mind the image of her toned skin beneath. Irrelevant. Definitely irrelevant.

'Everything okay?' she asked.

That her first concern should be for him didn't sit well with him when he was the cop and she a civilian who'd been through more these past couple of days than anyone should. And then to be left here to wait in the sterility of the police station, all stainless steel and white linoleum and coldness.

'Yes. Sorry to keep you waiting so long. Standard procedure takes a while to work through. I hope you've been treated well?'

'Perfectly fine.' She held out the envelope to him. 'I need to give you this.'

An envelope with Hugh's handwriting on it.

She glanced at the reception desk, stepped closer to him. 'Shelley had to leave before you'd finished your meetings,' she said, quietly. 'Apparently their laptop cases are similar, and Hugh *accidentally* put this in hers, not his own.' Her eyes didn't waver from his. 'She left it with me; asked me to make sure you got it.'

Nick turned the envelope in his hands, both keen and reluctant to open it. *Files*, Hugh had said. And he'd 'misplaced' this envelope so that it wasn't among his personal belongings and computer records that the CI team would go through. Convenient. Very convenient. But a deliberate action on Hugh's part, or a true mistake?

Jo's thoughts must be running along the same lines as his. And she'd made sure the envelope reached him.

'Thanks, Jo,' he said simply. She nodded.

Voices out in the corridor – Carruthers, Aaron – came closer, passed by without pausing.

Nick folded the envelope. Later. He'd read it later. 'We need to get you somewhere safe, Jo.'

She accepted the change of subject without comment. 'That's pretty much in hand. I had a phone call a few minutes ago, and apparently a number of my colleagues have been planning. Simon and a couple of the field staff have been out at the homestead today doing some maintenance work. They'll be cutting firebreaks tomorrow around the place, and so they're prepared to stay overnight. Erin's heading out there, too. Unless you object, I'll go home tonight.'

A possible solution – at least for tonight. She'd be among friends, and less than ten minutes from the police station at Goodabri. 'Are they people you can rely on? Sensible?'

'Yes, absolutely. Erin and Simon are both rangers, and are also involved in volunteer emergency services. Simon's a gentle giant at heart, but his size would scare off a few thugs. Robbo and Bruce are field staff and can pretty much turn their hand to anything. With three or four vehicles out front and five of us inside, it should be a solid enough deterrent, shouldn't it?'

There would be six inside. Until he knew more, he would not leave her without police protection.

He checked his watch – just past six. Plenty of time to get to the homestead and then out to Goodabri before eight. 'I'll take you home. I'll probably call back after tonight's briefing is over. If you don't mind, I can bunk down on the floor.'

She didn't appear to mind the suggestion, just raised an amused eyebrow, in that relaxed, teasing way of hers that he'd glimpsed sometimes. 'Don't you have a home to go to, Detective?'

A home? No. Places with a few belongings and pieces of furniture had never equalled a home. 'I'm still staying in a motel. Finding a place to rent isn't as important as ensuring your safety.'

Her head tilted slightly, studying his face, she said, 'Thank you.'

Sincere gratitude, delivered simply, and for a moment it almost floored him.

'It's my job, Jo.'

No longer joking, she challenged him. 'To be on duty for seventy-two hours straight?'

Damn. Cool cop with his colleagues, tough cop with law-breakers, courteous cop with members of the public – after years playing a ruthless criminal bastard, he'd slipped back into his police roles easily enough. But she had expressed more concern, more recognition of him as a person, than anyone had for a long time, and his repertoire of roles came up empty. Protector, yes, but circumstance had thrown them together, more than usual. Friend? How could he be a friend to her? He'd forgone friends years ago, not prepared to risk anyone being hurt by the violence he had to immerse himself in. He wasn't sure he even knew *how* to be a friend anymore.

'I do what needs to be done.' To soften it, acknowledge her concern, he added, 'I've had some sleep, both nights. Enough to get by.'

'Good.' She managed a smile. 'But let me know if you need me to drive, so you can catch a nap on the way to Riverbank.'

He needed to drive. To keep his eyes on the road, and not on her.

She sat beside him in the car, silent until he'd pulled out of the police station car park and around a couple of corners on to the main street. He heard her slow intake of breath, and in the corner of his vision he could see candid hazel eyes steady on him.

'I wasn't asked for details of what Hugh said in the church, and I didn't offer them,' she said. 'I figured that was personal, between the two of you. I just told them he was barely conscious. I'm not entirely sure why, and maybe I'm a fool, but I'm trusting you, Nick. I hope that isn't one enormous mistake.'

That explained why they hadn't grilled him about Hugh's dying words. Because Jo hadn't revealed them. If they'd asked her, she wouldn't have lied – he understood that about her – but she had decided to leave it up to his judgement what to reveal.

Jo trusted him, when his colleagues still regarded him with suspicion and doubt.

He had to clear his throat before he spoke. 'I'm grateful, Jo. I didn't tell them much because I need some time to piece the full truth together. I know you've got more than enough reason to doubt him, but whatever his failings, whatever he got caught up in, Hugh was a decent man at heart. I hope his letter gives me some answers to what happened.'

'I hope so, too – for all our sakes.'

She fell silent again, rested her head back against the head rest and closed her eyes.

He thought about the envelope as he slowed the car to turn on to the highway.

One glance at the familiar untidy scrawl against the white paper and he'd almost heard Hugh's laconic tone, saying his name, one last time. Now he saw in his mind's eye not the grown man, the detective, but the skinny, half-starved feral kid, surviving on cheek and attitude. An additional responsibility that he'd accepted, because the lad's fierce loyalty to Pat and Christie and Grace had earned him more than his share of fights, bruises and bloodied noses. And because Hugh, the irrepressible clown, had made them laugh, when his siblings, with their father in prison and mother gravely ill, had little enough to laugh about.

A few pages, Hugh had left him, judging by the thickness of the packet. Hardly 'files', but he had to hope there'd be enough information to lead to a break in the case, a solid direction to investigate.

He had to trust Hugh, despite the questions and shadows over his behaviour.

He had to trust Hugh, in the same way that Jo trusted him, despite her unanswered questions.

He'd return her trust by sharing as much of the information with her as he could. Just as soon as he made sense of it all.

THIRTEEN

The low sunlight cast long tree shadows, a constant flickering of bright light and shade across the road that strained her vision.

Closing her eyes, trying to relax, failed; her mind too occupied with the events of the day and the image of Nick, staring stony-faced at the road.

Sometime during the day, he'd changed his bloodied clothes for the navy blue search-and-rescue uniform. Fighting with Hugh, he'd been more than warrior enough, even in the civilised business clothes; now the dark uniform T-shirt shaped lean, hard muscle, a potent reminder of potential force and energy.

A complex man, Nick Matheson. Intelligent, courteous, intellectually and physically powerful . . . and an excellent actor, in control of all his outward expressions of emotion.

Yet she trusted him. If the interviewing detective had specifically asked her what Hugh had said, she'd have had to tell him. Although her personal code of ethics could accept –

just – the omission, an outright lie would have been a different matter. She'd have needed a lot more than instinct to justify that.

Instinct? No, she had more reason than that to trust Nick. His commitment to duty, to start with; he'd scarcely stopped since he'd arrived at the murder scene on Wednesday. His concern for her safety – even to the point of risking his own life to knock down a man with a gun aimed at her. And the glimpses she'd caught of powerful feeling beneath the controlled demeanour. Those facts all added up to a man with a strong core of integrity and dedication.

She wondered about his family; the siblings who had died, the sister he hadn't seen for years, the violence he'd hinted at in his youth. More than enough sorrow in those events alone to give a man reasons to build a wall around his emotions. But he'd also worked undercover, for a long time, it seemed. What did that do to a man? The roles he had to play, the kinds of people he had to live with, the things he had to do to survive? Not questions she could easily ask, not just now, despite the tentative friendship their shared experiences in the past few days had brought.

Neither of them bothered with small talk, letting the silence sit between them. There was only the rumble of the engine, the occasional sound of a passing car, and the clicking of the indicator as he slowed to turn off the highway on to the short-cut road to Goodabri.

'This is the right road, isn't it?' he asked.

'Yes,' she replied, then added almost without thinking, 'Watch out for kangaroos. There can be a fair few around, this time of day.'

'I will.'

The quietly spoken agreement made her realise how few *facts* she knew about him. 'I assumed you were a city type. My apologies if I got that wrong, and I just told a country boy the obvious.'

The silence returned for a moment before he answered. 'I've worked in all sorts of places.'

An answer, but not an answer. And no invitation to probe. She didn't press him for more details. If he'd wanted to tell her where he came from, he could have. He probably had far too much on his mind to engage in idle chat. Whereas she could have done with distraction from the worry of things she could do little about.

Distraction came when they arrived at Riverbank. Her workmates were still on the job, clearing the last of the old, straggling hedge from the garden perimeter, cutting dangerous low limbs off the eucalypt trees.

Not just cleared of fire hazards; cleared of hiding places. Little now obstructed the view between the homestead and the paddocks beyond the dirt road.

One of the work trucks was already loaded high with garden waste. Beside it, Rob and Bruce watched the car approach up the drive, visibly relaxing when they recognised her. As Nick parked in front of the garage, Erin came round from the back of the homestead, whipper-snipper in hand.

The heat hit Jo the moment she stepped out of the air-conditioned car, and in an odd way she was grateful for it. Alive, and back in familiar surroundings. If not alone, then with people she could relax with.

Erin greeted her with a concerned once-over, disguised with a grin.

'Good timing,' she said. 'We're just finishing up. Simon will have food on the table in thirty minutes. If you hurry, you can have first shower, before we hard-working types use all the hot water.'

A shower and food. Definitely good ideas. She'd had no appetite for the sandwiches offered at the police station, but that was hours ago.

Erin gave Nick the once-over, too, but in an altogether different way. Part protective-lioness, part twinkle-in-the-eye.

Jo introduced them, and they shook hands. Nick polite, serious, as though he hadn't noticed Erin's appreciative gleam.

Erin gestured towards the house. 'Simon's in the kitchen. Head on in and I'll join you in a few minutes.' Tucking the whipper-snipper under her arm, she strode away.

'Will you stay for something to eat, Nick?' Jo asked. 'It's been a long time since breakfast, and Simon always makes enough to feed a platoon.'

He glanced at his watch, and nodded. 'I will, thanks. I'll get my laptop.'

The rich, hearty aroma of Simon's Bolognese sauce wafted out through the screen door, setting her stomach rumbling even before she'd stepped inside. She paused in the hallway.

'You'll want some quiet to read Hugh's letter. Use the office. No-one will disturb you. I'll knock when dinner's ready.'

'Thanks, Jo.' He looked, for a moment, like a man who'd been on the go for three days straight. 'I'll have to eat and run, though. The briefing's in Goodabri at eight.'

No rest for him yet, apparently.

'Use whatever you need in the office. Phone, internet – the wireless password is "Riverbank".'

She closed the office door and left him, giving him the little privacy she could. It was all she *could* do, just now, and the inactivity and lack of control over her own life and decisions gnawed at her, a constant restlessness and whirring of frustration in her thoughts mingling with the growing fear that she had been trying to ignore all afternoon.

In her bedroom, she stood in the centre of the room, suddenly so tired she could scarcely think straight. Simon clattered pots and whistled in the kitchen, Robbo and Bruce talked out on the veranda as they sharpened the chainsaw, and the whipper-snipper buzzed in the direction of the small shed.

All of them doing their almost-normal work, while her routine had been thrown topsy-turvy.

A shower. Although she'd had a good scrub with disinfectant at the police station and changed into a fresh T-shirt, the memory of a dying man's blood spattered on her body couldn't be easily washed away.

Hugh's blood. Hugh, lying dead on the floor of the church . . . She felt the shock of reaction finally hit, wrapped her arms around her body to stop the trembling radiating out from her centre, rocked backwards and forwards on her feet and tried desperately to hold back the tears that burned her eyes.

Damn, she couldn't break down now. Couldn't, wouldn't. Had to hold everything together. She sucked in air, concentrated on deepening, slowing, her rapid shallow breathing, biting her lip so that she'd breathe through her nose, not her mouth.

Counting her breaths, blocking out wild thoughts with the steadily building numbers.

She'd reached a hundred and thirty before the trembling slowed right down.

Her still hands shook when she unclasped them, and she had to think to make them undo the band holding back her hair.

She needed to move, act, do *something* other than rock in useless whimpering.

A shower, clean clothes, a meal, and she would be functional again. Mostly. And then . . . ? She'd have to think about what she could effectively *do* towards solving these crimes. She knew the landscape. She'd built up a reasonable amount of trust and respect with the locals. She had to be able to contribute *something*.

Considerate of the others, she didn't spend long under the shower, despite the temptation. But she shampooed her hair, and she unwrapped the rose-scented soap her mother had sent last Christmas and lathered her skin with it.

Despite that feminine indulgence, she pulled on a linen shirt from the wardrobe and buttoned it up over a pair of comfortable, cotton trousers, slipping her feet into flat leather sandals.

As she combed her hair, Simon gave a general call-out that food would be ready in five.

The office door remained closed, all quiet beyond it. She knocked, opened the door when he said to come in.

On the desk, the pages of the letter lay face down. Nick stood by the window, his face hidden from her as he looked out between the gap in the curtains.

She remained just inside the doorway, partly to block the sight-lines of anyone passing, partly to give him space. Partly to give herself and her fragile emotions some distance from him. No sign of his usual impassive expression in the brief glimpse around as she'd come in.

'Dinner's almost ready. I'll bring some food in if you want some more time,' she said gently.

'No. It's okay.' He exhaled a long, slow breath and faced her, keeping some space between them. Weariness clouded his dark eyes, took the edge off the intensity of his usual control. 'He wanted to die. Believed he deserved it. The fight – it was to give me a reason to shoot him.'

'But you didn't,' she said softly. Words for Nick, not the furious words she'd have flung at Hugh, if she could have. How dare he try to force that decision, that responsibility, onto Nick? Reading the letter must have been harrowing.

She let her comment rest in the silence, didn't push him. If he needed to talk, she'd listen. If he needed something more – physical contact, a touch, a hug – then hell, she could do with the same thing herself. If not, so be it. Witnessing death together created a shared experience, the beginnings of a friendship, but they still hardly knew each other.

'No, I didn't. But I failed him, nonetheless.' His mouth a grim line, he scooped the pages of the letter together, folded them along the original fold lines.

Conversation over. He had experience with sudden death, doubtless had his own ways of dealing with his emotional reactions.

He fitted the folded pages back into the envelope and slid between them a small plastic bag containing a micro memory card.

He caught her glance at it. 'The files Hugh mentioned. He said everything he knows is on there. I just have to find a card adaptor so that I can read it.'

That problem could be easily solved. 'I have one,' she told him. 'My GPS uses a micro SD card. I'll get it for you.'

She deliberately didn't probe – about the letter, about what might be on the files, about anything. He had a heck of a lot more to deal with than her, and he'd tell her anything she needed to know, when he'd had time to process it.

She trusted him on that.

ை

By the time you read this, I'll probably be either dead or in a cell. If you shot me yourself, then everything's gone the way I wanted it to. If you didn't, by the time you get to the end of this, you'll wish you had.

Hugh's opening lines stuck in Nick's head, playing relentlessly over and over and over, charging his anger further with each repetition. Anger with Hugh, for a thousand reasons. For even thinking that he'd fire to kill him. For trying to put him in that position. For keeping secrets. For becoming so entangled that he could see no way out and *wanted* to die.

But the heat of his anger with Hugh had nothing on the searing anger at himself.

If he'd kept in more frequent contact with Hugh, he might still be alive. In protective custody, perhaps, but not lying cold in a morgue. If he'd contacted Hugh once his own case was over, he might have uncovered his problems: the desperate cocaine use, the blackmailing scum who'd supplied him and the bastard they'd sold their information on to. He knew from the inside how those networks operated: target a cop on the edge of a breakdown, gather information to hold over them. If he'd known Hugh was in deep, he could have acted. The bastard behind the John Doe murder in Coffs Harbour might have been arrested, and Travis Mitchell might still be alive. Grace would be safe. Jo would be safe.

Failure sat heavily in his chest.

He seriously considered making some excuse, avoiding the shared meal, but it would be a long night and he needed to eat. His hurried breakfast toast, here in this kitchen with Aaron and Jo, seemed a whole lot longer than thirteen hours ago.

He wasn't sure what he'd expected of this meal – maybe a camp-out mood, beer and frivolity. But no, these were professionals, taking their task seriously, determined to assist a colleague and friend in need, and although there were some jokes and teasing, the underlying mood when they all sat around the table was sober.

Simon's culinary skills matched his professional confidence and leadership, and the two other men, while quick to give cheek, deferred to him in a good-natured way. Despite Erin's sassy scrutiny when they'd met, her attention – when it wasn't on Jo – was all for Simon. An interest that the man returned, although there was little overt about it, as if he was ill-at-ease with his own attraction.

And that, Nick could relate to. Across the table from him, Jo joined in the conversation as warm damper and steaming bowls of spaghetti Bolognese were passed around, comfortable in the company but with the underlying tension of the situation showing in her quiet manner and the strain around her eyes.

A close-knit team, who genuinely liked and cared about each other. And who were all, in no subtle way, assessing him.

Once they'd finished serving and started eating, Jo unfolded a map in front of her on the table.

'Let's think about this. Three incidents in the past few days, all between Derringvale and this point in the park, which can be accessed off the Derringvale Road. We all drive along that route often.' She glanced up at Nick to add in explanation, 'There's another park on the other side of Derringvale, to the north-west. Now, if we all go over the past couple of weeks, think about who's been out in any of the parks, any incidents or unusual happenings, anything even vaguely out of the ordinary, then we might come up with something that can help the police.'

Nick nodded his agreement, inwardly respecting Jo even more for pushing her own fears aside to focus on ways to move the investigation forward. These people knew the district well, both on-road and off-road, and interacted with a variety of people, out and about. 'Good idea. That photo you took of Bradley Coulter last night, Jo – pass it around. Travis Mitchell's sister supplied a photo of him, taken a few weeks ago. I'd like to know if any of you have seen either of them, and if so, when and where.'

He took out his phone, started scrolling through emails with one hand while hurriedly eating a few more mouthfuls with the other. When he found the email with the image of Travis, he passed the phone to Simon, on his right. Simon took a few moments to study the picture, and handed it to Erin.

Erin's fork stopped halfway to her mouth, hit the bowl again with a clatter.

'Him. Yes. I know him. I'm sure it's him. Robbo, take a look.'

The phone shook in her hand as she passed it across the table, but she pulled herself together enough to explain.

'A few months back, maybe July? It wasn't long before you came here, Jo. Anyway, Nick, sometimes we get groups from the low-security prison out doing projects for us. It's a government-organised program. They've got their own specially equipped van, and they stay on site. That guy was part of a group that re-did the fencing along the southern boundary of the park. I was liaison for that project and I remember him, because he was forever trying to chat me up.'

'Yeah, it's him all right,' Rob agreed. 'Brash young hoon, full of himself. Not much of a worker.'

Her face pale, Jo pushed the map closer to Nick. 'The southern boundary of the park crosses the Derringvale Road at Eight Mile Creek, near the McCulloch woolshed. Then it roughly parallels the road west –' she stretched to trace a path on the paper with her finger – 'to here, where it turns north. Not far across the river from Church Lane.'

She watched him to ensure he grasped the significance.

He did. 'Travis Mitchell knew at least two of the three crime sites. But he died at the first one.' So others had known those two sites – and their abandoned buildings – well enough to make plans to use them.

She followed his line of thought as if he'd spoken it aloud. 'Plenty of people would know the Derringvale Road. Locals, regular travellers from the north-west to Goodabri or beyond. Some people head down Church Lane to fish in the river. But it's still a possible link, isn't it?'

'Yes. We're following up Mitchell's contacts in prison. I'll make sure we find out who else was on that work gang. Thanks for that lead, Erin.'

'I'll get the photos of Bradley Coulter in a minute,' Jo said. 'In case he was one of that crew, too.'

Rob passed his phone back to him, and Nick registered the time on the display. 'I'll have to get moving. I expect to come back later on – I'll use the police lights on the car as I approach. In the meantime, if you can, as Jo suggested, go over any recent events, that would be useful.'

Travis Mitchell's previous visit to the district added another sliver of information to the hazy, incomplete picture. Hugh's letter had added a little more, and answers, if there were any, might well be in the files.

Jo left the kitchen with him to get the card adaptor, silent beside him when she had every right and plenty of cause to demand explanations. But to explain to her meant to reveal more of himself than anyone, other than Hugh, had ever known.

He'd do everything in his power to keep her safe, but by the time she read Hugh's letter, and he explained the history between them, she would know that he'd failed, repeatedly, to protect those for whom he was responsible. He doubted he would hold on to the fragile beginnings of trust she had placed in him.

He'd give her the letter and let her make her own choice, fully informed.

When she brought in the card adaptor, he held out the letter to her. 'I'll answer your questions after you've read it.'

She brushed it away. 'It's personal, Nick. Between you and Hugh.'

Personal, yes. And there was one paragraph in there, with no bearing on the case, that he'd rather she didn't read. But he could hardly take scissors to it.

'You were there when he died. You heard what he said. That must have raised questions in your mind. You need the truth so you can decide whether to keep trusting me with your life.'

He placed it on the desk, took his laptop and left the room without looking back at her, without knowing whether she'd picked it up or not.

The last of the day's light was fading as he drove towards Goodabri, the narrow road darkening with shadows, the moon not yet rising.

Alone for the first time since he'd read the letter, its implications occupied his thoughts, and he could visualise the words on the pages, hear them in his head as clearly as if Hugh spoke beside him.

I never told you about me and Christie, because you and your father could be right scary bastards, and I knew she deserved better than me.

Hugh had blamed himself for Pat's and Christie's deaths, when the real blame lay with the criminal mob their father had become mixed up with on the docks, and the shifting loyalties and betrayals when they'd come under police and government scrutiny.

Nick could all too easily imagine his father's reputation terrorising the young Hugh into silence. It didn't matter that the reputation exceeded reality. Archie Matheson had been a fighter, an unbeaten champion of no rules, no holds barred back-street fighting that nobody dared cross. Fear had beaten more people than his fists – exactly the way he intended. Until the crime bosses framed him for an assault he didn't commit, and he'd gone to prison.

When it came to reputation management, Nick had learned from his father's example. A survival skill, not one that made him proud. But he'd learned it young, and he'd used it, as deliberately and as ruthlessly as his father had, to protect his siblings.

He couldn't recall Hugh ever visiting their father in prison, but he'd have heard enough on the streets to fear him. And although their father had never abused or intentionally terrorised his kids, he'd probably grilled Christie about boyfriends on her visits, all protective father, despite being behind bars.

But Hugh hadn't been the danger, and Christie and Pat had paid the price for their father's decision to give critical evidence for the prosecution in the high-profile murder trial of mob boss Victor Zinchenko. Their father had been relatively safe, in solitary confinement – but two of his children had been gunned down at a bus-stop, in a drive-by shooting.

Nick hadn't understood, until he'd read those handwritten pages, how deeply Christie's loss had affected Hugh.

Even now, I still can't get her out of my head. The psychs would probably have a field day with that. They'd have a full-on fucking festival with all the shit in my head.

Typically Hugh, that sardonic black humour, and yet . . . And yet a call for help, for comprehension, beneath it.

A call he was too damn late to do anything about.

ॐ

Jo closed her bedroom door to shut out the noise – Rob and Bruce unrolling sleeping bags in the bunk room, Erin and Simon talking quietly while they washed dishes – and curled up in her large wicker chair, reluctantly opening the envelope.

A confession of sorts, the raw honesty of the letter told her as much about Nick as it did about Hugh. Hard to read, not because of the untidy, inconsistent lettering, but because of the raw emotion layered beneath the self-deprecating tone.

Some of the references went over her head, but with the bare bones Nick had told her about his siblings, and what she knew of both men, she made sense of most of it. The 'too-young' Hugh, hiding his relationship with Christie because 'she deserved better than me', almost broken by her death. The longing that had seen him visit Grace time and again after she'd contacted him a year ago, because he 'wanted that time back, before Christie and Pat were killed'.

No wonder Nick had looked so shaken, his control cracking, when she'd gone into the office earlier.

Hugh's respect for Nick came through strongly.

I still wish, sometimes, that I'd died instead of them. You probably do, too. But you kept me out of the gutter, and you and the police force gave me a purpose to keep going.

But there came the confession of a worn-out cop who'd seen 'too many drive-by shootings' and found alcohol and sex no longer enough to allow him to forget. A line of cocaine, a dealer who sold that information to others, and 'my life hasn't been my own since'.

He feared for Grace, trusted Nick would ensure her safety. *You're her brother . . .*

She very nearly folded the pages back up, the rest unread. When she read the next sentences, a part of her wished she had.

. . . will you ever get your own life together? I've never seen you look at a woman the way you look at Jo. I didn't really think she was guilty of anything – I was just trying to prod some response from you. If she's right for you, don't throw it away on some rubbish notion of duty . . . The undercover shit is eating you alive.

She forced a long, deep breath, telling herself not to put much credence in the observations of someone in such an unstable state of mind.

She closed her eyes briefly, shut out the scrawl and the confusion it was creating in her. Regardless of whether Hugh was right or way off base, this stuff was too personal, too intrusive into Nick's private life. She understood he wanted her to read it because she'd witnessed those last words of Hugh's, but he couldn't have been comfortable about this.

She began the last page – case-related, a reference to the 'John Doe up the coast' being connected, and the admission he'd been ordered to compromise the Mitchell investigation.

Eliminating her had been one of his orders, presumably. Her skin cold, her fingers stiff, she could scarcely hold the paper any longer as she skimmed the last lines.

If I've done any decent, worthwhile things in my life, they're because of you. The screwed-up shit is purely my own doing.

The writing blurred before her eyes, her chest tight.

What she'd seen of Hugh, and now what she'd read, began to fit together into a whole that made sense. A man who wore a confident, devil-may-care mask to conceal a soul scarred, traumatised; compromised by a stupid action, weighed down by guilt, and desperate to escape it and see things made right. Desperate enough to plan to force a situation in which Nick would shoot him . . . *because that would be quicker and more fitting than what the bastard's minions would do to me.*

Hands shaking again, she dropped the letter onto her desk, went into the bathroom, splashing cold water onto her face, staring at herself in the mirror as water dripped to the basin.

Eyes wide, skin pale, breathing shallow . . . *shit*, she had to master herself, stop the panic from taking over again.

She was safe here, and despite hating the confinement, the drawn curtains, the lack of freedom, she wasn't going to do anything to put herself in danger.

She'd seen what they'd done to Travis.

She would focus on helping Nick; the sooner he sorted out this case the sooner she would be safe, free, and then she could think about everything else. She would go through the camping permits records. She would go through her photos. She would compile everything the others remembered into a list, a map, and look for links. If there was anything she could find to help Nick's investigation, he'd have it before morning.

FOURTEEN

The dark, empty streets of Goodabri contrasted with the Ferris-wheel lights and the noise from the showground at the edge of town, where most of the locals had congregated. Only a few cars stood in front of the pub; other than that, the main street was quiet, except for the cars parked around the temporary incident base. More than he expected.

With only ten minutes to spare before the briefing started, and Hugh's files to look over, he avoided time-wasting conversation by staying in the car, connecting Jo's card adaptor to his laptop and inserting the micro-card.

He found a single, encrypted folder.

Hugh had written in the letter: *Everything I've got so far is in the files. What happened on Pat's birthday will get you into them.*

What happened on Pat's birthday . . . He remembered. Jesus, he remembered, couldn't forget. The day that should have been

Pat's sixteenth birthday, a month after they'd died, riddled with bullets. An empty, grief-filled day.

He'd worked, worked for fourteen hours straight, two shifts on a demolition crew, carting and stacking and tearing apart anything of value in an old factory, working himself to exhaustion to forget . . . so when the police came to question him, it had taken a while for the news of the Zinchenko brothers' deaths in a car-bomb explosion to sink in. The Zinchenko brothers, widely suspected of being the ones who'd killed Pat and Christie, in revenge for Archie Matheson's evidence against Victor Zinchenko.

The box on the screen prompted him for a password.

Another line in Hugh's letter became meaningful.

What happened on Pat's birthday will get you into them. And if you're wondering about that, the answer is yes.

Grinding his teeth, he typed 'revenge'. Nothing happened. He typed 'explosion', 'car bomb', even, thinking of Hugh's warped sense of humour, variations on 'kaboom'. None of them worked.

How would Hugh define it? He'd taken no pleasure, made no black jokes, simply said, as exhausted and dispirited as Nick was, 'That's justice, isn't it?'

Not revenge. *Justice.* Nick didn't agree with the means, could never have condoned it and was damned glad he'd never known, but he could at least understand the young Hugh's actions, when the law had been helpless to act.

Nick typed the word, giving it a capital letter, and the folder opened.

Files . . . yes, Hugh definitely had made records. More than a dozen sub-folders, with notes, images, audio and video recordings.

With little time to spare, Nick copied the folders across to his laptop.

Inside, the main room bustled with people rearranging tables, desks and computers, making more space for those gathered. Some he knew – officers who should have been off-duty, like Matt Carruthers, Dee Edwards and Aaron Georgiou. Murdoch stood at the front of the room, in discussion with two officers in plain clothes. The additional detectives, Nick assumed.

Murdoch beckoned him, and one of the two detectives turned as he approached. Leah Haddad. Her dark hair cut short, no longer quite as skinny as she'd been, and a wedding ring on her finger.

She greeted him with genuine warmth, and a handshake that lasted a fraction longer than necessary.

'It's been a while, Nick. And I would have preferred better circumstances.'

Sixteen years since basic training. Twelve years since they'd worked together in Cooma. And ten years since they'd posed as a couple on the north coast, and arrested a drug-dealing cruise-boat operator. They'd crossed paths briefly a few times since then, but never for long.

'It's good to see you, Leah.' He meant it. Dedicated, ambitious, and hardworking, she had a reputation for getting things done. 'Last I heard, you were in Wollongong.'

'Still am, officially. But I was seconded to Homicide in Sydney three months ago.' She regarded him with concern. 'I heard about the Melbourne business. Is everything all right for you?'

He nodded, grateful for her unspoken vote of trust. She knew undercover ops, had done a stint in the specialist unit and had plenty of connections. Even with most of the details of the Melbourne case still suppressed for operational reasons, she would have her ways of finding out information.

Murdoch called the room to order and began the briefing as Nick expected, with the introduction of Leah and her partner, some respectful comments about the shock of Hugh's death and a summary of the CI team's preliminary report, the forensic evidence confirming their witness statements that a sniper's bullets had killed Hugh.

'Please note that Detective Dalton's name must not be released to the media until his next of kin are informed. Unfortunately, his nominated next-of-kin contact is currently on a London-to-Sydney flight and is unaware of his passing. My counterpart at HQ will meet her at the airport in the morning.'

Her, Nick noted. But not Shelley. Most of Hugh's affairs lasted no more than a few weeks. The only things he'd stayed committed to were his career and his martial-arts training.

Until Grace had come back into his life.

She hadn't answered the phone when Nick had tried calling from Jo's place . . . possibly because she was on a London-to-Sydney flight. Grace used her adoptive parents' surname, not Matheson, so Murdoch wouldn't have connected her to Nick.

'Funeral arrangements will be advised in due course,' Murdoch continued, and although his gaze swept the room, encompassing them all, it finished on Nick, with an unspoken question. A police officer killed in the line of duty traditionally received a full police funeral with honours. Nick gave a very small shake of his head, a gesture only Murdoch would notice and understand.

There would be no such honours for Hugh. The confessions in his letter would have to come out. They might avoid publicity, but Murdoch and others had to be informed.

Murdoch went on smoothly, 'I've accepted the CI team's preliminary recommendations, and as there appears to be a clear connection between Dalton's murder, the stolen weapons and possibly Travis Mitchell's murder, I'm authorising Nick Matheson to continue heading up the investigation, liaising with Detective Haddad. Matheson, I'll hand over to you now.'

Not a popular decision, judging by some of the glances exchanged as he strode the few paces to face the gathering. The shooting death of a second police officer in his presence in the space of three months would only add fuel to the conspiracy theories. But he'd never earn trust or respect from them if he let that sway him.

On the whiteboard, in Hugh's scrawled writing, the tasks allocated at the briefing that morning remained. The routine of working through those, getting reports, following up, would keep them all focused and on task.

'Let's start with Garry Coulter's nephew. We suspect he spent a night or two at his uncle's house in Strathnairn recently. Any progress on his background and current whereabouts?'

'I did some digging this arvo,' Aaron said. 'Bradley James Coulter was sentenced in Sydney last year to nine months for a break and enter. He served the last three months at Glen Innes – it's a minimum-security facility. He's been out since August.'

Nick nodded. 'That's a lead. Mitchell was on a prison work crew in the National Park in July. They did fencing from here,' he traced the line on the map, between the pins designating the crime scenes, 'to here. Find out from Corrective Services the name of every man in that work crew, and exactly where they went while they were there.'

'Will do. I don't have another address for Coulter yet. His driver's licence lists an address in Sydney that was demolished six months ago. Corrective Services has the same one.'

'Finding Bradley Coulter is a priority. Contact Social Security. Do whatever you need to.' Confident Aaron would handle all that, he moved to the next item on his mental list. 'The truck this morning – who ran the rego?'

'I did,' Dee Edwards responded. 'Plates had been changed, so it took a while to find the real rego details. It was reported stolen from a property west of Moree yesterday. The owner came back from a few days in hospital to find his shed broken into, and the truck and two farm bikes gone.'

A truck and two farm bikes. Transport for stolen goods and getaway in one job.

'Who went after the sniper? What do we have on him?'

'Not much, Sarge,' Carruthers answered. 'He rode off on a bike straightaway, across the paddock. Not a powerful bike – the engine sounded a bit dodgy, but he was pushing it hard over rough ground. No helmet, brown hair, brown T-shirt, but other than that I don't think any of us got a good look at him.'

Nick knew the rest of the story, from the hurried updates he'd gleaned at the church. By the time they'd got to the cars, and over the river, the sniper had had too much of a head start.

Aaron had organised road blocks on the surrounding roads, but there'd been no sign of the biker.

Brown hair and brown T-shirt could describe around sixty per cent of the male population of the district. But that description and the dodgy bike engine didn't match the biker Jo had seen the day before Mitchell was murdered.

'Forensics were still processing the site late this afternoon,' Murdoch said. 'They've promised an initial report in the morning.'

Nick read between the lines. If there'd been anything significant – like a dropped rifle, or a piece of clothing or a drink bottle potentially swarming with DNA – forensics would have reported it immediately. Fingerprints on the truck or the remaining guns might be their best hope.

That and good old-fashioned police work. 'Right – Travis was young, and so is Bradley Coulter. It's Friday night. Divide up the pubs – here, Derringvale, Strathnairn and any other communities in the district – take a copy of their photos, and the composite of the man Jo Lockwood saw, and show them around. Find out who's seen them, when, who they were with – names, descriptions, whatever you can get.' He remembered the bright lights at the showground. 'Ask around at the Show, too. Locals and stall holders, especially around the sideshows. If you find Coulter, arrest him and notify me immediately.'

He dismissed them, and Aaron took over handing out photographs and coordinating teams for pub visits.

'You haven't got much to go on yet, have you?' Leah challenged lightly when he joined her and Murdoch at the back of the room.

Although she'd taken a back seat in this briefing, her challenge confirmed that her ambitious nature hadn't changed, and she wouldn't be content playing second fiddle for long. She would want to make it her case, her success.

He only wanted what he'd always wanted – to get criminal scum off the streets, preferably while keeping his name and his face out of the media. So he'd take her contribution, use her skills, work with her to solve the case, and she could have the credit and the media appearances.

'We have a name and a face for one suspect, and a face for another. When we find Coulter, we'll have more. If you've got other leads to follow, I'd be happy to hear them.'

'The one notable omission from your lines of enquiry is into Hugh Dalton himself. Why was he targeted? Why not you or any of the others?'

That question couldn't be answered in a room full of police. Word would get out eventually, but it should be through official statements. He waved Leah and Murdoch into a small office and pulled the door closed behind him.

He could not protect Hugh. Hugh must have understood that, must have expected it, the moment he'd left the letter in Shelley's laptop bag.

But it still felt like a betrayal to say to his commander, to say to a senior detective from Homicide, damning words that could never be taken back. 'Hugh was compromised, initially blackmailed about his drug use, but he'd been acting under coercion for a while. With someone he cared about threatened, I think he got to the point he could see only one way out. He set up that confrontation, intending to provoke his own death, because he refused to eliminate Jo Lockwood as ordered.'

Leah whistled. Murdoch propped on the edge of the desk, arms folded. 'You're sure about that, Matheson? You have evidence?'

'Yes. He said a few things during the fight. And before he came in this morning he arranged for a memory card containing files to get to me; I received it late this afternoon. It seems he wanted it all over, one way or another, today.'

'Why not just hand himself in?' Leah asked.

'Because that wouldn't have protected his . . . his friend. If they thought he was spilling information, she would be endangered. I believe he saw an opportunity to escape an untenable situation, and took it, making it look – more or less effectively – that he'd been thwarted in an attempt to kill Jo. Arguing with me, coming at me with a knife, almost guaranteed that one of us would fire at him.'

'But the sniper at the river silenced him first,' Murdoch observed. 'Where is his friend? We'll need to protect her.'

Hugh's 'friend'. Neither sister nor lover, but the word 'friend' seemed inadequate for the deep longing revealed by the letter. *She's beautiful, Nick, and sane and gentle and so like Christie I kept going up to Brisbane to see her . . . I swear I didn't touch her, but I couldn't keep away.*

Certainty settled in his gut. 'I don't know for sure where she is. But if his next-of-kin contact is Grace Anderson, then that's her.'

'Yes. None of us in Sydney knows her, though. He went out with various women, but he didn't speak of her. Do you know who she is?' Leah asked.

'Yes.' He couldn't let them see the effort it took to speak as if it didn't matter to him. 'She's my sister. Hugh knew her when he was a teenager, and has been in contact with her recently.'

'Your sister?' Leah queried, eyes sharpening on him. 'I shared a house on a job with you for two months, and you never mentioned a sister. I thought you had no family.'

He'd never mentioned a great many things to her, despite the intimacy of pretending to be a couple, and long hours of close proximity.

But he needed to ward off any suggestion that Grace's connection to him compromised his involvement in the case. He needed to stay involved to keep her safe.

'I haven't seen her since I was eighteen and authorised her adoption by her foster carers,' he said, blunt and hard and factual in spite of, maybe because of, how much it hurt. 'She was twelve. I doubt we'd even recognise each other.'

CஓS

Jo studied the maps spread on the table, and compared the highlighter dots to the list on the notepad. Outside, the three men did another tour of the grounds, flashlights casting occasional arcs around the edge of the curtains. At the kitchen counter, Erin added ice to a jug of water. The draft from the overhead fan tugged at the edge of the notepad paper as Jo turned to the second page, and checked off the remaining points on the list.

'Are you seeing what I'm seeing, Erin?'

Erin brought over the jug and a couple of glasses and sat down again.

'I'm seeing a lot of fluoro-coloured dots on photocopied maps. Isn't that what I'm supposed to be seeing?'

'If you were going to commit a crime in this park, or hide something, where would you do it?'

'I don't know. Somewhere isolated, I guess. The old hut on Johnson's Fire Trail. The hollow tree at Sandy Creek. The rock overhang at Diggers Falls. There's plenty of places off the beaten track.'

'Exactly. Each of those places is marked on a park map, even the old state forest map. You can get to them all with a two-wheel-drive. But none of them have facilities yet, and they're off the main park loops.'

'And none of them,' Erin said, finding each place with her finger, 'have fluoro dots on them.'

'Every instance of loutish behaviour we've recalled, every BMW bike rider, every overnight party we've cleaned up after, has been in one of the other parks, or in one of the two camping grounds the prison crew used in July.'

Erin leaned back in her chair, sipping water, her eyes still on the map. 'If they're all the same lot, they don't know this park well, do they?'

'No, they don't. More like tourists passing through than local bush lads. If you were going to murder someone, why risk doing it in such a public place? Leaving the body so close was a risk, too – it might not have been found soon, but it would have been eventually. Anybody who knows the area at all could think of a heap of places it wouldn't be found. I mean, people hiding garbage can be more creative than that.'

A yawn cut her short, and she screwed up her eyes, sucking in oxygen.

'You should get some sleep, Jo.'

'No, not yet. I'll wait until Nick gets back at least. He'll want to see this.' And she wasn't likely to sleep much, anyway, so she might as well stay up.

'Interesting guy, your Nick,' Erin observed.

Frustration and tiredness made her irritable, despite the relative innocence of Erin's comment.

'There's no "my" Nick about it, Erin. He's a workaholic cop doing his job.' *I've never seen you look at a woman the way you look at Jo* . . . Damn Hugh for sticking that into her head. Nick knew she had read it, and now it would hang between them, like whatever else it was that was developing. But still, she had no reason to be cranky with Erin. 'Just don't go imagining something that isn't there, okay?'

'Sorry. I'm just a romantic at heart, and I'd like to see you have a happy-ever-after.'

'I had a happy-for-five-years, which is more than a lot of people get.'

'Would you get involved with someone again? Or was Leon your one and only?'

Damn. If they were going to talk about this, she needed alcohol. Or chocolate. Since she had to keep her head about her, chocolate would have to do.

She tugged open the fridge door and rummaged in the back for the block she'd bought a few days ago.

Erin misread her silence. 'Sorry, Jo. None of my business. You must still miss him.'

Yes, she still missed him. Sometimes. His ready grin, his bear hugs, his full-on energy. But sometimes days passed now without memories catching her unawares. And as she said to Erin, 'It's okay,' she accepted that it was. Really. All of it. Even the days passing without thinking of him.

She broke off a row of chocolate and tossed the rest to her friend. 'As for being my one and only, I don't know that I believe in the soul-mate, one-true-love destiny thing. There's more than seven billion people on the planet. If there were only one for each person out of all those billions, the statistical chance of finding them is pretty low.'

Erin snorted while chewing her chocolate. 'Trust you to bring love down to logic and statistics, Doctor Lockwood.'

'Oh, love's rarely logical. Pheromones and anxiety and ego can royally derail logic and sense.' And loneliness. Yes, that could do it, too. 'But I'm telling you, Erin . . .' She smiled, spoke lightly, as if it were just a bit of play. 'If I get involved with someone again, it will be a guy with a nice, safe occupation, and even safer hobbies. A stamp-collecting music teacher, maybe.' Not a man who thrived on the adrenaline rush of extreme exploration in the wilderness, caving and white-water rafting and abseiling and hang-gliding. And definitely not a man who knew violence and crime and who on any day could be shot in the line of duty. The thought of losing anyone again, of the abyss of emptiness, terrified her.

Before Erin could respond, the thump of footsteps sounded on the veranda as Bruce, Simon and Rob returned from a security check outside. Under their cheerful smiles they all cast her less-than-subtle glances, each assessing her, checking her, concerned for her, doing what they could to keep her safe and calm.

She moved towards the kettle. 'Coffee, anyone? I'm afraid all the chocolate is gone.'

'Not for me, thanks, Jo,' Simon said. 'I'm going to catch a bit of shut-eye for a few hours. Boz and Rob are planning to stay up and watch the cricket. I'll get up again around two.'

Like Nick and Aaron last night, they'd sorted it out between them. Keeping watch over her.

'You go and get some sleep, too, Erin,' she said as she filled the kettle. 'I'll be awake for a fair while yet. I've got some photos to look through.'

Hundreds of images she'd taken of camping grounds, viewing spots and walking trails, potentially to use in brochures and on the website. The chance that she'd inadvertently photographed any of the perpetrators was a very slim one, but she had to do whatever she could. She had to stay busy, fill her mind with something other than thoughts about who was targeting her, and what she would say to Nick when he returned.

☙

The moon hung almost directly overhead, bright in the night sky, as he drove along the gravel road towards the homestead.

After midnight. Another day gone, and he wasn't much closer to cracking this case. But now with Hugh's information, he had some idea of the type of ruthless, violent bastard behind the murders of Travis Mitchell and the Coffs Harbour John Doe.

The type of man who could order multiple murders – two youths, an elderly couple, a police officer, a National Parks ranger – without blinking an eye. The type of man who would punish those who failed to follow orders. The type of man Nick had pretended to be for the past two years.

Hugh only knew a surname – Ramirez – and suspected a South American drug connection, perhaps an attempt to establish one of the cartels in Australia, but he had little hard evidence. Nick had added the two images in Hugh's files to the artist's sketch of the man Jo had seen, and emailed the lot to Interpol for a facial recognition scanning. There might be an answer in the morning.

The dark shadow of a car parked at the homestead gate became eerie as it started to strobe red and blue lights at his approach. He flicked his lights on in response and pulled up beside it.

'It's all quiet here, Sarge.' Nate Harrison, pulling a long shift. 'Now you're here, I have to head back to town, make sure the crowd at the Show go home without trouble. I'll come back out later, check on things again.'

'Did Inspector Murdoch send you?'

'Yes. He said to swing by here a few times, keep an eye on the area.'

Nick left the police lights on as he drove slowly up to the homestead. A curtain flicked at the living-room window, then another at the bunk-room window. The automatic security lights switched on, then the stronger veranda light, illuminating the area in front of the main door where he parked. Out of the car, he paused so he could be clearly seen.

The front door swung open and Bruce waved him inside.

'That your mate at the gate heading off?' he asked, without waiting for an answer. 'Only thing moving out there's been a possum. Over near the fence, though, so it didn't even trip the security lights. Jo's in the kitchen, if you're looking for her.'

Nick glanced into the living room as he passed. Rob still stood at the edge of the window, and the television showed the cricket test match, with the sound muted. An empty crisp packet, two coffee mugs and soft drink bottles were on the side table. No evidence of any alcohol, despite Australian sport-watching traditions. A couple of decent, responsible blokes taking their self-appointed role seriously.

In the ten paces to the kitchen door, he mentally braced himself for Jo's questions. She'd have plenty, after reading Hugh's letter.

At the end of the kitchen table, she looked up from her laptop screen as he entered. She had let her hair fall loose, and the overhead fan wafted strands gently around her face. Above her strong cheek bones, dark smudges of tiredness underlined her eyes, but the smile she gave him, though subdued, had both warmth and welcome.

He smothered the instinct to smile back. He needed to put distance between them, keep it that way. Show her she had no reason to be concerned about Hugh's unfortunate comment.

'Any news?' she asked.

Not enough and too much. 'Nothing definitive. I'm still working through the files.'

Laying his laptop on the table, he opened an image on the screen.

'Have a good look at this and tell me if it's the man you saw.'

He took a glass from the dish drainer and poured some water from the tap, leaning against the kitchen bench while she studied the image.

'Yes, I think it is. It's very like him. This was in Hugh's files?'

Not the answer he wanted to hear. He had to concentrate to swallow the water past the tightness in his throat.

'Yes. His name is Ramirez. He's the ruthless, violent bastard Hugh wrote about, the one pulling the strings. Possibly with connections to a South American drug cartel. Hugh believed he's behind another murder, a few months ago.'

'The John Doe he referred to, on the coast?'

'Yes. A similar case to Travis.'

She grimaced. 'Poor bugger. One's bad enough. Two . . .'

'Hugh believed there may be more. So do I. There are a few young men missing who match the profile. Jo, I don't want to scare you, but if Ramirez *is* part of one of the South American cartels, then he's extremely dangerous. They're moving into Australia, and their methods are brutal. If you can ID Ramirez, you're a problem for him. Hugh was ordered to eliminate you. With Grace under threat, he ran out of options.'

She shoved back her chair and circled a few paces around in the corner between the table and the wall, like a trapped animal with nowhere to go.

He stayed by the bench, letting it take some weight from his aching leg, but more importantly, keeping a physical distance from her. He didn't know how long he could avoid the more personal conversation, but sticking to the case for now gave him some emotional distance, which he needed if he was going to answer the tougher questions.

She came to rest against the wall, hands in her pockets, facing him across the table. 'Jesus, Nick, you do know how to make a bad day worse. Did Hugh have definite proof against Ramirez? Do you?'

'Not yet. But I'll find it, Jo. I know criminals, organised crime, gangs, and how they operate. So did Hugh. From long before either of us joined the police. That's why I've been doing the undercover work for so long.' He drew in a silent breath, and said the truth bluntly, with no padding or preamble to diminish the ugliness. 'I grew up on the docks in Newcastle. My father worked there during the last years of organised crime in the Painters and Dockers Union, when the police were cracking down and the turf wars were bloody and violent. My father was a fighter. When I was twelve, he went to prison for six years for aggravated assault, for some standover work he did for his union mates.'

The only thing confession did was leave a bad taste in his mouth. That, and a frown on the face of a woman he respected.

The fan overhead swung around and around with an uneven *fwap, fwap. Fwap, fwap.*

'That must have been hard on your family,' she said finally.

'Yes. My mother was ill. When she died, I couldn't look after the girls – I was sixteen – so they went into foster care. Teenage boys are hard to place in foster care, so I made sure Pat and Hugh and I managed the house and routine fine, and Community Services let us stay at home. Easier for everyone.'

'What happened to Christie and Pat? How did they die?' she asked finally.

'My father gave evidence against Victor Zinchenko, one of the crime bosses.' A mouthful of water made no difference to the shards of glass in his throat. Show no weakness. Report the facts. Tell her, say aloud, what he had not spoken of for years. 'Pat had just met Christie off a bus, when a car sped past and sprayed them with bullets. They both died instantly.'

'Oh, Nick.'

She offered no platitudes, but he had to look away from the horror and hurt and sympathy in her eyes.

He would have preferred platitudes.

He drained his glass as if it were hard liquor, wished it was. He couldn't act as though it didn't matter to him. Even if he could, she wouldn't have believed it. He sought for the anger within. Anger for Pat, who should have had computers to exercise his geek brain and a future in programming or mathematics or something. Anger for Christie's lively, generous soul, a girl who never made womanhood. Anger now for Hugh.

The sudden buzz of the phone on the wall made them both start.

'Who the . . . ?' Jo muttered, reaching for it, answering it as Rob and Bruce pounded in from the other room.

'Yes, Mal.' She held up a hand to silence them, and Nick loosened the instinctive grip he'd taken on his Glock. 'Shit. Okay, where? Off Blackberry Road? Yes, we'll bring the truck from here. We'll be on our way in five.'

She was on the move the moment she replaced the handset. 'There are several fires on Blackberry Road. Get your gear and the tanker, guys. Mal's sending Craig and his crew out there with the Strathnairn truck. I'll wake the others and get my gear.'

Fires? And she intended to go out, into the wild, to fight them. Logical thought left him as he moved to intercept her at the door, his hand on her arm. 'No. Jo—'

Their eyes met, and she gave his hand a brief squeeze before shoving it aside. 'This is my job, Nick. They're forecasting strong westerlies, high temps and firestorm conditions by morning. If we don't get these fires under control before then, we're all in deep shit.'

FIFTEEN

Her brain whirling madly, jumping about from one thing to another, she hurried down the passage to knock on the bunk-room door. Too much happening, tonight. His revelations. His closed, controlled, denial of emotion. His insistence on protecting her. Her mental checklist of things to gather before she left. Things she needed to tell him, about the case, about his pain, her pain. About the distance he insisted they keep from each other, giving her no say at all.

Too much to say, too little time.

After a brisk knock, a call-out at the door and Simon's confirmation, she turned towards her own room, her fingers already on the buttons of her shirt.

Nick faced her in the passage, tall and tough and all cop in his uniform, the weapons belt bulky on his hips. 'It isn't safe, Jo.'

'Of course it isn't safe,' she said over her shoulder, aware he followed her a few steps and stopped in the doorway. She yanked off her shirt, reached for a merino T-shirt. 'Did you think of "safe" when you carried Hugh into the church with a sniper around?' She didn't wait for an answer, kept talking while she stripped off her light trousers and pulled on her firefighting uniform. 'We can't wait until tomorrow, or there'll be far more people at risk. There's a lot of dry timber between Blackberry Road and Goodabri.'

He spoke firmly. 'You should be protected. Not out there in the open in the dark.'

She sat on the edge of the bed to pull on thick socks. 'There'll be plenty of us, all in uniform fire gear. If anyone's stupid enough to chase a fire to come after me, they won't be able to pick me from the others, especially in the dark.'

'But if he wears fire gear too, you won't recognise a killer. I'll follow you out there in my car.'

He was right about the first part, but she knew the parks staff, the Rural Fire Service crews and the State Forests team. His second statement concerned her more. Tugging at the laces on her boots, she spoke bluntly. 'You'd need a vehicle with better clearance on those tracks. And unless you've done advanced fire-fighting training, or have your chainsaw licence, then you belong on a fire ground as little as I belong in a police shootout.'

She sighed, her bluntness falling away under his steely glare. 'You have to trust me, Nick. I know fires, and they scare me more than human killers. There's three, possibly four fires out there already. No lightning tonight, not much of a breeze to spread spot fires – it's most likely deliberate. If you can get some patrols out on the roads, there's a chance of catching the idiot. Not to mention any other bad guys lurking.'

She watched his usually unreadable face work through several responses before he finally nodded. 'I'll get on to it. We'll get some road blocks up and patrol the access roads. I presume Blackberry Road is on a map?'

'Yes.' She stuffed keys in her pocket, grabbed the satellite phone and GPS, caught sight of Hugh's letter on her desk and handed it to Nick. 'Regarding the other case, I've left some notes on the table – all places we've seen evidence of hoons in the past couple of months. Some instances of illegal shooting, vandalism, that kind of thing. The only ones in this park are in the southern end of it. They're marked on the map. There are also some photos printed out that I took for brochures. They may be nothing, but there are some bikes, vehicles and young men in them. None I recognised.'

He took the letter and hesitated an instant before replying. 'Good. I'll have someone look at them.'

He moved aside as she passed through the doorway, and with the adrenaline starting to pump through her arteries and her sheer relief at being active, doing *something* after days of passivity, she grinned up at him. 'Go catch me a firebug, Detective.'

Along with the State Forest land, National Parks had acquired a Forestry department dual-cab fire-fighting tanker, and Bruce and Rob had it out of the shed, ready to go. By the time she'd grabbed her protective jacket and helmet from her own vehicle, Nick was stowing his laptop in his car, and Simon and Erin were on their way from the house.

The trouble with fires on the east side of Blackberry Road, fanned by a westerly breeze, was getting safe access to them. Sandwiched between Bruce and Rob in the truck on the fifteen kilometre trip out, Jo compared the printed map to her recent GPS recording of the area's tracks and fire trails.

'I've only been on these roads a couple of times since the handover. I don't suppose any of you guys are more familiar with them?'

They topped a ridge, out of the trees, and Bruce stopped the truck while they surveyed the fires, visible in the distance among the trees and smoke. Three, Jo figured, a kilometre or so apart, each already covering more than a hectare. But not crowning yet. Manageable. Probably.

She reached for the radio and reported the situation concisely to the fire communication centre. As leader of the first crew to arrive, standard procedure made her Incident Controller. 'Strathnairn One Alpha, this is East Ridge Control in Riverbank One Alpha. You guys take the first fire, near the Blackberry Road corner. We'll go along the East Ridge fire trail and tackle the second. The third's close to the river, might slow down there. Firecom, we'll need RFS and Forestry crews on alert. If the fires aren't easily containable, they'll spread out of the park.'

'RFS Goodabri Two Alpha leaving base now,' an RFS crew responded. 'Where do you want us, Control?'

Three crews for three fires. That evened up the odds. And the RFS crew could go to the fire closest to the park boundary. 'Goodabri Two Alpha, take the north end of Blackberry Road, at the junction with the river,' she instructed. 'Report in when you get there.'

The East Ridge fire trail wound along the crest of a low line of hills, with dry scrub and rough, rocky ground on either side. Here and there, they caught flickers of red flame, eerie in the dark night.

'Stop here, Bruce,' Jo said, comparing her GPS data to the shadowed landscape. 'We'll follow this old fence line and have a look on foot.'

She and Simon walked in a couple of hundred metres, their boots crunching on thick layers of dry leaves, bark and grasses on the scattered rocks, the ground too rugged to drive the truck across.

'It's crossed the creek,' Simon said, pointing to a tongue of flame visible among the trees, still some distance off.

'Creek's as dry as a bone, has been for weeks, and it's too tiny here to halt anything.' The breeze stirred a branch overhead, and she checked the wind direction, relative to the lights of the truck behind her. The fire front ran roughly parallel to the trail, the breeze driving it directly to it. 'Best bet's probably to back burn up to the fire trail. That will make a decent firebreak.'

'I agree, Captain.'

Simon's grin flashed in the moonlight, a show of support she appreciated.

'Let's get started, then, before the wind picks up any more.'

Heat, smoke, the garish light of flames dancing in the night, the rumble of the pump and the crackling voices on the radio made up the entirety of her world for the next few hours. Hard physical and mental work, hauling hoses, clearing scrub, keeping track of fire and people and constantly assessing, planning, acting and reassessing.

Not the worst fire she'd fought – there had been plenty hotter, wilder and more dangerous than this one – but an overwhelming weariness dragged at her body by the time the firefront reached the firebreak, around sunrise.

With the sun came the heat, and the breeze strengthening to wind blowing ash, smoke and glowing cinders as they worked to extinguish the last of the flames and embers.

Stopping for a few minutes to check in with the other crews, she sat on the step of the truck, gulping water from a bottle in one hand, the radio in her other.

She watched her team as she listened to each crew report. Rob and Simon hosed down stumps to her right; to her left, Erin raked debris away from the base of a tree, and Bruce . . . She caught sight of him just as he staggered backwards a step, raised his hand near his chest, and toppled face first to the ground.

Heart attack, she thought as she raced across the blackened ground with the first-aid pack. He'd been looking grey and tired.

She reached him at the same time Erin did, and let loose a string of desperate swear words as she rolled him over and yanked open his jacket. His T-shirt, like hers, was soaked with sweat, but when she pushed it up, blood stained his skin, seeping from a hole beneath his ribs.

cҩ

The old guy they'd picked up with a lighter and thirty dollars in his pocket and a few clothes in his swag wouldn't give his name, and emphatically denied that he had anything to do with lighting fires. Nick believed him on that. He didn't believe that he'd seen no-one else in the vicinity.

His judgement distracted, he'd come down too heavy on the man initially, thinking him guilty before realising that he was already spooked by something even scarier than an aggressive cop. So, he'd handed him over to Aaron.

Now, with a hot pie fresh from the bakery across the road, and some soft drink, he went back into the small office they were using as an interview room.

The man had been living rough, and although they'd already given him sandwiches and tea, his eyes lit up at the sight of the pie.

Nick straddled a chair and faced the guy. He couldn't hold him much longer without a formal charge, and there wouldn't be anything to charge him with. Time to be the good cop. 'Listen, mate, I'm sorry I was tough on you when I picked you up. The thing is, I've got friends out there fighting those fires, and I was angry that some pyromaniac idiot had put them in danger. But it wasn't you, was it?'

The man blew on the hot pie filling, and gave a minute shake of the head.

'I believe you.'

He was good at concealing his emotions, but the small inhalation of breath gave him away, and the determined focus on the pie that didn't hide the relief in his eyes.

Nick had run images of recent missing adults, and found no match. From the look of the old bloke's well-worn clothes – patched moleskins, checked shirt and battered hat and boots – he'd seen a lot of miles; one of the men who still travelled the back roads permanently, camping out, working odd jobs here and there for a few dollars or a meal. A man who may have seen more than the dust beneath his feet.

'You haven't committed any crime, so I don't need to know your name or anything about you. As soon as you've finished eating, you can walk out that door. But look, mate, before you go, you might be able to help me with something.' He took up the small stack of photos from the folder he'd brought in. 'I think these people might have been camping out in the bush. Have you seen any of them lately?'

He placed the photo of Travis Mitchell, alive, on the table. The man pretended to concentrate on the escaping filling of his pie, tried not to look at the photo, but after a moment, his eyes flicked towards it. No recognition.

Nick placed the second image on the table. Bradley Coulter. This time, the man's glance skidded across to the photo twice. Recognition? Maybe. He wasn't sure.

The third image – Hugh's photo of Ramirez – drew more of a reaction than the other two, the instant shake of the head too vehement a denial.

Fear.

Fear in the difficulty swallowing a small mouthful of food. Fear in the briefly closed eyes and in the fingers grasping the pie so tight gravy squeezed out.

'I need to find this man. We know he rides a motorbike sometimes – a BMW. I think you've seen him, and he worries you. Is that right?'

No response, at first. Then a sniff. 'He's been around. Over near Derringvale a week or two back. Some blokes I yarned with up at Rocky Creek in the forest reckoned he'd been out there with some lads, shooting. That'll have been a week ago, maybe. There's a cave I sometimes camp in. He was near there this afternoon, by the creek with a mate. Saw them from across the creek. He saw me, and he pointed a rifle and told me to get lost. I scarpered. He's mad, that bloke.'

'What time was that?'

'Couple of hours before sunset, maybe. I walked through the scrub. Didn't want to meet any of his lads on the road.'

'If I get a map can you show me where the cave is?'

'Yeah. Reckon I can. But don't tell him I told you, when you catch him. Don't want any of his lads coming after me.'

'I won't.'

When Nick brought the map in, the man fumbled for his glasses in his pocket and propped them on his nose, studying the map carefully to get his bearings.

'Just give me a minute,' he mumbled, adjusting his glasses. 'Here. Must be round here. Yes. The creek here, where Blackberry Road ends.'

Ramirez. Blackberry Road.

'Nick.' Leah knocked lightly on the open door, grim faced. 'A moment?'

She would only interrupt for an emergency. Preoccupied, he excused himself to the old man, and followed Leah to the main room, where she handed him headphones. 'There's been a call in to Crime Stoppers you need to hear.'

He put on the headphones as she started the audio file on her computer.

A male voice, racing, speed and desperation giving it a high tone, the words strung together in a rush, ignoring the operator's questions.

'We shouldn't have done it. The drugs screwed our heads . . . really weird stuff, sick and weird and wired and I don't know if I remember straight. She's screaming still, in my head. It wasn't right, what we did. She didn't know anything. She begged and begged but we didn't stop. Mitchell deserved it but she didn't. You have to stop him. He'll do it again. He'll make us do it. You've got to stop him. You've got to—'

The call ended abruptly on a swear word, the silence afterwards chilling. With what they knew of Mitchell's death, Nick wouldn't bet much on the caller's chances. Or those of the woman he'd been speaking about.

His gut clenched tight. 'What time was the call?'

Leah wrapped the cord around the headphones with slow, deliberate movements. 'About eleven last night. Crime Stoppers didn't have much to go on, they thought it might be a crank call, until somebody cross-referenced the name. They sent it to us just a few minutes ago.'

'Can they pinpoint the call origin?'

'Not exactly. But a mobile phone, somewhere in this general area.'

Ramirez had been seen near where the fires started, with at least one other man. And a woman, by the sounds of it, had been raped, probably worse, sometime before eleven last night.

Ramirez was on Blackberry Road before Jo had gone out there, he reminded himself. Hours before. And he'd been listening to the fire service radio channel half the night, had heard her voice, calm, professional, capable in her job.

The uneasiness winding around his spine wasn't listening to logic.

Around him, the hum of conversation ebbed and flowed as the night shift handed over to day shift and officers arrived and left. The police radio at one end of the room continued the normal incidents for a Saturday morning in a regional area, but the portable radio on his desk kept at least half of Nick's attention.

'Firecom, this is Riverbank One.' Nick stopped breathing, focusing totally on the radio. A male voice, not Jo. Simon? 'Emergency sitrep. Request ambulance and police assistance. Repeat, ambulance *and* police. One injury.'

Emergency sitrep. Ambulance and – he'd emphasised the 'and' – police. One injury. But who the hell was injured? Why was Simon, not Jo, reporting?

A serious injury requiring urgent attention would be Code Red. But Simon had called an emergency, the code for life-threatening danger to the unit. And they'd only need police if . . . He snatched up keys, radio and phone, and ordered everyone in the room, 'East Ridge fire trail. I want every available vehicle heading up there now. Jo Lockwood's fire crew is in life-threatening danger, from something other than fire. Somebody's –' *Please don't let it be Jo. Not Jo –* 'already injured.'

☙

They all crouched, partially protected by a low pile of rocks, Simon and Rob half-supporting Bruce while Jo wrapped a bandage firmly around his abdomen over a thick dressing pad. Bruce's blood smeared the surgical gloves she'd taken precious moments to pull on, to protect the wound from the ash and grime that coated her hands. Red against the opaque white on

219

her fingers, it still reminded her too much of yesterday. Twice in two days . . .

Think, she inwardly screamed. Breathe and think how she'd get them safely out of this situation. Help would be at least twenty minutes away.

'The shot came from the north,' Jo told the others. 'We need to get Bruce into the truck, and get out of here.'

'I can walk,' Bruce muttered.

'Not fifty metres on rough ground with a trigger-happy sniper, mate,' Simon said. 'You all stay here, with your heads down. I should be able to get the truck pretty close in, probably to just over there. That will give us cover to load up.'

A good plan, but as captain it was her responsibility to take risks, not his. And she was the most likely target. 'Simon, you can't—'

'I can. Ex-army, remember?' His wry grin softened the way he took charge. 'I've had years of practice in evading snipers. Keep your heads low, and be ready to move as soon as the truck's in position.'

He didn't wait for an okay, but spun up onto his feet and bolted to the truck, his yellow jacket vivid against the scorched ground.

'He's been in Iraq and Afghanistan,' Erin said, flat and toneless, her gaze fixed on Simon, yanking the door open and leaping up into the cab.

Jo blew a breath out, sucked another long breath in. He still had to drive across rough ground, among rocks, tree stumps and fallen logs, with the driver's side north-facing, leaving him exposed to the sniper.

Iraq and Afghanistan. He didn't talk much about his army service. Not generally. Not to her. He was friendly, reliable, solid . . . and elusive when it came to his private thoughts. Interesting that Erin knew something about it.

He'd better not get himself injured or killed. The two of them deserved a chance to resolve whatever was keeping them apart. Whatever she had to do to ensure it, she would do. No matter the risk to herself.

Bruce groaned, tried to move and muttered a curse.

'Hold still, Bruce. Won't be long before we have you out of here.'

Nick had said similar words to Hugh. There had to be a better outcome this time. Had to be. She couldn't do it again, couldn't bear it if . . . No, Bruce had only one wound, to the side, hopefully missing critical organs. As long as he didn't bleed out internally, he had a chance.

Simon brought the truck to a stop about five metres away, keeping out of the sniper's gunsights by clambering across the front seat and out the passenger door.

Together they lifted Bruce and transferred him with some difficulty to lie on the back seat of the truck. Jo hated moving him, but they had little choice.

'Rob, you stay on the floor in the back with him,' Jo said. 'As long as we don't crash, you'll be safer there, and you can watch him. Erin, you too.' She continued, right over their protests. 'Rob, you've got a wife and kids to get home safe to. Erin, if he needs CPR, you can do it.'

She hoisted the first-aid pack in after them, and swung up into the front seat after Simon.

'Head down,' Simon said, shoving the truck into gear.

She grabbed the radio mike off its hook and spoke into it while bent over almost double to keep below window level, one hand against the dashboard to steady herself as the truck lurched across towards the track. 'Firecom, this is Riverbank One. Emergency sitrep. We are evacuating and will rendezvous with ambulance and police at Becketts Corner. Request rescue helicopter for medical evacuation. Repeat, rescue helicopter for medical evacuation required. Read back.'

Firecom repeated the request to confirm receipt, and Jo breathed a little easier. The rescue chopper could fly Bruce directly to a Tamworth or Newcastle hospital – or to Sydney, if they deemed it necessary. Strathnairn Hospital was smaller, with fewer specialists, and too far away by road.

As they approached the fire trail, two loud bangs hit in quick succession off her side of the truck.

Simon swore. 'Hold on, everyone.'

He put his foot down harder and swung the truck onto the trail, hitting it with a thump that banged Jo's chin hard against her knees.

The shots had come from the north; they were now heading south along the trail, the gunman behind them.

She clicked the radio button on. 'Riverbank One to all East Ridge units. Strathnairn One, withdraw to staging area at Becketts Corner. Goodabri Two Alpha, return to base via Cattlemans Creek Road. Do not, repeat *do not*, proceed along East Ridge Trail or Blackberry Road. Rifle shots fired and unit directly targeted in this area. Firecom, please advise sitrep to police.'

More than likely, the police were already listening in. Nick might be listening. She didn't think he was the type of man to say 'I told you so' out loud, but he had to be thinking it. She'd weighed up the risks, made her decision. Would Bruce have been wounded if she hadn't been there? Her gut coiled tightly at the thought, until logic argued that it was impossible to know at this stage. She'd probably have been an easy target, on the radio by the truck, but the sniper had shot Bruce, not her. What kind of rationale was that? Unless he'd planned to pick the others off, one by one, leaving her alone . . . No. They had to get away. *Would* get away.

The truck leaned as Simon rounded a sharp bend, and she sat up straight, the vehicle now out of the line of sight of the shooter. In among the trees she caught glimpses of grey–brown smoke in the sky.

'You didn't mention the smoke ahead.'

'Nope,' Simon said. 'I don't think it's near the trail. Must be a spot from the first fire.'

'The wind's a westerly. The first fire is south.'

'Yeah.'

She kept a watch for it, scouring the fractured views as they twisted and turned along the tree-lined crest road, trying to pinpoint the location.

'Might be one of the gullies,' she said.

'Yeah, I think so, too.'

A couple of gullies ran west–east, carved out of the ridge they drove along. The wind would funnel any fire straight up a gully.

'How much water have we got left?'

'A little over eight hundred litres. Enough.'

Enough to protect them for a short while in a mild burn-over. Mild being a relative term. If the wind picked up any further, if the temperature kept climbing, there would be nothing mild about this fire.

But they couldn't stop, couldn't go back. Bruce's breathing was becoming more laboured.

The road dipped, the top of the ridge to their left an impenetrable rock cliff. She could see the location of the fire now.

'It is in one of the gullies, but it looks like it's not up to the road. We'll be right,' Jo said, as much to encourage herself as those in the back.

Smoke curled over the road, filling the air as they came closer, and Simon slowed the vehicle.

'Keep a watch on the fire, Jo. I have to concentrate on staying on the road.'

The rocky bluff formed a wall to their left, dotted with trees, shrubs and grasses. To their right, off the narrow track, the gully sloped away steeply.

With the binoculars, Jo managed to discern some flames through the smoke. 'The fire front is about five hundred metres away.'

Simon threw her a relieved grin. 'No worries, then.'

Nothing to stop the fire from rushing up and cresting the ridge. But they'd be through before then. Ten, fifteen minutes later, it would have been a different story.

Crossing the head of the gully, Simon rounded a bend . . . and slammed on the brakes.

Rob shouted, Erin gasped and Jo braced herself as the truck skidded slightly in the gravel. They came to a stop a metre from a large eucalypt tree, fallen across the road, the trunk a good two metres in diameter, branches and leaves thick around it.

No way around the tree, no way over it. They'd have to cut it up with chainsaws.

And they'd have to do it before the fire reached them.

SIXTEEN

At the staging area at Becketts Corner, the Strathnairn National Parks fire truck arrived at the same time as the third police vehicle from Goodabri.

Nick had an ordinance survey map spread on the car bonnet, the large sheet giving a much clearer idea of the area than the small screen of his GPS. A huge area of wilderness for a killer to hide in, and only two access roads into it.

'Is Blackberry Road clear of fire?' he asked the firefighters. 'Can I send police cars right along it?'

'Yes,' one of them said. 'They need to stay alert, in case the wind changes or the bastard bug lights more, but all three fires are mopped up.'

'Carruthers and Edwards, you take Blackberry Road. Georgiou and I will take the fire trail. We'll meet up down here—' He broke off as the portable radio gave its warning hiss before Jo's voice came through.

'Firecom, East Ridge Control emergency sitrep. Road blocked by fallen tree at grid . . .' A voice in the background spoke, and then she repeated the map grid numbers. 'Medium fire approaching along gully approx four hundred metres west of position. We will attempt to clear the road for ten minutes, then withdraw approximately five hundred metres north.'

'Jesus,' someone muttered.

The wind tugged at the map under Nick's clenched hands. The same wind sending a fire towards a trapped crew. Towards Jo. His initial relief at hearing her voice earlier evaporated, leaving only cold dread. He couldn't battle a fire. Couldn't threaten it, throw it to the ground, shoot it.

A yellow-clad arm reached over the map for the radio.

'Firecom, this is Strathnairn One. We will proceed to assist Riverbank One.'

Nick took the radio from the ranger's hand. Disregarding protocol, he depressed the button and spoke. 'East Ridge Control, police assistance proceeding from north, ETA twenty-five minutes, and from south, ETA ten minutes.'

He couldn't battle fire, but he might be able to protect her – protect the crew – from other dangers.

'All units proceed with extreme caution,' Jo ordered, her voice sharp with a rough edge of desperation. 'Obstacle intentional, not natural. I suspect at least two malicious individuals, north and south. Repeat, danger north *and* south.'

Obstacle intentional. Some bastard had felled the tree *on purpose* to trap them.

'Carruthers, Edwards, get onto the trail from the north, make sure it's clear and escort them out that way if necessary.'

The long way around, more than thirty kilometres; they'd take a while to get there. If Jo and her crew decided to risk escaping back that way, they'd not only be running the gauntlet of the sniper, they would be taking a wounded man needing urgent medical attention much further from it. A tough choice for them to make.

'If you see anyone on the trail,' he added, 'arrest them. Do whatever you need to do to apprehend them.' Looking as grim as he felt, Carruthers and Edwards nodded in understanding.

He folded the map up roughly. 'Aaron, we'll follow the tanker in from the south. When the ambulance arrives, it should come after us as far as it's safe.'

The whole way down the narrow dirt track through the dry, scrubby bush, Nick kept immediately behind the tanker, willing it to go faster, letting loose a string of swear words when smoke obscured visibility, slowing them down further.

The minutes ticked away, and the fear they'd get there too late pounded against the thin thread of his control.

c&

Choking smoke, ash and burning leaves swirled all around, and the growing rumble of the fire and the roar of the wind almost drowned out Simon's chainsaw. The fallen ironbark – felled at the base by someone else's saw – was huge and tough, its many branches obstructing the road as effectively as the trunk itself.

A cough racked Jo's burning lungs as she and Erin dragged each end of a three-metre branch off the road.

Flames licked at the base of a tree fifty metres away.

No more time.

'Tell them to quit,' she shouted to Erin. 'We're getting out of here.'

At the truck, she sprang up into the driver's seat and started the engine.

'How are you doing there, Bruce?' she asked, talking for reassurance rather than expecting an answer, twisting around to see into the back. His chest rose and fell slowly. 'You just keep breathing, Bruce. You're going to be fine. No other outcome is permitted. You got that clear?'

His closed eyes flickered behind his eyelids, mouth twitched a fraction. 'Nag, nag,' he muttered.

Conscious, coherent, and attempting humour – all good signs.

The flashing lights of the Strathnairn truck approached through the smoke on the other side of the tree, shadowy figures moving in front of it. Simon, Erin and Rob were all closer to it than to her. But no way could they get Bruce out of her truck and over the hurdle of the tree in time.

'Strathnairn One, position not defensible. Take three Riverbank crew and withdraw immediately,' she ordered over the radio. 'I will retreat approximately five hundred metres north.'

'Jo, you can't—'

Craig? Simon? The call broke off with an oath as a fireball swept up the slope, exploding the pile of cut-off branches near the road into a wall of searing flames.

She repeated her instructions loudly. 'This is East Ridge Control in Riverbank One ordering immediate evacuation in nearest vehicle.'

She thrust the truck into reverse, straining to see anything of the track behind her in the swirling smoke. She began edging backwards anyway, using the rocky wall of the bluff to one side as a guide to the track's location. Glancing continually between the rear-vision mirror, the bluff and the fire, she caught sight of a figure in a yellow jacket and helmet running through the smoke. She stopped and he leaped up onto the truck's running board, yanking the door open.

Nick, not Simon. *Nick.*

'They're all on the other truck,' he said. 'Go.'

The radio crackled. 'Control, we have three Riverbank crew on board. Evacuating now.'

Nick breathed heavily beside her.

Anger and relief battled it out in her mind, neither winning. As she started reversing again, she let him have the anger. 'What the *hell* did you think you were doing? Don't you know what fire can do? You could have been killed or badly burned. You were damned lucky.'

'Yes. I *was* lucky.' Calm, steady, not arguing. When she turned to see past him to the mirror, he was watching her, and answered her, eye-to-eye. 'I was thinking that I couldn't let you do this alone.'

As if she didn't have enough to unsettle her already, his straightforward honesty erased her anger but threw her brain into confusion. No, she didn't want to do this alone. Any of it. As for Nick . . . she focused on edging the tanker backwards, checking the driver's side mirror, the rear-vision mirror, anywhere but him.

'How's Bruce?' he asked, after a moment.

'Breathing,' came the rasping reply from the back.

Breathing. Just. But he'd made it this far and she had to believe that he'd be okay. Probably. As long as she could get them out of danger. As long as the maniac shooter wasn't waiting just down the road. As long as the ambulance or the rescue helicopter made it in time.

'Get over the back and keep him alive,' she murmured to Nick.

Twenty metres in front of the truck a wall of flame poured over the dirt road, lighting the straggling bushes on the bluff, the heat and wind surging it upwards and outwards. Her foot heavier on the accelerator, she reversed as fast as she dared.

ॐ

Despite his height and size, Nick managed to climb over into the back of the cab without hitting Bruce, prone on the seat. Crammed into the small space between the seats, he began an assessment – pulse faint and thready, breathing shallow and uneven, complexion pale and skin cool to the touch.

Not good. But not desperate yet, either. He'd lasted half an hour or more since the shooting. Blood soaked the wound dressing, and still seeped from his side, but not in any volume. Although in his late fifties, his physical fitness had to give him more of a chance.

'It bloody hurts,' Bruce muttered, as Nick examined the wound.

'I know. I've done a couple of these myself. They hurt like hell.' And, crouched awkwardly as he was, the shredded muscle of his thigh still throbbed with pain, almost three months on.

The truck slowed to a stop. The little he could see outside the window showed blue sky and sunshine visible through the thinning smoke.

'I can turn around here,' Jo said over her shoulder. 'Just as well, because I hate reversing.'

Half a kilometre or more in a large vehicle down a narrow hillside track with severely limited vision – no easy task for anyone. Yet that had been her only words of complaint. Staying with Bruce and the tanker in the face of fire and snipers, then making that dangerous backwards drive, had taken courage and sheer guts. No ordinary woman, Jo Lockwood.

The three-point turn accomplished efficiently, they moved forward at a faster speed. 'We're out of that fire range, guys,' Jo said. 'You can breathe easier.'

'Riverbank One, this is Firecom,' the radio interrupted her. 'Emergency rescue helicopter is en route, ETA ten minutes. They will attempt landing four hundred metres south of Diggers Creek junction.' A grid reference followed, and Jo passed a map over the seat to him before she answered.

'Wilco, Firecom. ETA thirteen minutes. Confirming grid—' She recited the numbers, while Nick quickly found the place on the map. Beyond where Bruce had been shot. Closer to where Carruthers and Edwards would join the fire trail.

With his portable radio tuned to the police channel, he instructed the other two vehicles to rendezvous with them there.

'It's a cleared paddock,' Jo explained when he'd finished. 'Probably the closest decent landing place. The chopper must have already been out this way, to get here so quickly. It's based in Tamworth, serves the whole north-west region.'

Bruce had drifted into unconsciousness again, and Nick kept fingers on his pulse, willing it to keep beating.

'Not long now, Bruce. The paramedics will have pain killers for you.' Déjà vu. Yet he had far greater hope now than yesterday with Hugh. Hugh had died, probably bled out, within minutes. Bruce had only one wound, to the side, and if any major organs or arteries had been hit he'd have been dead already.

The strain on Jo had to be immense, but she kept driving, kept going as she'd done throughout the night and morning, and not once in any of her radio calls or his brief conversations with her did he detect panic or loss of composure.

The distinct sound of a helicopter rose over the rumble of the engine.

'There she is, doing a flyover,' Jo said. 'Only a minute or two and we're there, Bruce.'

Bruce made no sign he'd heard.

Within three minutes Nick surrendered his place in the cab to a paramedic. Within five they had Bruce out, on a gurney, fitting a cannula for a saline drip.

Jo remained in the truck, reporting in. Superfluous to the medical needs, and aware they were in a large open paddock edged by thick bush, Nick scanned the land around.

'Did you see any vehicles, bikes or people as you flew over?' he asked the helicopter pilot.

'Your blokes, coming in from the north. They're not far away. Bloke on a quad bike, heading west cross-country, probably a couple of klicks from here. Other side of that other road – Blackberry, is it?'

Nick nodded, processing the information. A quad bike heading west across country – a needle in a haystack without air surveillance, and he'd not be able to get that into the air in time. He knew the rough lie of the land from here – much of the park to the west and north, and only a few roads and tracks through the scrub and farmland for a hundred kilometres in those directions.

On a quad bike a rider could easily carry a chainsaw and a rifle, maybe could have travelled between the site of the shooting and the place where the tree had been felled. There could be two of them, but the fact that this one was travelling west, away from them, eased a fraction of Nick's concern. He radioed instructions for nearby cars to be on the lookout and pursue.

Jo's door opened, and she swung down to the ground, wavering slightly as she landed so that she had to steady herself with a grip on the door frame.

Nick held out a hand to her. 'You okay?'

'Yes.' She made a brave effort at a smile. 'Just a shaky leg there for a moment.'

Shaky leg, and reaction to the stress setting in, if he read the tenseness in her body right. But she walked steadily enough over to where the paramedic worked on Bruce, gave details of his name and age, and the circumstances of the injury.

'Where will you take him?' she asked.

'The John Hunter Hospital in Newcastle,' the medic told her. 'I know it's further for his family, but until we know what injuries there are, it's better that he has access to a good range of specialists.'

'I'll let his wife know. They've got a daughter in Maitland.' She took hold of Bruce's hand. 'Did you hear that, Bruce? I'll phone Mary. I'm sure she'll be down with you as soon as she can. And you'll probably get to see Rachel and your scamp of a grandson in a day or so.'

Maybe Bruce didn't hear her reassuring words, maybe he did. Nick had vague memories of his own state by the time the ambulance arrived after he'd been shot in Melbourne; in too much pain, too groggy to open his eyes, too weak from blood loss to move, just aware of movement and voices and one kind, direct voice who'd spoken to him by name, as if he was there. He had no idea if he'd actually responded, or only thought he had.

Jo moved aside so the paramedics could transfer Bruce into the helicopter. The sun, moving up in the sky, beat down on them, the freshness of the early morning long gone, and she took off her helmet and shrugged out of her firefighter's jacket, tossing them on the seat of the truck.

Long hours of hard, physical work and perspiration made her T-shirt cling to her, and strands of damp hair stuck on the sides of her face and neck, mixing with ash and smoke grime.

The sooty, sweaty dirt did nothing but highlight the strength of character in her face, and her beauty, authentic and sincere. No pretence, no being anything she wasn't.

Unlike him.

His chest as tight as if he'd been shot again, he took off the jacket he'd borrowed from Simon in those mad, desperate seconds before the fire struck, concentrating on folding it neatly and avoiding watching Jo's throat as she gulped water from a bottle.

But when she offered the bottle to him, her hand trembled noticeably.

'Sit down,' he said, taking the bottle before she dropped it.

235

She perched on the step of the truck, the shakes setting in. She hugged her arms around herself in a fruitless attempt to stop them.

'Sorry. Reaction, I guess.' Her teeth chattered but she tried to grin regardless. 'Can't imagine why.'

He played along with the gentle humour. 'A murder attempt, an injured friend, a couple of bushfires, a too-close call, and all before breakfast – nope, nothing there to stress anyone.'

Behind him, the rotors on the helicopter started to whirr and he heard car engines approaching on the track. He spared only a quick glance to check they were the police cars.

Another shudder racked her, but still she tried to joke. 'Actually, the driving backwards was the worst. My spatial sense is lousy.'

He wanted to touch her. One of those reassuring touches on the arm, the hand, that she gave so naturally to him and to others. Hell, he wanted to take her into his arms and hold her until she stopped shaking.

He did neither, just pulled some words from the mass of unfamiliar thoughts crowding his mind.

'You did an amazing job, Jo.'

Her head jerked up, all humour gone. 'No, Nick, I didn't. I came out here despite your warning not to. And now Bruce is being flown to hospital.'

He *had* warned her not to go. But how much of that had been about legitimate operational considerations, and how much about his personal fears for her? And how much of the motivation for his mad dash over the fallen tree, past the burning debris, had been a rational decision to protect a witness and an injured man from snipers, rather than pure desperate need to be with her?

'You made a professional decision based on facts and probability. I had no right to try to stop you. There was no evidence, no firm reason, to assume a specific danger for you.' Not then. He had plenty now.

'Yeah, well, firm reasons or not, Bruce was shot instead of me.'

'I'm not convinced you were the target.' Worried, yes. Convinced, no. 'Bruce is close on six foot tall, and a big man. Even in fire gear, it would be hard to mistake him for you. Even assuming it's the same group, they may not have known you were out here.'

'Oh, come on, Nick – anyone tuned to the radio channel knew. I was broadcasting my position, right down to grid references, all night.'

'Without mentioning your name. They'd have to be pretty close to the local community to know who captains which tanker. Other than Bradley Coulter, we've got nothing so far that suggests they have local connections.'

She fell silent, but not necessarily in agreement.

The chopper's rotors spun at high speed, sending a hail of dust and dry grass over them as it rose off the ground and moved forward, making a graceful curve as it gained height to fly over the two police cars pulling up nearby.

Nick waited with Jo in the shade and relative protection of the fire tanker while Carruthers and Edwards came across to join them.

Their first question was, 'Who was hurt?'

A blunt reminder for Nick that everyone knew almost everyone here. With no phone reception and no names used over the radio, it had to have been hard on the locals to know one of the crew had been injured, but not which one.

Jo rose to her feet. 'Bruce Lockyer. He was shot.'

Carruthers swore. 'Bozza. Shit. How bad?'

'They're taking him to Newcastle.' She didn't elaborate. On a scale of severity, Newcastle ranked just behind Sydney. That said enough.

Beside him, she wavered a little on her feet. She had to be close to the end of her endurance. If he was honest about it, so was he.

'We'll take you home, Jo. It's probably best if you pack some things and stay somewhere safer in Strathnairn for a few days.'

She nodded wordlessly, and climbed back into the tanker to collect her gear.

He beckoned his colleagues a few metres away. 'Dee, I need you to drive us back to Jo's place and then to Strathnairn. We'll leave the tanker here to be picked up later. Matt, there's a site down by the river that needs to be checked. That man we picked up earlier saw our key suspect, Ramirez, and another man there yesterday afternoon, and a report to Crime Stoppers suggests a sexual assault took place in this area – I suspect in the same place. Meet Aaron there, and be careful.'

As soon as she was seated in the back of the police vehicle, Jo used the satellite phone to call Malcolm in the comms centre.

'Simon's spoken with you? Good. They're taking Bruce to the John Hunter. Can you phone Mary and let her know? She'd probably rather hear it from you than me. But look, tell her that he was aware and talking some of the time. Joking, in

238

fact. Yes. Thanks, Mal. I'm going to take a few days off. Seems wisest in the circumstances. I'll give you a call on Monday.'

He looked over from the front when she finished the call, but she'd let her head fall back against the seat and closed her eyes. Not resting; creases tightened around her eyes and she bit her lip, drawing in a deep breath, then another. She fought for composure, and he gave her silence and space to find it.

With Dee driving, the radio a familiar, non-urgent chatter in the background, and his phone without a signal, he closed his own eyes, trying to still the thoughts racing around and around.

He needed order, and clarity, and unemotional strategies and decisions.

Order? As soon as he had Jo somewhere protected in Strathnairn, he'd find Leah, Murdoch and a large whiteboard, and they'd map out everything, including the information from Hugh's files and this morning's events. Then they'd prioritise, plan, and allocate teams for a multi-pronged strategy.

Clarity? He let his instinct feel around what he knew, and what Hugh had gathered. Ramirez was building a gang. Drawing together restless, unemployed, disconnected young men. Rewarding them with drugs and money. Binding them with violence. Making them punish those who transgressed, symbolically and viciously. According to Hugh's sources, the John Doe had tried to run – and lost a foot. What about Mitchell? A hand cut off for what? Stealing? A nervous Coulter adding a gun to the cache at the last minute fitted that scenario.

Ramirez manipulated them, owned them, watched them carry out his orders – and thus left no DNA or fingerprints of his own. And they may have gang-raped a woman last night.

Immediately he thought of Jo, of her vulnerability, and he jerked open his eyes. Unemotional strategies? No. Where Jo was concerned, he could not be unemotional.

There had been a time when he'd gone out with women, had friends, occasional lovers. Then he'd gone into covert operations full-time, living lies for ten years, these past few constantly walking a thin and dangerous line between playing cold-blooded, controlling, immoral bastards, and actually becoming one. With his cover potentially blown in the aftermath of the Melbourne job, he'd asked to return to normal duties. But he knew there never had been, never would be, any vestige of 'normal' within himself.

So, he would do nothing about his feelings for Jo other than protect her, by doing his job. She'd loved a good man, probably still grieved for him, and she deserved far better than a cop who'd forgotten the little he'd ever known about how to function in ordinary society without donning a mask and hiding behind a lie.

Dee turned through the homestead gate. The old house with its white-painted timberwork verandas shone in the bright sunlight. A rambling country home, with small birds flittering through the bushes, serene and peaceful.

The bushfire and shooting priorities had reduced the number of patrols during the night and morning, and despite the undisturbed appearance, he planned to be cautious.

'Check around the back,' he told Dee. 'I'll go with Jo through the front.'

Jo got out of the car, her face set, closed, her voice lacking emotion as she said, 'It won't take me long to pack.'

She was almost stumbling as she walked beside him across the grass. But still she pushed herself on.

Now they were within range, his phone beeped with multiple text messages and he slowed, his attention split between it and Jo.

He'd missed three calls. He opened the text from Leah, and stopped dead as he read it.

Brock not home in Sydney. Airline says not on flight. No message, no response on phone.

Already at the door, Jo unlocked it, pushed it open, and he called for her to wait, sprinting across the drive and up the steps after her.

She was at her bedroom door when the scent hit him. Faint, but that distinctive mix of urine, shit, blood and death.

She pushed open the door as he reached her. Frozen, rigid, a strangled cry dragged from her throat.

'No!'

She turned, straight into him, burying her face in his chest, banging her head, her clenched fist against him in desperate denial, sobbing 'No, no, no, no,' with each hit.

He held her tightly against him, keeping her from looking again, from seeing Bradley Coulter's battered and bloodied corpse sitting on her bed, tied to the wrought-iron bedhead, her camera hanging around his neck, his eye sockets a mangled, bloody mess where his eyes had been.

SEVENTEEN

In the shower room in Strathnairn police station, Jo stripped off her grimy, stinking clothes and stepped under the water, turning it hotter, letting it pour over her to warm her and wash away the cold shivers that kept racking her body. Uncaring how many litres of water she used, she stayed there. Eventually warm enough to think, she squeezed soap from the dispenser into her hands, scrubbed and scrubbed her hair and her body to be free of soot and dirt and the taint of death.

Nothing could scrub her memory of the nightmare of Bradley's corpse on her bed.

The soap dispenser empty, she leaned her forehead against the tiles beside it, suds swirling down the drain at her feet.

Breathe. Control. Let emotion drain away like the suds. *Breathe. Control.* Hold it together.

Someone tapped on the door, and Dee called, 'Are you okay in there, Jo?'

'Yes.' The word scraped in her throat.

'I've left some clothes just here for you. Sorry, it's only my gym gear. But it's clean.'

'Thank you.' She made an effort, pushed herself away from the wall. 'I'll be out in a minute.'

White T-shirt, navy track suit. Jo pulled them on, the warmth of the clothes doing nothing to stop her shivering in the airconditioned bathroom. With wet paper towel, she wiped dust and soot off her boots before lacing them up over Dee's cotton socks, then stuffed her clothes into the plastic bag Dee had left for her.

In front of the mirror, she finger-combed her wet hair into some semblance of order, and stared at her haggard reflection. Dark smudges under eyes still red from stinging smoke. Or maybe from crying.

She had to make sure she didn't fall to pieces again. Almost everything after walking into her bedroom blurred in her memory, only a few things remaining clear. Nick's strength, holding her up when her knees buckled, steering her from the house, keeping a supportive arm around her when she dry-retched into the garden, protecting her head with his hand as he guided her into the rear seat of the car.

And she remembered the harshness of his voice as he'd called for back-up.

He'd stayed at Riverbank, sending her to Strathnairn and safety with Dee as soon as others arrived. She didn't know how long he'd be out there, whether she'd see him again today, or who would be advising her of the next steps from here.

Squaring her shoulders, she opened the door and went to find out.

☙

'Bloody hell,' Leah said, joining him in the doorway of Jo's room. 'They sure did a job on him, didn't they?'

'Yes,' Nick agreed. 'That phone call last night – it might have been him. The timing fits. And that could be a phone in his pocket.'

'CSOs can check it. But yes, it's likely.'

He'd seen all there was to see, but he didn't move away from the doorway. What they'd done to Coulter angered him, but what they'd done to Jo affected him at least as much, maybe more.

They'd not completely trashed her room, but they'd tossed things off her bed, searched to find her camera and scarves to tie Coulter to the bedhead, and left drawers and wardrobe open. A vicious, nauseating invasion of her space, her privacy, and a warning and threat to her safety.

The blue robe she'd worn the other morning lay crumpled on the floor, a large dusty boot print dirtying the bamboo pattern. An image that would haunt him, as if they'd trampled on, violated, Jo herself.

They would, if he couldn't protect her from them.

He had to find them, before they found her. Had to push his feelings aside and get on with his job, work with his colleagues to track down and catch the bastards.

'I've notified the coroner's office and called in the forensic team,' he told Leah. 'They're on their way, should be here in an hour or so.'

'Good. He didn't die here, by the looks of it.'

'No.' He'd made his observations already. There'd have been more signs of struggle, more blood, if they'd killed him here. 'There's dirt and leaves on his clothes, and on him. See his hands? He clawed in the dirt.'

'We're looking for another crime scene, then.' She turned away, and they moved to the fresher air outside. 'Have you heard from Aaron yet?'

'A radio report that they're searching the bushland near the river, close to where one of the fires started.' Frustrated by the necessary inaction of waiting, he leaned his elbows on the railing, pointing his phone in different directions, searching for a signal.

Leah propped against the veranda rail beside him. 'I'm worried about Shelley. If you told me that she could be in on this, if you thought she was compromised somehow, like Hugh was, I'd have more hope for her.'

'I doubt it.' He'd already considered that, dismissed it. Shelley had passed Hugh's letter on; not the action of an accomplice, or an enemy.

'Maybe she's just run home to her mother,' Leah suggested, grasping at straws.

'Would you? She's young, ambitious, just earned her detective badge.' Like Leah herself had been, years ago.

Leah sighed. 'No, I was too driven to run home. It would have been an unforgivable weakness. But I wasn't one to fall in love, either, and Shelley was. I had lunch with her last week.'

Neither of them voiced the other possibility, but confirmation of it came within minutes: the radio notification a coded request for back-up, the text message from Aaron that beeped onto Nick's phone moments later more precise.

Homicide located. GPS coords following. Prelim ID DC Shelley Brock.

A heaviness weighing in his chest, he passed the phone to Leah, staring at the tree shadows on the lawn as she read it, his thoughts echoing her bitter, defeated swear word, repeated again and again.

'Do you want to go, or stay with this one?' he asked her. She'd known Shelley, worked with her, even if only for a few weeks.

'I'll go.' The catch in her voice didn't stop her. 'I owe it to her, Nick. But you've done all that's needed here – the uniforms can wait for forensics. You're dead on your feet, so I'll drive. We'll have to go via Goodabri, though – I need to phone my boss, and you'll need to inform Murdoch. And get some caffeine.'

In the ten minutes at the Goodabri incident room, Nick reported Shelley's death to Murdoch in Strathnairn, scalded his tongue on strong black coffee, and left a message with the witness protection unit requesting protection arrangements for Jo.

'You think she's that much at risk?' Leah asked as they returned to the car.

'Yes. I think the sniper shooting this morning, and Coulter's corpse, are both specific warnings to her – they know she can ID Ramirez, and they want her to know fear before they take her. So until we arrest them all, I want her well away from here, in witness protection.'

'Probably wise. She won't thank you for it, though.'

No, Jo wouldn't thank him. She'd been restless enough confined to her office, and her home, for just a couple of days. Days, weeks, perhaps even months inside a rented apartment in another town or city, far from the bush she loved, denied contact with friends and family, with nothing meaningful to do – she'd hate every moment of it.

She'd probably end up hating him.

But when he saw what they'd done to Shelley before dragging her body into the bush not far from the river, he knew Jo's hatred would be a price he'd willingly pay a thousand times over to ensure her safety.

ॐ

The interview room was daunting enough even though Dee left the door open, Jo hadn't done anything wrong and she knew she was welcome to wander to the meal room and the bathrooms whenever she wanted to. She couldn't imagine being closed in here for hours and being questioned about a crime. She didn't want to imagine it.

She'd done every Sudoku puzzle in the stack of old magazines Dee had left, and at least half the crosswords. She also knew more about the personal lives of famous people she'd scarcely heard of than most people knew about hers.

But she kept ploughing through the articles, desperately trying to keep her mind off the horror in her bedroom, never quite succeeding. Hours ticked away, and although Dee kept stopping by with upbeat words, Nick hadn't returned, and the station was eerily quiet, only a few staff remaining.

Her mood improved slightly when she heard Erin's voice with Dee's in the corridor, and she was out the door in seconds.

Erin dropped the duffel bag she carried and gave her a hug. 'I'm so glad you're all right,' she said. 'What a shit of a day for you.'

'I'm okay. But yes, a shitty day.' An understatement of epic proportions.

'Nick just called,' Dee said. 'He's on his way back now. He'll be here in half an hour or so.'

This time, Dee's smile was forced, and she hurried away without any further comment, leaving Jo wondering what had upset her.

Erin handed her the duffle bag. 'I gather you couldn't bring anything from your place, so I went shopping for you. Clothes, PJs, toiletries, phone charger and . . .' She drew a small plastic bag out of a side pocket and waved it like a trophy, 'Leaf tea and infuser.'

Jo had to blink away tears. Erin had solved one immediate problem for her; even if she could have retrieved some of her own clothes, the thought of wearing anything that had been in her bedroom made her skin crawl. 'You're an angel, Erin. Thank you.'

Erin grinned cheekily. 'Don't thank me until you see what I chose. I went for plain and functional – well, except for the PJs; I thought you needed a little bit of spoiling – but all the receipts are in there, so if you don't like anything, I can return it.'

'When I can get to a computer, I'll transfer some money to repay you. I've only got my driver's licence and ten dollars on me.' Another logistical problem to deal with. She'd have to ask Nick if her wallet was still in her room, or if it had been stolen. Where she'd be staying the next few days, how to access her money, replacing cards and documentation if necessary, salvaging some belongings and finding a new place to live without nightmare reminders . . . all issues she'd have to deal with, soon. Before she could get on with her life again. Assuming the twisted, murdering bastard criminals were arrested so that she *could* get on with her life again.

The nausea that had plagued her all afternoon made her gut do another somersault.

'Come into the break room,' she said to Erin. 'I'll make a cuppa. Unless you have a bottle of Scotch in here,' she added, 'in which case we'll drink it.'

Unlike the interview room, the staff break room had windows to the outside world, a few armchairs as well as the standard-issue table seating, and some photographs decorating the white walls. A fraction less sterile and claustrophobic, and the armchairs definitely more comfortable for her weary body.

Erin stayed fifteen minutes, and in quiet conversation, mutually avoiding the worst of it, they caught up on some of the happenings of the day. Mal was driving Mary to Newcastle; they expected news of Bruce's condition this evening some time, after surgery.

When Erin left, Jo drew her knees up and curled in the armchair, closing her eyes and breathing deeply, slowly, to calm her mind. Positive, constructive thoughts would get her through. She could, *would* cope with everything. She had the support of friends, dedicated police officers investigating the case, and chances were they'd remove the threat to her soon.

She'd find another place to live and settle into the district properly; instead of marking time at the homestead, she'd make her own home.

⬥

From the doorway, Nick saw her dozing in the chair, arms around her tucked-up legs, head resting against the cushion. Safe and whole, and peaceful, at least for now. He needed to keep her that way.

She'd had an exhausting and traumatic night and day, and he would not disturb her much-needed rest to tell her about Shelley.

He pulled the door closed quietly, flipped the sign to 'Meeting in Progress' and continued down the corridor to brief Murdoch on what they had found.

Accepting the chair Murdoch offered in front of the desk, he gave a concise report on the visible injuries he and Leah had observed.

Murdoch didn't interrupt, and he stayed silent for a long moment when Nick finished, his forehead resting on steepled fingers. 'There are days I hate this job,' he finally looked up and said. 'She must have suffered a great deal.'

Nick's mouth felt like sandpaper. 'Yes.' Even without full forensic examination, that much had been grimly obvious. 'From the phone call, it sounds like there was a group of them, and they were demanding information from her.'

He could almost see Murdoch's thought processes, racing through the possibilities and implications. 'We can presume they knew of the relationship between Dalton and Brock and that's why she was targeted. How well known was Dalton's connection with you?'

'Not very. We were in the same intake for basic training in Goulburn, but after that we were posted to different areas. I trained with him at a dojo sometimes when I was working out of Sydney, but other than some shared history, we don't really have a lot in common. Until this week, I hadn't seen him for a couple of years.'

'What if Brock told them about his letter to you? Would she have revealed that?'

He considered it briefly. 'If they were asking questions like that, then yes, it's likely. I don't believe that she understood the significance of it, and she didn't know me.' So she'd have had no reason to endure pain to protect him. His gut tightened at the thought that she might have tried.

Murdoch paced to the window. 'If they even suspect that Dalton passed information to you, that would make you a target.'

'Possibly.' It didn't rate high in his concerns. At any moment in the past ten years his cover could have been blown and he'd have been a dead man. 'There's no evidence of it.'

'Nevertheless, with two murdered police in two days, we're not going to take chances. You need to be rested and alert, so I'm ordering you off-duty, Nick.'

'I can't go yet. I still have to arrange—'

Murdoch overrode his protest. 'You *can* go off-duty and you *will.*'

A direct order Nick would have to obey. Or find some way around.

'I value your dedication, Nick,' his commander continued, resuming his place at the desk, back ramrod straight and tone formal, 'but I will not have you risk your health and safety or that of your colleagues, or the public. You are not working alone on this case. You will remain off-duty for at least twelve hours and you will get some rest.'

Nick didn't object. No use denying that he *was* exhausted. If he'd been sharper, he'd have handled Murdoch better, not pushed him into pulling rank.

'We still need to arrange protection for Jo Lockwood, sir. I can't get her into witness protection until at least tomorrow.'

'There isn't a safe house available in the region at present for Jo. However, as this case has now become a major incident, there are additional officers from Sydney and the region and twenty trainees from Goulburn due to arrive shortly. They'll be accommodated in the Police Youth Club. It will be basic, but I think it's the safest solution for Jo to stay there with them tonight. Given the possible threat to you, it might be wise for you to stay there, too.'

Nick nodded in agreement, his decision made before Murdoch had voiced the suggestion. Whether intentionally or not, the Inspector had given him what he needed – relative peace of mind about Jo's safety overnight, and enough assistance in protecting her that he could allow himself a few hours' sleep.

Assuming he could switch his mental activity a notch or two below frenetic in order to let himself sleep.

Murdoch's phone rang, and Nick rose to leave but the Inspector signalled him to stay as he answered it. A senior officer, going by the number of 'sirs' Murdoch used.

'That was Assistant Commissioner Fraser,' Murdoch said when he'd finished the brief call. 'He's confirmed the establishment of a formal Strike Force to investigate the murders of Brock and Dalton. There's a media release going out now announcing it, and HQ is flying up a DCI to lead it. Goodabri doesn't have sufficient resources, so we'll move the incident centre back here.'

The decision came as no surprise. He'd discussed the likelihood with Leah already. Two murdered detectives made it a high-profile, priority case. Although it meant he'd no longer have charge, the additional resources a declared Strike Force brought might make the investigation quicker.

They needed it resolved quickly. *He* needed it resolved quickly. The escalation of violence overnight – the torture and murder of both Bradley and Shelley within a few hours of each other – suggested a significant psychological shift in the gang. The bodies of Travis Mitchell and the John Doe had been hidden; but for the dingo and Jo's observation skills, Travis would not have been discovered for weeks or months. Not so with Shelley and Coulter.

Ramirez had cultivated in his gang a taste for torture and murder, an addiction to that power and contempt for the police.

What alarmed Nick most – what set every muscle in his body tense for action – was that the placement of Coulter's tortured, blinded remains in Jo's bedroom was a clear and confident message that they intended to do exactly the same thing to her.

EIGHTEEN

The trouble with drifting to sleep wasn't so much the sleeping, but the waking. Bad dreams danced in her subconscious until she jerked awake; nightmare images of faces with empty eye sockets laughing at her from the depths of a fire.

Over-used muscles had stiffened while she dozed, protesting when she pushed herself out of the armchair and hobbled to the sink. She splashed her face with cold water and drank two glasses of it, the cold liquid refreshing the staleness in her mouth.

Someone had closed the door, so the break room was empty, but she could hear a few voices down the corridor somewhere, and went to find out if Nick had returned, and if there was any news.

She was just a few steps down the hallway when Nick walked out of a room and saw her. His attempt at a smile didn't work, overwhelmed by the tightness in his face as he motioned her to follow him into his office. He offered her a chair and waited until she was seated before drawing his own chair up to the desk.

'I'm sorry I kept you waiting so long this afternoon. And I'm sorry that I have more bad news to give. I don't know if you've heard, but Shelley Brock didn't get onto the plane last night.'

Her heart had sunk at 'more bad news'; at mention of Shelley's name dread tightened fingers around it. 'She's not all right, is she?'

'No.' His voice hardened, his dark eyes clouded, world weary. 'Her body was found this afternoon, near where one of the fires started. Her death . . . it wasn't quick, Jo. Forensic and autopsy reports will take a while, but what we saw is indicative of multiple injuries, and multiple sexual assaults.'

The chill settled in her bones again, and those fingers dug into her chest, made it hard to breathe. He hadn't used the blunt, more emotive terms. Gang rape. Torture. Murder.

Her brain couldn't, wouldn't accept it. Her voice shook. 'I saw her. Spoke with her. About Hugh. She loved him even though he couldn't love her. The taxi arrived out the front and she dashed out, saying she was late.'

She clutched her arms around herself, tried to resist the urge to rock back and forth. She wanted to be held, to draw strength from him, but he sat behind the desk, unmoving. Not unmoved. Something beyond the clamour of her selfish need registered the whites of his knuckles clenched around a pen, and his eyes. Eyes that had seen Shelley in death. Could still see her.

She had to pull herself together. Deal with it, be strong and help him, not drain from him. What could she remember that might help?

'She thanked me for trying CPR. She said I could trust you, that Hugh thought the world of you. Then she remembered the letter just as she rushed out the door. I didn't see the taxi driver.' She was babbling, and nothing of use. 'I'm sorry.'

'The taxi was left behind the depot. But we can't contact the driver who was rostered.' He exhaled a slow breath, as if trying to temper frustration.

What could she say to support him?

'This isn't a densely populated region, Nick. You're going to get a break soon. Someone will know something, have seen someone. Even if they've been camping out in the wilds, they'll have to buy supplies somewhere. People around here often remember strangers.'

'We'll start publicising the photos we have of Ramirez and Coulter and Mitchell. If we can find out who they've been hanging out with, that will help.'

'And it will help if I get out of your way and lie low for a while. Where do you recommend I go?'

'There are additional police arriving this evening, including a bus-load of cadets from Goulburn. They'll be accommodated at the Police Youth Club. I want you to stay there as well, for tonight, Jo. It won't be luxury accommodation, but it will be safe.'

Mats on the floor with a bunch of young trainees. She could do that. 'I don't need luxury. You said for tonight. What about tomorrow?'

'I'm making arrangements for you to go to a safe house under police protection for a while.'

The determined edge in his tone put her on alert. No consultation, just a decision made for her. Not his usual style with her. 'Can you define "a while"?'

He held her gaze, unflinching. 'Until it's safe.'

'Why don't I just go and stay with my mother in Sydney for a few days? Her apartment block has good security.'

'No. Under no circumstances contact your mother, Jo. Or anyone else in your family, or friends. No-one. No phone calls, emails, nothing.'

The severity of his orders scared her. 'Are you talking about witness protection?'

'Yes.'

'I can't just disappear, Nick,' she argued. 'I have friends. A family. I speak to my mother at least once a week. If I vanish, she and my brother will assume the worst.' Her mother would be sick with worry, her brother would be pounding on the police station counter, demanding action and answers.

He tapped his pen against the desk a couple of times, taking a moment before replying. 'You could phone one of them from here. Tell them you might be out of contact for a week or so. Give them Inspector Murdoch's name as a contact. He'll be able to pass on any urgent messages.'

She sighed, too tired to argue. 'Thank you. I guess I'll need to switch off my mobile.'

'Yes, and keep it off. Better still, leave it here. And I mean it about no email or internet, Jo. Your laptop wasn't on the table where you left it. You have to assume they'll have access to sites you regularly visit, your usernames and passwords, and that anything you do electronically could be tracked.'

Panic overtook tiredness for a moment, her family in her thoughts. But it dissipated slowly as she worked through the implications. Other than email addresses, she kept her family's contact details in her head, not on her laptop. And none of them used email addresses with identifying surnames. Her mother scarcely used email at all, preferring phone contact. Todd might be on social networks, but Jo had steered clear of them.

Nevertheless, she'd ask Todd to go and stay with their mother for a few days.

That contingency planned for, she considered her own situation. No access to her belongings, no contacts, no work, no internet.

She tried to smile, but didn't quite succeed. 'I'm going to be bored stupid, aren't I? Any chance of some books to read?'

'I'll arrange some for you. What would you like?'

She preferred to browse, to take time deciding about books, but he had a multiple murder case to work on and she'd taken up enough of his time. She thought quickly. 'Maybe something chunky that will keep me going for a bit? Science, philosophy, history? Or perhaps a novel or two – but nothing gruesome or depressing, please. Cheerful ones. Where the good guys win and everyone lives happily ever after. I think I'm going to need to believe that.'

CB

He'd been twelve, the first time he'd stepped into a Police Youth Club. Twelve, self-conscious in the unfamiliar karate uniform, angry, and convinced he didn't belong, that they'd toss him out after a good beating as soon as they discovered he was Archie Matheson's son.

He carried that same tension between his shoulderblades twenty-five years on, walking into the Strathnairn Police Youth Club. In his youth, he'd come to belong, to trust in individuals, to bring his siblings into the classes and safety of the local club. But the taint of the places he'd been since then, the bars, drug warehouses and clubs where people fought to maim and kill, the things he knew that no youth should know, the things he'd seen, pretended to be . . . he'd come full circle, and no longer belonged.

In the main hall, a half-dozen young kids in martial arts uniforms hauled gym mats from a storage room, dragging them into low piles. Nick scanned the layout of the place; change rooms and a fitness centre to one side, and stairs leading to a second storey above, looking over the main hall, with maybe an office or two and an activity room. A sign near the entrance indicated that squash courts were on the other side of the central block. A kitchen at the rear of the hall. Three exits, that he could see: the front one they'd come through, a side door and a back door out of the kitchen.

A man wearing traditional white uniform and a dark blue *hakama* carried a broom through the breezeway between the change rooms, his attention on the kids. The shaft of envy hitting his gut at the sight of the formal pleated trousers of the Aikido uniform he'd once worn took Nick by surprise. So did the flood of memories when the man registered their presence and glanced across, recognition dawning in his eyes at the same moment Nick placed his face.

In a subtle transformation of focus and purpose, David Thomson laid down his broom, straightened his back, and bowed. 'Sensei! Welcome. I'd heard you were in town, wondered when you'd have time to visit.'

Out of the corner of his eye, Nick caught the enquiring glance Jo cast him. Behind David, his young students scrambled into a crooked line, not quite sure what was going on, or of etiquette, but one of the bigger students bowed so the others followed suit.

Nick almost froze. He'd been a different person when he'd taught David in Sydney. Eleven years younger, inspired after six months training at the head dojo in Tokyo, and optimistic that he could, maybe, make a difference. Something stirred in his gut – yearning, nostalgia, he wasn't sure what it was – but despite the grimy uniform he'd been wearing for days, and the preoccupations and worries crowding his thoughts, he returned his former student's bow as if he too stood, grounded and balanced, in a *hakama*.

Respect for them, not for himself. The man he'd become over the past ten years made a mockery of the principles he'd once tried to live by.

'David. It's been a long time.' He indicated the class, watching with curious, wide-open eyes. 'So, you're teaching now.'

David grinned, coming forward to shake his hand warmly, as easy and as carefree as Nick remembered him. 'Yes, I moved up here a couple of years ago. There was no-one else, so I started teaching. I still aspire to your discipline and skill, Sensei.' He held out his hand to Jo. 'You must be Jo. Keith Murdoch said you'd be coming over. I'm David, the centre manager, and occasional Aikido instructor. Nick was my teacher, some years ago when we both lived in Sydney. I hope he will be again.'

'I haven't trained properly for a while, David. I'm very rusty.' And unfit. Not so much in body, because he'd trained hard in other fighting forms until his recent injuries slowed him down. But unfit in mind, in spirit.

Before David could utter an invitation to train with him, Nick changed the subject and asked directly, 'Do you mind if I take a look around? I need to ensure that Jo will be secure here.'

David gave little sign he'd noticed the lack of courtesy. 'Of course. I've been told to expect about thirty officers and cadets. They should all fit down here. There's an empty office upstairs. If you'd like some privacy, Jo, you're welcome to use that.'

'Thank you,' Jo said, and Nick thought he detected some relief in the words. She'd been remarkably uncomplaining, all along. Yet this upheaval of her normal life, the very threat to it, had to be unsettling in the extreme. Instead of somewhere quiet and peaceful to retreat to, he was throwing her in with a mob of strangers.

The office, although small, was uncluttered and recently renovated, with fresh paint and carpet, blinds on the internal windows, a desk and filing cabinet in a corner. And a solid lock on the door.

'I'd take this, if I were you,' he suggested to Jo.

She nodded. 'It might be quieter. And I'm more used to being alone.'

The upper level overlooked the hall on one side and squash courts on the other, with seating for spectators. In the first court, a couple of men had just finished a game. The second was empty. He walked along the balcony to check the last courts. They'd been converted into one room, the floor fitted with a large mat centred in the space, and a portrait of Aikido founder Morihei Ueshiba on the far wall.

Up here in the viewing area, he had not technically entered the dojo space, yet he had to consciously restrain the instinctive bow that etiquette and habit required.

Perhaps Jo had seen his instinctive movement. 'You used to teach Aikido?' she probed.

'I've taught a lot of different forms of fighting. Many of them incompatible with Aikido's minimal-harm principles.' Not relevant to the situation now. Not a priority to consider the reasons for the unsettling nostalgia. He changed the subject briskly. 'There's a fourth exit down there, past the last squash court door. I'll check to make sure it's alarmed.' And he'd sleep upstairs, near the office she'd be in. Four exits were good from a fire safety perspective; four *entrances*, one of them away from the main hall area, were less safe from a protection perspective.

Voices came from downstairs, and within a few minutes the hall was busy with police cadets and their duffel bags. Some Rotary Club members arrived with a portable barbecue, which they set up out the front of the building, and a couple of cars of officers from other areas arrived shortly after. With over twenty armed police in the building, and four apparently reliable and dedicated Rotarians in their sixties nearby, Nick considered it safe to leave Jo for a short while.

In the motel room he'd scarcely seen this week, he quickly peeled off his dirty clothes, washing them under the shower as he cleansed sweat, ash and dirt from his body. He wrung his clothes out and draped them over the shower screen; in the harsh summer heat, they'd likely be dry by the morning.

Stacked in the corner of the room, the four removalists' boxes he'd brought from the storage unit in Sydney contained the limited elements of the life he led between undercover jobs. Not much. He rummaged in a different box for the clothes he'd bought after his release from hospital, and dragged on jeans and T-shirt.

Showered, dressed and shaved, he felt marginally better than dead beat. Preparing for whatever the next few days might bring, he packed an overnight bag, and then he ripped open the tape on one of the storage boxes. Books, Jo had asked for, but the shops in Strathnairn closed by five on a Saturday afternoon, and few were open on Sunday. He hadn't labelled the boxes properly, could hardly remember packing them over twelve months ago, but there were books somewhere.

Coffee maker and basic kitchen equipment. No, not that box. When he opened the second box, the memories he'd been struggling to supress all evening surged back. On top, wrapped in tissue paper and still in its precise folds, lay the indigo *hakama* he'd put away years ago. Hardening his heart, he put it and his dojo clothes to one side.

Under his Aikido books and the few texts he'd kept from his university studies, he found the small pile of paperback books he'd lugged from one rented apartment to another until he'd finally put them in storage. Some Terry Pratchett novels that had belonged to Pat. A couple of Ursula Le Guin books that Christie had struggled with on first read but declared 'awesome' after the second.

He drew out one of Grace's *Little House on the Prairie* books and flicked through a few pages, the black-and-white illustrations meticulously coloured-in with pencil blurring in front of his eyes before he snapped it closed it again and replaced it in the box with his mother's Bible and the theological texts she'd bought in her search for answers.

Not much left of his family, and all of it from a used book store.

But he didn't have time to remember, and what good would it do, anyway? He packed the Pratchett and Le Guin books into his bag for Jo, and on the spur of the moment he added in his Aikido uniform. Rebuilding his physical fitness made sense. He didn't allow himself to consider anything more than that.

He had a job to do, killers to arrest and charge and a witness to protect. Being ordered off-duty wouldn't stop him doing it.

One of the things Jo appreciated about smaller towns was the way people simply pitched in when need arose. In most communities, the Rotary or a similar service club could start up a barbecue, chop up salads and feed steak sandwiches to thirty or more hungry police officers with little notice.

With nothing else to do, and feeling out of place among the young cadets, Jo offered to help in the kitchen. The rhythm of slicing lettuces and tomatoes, buttering bread, and the easy, getting-to-know-you chat with Rotarians Helen and Frank distracted her thoughts from darker subjects, at least for a while. Maybe someone had told them why she was there, because they never asked, and they avoided any mention of the murders.

They found common interests easily enough, mostly to do with the land and environment. By the time they'd cleaned up, she had invitations to speak at one of the local LandCare groups about her PhD research on microbats, and to visit Frank's garden of local native plants. Fairly typical of the welcome and genuine interest in her work that she'd experienced in the last four months from the locals. She liked the town and the broader community, could see herself staying some years here.

Assuming the killers were caught. Why the hell did she keep remembering that caveat, and the threat to her?

Out in the main hall, Keith Murdoch and a dark-haired woman – one of the Sydney detectives, someone had said – were setting up a computer projector for a briefing. After being introduced to Detective Leah Haddad and invited by Murdoch to attend the briefing, Jo found a place at the back of the room and leaned against the wall. Not that she wanted to hear and see graphic details – she had enough fodder for a lifetime of nightmares in her head already – but if her life and the lives of others were at risk, the more information she had, the safer she might be.

Nick came in through the side door during Murdoch's introduction, standing to the side and scanning the group. Looking for her, she realised, as he made his way across the room and stood beside her, his attention, after a fleeting, drawn smile at her, on the briefing. But she was glad he was there, by her side.

Murdoch acknowledged her in his outline of the key events, and she felt herself flush as most people turned to take a look at her. Some curious, some with sympathy, some just impersonally processing relevant information about the what, who, where

and how of the crimes. She might as well be wearing a label –
Exhibit 1: National Parks Ranger.

Yep, that would be the National Parks ranger who regretted changing her roster and going in to work on Wednesday. On Tuesday, too, come to think of it. If she hadn't seen Ramirez, she might have avoided the bullseye on her forehead.

She studied her boots while images of the murder victims were screened. Gutless of her, but she couldn't quite rally the scientific neutrality to view them unemotionally. Not when the killers apparently planned to do the same kinds of things to her.

Nick touched her shoulder, murmured, 'You okay?'

'Yes,' she whispered back, trying for lightness. 'I never did like horror movies.'

Being stuck in a real-life one was even worse.

There was little in the briefing she didn't already know – until Leah Haddad mentioned the old man, and where he'd been picked up. In the middle of everything else today, she hadn't heard about that.

'One of the sites we'll have you cadets search tomorrow is here,' Leah said, using a laser pointer on the projected map. 'According to an informant, our chief suspect was here yesterday afternoon. It's only a few hundred metres from where Detective Brock was found.'

'Older gentleman, with a white beard and a gruff manner?' Jo asked Nick in an undertone.

'Yes. Do you know him?'

She nodded. 'Met him in that area a few weeks ago. Nice old guy – a bushie from way back.'

She'd shared a cuppa and a long yarn with the old man, deep in the bush, learning about the district from his rich knowledge of history and stories. If he was out there, alone, he'd be almost defenceless against thugs.

'Leah arranged a lift for him to Strathnairn,' Nick added quietly, as if he read her concern. 'He'll stay in town for a few days.'

One weight off her mind, at least.

'The bus will leave for the search site at six in the morning,' Leah was saying. 'You need an early start, because it's over an hour out to the site, and it's going to be hot later in the day. Jo, if you wouldn't mind, can you tell us something about the terrain and if there's anything they should be wary of?'

A little more notice would have been good, but this was her work, her expertise and she appreciated that recognition. Far better than being a witness or a target.

She walked through the assembled police to the front, and accepted the laser pointer from Leah. The projected topographical map detailed familiar ground. 'The river in that area is close to the north-east boundary of the National Park. The other side of Cattlemans Creek Road is State Forest. In the park, there is a series of low granite hills with creeks in between that flow into the Nyland River. However, none of the creeks are flowing at the moment, and the river is very low. The river flats aren't very wide at this point, and there are low, rocky rises on either side. Be aware that there are a few old mine shafts in this area of Diggers Creek, but that's a little way up from the junction where you'll be working.'

She drew breath and swallowed, wishing she'd grabbed a bottle of water earlier. 'As far as other things to be wary of

– it's going to be stinking hot tomorrow. Drink plenty of water tonight, so you're fully hydrated, and take several litres *each* tomorrow. Also, because we had a wet winter, there's a lot of dry grass and undergrowth, and it's a bumper year for snakes. I appreciate that as you're looking for evidence you'll be watching the ground in front of you, but please do take extra care, particularly among the debris from last year's floods. Most of the snakes here are highly venomous, and you'll be a long way from medical care.'

At least they'd be properly dressed for it, in solid boots, long trousers and protective gloves. But she'd check with the supervising officer that their first-aid kit included long, wide bandages suitable for snake bites.

She got caught after the briefing was over, answering more questions than expected from the cadet's supervisor, so that when she looked around for Nick she couldn't see him. With those in the hall starting to arrange gym mats and preparing to settle for the night, she found a small mat for herself and carried it upstairs.

Nick stood near the office door, his bag at his feet, staring at the phone in his hand so intently that he didn't hear her approach.

'Nick?'

He looked up swiftly, too swiftly to conceal the pain darkening his eyes.

'What's wrong, Nick?'

He shook his head as if to clear it. 'A message from my sister.'

NINETEEN

Murdoch's text message simply read: *Grace Anderson trying to contact you* – and a mobile phone number.

But there was nothing simple about it. Nothing simple in the mix of raw emotion assaulting him. Emotion he'd convinced himself he'd left behind, dealt with, close on two decades ago.

Definitely nothing simple about dialling that number and talking to Grace. When he'd dialled her home number last night, emotion dulled by sheer adrenaline overload, even then he'd been ashamedly relieved when she hadn't answered.

Facts. Straightforward facts. 'My youngest sister, Grace, is trying to contact me.'

Jo waited, watching him, as if she expected more. Of course she expected more. That one sentence hardly explained anything. Anyone but Jo and he'd have left it there. Wouldn't have even revealed that much. But he needed her to understand. Needed, perhaps, to draw on her strength.

'I told you I haven't seen her since I was eighteen.' *Breathe, control, focus.*

He expected her to ask why. Instead, after a long moment, she said, 'That must have been hard for you.'

Hard? He'd done what he'd had to do, for Grace's safety. No regrets. The cost to him – the emptiness, the sorrow – had been bearable, for her sake.

Never show weakness. He'd blown that rule multiple times, with Jo. But to earn trust, he had to give trust, and he trusted her. She knew almost the worst of him already, and she hadn't judged him harshly.

He had to steady himself before calling Grace. Perhaps explaining to Jo, putting spoken words to the tumult of memories and emotions and arguments in his head, would give him clarity and the emotional composure to make the call. Maybe Grace already understood how willingly he'd ripped a hole in his heart to protect her. Maybe Jo needed to understand how far he'd go to protect those he cared about.

'Let's go over here where it's quiet, and I'll explain.' He walked away from the noise and the curious eyes of those below, to the balcony overlooking the squash courts, his mood drawing him along the railing to where they looked into the dojo. The lights from the main hall hardly reached here, only a few security lights glowing in the dimness.

Arms resting on the railing, Jo shoulder-to-shoulder beside him, he began. 'The day Christie and Pat were killed, I was visiting my father in prison. He'd called me in to tell me he planned to give evidence. Vinchenko was powerful, influential, and my father feared reprisals. Word must have already got out,

270

though, and I was too late. I identified their bodies there at the bus stop. Then I went to Grace's foster home. I hadn't been entirely happy with the carers, and I knew she was putting on a brave face. Anyway, I packed some clothes for her, and took her as far away from Newcastle as I could afford train and bus tickets for.'

She'd cuddled into him the whole way, crying a little, sleeping a little, small and fragile under his arm. Trusting him completely, reliant on him to protect because his father hadn't.

Facts, not emotion. 'I left her with the Child Protection office in Toowoomba and told them it was too dangerous for her to stay in Newcastle, to find somewhere safe for her. They did. I made sure she was happy before I signed the papers allowing her adoption by her foster parents a year later.'

'Were you close to her?' Jo asked quietly.

'Close?' he repeated. Yes, 'close' probably described the powerful mix of affection and love and fraternal protectiveness he'd felt for his sister. 'She was the youngest by several years, small for her age, a tiny doll of a girl. We were all close. When our father went to prison, we Matheson kids became targets. We stuck together and we looked after her. But Grace was the most vulnerable of us, and after the others died, I had to get her out of there.'

He cleared the roughness in his throat. He'd been staring ahead into the dusky dojo as he spoke, aware of Jo's presence, telling his story to her, yet not quite courageous enough to watch her response.

Within his field of vision, her hand, tanned and calloused from outdoor work, lean and strong, closed over his.

'I've never had to deal with the kind of violence and loss you've experienced, Nick. I've never had to make such difficult decisions. Nobody should have to, especially not a teenager. You haven't seen her since you consented to her adoption?'

He took her hand in his, brushed his fingers gently over hers, over the back of her hand, as if the connection with her decency could ground him and counter the violence of his life. And then he drew his hands away, abruptly, as if it had been no more than a mere touch between friends.

'No, I haven't seen her. For a long time I couldn't be sure that there was no threat. Grudges last a long time in that kind of culture.' Instead of connecting with hers, his hands gripped the cool metal of the railing. 'When I started working undercover, my background and the fact that I had no close family or friends made me a suitable person to infiltrate gangs and underworld mobs. So I kept it that way.'

She turned to face him. 'You're a remarkable man, Nick.'

'No, I'm not. Two of my siblings are dead. Three, if you count Hugh.' He was never sure if he did, in fact, count Hugh as a sibling. 'And now Hugh has involved Grace in this nightmare.'

Jo sighed, and said gently, 'So, go call your sister, Nick. If you need a friend afterwards, you know where to find me.' She brushed his cheek with her lips, as easily as Christie and Grace used to, and walked away, leaving him alone.

The screen on his phone glowed in the dim light, and his finger hovered over Grace's number. One touch, and he'd be dialling it. Just as soon as his pulse stopped battering his ear drum.

The drumming banged some sense back into him. He would dial it. But not on this phone. Not on a phone connected to him where the contact might be traced. The fewer people who knew of her relationship to him, the better.

He went downstairs, borrowed a cadet's phone and took it to the privacy of the unused squash court.

Grace answered immediately, as if she'd had her phone in her hand. A woman's voice, not a girl's, but retaining the hint of a lilt like their mother's.

'It's Nick, Grace.' The words came out almost even.

'Nick! God, is it really you? Are you all right? They told me about Hugh. But I don't have your number, and the Inspector wouldn't tell me anything about you. Are you okay?'

'I'm fine. It's good to hear your voice, Grace. I'm . . .' he trailed off, then forced himself back on track. 'How did you know where I am?'

'Hugh phoned me, days ago. He was in a strange mood, he said something about your new job, something about arranging it. Sometimes I can't tell when he's joking and when he's not, and it worried me. He hasn't let me get in touch with you, Nick, even though I wanted to. He said you couldn't contact me.'

Hugh had *arranged* his posting here? It couldn't be possible. Or could it? There'd been a distinct lack of available positions on offer when he'd spoken to HR. Hugh wasn't the only officer in the police force who disregarded rules and policies at times, preferring the informal network of mates and favours. Something else to look into, later.

'Were you there? When he was shot? Are you all right?'

'I was there.' He swallowed, and narrowed in to the most significant issue. 'He was worried about you, Grace. About your safety. So I'm worried about you. Where are you? In Brisbane?'

'No. I flew into Sydney this morning, and they met me and told me about Hugh. I'm going to stay in Sydney for a few days. His lawyer is here, and his apartment, and there will be things that need doing.'

His brain raced through options, possibilities, strategies. He had contacts in Sydney, police and others who owed him a good turn. 'Don't stay in his apartment. Stay in a quality hotel, somewhere secure at least for tonight. I'll pay for it, if you're short of funds. And I'll arrange someone to stay with you.'

'I'm not in his apartment. I don't know how much he told you, Nick, but we weren't lovers. Never were. Anyway, he had a new girlfriend. One of his colleagues.'

Nick kneaded the tension in the back of his neck. 'I know. Shelley Brock. Listen, Grace, she was murdered last night.' He heard his sister's gasp, hated scaring her. 'I don't know if there's a danger for you, but he spent time with you, and if they are harming people who were close to him . . . I need you to take extreme care. Tell me where you're staying, and I'll ensure there's extra protection there.'

Whether they'd been lovers or not, according to Hugh, Ramirez and his gang had believed it. Even with Hugh's death, Nick couldn't be sure the danger had passed.

He noted the name of the hotel and her room number. Not far from a dojo he knew well. He could have people he trusted watch her floor tonight.

'I'll be careful, Nick,' Grace promised. 'And you have to be, too. It's past time I saw you again. There's so much more to say. I've missed you.'

'I've always missed you.' Saying it aloud, at last, dissolved some of the hard lump in his throat. 'I'm sorry, Grace. I only ever wanted you to be safe.'

She sighed, not bothering to stop the tears showing in her voice. 'I know that. I understand. There's nothing to forgive, never has been. I'll see you soon, okay?'

'Yes.' He disconnected the phone. He'd lived too much of his life unsure about tomorrows. And he still couldn't promise his sister that he'd see her again.

❧

Jo lay on a gym mat on the floor in the corner of the office and contemplated the ceiling. Downstairs, most of the police were sleeping, a few talking in low murmurs audible under the hum of the airconditioning.

Silk pyjamas, Erin had bought her. Soft and smooth and sensuous on the skin, and oh, so unsuitable for sleeping on a gym mat with thirty cadets nearby. She smiled at the thought of them. Maybe sometime soon she'd pamper herself and wear them, but not tonight. She'd changed, instead, into a camisole and cotton pants lighter and cooler than Dee's track pants.

Nick had been in a while ago. He brought her some books, gave her a brief summary of his conversation with his sister and said he'd be working for a while. Then he'd wished her goodnight and walked away, closed, distant, as if they hadn't shared anything at all. Worrying about the case perhaps, all detective.

She'd tried to read for a while but couldn't concentrate.

She might as well close her eyes, focus her mind on relaxing and try to sleep.

Breathe in. Relax. Breathe in. Relax. Don't think of bodies, or fires. Don't think of the pain in Nick's eyes. Think of beautiful things, peaceful things. Early morning sunlight shafting through trees. A little joey kangaroo, small and fuzzy, peeking at the world from its mother's pouch, warm and safe. Safe. Protected. Nick's arms around her. Strength. Comfort.

She woke suddenly, striking out at a nightmare, panic driving her heart rate fast and confusion clouding her thoughts about where she was until she recognised the room, different in the darkness with only ghostly, dull shadows from the security lights and the moon shining through the skylights.

She checked her watch. Just past midnight. Her heart rate still raced and the images from her dream still lurked, only barely in the background. She needed to wake up properly, clear them from her head, before she could rest again.

Muscular aches dug tentacles deep into her legs, shoulders and spine as she rolled over, almost making her groan aloud. Damn, but the after-effects of hard fire-fighting could *hurt*.

She'd have to stretch before she totally seized up. She had the space in this office, nothing and no-one to trip over. Standing, she reached upwards, bent slowly over to touch her toes. At least half of her muscles protested. Another gentle stretch upwards . . . she looked through the internal windows. Nick's bag was out there, and the mat he'd found. His boots stood beside his bag, neat and straight. But he wasn't there.

She swore under her breath. He needed sleep even more than she did. He'd been walking around looking like a ghost for days. And she would feel better, safer, knowing he was nearby.

She went in search of him, but didn't have to go far. Small sounds came from the martial arts room: the brush of bare feet on a mat, deep, even breaths.

The skylight above him shed enough illumination into the room for her to see him from the balcony. The full, pleated trousers of his Aikido uniform swished softly as he worked through an exercise with a wooden staff in the semi-darkness. Graceful. Powerful.

His back to her, he didn't see her, and she sat in the shadows, watching silently, as all her impressions and experiences of him swirled gradually around like the staff he swung, and began to form into a cohesive, multifaceted whole. She'd thought his police uniform and gun belt made him look like a warrior. But compared to this, they were . . . *ordinary*.

He finished the routine, bowed from the kneeling position and then sat, motionless, for some time – she didn't know how long – before he began the exercise again.

This time, something had changed. The grace and power were qualitatively different, both smoother and more intense. Incredible masculine beauty, strength and harmony distilled into a precisely contained but unbroken flow, each movement effortlessly following the last, the whole perfectly balanced.

She had no doubt that armed only with a wooden staff he could be lethal – if he chose. But she also had no doubt that at every moment of every movement, he had complete control over where and how the staff moved, where and when it started and stopped.

She'd never understood, until these moments watching him, why traditional martial-arts training and discipline were so respected and awed.

Despite all that he'd suffered and lost, she saw no anger, no aggression. Self-discipline, self-control, internal strength, rather than enforced power over others.

That strength of mind, honour and dedication earned even more of her respect.

More than her respect, if she was honest with herself.

His guarded reserve couldn't be more different to Leon's outgoing, easy way with everyone, his boundless energy and enthusiasm. But in all the ways that mattered to her, in that solid, central core of respect and commitment to others, they were similar.

All her efforts to keep emotionally distant had failed, and the attraction to him – far more than physical – could no longer be denied.

But the power of it frightened her.

༂

Nick completed the kata, the wooden staff smooth and solid in his grip, the mat cool and springy under his bare feet.

He returned to the kneeling position and bowed to the portrait of O Sensei, the great teacher and founder of the art, with gratitude for the discipline and the awareness, and for the strength and balance they gave him.

In the last time through the kata, the discordance in his mind and body had eased. He had found his centre of calm, of clarity and determination, a certainty that he'd not felt since before the undercover work, since the six months he'd spent, at twenty-five, in intensive training at the head dojo in Tokyo.

He could protect, would protect. That was the heart of who he was, who he'd been since he was twelve years old and had stepped up to look after his family after his father's imprisonment.

He had no illusions that right always prevailed, but if he hadn't always succeeded, it had not been for lack of commitment.

The doubts that had assailed him these past few days dissipated and settled into their proper perspective, and the fatigue in his body became just that: fatigue from lack of sleep, not nerve and muscular weakness from a poisonous biochemical cocktail of emotional and physical stresses.

He would sleep for a few hours, and then he would be better equipped to find, confront and neutralise the current threats. And when that was achieved, he would consider his future.

The undercover shit is eating you alive.

The memory of the letter sounded in his mind as if Hugh was there, saying the words. And Hugh was right – the half-life he'd led for almost a decade, his own life subjugated to the roles he'd played, had sucked him dry. He'd been right to request a return to normal duties. He'd have to make sure it stayed that way, so that he could finally *be* Nick Matheson.

As he climbed the stairs, a figure rose from the bench seats on the balcony. Jo. He knew her profile, the easy way she moved, her slim body softly shaped by some light clothing, white in the dusky light.

She came forward to meet him. 'I think I've just seen the real you,' she said quietly. 'And I think I'm beginning to understand who you are.'

Her presence should have disturbed the equilibrium he'd found, but it didn't. He gave that a small test.

'I've spent much of the past decade playing different people, Jo,' he said, his voice low. 'Why do you think this isn't just another performance?'

She answered him slowly. 'Consistency. Authenticity. And the fact that you seemed . . .' She tilted her head, searching for a word. 'Whole, I guess. At peace with yourself.'

Whole and at peace? 'I'm working on it,' he said. 'I've missed Aikido. I studied it seriously for some years, but while I was undercover I couldn't practise it openly. When I couldn't sleep, I thought I'd start to fix that.'

She reached out a hand, fingers brushing against the side of his face. Brief, gentle, and he didn't move away from it. Had no desire to move away. 'Seems to me you've fixed something. Will you sleep now?'

'I think so.' The sense of peace still infused him, but sleep . . . No, he wanted more than sleep. 'How about you? Couldn't sleep?'

'I had bad dreams.' She gave a small, rueful smile. 'My subconscious can see right through my pretence of bravery.'

'You've had one hell of a few days, Jo.'

'Yep. I'm trying to keep calm and rational about it, but underneath . . . well, underneath I'm scared. I'm not keen on the whole possibly dying thing.' She tried to smile again, but the strain made it waver, and she bit her lip, still trying to keep it in place.

And that was the end of him. He'd been fighting his feelings for her since that first day. But to deny that, to deny her, would be a lie, and he was through with living lies.

He drew her into his arms, and she came easily, rested her forehead against his shoulders, her fingers splayed on the cloth over his chest. When she'd turned into his hold earlier today, she'd been in shock, traumatised, and he could have been anyone she trusted. She might not even remember it. But this time was different.

He held her close, rested his face against her hair, aware of every point of touch, of her body against his, the curve of her shoulders and the small of her back under his hands, the soft fabric of her camisole scarcely concealing the warmth of her skin.

Aware, too, of his responsibility, and her need for reassurance. He tried to give her a solid foundation for some hope. 'You're not the only one who's scared, Jo, and I can't promise happy endings for everything. But these thugs are making mistakes. We're going to track them down quickly. I can promise that you'll be under police protection until we do.'

'Thank you.'

She didn't move, stayed in his arms, and he could feel, hear, her deep regular breaths as she struggled for calm.

He matched his breathing to hers. Authenticity, she'd said. Wholeness. He couldn't be authentic and whole if he hid from his emotions.

'I'd give my life to keep you safe, Jo.'

She drew her face away just far enough to look up at him. 'I know that, Nick.' Holding his gaze, she brushed her lips against his, once, and again.

Sensual, yes, but more than that. Intimate. Trusting. Honest.

He'd played so many roles over the past decade, had sex when the job required it, always in character, hard and hot and often controlling and never gentle and definitely never emotionally intimate or honest.

Never himself.

In the semi-darkness he held her close, and he returned her trust, allowed her to know his vulnerability, with soft tastes of her lips, her mouth, the line of her jaw, the pulse at her temple. Her body pressed against his, lithe and soft yet strong, fuelled a longing for something more than the physical release of sex. More intimate, more giving than simple sex.

They paused eventually, their breathing ragged, and Jo tucked her head into his shoulder, one hand resting on his waist.

He didn't need the awareness of the timber floor, cool and firm, under his bare feet, to have the sense of being grounded. Here, holding Jo, he was in the right place, steady and grounded and completely himself.

She lifted her head, raw honesty in her eyes, in the solemnity of her voice. 'I told Erin I wouldn't get involved with a man who might get himself killed. That terrifies me, Nick. When

Leon died, grief – it eroded everything I was for a long while. I was petrified I'd lose myself.'

The ground beneath his sense of certainty tilted. Jo. *Her* needs, not his. 'But you didn't lose yourself.'

'Not entirely. Not forever. Not something I want to go through again, though.'

Still holding her close against his pounding heart, he loosened his jacket, and taking her hand, guided it to the puckered skin between his lower ribs where Terry Costello's bullet had ripped into him. His voice felt just as rough as he said, 'I can't promise not to die, Jo.'

He half-expected her to recoil, but her fingers on his skin were feather light, with a gentleness that soothed the still-healing nerves around the wound. Then she covered it with her palm, protecting, and her eyes met his.

'I don't know what's between us, Nick, or where it's going. The intensity scares me. But I won't deny it. I want you. I want you to stay with me tonight. No promises, no assumptions, no complications. Just stay with me.'

He grazed her mouth with his, closed his eyes to absorb every sense, every taste, touch, impression of her hands, her mouth beneath his, her body with his. Heat and need and longing roared to life within him, and his focus narrowed. Just Jo. Nothing but Jo and the craving to be with her, to give himself to her, completely.

⁓

That a man so strong, so hardened, could be so gentle scarcely surprised her. That she could want him so intensely did.

Firm muscles flexed under her hands. Back, shoulders, waist and chest. Hips against hers. A hard body, powerful, but not threatening. She tasted, explored, his mouth, his face, the hunger for connection acute, his hands on her skin drawing her deeper, further into pure need.

Somewhere, downstairs, someone coughed a few times, awareness of the sound only slowly registering in her brain as Nick stilled, alert.

Upstairs, in the shadows, they could not be seen, but without speaking she took his hand and drew him towards the darkened office, where the blinds on the windows would provide privacy.

His hand still in hers he stopped by his bag, crouching for just a moment as he reached into it and found something, a small rustle of plastic in his hand as he rose again.

She smiled in the semi-darkness. Protection, in all its forms.

She clicked the lock closed on the door. Moonlight drifting through the skylight fell on him, tall and rock steady.

His breathing rasped quietly, as uneven as hers.

With his fingertips, he slowly traced a fiery sensual path down the side of her face, her throat, lightly over her breast to her waist, and she trembled, stepping into his arms again for the closeness she ached for.

While his hands slid up from her waist and slipped the camisole over her head, making nerves come alive in every inch of skin, she pushed his jacket open, pressed her lips against his chest, trailed fingers around his hips where the *hakama* tied.

'You're a little formally dressed, Nick,' she murmured. 'I want to touch you. All of you. Skin to skin.'

With a gentle hand he lifted her head, let her see the desire in his face. 'We will,' he said, and lowered his mouth to hers.

Need seared through her as his left hand closed over her breast, and she claimed his mouth again, hungry for him, for every sensation, desperate to give him the same sublime pleasure he gave her.

His fingers teasing her breast obliterating coherent thought, she fumbled with the ties on his *hakama*, but with his other hand he brushed hers aside, nimbly dealing with the knots.

'Wait,' he said against her mouth. 'Don't move.'

He stepped back only far enough to remove the *hakama*, but his intense, all-encompassing focus never left her.

Her heart full, she pushed the jacket off his shoulders, laid her hands on his chest; warm skin, firm flesh, the scars he carried, and all of it, all of him, hers for this brief time. Hers to share with, to gift with her care and honour and love.

'I want you, Nick. Completely.'

The last of their clothes fell to the floor, and the mat pressed cool against her back, but Nick's face filled her vision as his touch overwhelmed her senses. His eyes, dark and deep, locked on hers as she drew him in to her, again and again and again, until he threw his head back and let go his control and his release, deep and strong, triggered wave after wave of exquisite sensation.

When it finally faded enough for thought to return, he rolled her into his arms, holding her close, his lips against her temple.

Nick stayed with her, and she slept cradled against him on the mat. Her subconscious must have been either exhausted or reassured, because when she woke it was slowly, when he moved in his sleep. A long time since she'd shared a bed, listened to a man's breathing beside her, felt his body warm against hers.

No promises, she'd said. No complications. And two unattached adults physically attracted to each other should be able to have sex without it becoming a 'complication'.

But what they had shared was more than just sex. They'd made love, shared love, given each other love and tenderness and acceptance.

Definitely not *uncomplicated*.

She was falling hard for him – had fallen already – and she knew he'd do everything he could to keep her safe from external threats. But could she be safe with him, afterwards? A dangerous job, a traumatic background. If she allowed herself to be close to him, how would she cope if he was killed on duty? How would she cope if the trauma of his past became too much for him, and he went off the rails, like Hugh? Or if he gave up and walked away one day, put a gun to his head and pulled the trigger?

Nick brushed a thumb against her temple, kissed her forehead lightly. 'Go back to sleep,' he murmured drowsily. 'You're safe with me.'

There was no way he could have read her thoughts. But she closed her eyes again, felt her mind relaxing despite the irrationality of it. He wasn't Leon. And she was stronger than the young woman she'd been years ago. They just had to stay alive through this crisis. The rest she would find a way to deal with, in the future.

When she woke again, he was gone. The muted daylight of early morning glimmered through the skylight and a steady hum of voices and noises drifted from downstairs. Not quite six o'clock.

She selected jeans and a T-shirt from the clothes Erin had bought her and dressed quickly.

The cadets were loading onto the bus as she went downstairs, the other officers in varying states of readiness for the day ahead, some clutching paper coffee mugs. Through the open front doors, the smell of bacon wafted in from the Rotary barbecue.

Nick had his laptop open on a table at the back of the room, a coffee cup beside it, but he paced nearby, speaking on his phone, and any peace he might have found last night had vanished. Too far away to hear his words above the noise of the television, she could see the conversation consisted of intense, urgent, short exchanges.

Frank brought in a platter of bacon-and-egg rolls, and she accepted one from him although she had little appetite. Given the uncertainty of the day ahead, taking advantage of breakfast to shore up her energy levels made sense. But as she juggled eating it without egg dripping on her T-shirt, she kept an eye on Nick. He finished that call and made another – he must have left a message for it was only brief.

He came across the room to meet her, all detective, with no evidence of the lover she'd been close to in the night.

'Can you be ready to leave in five minutes? I'm going to take you back to the police station. It'll be more secure than here today.'

'I can be ready in two. What's happened?'

'I'll tell you in the car. If you can bring down my gear, I'll pick you up at the back entrance in a couple of minutes.'

She flew up the stairs, put the books Nick had loaned her in her bag, picked up his and was back down again, waiting by the kitchen door when he reversed out of the parking area and swung around to pick her up.

On the short, two-block trip, he kept his eyes on the road, tense and alert, as he briefly explained.

'That was Interpol on the phone just now. They've confirmed, from both fingerprints and facial recognition analysis on the photograph, that the man you saw on the bike is Eduardo Guerrera Ramirez. The Ramirez family runs one of the major Mexican drug cartels.'

Mexican cartels. She read the news, knew of the ongoing violence in Mexico and drug wars in other parts of South America, had felt sorrow for the terrible cost inflicted on ordinary, decent Mexicans by the drug lords and their cartels. 'They're here, in Australia?'

'Yes, they've been coming in recent years because prices are high here and it's lucrative compared to other places. I've seen a lot of different organised-crime groups. Many of them can be very violent, but it's mostly towards their rivals. In Mexico cartels have enormous influence, through corruption, intimidation and fear. Anyone inconvenient is eliminated. What concerns the Australian police is that the cartels are bringing those same attitudes and practices here.'

He turned the car into the police station parking area and swiped his access ID to open the security gate. While it gradually opened, he turned to her. 'Jo, I can't overstate the risks. I've told you before how dangerous Ramirez is. You're the only one who can place him at the scene of Mitchell's murder. I know it's going to be hard on you, but you need to stay in witness protection for as long as it takes to get him and all his associates locked away.'

TWENTY

After escorting Jo to his office, Nick found Murdoch had already arrived, despite the early hour. Clean shaven and parade-ground straight, only his tightly drawn, pallid face reflected the strain.

'I saw the Interpol email you forwarded,' he said. 'Have you spoken with them?'

'Yes.' Although Murdoch indicated the chair, Nick remained standing, too wired to sit. 'They're sending a report on Ramirez with the information they have. The family cartel supplies the drugs but he runs more as a lone wolf. Modus operandi may be similar to when he set up operations in Canada: targeting regional areas for cocaine transportation routes, attracting a gang of disaffected youths by promising money and drugs, training them up in violence and intimidation. It seems to fit the pattern here.'

Murdoch didn't disagree outright – just worked through some of the questions he had aloud. 'There's not much of a market out here. And we haven't seen an increase in drug-related crime. A reduction, in fact, since the Mafia bust a few months ago, south of here.'

'I doubt much is intended for this district. I'm guessing they're bringing it in somewhere along the Queensland or Northern Territory coasts, and using inland roads to shift it to the southern states. But I'm also guessing – hoping – that the operation is still in its set-up phase. The Federal Police haven't got a file on him, and according to Interpol he was last sighted in Vancouver in July. The John Doe up near Coffs died in late September.'

In the midst of his increasing concern, Nick held on to that sliver of hope. If it was early in the establishment of the local mob, they might have a chance of catching them before the web had spread too far. Ramirez might not have earned the fierce loyalty that would make the ring hard to crack – or that would make his associates remain dangerous to Jo, and other witnesses after they arrested Ramirez. If, if, if . . . He needed that hope, because the thought of Jo hidden away for months or years terrified him.

Murdoch pulled up a window on his computer. 'Some reports have come in from Crime Stoppers since the photos were released to the media last night. I'll forward them on to you and Haddad. I've just scanned through them – a few likely sightings, some descriptions of men with them, and there might be a location – there's a report of a shooting party staying in an old hut, north of Derringvale.'

'I'll get Leah to follow them up. I'm going to take Jo Lockwood away today, and I'd like an escort car at least as far as the New England Highway.' Over an hour away, that would see them escorted out of the district and, he hoped, away from any immediate threat. 'Witness protection officers will meet us further south at Singleton, and arrange a safe house and police protection for her. I'll be back later tonight.'

He didn't mention Grace, and Murdoch didn't ask him about her. Nick would arrange whatever she needed for safety.

'Keep in touch with Haddad during the day, Matheson—'

There was a sharp rap on the door, and Leah poked her head in without waiting for an invitation. 'You need to come and see this news report now, sir. You too, Nick. Some idiot is trying to stir up trouble.'

Someone had turned up the sound on the television in the break room, so Nick heard the newsreader's overly dramatic voice, heard his own name even before he saw the screen. When the dozen or so officers watching it stepped aside for him, his own face filled the screen, in the years-old newspaper article hinting at his dismissal from the police force – the story that had been planted to build his cover as a corrupt former cop, to ease his entry into the underworld.

In fewer than three minutes, the newsreader breathlessly twisted together a handful of facts with rumour and outright lies, citing the 'ongoing investigation' into the Melbourne incident, Nick's aliases and 'well-known links' with organised crime, and quoted speculation from unnamed police sources that he'd been too convincing as a criminal not to be one, that he'd been fighting with Hugh immediately before his death, managing to imply, without actually saying it, that he was involved in the murders of Hugh and Shelley.

The whole piece implied an inept local investigation, relying on a corrupt cop – *him* – and hence doomed to failure.

Murdoch jabbed off the power button on the television, his usually composed face reddening with rage.

Nick's anger ran deeper, colder. He turned and grimly surveyed his colleagues. Most were locals, just come on duty for the day shift, gathering for a 6.45 a.m. task allocation. Some shifted uncomfortably on their feet, one or two edging to the door. A couple of them returned his glare with a coolness that could have been contempt. A few avoided looking at him at all. Aaron fumed silently, scanning the group himself, looking for guilt.

'Nobody leave,' Murdoch commanded those near the door. 'That was the most atrocious and blatantly irresponsible piece of pseudo-journalism I have ever seen. I will be in contact with headquarters the moment I return to my office, and you can be sure that the Commissioner will immediately lodge a formal complaint with the broadcaster.'

Murdoch scanned the room, his anger still evident in the veins pulsing at his temple. 'I will also recommend that the Ethics Branch launch an immediate investigation into the leaking of sensitive operational information to the media. This is a very serious matter, and anyone who is found to have transgressed the rules will face disciplinary procedures.'

Being identified as an undercover officer on national television was serious enough – the permanent end of his covert work. Having his name, face and aliases publicised gave a whole lot of criminals he'd crossed exact directions to find him. Not that it would have been impossible before – the underworld had access to technologies most police could only dream about – but it made it much simpler.

Murdoch wiped his forehead with a handkerchief. 'Detective Senior Sergeant Matheson has served the New South Wales Police Force for more than fifteen years in a distinguished and decorated career, often at significant personal cost. He has my complete confidence and support.'

Significant personal cost? Oh, yes. And the cost had just gone way up. Any thoughts he might have dared last night about a possible relationship with Jo were now smashed. He'd told her he couldn't promise not to die on the job, but he'd figured that returning to normal duties at least reduced the risks. Not so now. She'd lost enough, with Rossetti's death. He could never ask her to run the risk of that kind of grief again. And he could never put her in the position of being harmed in order for someone to get to him.

So that one night, the few hours together, would be all he'd share with her. And this afternoon, witness protection officers would take her away, for days or weeks or months, and he might never see her again. A wave of harsh, bitter anger threatened to consume him.

Murdoch marched back to his office but Nick stayed, giving each of the assembled officers a hard stare, seeking any sign of guilt or contempt. 'Somebody leaked that information about my fight with Hugh. That wasn't in any media statements. And someone knows someone who had already put together a dossier with details of my jobs and aliases. And somebody – probably the same somebody – then contacted the journalist or producer of that news show and fed them a story of half-truths and lies. And that somebody better damn well pray that when the hitmen start coming for me, they don't take out anyone else in the spray of bullets.'

His gut a hard ball of despair and loss, he pushed past them out of the room. Leah followed him, and although he didn't acknowledge her she caught up the couple of paces to stride beside him.

'I hope you actually manage politeness with your new colleagues sometimes, Nick. Because that was an impressive deployment of your I-know-ten-ways-to-kill-you-with-my-little-finger glare.'

'I'm not in the mood to laugh it off, Leah. You know the implications as well as I do.'

'I do. And you're going to need your colleagues to back you up, so you might try trusting them and treating them as though you're on the same side.'

'Trust?' He stopped walking and spun around to face her. Some of the others had left the break room and were following at a cautious distance. He didn't care. 'I trusted my partner in Melbourne, Leah. Terry Costello was supposed to be my back-up. Instead I found he was blackmailing and raping the target's mistress. That was just before he blew my cover and shot me. And I trusted the covert unit at HQ, but now details of the past few years' jobs and aliases are on the breakfast news. So, I'm not inclined to trust *anyone* right now. Including you.'

It had flickered through his mind that she might be responsible. She knew something about his work, knew about this case and could potentially have had the contacts to find the rest. If ambition had corrupted her, or maybe some threat . . .

Instinct said no, but perhaps he just couldn't bear to consider the possibility of another betrayal.

As he turned to continue down the corridor, he saw Jo, standing in the doorway of his office where he'd left her.

She'd likely heard a fair amount of that. Good, because she needed to know the truth.

Although his mind raced with possible strategies to deal with the new threats, concern for her overrode all of them. Eliminating any threat to Jo – and to Grace – had to be his first priority. He just needed to stay alive long enough to see it through. And he had to ensure that no-one ever suspected his feelings for Jo. He could not risk her becoming a target to get to him.

Details of the past few years' jobs and aliases are on the breakfast news.

She'd heard the hurried footsteps a few minutes ago, the growl of raised voices from the break room. But she'd not heard enough to grasp what had happened until she'd come to the door and heard Nick's words.

The icy expression on his face stayed in place as he strode the fifteen metres down the corridor to her. He waved her inside, closed the door, and leaned against it. His face tightening, he closed his eyes for the length of a breath in and out.

She had never seen him reveal that much stress.

'Your aliases were on the *news?*' Impossible. She had to have misheard, misunderstood.

She listened, horror constricting her heart, as he repeated details of the news broadcast.

'But they can't do that. There are journalistic standards—'

'Oh, I'm sure there'll be a retraction and an apology before the end of the day. A couple of heads may even roll. But the effect won't change.' He sank into his chair at the desk, dragged his hands through his hair. 'The segment will have been downloaded plenty of times already and will be in wide circulation among criminal organisations by lunchtime.'

Who would, now they could connect his aliases with a real name, know exactly where to find him.

She stood by the window, staring out while she tried to control her voice enough to ask, 'What will you do?'

He came to the window, gently guided her away from it and closed the blinds, shutting out the early summer sunlight. And any peering eyes. 'I'll take you away from here as planned. Then I'll come back and find Ramirez and his mob.'

'But shouldn't you go into witness protection yourself?'

He shook his head wearily. 'It's like you and the bushfire the other night, Jo. This is my job, my responsibility. I have skills and knowledge that might help solve the case. So I'm coming back here to do that.'

'Where they can find you.' She looked directly into his eyes, and he didn't look away.

'Yes.'

'I hate the thought of that.' Anger began to burn through the numbness. Anger at everything, at Ramirez and Judases and the whole situation that was tearing her heart apart. She wanted to cry, couldn't cry. She wanted to fall apart on him but she had to stay strong and in control. But she also had to be honest. 'Dammit, Nick, I know we said no complications, but my head and my heart aren't in agreement. I hate the thought of you dealing with this alone. Of *us* dealing with this alone. I'm afraid for you and I'm afraid for me.'

Afraid of falling apart, of the chasm of grief. Afraid – terrified – of losing herself and sense and meaning.

He didn't answer immediately. Didn't hold her and lie to her that it would be all right. He paced across the small office, back again, stood just beyond touching distance from her, his hands thrust deeply into his pockets.

He swallowed. 'We're both doing a lousy job of "no complications", aren't we?' Without waiting even a breath for an answer, he went on, 'Jo, I'm going to walk out that door shortly, and from that moment I will treat you as nothing more than an acquaintance, a responsibility. Maybe even an inconvenient one. I want you to know . . . I need you to know that it will be a lie. The closeness we shared means more to me than I can explain. But for your safety, no-one must guess or even suspect it.'

I'd give my life to keep you safe, Jo.

New layers of meaning sank in. He wouldn't just throw himself in front of a bullet for her. If she was held hostage or threatened, he would give himself up for her.

Except that she would not allow that to happen.

'I understand, Nick. But you need to understand this: for your safety, I will lie, cheat, steal, kill, or die if necessary. I will also follow all precautions and I'll stay in police protection for as long as it takes. I will not allow anyone to use me to get to you.'

He reached out a hand, stepped forward. 'Jo—'

She'd go to pieces if he touched her, and she desperately needed to stay strong, for them both. She moved aside, away from him. 'Nick, please,' she protested. 'Since we're both doing a lousy job on "no promises", as well, we'd better avoid making any assumptions about why that is, and any further complications, and just get on with the pretence. Please.'

He nodded wordlessly, turned away. About to open the door, he paused. 'I'm sorry,' he said quietly. Then, his shoulders straightened, his head lifted higher, and he breathed in deeply, once.

As he stepped out of his office, he looked back at her, and there was nothing of the man who'd caressed her with tenderness and held her gently in the night. Only a crisp, cool professional. 'We'll be leaving within the hour, Jo,' he said firmly but politely. 'As I mentioned, all your basic expenses will be covered. You may switch your phone on while you are still in the police station in order to get any necessary data off it, but you must switch it to airplane mode before you turn it off, and then leave it off.'

'That's already done.' Turning off her emotions was far harder. As she walked out the door in front of him, she forced some impatience into her tone and added, 'I'm well aware of the traceability of phone signals. I've also turned off location services and disabled the GPS functions.'

'Good. You can wait in the interview room you used yesterday. I'll have someone come and get you when we're ready to leave.'

Aaron emerged from a nearby room and Nick immediately turned away from her as if he'd already mentally dismissed her. 'Aaron, I need you to follow up some Crime Stoppers reports ASAP. I'll forward you the details now.'

In the interview room she pulled up a chair to the table and dropped her head on her folded arms. An empty room, nothing to do but think.

She'd better get used to that.

Without work, without contact with friends or family, without Nick . . . without access to her research materials or scientific journal databases, just shut into a small apartment all day every day, she'd have to find *something* to do to occupy the time. Something other than finding out if Bo and Hope had ever managed to stick together on *Days of Our Lives*. If her minders could bring her books, she could catch up on some of the classics she'd never read. Or maybe they could bring her yarn and knitting needles, and she could knit squares into blankets. Or get adventurous and try socks.

For an independent woman accustomed to running her own life, it would be a challenge. But she'd cope, somehow. She had to, because it was as much about Nick's safety as her own.

⤐

Bordered by trees, with dry paddocks beyond, the road ran mostly straight east, now and then curving in a ninety-degree bend to zigzag around century-old property boundaries. Nate Harrison and one of the junior constables were the escort – they wouldn't have been Nick's choice, but resources were short and they had to go to Tenterfield, anyway.

Nick kept a hundred metres behind the escort car and they travelled together at the speed limit. There was little other traffic around, only the occasional car from the opposite direction.

Jo hadn't said a word since they'd left Strathnairn. She stared determinedly out the window, hands gripped together on her lap.

He could have pushed some conversation, but what would be the point? Nothing could be changed, and to add anything else to what they'd already said to each other would cause nothing but pain.

About forty kilometres out from Strathnairn, a mob of cattle spread across the road, ambling along, forcing him to slow to a crawl. They should have had warning signs out, but in the dry, dusty summer there were plenty of mobs of cattle moving up and down the stock routes, some of the drovers more efficient than others in placing the signs. On another day, he might have thought it peaceful, the placid beasts mooching along in the sunshine.

The escort car inched through the mob, making slightly better speed, drawing further ahead. The road curved here, a sharp bend around a huddle of old deserted farm buildings.

A couple of guys on farm bikes rode without helmets on the verge alongside the mob, and two kelpie-like dogs raced with them, barking madly, spooking a group of half-grown calves into running directly in front of his car.

Nick had to jam on the brakes to avoid them. The escort car disappeared around the bend, sight of them obscured by trees and the old buildings, and his gut instinct kicked in with a warning adrenaline shot.

'Nick,' Jo said, low and urgent. 'This isn't right. Those guys don't know the first thing about cattle. Neither do the dogs.'

TWENTY-ONE

Alarm bells jangling loud in his head, Nick checked the rear-vision mirror, about to yank the gear into reverse. Stock milled across the road behind him, and an old, large four-wheel drive approached, driving up the centre of the road, nudging cattle out of its way. Not a farmer.

He radioed an emergency order for the escort car, and blasted on the car horn to scare the cattle, but another four-wheel drive roared from behind a farm building out onto the road ahead.

He yelled at Jo to get down as a figure with a rifle leaned out of the four-wheel drive ahead, spraying the cattle with bullets. Several fell. The rest, panicked now, raced towards him, and accelerating into a mob of panicked, half-ton cattle made as much sense as ramming into a tree.

Ahead, the vehicle and the two motorbikes blocked the road. Behind him, the other four-wheel drive – an old Patrol – had stopped in the middle of the road, blocking any escape that way, and the driver sprayed another round of bullets into the mob. More cattle fell, blocking the road.

Jo hunkered low, but she twisted her head to see him. 'That's the missing semi-autos, by the sounds of it.'

'Probably. There are six men: two in each vehicle and two on bikes. The escort car should be here any moment. Stay in the car and stay low. I'll try to bluff them until the others get here.'

The cattle were mostly past them now. The live ones. The dead and dying created a road hazard, and the two guys on bikes wove around them to come closer.

Where the hell was Harrison? They couldn't have driven more than a few hundred metres ahead, had to have heard his radio call – and the gunfire.

If any civilians were about to drive into this it could become a bloodbath. Guys who dropped cattle for fun probably didn't care much who else they hit.

Jo reached for the radio. 'I'll turn the sound down, but keep calling on it,' she whispered. 'Be careful.'

'There's a second gun under the seat. Any chance you get to escape, Jo, do it. If I can get them into position, I can deal with them. If you see me scratch my head, blast the horn as a distraction for a second.'

He left the keys in the ignition, engine idling. Taking his Glock from its holster, he opened the door slowly, letting them see the weapon. Closing the door, he left the weapon casually on the roof of the car as if it were a statement of trust.

'Rather messy, guys.' He strolled forward as they rode to within a couple of metres of him, everything in his stance, his expression, his language reflecting an unhurried, amused, hardened criminal. Exactly the kind of role he'd played for years. 'Hasn't Ramirez trained you lot better than this?'

Late teens or early twenties at best. Glancing uncertainly at each other, the one in a heavy-metal T-shirt drew a pistol. Nick couldn't see a weapon on the other but that only meant he didn't have a rifle. Knife, pistol, nunchakus – a range of deadly weapons could be at his waist under the sleeveless checked shirt or in his boots. Thirty metres ahead, the occupants of the Pajero walked towards him, carrying rifles. One dark, average height, mid-twenties, black leather vest; the other with a shaved head, arms covered in tattoos, and a steroid-assisted build.

Still no sign of the escort car.

'What have you done with Harrison?' he continued. 'You know, if he's in on this, we could have saved a lot of fucking bother.'

They weren't convinced yet, but he was unsettling them. Good. Their uncertainty gave him a slight edge.

One against six. To have any hope, he needed them closer together, needed those semi-autos within reach. And he had to get them further away from Jo.

'Your mates are going to meet with a little trouble,' heavy-metal guy with the pistol gloated. 'Couple of blown-out tyres or something like that.'

So Harrison was involved. No help there. He just hoped they had the sense to keep any civilians away.

He shrugged. 'Waste of fucking effort if you ask me. I was bringing the woman to Ramirez anyway. Although shit knows what he wants with the hysterical, complaining bitch. Besides,

I've compromised her already, so no way will she be a credible witness against him.'

From behind him he heard a shout in disgust and a complaint about 'fucking cow shit'. Keeping his attention on the four in front of him, three of them now definitely confused, he threw up his hands in disbelief.

'Jesus, you don't fucking get it, do you? My cover was royally fucked this morning. I thought that might have been Harrison's doing, but maybe he's not that bright. I did the righteous indignation shit, bought a few hours, but I figure it's time to pull the plug on that lark and fuck off to Canada.'

He took a few steps closer to them, thumbs hooked into his pockets, casual and relaxed. On the surface. Underneath, he recalculated the odds. He almost had them believing. The two on bikes, yes. Younger, slightly awe-struck by his unflustered attitude, they'd be slower to react. Not so much Leather and Shiny on foot beside them, with rifles still pointing his way. Pump action and semi-auto. The two from the Patrol behind – one a little older, one younger – had come around his side of the car, not Jo's side. An advantage, because it kept them in range. But not one he could make use of, yet.

'Anyway,' he continued his casual chat, buying time, 'since Ramirez is starting up here, I can give him some gold tips about who's who and who's rotten. Trade him for the same info on the Canucks.'

'That's enough bullshit.' Leather, pump-action man stepped forward, but not close enough. 'The boss wants to see you both. Alive. At least for now.' Trace of an accent. A grin reading as a clear threat. 'But he sure ain't planning to fucking trade or pay for what he wants from you.'

Alive. That one word improved the odds. Nick shifted his weight to spring and frowned in pretended puzzlement as he scratched his head.

The explosion of a shot shattered the windscreen to the left behind him, hit Leather, and in the moment of distraction, Nick dropped the young guy on his right with a vicious uppercut to his neck, sidestepped and tossed the older one as he charged, used the momentum to kick the bike out from under checked-shirt biker, and grabbed the muzzle of the rifle as Shiny swung it, ducking under and pushing with the force of the swing up and out so that the round went into the air and Shiny went onto his back.

Another shot had toppled the other biker. A third shot went wide and as he heard a car door and a harsh, 'Drop it, bitch,' Nick spun around to check on Jo and grab his gun if he could. The far side back door open, a seventh man – where the hell had he come from? – held a pistol to the back of her head.

For one heart-seizing moment he thought she wouldn't obey the order to drop the gun, that she'd fire at her target before the thug blew her head apart.

He raised his hands high in surrender, and she read his message, letting the gun fall forward onto the dashboard.

Two of the guys he'd put down, Shiny and checked-shirt, were scrambling to their feet, swearing, Shiny already lifting his rifle. The first he'd hit, the young one from the Patrol, was still half out of it, and his mate was rising slowly. Not experienced fighters, except maybe Shiny, if it took them seconds to recover from a fall. The two Jo had shot, Leather and the heavy-metal biker, bled on the ground, the biker writhing and groaning.

Five seconds it had taken, maybe ten, and with that element of surprise they'd almost won. If Ramirez wanted them alive, then there might be another chance, other chances. He had to believe it, and be ready. But as he watched in silent fear and rage as the seventh man dragged Jo from the car, a handful of her hair twisted in his hand, gun in his other hand close to her head, Nick vowed that he'd find that chance before they did to Jo what they'd done to Shelley – even if, as a last resort, he had to kill her first to prevent her suffering.

∝

She fought, kicking, yelling, striking out at the body behind her, partly an instinctive response to the blinding pain in her head, partly in desperate hope that the distraction might give Nick an opportunity to fight some more.

She thudded out of the car to the ground, but her captor hauled her up by her hair, the moment of relief when he let it go obliterated in the punishing back hand across the face, so hard she hit the ground again, gasping for air, her head screaming, and hating every breath that caused such agony.

'Restrain them and load them,' a harsh voice ordered, above her, around her, right inside her skull. 'We've taken too long here.'

'What about these guys?'

'Put the kid in the Pajero.' He pronounced it in the Spanish way, not the Australian. 'Finish and leave the others.'

Her eyes closed, she lay still, ear against the ground, and as the pain in her head faded to a shriek she became aware of a vibration, a faint, low rumble somewhere underneath her pounding pulse and the distant braying of cattle. Either her head was about to explode, or she could hear an oncoming vehicle. Police? *Please, please, let it be the police.*

Another short, sharp sound registered, loud in one ear, a dull thud in the other. Then another.

Finish and leave the others.

Nausea swamped her, and she pushed herself up just enough to vomit into the dirt. Shooting armed men in self-defence as she'd done was one thing; they'd given her little choice. But callously shooting unarmed, injured comrades instead of helping them, or leaving them where others might help them – that was another thing entirely. Violence and brutality, not mercy.

She struggled to her hands and knees, tried to open her eyes but the bright sunlight made her head swim, and when she gasped for air, a nauseating mix of cow shit, blood, heat and dust hit the back of her throat and made her throw up again.

'Get a move on!' the voice shouted.

Rough hands hauled her to her feet, and it was all she could do to stay upright, her body shaking. She forced her eyes open to find Nick.

The man with the shaved head smashed Nick's face into the car roof as her captor pushed her against the other side of the car, his grip tight around her neck so she couldn't move. Nick's eyes opened, looking straight into hers. Aware. Focused. So there had to be a reason why he wasn't fighting now, why he let the man hold him there while another bound his hands behind him with plastic restraints.

Taking her cue from him, she let them cuff her hands behind her back, and endured the groping search for weapons before they pushed her towards the Patrol. Nick's captor yanked Nick around to face him, and she heard the thuds of hard punches into his gut, his grunts, and Shaved Head's order to walk.

The wild leap of hope when she saw the approaching car dived into sickening disappointment when she realised it was a beat-up utility, with two men who greeted the others. At the rear of the Patrol, her captor taped her mouth and dragged a dark hood over her head, pulling the drawstring closed around her neck. She fought to breathe through the instant panic, writhed as hands lifted her at the waist and half-threw, half-shoved her into the cargo area behind the back seat. Her shoulder rammed into something sharp and hard, spearing pain into her spine and head, her cry smothered by the tape.

She tried to wriggle into the corner, to draw her legs up close. They were bringing Nick now, their movements hurried, voices in the distance urging speed, doors slamming, engines revving.

'Get the fuck in,' Shaved Head barked, with another thud of fist on flesh.

Her legs were jostled, bumped as they pushed Nick in, and she curled in tighter, her back against the side wall of the car, trying to give him space.

The door slammed shut on them, the engine of the Patrol started and two other doors shut.

Her head throbbed, her mouth tasted of bile and her instinct fought against the hot blackness of the hood, but she could not let herself cry, because if she clogged up her nose she would suffocate.

She had to calm herself, try to still the spinning in her head and be ready for whatever came.

Nick's boots nudged hers, slid beside them, his leg pressing gently against hers. Deliberate contact.

Unable to see him, talk to him, touch him other than in this one way, she found the gesture comforting, reassuring, and she uncurled her legs enough to increase the contact.

She concentrated on breathing, on lowering her pounding pulse rate, on being aware of surroundings and sounds. They'd done a U-turn, back towards Strathnairn, and were travelling fast. The men in the car had hardly spoken.

A right turn on to a dirt road, a sharp bend to the left. She knew where they were. Now she could start counting time and measuring how far they went.

⁂

They travelled for perhaps an hour, mostly on dirt roads, rough and jarring on the hard floor of a vehicle that needed new shock absorbers, made worse by a driver who travelled too fast, with no respect for the vehicle or the road.

The men didn't talk much, but when they did Nick listened to their voices, their words, their manner. The dark-haired, dark-eyed, accented man who'd held the gun to Jo's head might be Mexican, and he carried some authority. Not as much as 'the boss'. He growled at the driver to slow down on two occasions, received a mumbled apology and a slight reduction in speed in response.

The driver, the man who looked around thirty, tried to cover his nervousness and didn't succeed. He wondered aloud how 'the kid' was. No answer. Reckoned they'd got away with it pretty well, hadn't they? A noncommittal grunt in reply.

The driver persisted. 'If it wasn't for the bloody bitch – who'd have thought she'd be such a good shot?'

'Shut the fuck up, Gibson,' the other guy growled.

Nick pressed his leg against Jo's, and she responded with an answering pressure.

Gibson would be an easy target. Back on the road, he'd charged blindly, been thrown easily and fallen hard. Later, he'd hesitated on the order to shoot the two wounded men, screwed his eyes shut when he did it. New to the gang, Nick figured. Excited by the promise but starting to worry about the cost.

Nick ran through his assessment of the others again. Nine of them initially. Seven now, including the kid, who might well be concussed. The Mexican and Gibson in the Patrol with a handgun and a semi-auto; Shiny and the kid in the Pajero, with a semi-auto and the pump-action; Checked Shirt on a bike, and since Nick had heard two bikes overtake them, one of the guys from the ute must have picked up Heavy Metal's bike – and, presumably, his gun. Which left one guy in the ute.

Shiny was dangerous, a brute who took pleasure from violence. Probably had already served time for a violent crime, not in minimum security. Checked Shirt was cocky, and pissed off that he'd been tossed from his bike so easily. The kid and the two guys from the ute he didn't know enough about, yet.

The vehicle slowed, and the Mexican mumbled something as he clambered out. They edged forward a few metres, stopped again, and the Mexican climbed back in. A gate. They bumped for a little over rough ground, bushes scraping against the vehicle's side. North of Strathnairn, he figured from what he could tell of the direction they'd taken. North-east or north-west, he wasn't sure.

They stopped again, and swung around in reverse. The men left them, slamming doors but not locking them, and within minutes the temperature in the vehicle began to rise. It had been warm enough before, but parked in hot sunshine without airconditioning, he soon felt sweat dripping down his neck, soaking his shirt.

Jo pressed her leg against his. She would know as well as he did that if they weren't let out of the literally baking heat soon, they'd be too weak to function, let alone to take advantage of any opportunities. People died in less than half an hour locked in cars like this.

Voices. The uneven, medium-pitched engines of the farm bikes. Footsteps crunching on gravel.

The back door yanked open, a rush of warm air on his shirt marginally cooler than the air inside.

'Put them out the back and give them some water.' The Mexican's voice, some distance away. 'But don't rough them up. He wants them in good shape.'

Despite the instructions, the arms that yanked him out weren't gentle, and unable to see, Nick stumbled finding his feet and rammed his bad thigh against the towbar, sending blazing pain down his leg.

Jo's exit was just as quick, and she staggered against him. But here the air was fresh, although hot; they were outside, the breeze fluttering the hood over his face, the sunlight piercing the cloth enough to make out light and shade, broad shapes.

'Out the back' was behind a building, under some kind of shade.

'There's a post there,' Gibson said, pushing them against it. 'Sit, both of you, with your backs to it.'

His back against the solid, round wooden post, he touched hands with Jo, before they both eased down to sit on the ground. One of them – probably Checked Shirt – looped cord through the plastic restraints and around the post, pulling his restraints tight against his wrists.

Checked Shirt came back a few moments later, loosening the cord around Nick's neck and dragging the hood over his head. The light hit his eyes, momentarily blinding him. He blinked a few times, the glare easing so he could see the rough machinery shed they were in: earth floor, no walls, only a bent and twisted corrugated-iron roof supported by thick posts and railings. An old hut stood some metres away and dry scrub surrounded them. The Pajero, the Patrol, the bikes and the ute were all there, the ute with a quad bike loaded on the back and the dogs tied to the towbar, sheltering underneath from the sun.

Beside him, Checked Shirt took off Jo's hood, leaning too close in to her, ripping the tape off her mouth in one hard jerk, leaving her mouth bleeding. Leering into her eyes, inches from her face, he wiped the blood off with his finger and licked it suggestively.

Nick tugged at his restraints, tempted to try to rip them apart, and then the man.

Gibson stomped into view with a couple of bottles of water. 'Leave her, Hayes. That's for later. Take his tape off and give him some water.'

Hayes tore the tape off Nick's mouth, jammed his head back and upended the bottle of water into his mouth, almost choking him. He jerked his head down and away, coughing water up while Hayes laughed.

Gibson went more slowly with Jo, giving her a chance to drink, but then drawing the bottle back from her mouth and tipping water down her T-shirt, soaking it over her breasts.

'Oops, bit of an accident there. Sorry, bitch.'

Someone called from the hut, and both men left, leaving the water bottles on the ground, unreachable.

Nick wriggled an inch or two closer to Jo and linked fingers with her despite the restraint cutting into his wrist.

'I know exactly where we are,' she murmured. 'This is Dyson's Hut. It's private property, used as a shooting camp. The National Park boundary is about four hundred metres that way.' She nodded away from the hut, roughly towards the mid-morning sun. 'East-ish. We're on the north-west side of it here.'

'About forty kilometres from where the cadets are searching today?'

'As the crow flies across wild country and two rivers, yes. As roads go, over a hundred.'

'Any roads or properties close by? Anywhere for help?'

'Not much. It's about fifteen k's west to the main Strathnairn–Queensland road. Park is to the east and the south, and most of the north is State Forest. There's not much in the way of phone reception, even if we had one.'

'Shiny took mine. And my weapons.'

He gripped her fingers, leaned his head over to touch hers. 'There will be a search for us underway already, Jo. Even if

Harrison lies his head off, there's no way he could make that scene and our disappearance look innocent. I'm fairly sure I heard sirens in the distance when we turned off the road.'

'I hope so. But we're a long way from there now, and they won't find us easily.' She rubbed her head lightly against his. 'Listen, Nick, if we can't stop them, Ramirez and this lot will keep killing – directly and through drugs. So if it comes to another situation where you can fight, but I've got a gun against my head, then keep fighting. Take every chance you have to beat them or to escape to beat them later. I'd rather have a bullet through my head or whatever, than have more people die.'

The 'whatever' worried him far more than the bullet. Haunted him, but he had to keep a strong front for Jo. 'I made a snap judgement this morning, Jo. Some of them had to be blocking the road further back, as there'd been no traffic through. So, even if I'd been able to deal with the remaining men, there was no escape. Ramirez wants us alive, so I'm banking on us getting another chance, maybe with fewer of them around. This isn't over. And no matter what happens, I'm not leaving you.'

They both fell quiet, listening to the deep rumble of a motorbike engine approaching the house.

TWENTY-TWO

Ramirez kept them waiting at least another hour. The sun shifted high in the sky, close to mid-point, and the temperature continued to rise. Even in the shelter of the shed, with a cross-breeze blowing through it, Jo sweated precious fluid away. But it gave them a rest, breathing space; a chance to build strength for whatever lay ahead and to discuss possible strategies.

Eventually Ramirez emerged from the hut, the others following him, each carrying a rifle or a handgun. Nick straightened, releasing her fingers, shifting away from her and feigning indifference, as they'd agreed.

White T-shirt, jeans, sunglasses – if she hadn't remembered those eyes behind the glasses, Ramirez might have seemed a fit, attractive man. A successful businessman, enjoying the challenge of the great outdoors in comfort. Not a man who incited others to monstrous crimes.

His offsiders – six of them – shifted into a curved line behind him. The kid was there, pale and unsteady on his feet. The other Mexican man wasn't – the one who'd held the gun to her head and belted her.

Feet braced apart, arms folded, Ramirez looked down on them, his eyes obscured by the sunglasses. Determined not to show fear – that would give him too much power over her – she stared back at him, head held high. But Hayes stepped forward and whacked her across the face, the sting making her eyes water.

She got the message. No insolence to the boss. If there'd been any point continuing, she'd have done it, but with both of them disabled, helpless, it made no sense. She lowered her head slightly, and concentrated on the movements and sounds of the men around her.

Ramirez's black leather boots turned away from her towards his louts. 'I gave you a simple extraction task, and you morons totally fucked it up. You lost two men, and left Harrison alive to talk. We'll have police crawling around here before long. I should shoot the useless fucking lot of you now and leave you for the crows and the cops.'

A few of the men shuffled their feet, shifting backwards, maybe ready to run.

'I'll give you one last test to prove yourselves,' Ramirez continued. 'Gibson, Saunders, get them up and uncuff them.'

Under the watchful eye of Ramirez, Gibson didn't grope her as he cut the cord and dragged her upright. But he did twist the restraint tight before he cut it, digging it painfully into her wrists. Bringing her arms forward at last, restoring proper blood flow, she had a moment of light-headedness. Nick stood tall and straight, showing no evidence of weakness.

He stayed half a pace away from her, not touching her and scarcely acknowledging her as he faced Ramirez.

'I've got plenty of information you'd find useful, Ramirez. Business tips. What say we cut a deal?'

No-one stepped forward to hit Nick. Standing with equal confidence and menace as the boss, no-one dared.

Ramirez regarded him coolly. 'I already have my sources, Matheson. I doubt you could provide much additional value. But I assure you, I do intend to have your information, later.'

'What are your plans for us?' Nick asked, as easily as if Ramirez hadn't just alluded to torturing him.

'A test. Since you almost bested these idiots, they need to have another round with you and show me all they've learned. Hayes, handcuff them together.'

Proper handcuffs this time, but they still rubbed on the raw skin where the restraints had chafed her wrists. Her left hand, Nick's right. At least they were side by side, not looped together in a more limiting way.

'I'll give you a five-minute head start,' Ramirez said, 'and then send them after you.' He turned and looked at each of the men as he continued. 'The ones who bring them back – alive – win. The ones who don't, lose. Matheson is mine. The winners can have the woman.'

So, Nick would be tortured for information and she was the prize for the winners. Adrenaline pumping, she had only time for one train of thought: she mentally pictured the water bottle on the ground, and decided which direction to run.

'When does our time start?' Nick asked, his voice cool, unperturbed.

Ramirez glanced at his watch. 'Ten seconds ago,' he answered.

Jo grabbed Nick's hand, swooped up the fullest water bottle and sprinted for the scrub behind the hut, hoots of laughter following them.

Boots thudding, they quickly shifted into a rhythm, keeping pace side-by-side across the paddock. Once among the trees she took the lead, pushing through the scrubby undergrowth, weaving between the taller trees, jogging rather than sprinting because of the obstacles, and trusting that the hard vibrations of their steps would send any snakes slithering in the opposite direction.

'Why this way?' Nick said.

'They can't follow on the bikes, and we'll be hard to see. Plus, this is my territory, not theirs. They mostly stay near roads.'

Branches whipped into her face, scratched her and tugged at her hair, but she kept going, the water bottle in her free hand shielding her from some of it, Nick's hand tight in hers.

Not straight to the park boundary – that might be too obvious, if they knew the area. She turned more south, angled towards it. She had an idea for a hiding place, if they could reach it undetected.

Under the noise of their progress, she heard shouts. Head start? Apparently not.

Another branch struck her face as, among the shouts, dogs barked.

She picked up pace, desperately trying to remember the topographic details beyond the key features. The river carved down into a rugged gorge about four kilometres away. She'd walked part of the length of the gorge, but not every hectare of wild scrub around it.

Rocks. Granite hills or tors made of huge boulders. Boulders that might be both vantage points and hiding places.

She checked the position of the sun, and veered further east. If she remembered the satellite photos correctly, there might be a large tor about halfway to the gorge.

Nick kept pace with her, but he'd received plenty of punches, and the bullet scar on his side was only a few months old. Still healing.

'How's your fitness? Can you run uphill in a while?'

'Yes. Assuming we're not talking Everest.'

Another advantage. Her familiarity with the territory, their physical fitness.

'Are those dogs going to be a problem?' Nick asked, slightly gasping.

'I doubt it,' she replied, her breathing matching his. 'They weren't working the cattle at all – not even an ounce of instinct. All the scents out here will excite them, but I'd be surprised if they stuck to one.'

She ducked under a low-hanging branch, but not quite far enough, her hair catching in it and bringing them both to a sudden stop. She raised their joined hands to deal with it, the handcuff scraping her raw wrist.

Nick saw her wince. 'Hold still. I'll do it.'

Stepping in front of her, close, he reached over her shoulder with his free hand to untangle the snarl, his cuffed hand cupping her face, tender and soothing against the bruises. 'I'll go in front now. Just keep pointing me in the right direction.'

The sharp report of a rifle, loud and reverberating, sent them running again, and she let him take the lead. The tree cover was changing here – less low undergrowth, fewer native cypress pines, more ironbarks, many of them tall and strong. Faster going, but easier to be seen in.

Another rifle shot cracked through air. Close, but not aimed at them. Maybe a roo. Excited yelps sounded a couple of hundred metres away, but headed in the other direction.

She caught glimpses of the granite tor through the trees, rising above the plateau, and they gradually started an uphill run.

'Go around to the east of the tor,' she told Nick, gasping the words. They'd come a couple of hard k's, in stinking heat. They both needed a rest.

She'd not been to this particular section of the vast park, but she'd chosen the east side for two reasons – because she hoped it would give them a view of the direction she planned to take and because she wanted their pursuers to assume they were going past the tor, not up it.

They reached the base of the tor, the huge rocks towering in a pile a good sixty metres high, trees and shrubs growing out at angles among the granite. They continued almost past it, before Jo turned them back.

Halfway up, a large split rock, its entrance shaded by an overhang, offered a possible shelter. She searched for a way to access it, while avoiding the natural paths where sand gathered between the rocks, and tracks would be too visible.

'Up this way. We should be able to manage this.'

Clambering up and over granite boulders while handcuffed required fitness and coordination – fortunately, they had the first and they had developed the second quickly. But she noticed, once or twice, Nick's gritted teeth, slight hesitation, as he used his left leg on large steps up.

'You're hurt. You should have said.'

'It's nothing major. An old injury – exercise will do it good.'

Nothing major. Right. Where she could, she selected a path upwards that put less strain on his left leg.

A small group of wallabies, resting in the shade, leaped up and away from them, and twice lizards scurried off their path. Getting close to the middle of the day, the time most animals and birds hid from the heat. As humans should be doing, too, Jo thought wryly.

The gap in the split rock was just enough to walk between, and opened out to a width inside of a couple of metres. She broke off a branch from a bush before they entered, and brushed away their footprints in the sand near it and as they ventured in.

At the end of the passage in the rock, about five metres long, light spilled into a larger area, and they found a cavern of sorts, made up of vast, tumbled rocks and slabs at all angles, with several gaps leading out to the light. Cool and quiet.

She indicated a flat rock, complete with an almost-even back rest.

'Sit,' she whispered. 'And keep your voice low. Sound carries in these places.'

She unscrewed the cap of the water bottle and offered it to him. Less than a litre between the two of them. Not nearly enough, given the heat.

He glugged a few mouthfuls and then tried to hand it back.

'No. Have some more. Drink half of it. We'll get more at the river.'

Assuming they reached the river. Another shot sounded, close, and a jubilant shout. Voices, laughs and a dog's yelp.

She finished the water in the bottle, listening beyond her gulps, concentrating on where and who and how many. She screwed the cap on the bottle and laid it between them. They held still, silent, hardly daring to breathe, fingers gripped together.

Voices came closer, drifting into the cavern so that she couldn't tell which direction they came from.

And a dog trotted in through the cavern, panting and snuffling, curious rather than particularly following a scent. She held her breath, dead still, while it explored and peed on the wall. But it finally noticed their scent, yelped excitedly and ran over to leap on top of them.

TWENTY-THREE

Four of them pounded in, from two directions: the kid and Gibson through the split, Saunders and the other bloke from the ute through the cavern. Two rifles, two handguns.

Nick hadn't heard Shiny's or Hayes' voices, but that didn't mean they weren't out there.

He and Jo literally had their backs against a wall, and nowhere to run.

He'd finished his scan for his weapon options. The leafy branch Jo had brought in. He passed a short stick broken off it into Jo's cuffed hand. 'Neck or eyes are best,' he'd whispered. 'Or anywhere you can reach.'

The stupid dog, panting and leaning happily against his leg for pats while ripping apart the plastic water bottle, gave Nick two more weapons: sharp shreds of plastic, and a studded leather collar with a metal pin in the clasp, now in his pocket.

He concealed a two-inch piece of plastic in his hand as he and Jo rose to stand, and he purposely unbalanced her so it appeared that they were awkward in the cuffs.

Saunders jeered. 'Look what we have here. The big-shot detective and the interfering ranger. Cute enough bod, I suppose, but a bit old and scrawny. The copper-woman was sexier.'

His mate from the ute laughed, and Gibson grinned, not quite effectively.

Jo tossed her head in disgust. 'Look what *we* have here, Nick. Gutless, low-life scum. They probably even piss where Ramirez tells them to. No wonder he doesn't want to take any of them with him.'

On the slab rock, they had a height advantage, so Saunders had to step up knee-high to belt her across the face with the rifle butt, and he swung it right to left.

Grounded, his strength centred, Nick caught the rifle before impact, using Saunders's own force to twist it out of his hands, topple him sideways and backwards off the rock. Jo's arm, relaxed, flowed with his easily.

The dog yelped and ran out, cowering.

Saunders landed with a thud on his back. He immediately starting swearing and rising, but Nick already had the rifle pointing at him, holding it left-handed so that Jo's wrist carried less strain.

Gibson and the other man had their weapons raised, handgun and rifle.

'Looks to me like you've got a choice, guys,' Nick said. 'You know Ramirez intends to kill most of you, don't you?'

Gibson cast an uneasy glance at the other man, who shifted a little on his feet. Maybe they needed drugs to be brave. Too bad Ramirez hadn't given them any yet today. No reward for this morning's events. Nick worked on the fear, drilling it harder. 'I'm guessing he'll make you draw lots. Or maybe fight it out. I gather he likes to watch, likes to see what the drugs do to you, what kind of animal they turn you into. He likes the power – over you, not just over the poor sods you kill. Oh, and the punishment-fitting-the-crime thing – Mitchell's stealing, Coulter's mistake in being seen – what will he apply to you, do you think?'

'Castration for being wankers and losers,' Jo suggested.

'He's bullshitting,' Saunders said, yanking the handgun from the kid's drooping hand. 'If we take the bitch back, we'll be fine. And she'll pay for her fucking shit.'

Jo moved in close, closed her right hand on the rifle grip, and Nick let her take it, sliding his free hand to his pocket for another weapon. They wouldn't kill her yet, and they didn't want to wound her and have to carry her, although they'd be happy to kill him. But while she had the rifle she had the power to reduce the threats to both of them, and he had his own weapons.

'"Bitch" is such an empowering word,' Jo said. 'No pressure to be "nice". And yes, this bitch can shoot. Feral pests and predators are my speciality.'

The kid collapsed and vomited, and Gibson dropped beside him to lift his head from the dirt, rifle on the ground.

Nick found it easy to feign exasperation. 'Oh, for fuck's sake, Gibson, if that boy means anything to you then get him out of here to a hospital. He's concussed, probably bleeding in his brain. And you know damned well this lot aren't going to let him see sundown. Show some courage and do something decent for once.'

Gibson slid an arm under the lad's shoulders to hoist him up.

'Leave the rifle,' Nick ordered, as he tried to reach for it. 'You'll have your hands full with the boy.'

As Gibson started half-carrying, half-dragging his young mate out of the cave, Saunders charged forward, the other man following suit a moment later, a little to one side.

Aiming to topple them, betting Jo wouldn't shoot.

Not a bet Nick would have made.

She fired as Saunders came close, and he went down with a howl, but the other guy threw himself forward, tackling her legs, toppling her. Nick followed the pull of her arm down, falling on to the man's body, gripping his hair and pounding his head against the stone twice.

Saunders writhed on the ground, a bloodied hand on his knee. He wouldn't be walking far anytime soon.

Nick helped Jo to her feet. Saunders spat foul curses and tried to fight, but Nick kicked him back, held him still with a knee on his neck and a threat to break it while Jo restrained his hands with the dog collar and wrapped a makeshift bandage from the other guy's shirt around his knee.

'If we make it out alive, Saunders,' Nick told him, 'we'll let the authorities know you're here. So you'd better just hope your mates don't find us.'

He searched both of them, found switchblades and brass knuckles. Not well-trained street-fighters, since they hadn't used them, but a welcome addition to his range of weapon options. Weapons he abhorred using, but they were fighting for their lives. For Jo's life. He'd use whatever he could.

Jo tucked a handgun into the back of her jeans, as did he, and they took a rifle each.

'Ready?' Nick asked her.

She nodded, grim and pale. This wasn't her place, her life, but she'd stepped up, held her own when tough men might have failed.

He touched gentle fingers to her scratched and bruised face. 'You've been fantastic, Jo.' He grinned, aiming to bolster her spirits. 'But do remind me never to get on your wrong side.'

He went in front through the split rock, rifle tucked under one arm. Shiny and Hayes were still out there, somewhere. He hoped they weren't waiting, just outside, to steal the prize when the victors emerged.

༺

Past midday, fast heading to the hottest part of the day. The sun beat down on the rocks of the tor, and there was limited shade – or cover – on the path they ran down.

They'd need water and shade, and more rest, once they'd found them. Dehydration and heat stroke loomed as real possibilities if they weren't careful.

From the tor she'd checked the direction of the river and gorge. Due east. Maybe two kilometres. Half an hour, if they kept moving and the scrub wasn't too rough.

They heard no gunfire, no shouts, no dogs.

The breeze strengthened to wind. Another westerly, but this time she was glad it was at her back, if not actually aiding them, then at least not making it tougher.

Everything ached – head, legs, body, arms – and despite Nick's grip on her hand, reducing pulling on the cuffs, the jostling of the metal rubbed her skin even rawer.

The bush became denser and they had to slow, too much undergrowth, too many rocks and tree branches threatening to trip them on the uneven ground. They both ditched the rifles, needing their hands to push aside branches and climb over fallen tree trunks.

Tiring, her feet heavy and clumsy, she fell once, dragging Nick half-down with her, wrenching her arm and, she feared, his leg.

As she rose to her feet, several crows flew overhead, cawing harshly. She couldn't see far back the way they'd come, but a few wisps of white drifted above the trees. Facing west, she breathed in deeply.

Smoke. Definitely smoke.

'Keep moving. There's a fire. Let's hope we can outrun it.'

Only a kilometre or so. Ten minutes. Ten minutes in which the wind became stronger and the smoke more evident, and burning leaves and embers blew past them.

She veered fractionally to the south-east. Not to the gorge itself but above the falls, where the river flowed more slowly and the land sloped more gently to it. Where they could wade across it at this time of year, and there was a camping area, a cleared parking ground and an access road on the other side.

They were gasping for breath and clear air by the time they made it, the smoke thickening around them.

About to plunge down the slope towards the river, Nick stopped so suddenly she rammed into him.

In the parking area on the other side was an older white Pajero, two men with rifles standing beside it, watching the river.

TWENTY-FOUR

Nick drew her back into the trees, low to the ground, and they crawled behind a stump. Shiny and Hayes. They'd be harder to beat than the others, and they held all the advantages.

'Bastards,' Jo muttered. 'I'm assuming they lit the fire to drive us this way.'

'Likely. What's down this way?' he asked. The river curved over rocky pools, and through low scrub.

'About two hundred metres further down it drops into a steep gorge. Almost cliffs on this side. There are ways down, but they'd be tough in handcuffs, and we'd be visible targets.'

'Not much of an option, then. South?'

'More of this. The river's slow and shallow, but the vegetation is mostly low scrub. Not much good for cover or for a fire break. We'd have to go a fair way along so they couldn't see us.'

'South it is.'

If he wasn't cuffed to her, he'd have tried a decoy, directing their attention elsewhere so that she could get across safely. Not a possibility. They would have to cross over further up, detouring around through the bush to join the access road some distance from the Pajero.

'No. We need water, we need rest and we need to get away from the fire front. The vehicle and the handcuff keys would be bonuses. What are our chances for a bluff?'

Instinct said no, roared to just keep her away from them. 'I want you safe, Jo.'

'That makes two of us. But I can't go much further, Nick. Not another four or five kilometres even before we get back to the access road, and who knows what, then? Hayes wants me. I'm not sure Shiny cares, but he probably would like to thump you a few more times. If this fire is their work, then they had to drive about forty kilometres to get here, so they probably don't know about the others. If they see us crossing, clutching each other, limping, surrendering and begging for our lives, then I bet they'll wait for us to get to them rather than get their feet wet. And they don't know we're armed.'

'It's a risk, Jo.' He ran scenarios through his mind, could see some succeeding, some failing, all dependent on luck.

'Whatever we do is a risk. You could try the I-brought-you-the-woman story again.'

The thought of what they would do to her terrified him so much he doubted he could be convincing, this time.

But he could try to deal with them. Tempt them to quit Ramirez. Offer them information. He could do that convincingly. And they only had to get close enough for him to strike.

'If you're sure you want to risk it, then we'll try it. Can you do a terrified, weeping woman? And if I'm a total bastard to you, will you forgive me?'

She turned on her knees to face him, her scratched and cut hand against his cheek. 'Nick, do whatever it takes. If I'm still alive tomorrow morning, I'll forgive you anything. And if I'm dead before they get their hands on me, I'll forgive you that, too.'

&

It wasn't hard to cry, to cling to Nick, to stumble through the knee-high water and threaten to fall. Harder to actually *not* fall on the slippery stones below the surface, but he only tugged her impatiently when they were on smooth rocks between pools. The water might be refreshingly cool on her legs, but it wouldn't do much for the gun tucked into her jeans, with a wet T-shirt advertising its presence.

She loudly begged him not to do it, to save her, but he just yelled at her to shut up, raising his hand in a threat to hit her so convincing she flinched.

The whole way across the river, the two men stood on the far bank, watching and waiting for them.

'For fuck's sake, will you take this bitch off me?' Nick demanded as they made their way the last few metres. 'Get the bloody key, Hayes. If you get this bitch off me you two can have the deal I was going to give Ramirez.'

'What deal?' Hayes asked.

Jo sobbed more, struck out at Nick. 'You're a bloody traitor. And people *trusted* you.'

He grabbed her flailing hand, twisted it lightly behind her back, held it there with his cuffed hand as though restraining her. Near her gun. She didn't reach for it, yet. Shiny and Hayes were still suspicious, their rifles ready. Interested, but not convinced.

'Information about rivals,' Nick said. 'I know most of the major players, from the inside and the official surveillance. Dates, places, methods for shipments. And I can tell you date and place for a shipment Ramirez has coming in through the north soon. He's not had much luck setting up his network here, doesn't have much decent back-up. He prefers having them murdered to keeping them. You could be next – or you could have the shipment for yourselves.'

His hand, covering the brass knuckles on her fingers, squeezed a warning, and he half-dragged her, stumbling, the last few steps out of the water.

She jerked her head around to Hayes and Shiny, screaming at them. 'You murdering, filthy bastards. You think you're men but you're nothing but cowards.' Hayes came forward, arm rising. Nick released both her hands, and she flicked the safety on the pistol. Her throat flamed but she kept on screaming, holding Hayes' focus, moving her arm around slowly. 'Gutless, no-balls wimps, not even worth spit.'

She pulled the trigger as his blow landed on her, her head jerking one way, her cuffed arm another as Nick rammed a punch into Shiny and another shot exploded.

They all hit the ground. Her head spun and she could hardly see anything before her eyes, nausea bubbling in her throat. But pure panic and adrenaline flooded her system. Something grabbed her ankle and she kicked out, her boot meeting spongy flesh. Another shot echoed in her head as Nick's body rolled into her, and jerked away. The body underneath her pushed up and Shiny's scalp came into focus. She rammed her cuffed hand under his chin. A vice gripped around her upper right arm and she bore down from the elbow with the pistol, squeezing her whole hand and the gun in it as agony tore into her shoulder. The reverberation of the gunshot cracked so loudly near her she dropped her head in shock and pain.

කෘ

His left leg burning, Nick eased up on to his right knee, uncaring as his weight pressed on Shiny's chest. Shiny was out, breathing but not conscious. Hayes moaned. Jo lay half over both of them, her face between them, still and silent.

Other than Shiny's bullet in his already-damaged leg, he'd lost track of shots, had no idea who'd shot whom.

Awkward to lift her, with one leg useless and their hands cuffed together, but she groaned and moved herself, yelping as her free arm refused to take any weight. Blood covered half her T-shirt.

'Jo, be all right. Please, be all right.' He moved closer so their joined hands could take her weight.

'I'm okay,' she murmured. 'It's his blood. I think.'

She pushed off Hayes, and he groaned, swore at the bitch, tried to move and swore again. Nick stretched to grip the pistol he'd dropped, raised himself up on his knee again and aimed at Hayes. Blood covered one hip, and his opposite shoulder.

'Hayes, the only move you make without me shooting you is to get the handcuff key. You've got no choices. Shiny won't be any help to you. If you don't have it in your right hand in five seconds I'll starting putting more holes in you. '

He managed it in seven seconds, holding out his hand with the key in his fingers. Nick couldn't quite reach it, without dragging Jo's hand, and with the shoulder of her free arm held immobile, she wasn't able to help.

'Toss it lightly towards me,' he ordered. 'And remember I have the gun.' Hayes's rifle wasn't far from his left hand, but his left arm wouldn't be gripping anything for a while.

Hayes obeyed, and the key dropped within reach. Nick made quick work of unlocking the cuffs, freeing Jo's wrist carefully, yanking his own out of the restraint.

He dragged his shirt off, ripped it into a couple of strips and bandaged his leg as best he could. If an artery had been hit, he'd be dead by now. But he could survive this. He'd done it before.

Now all they had to do was get across the car park and into the Pajero.

'The Pajero keys – who has them?' he demanded of Hayes.

'He does.'

Nick shuffled up a few inches to reach Shiny's jeans pocket, found the keys first try and stuffed them in his own pocket.

With the gun trained on Hayes again, warning him not to move, he snapped the cuffs around his ankles. The handcuff key went into his pocket with the car keys.

'You can't do that! The fire's coming!'

'Too bad. I'll call for help for you. If you're lucky, it will arrive in time. If not, consider who to blame as you choke on the smoke.'

His mouth tasted bitter. He'd have taken them somehow, if he'd had the choice. But with neither Jo nor him in good shape, he couldn't risk another fight.

The smoke was becoming thicker, adding to the effort of breathing.

'My shoulder's dislocated,' Jo said, her voice beginning to betray the pain and shock. 'If you can push it back in, I should be able to help you walk.'

He'd seen dislocated shoulders a number of times, knew the theory. He'd have to do it, now. Her face white with pain, she knelt on the ground, holding still while he gripped his hands around the joint, felt with his fingers for the correct position.

He exhaled a breath. 'Are you ready?'

'Do it.'

With one quick movement, and a smothered cry from Jo, the joint clicked back into place.

'Hope it never heals properly, bitch,' Hayes said.

She ignored him, and rose to unsteady feet, biting her lip, her arm pressed into her stomach. She looked around the area.

'There's a good-sized stick over there. With it and me, you should be able to walk.'

He worried that her voice was flat, her eyes clouded with pain, but she retrieved the stick from near the trees and brought it over. Two inches thick, over a metre long. He wouldn't need to lean on Jo.

Agony as he used the stick to lever his weight up on his good leg, his twice-wounded leg dragging. He breathed in slowly through his nose, out through his mouth. In, out. *Strength. Conviction. Control.* He could do this. Had to do it.

'If you give me the keys,' Jo said, 'I'll bring the vehicle closer.'

He passed the Pajero keys to her. 'Can you drive, with your shoulder?'

She nodded. 'I have to.'

But when she was halfway across to the vehicle, engines roared not far away. Motorcycle engines.

His gut twisted in fear and despair. No, not now. Not when they'd come so close to freedom.

She heard them at the same time he did, and ran for the Pajero.

'Get out of here, Jo!' Nick shouted. 'Get away!'

He could scarcely move, every step a nightmare. Better to have a weapon, ready to aim.

They roared in, two of them, so fast he couldn't get a decent shot, one screeching to a stop beside Jo as she tried to haul herself up into the driver's seat, the other spinning a cloud of sandy dust into Nick's eyes, before knocking him down again with the back wheel.

When the dust subsided, Ramirez held Jo against him, a knife at her throat, and his offsider stood over Nick, a pistol by his side, his boot on Nick's gun.

Nick curled his fingers around the stick. Roughly the size of a staff, he might be able to do something with it. If he could work out a distraction, get that knife away from Jo's throat.

'Get up, Matheson,' Ramirez ordered. 'Or I slice her throat. I want some information from you before I kill you.'

Up. He used the stick to drag himself to his feet. He'd have to master the pain if he was going to do this, make it of no importance. He shifted his feet slightly apart. *Breathe. Balance. Centre.*

The second man took a casual step back, his gun pointing directly at Nick. Good. A better position to strike.

'What do you want to know, Ramirez?'

'What you offered me this morning. Names, people, who's crooked and who can be eliminated. Information is power.'

Jo held still, watching him, the knife resting against her skin. She opened her eyes a little wider – a question.

He gripped the staff tighter, hoping she saw the answer.

'Let's go where I can sit down, Ramirez, and I'll give you all I know.'

Ramirez grinned, and in that same moment Jo gave a small sigh and turned into a dead weight in his arms. Instinctively he gripped her to stop her falling, his offsider turned to see what had happened and Nick struck. The thick stick balanced perfectly in his hand, he hit the gun out of the man's hands in one movement and swept around to land an upward blow under his chin in the next, followed by another crack on the side of his head that sent him toppling.

Four steps, and he would reach Ramirez, bending over Jo, hand in her hair, bringing the knife closer. But Nick saw her hand scrabble in the sand, and she threw the sand in her attacker's eyes.

While Ramirez howled, he made those steps, the pain a hum in the background, not belonging to him.

He struck Ramirez's head, but he still had Jo's hair in his grip, and he slammed her against the car before he turned to circle Nick with the knife.

'I'll kill you, Matheson,' he snarled, keeping just out of reach of the stick, and Nick let him believe that for a few moments.

He turned on the spot as Ramirez circled. *Breathe. Balance. Centre.* Pain did not matter.

'No, you won't,' Nick said. 'You're nothing, Ramirez. You're so twisted you can't function properly. No-one matters to you, and you matter to no-one.'

Ramirez lunged, but Nick was ready. The stick landed with a loud crack against the Mexican's arm, and the knife went flying. Two fast jabs to the knees brought the man down, two quick blows to each side of the head sent him first one way then the other. He finished with an uppercut under the chin, and Ramirez fell backwards on to the sand.

He lay silent, motionless. His companion remained the same.

Nick didn't particularly care if they were alive or dead, as long as they didn't move.

Jo slumped against the tyre where Ramirez had slammed her.

Nick limped across to her, felt for a pulse in her neck, breathing again as she made a small sound, murmured his name.

'I'm here. Everything's all right. We're just going to stand up now.'

She seemed barely conscious. He had to get her into the Pajero, up on to the back seat. And he had to get himself in so he could drive her away from here.

Agony struck his leg again as he pulled her weight up and leaned them both against the vehicle. Agony as he dragged his leg, inch by precious inch, to the door, Jo hanging in his arms. Agony as she jarred her leg against his, trying to find her feet. He stopped, all his weight on his undamaged right leg.

'Can you get into the back, Jo?'

'Think so. Woozy.'

'Lean into me. We'll take it slow.'

Slurring words, dizziness – how many blows had she taken to the face and the head today? He had to get her to a hospital. The Pajero had radio antennas – a functioning radio had to be inside.

He held her to his right, still half-supporting her, but not as a dead weight. He breathed deeply again, made his muscles relax. He would beat this. Pain was only pain. It wouldn't kill him.

She helped him lift her on to the back seat, took some of her own weight and edged across so she could lie down along the seat. There was a towel on the floor, grubby and dusty, but Nick rolled it into a makeshift neck brace and carefully wrapped it in place.

Once in the driver's seat, he started the engine, grateful for the automatic transmission. Unable to reach the police channel from a private radio, he found the emergency channel and sent out a call, requesting urgent medical assistance for a head injury, and ambulances for other injuries, and reporting the fire. He gave directions as best he could.

He turned the vehicle around, stopping a little nearer to Hayes to toss him the handcuff key. Not intentionally, it fell a few metres short. If Hayes needed it badly enough, he'd reach it.

He took the dirt road slowly, juggling the necessity to get to an open, fire-free area for a chopper to land with the need for minimal movement for Jo's head injury. He clarified a few details on the radio, was assured help was coming.

Jo lay silently in the back, unconscious.

ᗄ

There were people and voices and noise and flashing lights in her head and something on her face and she couldn't get any of it straight. Only the throbbing pain was clear and constant, and the nausea.

But there was one voice . . . she listened for it, heard it, lost it . . . heard it again, close. Quiet, near her. Somebody held her hand, very gently. She tried to curl her fingers round it. *Hold on to the hand.*

'Jo, it will be all right. They'll take care of you. You're strong and courageous and you will get through this.' She felt a breath near her cheek, a kiss, feather light. And a whisper, 'Goodbye, Jo. I'll never forget you.'

No, she tried to say. *No. No. No.*

TWENTY-FIVE

'It's okay, Jo. You're in hospital. You're just waking up from an operation.'

Hospital? Operation? She forced her eyes open. Yes. Lights. Faces. Electronic beeps. A bed under her.

'What operation?' She couldn't make her voice work.

'Don't try to talk, Jo. You've got a tube down your throat to help you breathe. You had a bad bang on your head, but the doctors are very happy with you.'

A bang on the head. Yes, she remembered that. Remembered all of them. Remembered running and fighting and being terrified for her life. And she remembered Nick, beside her the whole time, his hand in hers.

She tried to lift her hands, could move but not lift them. They were covered with tubes, and bandages holding them to the bed frame.

'It's okay, Jo.' Someone held her hand, but not the right person. 'We just need to make sure you don't take the breathing tube out. The doctors will come and do that soon, I promise.'

She nodded, understanding. They'd operated on her brain, presumably to relieve some bleeding. But she was okay – she could think and she could understand and she could move both hands and her feet, and when they took the damned tube out of her throat she'd be able to talk.

And the first thing she'd ask would be, 'Where's Nick?'

***

They gave him a private room in Strathnairn Hospital. A private room with a police officer on duty outside the door. They also gave him pain meds for his leg, a drip to re-hydrate him, and endless forms to fill out.

What they couldn't give him, for far too many hours, was news on Jo.

Outside his window, Strathnairn's lights shone into the night. He'd heard hospital visitors leaving a while back, and the voices of nursing staff, beginning to ready patients for sleep.

Nick shifted, trying to find a more comfortable position, his leg protesting the movement. His left leg ached, his head ached despite the pain meds, the cannula in his hand for the intravenous fluids ached. Though he strived for any vestige of centred, balanced calm, it eluded him, his mind far too restless.

When Leah poked her head around the door to see if he was awake, he beckoned her in.

'Jo's out of surgery,' she said, in response to his first demand. 'Murdoch spoke with her mother. There was some bleeding in the brain, so the docs have relieved the pressure. "Stable" is the official statement at present, but her mother is pretty optimistic, apparently.'

Bleeding in the brain . . . Hearing the words confirmed the fears he'd endured for hours. Not his worst fears – she was still alive – but 'stable' still covered too broad a range of possibilities. Optimism was good, probably the best he could expect at this stage, but he desperately wanted to hear 'full recovery'.

Leah pulled a chair towards the bed and dropped into it. 'Nick, they do that kind of surgery every day. I had a constable whose head met a brick wall a year or so back. Same kind of op, and he was out of hospital in less than ten days. Jo's young, fit and tough. Trust that she's not going to give up easily.'

No, she didn't give up easily. She'd kept going, kept fighting, all day, facing guns and fists and heat and dehydration and still – even with bleeding in her brain and an injured shoulder – she'd battled Ramirez, struggled to get herself into the Pajero. But now she lay unconscious, far away in Sydney, and all he could do was lie uselessly here and hope she had the strength to keep fighting.

'I guess there won't be any more news until morning.' He spoke the thought aloud.

'No. You know how hospitals are. I'll make sure you're told as soon as I hear anything.'

She didn't ask, didn't tease or comment otherwise on his worry for Jo – just the brisk, practical understanding that characterised their relationship; respect and friendship without emotional closeness.

'Thanks, Leah.' He trusted that she would understand his gratitude. 'So, what's happened? Did you find Ramirez?'

'We've found them all. Most of them are in Tamworth Base Hospital, and some of them are talking, busy blaming each other.'

Nick's chest relaxed, the tight band around it and his spine loosening a little. He'd do the same things again if he had to – he'd been fighting for survival – but leaving injured men out in the wilderness had weighed on his conscience.

He tore a dozen pages off the notebook he'd borrowed from a nurse, and passed them to Leah. 'I've written out my statement, everything that occurred. It should help you piece it all together.'

'Thanks.' She settled back in the chair, skimming down the first page before she glanced up again. 'We've got Harrison. He bullshitted for a few hours until I put him through Haddad Hell.'

Nick had seen it, a few times – the relentless, scathing verbal cyclone that she could keep up for hours if necessary.

Leah grinned. 'Now he's babbling like a baby, trying for reduced charges. Not a bloody chance. He's been in with Ramirez for weeks, probably longer. That coke Jo found at the lookout? It was left for him. The coordinates were in a text message on his phone.'

'Reward for stonewalling the vandalism investigation? It makes sense. If Jo hadn't found Mitchell's body, Harrison might have been the only one to go out there to look into the damage.'

'Yes. Ramirez wasn't happy about the damage. Even less happy about the rifle Mitchell took. I'd say it was the beginning of the end for that group of louts, as far as he was concerned.'

So he'd let them loose, punishing Mitchell and Coulter, silencing Hugh, torturing Shelley for information – keeping his distance, letting them commit the crimes. 'Will we be able to get enough on Ramirez?' Nick asked. He couldn't contemplate the possibility that the man might walk free.

'Even without the rate they're all talking, yes. We have his laptop and his phone, and although his filing system is, shall we say, unique, and half of it's in Spanish, there's plenty there already. Including his file on you, which he gave Harrison to leak. Drugs, money laundering, conspiracy to murder, perverting the course of justice – we'll get him, Nick.'

They had to. He'd be officially off the case now – witness rather than investigator – but if Leah and the team couldn't do it, he'd find a way. 'Where is he now?'

'Royal North Shore Hospital, under armed guard. Don't worry – Jo's at Royal Prince Alfred, not North Shore. If he's conscious in the morning, he'll be charged, and transferred to Long Bay prison as soon as he's out of intensive care.'

She yawned, and checked her watch. 'I've got paperwork to finish, and I should let you get some rest.' Using the armrests of the chair for leverage, she pushed herself to her feet.

She had a long night ahead of her, and although he could – theoretically – rest, probably should, being sidelined by injury sent his frustration levels soaring. With so much to do, cases to build and document, strategies to decide, aftermath to deal with, he doubted his brain would let him rest.

'The two guys on the road yesterday,' he said before she left. 'Can you make sure, when the official autopsy comes back, that Jo is told that their gunshot injuries would not have been fatal?'

'Yes, I saw them. I'll have to wait for the official report of course, but if it confirms that, I'll make sure she knows. She's had enough to deal with, without guilt on top of it.'

Nick could only agree. She was going to need her strength of spirit, her courage and her good sense; all that and more in the weeks and months ahead.

Leah stopped at the door. 'Before I forget, the youngest lad – his name's Jared Gibson – he's here. His brother brought him in early in the afternoon, and at that stage we didn't know the connection. Concussed, and having a reaction to some drugs, but they haven't shipped him elsewhere so I guess he's all right. His brother flagged down the team that went to check Dyson's Hut, and gave himself up. He helped us find the others, and he's given a full statement. He said to tell you that he'd finally had the courage to do the decent thing.'

After Leah left, with little to do and plenty *not* to think about, Nick stared at the ceiling. He was neither glad nor sorry that Ramirez's injuries were serious enough for intensive care. The man had made his choices, manipulated people, tortured and killed – and he'd threatened Jo with the same. Nick had defended her, and Ramirez had reaped what he'd sown.

Now she should be safe from him, wouldn't have to live her life looking over her shoulder, or under police protection.

Unlike him.

He would do what had to be done, but it wasn't a life he wanted to live.

He wanted a life where he could be himself, fully and completely, authentic and *whole*.

He just couldn't see, with the exposure that Ramirez's leak had caused, how it might be made possible.

&

After a couple of days in intensive care, they moved her upstairs to a ward, and for Jo a distinct advantage of the ward was the large window with a view outside – a view of Sydney, the crowded cityscape not as beautiful as a bush landscape, but she was counting positives, not negatives. Alive, in one piece, with no lasting damage; she'd recover, and be back in the bush before too long. For now, she sat by the window, enjoying the freedom from tubes and monitors, resting, occasionally sleeping, and looking forward to a walk to the cafeteria when her brother arrived later.

A reflection in the window caught her eye, and she turned to the woman hesitating in the doorway, an arrangement of flowers in her hands.

Slim in a simple sundress, dark hair brushing her shoulders, she was distinctly feminine, and yet . . . one look at those familiar eyes, and Jo guessed her name before she introduced herself.

'I hope I'm not intruding. My name's Grace Anderson. I'm—'

'Nick's sister,' Jo finished for her. 'Please, come in, take a seat. I'm so glad to meet you. Have you heard how Nick is? I'm only getting official statements.' And if she didn't get more news soon, now that she was out of intensive care she'd be on the phone herself, hassling Murdoch, Aaron, *anyone* until they gave her a direct number for Nick.

'He's okay.' Grace placed the flowers on the bedside cabinet, and sat on a nearby chair. 'He's out of hospital. He's supposed to be taking it easy, but he's back at work, dealing with the aftermath. The police want detailed statements to support all the charges they'll be making. I'm so sorry that you – that both of you – had to go through such a horrific experience.'

'I survived, thanks to Nick. A detective came to see me yesterday, and I told him all that happened.' She swallowed to moisten a dry mouth, the memories fresh again in her mind after a day or so of post-anaesthetic blurriness. The detective would be back, later today, for a formal statement. She had to make sure she gave it clearly, so there could be no doubts, no loopholes enabling blame to be cast other than where it belonged.

'From the little Nick told me, I gather it was a team effort. He's worried about you, Jo.'

'Everything works fine. I'll be back to normal before long.' Jo pointed to the telephone beside her bed. 'I could tell him that myself if he phoned me. Or if you can give me his number, I'll call him.'

'He's not giving me his direct number.' A small smile didn't quite succeed in disguising her sadness, her pain. 'He said he hasn't replaced his mobile yet, but I can read between the lines. That television report has him worried. So he's protecting me. Protecting you, too.'

I'd give my life to keep you safe . . . He hadn't just meant his physical body. He'd given up his sister, this lovely, compassionate woman, to keep her safe. He would give up . . . she didn't know how to define the bond between them. No promises, no commitments, they'd said, but he'd made that promise to protect her, and he'd meant it.

Jo brushed moisture from the corner of her eye. 'I wish . . . God, I wouldn't wish your brother any less than he is, Grace, but I wish his protective streak didn't come at such a cost to him.'

Grace passed her the box of tissues from the bedside cabinet. 'I know. It's what I remember most about him. Where we grew up was an ugly, violent place. When the police smashed some of the organised crime, *dis*organised crime and turf wars filled the vacuum. For many of the kids – even the little ones – bullying and fighting was just the way of life. Nick learned to fight to protect us, not because he ever enjoyed the fighting. And then he joined the police force, and he seemed to have found somewhere he could use his skills for good work. I hoped, when Hugh told me he'd given up the undercover jobs, that he might finally build the life he deserves – that I might get my brother back.'

Tears brimmed in her eyes, and Jo offered her the tissue box.

'I'm sorry,' Grace said, wiping her eyes. 'Some doctor I am. I'm supposed to be cheering you up, but here I am crying into your tissues. I must seem so weak, but I'm just so afraid of losing him again.'

'It's not weakness. I've only known him a few days and I don't know—' She clutched a tissue tight in her hand. 'Grace, I don't know exactly what's between him and me, what we might want. But I'm afraid. Afraid of the threats to him and afraid that if he thinks either of us will be safer without him, then he'll leave. Witness protection, hiding, a new identity – it doesn't matter which, we'd still lose him.'

And she could no longer imagine which might be more

unbearable – losing someone she cared about after only a few short days, or losing someone she loved after five years.

☙

Two evenings later, with the ward emptied of visitors and the evening hush starting to settle, she took her usual chair by the window, browsing the internet on a laptop she'd begged from her brother to catch up on media reports. Given the lack of contact from Nick, the bare slivers of information she and Grace had gleaned had come from the media.

One headline from the morning caught her eye: *News team sacked.*

She raced through the brief article. A news presenter and a producer sacked. A 'full and unreserved apology' to 'the detective concerned for the misrepresentation of his character and his career'.

They acknowledged multiple errors of fact and judgement, and again, without naming him, stated that the detective had 'no connection to any of the persons named in the original report'.

She rested her head against the back of the chair and watched the lights sparkling across the city.

It had to be some kind of damage-control strategy, not just an apology. But would it be enough?

Goodbye, Jo.

That was the bad dream that woke her from every sleep. Not killers or fires or fighting or running through the bush she loved, scared for her life. Just two gently whispered words.

No. Not goodbye. There had to be a way. They would have to find a way.

Three framed photographs stood on top of the coffin. Hugh in dress uniform, receiving a commendation for bravery. A much younger Hugh, in far less tidy high-school uniform, grinning with Pat and Christie at the camera. And the last, taken just weeks ago, of Hugh and Grace enjoying dinner in a restaurant.

Nick steadied himself on his crutches and faced the small graveside gathering. Very small, the request for a private funeral respected. Three of Hugh's Sydney colleagues stood to one side in dress uniform, with Keith Murdoch and the head of Homicide representing the Police Force officially. A sign of respect. And Grace.

Fresh flowers rested on the graves beside the new plot: Christie, Pat, their parents. It was right that Hugh would lie here with the Matheson family.

Nick drew his inadequate notes from his pocket. He had to start, but he wasn't ready.

A taxi stopped in the lane nearby, and a woman alighted. She wore a simple jade-green dress, classic and unadorned but for a pendant, and flat sandals. A silk scarf was tied around close-cropped hair.

She crossed the lawn towards them.

Beautiful, natural, herself. Discharged from hospital only this morning, and she'd travelled up to Newcastle.

Grace held out her hand in welcome and drew Jo into the small circle.

Nick met her gaze and held it. Everything was right, and he could do this now. Authentic. Whole.

He could honour Hugh as a man who'd risen above a tough childhood, made something of himself through hard work, who'd lived with passion for life and unwavering loyalty to his family and friends. An imperfect man, a complex man who had suffered and feared and loved and made mistakes but also a man who had saved lives and put his life on the line for others, time after time.

Nick looked across the casket at Grace and Jo, and told them, told them all, that he could honour Hugh as his colleague, brother and friend.

ॐ

She walked with him after the service, a short stroll to a bench under the shade of a tree, peaceful and quiet. The sky huge and blue above them, the sun starting to angle, golden, catching tiny sparkles in granite here and there, birds flitting through trees and graves, chattering contentedly.

He stretched out his injured leg, easing into a comfortable position.

'How is it?' she asked.

'I'll have to take it easy for a while, but it will heal, again, given time. And you?'

Ordinary questions, necessary questions. She looked out over the view, content that they would get to the deeper ones.

'Time and rest, and I'll be fine. The doctors are very happy with me. It's pretty amazing what they can do.'

Time and rest and care, and most things would heal. Bones, muscles, tissue and nerves; hearts and spirits.

But hearts and spirits required different forms of medicine. She reached out a hand, linked her fingers through his, saw his close around hers, still bearing scratches and scars like hers, but strong and sure.

'I read the apology in the news. Will it work to protect your identity? Will you be safe now?'

He nodded. 'Relatively. Nothing's guaranteed. Apparently the original report never streamed out, the file never went online. One of the technical people was on the ball, and pulled it after the first few seconds. HQ ran a risk analysis. A short segment at six-thirty on a Sunday morning that never went online – the initial feeling is that the risk might not be immense.'

It never went online. Relief relaxed muscles she didn't know she'd been holding tense.

'So you're here, not in hiding.'

'Yes. They've put a few other protective strategies in place, as well. Nick Matheson's been doing things, according to official records, when some other people were elsewhere. So, I'm here.' He smiled, and the depth in his dark brown eyes wasn't the dark of fear or despair. 'All of me. Nick Matheson.'

Her smile stretched the tight skin on the side of her scalp, and she didn't care. 'Hello, Nick.'

'Hello, Jo.'

She lifted his scarred hand to her lips, kissed each knuckle, one by one. Hands that fought when needed, to protect, but could be gentle, giving. Strength, for all the right reasons.

'I know I've mentioned it before, but you are a remarkable man.'

He didn't protest, as he'd done before. Dark eyes, peaceful, held hers as he kissed her fingers. 'You're pretty remarkable yourself, Jo.'

She leaned her head against his.

'Do you think we should make time, while we're resting and recovering from our various wounds, to get to know more about each other?'

He folded his arms around her, drew her close. 'Good idea. What do you want to know?'

'The kinds of things we haven't had time to discover yet. Interests, passions, dreams, plans. Although I've already figured out that you probably don't collect stamps.'

'Stamps? As in postage stamps? No, I don't collect them.' He was silent a moment. 'I practise Aikido,' he said quietly. 'It's self-defence, based on a philosophy of minimal harm. That's important to me. I'm thinking seriously about returning to teaching it.'

Protection, minimal harm. The heart, the centre of him. A powerful strength.

'I love the outdoors,' she said. 'Nature awes me – the environment, wildlife, the balances, the way things gradually change yet remain strong. There's so many questions, so much to study and discover. But I also love home and simple things. Friends, family, community ties. It's time I found somewhere to live, not just camp. Maybe a few acres near Strathnairn.'

'You'll stay in the district? I didn't know if . . . whether there'd be too many bad memories, to go back to work there, live there.'

She pulled away just enough to see him properly.

'The land has never scared me. Landscape isn't good or bad or evil or confused, it just *is*. It's beautiful and intricate and incredible. People scare me sometimes, but most astound me with their resilience and hope and their ability to dream and love and to continue on, despite the inevitable challenges. Like you.'

His arm, gentle around her shoulders, drew her close to him again. 'Like you,' he said.

ACKNOWLEDGEMENTS

I wrote this novel while waiting for and recovering from brain surgery, and I am grateful to many people who have supported me throughout the medical and writing journeys. Doctor Rodney Allen and the entire neurosurgery care team at Royal Prince Alfred Hospital have ensured that I am still here to write many more stories, and cared for me throughout with dedication, compassion, and good humour.

My agent, Clare Forster, and publisher Bernadette Foley of Hachette have been patient, understanding, and accommodating, and their encouragement helped me through the rough times. Editors Sara Foster and Claire de Medici took great care in reading the manuscript and their thoughtful suggestions and feedback have improved the book a great deal.

Sergeants Gemma Gallagher and Simon Meehan have again provided very helpful advice on police procedures, and National

Park Ranger Emily Ingram generously shared her experiences and answered many questions about the realities of the job.

I am grateful, too, for the ongoing love and encouragement of family and friends, and to the many readers who sent messages and who have been waiting, eagerly but patiently, for a new book from me.

Gordon has been by my side throughout the journey. He endures an untidy house, my distracted writer's brain, and my late night writing timetable, and still believes emphatically that I am a good writer. But, most importantly, he held my hand and talked to me when I was unconscious after the brain surgery, and was there by my side when I woke up. Thank you, joy of my life.

Storm Clouds

Storm Clouds
is dedicated to the memory of three
inspirational friends, lost far too soon:

Kerry Hawkins,
with whom I shared many visits to national parks, a love of
sewing and textiles, and a rich and wonderful friendship;

Deborah Anderson,
influential friend of my youth, who encouraged me – and
so many others – not to let uncertainty stop me from
trying something new and reaching for my dreams;

Matt Richell,
CEO of Hachette Australia, who believed in
my books right from the beginning.

CHAPTER 1

The late afternoon sun shone straight at the dusty windscreen, semi-blinding Erin so that she didn't see the small landslide of rocks and dirt across the rough fire trail in time to avoid it. The four-wheel-drive Hilux utility tilted as one wheel mounted the edge of a rock, and then dropped suddenly as the rock spun off to the side. Metal scraped on stone, the steering wheel dragged to one side and the right front wheel went *thunk, thunk, thunk* before the vehicle stopped.

She swore as she switched off the ignition. A flat tyre. The last thing she needed at the end of a twelve-hour workday. She swung out of the ute, knowing exactly what she'd see. Sure enough, the Hilux had thrown a tyre off the rim.

Changing a tyre? No worries. As a National Parks ranger

working in rugged country, she'd changed a fair few, and she methodically chocked the other wheels securely and gathered what she'd need – the jack, the wrench and the spare tyre from beneath the truck.

But changing a tyre on an isolated bush track miles from anywhere when the wheel nuts were so frigging tight she had to battle for minutes to loosen them? Despite her strength and fitness, Erin ran through her entire vocabulary of swear words twice before she'd removed the first one. She brushed hair that had escaped her ponytail out of her eyes.

'Where the bloody hell are you when I need you, Kennedy?' she muttered into the silence.

Simon Kennedy. Fellow National Parks ranger. Friend. And army reserve soldier who'd been gone on deployment for close on two months. Maybe in Afghanistan. Or Iraq or some other war-torn hellhole. He had to be overseas somewhere, because in the two months since he'd been abruptly called up for army reserve service there'd been no word from him. Two months without an email, a text. Nothing.

She used her pent-up frustration as well as her boot on the wrench and the third wheel nut finally loosened. Hallelujah. She might get this tyre off sometime before nightfall.

She wouldn't make it home before dark, though. Twenty kilometres back to the Goodabri National Parks office to leave keys and swap the work truck for her own ute. Seventy kilometres back to Strathnairn. She *should* go into the National Parks district office there and return some borrowed equipment, but no one would need it before morning. And she just wanted to go home to the cottage she rented on the edge of Strathnairn, pig out on some comfort food – she'd done more than enough physical work this week to justify a dozen cheese-laden pizzas – watch some mindless TV, and have an early night.

Assuming she could get this tyre changed.

A stick cracked in the undergrowth and she stilled, gripping the handle of the wrench. She spent most of her days out in the bush alone and had never scared easily – until three months ago, when her colleague Jo had stumbled across a body, and a drug lord's minions had terrorised the park. They'd all since been arrested, but Erin still responded warily to any sudden sound. Now she scanned the bushland around her for the source of the noise.

Ten metres away among the trees, a six-foot, well-muscled male watched her. Fortunately not a human one. A full-grown red kangaroo, powerful and dangerous if threatened. But this one only studied her, his upright posture showcasing his height and strong shoulders, until he decided she was no threat and resumed grazing the native grasses in the scrub.

'Good decision, big boy,' she murmured. 'You stay over there, and I'll stay over here.' Unlike the time a few months ago when she'd inadvertently disturbed one and Simon had stepped between her and the kangaroo to protect her. No Simon to step in this time, but she could always jump into her utility in the unlikely event that the roo changed its mind about her. Very unlikely. She had far more chance of being bitten by a venomous snake than being attacked by a kangaroo.

The fifth wheel nut defied all her strength and curses for a good five minutes. Giving in wasn't an option – she was going nowhere until she changed the tyre. They were so short-staffed she had no colleagues closer than an hour away, and they'd both be finished for the day anyway, so she'd just damn well have to manage by herself.

By the time she'd removed the last nut her shoulders and back ached from the exertion. She replaced the wheel, fastened the damaged tyre in place of the spare, put away the jack and the wrench and removed the rocks she'd used to chock the other wheels. Climbing into the driver's seat, she stretched her neck and rubbed her shoulders before turning the key in the ignition. There'd been way too many long, lonely days with too much work.

No point whingeing and moaning. She put the truck into gear and eased her way over the loose rough ground. Home, a hot shower, and pizza. Definitely a good plan.

In the small town of Goodabri – population barely three hundred – she parked in the yard behind the National Parks office, closed and silent after hours. It took her only a few minutes to leave the work ute keys, collect the paperwork she'd need for a meeting tomorrow, and lock up again. In her own ute, she reversed out into the back lane, on her way home at last.

Only one other vehicle moved on Goodabri's main street – a white LandCruiser, a block ahead as she turned into the street.

She caught her breath. A white LandCruiser with two spare tyres on the back, and indicating a left turn.

Simon. Simon Kennedy driving back into Goodabri as unexpectedly as he'd left two months ago.

The rush of pleasure at his return dragged with it the undercurrent of uncertainty that had plagued her during those two months of silence. She'd regarded him as a friend – a good friend. But what good friend didn't happen to mention in almost a year of working together that he still served in the army reserve? Dammit, she'd liked him. More than liked him, although – for reasons that had nothing to do with him – she'd quashed any errant fantasies of anything happening between them. And she still couldn't quite believe that she'd never known, that he'd never told her, and worse, that she'd never suspected he hid something so important. So much for being able to read people.

And there she was again, on that round-and-round-and-roundabout of emotions and second-guessing and trying to work out how to make sense of her feelings.

She shook her head, as if she could shake the confusion out of it. Her hang-ups, not his. Plain and simple, they were friends, and he'd been away, serving the country. So she'd do the friendly thing and go welcome him home.

Goodabri had only a few streets, and she followed Simon's route left off the main street then right into the next, and pulled up five houses down in front of the weatherboard house he rented.

He stood at the back of his LandCruiser in the driveway, a kit bag resting on the tray. Old Snowy McDermott, his neighbour, leaned on the fence post between them, settling in for a good long yarn. Snowy could talk the hind leg off a horse and usually missed most social cues, but Simon saw Erin and excused himself to Snowy as she got out of the ute.

As they walked the fifteen paces towards each other, the light cheeky comments she might normally have made turned to dust on her tongue. For months they'd worked side by side in the relaxed way of equals, trusting and relying on each other in their physically demanding duties for both their National Parks jobs and volunteer SES service.

He wasn't in uniform now. Not the army uniform she'd never seen him wear. Not the National Parks uniform, nor the SES uniform they both wore often enough outside work. Just faded jeans and a white t-shirt that stretched over his fine physique and highlighted the deep hazel of his eyes. Eyes that reflected the warmth of his easy grin and gave little hint that he'd been anywhere but a relaxed holiday away.

The early autumn sun had started to set, casting a golden outline around him, almost as if nature wanted to make a gilded statue of the soldier hero. Whereas she . . . she was no hero.

They stopped half a metre from each other, within touching distance, but neither of them made a move to touch. He was out of her reach in too many other ways. Maybe the caution that had stopped her making a fool of herself in the months before he'd left had been good sense, rather than cowardice.

She resisted wiping suddenly sweaty hands on her uniform trousers and summoned up a grin, aware of Snowy watering his garden close by. Keep it simple, keep it light. Just the warm, familiar teasing she'd missed in his absence.

'If I'd known you were coming back today, I would have volunteered you for the regional planning meeting in Moree tomorrow.'

His eyes sparkled. 'Phew. I've had a lucky escape then. Who drew the short straw?'

'Well, since Jo's on light duties and not allowed to drive, I got the long straw, the middle straw *and* the short straw.'

'Jo's back at work?'

'Yes, working half-days. But it's not quite three months since her craniotomy so she's not allowed to drive yet.'

'So you've been doing all three of our jobs, all this time.'

'Yeah. You owe me. Although I suppose if you've been off saving the world, that might cancel the debt, soldier.'

His cheerful, relaxed expression slipped and the light in his eyes dimmed for a moment before he gestured with a jerk of his thumb towards the house. 'Come on in and tell me the news while I dump my gear, and then I'll shout you dinner at the pub.'

Back at his LandCruiser, he grabbed his kit bag with one hand and then slid a metal case out. His rifle. Invaluable in feral animal campaigns. She'd usually managed to put out of her mind that in the army, his targets didn't have four legs. His past army service had been abstract in her head, something she rarely considered in detail, because on the few occasions he'd spoken of his experiences he'd sounded carefree, as if his deployments, even in Iraq and Afghanistan, were barely more adventurous than an outback camping trip. But then he'd gone again, between one shift and the next, with scarcely a word of explanation to her. Nods and murmurs from senior National Parks staff who'd known him longer suggested there was more to his role than he'd ever let on, leaving her with the distinct impression that he'd been – was still – a commando with significant experience in covert operations.

No wonder he was such a valuable member of the volunteer SES squad and a capable National Parks ranger, especially in dealing with the law-enforcement aspect of their roles. Maybe the signs had always been there, and she just hadn't recognised them.

But the fact that he was still in the army – that changed things, changed how she felt, although she'd spent the past few weeks trying fruitlessly to put a finger on how and why. Not that there was any point in trying to understand it, since she mattered so little to him that he'd not contacted her once since his abrupt departure. They were friendly colleagues in a small community, nothing more. So she'd keep things at that level.

She grinned with a good imitation of her usual cheekiness. 'Well, since you apparently couldn't remember my email address all this time, I'll let you shout me dinner.'

She'd not often seen him discomfited, but now he grimaced. 'Sorry. Not much internet access where I've been.'

Obviously not a local army base, then. But he headed towards the house without any further explanation. He set down his bag and the rifle case to unlock the front door and from behind she saw the sudden wariness tensing his spine as he pushed it open.

The odour hit her. Pungent, nauseating, *dead*. 'Sheesh, Simon, did you leave dead fish in your —'

'No.' His hand moved towards his hip, reaching instinctively for a sidearm that wasn't there. 'Keep back, Erin.'

She stayed on the doorstep while he entered, as alert and cautious as if walking into a terrorist's hideout instead of a typical Australian colonial cottage. There were four doors off the short central passageway, two on each side. In the dimmer light inside she watched as he approached the second on the right, the only door not closed. Although he had no gun to hold ready, he used the partially open door as cover to glance into and check the room.

Whatever he saw startled him with a visible jolt. He swore and dropped his guard, striding into the room.

In a few steps Erin covered the length of the passage and followed him through the door. His study had been ransacked, computer equipment smashed, books and DVD cases torn apart and thrown on the floor. But she stopped hard when she saw what Simon had discovered, and nausea rolled in her stomach so violently that she barely resisted the urge to turn and run.

He knelt by a woman sprawled on the floor, his hand on her wrist to check her pulse. But there could be no pulse. There had been no pulse for hours, maybe days. Numerous wounds on her torso had stained her white dress dark red, and blood from her slit throat had dried in splatters all around her on the polished wood floor. Her eyes stared blankly at the ceiling.

'How . . . ? What . . . ?' Erin's throat wouldn't make a full sentence.

Simon turned his head slowly to look up at her, eyes shadowed, his mouth a hard line. 'I don't know how she got here, Erin, or why. I haven't seen her for years.' But he didn't move away from the woman, and there was an intimacy of sorts in the way his fingers rested loosely on her wrist.

The closeness of the room, the stench, the buzz of flies filled Erin's head, almost suffocating rational thought. 'Who . . . ?'

'She's . . .' His voice came out as ragged as a storm-ripped tree. 'She's my wife.'

CHAPTER 2

'Your *wife?*'

The disbelief and hurt in Erin's voice cut him like a whip. Pain he deserved, for betraying the trust and friendship they'd built. But the slim hope he'd held on to for months – that a relationship with Erin might eventually be possible – had already shattered the moment he saw Hayley's body on the floor.

That Hayley could be *here*, after all these years, made no sense. That she could be here, and dead . . . he couldn't even begin to process it in his mind. Logic eluded him, and grief, anger and shame boiled together, caustic in his gut. Anger with Hayley, for being absent so long, denying him the chance to make things right between them. Anger with the bastard or bastards who'd murdered her. Anger with himself, for failing his wife yet again, in the worst way possible. And for failing Erin.

But he couldn't disintegrate, couldn't give in to the emotion and sit there on his knees and howl like a wounded animal. He was a soldier and he needed to send Erin out of there. So she'd be safe.

'Get out,' he rasped. He didn't dare look at her, couldn't bear to see her stricken eyes again. 'Go to Snowy's. Call the cops.'

'No.' Her hand closed over his shoulder, her fingers warm through his shirt. 'Simon, you have to come outside with me.' A hitch in her breathing unsteadied her voice but she continued, more in control than he was. 'We'll call the police from outside.'

'I can't . . .' *Leave Hayley like this. Leave her alone.* Because he'd left her alone far too many times, despite her pleas, despite her need of him.

'We can't contaminate the scene. Simon, I'm sorry, I know this is a shock, but we have to *think*. The best thing we can do for her now is leave the room as it is for the police.'

Erin's strength – considering *him*, when she had every right to be angry – hammered logic into his brain. She didn't know, and would never know, that his grief was as much for her and for his dreams of them as it was for Hayley. But she was right. He couldn't do a damn thing for Hayley now except help find her killer.

As he rose to his feet he scanned the room again, alert, wary. Soldier, not husband. Protector, not friend.

'They're probably long gone,' he said to Erin. 'But keep close behind me.'

Nothing stirred in the house as Simon listened briefly at the closed door of each room on their way out. He didn't touch the front door handle but instead hooked the door with his foot to draw it partly closed, a small barrier against the prying eyes that would doubtless start to gather once the police cars arrived. In the way of small towns, word would spread faster than a bushfire on a hot gusty day.

But right now the sun had sunk below the horizon, Snowy must have finished his watering and gone inside, and the street was as quiet and lifeless as the house. Simon's training nagged at him to do a circuit of the house, check for anyone lurking, or evidence of who, when and how, but Hayley's death must have occurred hours ago and the perpetrator was unlikely to still be around. He'd stay by Erin's side and let the police scour the house and surrounds for evidence.

Erin had her phone out before he did. Her usually lively face pale and drawn, she flicked rapidly through her contacts. 'I'll call Tess. She can be here in just a few minutes, and she'll know how to set things in motion.'

His thoughts still reeling, he didn't object or insist on making the call himself. The new police officer had arrived in Goodabri only days before his abrupt departure, so he scarcely knew her. Better for Erin to talk with her.

He leaned two hands on the roof of his vehicle, dropping his head down while she made the call beside him. Professional, not panicking. Capable in a crisis. Unlike Hayley's doe-eyed dependence.

'Tess? It's Erin Taylor. We've got a situation at Simon's place in Grey Street . . . Yes, he only just got back, about ten minutes ago. I went inside with him. We found a . . . a homicide. Hours, maybe a day or so gone. A woman. Simon's . . .' Her breath caught and she didn't say the word 'wife'. 'Simon knows her.'

Did he know her? Know Hayley? He might have once. Fourteen years ago. Perhaps not even then, despite three years of marriage. They'd married too young, too inexperienced to make the marriage last. And his career – he'd always put it first. Before her. Before anything. He could make sense of himself as a soldier, but a husband? Jesus, he'd made a mess of that.

And after all this time she'd come to him, out of the blue, and now she was dead because he hadn't been there to look after her as he'd vowed on their wedding day.

Someone had killed her. A random attack? Someone she'd brought with her? Or had a killer come for him, and found her?

•

Erin finished the call and slipped her phone back into her pocket. 'Tess is on her way,' she told Simon. 'She won't be long.'

She had no idea what else to say, and her mind raced with questions she didn't want to ask. Simon stared at the ground, his face tight. Hands thrust into her pockets, Erin leaned back against the LandCruiser, huffing out a breath, and the silence hung between them.

Simon had a wife. One he'd never mentioned in her hearing in ten months of working side by side. His wife, his army reserve membership . . . come to think of it, she couldn't recall him talking about family either, or where he'd grown up, or any of the other aspects of his past that people usually talked about, at least *mentioned*. Not that she'd told him anything about her family. Her family wasn't relevant to her, hadn't been for almost twenty years.

But Simon had a *wife*. A pretty woman, from Erin's glimpse of the body. Long brown hair, delicate, girlish features, slim build. Murdered. The multiple injuries meant it had to be murder. Despite the warmth still in the air, Erin's skin prickled. Sometime in the past day or so, a killer had entered Simon's home and attacked the woman with a knife or something similar. The injuries, the amount of blood – she hadn't died instantly, she must have been terrified and in pain in those last minutes. *She.* Simon's wife, lying dead in his house, and Erin didn't know what to call her.

'What is her name?' she asked him, the words stilted in the silence.

He lifted his head slowly, and his eyes took a moment to focus on hers. 'Hayley. Hayley Munro.'

Hayley. A pretty name for an attractive woman.

A police car rounded the corner into the street. No time

to ask Simon more, even if she could untangle her thoughts enough to frame questions beyond the most basic.

The police car parked across the road. Erin knew the day shift usually finished at seven, but Tess was still in uniform. Still in uniform, and alone, because she was the only officer stationed in Goodabri, with the rest of her colleagues fifty minutes' drive away in Strathnairn.

'What have we got?' Tess asked without preamble as she strode down the driveway. Brusque, focused, not a woman who easily relaxed – but Erin respected her, her commitment and her skills.

Simon straightened up, and although he didn't quite snap to attention his unguarded moments were over. He answered the policewoman's question in short, clear sentences. 'A murder. In the bedroom I use as a study, on the right. I've been away for weeks, only just arrived home. The victim is my wife, Hayley.'

Tess raised an eyebrow. 'You have a wife? Ex?'

'Separated. For fourteen years. I haven't seen her in almost that long.'

Fourteen years? Fourteen years he'd not seen her? Erin had never read him as a man who'd just up and leave, ignore his responsibilities. But that was a hell of a long time to be apart and not divorced.

'So what was she doing —' Tess broke off, her interrupted question echoing Erin's thoughts. 'Time for questions later. I'll go take a look.' She rested her hand on the weapon at her side. 'Any signs the perpetrators are still around?'

'I didn't check the back of the house, but I think not. I'll come in with you, just in case.'

Tess considered for a moment before nodding. 'Okay. Only as backup. Don't touch a thing. Erin, stay out here and make sure no one else comes onto the property.'

Erin waited beside her own ute as the blue of the sky deepened and Venus glowed, the first star low on the horizon. No cars or people came along the street. The sounds of a television drifted from Snowy's front room, the canned-laughter decibels louder than the actors' dialogue. Tess would likely ask him if he'd seen or heard anything next door, but given his propensity to leave his hearing aids turned off, Erin doubted he would have.

Just a quiet street in a small town, twenty or so houses on large blocks that once would have boasted well-tended gardens, a couple of dogs in the backyard, chook sheds and veggie patches. Some of them undoubtedly still did. But Goodabri's population was ageing, many of the younger generation leaving for jobs and opportunities in larger towns, and a number of these houses were empty, or their residents were elderly, like Snowy, and not up to as much outside work as they'd once been. Had anyone seen Hayley arrive? Or her killer? Or heard her cries when she was stabbed?

Erin rubbed the goosebumps on her bare forearms. If Snowy had seen or heard anything, he would have mentioned it to Simon. That was Snowy, full of friendly curiosity. If he'd seen anything, he wouldn't have been able to resist saying something about it.

A white sedan came around the corner and slowed. In the dimming light, Erin couldn't clearly see the driver, but she knew the car. The detectives' car, from the Strathnairn police station. Aaron or Nick . . . ?

She breathed a little easier when Nick Matheson stepped out of the car. Aaron would make a good detective one day but Nick had years of experience, senior rank, and well-honed investigative instincts. In the past few months, since he'd fallen hard for her colleague Jo, he'd also become a good friend. She wasn't used to seeing him in uniform, but he'd been appointed acting inspector for the district recently, and he wore it with natural authority.

'You got here quickly,' she said. Even if Tess had called him before she'd arrived, he couldn't have made the seventy kilometres from Strathnairn so fast.

His smile was brief, distracted. 'I was on my way back from Tenterfield. Tess is inside?'

'Yes. With Simon. I'm staying out here to keep the crowds under control.' Erin waved her hand at the deserted street. 'Would you like me to phone Jo, tell her you'll be late?'

'That bad, is it?'

Of course he hadn't seen yet, presumably only received a coded message from Tess over the police radio about a death. The image of the dead woman floated into Erin's memory again. Because this wasn't the first murder in the district in recent times, she had a fair idea what it would entail for a local detective with few resources nearby. Additional officers from Strathnairn were at least fifty minutes away. Forensics from Inverell an hour, minimum. More likely two. As acting inspector, Nick would be heavily involved, overseeing operations and allocating and approving resources.

'Yes,' she told him. 'You're definitely going to be late.'

'Shit. Okay, yes, phone her. Thanks.'

Erin had the number dialled before he'd reached the door of the house, but when her friend answered she realised she hadn't thought about what to say. She couldn't discuss a murder, even with the discreet Jo, in the middle of the street and before official announcements were made.

'Simon's back but there's been some trouble at his place,' she said quickly. 'Nick asked me to phone you.' As Jo asked an anxious question, Erin hastened to reassure her. 'No, no, they're both fine. But Nick wanted me to tell you that he'll be here for a while.'

'Somebody's hurt?' Jo asked. 'Or . . . ?'

'Nobody we know,' Erin said. 'Not a local.'

Jo must have heard the brittle edge to her composure. 'Are you okay? Do you need to talk about it?'

Yes. Erin bit back the plea. She let few people close, but if she could lean on anyone, it would be Jo. *Simon's come back and his wife has been murdered here in Goodabri and did you know he had a wife? Because I sure as hell didn't.*

No, she'd deal with this alone. She made herself smile so her voice didn't come out tight. 'No. I'm okay. I'll see you tomorrow.'

Another police car turned into the street, and Erin set her shoulders back and walked forward to meet it. As a National Parks ranger she worked closely with the police, knew everyone in the district command, and her responsibilities in the SES also involved helping out in emergencies. In a small community like Goodabri, a murdered woman was an emergency. There'd be an influx tonight of police, forensic officers and the coroner's deputy. They'd need the crime scene secured, they'd need food, a place to work other than the tiny, cramped police station, and some of them would need accommodation overnight.

She shoved aside her personal confusion, all the questions going through her mind. Later she could deal with the emotional chaos. Right now, she had work to do.

•

Hayley lay dead in his house, murdered with one of his kitchen knives, which doubtless had his fingerprints all over it, and he probably had no alibi for the last seventy-two hours.

Simon waited in the claustrophobically small interview room of the Goodabri police cottage and steeled himself for the interrogation to come. A husband was always the first suspect. An unsuccessful marriage and a soldier husband who had reason to want his wife out of his life? That made means, motive and opportunity. He could almost feel the handcuffs closing around his wrists.

The hands of the clock on the wall crawled slowly around the dial. Nick Matheson must have called in the homicide specialists from Sydney. Standard practice with a crime like this. He'd heard the thud-thud of the police chopper flying in to land at the showground half an hour ago, although it seemed longer. He'd checked the time against his watch several times, in case the clock batteries were dying.

Eventually cars pulled up outside, doors slammed, footsteps and voices entered the station.

'You've got the husband in here? Have you cautioned him?' A woman's voice, clipped, brisk, authoritative.

'He's come voluntarily, Leah, to tell us what he knows about the deceased.' Nick's tone packed just as much firm authority into his reply. Simon hadn't known him for long, but he liked and respected what he'd seen in those few weeks. Their nascent friendship wouldn't cloud Nick's judgement, and the detective could well suspect him, but at least he'd get a fair hearing.

Nick opened the door and showed in the woman and another plainclothes cop. There was no sign of the man he'd shared a couple of drinks with in the Strathnairn pub in Nick's unsmiling face and formal introductions. 'This is Detective Senior Sergeant Leah Haddad from Homicide in Sydney, and Detective Sergeant Steve Fraser. They will be leading the investigation.'

Simon recognised Haddad from the murder investigation at the beginning of summer when Jo had found a body in the park and all hell had broken loose. In their brief encounters back then he'd pegged Haddad as a career cop, capable and hard and determined.

Although he stood and offered his hand, she ignored it.

Fraser he found harder to size up. Around his own age, with enough experience to put a sharpness behind the brown eyes. Suit, white shirt, dark tie, and a handshake firm enough to challenge his own. Although Fraser played it relaxed, straddling a chair and loosening his tie as though they were sitting down for a friendly drink in a bar, Simon's instincts heightened to alert. He'd be a fool to think of Fraser as some kind of devil-may-care detective. The rigid formality of the senior woman detective contrasted with Fraser's relaxation, but he'd bet they were running the good cop/bad cop routine. Either that, or they were trying to piss each other off.

Haddad fixed Simon with a cool, dark-eyed stare that might have intimidated a less hardened man. 'Mr Kennedy, I understand that you have identified the deceased as your wife?'

'Yes. Her name is Hayley Elizabeth Munro.'

'Munro?'

'She took her grandmother's maiden name when she was eighteen and kept it when we married.'

'Did that bother you?'

'Bother?' What was she trying to suggest, that he was some Neanderthal prick who wanted total control over a woman?

'It's the twenty-first century, for chrissakes. Of course it didn't bother me.'

'How long have you been estranged?'

'Separated,' he emphasised. 'Estranged' implied hostility and resentment, and he wanted to correct that impression. 'Hayley needed some space, needed some time to herself. She was only nineteen when we married, I was barely twenty-one. I was in the army, and often away on exercises or deployments. That's a hard life for a young woman. After about three years she left to go on some kind of alternative-lifestyle healing retreat when I was deployed to East Timor. Other than one brief visit, she didn't come back.'

'When was that?'

'We separated fourteen years ago.'

Haddad raised a defined eyebrow. 'Fourteen years? And you never divorced?'

'There was no pressing reason to. I cared about my wife, Detective. I had a responsibility towards her. Her life had not been easy and she was . . .' He struggled for words. *Not like Erin.* Yeah, that'd go down like a lead balloon. He shoved thoughts of Erin away. 'Hayley wasn't emotionally strong.'

Despite the late hour, the room was stiflingly hot, and while Haddad was distracted by a text message on her phone, Fraser rose and filled three plastic cups from the water cooler just outside the door.

Passing a cup across to him, Fraser asked, 'When was the last time you saw Hayley?'

Simon let the water cool his throat before he answered. 'About eighteen months after she left. She'd been travelling with a girlfriend. I'd had sporadic postcards from her, the occasional phone call. I wasn't in the country myself a whole lot at the time. She came back to Sydney once, to collect some things. She was heading back to the north coast for a job as a nanny at some kind of retreat place. She was excited about it – she'd always loved being with little kids. She gave me a phone number and a post office box address before she went.' And a kiss. She'd given him an affectionate, casual kiss before she'd hurried off to catch her train. A kiss on the cheek. Like a sister. 'She said there wasn't anyone else, but she needed some more time to become stronger before she came back. That she still couldn't cope with being an army wife with me so often away overseas. But she said she was happy and peaceful within herself.'

'You're telling me you haven't seen your wife since then?' Haddad, finished with her text message, glanced at her notes. 'For over *twelve years*?'

Simon kept his gaze steady. 'Yes.'

'But you never divorced,' she said again.

'No.'

Haddad clearly couldn't comprehend it. Perhaps a woman like her wouldn't tolerate anyone lingering in her life if she didn't have a use for them.

He searched for words to explain. 'Look, I was – am – a soldier. I've almost lost count of the number of tours of Iraq and Afghanistan and other places I've done in that time. I stayed in the reserves after I left the full-time army and I'm still sent on active service. In between studying for a science degree, earning a living and my army service, getting a divorce I didn't need hasn't been a high priority. Until —' He broke off. *Until Erin walked into the National Parks office.* He had to keep her right out of this. 'About five months ago, I wrote to her, with the divorce papers and a settlement offer. I sent my new contact details when I moved here to Goodabri. But I didn't hear anything from her before I was called back to service again.'

'Not even an email or phone call?'

'No. I'm not even sure she has an email address. She's only ever contacted me by mail or phone. But I only got back to town tonight. I haven't had time to see if there's a letter.' He'd shoved the small pile of mail Snowy had collected for him into the pocket of his kit bag without flicking through it. 'I had no idea she was coming here. Last I heard, she was living in a community on the north coast and loving it. I don't know where she's been since then, what she's been doing, who her friends are. And I don't know who killed her, or why. Maybe it was someone she knew. Maybe it was someone trying to get at me.'

'I'm not interested in conjecture,' Haddad said curtly. 'Can you account for your whereabouts for the past few days?'

'I arrived back in Australia on the weekend. I left the regiment's headquarters on Monday morning. I called in to see my stepfather in the Hunter Valley for coffee. And then I drove north and camped in an isolated valley in the Oxley Wild Rivers National Park for three nights. I left there earlier this afternoon and drove back here.'

'Can anyone vouch for your presence there?'

'I doubt it.'

She zeroed in on that. 'So you have no alibi for the past three days.'

Fraser leaned forward, ignoring Haddad's scowl. 'Come on, surely someone knows you were there. You're a park ranger, right? You didn't meet up with the local rangers at all? Have a yarn at your campsite?'

'I'd just come home after seven weeks in Iraq. I wanted a few days alone to . . . readjust.' To stop being Sergeant Kennedy, with responsibility for a small group of highly trained men and a near-impossible mission deep in extremist territory, and become easygoing Simon, with a new national park to develop and a team of colleagues who weren't trained to kill anything other than feral animals.

He always needed at least a few days alone to reset his equilibrium. It took time to strip himself of the discipline, the harshness of war, to bridge the chasm between one half of his life and the other. This time he'd wished for a month but had to make do with three too-short days and nights of solitude in the wilderness.

'There's a locked gate on the road into the area. I collected the key from the depot at Walcha late on Monday afternoon.

I spoke briefly with the local ranger then. But the area I camped in is almost two hours from there. And I just dropped the key in the lockbox at the gate when I left.'

'But surely the local rangers would have been out there during that time?' Fraser persisted.

'It's wild country that few people go to, so they don't make the trip out often. The only person I saw was an old army mate. Gabe McCallum. Must have been Tuesday morning. He lives up on the tablelands but sometimes musters brumbies down in the gorge country. I met him by the river and we talked for a short while. But he left to track a mob of horses. He stayed in the area – I saw the horses a few times and signs of him – but a couple of hikers came down the river and neither of us was looking for company. I'm a commando, Detective, and he used to be one. Even a raw recruit could be invisible for days.'

'You're a commando?' Fraser asked. 'I grew up near the Holsworthy base. All the girls had their sights set on the 4 RAR commandos. Damn tough competition for us ordinary mortals.'

'Yeah, I was 4 RAR,' Simon conceded. Not that he'd had much to do with the local girls. Even then, he'd understood that the job put pressures on any decent relationship. 'I'm in the 1st Commando Regiment now. It's a mix of full-time and reserve soldiers.' When he'd agreed to stay on in the reserves, he'd envisaged more of a training role. It hadn't worked out that way.

'So can your friend verify your presence in the national park yesterday and this morning?' Haddad demanded.

'On Tuesday, yes. Whether he saw me after that, I don't know. I'll give you his contact details but he's usually out of mobile range.'

Fraser passed a notepad and pen across the table and Simon noted down Gabe's name and phone number. Maybe Gabe could give him an alibi. If they could get hold of him. Cutting promising foals out of the herds of brumbies in the gorge country gave him a reason to avoid civilisation. Since a mission had gone badly wrong a few years ago – no fault of Gabe's – he preferred the company of horses to people.

'Thanks,' Fraser said. 'We'll get on to him asap.'

Despite Fraser's matey routine, Simon didn't relax. Nor did Haddad. If it wasn't for the fine worry lines on her forehead he'd have judged her a cold-hearted woman, but she clearly took her work seriously and that suggested at least some emotional commitment. Her phone vibrated again and she glanced at the message.

'Forensics have finally arrived,' she said. 'I'll go meet them. Steve, you check on the incident room set-up. We can't work in here. Mr Kennedy, I may have some more questions for you after I've spoken with the forensic officers. Please wait here.'

'Am I under arrest?'

'Not at the moment. But your wife is dead in your house and by your own admission you probably have no alibi.' She stood, looking down at him, exuding suspicion and determination.

'As you'd expect, we need to ascertain your whereabouts for the last few days and investigate all the possibilities.'

Hands flat on the table, Simon rose to his feet. With the table between them he didn't tower over her, his intention assertion, not intimidation. 'I expect that you *will* investigate all the possibilities, Detective Haddad. I expect you to establish whether this was a targeted crime or a random one. I expect you to find out where Hayley has been, who with, and whether anyone she knows would have a reason to follow her here and kill her. And I expect you to contact army intelligence and ask them if anyone I may have pissed off in Afghanistan, Iraq, or East Timor could possibly have identified and found me.'

He deliberately, neatly, put his chair in place under the table. 'Now, if your forensic officers are searching my home I believe I have a right to be present. And since I remember what state I left the place in two months ago, I should be able to show them what, if anything, has been disturbed. So, that's where I'm going.'

He held the door open for her before he followed her out.

●

The empty half of the old double-shopfront building National Parks leased in Goodabri's main street had seen use in emergency operations before – for a joint emergency services training exercise not long after Erin came to the district, and three months ago as a police critical incident room when Jo's discovery of a body in the park had revealed a violent criminal gang operating in the area. So when Erin phoned her boss in Strathnairn to report the evening's events, Malcolm didn't hesitate for a moment in approving the cooperation between services.

'I'll call Nick now and formally offer use of the building,' he said. 'Do you need me to come out there tonight?'

Drive seventy kilometres each way to open up a building when she was already on the spot? 'No, I'll deal with it, Mal. I'll see you tomorrow.'

Yet when she parked behind the deserted building she wished she had asked Mal to come. Walking into a dark, empty building at night when a murderer was out there, somewhere . . . She glanced back at the shed where the folding tables and chairs were stored. The shed she hadn't been into for over a week. The main building itself should be safe enough – the other staff had been in and out of there all day, and she'd been in an hour or two ago to drop off the keys – but she'd wait until someone else came before she went to get the tables.

She unlocked the back door of the empty side of the building first, and without going in, called out, 'If anyone's lurking in here, you've got five minutes to escape before I come in. The police are on their way, so be quick.'

Silly, perhaps, but it couldn't hurt and at least there were no neighbours around to hear her being paranoid. Inside the National Parks office, she collected the basic essentials for people working late into the night – mugs, coffee, milk and sugar.

She didn't spook easily, but she'd far rather be out in the bush alone than walking into the empty rooms of the office next door, especially with her hands full. The mugs clutched in her fingers clunked against each other as she reached to thumb the light switch inside the rear door. The bare bulb flared to life, and her pulse skipped a beat as she caught movement out of the corner of her eye. A huge huntsman spider scuttling up the wall. It stopped at eye level, watching her. Harmless enough, but she gave it a wide berth, dumped the mugs on the table in the kitchenette, and found a broom to encourage it out the door.

The mirror image of the National Parks side of the building, this side likewise had a tiny bathroom, a windowless storeroom, and a small office tucked in behind the large front room that had for over a century housed a general store. Now it waited, echoing and empty, dust coating the wooden floor, for the few times it came to life when space was needed to coordinate emergency responses: fires, readiness exercises, murder investigations. An old ice-cream poster on the wall watched over it all, a reminder of normality.

Mal must have got on to Nick and the police authorities quickly, for Erin had only just opened the blinds on the large front windows when a police car pulled up outside. Matt Carruthers, one of the constables from Strathnairn. In his early thirties, Matt had plenty of country policing experience, handling the job with dedication and a sense of humour, and reliable in a crisis.

'Nick sent me over to start getting things sorted,' he told her when she unlocked the front door to let him in.

Erin handed him the broom. 'If you can sweep up the dust, I'll bring over the urn from our office and get it heating for coffee. Then you can give me a hand getting the tables from the shed.'

Matt grinned. 'Caffeine first. I like your priorities. It's going to be a long night. Homicide in Sydney have sent DS Haddad here again. Do you remember her?'

'I saw her in action last time. She's very . . .' Erin sought a polite word, '. . . determined, isn't she?'

Matt didn't bother with polite. 'Hard-ass Haddad. Rumour has it she can bust balls with a telekinetic glare.'

'I wouldn't let her hear you say that, if I were you,' a male voice drawled at the doorway. 'Or you might find out if it's true.'

Matt straightened to attention, the broom still clasped in one hand. 'Sorry, sir.'

The guy strolled in, his suit jacket slung over one shoulder and a laptop bag in his other hand. He glanced at Matt's nametag. 'Relax, Carruthers. I won't tell her. I'm DS Steve Fraser.' He turned a hundred-watt grin on Erin. 'Did I hear someone mention coffee?'

'Coming soon, courtesy of interagency cooperation.' Erin indicated the National Parks and Wildlife Service badge on her uniform sleeve. 'I'm Erin Taylor, one of the rangers. Our office and visitor centre is in the other half of this building.' She matched the firmness of Fraser's handshake. Despite the boyish grin, he had a few years on her – she'd place him in his late thirties, perhaps even early forties.

'You're a colleague of Simon Kennedy's?' he asked.

'Yes. Our district office is in Strathnairn. We manage four parks and three conservation areas, most of them closer to Strathnairn. But we have this office for the new Goodabri Rivers park nearby. I've been overseeing the park and its development while Simon was away.'

The cheerful grin had softened, replaced with a relaxed but professional regard. 'Inspector Matheson – Nick – said you were with Simon when he found the victim.'

'Yes. I'm happy to answer any questions you or your colleagues have.' She'd gone over those few minutes in Simon's house with Nick already, but once the preliminaries were established he'd said he wouldn't be running the investigation, because of Jo's friendship with Simon, and because as acting inspector he was overseeing all police operations in the district. So she'd tell the little she knew again, to Fraser or the other detective, however many times it took.

'Thanks, Erin, I appreciate it. We'll have a chat as soon as things are set up here.' Fraser turned to Matt, systematically wielding the broom along the length of the main room. 'Any idea of the arrangements for comms, Carruthers?'

'Techs are coming from Tamworth but they'll be a while yet.'

'Data coverage is fairly patchy out here on the mobile network,' Erin told Fraser. 'And even satellite broadband won't be anywhere near what you're used to in Sydney.'

'Sydney? Oh, I'm not from Homicide. I'm just a country detective. I work mostly out of Birraga these days. But I happened to be at the same meeting in Tenterfield as Nick today, and he's roped me in to this one.'

Birraga, a couple of hours south – she knew the name, had seen it in the news not so long ago, with a series of violent crimes. Fraser had described himself as 'just a country detective', but if he'd been in Birraga this past year or so, he'd have notched up plenty of experience in murder investigations.

He didn't seem to mind turning his hand to anything, though. When she returned from next door with the urn, he and Matt had fetched the first of the large folding tables from the shed and were wiping off the dust with damp handtowels from the bathroom.

'We have a whiteboard you can borrow if you need it,' she offered. 'I'll need a hand moving it, though.'

Fraser volunteered before she finished speaking. As they manoeuvred the large, awkward whiteboard out of the Parks office via the front door, he asked casually, 'How long have you and Simon worked together?'

The very casualness of the question put her on alert. 'I joined the Strathnairn office about ten, eleven months ago. I'd met him a few times before that, though, at meetings and training sessions – I worked out of Armidale before here.'

'Did you ever meet his wife?'

A trick question? Trying to find holes in whatever Simon might have said in their interview? She could only assume he'd told the police what he'd told her. She kept her answer simple and honest. 'No.'

He waited until they'd angled the whiteboard in through the next door before he asked, 'Do you know him well?'

'We work together in a demanding job. We're also volunteers with the SES. We're friends as well as colleagues, but there's nothing more to it than that.'

'You're both in the SES? So you'll have seen him in some stressful situations?'

No mistaking the direction of his questions now. The friendly help in lugging things around was just an excuse for an off-the-record interview. All the questions about Simon meant he had to have some suspicions. Suspicions she planned on dispelling, fast.

'Yes, I've seen him in plenty of stressful situations.' She shoved her end of the whiteboard against the wall harder than she'd intended and locked the wheels with a stamp of her boot before she faced him. 'I don't know what you think we do, but National Parks work isn't all about picnics and possums. As well as project planning and park management, we deal with illegal shooters, bushfires, search and rescue, floods, the works. Sometimes,' she gave him a sardonic smile, 'all on the same day. And I can assure you that if I'm going to be abseiling down a cliff to reach a kid stranded by a bushfire, then the person I'd most want to have with me is Simon, because he's damned calm and cool-headed in a crisis. I have never, ever seen him lose his temper.'

Unlike herself. She'd barely kept hers from exploding. Tiredness and the emotional toll of the last couple of hours were undermining her self-control. Shit. She had to get on top of it, concentrate on answering Fraser's questions without being snarky. For Simon's sake – and for Hayley's.

'He's a soldier, seen a lot of active service. What about PTSD?' Fraser must have noticed her over-reaction, but he kept his manner casual, curious, as if he wasn't grilling her about a murder suspect. 'Any signs of that?'

Post-traumatic stress disorder? Erin couldn't think of any occasion when she'd had cause to doubt Simon's emotional or mental stability. 'I know he's served in war zones. He doesn't talk about it much, other than in passing. But he's a very together person. Very . . .' How could she say what she meant? Explain her sense of the solidity of Simon's character? 'Very . . . grounded. Level-headed. Look, talk to Nick. He's become friends with Simon. They're both martial-arts types. Nick's done years of undercover work and I guess that's not so different from the military. I'm sure you'll trust his judgement more than —'

A sharp, loud crack sounded behind her and she spun around, heart stalling.

'It's okay,' Fraser said, his hand steadying on her shoulder for a moment. 'It's just Carruthers.'

Adrenaline flooding her body, Erin tried to breathe slowly. Just Matt, carrying in a stack of chairs from the shed, letting the flyscreen door at the back thwack hard against the frame as he came through. Just Matt, and she'd jumped almost to the ceiling, in front of the detective.

'I'm sorry,' she said to Fraser, embarrassment making her laugh thin and strained. 'I'm edgy, I guess. Knowing there's a murderer lurking around, somewhere out there. I'm going to be wary of every sound, every dark place, every stranger until you arrest the bastard, Detective.'

His brown eyes watched her, not unkindly, but not softly, either. 'Stranger? Be careful, yes, but be aware, too. Far more often than not, murder victims are killed by people they know.'

She stared back at him. 'You can't seriously believe Simon killed her. It's impossible. He wouldn't kill any —'

Fraser raised an eyebrow and her voice trailed away as reality hit.

Simon was a soldier. A commando. Had been for years. Her easygoing, reliable friend was very capable of killing a person, in any number of ways.

She swallowed against a dry throat and turned away from the detective, unexpected tears burning her eyes.

CHAPTER 3

A few neighbours and other townspeople had gathered at a curious but respectful distance from his house, beyond the police tape and the growing collection of official vehicles.

Simon walked down the driveway beside Nick and Haddad, aware of the eyes watching him. Conjecture would be running wild, transforming quickly into rumour and gossip. After all, they barely knew him. He'd moved here from Strathnairn only a month before his latest call-up, and although some of them already knew him through his National Parks and SES work in the wider district, he was still a newcomer, a stranger in their midst. Unless someone had seen Hayley, or her killer, they had no reason to trust him or believe in his innocence.

The senior forensic officer who met them at the door wasted few words on polite sympathy. 'Can you tell me exactly what you did when you arrived earlier?' he asked. 'How you came in, where you walked, what you touched?'

No longer on alert for danger, as he entered his house this time Simon immediately began looking for anything out of place. Not easy, with detectives on either side of him, and forensic officers already moving methodically through the rooms. He described his earlier movements, answered questions, all the while fighting the urge to drag the officers standing around Hayley's body away from her, to protect her from their impersonal scrutiny.

Small, fragile and defenceless, but he hadn't been there to protect her from the killer who'd stabbed her multiple times. He couldn't even protect her from the man who photographed the wounds and described her condition into a voice recorder.

He'd caused her so much grief, when he'd only wanted to keep her safe from harm. If it turned out someone had come here looking for him and found her . . . He pushed past Nick and walked out of the room, hardly able to draw air into his lungs.

In the kitchen, one of the forensic officers lifted out the plastic bag lining the swing-top rubbish bin beside the sink. A bag hanging straight, lightly weighted with rubbish.

Simon reached out a hand to take it but the woman held it back. Of course. They weren't going to allow him to touch anything. 'I emptied that before I left,' he told her. 'I put in a clean bag.'

There was a soft metallic clink as the officer lowered the bag to the floor and opened the top to peer inside.

Nick must have followed him and overheard. 'What's in there?' he asked from behind Simon.

Her glance darted to Simon before she answered the detective. 'Cans. An empty packet or two.' She reached in with a gloved hand, carefully shifting the contents. 'One tin was sliced peaches. There's a salmon can, too. And . . .' She pulled out three plastic wrappers, uncrinkled them to see the labels. 'Skim milk powder. Nuts. And a muesli bar.'

Long-life food. Nothing perishable. 'I had all those things in the pantry,' Simon said. 'I emptied the fridge before I left and switched it off.' His thoughts racing to process the possibilities, he turned to Nick. 'Hayley must have needed food. You saw how skinny she is. And her clothes . . .' That simple white dress, the scuffed and worn leather sandals. 'She can't have had much money.'

Haddad crossed the passage from the study to join them. 'Is there any drug paraphernalia?'

Simon's anger flared as the forensic officer started to go through the rubbish again. 'Hayley didn't do drugs,' he insisted.

'You have no idea what she did or didn't do in the last twelve years,' Haddad retorted.

The truth of it stung, but Simon didn't let Haddad see it. 'No. But I knew her for years before that. Her mother was an addict. Hayley was determined not to be like her and avoided all drugs. She wouldn't even take a painkiller.'

'People change. Make sure you collect the bathroom bin contents, too,' she instructed the officer.

'Do you always believe the worst of people?' he grilled Haddad as he followed her out.

'Yes. It's quicker and easier. I'm rarely pleasantly surprised.'

Easier? Haddad possibly didn't realise how much she'd revealed with her use of the word and with the almost inaudible sigh that followed it. Not as hard as the persona she projected. That gave Simon more hope. If Haddad genuinely cared about victims, then she'd care about truth, too, and about justice.

In his bedroom, his bed was as neatly made as he'd left it, the light summer blanket unrumpled. The clean jeans and t-shirts that he'd hurriedly brought in from the washing line and dumped on the end of the bed had been neatly folded. A lump formed in his throat. But then he caught sight of an orange blanket and a pillow on a beanbag in the corner and it almost undid him, the shock a sledgehammer to his gut, making him grip the doorframe for stability while the room wavered in front of him.

'What is it?' he heard Haddad ask.

A memory. A memory of a rushed marriage, a hurried move from barracks to an apartment, a delivery van that failed to arrive with a new bedroom suite and bedding . . . His wedding night he'd just been able to afford the honeymoon suite in a Parramatta hotel, but the second night of their married life they'd curled up together on the beanbag on the floor of the empty bedroom of their new apartment, cuddling under the orange blanket they'd found at an op shop minutes before it closed.

Whenever he'd come back from deployments, Hayley always had that blanket on the bed, a bright splash of colour against the subdued blues in the room. He'd kept both the blanket and the beanbag, all these years, because it never seemed right to get rid of them.

'Kennedy? Are you okay?'

'Yeah,' he lied. He cleared his throat. 'Hayley loved that blanket. She must have found it in the wardrobe. The beanbag was over there, under the window, so she's moved it.' To the corner between the bed and the wall. Tucked in where no one could see her from the window, and barely from the door. 'She could have used my bed, or the bed in the other room. So why huddle down there?'

Haddad folded her arms and studied him coolly. 'Some men treat their wives like dogs,' she said.

He silently counted to three before he answered, crushing his anger for a more reasoned response. 'You must have seen some atrocious things in your career, Detective. But most men respect and do their best to care for the people they love.'

'Did you love her?' Haddad challenged.

No clear answer sprang to his mind. His gaze drifted back to the orange blanket, the memories of the first days of his marriage vivid. He made an attempt to answer the question honestly. 'I thought I did,' he said. 'But I'm not sure anyone really understands about love in their early twenties. And the army demands a lot from any marriage. I meant my vows, though, and honouring them was important to me.' And he'd kept them, all of the formal ones of the marriage service. It was his own vow to protect her that he'd failed in, too many times. He'd protected her from her father, in those early years. But that hadn't been enough.

'You should contact her father,' he said to Haddad. 'He is . . . at least he was . . . involved in drug dealing. He served a few years in prison in Victoria. Hayley's evidence – she was only fifteen – helped put him there. He never forgave her, and when he got out he threatened to kill her.' That's why she'd run to Simon, terrified, catching an overnight bus from Melbourne to Sydney to find him at Holsworthy army base. Only his own threats, backed up by four of his army mates who joined him in a desperate drive to Melbourne on a few days off, had made the bastard keep his distance from Hayley.

Haddad looked doubtful, as though she still wanted him in the frame. 'I'll need a name, address, whatever you know about him.'

'I kept a file for a while. He was convicted of a series of aggravated assaults about ten years ago, and went back to prison. He might be out by now.'

'You kept a file? What kind of file?'

'Just a few records, mostly media reports of the second conviction. I had a private investigator check on him, years ago, to make sure he was still in Victoria, away from Hayley. It's all on my computer.' The one smashed on the floor of his study. 'The hard drive is backed up online. I can get the file for you.'

'Hmm. Forensics may be able to get it off your hard drive.'

Shit, she was trying his patience. He blew a long breath out through his nose to try to keep his anger in check. 'Detective Haddad, examining the scene of a murder is one thing. But I believe searching my computer files requires a warrant.'

A quick gleam in her eyes almost made it to a smile. 'Do you have something to hide, Kennedy?'

He briefly considered handing her the drive there and then. If she expected gigabytes of porn and other suspect activity then the actual contents would disappoint her. But principle and procedure mattered.

'Private doesn't equate with criminal, Detective,' he reminded her. 'My personal correspondence, papers and journals are private, and not relevant to this. Except . . .' Yes, except one. 'I can give you a copy of the letter and the settlement offer I sent five months ago to the last address I had for Hayley, from years ago. I assumed she hadn't received it because she didn't respond.'

Until now. She'd come to him and he'd not been there for her. So she'd clung to the orange blanket with its reminders of youthful love and optimism, just as she'd clung to it through his long absences during their marriage, and as usual he'd returned too late.

He'd never be able to sleep in this room again without the bright image of that blanket haunting his dreams. But then he'd likely never be able to sleep in this room again at all.

'Your computer is part of a crime scene, Kennedy,' Haddad said bluntly. 'I have every right to take it into evidence and search it.'

He shrugged and didn't object further. His privacy didn't matter that much in the circumstances.

Out in the passage, he hesitated, undecided which way to go. Not back into his study, where Hayley lay. Nor the kitchen, where she'd fed herself meagrely from his cupboards. Needing space and air, he headed for the front door. After one last glance around the bedroom, Haddad followed him, until a voice calling his name halted them both.

He turned. The senior forensic officer – Simon couldn't recall his name – apologised for interrupting. 'I'm going to need your fingerprints, Mr Kennedy. It's just routine. We need to be able to determine which prints are yours and which prints . . . aren't.'

'No worries,' he answered without thinking. Stupid thing to say, when of course he had worries.

He followed the man outside to the forensic van.

'My fingerprints will be all over the knife,' he said, while the officer – Cunningham, his nametag read – pulled out a case from the back. 'It's one I use regularly.'

Cunningham made no comment, but Haddad, Simon noticed, hovered nearby, listening and watching.

'It's your favourite, is it?' she asked.

If she was trying to trip him up, she wouldn't succeed. In eighteen years as a commando, he'd been through advanced interrogation training and exercises multiple times. Nothing she did or said could approach the treatment he'd received from the trainers. He could stick to name, rank and number through days of the harshest handling. But they were supposed to be on the same side, so he'd give her more than that. 'I do a lot of cooking,' he answered.

As he laid out his equipment on a folding table from the van, Cunningham asked, 'Would Hayley have had a house key? Or would the house have been left unlocked?'

'No. I definitely locked all the doors before I left. And Hayley doesn't have a key to this house. I only moved in ten weeks ago.'

Haddad stepped closer, hemming him in between Cunningham and the van door. 'There's no sign of forced entry, Kennedy. Can you explain how your wife got inside?'

'Not for certain.' He held her gaze while the forensic officer pressed his finger against the scanner. 'But there's a spare key on a magnet under the table on the back veranda. We had a different table in Sydney, but that's where we kept the spare key then.'

'Mr Kennedy . . .' Cunningham began, but although he maintained his courteous manner, he gripped Simon's hand more firmly and didn't press the next finger onto the scanner. 'Is that blood around your fingernails?'

Blood? Simon looked down at his hand, at the traces of a dark substance around the edges of the nail and under the blunt, work-short tips. How the hell had blood . . . ? The memory of his journey back this afternoon re-formed, although hazily, as though it was days rather than hours ago. 'I found a wallaby on my way out of the national park. A wild dog had got it, started ripping into it. It was dead, but only just, so I checked its pouch for a joey. I didn't have a lot of water left to wash my hands thoroughly afterwards.'

Haddad snorted. 'Oh, nice story, Kennedy. Quite original. I just don't happen to believe it.' She drew herself up straighter, and although she still had to look up at him, her face hardened and the solidity of her stance became a warning. 'I'm arresting you on suspicion of murder. You do not have to say anything. However, anything you say or do may be noted and used in evidence. Do you understand that?'

He could have protested, but he remained silent and allowed her to snap the handcuffs on his wrists. Clearly she wanted to secure the evidence on his fingernails before he could scrub it off. They would find the truth of the blood soon enough – assuming their analysis could tell the difference between macropod and human blood. But as for all the other evidence . . . yeah, not surprising she'd focused on him.

He'd just have to clear his name, somehow, and fast. Because whoever had killed Hayley was still out there, and if they were targeting him, it might not take them long to discover his close friendship with Erin.

•

Erin waited in the Parks office, half-heartedly attempting to work while all the time her attention was split between the activity next door and keeping watch for Simon. Even if he didn't call her to check on her – and she expected her phone to ring any moment – he'd see the lights on and come in. He'd have to. He had nowhere else to go, with his house a crime scene and Goodabri's small hotel booked out with detectives and forensic officers.

When a car pulled up outside, she hurried to unlock the door . . . but it wasn't Simon. It was Bruce Lockyer, one of the National Parks staff who'd worked a few days a week in the Goodabri office since an injury took him off fieldwork. A colleague she regarded as a friend. In his sixties, he had a gentle way about him and a respect for women that might have had something to do with his long and devoted marriage and the two adult daughters of whom he was immensely proud. Although she didn't think of him as a paternal figure, Erin sometimes wished her own father had been more like him.

'What's going on, Erin?' Bruce asked as soon as she let him in. 'I was at a Lions Club meeting at the pub and rumours are flying. The police have blocked off Simon's street. I saw the lights here. Tell me he's all right?'

'Simon's not hurt,' she assured him. 'It's . . .' She didn't know how much she could, or should, say. Or how to say it.

'The police are setting up next door. It's something bad, isn't it?'

In a small community like Goodabri, everyone knew the police would only come in numbers for a major crime. And if the mortuary van hadn't driven through town yet, it would soon. News would fly that there'd been a murder, and where.

Erin nodded. She led Bruce into the office kitchen, and dragged out a couple of chairs from the rickety table. The fatigue draining her body made her grateful to sit.

'Simon just got back tonight. I was with him when he went into his house, and we found . . . a murder victim. A woman. Simon's . . .' She might as well say it. 'Simon's wife.'

'His wife? Simon's not —' Bruce shook his head. 'He's never mentioned being married.'

'Yes, well, he is, apparently. I didn't know either.'

'You didn't know? But you two are —' He broke off, his cheeks flushing.

The warmth in her own face might have just been from the stuffiness of the kitchen. 'We're friends, Bruce. That's all.' Maybe if she kept repeating it, she and everyone else might believe it. 'He said they've been separated for a long time.'

'And she was murdered? In his house?'

'Yes.'

'No. No. I don't . . .' His face paled to grey, his hand shaking as he rubbed his head, and he suddenly seemed much older than his years. 'Listen, you said you saw her. Was she . . . was she a skinny woman, doll-like? Young? Maybe thirties? Long hair? Hippy-type dress?'

'Yes. All that.' Concerned about his stress, Erin laid her hand gently on his across the table. 'Bruce, did you see her?'

He dropped his head and nodded. 'It was on Monday afternoon, not long before I closed up here. She came in, looking for Simon. I told her he was away and we weren't sure when he'd be back. She was a little thing, quite shy, just said he was an old friend and she was passing through town. I didn't think anything more of it, assumed she'd just gone on her way. But it must have been her.'

He'd gripped her hand almost painfully tight, but Erin didn't move it. The chance of the woman he'd seen being someone else? Close to zilch. On Monday afternoon, Hayley had been here. Today was Thursday. And she'd been killed maybe yesterday or this morning.

'If I'd only done something . . .' Bruce muttered.

'Bruce, you couldn't have known.' Who was she trying to convince – him or herself? She thought it through, aloud. 'She didn't tell you who she was. Simon had never told us she existed. If she'd asked for help you would have found a way to help her.' He'd have taken her home to his wife and they'd have looked after her as though she were their own. 'If she was in town for a few days, surely other people must have seen her or spoken with her.'

Restless, driven to do *something*, she went to the sink, filled the electric kettle with water and dumped a couple of tea bags into mugs. Tea. A good strong cup of tea might give Bruce enough composure for his drive home on dirt roads to his wife. Eventually. And she could do with one herself. 'I'll go next door, tell the detective you saw her. Are you okay to talk with him?'

'Yes.' He cleared his throat and repeated it more strongly. 'Yes. I'll just phone Mary-Rose. She'll worry if I'm late.'

Lucky Bruce, to have someone like Mary-Rose to worry about him. She shoved aside the thought and left the room to do something useful.

Next door, someone from the pub had delivered the platters of hearty sandwiches and pizzas that Erin had arranged earlier. Matt was still there, setting up a computer with the IT guy from the Strathnairn station. Steve Fraser munched on a slice of pizza held in one hand while he typed rapidly on his laptop with the other.

Hearing Matt greet her, Steve glanced up, and that rakish, all-charm grin dissolved the frown he'd been wearing. He waved the slice of pizza. 'I gather we have you to thank for organising this. Caffeine *and* food. You're a goddess.'

Erin disguised the swift rush of pleasure at the unaccustomed compliment with an indelicate snort. 'Definitely not a domestic one. But if you've got a feral goat problem, or you need a firebreak burned, that's my realm.'

He laughed outright, but when she told him why she'd come, he was all detective again, the frivolity swiftly erased. 'He saw her on Monday? Is he sure of the day?'

'Yes. He's only working Mondays and Fridays at the moment.'

'Right. I'll need to talk with him. Is he still around?'

'Next door. He's a bit shaken.'

'Grab some pizza and sambos and we'll go and have a chat with him.'

Erin glanced at the food, too keyed up to feel hungry, although she hadn't eaten much all day.

'Take some while you can,' he urged. 'Forensics and the rest of the horde will be here shortly and there won't be anything left after that.'

She wrapped a couple of sandwiches in paper serviettes. She might be hungry once she stopped. Simon might be hungry, too. Not quite the pub meal he'd suggested hours ago, but there'd be nowhere open to get food later, either here or in Strathnairn, and her own fridge was pretty bare.

Bruce had filled in the time she was gone making some notes on a writing pad and drinking his industrial-strength tea.

'I wrote everything down,' he told the detective, tearing the sheet off the pad and passing it to him. 'It's not a lot. What she looked like, what she said, as best as I can remember. There were a couple of other people here when she came in, so I didn't have a lot of time to talk with her.'

Fraser pulled out a chair and sat down at the table, genial and approachable. Erin watched him from where she leaned against the kitchen bench, trying to gauge if his manner was genuine or calculated.

'Did you see her around town after that?' he asked. 'At the pub, maybe, or even in the distance?'

'No. No, I'm sure I would have noticed. But I live out of town on the Strathnairn road, and I've hardly been in Goodabri since Monday.'

Fraser glanced between Bruce and Erin, including them both. 'So, if we want to find out if anyone else saw her, what's the best way of getting the message around town? Is there a local radio station or newspaper?'

Erin gave him points for asking advice, consulting community members, but it still could have been a practised performance rather than genuine interest. Her once well-developed bullshit detector had been idle for a while, and she no longer knew if she could rely on it.

'Tomorrow's newspaper has already gone to print,' she said. 'They could probably put something online in the morning, but posters around town would be more effective. In the pub, in the bakery, at the service station. That would get people talking.'

'Good. I'll get some posters made, and we'll try that.' His phone buzzed and he pulled it from his pocket and glanced at it in a smooth, quick move. And then he swore.

He muttered an apology, but she wasn't sure if that was for swearing, for the loud scrape of his chair as he pushed it back, or for his abrupt departure from the room, already thumbing a number on his phone and putting it to his ear. Before the front door closed behind him she heard, 'Why the hell did you arrest him?'

Arrest? Erin's brain raced. Whose arrest, so early in the investigation, would Fraser be shocked by? She went to the window to try to hear his side of the conversation, both desperate for and afraid of the answer. Only one answer made sense – but it didn't make sense. How could they have arrested Simon? *Why* would they?

Through a gap in the blinds, she could see Fraser pacing up and down under the streetlight, the road deserted. She stopped short of going outside, but he spoke loudly enough that she heard his words, and the vain hope that he might have been discussing an entirely different case – or man – dissolved.

'*Shit.* Yeah, well, you'll have to bring him here for now until we can take him to Strathnairn. The local station doesn't have holding facilities.'

The old wooden floorboards creaked behind her and she spun around, but it was only Bruce, entirely harmless in his checked shirt, his hand around the stoneware mug.

'I think they've arrested Simon,' she said, keeping her voice low.

Bruce's frown creased his face. 'Simon? But he couldn't have . . .'

'That's what I want to think, too.'

Bruce gave her a sharp glance, but she didn't say any more. She wanted to believe in Simon, to believe in the friendship they'd shared, in the trust she'd placed in him again and again in multiple dangerous situations. But fingers of doubt clawed at that belief, scraping away certainty. He might not have lied to her, but he'd lied by omission. Despite their friendship, he'd kept secrets. His wife, his active army service, his commando expertise.

How could she trust, how could she believe in a man who hid that much of himself? And how could she know what else he hid, and what he was capable of?

•

To be arrested and cuffed in full view of his neighbours was bad enough, but walking from the police car to the makeshift incident room with Erin watching . . . that was a humiliation Simon found hard to bear.

He met her gaze, tried to convey with an attempt at a smile that it would all be okay, but the pain in her eyes gouged him and he feared that even if proof of his innocence came quickly, nothing would be the same between them again. Shame ate at him – not so much for the cuffs on his wrists, but for the hurt he'd caused her, when he'd only wanted to do the right thing. He'd been so determined not to betray Hayley, he'd betrayed Erin instead.

He saw Bruce standing behind Erin in the open doorway of the National Parks building, and despite Haddad's firm grip on his arm he stopped on the pathway. 'Erin, can you stay with Bruce tonight? It might be safer if you don't go home alone.'

She glanced back at Bruce, who nodded, before she demanded, 'What the hell's going on, Simon?'

Simon shook his head. 'I don't know. But this —' he raised his cuffed hands slightly, 'will be sorted by morning. I'll come into the Strathnairn office then.'

Haddad huffed an irritated breath and he succumbed to the pressure on his arm to go inside. He didn't look back at Erin. She hadn't rejected out of hand the idea of going to Bruce's, and he had to hope she'd agree to it. But after Haddad had instructed him to sit at one of the tables while they arranged transport to the larger station, he considered enlisting help in persuading Erin.

Matt Carruthers and three other officers from Strathnairn – cops he'd worked alongside on various rescues and incidents in the parks – carefully avoided looking at him, concentrating on results from a doorknock around town. Cunningham and his crime scene offsider were occupied with preparing to take samples from the blood around his fingernails. Haddad entered data on a laptop, presumably logging details of his arrest.

Only Fraser acknowledged his presence. 'Can I get you a coffee? Or some not-quite-congealed pizza?'

'Just coffee, thanks.' The burger he'd bought at the Macca's drive-through in Glen Innes hours ago still sat heavily in his gut.

They'd handcuffed his wrists in front, not behind his back, and he took the large mug Fraser brought him in both hands and breathed in the caffeine fumes.

The detective propped himself against the table. 'We've got this whole procedure we have to do when someone's arrested.

The custody sergeant at Strathnairn will go through it with you, but since that's a little while off, is there anything we should know now? Medications? Allergies? Other medical conditions?'

More of the good-cop routine. Perhaps hoping he'd relax and let something slip. Or perhaps not.

'No medical conditions.'

'Good. Won't be long before they take you to Strathnairn – just waiting on a car from there. The custody sarge will allow you to contact a lawyer. Nothing else worrying you?'

On a hunch, Simon decided to take the good-cop persona at face value. 'Have you met Erin?'

'Your colleague next door? Yes.'

'Can you persuade her to stay with friends tonight? It may not be safe for her to go home alone.'

'Not safe? Why?'

Simon looked him straight in the eye. 'Because Hayley was brutally murdered in my house, and I'm not the killer. Erin lives alone, and this whole district knows that we're workmates and friends. If someone's trying to get to me, they might target her.'

Fraser appeared to be considering the request, but before he could respond a car pulled up outside, a door slammed, and Nick strode in, his face troubled.

'We need to get a team together quickly,' he announced to the room in general. 'Campers in the Goodabri Rivers park have phoned in an emergency call – they saw a woman go over the falls at the Niland Gorge about an hour ago, and they think she might have been pushed.'

Simon's mind raced through implications and possibilities. Three waterfalls in the park, and it had to be Angel Falls – the least accessible. 'It's very rocky at the base and there's not much deep water,' he told them, 'but there's a chance she survived the fall. There's no vehicle access, though – it's a four-kilometre walk in. You'll need a guide. I'll —'

Haddad didn't let him finish. 'I'll take Kennedy into Strathnairn and keep things going on the case, as we can only hold him for a limited time. Steve, you lead the team into the gorge. Get one of the other park rangers to go with you.'

Simon clenched his hands around the mug. With Jo on restricted duties, there were no 'other' rangers familiar with that park, except for Erin.

As if reading his mind, Nick asked quietly, 'Does Erin know the area, Simon? Or one of the field staff?'

'Yes, she does. We surveyed for a new track there a little while ago.' The day before his call-up came. A day of sunshine, rewarding work and companionship, and he'd held on to the memory through long nights in frigid, barren mountains in northern Iraq. 'But I probably know the river access better, and you'll need to search all along the gorge. Nick, let me take them out there. Please.'

Despite his senior status as acting inspector, Nick turned to Haddad. 'Detective?' The formality of his address when he'd known Haddad for years signalled that he wouldn't use his rank to override her. At least, not in public, and perhaps not so early in an investigation he'd put her in charge of. In the short time Simon had known Nick, he'd seen that fairness and respect again and again.

Haddad glared at Nick as if daring him to challenge her. 'No, Nick. I'm not releasing him now. The evidence we have so far points to him, and I need what's on his hands. Plus out there, where he knows the land, he's too much of a flight risk.'

Nick gave no indication as to whether he agreed or disagreed. 'Steve, if Erin's still next door, ask her if she's willing to go. She's SES as well as Parks, so she'll know the drill.'

Simon considered arguing, even momentarily imagined leaping to his feet and fighting his way out the door. But no matter how easily he could do it, even with the handcuffs, it would be stupid. Haddad wore a handgun on her hip – they all wore them, but Haddad wouldn't hesitate to fire at him.

His injury or death wouldn't protect Erin, out there in the wilderness in the dark night. She was capable and professional and he had to let her go and do her job, no matter that the access down the gorge was narrow, steep and dangerous in daylight, let alone darkness; no matter that at least one killer still roamed free, and perhaps another had pushed a woman over a cliff.

CHAPTER 4

Urgency and its accompanying rush of adrenaline stifled, at least for now, the tiredness that had been dragging at Erin's mind and body.

'The falls are only about forty metres high,' she explained to Steve Fraser as she hastily pulled equipment from the storeroom shelves and handed it to him to stack. 'But they're at the top of a narrow and rocky gorge. The river's flowing reasonably well at the moment. If she fell into the waterhole at the base, she might be okay. But if she hit the rocks, we'll be carrying her out. Or winching her.' She passed him a couple of bags of abseiling gear. 'Have you done much hanging off cliffs?'

His mouth quirked in a quick grin. 'Yep. Did a stint in search and rescue. I have all the certificates somewhere in a drawer.'

'Good. But you aren't going to be abseiling in those clothes.' She nodded at his grey suit trousers and leather shoes as she hoisted a bag of ropes onto her shoulder.

'I've got overalls in my car,' he said. 'We'll load this and I'll change while you're briefing the others.'

A few minutes later, the small group gathered around the map spread on the information counter. Bruce, Matt, Tess, Nick, a couple of other constables from Strathnairn, and Fraser at the back, stripped to his jocks and t-shirt without inhibition and dragging on overalls while she talked. She didn't officially have charge of this operation – that responsibility lay with Nick – but they all looked to her for her knowledge of the area.

'The Niland River campground is the closest vehicle access. That's the best place for a staging ground. Nick, I suggest the officers you've called in and the SES from Strathnairn meet us there.'

He nodded agreement. 'I'll coordinate things from there. What's the access like to the river?'

'There's a walking track up to the falls lookout here —' she followed the line of the track on the map with her finger, 'but we've really tried to discourage people from going to the falls themselves, so the old track beyond the lookout is closed.'

'The witnesses said they'd just got to the lookout when they saw her at the edge,' Nick said. 'Just before she fell.'

'It's dark,' Fraser commented, buckling a police equipment vest over his overalls. 'How can they be sure of what they saw?'

'There's a full moon. They're not sure if they saw one or two people at the edge, but they're agreed that they saw a woman fall.' Nick paused for a moment before he added, 'A woman in a white dress.'

A woman in a white dress . . . Erin swallowed. Two in one day? It had to be just coincidence – but she hadn't noticed white dresses suddenly becoming super fashionable.

Fraser raised an eyebrow at Nick, evidently also noting the coincidence, but he asked nothing more and she silenced her own questions. Her job was finding the woman; the police investigation could make the connections if any existed. She reached for a photo she'd taken off the display board. 'This is the view of the falls from the lookout. You can see there's a fairly wide, flat area at the top – when it's not high, the river breaks into numerous channels through the rocks. You can often rock-hop across it. But a few of the channels are deep, and can be fast flowing. If she fell from this area, here, she may have hit the water below, where it's deepest. But if she fell from either side of that . . . it's rocks below. There's some water in places, but not enough to break a fall from that height.'

She didn't have to spell out the rest for them. Unless the woman had been very lucky, they'd be carrying a body bag out of the gorge. And if by chance she had survived the fall, her injuries were likely to be severe and time-critical.

'There's a walking track from the campground that goes about two kilometres along the river bank,' Erin continued. 'Not up as far as the gorge, though. Nick, if you send the SES team along there, they can check that downstream section. Just in case she's made it that far.'

'What's on the other side of the gorge?' Fraser asked. 'Is there easier access from that side?'

'Up here near the falls,' Erin circled the area on the map, 'the national park boundary is only about two hundred metres away. Beyond that is private property, a few thousand hectares, but a lot of it is scrub and there are no access tracks to the falls that I'm aware of. I gather the property was sold some months ago, but I haven't had any contact with the new owners.'

Nick considered the map. 'The campers said they hadn't seen anyone at the campsite, and no vehicles. So the woman could have come from that property to the north.'

'Possibly,' Erin agreed. 'Or from the state forest next to it, here. There's an old fire trail that runs parallel with the gorge on that side, but it hasn't been cleared for years.'

If someone *had* pushed the woman, Erin couldn't help hoping that person had gone north, rather than back towards the camping area. Even with armed police in the team, she didn't want to encounter a killer in the dark on a rough bush track.

•

'Detective Haddad, you have already asked my client these questions at least twice, and he has answered them. By my calculation, you have less than three hours remaining before you must either release or charge him. May I respectfully suggest that you are wasting everyone's time going over the same ground.'

Simon watched the silent battle of wills between the two women facing each other across the interview table. His lawyer was at least ten years older than Haddad, and her assertive, no-nonsense manner gave the impression of decades of experience in a demanding profession.

Despite the detective's obvious confidence and determination, they all knew she had little solid evidence against him. Haddad had continued with her earlier tactics: trying to wear him down, find inconsistencies or contradictions in his story. Those tactics might even work – on a guilty man. Simon simply repeated the truth, again and again, and could keep doing it as long as she wanted to. But he battled not to let his frustration show. While she persisted here, grilling him, Hayley's killer remained free, and Erin was out searching rugged, isolated country through the night to try to save a life.

'We'll take a short break,' Haddad conceded abruptly. 'I'll have the custody sergeant bring you some refreshments. Interview terminated at eleven-fifteen p.m.,' she added, and switched off the recorder before walking out without another word.

Aware that the custody sergeant was keeping an eye on him through the observation window and would be noting his behaviour, Simon channelled his pent-up energy into standing and stretching tense neck muscles, rather than pacing the floor of the small room and pounding his fists into the wall as he wanted to. Control, patience and focus. He didn't intend to give Haddad any justification for her evident belief that he'd murdered Hayley in a fit of anger.

Massaging an obstinate muscle in his neck, he watched his lawyer write up the last of her notes. 'What happens now?' he asked.

'She can apply to hold you for another eight hours while investigations continue. She won't be able to get the blood analysis back in that time frame, though. That will take around twenty-four hours, by the time they get it to the lab in Sydney and run the tests. She could well argue that because that could potentially be very strong evidence, you are likely to be a flight risk and she should be given the extended time to find additional evidence that puts you at the scene at the time of the murder so that you can be formally charged.'

'Will the extension be granted?' The prospect of being detained until well into the morning concerned him. The confinement itself didn't particularly worry him, and under normal circumstances he'd be patient because it was only a matter of time before they cleared him of having Hayley's blood on his hands. But in normal circumstances Erin wouldn't be out in the bush in the middle of the night, already exhausted from doing his job on top of her own for weeks, risking her life when he should be the one guiding the search.

'I'll argue against the extension, of course,' his lawyer said. 'But yes, I think in the circumstances it's likely that it will be approved.'

Simon dragged out his chair and sat down again. He needed to think, needed to go through everything so that he could find some way to *prove* he hadn't murdered Hayley. Because with Fraser caught up in the search at the gorge, and Haddad focused on him, no one was looking for the killer.

•

The full moon almost directly overhead lit their way as Erin led the first search team along the walking track cut through the scrub, the path just wide enough for two to walk side by side. Steve Fraser kept an even pace beside her, with Matt and Tess following behind.

They scarcely spoke. Erin's thoughts buzzed with questions she wished she could ask the detective, but even if he had answers, she doubted he'd share them. And there were questions she could scarcely dare to ask, even in her own mind. Questions about Simon; questions about her own feelings and her knowledge of him. She couldn't believe him guilty of murder, but with every trudge of her boot on the ground, a small voice of doubt taunted, *What if . . . ?* What if he was guilty?

They'd walked in the moonlight most of the way, but as they neared the lookout platform the tree cover became thicker and the breeze picked up, dancing eerie shadows across the dim path. Erin flicked on her head torch. Time to concentrate on the questions she might have a chance of finding answers for soon.

The clunking of four pairs of boots on the steel base of the lookout platform echoed in the darkness, briefly drowning out the background sound of the waterfall. The rocky gorge fell away beneath the struts of the platform, moonlight catching on the water below.

Erin swung her backpack off and took out a powerful spotlight. 'Let's see what we can see from here. With any luck we'll spot her quickly.'

Fraser paused with his water bottle half raised. 'And without luck?'

'Without luck it will be a very long night.' Even longer for the woman, if she was still alive. And if she was, Erin just hoped she'd see the searchlights and know that help wasn't far away. 'Okay, we'll just use two of the searchlights for now, to preserve the batteries. So pair up. Two sets of eyes per light. We'll start directly below here and sweep the area methodically, from one side of the gorge to the other. Matt, you work downstream, I'll work upstream. She's wearing white, so that should make her easier to spot.' Unless she was under the scrubby trees or rocky ledges, or had become wedged in among the boulders. If they had to search every inch of the river gorge on foot, they'd have to wait until daylight.

Matt went to the opposite side of the lookout, and his searchlight flicked on, glinting on the water below. While Tess tightened a bootlace, Fraser stepped to Erin's side.

She'd said to pair up, and he'd picked her. She'd have preferred Tess with her. She liked Tess's resolute focus and dependability; she knew where she stood with Tess. With Steve Fraser, she wasn't so sure. When he'd shed his suit earlier to change into his dark blue police overalls, it seemed that he'd also cast aside the suave, smooth persona for an altogether more rugged, down-to-earth practicality. His air of competence should have been reassuring, but she couldn't forget that he was actively investigating, and his colleague had arrested Simon.

Erin turned on her searchlight, resting both arms on the railing of the lookout to steady it. With her light beam beside Matt's, she began the first sweep from directly below them, down across the rocky river and up the steep side of the gorge opposite. The river wound among boulders and straggling scrub, the water low and sluggish now, but the evidence of the last flood was still tangled in the branches of the trees.

'The water can come up high,' she commented to Fraser as she began the next slow sweep with her searchlight, grasping at anything easy and straightforward to say. 'If it rains heavily in the district, or on the hills to the east, the river can rise quickly, and the gorge acts as a choke. You don't want to be down there if it's raining anywhere nearby.'

'They're not forecasting any rain, are they?'

Erin kept her eyes on the illuminated patch of river. 'Chance of storms at the weekend.' The weather forecast she'd checked before leaving town had only heightened her sense of urgency. All the more reason to find the woman and get her out of there as soon as they could.

They fell silent, but within moments Matt muttered something and Tess drew in a sharp breath.

'What . . . ?' Her own breath catching, Erin swung her searchlight around to join Matt's, hovering on a patch of something pale-coloured near a rock. Hope died as soon as she saw the shape. 'It's a goat,' she said. 'Just a dead goat. That's one less feral animal I'll have to worry about.' That probably sounded more callous than she'd intended. She hated to see any animal suffer, but feral goats did huge damage to the environment, competing with native species for water and feed. The surefooted animals didn't often fall into gorges, but like every other animal, sometimes they had a run-in with a venomous snake, or were injured in a fight, or simply died of old age.

'Errgh.' Matt flicked his light away. 'Let's hope we don't have to wade in goat soup downstream of it.'

Erin turned her spotlight back to where it had been to resume the search. 'Nope. It won't be there long. A fox or dingo will likely drag it out tonight.' And might have a go at the woman, if they didn't find her soon. Yet another reason to hurry.

Within minutes, Erin's spotlight caught a patch of white just visible through some scrubby foliage not far from the base of the waterfall.

'I think that's her.' She thrust the light at Fraser so she could focus her binoculars with both hands. 'But I can't see if she's in the water or not.' Matt's spotlight joined hers, brightening the area, but with the shadows of the scrubby trees in the gorge she still couldn't see clearly enough. 'We'll have to walk up along the edge of the gorge. See if we can get a better view further along.'

'Is there a track along the edge?' Fraser asked.

With no time to waste, Erin hoisted her pack onto her shoulders again. 'There's an old track that we closed because there were some landslides. It's fairly rough in places. Not easy in the dark, but we'll just take it slowly and carefully.'

'I assume,' Tess said drily, as Erin unlocked the steel gate across the old, overgrown track, 'that as we're about to start clambering around the edge of a gorge at night-time, no one saw the assistant commissioner's email this morning about occ health and safety procedures.'

Even as she spoke, Tess helped Erin swing the heavy gate open. Whatever the police boss's email had said, it obviously wasn't going to keep her from the search, whether it contravened health and safety regulations or not. But Erin caught the edge of a challenge in the glance Tess tossed Fraser.

'I didn't happen to see it, Constable,' he said, with the air of a cheeky schoolboy pretending innocence. As Erin moved off down the track, he followed, walking beside Tess. 'Anything in the email I should be aware of?'

'The usual, sir. A stern reminder to undertake risk assessments and follow procedures. And a note about disciplinary processes for those who fail to do so.'

As far as Erin knew, the two of them had only met tonight, but the touch of amusement in the detective's voice and Tess's manner suggested an undercurrent of . . . well, she didn't have a clue what, but since neither of them seemed to have any inclination to stop the search, it didn't concern her right now.

'Well, let's agree, Constable,' she heard Fraser say, 'that an informal risk assessment has taken place. We're searching a specific location for a woman who may be seriously injured.

We have radios and emergency equipment, an experienced guide, and there's backup at the campground. But I'm not ordering you, so if you consider it too dangerous . . .'

He deliberately trailed off, and Tess snorted. 'Oh, don't worry, sarge. I make my own decisions and take responsibility for them. If I thought this was beyond average crazy, I'd definitely let you know.'

He laughed. 'Oh, I can assure you that if it all goes pear-shaped, AC Fraser will be certain to make sure it's my head that rolls.'

Erin half turned as she held back an overgrown branch for them. 'AC Fraser?' she asked. 'Family?'

'Only genetically.' He made light of it, as if he didn't care.

Oh yeah, she knew about that kind of family. But the detective's family was none of her business, and sure as hell not her priority right now.

'We're coming up to the area where the landslide was,' she told them. 'The track's pretty dangerous – part of it's gone and there's a sheer drop – so we'll have to bush-bash around that section.'

The overgrown track had been easy walking compared to the rough ground and dense scrub she led them through now. In the darkness, she moved slowly to reduce the risk of any of them losing their footing on the rocky ground. But fine branches she could barely see whipped her cheek more than once, and when she walked face-first into a spider's web, she swore and stopped so suddenly that Fraser collided with her from behind.

Strong hands, warm on her shoulders, steadied her. *Male hands*, her body noted, with a flicker of longing. *But not Simon's*, another small voice quickly said.

'You okay?' Fraser asked.

No. I hate this confusion. She stepped out of his touch, scrubbed at her face to remove the clinging sticky web and concentrated on the here and now. 'As long as I've got no spiders crawling in my hair, yes.'

'A ranger afraid of spiders?' he teased, although he did quickly check over her ponytail. 'You must be in the wrong job.'

Grateful for his friendly manner, she responded, 'Oh, I'm not afraid of them. Fascinating creatures, spiders. And vital to the ecosystem. I just hate the creepy-crawling feeling in my hair.'

'I'm glad it's you out front clearing the webs, and not me,' Tess commented, and Matt made a clucking noise at her, imitating a chicken.

They all kept up the banter while they made their way through the scrub, Erin ensuring she contributed light-hearted comments now and then. Better to keep the darkness at bay and avoid thinking too much about the task awaiting them. She'd worked with Matt often enough, and with Tess once or twice, and Fraser's relaxed friendliness boded well for an efficient team. They might indeed have to work seamlessly together very soon, depending on what they found.

When they joined the track again, not far beyond the landslide, she signalled the others to stay put and climbed nimbly over the old fence that had never kept curious walkers away from the edge. Here a large flat rock overlooked the gorge, with a more direct view of the waterfall than they'd had from the lookout. Fraser followed her over the fence – that didn't surprise her – and joined her as she aimed the beam of the searchlight at the rock pools to the right of the base of the falls.

The woman floated in water fed by a rivulet, away from the deeper pool carved by the main channel of the river. A low-growing bush clinging to the rocks entangled her, keeping her from the flow of the water.

'I think she's . . .' Erin lifted her binoculars for a closer look. 'Yes. She's face up.'

Fraser echoed her thoughts. 'So she could still be alive.'

'Yes.' Perhaps she'd fallen into the deep water and managed to make her way out of it. Perhaps. 'It's a slim chance,' she added, 'but . . .'

'But we're going down there to find out.'

'Yes. I am, anyway.'

'We are. Two is safer than one. So, what's the best way down there?'

'We could go back along the top and work our way down, but the slope is steep and there are no tracks. Or we could abseil down the cliff here. I think that's safer, and it's sure as hell quicker. It's a fairly even rock wall, and with Matt and Tess at the top, they can help light our way down.'

It took very little time to unpack the equipment, find suitable anchor points and gear up. She'd been half worried that Fraser had been boasting when he'd said earlier that he was experienced, but as he quickly and calmly prepared she quit doubting his proficiency. She was beginning to suspect that the laid-back, devil-may-care image Steve Fraser cultivated didn't, in reality, go deep.

But as she checked her radio and the torch on her helmet and positioned herself at the edge of the cliff, she wished for the comfortable familiarity of Simon beside her instead of the detective who – despite his easygoing persona – might yet charge Simon with murder.

She pushed off from the edge before Fraser did. Tess and Matt held the searchlights steady as she descended, illuminating the rock shelf she was aiming for, devoid of scrub and a few metres above the water level. But the contrast between the dark and the light from the searchlights messed with her depth perception and she landed unevenly, the shelf not as smooth as the searchlight had made it appear. She almost fell, swearing as she regained her balance just before her knees hit the ground. Stupid, so stupid, to let other matters distract her.

'Careful! It's uneven,' she called to Fraser as he followed her down. Teamwork. Looking out for each other. That's where her head had to be. There was nothing either of them could do about Simon's predicament for now.

Fraser landed easily, unclipping from the rope within seconds and divesting himself of his harness as quickly as she did. They were still thirty metres from the woman, over boulders and rocky ground held together by straggling casuarinas and acacias.

'Take it slowly,' she warned Fraser as she set off, looking for what might be the safest way down off the ledge onto the boulders below. 'Believe me, you don't want to break an ankle down here.'

'Might be the only way I get any time off,' he quipped behind her. 'We're too short-staffed to take rec leave.'

'Yep, same with us. But if you're going to break a limb, do me a favour and do it back at the campground. 'Cos I don't want to carry you out of here.'

The beam from her head torch caught the white of the woman's dress and their idle chat dried up. Erin clambered down off the ledge and skirted around pools of stagnant water, remnants from the previous week's rains which had temporarily swelled the river. A few more rocks to scramble across, and then . . . then she'd just have to deal with whatever they found.

The main channel of the falls splashed a steady flow into the larger pool nearby, sending a light spray metres around and making all the rocks slippery. The woman floated in the pool below the trickling secondary falls, tangled in the branches of a dead casuarina that had toppled into the water, its roots still embedded in a rock crevice. Face up, eyes closed, pale, and still but for the gentle drifting of her long hair on the surface. Face up, but more than a metre from the edge of the pool. Beyond easy reach, and no way, from here, to tell if she still breathed.

'We have to get her out. Hell knows how.' Erin slid her pack off aching shoulders and began to tug open the fastenings on her SES jacket. The thin branches of the straggling casuarina wouldn't hold her weight. She'd have to go in to the water to reach her.

Fraser's hand closed on her arm. 'Hold on for a tick. Crime scene. I'll get a couple of photos for the record before we plunge in there.'

Her thoughts circling the problem, she shrugged off her jacket and started unlacing her boots while he snapped a few shots with his phone. 'No need for both of us to get wet. I can take her weight in the water, but I'll need you to pull her up here.'

He opened his mouth to object, but must have realised she was right. Smart man. 'How deep is it in there?' he asked instead.

'Less than two metres. I think.' In the stark contrast between torchlight and moon shadow, she couldn't see the bottom. 'The main pool's much deeper. Complete with whirlpools when it's flooding. This one's fine.'

She stripped down to shirt and underwear. Although the autumn night wasn't cold, she'd appreciate dry clothes to put on afterwards. If Fraser noticed the totally impractical red lace G-string, he used his brain again and didn't comment. Dammit, she could almost like this guy. Except for the whole investigating-Simon issue.

Simon wouldn't have commented on a lace G-string either.

Shit, why the hell was she thinking that now? She tucked her hair under her helmet and slid from the rock into the water. Cold water. Cold enough to suck her errant thoughts away. She didn't touch the bottom, taking the few strokes necessary to swim to the woman. She found a footing on an underwater rock and, chest deep in water, took the woman's outstretched hand to feel for a pulse.

Nothing. Nothing but the gentle lapping of the disturbed water, the sound of the falls, and the scrape of Fraser's boot against rock as he moved to shine the light more directly for her. No moaning from the woman. No breathing. From here, Erin could see the jagged, broad gash on the side of her head, and the way her neck twisted, broken.

'You can radio Nick.' The cold had seeped into her throat, making her vocal cords stiff. 'Tell him we won't be needing the rescue helicopter.'

By the time she'd disentangled the body from the branches, she almost had her leaking eyes under control. Fraser leaned well over the water to lift the body up and onto the rocks, and then his two strong hands gripped hers and he helped her out. He handed her an unfolded space blanket. 'Wrap this around yourself. Are you okay?'

The night air chilled her wet skin and her teeth threatened to chatter so she just nodded, clutching the blanket close around her. She'd find her dry clothes in a minute, dig out the sweatshirt from her pack. When she stopped dripping.

Fraser knelt beside the woman on the cold stone, his fingers against her neck, confirming the death. A youngish woman. Perhaps thirty, thirty-five, her skin lightly tanned and her face devoid of makeup. But it was her dress that drew Erin's attention away from her face. Plain white cotton, a simple short-sleeved wraparound shift, tied at the waist with thin ties.

The damp fabric clung to her body but the top had skewed, exposing one breast. In an act of respect, Fraser drew the edge of the bodice closed and as he did so, Erin saw the stitching edging the fabric, and the delicate line of decorative flowers.

'Steve,' she said, making her tight throat work. 'Her dress – it's the same as Hayley's.'

'Yeah, that's what I thought.'

'No, I mean . . . not just the same style.' She knelt beside him, dropping the blanket enough to point at the edge of the bodice he'd just closed, keeping her eyes on that small detail. 'It's hand-stitched and embroidered. It's a home-made dress. I didn't see it for long, but I think Hayley's was, too.' She remembered spots of blood on Hayley's dress, like red flowers on the stitched leaves. 'They're both wearing embroidered dresses, and believe me, this isn't the latest fashion.'

'You think they knew each other.'

'Yes. They must have. The chances of two women making the same dress from the same fabric in the same area are pretty slim.' *And then being murdered . . .* The chill seeped into her bones. This woman's death *might* have been accident or suicide, but the timing, the circumstances, the report of someone else there with her . . . something was very wrong.

Erin reached for her own clothes, dragged on socks and trousers, then stripped off her wet shirt and rummaged in her pack for her sweatshirt. Fraser kept his back to her, taking a few more photographs of the woman. When she pulled her sweatshirt over her head, he was holding his phone in the air.

'You won't get a signal here. You'll need a sat phone.'

'I don't suppose you happen to have one?'

'Mal – our boss – insists we always carry one now, since we're usually out of mobile range.' She took it from its pocket on her pack and keyed in the passcode before handing it to him. 'I presume you're reporting in to Detective Hard-ass.'

'Thanks. Yes.' As he copied the number from his mobile into the sat phone, he said, 'Leah's a good detective. I worked with her a few months back in Birraga, just before she came here for that other case. She's tough but she's thorough and fair.'

A sudden clatter of falling stones startled Erin, and she spun around towards the sound, hearing the multiple soft plops as they hit the water in the pool below the falls. Not from the top of the cliff where Tess and Matt waited; no, they'd fallen down the steep slope on the other side of the falls.

Fraser grabbed the spotlight with his free hand and directed the beam at the slope. 'I suppose it's one of the goats,' he said.

It could have been a goat. Or a fox or a dingo or a wallaby. Except the silhouette she'd briefly glimpsed on the cliff edge against the night sky stood tall and didn't have four legs.

CHAPTER 5

Hours dragged by. Simon lay on the mattress, hands clasped behind his head, and stared at the white ceiling of the holding cell. Despite his fatigue – he'd slept rough the last three nights – he didn't plan on sleeping now. Custody procedure didn't allow him a pen and paper, so he worked mentally through possibilities, unanswered questions, and ways to find those answers.

But his thoughts kept circling back to Hayley, hiding in his house for days, sleeping on the beanbag, wrapped in the old orange blanket, and relying on his pantry for food. She'd been in the National Parks office on Monday afternoon but not said anything to Bruce about needing help. Going by

444

the food she'd eaten, she'd probably been in his house since sometime not long after that, waiting for him.

The harsh truth knotted his gut. If he'd come straight back to Goodabri after leaving Sydney, if he hadn't taken those three days in the wilderness, he'd have arrived home around the same time she came looking for him.

If, if, if . . . All the years of his marriage were littered with ifs and regrets, guilt and remorse.

She must have received his last letter, because she'd known where to find him in Goodabri. But why had she hidden like that? He'd seen no sign of a bag or purse, nothing belonging to her in his house, and no evidence of food other than his. He'd check thoroughly when they let him back into the house, but everything pointed to her having no money. No money, no clothes, no belongings. Had some hardship befallen her? Had she run in fear from something? If so, why hadn't she asked anyone in town for help? Bruce would have helped her. Snowy would have helped her, and Tess at the police station. Hell, at least half this town knew what it was like to fall on hard times and would have bent over backwards to do what they could for her.

She must have found the key to enter the house, but how had the killer got in? The absence of any evidence of forced entry indicated three potential explanations: that she'd let her killer in; that she'd left a door unlocked; or that her killer had been with her all along. The possibility remained that someone had come looking for him and found her instead, but the more Simon considered it, the less likely it seemed. He didn't rule it out, but given all the other questions around Hayley's sudden reappearance, his instinct leaned towards the killer being someone connected with her, not him. And if that was the case, then who or what had she become involved with that had cost Hayley her life?

Voices came from further down the corridor. He didn't catch many words, but he recognised the custody sergeant's broad ocker accent and Haddad's clipped tones. And then he *did* hear Haddad's sharp, 'I am well aware of the time.'

Because his watch had been taken from him for safekeeping in the custody office, along with his phone, wallet and belt, Simon couldn't be sure of the time, but it had to be close on three in the morning. Hours since Erin had left on the search, and he'd heard no news.

Restless, he got off the bed and dropped to the floor to begin a round of one-armed push-ups. He'd hardly done ten when footsteps stopping outside the door and the beep of the electronic lock alerted him to roll out of the way of the person entering. He rose from the floor and sat on the edge of the bed, making no moves to the door.

Not Haddad but Aaron Georgiou, the detective constable who usually worked with Nick, stopped just inside the door, leaving it wide open. A sign of trust? Caution? Procedure? Simon knew him, as he knew most of the police in the district. Although young, Aaron had the makings of a good cop; he was dedicated, hard-working and honest. Too honest to play power games. Whether that would help or hinder his career, only time would tell. But Simon trusted him.

They must have called him in at short notice, for instead of his usual business shirt and trousers he wore jeans and a light sweatshirt.

'You okay?' Aaron asked. 'For a moment there I thought you were writhing on the floor.'

'Push-ups. I can't sleep, might as well do something. Is there any news from the search?'

Aaron hesitated, glancing away as if unsure whether he should share information with a man under arrest, before he said, 'I heard they found her.'

'Alive?'

Aaron gave the smallest shake of his head.

Simon swore. 'Accident or . . . ?'

'Too early to tell,' Aaron said, his voice low. 'They'll bring her out once it's daylight. Forensics are heading there now.'

Simon wanted to ask about Erin. He didn't. He was still under arrest for murder, and he had to keep her right out of it. A lot of people knew they were friends – good friends – but he was glad, now, that he'd made no moves towards anything more. No one knew what she meant to him. None of this shadow over him would fall on her.

Aaron thrust his hands in his pockets and leaned against the doorframe, informal and unthreatening. 'Look, Simon, I'm not here for any official interview. The custody sergeant won't permit it at this hour. But since you're awake, he says it's okay to ask a question about Ms Munro that might help us. But you don't have to answer anything.'

'Ask.'

'Do you know of any other names your wife used?'

'I told you her maiden name. I guess she may have used my name, but I never heard her do so. Why?'

'Did she have a driver's licence?'

'Yes. I taught her to drive. She got her licence the first year we were married. Why do you want to know?'

Aaron gnawed on his lip for a moment. Things were definitely awkward. 'We need to find out where she was living, and who with. We need to establish her next of kin.'

Simon swallowed and nodded. He probably wasn't her next of kin. He couldn't be, after all this time. If Hayley had a de facto partner, that person would take precedence over a long-separated spouse. And Hayley was pretty and loving, with a warm heart and generous spirit – surely someone had valued that, and loved her?

'I gave Detective Haddad the PO box address in Lismore. That's the only address I have. She went to an alternative lifestyle retreat up that way. That's all I know.' Simon gripped the edge of the mattress. He couldn't pace in the small cell. Couldn't move much, couldn't walk out and try to assuage this helplessness with action. 'You should ask her father. I doubt she kept in touch with him, but perhaps he knew where she was. I've already told Detective Haddad about his previous threats of violence to Hayley.'

'Yeah, we're trying to locate him. The thing is . . . there's no record of Hayley that I've been able to find. Not under Munro, or Kennedy, or her birth name. No licence, car rego or electoral roll. No police record. Nothing I can find on the web either, or on social media. I'll get onto the post office in Lismore in the morning, check who rents the box. But for the moment, I've got no clues at all.' He dragged a hand through his hair. 'Did you know any of her friends? Girlfriends from when you were together? Maybe other army wives? Even old school friends?'

'Not really. She was always shy, didn't make friends easily. Her father was physically abusive. They moved to the town I grew up in when she was sixteen. She'd left school by then, and I don't think she had many friends other than me. After we were married and she'd moved to Holsworthy . . .'

He dredged through his memory, trying to recall what Hayley had been doing when he'd been absorbed in training. 'She was so shy we didn't have much of a social life. She studied for her childcare certificate. She did have a friend in the course.' He could picture the woman from the couple of times he'd briefly met her, when she'd come to pick up Hayley for a girls' night out. Hayley had spoken of her fairly often. 'Her name . . . it was something old-fashioned. Celia . . . no, Sybilla. Sybilla Braithwaite. When Hayley went on the trip around Australia, she went with Sybilla. But I don't know . . .' There was too much he didn't know. 'Look, I don't know if they stayed friends, if Hayley went to the north coast with her or alone. She might not have seen her for years.'

'It's worth asking her. Sybilla Braithwaite isn't a common name. That might make it easier to find her. If you think of anyone else, let me know.'

After Aaron left, Simon remained sitting on the mattress, dropping his head back against the wall, his eyes closed. He'd lived with Hayley for three years, and he could barely remember the name of even one of her friends. There must have been more, although other than the occasional mention of an acquaintance he couldn't recall her having friends. He'd encouraged her to go out, join groups, meet people and get involved in activities outside her studies, but she always found some reason not to. And although they'd socialised sometimes with the guys in his unit and their girlfriends and wives, she never seemed to feel comfortable with them.

Shyness, lack of confidence, her constant feelings of not fitting in – they were a big part of the reason why he'd not objected when she'd left to go travelling, why he'd given her space to spread her wings and find her own way. She'd had a shit of a life until he'd married her. He wasn't sure if he'd given her a better one, even if she'd been safer with him than with her parents or on the streets.

When it came down to it, he'd hardly known her. He'd given her money, safety, a place to live, gentleness and affection. They'd shared some good times – movies, picnics, renovating their apartment, quiet evenings together – but he'd always felt . . . yeah, he'd always felt as though he had to look after her. She'd deferred decisions to him, always asked for his guidance, initiated little herself.

She'd needed him in so many ways. Until she didn't, and she'd left. Even the withdrawals from their joint bank account had become fewer and further between, then they'd stopped.

Shit, he was just going around and around it all, and getting nowhere. Some sleep, if he could get it, might give his brain some clarity. Or at least get him through these interminable hours of uselessness in the cell.

He stretched out on the narrow mattress and punched the pillow into a semi-comfortable shape. He must have slept, because he dreamed, a jumbled, scattered jigsaw of memories and imaginings, experiences and fears; of Hayley and Erin, of his father, of war and shattered houses and a refugee child, crying and crying and crying.

He jerked awake, the child's cries still echoing in his mind. No stranger to bad dreams, usually he'd get up, walk around, drink a glass of water, and maybe read for a while to clear his mind of the clinging, spider-web strands of the dream. He swung his legs around to sit on the edge of the bed, but here he had nowhere to walk to.

The beep of the keypad sounded, loud in the stillness, and the door opened. Aaron again, tiredness beginning to show in the shadows under his eyes. He carried a cardboard coffee cup and Simon caught the scent immediately.

'I'm glad you're awake,' Aaron said, passing the cup to him. 'I've got some good news and some bad news.'

Simon wrapped his hands around the cup and inhaled the rich, steaming aroma. 'Coffee is good news.'

'I thought it might be. But even better is that your friend Gabe responded to my messages and confirmed your whereabouts yesterday morning. He saw you leave your camping spot. So we're releasing you without charge. You're free to go.'

Free. The word meant far more to him now after less than twelve hours in a cell than it had a day ago. 'The bad news?'

Aaron glanced out into the corridor as if checking for listeners. He dropped his voice. 'Hayley's friend Sybilla. We can't find her. No one can find her. The thing is, she was reported as a missing person eleven years ago. There's been no sign of her at all since then.'

•

Time moved slowly with nothing to do but wait for daylight. With the forensic officers deciding against rappelling down the cliff in the dark, Erin stayed at the bottom with Steve to protect the woman's body until they could lift her out of the gorge in daylight. Although Matt and Tess hadn't found anyone in their search for the figure Erin had seen, they stayed and kept an eye on things from the top of the gorge.

Her SES jacket provided little cushioning against the rock Erin sat on beside Steve, but at least it was a barrier between her butt and the chill of the stone. And the two episodes of

Doctor Who they'd watched on Steve's phone had helped them pass a couple of hours. The debate about which Doctor was best absorbed another half an hour. They both carefully avoided discussing Simon, or Hayley, or the corpse lying a metre away.

The full moon dropped gradually towards the west, beyond the walls of the gorge and out of their sight now, although the silvery light reflected on the top half of the falls. Most of the time they left the torch switched off to discourage mosquitoes and other insects, their eyes accustomed now to the moonlit night.

The bush around them rustled with small sounds – the grumbling hiss of a possum, the quiet whoosh of an owl overhead, the low, pulsing hoot of a frogmouth somewhere in the distance. And always the steady, soporific splattering of the waterfall nearby.

Steve yawned, and checked his watch for the second time in as many minutes. 'Sunrise is around seven, isn't it?'

'Yes.' An hour to go. Longer before the team up above carried a stretcher in and got it down to them. Erin delved in the side pockets of her pack, feeling for the two muesli bars she'd been saving. 'Here. Have some breakfast. Is there any coffee left in the thermos?'

He took the muesli bar and gave the thermos an assessing shake. 'About half a cup each. I'll ask them to send down some more. Preferably with bacon, eggs, and hot buttered toast.'

'I'm hankering after French toast. But fat chance of either, out here. You should get some sleep. I guess you'll still be working most of the day.'

'I'll be fine.' The plastic wrapper on the muesli bar crackled as he ripped it open. 'Wouldn't be the first all-nighter I've pulled. But why don't you take a nap?'

'I'll wait until I get home. The bedding's not exactly comfortable here.' Home, fresh coffee and her own bed – beautiful thoughts, but still hours away. An hour until daylight, probably another hour or more before they had the body strapped into a stretcher and ready to lift up the rock face. Then they'd be carrying her through the bush, back to the camping ground and the police team. Then another hour or so to Strathnairn and home.

Except she had to see Simon first, find out what had happened. If he was still in custody . . . No, surely he couldn't be.

She'd overheard parts of Steve's conversation with Leah Haddad on the satellite phone, hours ago. He'd wandered a short distance away to make the call, yet made no real attempt to hide his side of the conversation from her. But because it was police business, and she respected that, she'd said nothing about it since.

Now, after hours sitting side by side on the flat rock surrounded by the dark stillness of the bush and the gentle splashing of the falls, they'd established, if not a friendship, at least a working partnership, so when she finished eating the muesli bar she broached the subject hanging unspoken between them.

'Would you have arrested Simon? Do you really believe there's evidence against him?'

In the dim light she saw him turn his face to her. 'Would I have arrested Simon?' he repeated thoughtfully. 'I'm not sure I can answer that, or whether my answer would mean anything. I wasn't there at the house with him, Erin. I don't know what Leah saw, or thought she saw, or what was said to make her suspect him. But I do know that she's a good detective. She's thorough and dedicated and she wants to find the truth.'

Not what Erin wanted to hear, but she couldn't fault his honesty, or the way he spoke of his colleague. 'What does your instinct say?'

'Instinct? Instinct is highly overrated.' He leaned forward with his elbows on his knees and stared straight ahead. She assumed it was a dismissive comment, until he took a deep breath and continued, 'A couple of years ago I let "instinct" guide my judgement. I believed a man was guilty of murdering a child, and when his life was threatened I didn't rush to save him. He died at the hands of a mob, and a colleague – someone I care about – was seriously injured trying to protect him. But it turned out the man was innocent. My "instinct" in that case was nothing more than prejudice and anger.'

And he carried the scars, apparently. A man with a conscience, even if it hadn't always been uppermost. But he'd bared a painful part of his past candidly, and she unsuccessfully sought words to respond.

Again he turned his face towards her, and the starlight reflecting off the water danced silver across the angled lines of his profile. 'Erin, I'm much more cautious these days. We

455

don't have enough evidence yet. I don't believe anything in particular about Simon at this stage. I'd *like* to think that the killer is just some random madman Hayley opened the door to rather than a dedicated soldier, but they've got a history, and it isn't a happy one. I have to consider all the possibilities. Including . . .' His slight pause alerted her. 'Including the possibility that a woman who cares about him may have been incensed when his wife arrived in town.'

The fact that he'd guessed – read? – the feelings for Simon she'd tried to hide shocked her almost as much as his implication. 'You think *I* could have murdered her?'

'I said I had to consider all the possibilities.' His voice in the darkness was even, and although it wasn't harsh it wasn't light and teasing either. 'You work in town, and it's a small town. You could easily have met her since she arrived. You knew the house was empty and you're strong enough to have overpowered her. So it's a possibility.'

Put like that, she could see the logic. The decidedly uncomfortable logic. So much for professional friendliness and the good working relationship she thought they'd established. He'd probably been watching and assessing her the whole night.

'Should I be grateful that you haven't arrested me yet?' she asked, without much in the way of humour.

Five minutes ago, she would have seen the smile he threw her as simply light-hearted and friendly. She wouldn't make that mistake again. 'Theoretical scenarios aren't evidence,' he said. 'I've got a dozen or more of them. They give me options for the directions to start making enquiries. But I'll start pruning them when we have forensic data, post-mortem evidence, and witness and alibi statements.'

She kept her mouth shut. No use in protesting her innocence when she didn't have much of an alibi, whatever the time of Hayley's death. She mentally ran through her own movements. Wednesday afternoon and evening working alone in the park, before she'd gone to her home on the edge of Strathnairn – still alone. Yesterday morning she'd been up at the crack of dawn and out to check campsites and refill toilet-paper stocks before arriving at the Goodabri office around lunchtime.

If Hayley had been murdered on Wednesday night or Thursday morning, it would be impossible to prove to Fraser that she'd been somewhere else at the time.

•

The first rays of sunlight glinted on the tops of the trees outside the police station. Simon paused on the footpath and breathed in the fresh air. A light breeze fluttered the sun-gold leaves, bringing with it a few degrees of autumn chill.

With his vehicle in Goodabri and probably still being examined, he checked his wallet for his access card to the Strathnairn National Parks depot. Yep, he had it on him. He could take a work truck out to the search site.

He'd just started walking towards the depot when the police station door swung open again. Dee, one of the constables, called after him, 'We're heading out to the park now if you want a lift.'

Dee wore her search and rescue overalls, and introduced a new, very young probationary constable as they finished loading some gear into a four-wheel-drive police vehicle. He knew Dee from around town and from his work in Parks and the SES. She didn't seem perturbed by the fact that he'd been arrested and might still be under suspicion of murder. Her attention was on explaining procedure and the task to the new recruit, and Simon sat in the back, largely forgotten for most of the trip.

At the staging ground, Nick gave him an apologetic smile but made no comment about his arrest or release, launching straight into instructions for the morning-shift team of Dee and her offsider and a couple of cops from another station.

'The SES crew are up there with Matt and Tess, setting up the tripod to bring the victim out. Simon, can you take the basket stretcher and help them? Dee, take a couple of the relief crew and have a look at the top of the falls, now that it's light. Look for any evidence and for any signs of the person Erin and Fraser saw last night. Then relieve Matt and Tess. They've been out there all night.'

Erin had seen someone in the bush during the night? Simon interrupted to ask, 'Is Erin still there?' She had to be – her ute was parked near the walking track beside the Strathnairn SES truck.

'Yes,' said Nick. 'She and Fraser found the victim at the base of the falls. They're still there.'

She'd been at the base of the falls all night? The temperature hadn't been frigid, but it hadn't been warm either, and here at the campground a light morning mist hovered around the river. It would be denser – and cooler – in the gorge.

Simon went to the SES truck, unlocked as he expected, and found a spare helmet and a discarded jacket in the back. He dragged out the basket stretcher, ran a quick check over it. Designed to be used in difficult terrain, it separated into two easily-carried parts.

Dee and her offsider were still consulting the map with Nick, so he set off without them, both halves of the unloaded stretcher a fraction of the weight of a full military pack and weapons.

After the night in confinement both his body and his mind welcomed the jog along the track. The early sunlight, rising above the treetops, burned away the river mist and the chill. Somewhere in the vicinity, a group of kookaburras cackled raucously, proclaiming their territory, and as he rounded a bend near the lookout platform a couple of rock wallabies scattered into the bush. He had no time now to stop and enjoy it, but he never failed to appreciate the beauty and peace of the bush – and the fact that here, in a landscape unscarred by war, he had no need to be watchful for mines, snipers or ambushes.

The overgrown track from the lookout to the waterfall had been well trodden during the night by the police and SES teams, and he had no difficulty following where they'd left the path to skirt around the collapsed part. He heard voices well before he emerged from the tree cover, and fortunately caught sight of a guy rope before he jogged into it.

At the top of the cliff they'd made good progress setting up the tripod and rigging for the high-angle recovery. He received a couple of surprised glances from the police officers present, and grins from several of the SES crew, but nobody made an outright comment on his release.

'Hey, Kennedy,' one of the SES guys called. 'Whaddaya reckon about anchor points for this belay? The ground's as crumbly as a biscuit.'

There were enough cops around to protect Erin if last night's figure in the dark still lurked nearby, so for the next twenty minutes Simon turned all his attention to practical matters while they finished setting up the gear. Although the volunteer crew had trained for such rescues, most of the district consisted of flat plains so they rarely needed the skills for vertical extractions. He had more experience, gained mostly in a park in the high country further east rather than in the army.

He didn't mention Erin, and although Tess coordinated communication with her and Fraser in the gorge – via both radio and more informal shouts – he took no part in it. She might not have known he was there. But while others lowered the stretcher, he grabbed a harness and a helmet and clipped on to one of the ropes.

'What do you think you're doing, Kennedy?' Tess demanded.

'I'll go down there to bring the body up. The other two must be exhausted and chilled. It's safer for me to do it.'

'And you haven't been up all night?'

460

'I've been warm, dry and well fed, not sitting on cold rocks in the middle of nowhere.'

She could have ordered him to stay – the police had charge of the operation – but she didn't. Maybe she trusted him. Or maybe she trusted the judgement of her colleagues: Haddad, who'd let him go, and Nick, who'd sent him here. Or maybe she just figured that down in the gorge he had nowhere to run to, and there were plenty of police around to ensure he didn't do anything stupid.

He descended swiftly and easily, the rock wall sheer and without dangerous protrusions. Fraser met him at the bottom, having just finished unhooking the stretcher from the ropes used to lower it, and they carried it between them over the rocks to where Erin waited with the victim.

He didn't realise how much he'd wanted to see Erin's quick grin until he didn't see it. She just nodded a greeting and turned away from him, but not before he saw the dark shadows under her eyes. It should have been him down here all night. She'd worked her butt off for months, carrying the load of three staff, and although he'd always admired her fitness and strength, that kind of workload was too much for anyone.

They'd laid a first aid blanket over the dead woman. He hadn't given her a great deal of thought, except to curse the circumstances that necessitated Erin having to be out here. But when he and Fraser set the basket stretcher beside her, and Erin gently lifted the blanket away, he saw the similarities to Hayley's dress immediately. A mate's alibi couldn't count for much, so was this why they'd let him go? Because the two women – and their deaths – might be connected, and he'd been in the company of the police when this woman had fallen?

Strands of her long dark hair, dry now, fluttered across her face. A memory from long ago stirred, an image, hazy in remembrance. His focus had been on Hayley, the day they'd laughed over drinks on the balcony of their apartment. Hayley, laughing and relaxed, as he'd rarely seen her.

The woman's head was tilted to the side, away from him. He leaned over her to get a better view of her face. And then he rose and stepped away from her, his thoughts reeling.

For all she'd barely acknowledged him moments ago, Erin came to stand beside him. 'What is it, Simon? What's wrong?'

The water falling into the pool seemed louder, joined by the thudding in his ears. What the frigging hell was going on? First Hayley, now . . .

Both Erin and Fraser waited for his answer, Erin with worry creasing her forehead, Fraser in a ready stance, hands on his hips, watching him carefully.

'I think I know who she is,' Simon said. 'I can't be sure – it's years since I've seen her. But I think she's Hayley's friend, Sybilla Braithwaite. Aaron told me she's been missing for eleven years.'

CHAPTER 6

Her brain foggy with tiredness, Erin struggled to think through the implications. Hayley and Sybilla were friends. Simon knew both of them. The police already suspected Simon . . .

Simon's brain must have been functioning faster than hers, because he said to Steve, 'I was going to take the body up. But I guess you don't want me anywhere near her now.'

'Yeah, that's probably best,' Steve said. 'I know you've got a pretty solid alibi for when she fell, but you're the only link between them so far. I can take her. You look after Erin. It's been a long night and she's exhausted.'

Leave before the job was done? Erin shot Steve a glare. '*She* can both look after and speak for herself. Besides, unless you've got a Superman cloak hidden somewhere, you're going to need help carrying her to the cliff base.'

'Tess could come down. Or some of the others.'

'Tess has been out all night too.' Impatience and chill made her stamp her feet on the spot. 'Come on, let's get this woman onto the stretcher and out of here.'

Simon didn't touch the victim, but Erin and Steve transferred her to the stretcher without difficulty, strapping her in securely. Erin didn't let her gaze linger on the woman's face. Experience had taught her to keep things impersonal when dealing with the deceased. Respectful, careful, distanced. Emotions were too distracting, so she focused her attention on the mechanics of the task. Straps, ropes, clasps to keep the remains safe for the investigators and for her loved ones.

Steve didn't object when Simon stepped forward to help them carry the stretcher over the rocks to the base of the cliff. And although the woman was slightly built, they needed Simon's strength; even with it Erin's arm ached by the time they'd covered the short distance.

While Steve harnessed up and attached the stretcher to the ropes, she slid off her backpack and rubbed the painful muscles of her shoulder.

'Are you okay?' Simon asked quietly.

'Ratshit tired,' she admitted, because he was a friend and he'd never belittled her, 'but it's nothing a hot shower and a sleep won't fix.' And maybe a cry. A cry for two dead women, and for the mess of her own emotions that had only become more tangled since Simon's long-awaited return. So much for thinking that everything would be easier once he came back.

'What about you?' she asked. 'You've had a hell of a night.'

'I'm fine. I —' He broke off, changing his mind about whatever he'd been about to say. 'Come on, let's get geared up. We've still got to get back to the campground. But I'll drive you home from there. If . . .' He paused, and his voice thickened as if with discomfort. 'If you're okay with that.'

Was he ashamed about being arrested? Did he think she didn't trust him? She might be uncertain and confused about a heap of things, but she no longer had any doubts about his innocence. 'Let's get back to the vehicles. We can argue then about who's driving.'

She didn't argue, though, when he swung her backpack over his own shoulder. By the time she reached the top, she was glad she didn't have the weight dragging on her. She hadn't exactly been on the go for all of the past twenty-four hours – she'd just been waiting around half the night – but none of that had been particularly comfortable or restful.

'Between the SES and us, there's plenty of people here to carry the stretcher out,' Tess said as Erin divested herself of her harness. 'No point staying around. You and Simon should go home. I'm sure Fraser will be in touch later if he needs anything more from either of you.'

The walk from the campground had seemed long enough at night, although it was only a few kilometres. The return trip in daylight should have seemed shorter, but although Simon still carried her pack, weariness weighed her down. She had to concentrate on her feet to avoid stumbling.

Neither she nor Simon spoke much. They passed a few people on the track: the forensic officers returning to search the waterfall in daylight, and a couple of their SES colleagues heading up to relieve the crew who'd worked overnight.

When they emerged from the bush at the campground, they saw Nick and his detective offsider, Aaron, deep in discussion at the picnic table scattered with maps, radios and other equipment. Steve had returned her satellite phone, so unless Tess or anyone in the police team had one, he couldn't have reported the victim's possible identity yet.

'We have to tell them who the woman might be,' Erin said. 'Steve won't have mentioned names over the radio.'

'I'll go do it. Do you want to wait at your ute?'

Wait out of earshot? She shook her head. The only way she'd have any chance of working out what was going on was by staying informed. As informed as the police would allow, anyway. And since Steve had his suspicions of *her* – suspicions that Haddad would undoubtedly share – police information would likely dry up as soon as she was off the immediate scene.

'She's *Sybilla*?' Aaron exclaimed when he heard the news. 'She's been alive all this time?'

'You'll need to get her family or someone who knows her better to identify her. I only met her a couple of times. I could be wrong.'

'She has family,' Aaron said. 'Parents, and two sisters.' He turned to Nick. 'How do you recommend we contact them?'

Erin bit her lip to keep her composure as the mental blocks she'd held in place against thinking of the victim as an individual with a life and a history crumbled. Sybilla had a family, people who loved her. People who had worried and searched and hoped every day for the past eleven years for some news of her. And now they would hear this worst of outcomes.

Nick's grim face reflected how they all felt. 'It's Leah's case and her decision, but she'll probably first want to liaise with the detectives who investigated her disappearance. They may have fingerprints on file. That'll be the quickest way to confirm if it's her. When Fraser gets here, Aaron, you can go back to Goodabri with him to brief Leah.'

'Make sure the forensic people look at her dress and Hayley's,' Erin said. 'I think they're home-made, and they're very similar. Maybe they got them from a market stall or shared a pattern or something. If you can find who made the dresses, you might find out more about where they've been.'

All three men looked at her, evidently not entirely comprehending the significance of the dresses. Practical guys whose most taxing fashion decision was whether to wear a blue shirt or a white one. They'd probably never sewn a seam in their lives.

'Do people share sewing patterns?' Nick asked. 'Or maybe the design is some kind of internet trend?'

'Yes, people do share, and you can buy patterns online,' she said. 'But the odds of two women coincidentally making the same pattern out of the same type of fabric are very long. It's not even a particularly fashionable style, unless you're into alternative stuff. So, if you ask me, they've either bought them from the same place, or they've been living together somewhere and shared the pattern.'

'Thank you for that, Erin,' Nick said, grave and formal, befitting his acting inspector role. 'Thank you for all of your help in this.' He glanced from her to Simon. 'Both of you.'

She'd worked long enough in predominantly male environments to interpret the silent communication between the two men. Nick couldn't apologise outright or say anything implying criticism of Haddad, but it was there in his eyes. For professional reasons he gave Haddad the respect due, but Erin suspected that in private his conversation with the detective might well be blunt.

Simon gave a slight shrug. 'No worries,' he said, as if being locked up half the night was of no importance. 'I guess someone will let me know when I can access my house and vehicle again?'

'Yeah. I'm afraid it may be a day or so yet. Aaron, check with Forensics about their time frame for releasing the scene.' Nick considered Simon and Erin again. 'I guess I don't need to remind you not to talk to others about the case. Leah or I will be releasing a statement later today.'

Erin found a reassuring smile. 'Don't worry, Nick. We know the drill.' Don't compromise a police investigation – especially in a small town. And especially when the murderer might still be around.

Nick's face relaxed a fraction, and for a moment he wasn't a senior cop in uniform but a fast-becoming-friend, the man with the good sense to fall for her friend Jo. Lucky Jo. Lucky Jo to have found someone she loved and to be building a strong relationship with him.

Whereas Erin . . . yep, the one she'd found had turned out to be not quite who she'd thought him to be, and she still didn't know how she felt about that. Just as well they were only friends and she'd never made too much of a fool of herself. Just friends. She could keep doing that.

'Do you need a ride?' she asked Simon as they left Nick and Aaron. 'I'm heading home to Strath, but I can go via Goodabri if that's where you want to go.'

'No, Strath is good. I'll need to get a few things in town.'

'You know how I said we could argue later about who was driving?' She tossed him her keys. 'I'm so damned tired that I won't argue.'

Her limbs and head felt heavy as she climbed wearily into the passenger seat of her ute. It occurred to her that Leah Haddad might think she was stupid to get into a car with a man who'd been arrested for murder. But Leah didn't know Simon at all. Erin did – at least some aspects of him. So did Nick, and if Nick had held the slightest doubt about her safety he'd have done something about it, instead of raising a casual hand in farewell as they drove past him on their way out of the campground.

She had no concerns about her physical safety. But as she stole a glance at the man beside her, his mouth tight and eyes straight ahead as he negotiated the winding dirt track, she knew that her emotional safety had been in jeopardy for months. The things she hadn't known – his *wife*, his army reserve service – raised a stack of questions about what else she didn't know. She wanted to shake him, push for answers, give him hell for not being straight with her and for going off without a word. Fortunately, before she gave in to the temptation, she remembered that in the last sixteen or so hours he'd found and lost his wife, spent a night in a cell, and helped retrieve the body of another woman he'd known.

So what if someone being less than truthful pushed a few buttons in her psyche? She was a mature, intelligent adult, and it wasn't all about her.

•

He'd had no real time alone with Erin since those first few minutes after they'd discovered Hayley's body. Now they had at least forty minutes, just the two of them in the ute, and he had no idea where to begin, what to say. *I'm sorry* was easy enough. But before he could decide which of several apologies should come first, Erin broke the silence.

'I'm sorry,' she said. 'I can't remember if I said it earlier, Simon, but I'm sorry about Hayley. It must have been one hell of a shock for you.'

'Yes.' A shock, definitely. A sorrow? Oh, he had plenty of regrets, for sure, and sadness for Hayley, as well as anger that someone had murdered her and cut her life short. But grief? The raw truth was that she'd been out of his life so long that her absence would change little in his day-to-day life. Except . . .

'Erin . . .' He spared a glance from the road to look at her. '*I'm* sorry. I should have told you about Hayley. It's just that . . .' Damn, he had to pull together some coherent words. Honest, coherent words. 'I wanted to finalise things with her, make sure she was looked after properly, before I —' *Just say it.* 'Before I started anything with . . . anyone else.'

'Oh.' Silence for several seconds. He heard her slight intake of breath before she asked, 'Is there a particular "anyone" you have in mind?'

'Yes.' Would she understand what he meant? For a man who'd looked death squarely in the face plenty of times, he found he didn't have the courage to be completely upfront and face the possibility of rejection right at this moment. 'Yes, there is. But just now . . . well, I've got to sort this out. Hayley's death. The police investigation, finding out where she's been, funeral arrangements.'

'Of course that's your first priority now,' she said quickly. 'Anyone,' she put a very slight emphasis on the word, 'would understand that.'

Hope flared and he might have smiled at the tacit message, but as he slowed to turn at a T-junction, he had to give way on the narrow dirt road to the mortuary van, heading out to collect Sybilla's body, and the sombre sight made them both fall silent.

Had the van already collected Hayley from his house? It was likely. The idea of them moving her disturbed him more than he expected. Sweet Hayley, more helpless now than ever. He owed it to her to ensure that her killer was found and stopped.

Hayley murdered, Sybilla dead – how could those things be unconnected? The idea that Sybilla had murdered her friend and then thrown herself from the waterfall had occurred to him. Probably to the police, too. But that theory didn't explain the person seen with Sybilla at the top of the falls, or the figure Erin had seen in the night – likely the same person. That person had to know what had happened, at least to Sybilla.

'The figure you saw out at the falls – anything that might give a clue as to who it was?'

'No. Just a silhouette. Definitely human, not a goat or a kangaroo. But I couldn't say if it was male or female, old or young. It was dark, and from a distance.'

'Any campers in the area that you know of?'

'Only the couple who saw Sybilla fall. They arrived yesterday afternoon. The police and SES searched around the gorge last night and this morning but didn't find anything. Including any sign of how she got there. If there's a car, it's on a fire trail, or on the other side of the gorge, in the state forest or on one of the properties.'

'Unless she walked through the park from one of the other campgrounds,' he mused.

'She was only wearing sandals, and I didn't see any indication of rough walking. The police checked the picnic area at Casuarina Falls and the SES are doing the fire trail between there and Niland Falls. But that's almost ten kilometres.'

And only a fraction of the huge area of the park. 'The north of the gorge is more likely, isn't it?' he asked, thinking aloud. 'The state forest access tracks come in closer.'

'That's what I think. I suggested to Steve Fraser that they look around out there, speak with the landholders.'

'Will he?'

'I don't know. He's not easy to read.' She shifted in her seat, turning slightly towards him. 'You should know – he thinks I might have murdered Hayley.'

'He accused you of that?' Simon hadn't seen any signs of major tension between the two of them down in the gorge, but they hadn't been overly friendly either.

'Not as such. Just said it was one of the possibilities he's considering. And I don't have an alibi.'

'He doesn't know you very well, does he?'

'You don't think I'm capable of killing someone?'

He'd seen enough in war zones to know that given enough reason, everyone was capable of killing. But Erin murdering Hayley? No, that didn't add up at all. So far from possible, in fact, that he answered with a touch of lightness. 'You're far more likely to have taken her home and given her a good feed. Besides, you don't leave a job half-finished, Erin. If you had murdered her, you'd have taken her somewhere out in the bush where no one would find her. And you'd have cleaned up my place so there was no evidence at all.'

The corners of her mouth turned up in a wry smile. 'Thanks for the vote of confidence. I'm glad you're not doubting me, on top of everything else you have to worry about.'

He turned onto the main road from Goodabri to Strathnairn, still a minor road but sealed and smoother than the potholed sandy dirt of the road to the park. Easier on the tension in his neck. He took one hand from the steering wheel to massage the tight muscles.

'I'm sorry you've been dragged into this. Hell, I'm sorry about so many things, Erin. You've got more than enough reason to be angry with me already.'

She didn't say anything straightaway. He stared at the black ribbon of road and replayed their conversation in his head. She'd been more subdued this morning than usual. All her comments had been brief, factual. He'd put that down to fatigue, but maybe . . . maybe he'd misread her earlier statement about 'anyone' understanding.

They'd gone a kilometre or so before she spoke. 'The two weeks you went camping with your old army mates in November – you were really on reserve service, right?'

He'd not actively lied back then – he *had* been camping with army mates, on a training exercise. But that wasn't any excuse. 'Yes, I was.'

'Why the secrecy?' He heard curiosity rather than censure in her voice. 'Heaps of people are in the reserves and go off training a couple of times a year.'

'It's complicated.' But he had to find some way to uncomplicate it, fast, so he could explain and keep her trust. 'Erin, I'm a commando. It's not your everyday reserve service. Much of what I do, even as a reserve, I can't talk about. So when I started in Strathnairn it seemed easier to say nothing, other than to Malcolm, rather than have all the questions and conjecture from everyone.'

'So I guess you can't even say whether you were just training these past two months, or on some kind of operation. Active service. Whatever you call it.'

'Sometimes I'm sent overseas. We're often involved in training local teams, or joint ops, and occasionally special ops. Not as often as the movies suggest, though. And usually for me, now, not for as long as it was this time.'

'But you can't say where you were this time, or for what purpose.'

'No.' He could tell immediate family the general details of which theatre of operation he was being sent to, but Erin wasn't his family. He'd added his stepfather to his official army record of next of kin when Hayley didn't come back. He'd maintained a close relationship with Ray even after his mother's passing, and valued the older man's friendship. Ray didn't panic. Ray understood the risks and had a fair idea of the challenges in most of the places the army sent him, but he kept his worries to himself, and welcomed Simon back after each tour with a few perceptive questions that didn't require answers he couldn't give. In his quiet, undemanding way, Ray provided more support than Simon's wife had ever been able to give.

'That must have been tough on Hayley,' Erin said. 'But even tougher on you, I imagine. I hope they give you good support over there – wherever "there" is – and when you come back. Because I'm guessing it must be pretty damned lonely sometimes, if you're not able to talk about what you've been doing and what you've seen.'

The sunlit road in front of him became less distinct and he had to blink to clear his vision. If he hadn't already been head over heels for her, he'd have tumbled the last distance there and then. Lonely? Hell, yes. More so since he'd left the full-time army and the company of mates with whom he'd shared the adrenaline-pumping months and years. Achingly lonely since the day Erin had walked into the Strathnairn office with a cheeky grin, an intelligent, down-to-earth attitude and an easy way with people. And all the months since then, during SES training and jobs and the inevitable drinks at the pub afterwards. When he'd spoken of his previous army experience, lightly, as if it had scarcely impacted on him, she'd listened more closely than the guys had, and he'd brushed off her questions with simple answers that stopped a long way short of complete. Keeping the two halves of his life separate had been relatively uncomplicated – until Erin.

He slowed for the speed limit change as they drove into the tiny community of Derringvale. Smaller even than Goodabri, just a scattering of houses, a shop, a pub and a school. A few little girls played inside the fence of the school playground, skipping and laughing and unconcerned for their safety, racing each other as the bell rang for morning classes. So different from the little girls he'd seen in faraway places, kidnapped and executed for their 'crime' of seeking an education.

He gripped the steering wheel. Memories like that . . . yeah, exactly the kind of thing he couldn't talk about easily to anyone. Exactly the reason why he restricted himself to incidental, unimportant tales of army life and kept quiet about his continuing service. Shock a pub full of half-plastered emergency services guys with the brutal realities of a dozen murdered kids he'd been too late to save? See the light drain out of Erin's eyes to be replaced with horror? Hayley had had nightmares for weeks the one time he'd told her about an atrocity. Never again.

'Simon? Are you okay?' Erin asked, and he realised he'd not responded to her, not talked about not talking.

'Yes. Sorry.'

Neither of them came up with anything else to say while they covered the last fifteen kilometres to the outskirts of Strathnairn. He thought maybe she'd dozed off, but when he glanced across she was looking out the window, her face turned away from him.

When they turned into the lane to her cottage, she asked, 'Have you got somewhere to stay, since you can't go back to your place yet? You're welcome to my spare room, if you want it.'

Her spare room? In a cottage smaller than his? They'd shared huts sometimes, out in one of the parks, and the staff bunkroom at the Riverbank depot, but always there'd been at least one other person with them, usually more. Staying at her place when his wife had just died and they'd both already been tagged by the police as suspects would only complicate matters further.

'Thanks, but I'll just camp out in one of the park huts. Until we know what's going on – until the police make some progress – it's better if I keep to myself.'

'I understand,' she said, and he thought she did recognise what he hadn't said. 'Let me know if you need anything.' A deep yawn caught her, scrunching her face. She shook her head, adding when she could talk again, 'I'm going to sleep for hours. Do nothing today but . . . Oh, shit. It's Friday. The Goodabri rescue helicopter ball is tonight.'

A major community fundraiser for the vital service. He'd gone to it the last few years, not because he enjoyed formal social events but because if it wasn't for the regional rescue helicopter, people injured or taken seriously ill this far from major hospitals might not survive. Just a few months ago, he'd helped load Jo into the chopper when she'd been critically injured. And so a few weeks later, the day before his unexpected call-up, he'd happily handed over his hundred dollars for a ticket to the charity ball.

He turned into her driveway and stopped beside her cottage. 'Sleep all day. Then you'll be fine to dance all night.'

'Can't sleep all day.' Her grin flashed, and even though it didn't quite light her eyes, he'd missed it so much it served as an electric jolt to his failing spirits. 'I've been making a dress for months. It's stunning, but I've still got some sewing to do.'

He was already out of the ute and reached into the back seat for her pack. 'I didn't know you sewed. That's how come you saw the similarities between the dresses?'

'Yes. I made most of my own clothes, growing up.' For a moment her mouth tightened, but then she smiled again, although not as naturally as usual. 'I don't do much anymore, but this one's a special project. I've got nowhere else to wear it, so dammit I'm going to finish it and wear it tonight. Even if I yawn all through the speeches.'

He came around to her side of the ute and handed over her backpack and car keys. 'I'm going to hire a car for the next day or two. Would you like me to drive you?' So much for keeping to himself.

'You're going? But surely . . . You certainly don't have to go, Simon, under the circumstances. And there's no need for you to drive all the way back out here to give me a lift – I'll be perfectly fine to drive after a bit of a sleep. And you know me – I probably won't even have any wine tonight.'

Yes, he'd been at the pub with her and the SES crew often enough to know she seldom drank, and then only a glass. 'I bought my ticket months ago. And I need to be there tonight. Most of Goodabri and the district will be there. If anyone saw Hayley – if anyone knows anything – my presence will make sure it's talked about. Some useful information might come out of it.'

'Good point. But if you decide not to go after all, I'll be keeping my ears tuned for any clues, and I'm sure Nick will be, too.' She held out the keys. 'How are you getting into town now? Do you want to take my ute?'

'It's only a couple of k's. The walk will clear my head. I'll see you tonight.'

He waited until she was inside, and even then he paused at the end of her driveway, on the pretext of checking his phone, to make sure she'd encountered nothing untoward. He heard the water pump kick in – her old farm cottage was just outside the town boundary and water supply – and relaxed. She was either going for a cup of coffee, or a shower.

Thinking of Erin in the shower did absolutely nothing to clear his head.

He set off at a punishing pace towards Strathnairn's small business district. Practicalities. He had to keep his mind on practicalities. He currently had only the clothes he wore, his wallet and phone. His house and vehicle might be out of reach for a couple of days. He could buy a change or two of clothes from Dylan's, the men's clothing store in Strathnairn. He could probably even hire a dinner suit there for the ball, if they had one left in his size. Or he'd hire a standard suit, or a kilt if he had to. Being a rural ball in Goodabri, it wouldn't matter much what he wore. Some of the locals considered new jeans or moleskins to be formal wear.

He could shower and change at the Strathnairn National Parks office. There he'd also have computer access, and he'd start searching for any information he could find. Hayley hadn't had an online presence, but at the very least there'd have to be something in old news reports about Sybilla Braithwaite's disappearance. He only had the PO box address for Hayley, but he'd start scouring maps and records and calling in favours from contacts to try to locate any alternative lifestyle communities in the area.

He had to be able to find something, somewhere.

•

A long hot shower and five hours of sleep made Erin feel semi-human. A strong coffee almost completed the process. But the fragments of dreams still clung to her mind, catching her unawares and sending her mood spiralling down. Erotic dreams were one thing. Erotic dreams about a guy whose wife had just been murdered? Yeah, so not the right time. His comment about wanting to make things right with Hayley before starting something new with 'anyone' still applied, even though 'right' was no longer an equal, amicable divorce.

She had to give him time. She had to give herself time. Time to get to know him better than she did. And right now, this afternoon, she had a more urgent task to accomplish than worrying about a relationship that might or might not ever evolve.

She carried her coffee mug into the spare room, where her nearly finished dress hung on the back of the door. Little evidence remained of the bridesmaid's dress she had found in an op shop a year ago. A wealthy bride of the 1980s with more money than fashion sense had obviously decreed for her bridesmaid an ostentatious flummery of puffy sleeves and full gathered skirts in pale blue pure-silk lace. A travesty, really. But Erin knew quality fabric when she saw it, and over the last year she'd patiently unpicked the seams, rescued the yards and yards of lace, and overdyed and totally refashioned it into a dress as unlike its original form as it could possibly be.

And as unlike the simple white dresses of the two dead women as it could be.

The memory dulled her mood. Under the circumstances, she wasn't looking forward to tonight's ball with the same anticipation she'd felt a couple of months ago when she'd decided to finish the dress in time for it. But Simon was right – with many people from Goodabri and the district attending, Hayley's murder would be on everyone's mind, and likely a topic of hushed discussion. The woman had been in town for several days before her death. Surely someone had seen her. Or her killer.

Erin drank the last couple of mouthfuls of rapidly cooling coffee and set the mug down well away from the sewing table before she took the dress from its hanger. If work hadn't been so mad these past few weeks, it would have been finished already. But she had only another metre or so of scalloped lace edging to hand-stitch on, and a hook and eye closure at the top of the zip. Easy. Half an hour, max. Plenty of time to finish it and then spend some relaxing time pampering herself before she got dressed.

She deserved to pamper herself. She worked hard at a respectable career and served her community and she'd made it on her own. And this dress was no designer knock-off for her father to sell as the real thing. Nor was it one of the countless formal dresses for wealthy students that she'd made to support herself through university. She rarely sewed these days, because years of sewing for money had burned her pleasure in it, and because she preferred being outdoors rather than inside, but when she'd seen the silk lace in the op-shop window her old love of textiles had resurfaced and she'd vowed to make something special, purely for herself.

Pity, now that she was finally going to wear it, that she wasn't in the frame of mind to really do it justice. Pity that the one man she'd fantasised about impressing had so many other things on his mind that he probably wouldn't even notice she wasn't in uniform and boots. But she'd wear it with pride anyway, because this was part of who she was, alongside the practical, unfeminine career she'd chosen. It wasn't a part she showed her male workmates, because although they were great guys it was easier if she didn't remind them too often that she was female. But tonight, in this dress, they'd notice.

She sewed the last stitch, snipped the thread and returned the dress to its hanger, taking it through to her bedroom to hang on the front of the rickety old wardrobe. Done. Finished. She couldn't help grinning. Still a couple of hours before she was actually going to wear it, but she twirled on the spot anyway, as if she was already clothed in lace and silk instead of cotton yoga pants and a t-shirt.

Now she just had to do her nails, maybe a facial, decide how to do her hair . . . girly things she hadn't done for months. She kept her fingernails short and unpainted because the physical nature of much of her work would have wreaked havoc on a manicure, and her toes were usually invisible, encased in socks and boots.

In the bathroom, she found the solitary bottle of polish she owned, a deep crimson she'd last worn – when was it? Almost twelve months ago? Yep, the farewell party from her old job, before she'd transferred to the Strathnairn division of National Parks.

The lid of the bottle took some effort to open. Not a good sign. The brush was stiff, the remains of the polish clumpy, unusable. Either she needed to give up the stuff entirely, or wear it more often. A quick check of her makeup bag revealed a similar problem with her mascara.

She checked her watch. Not quite five o'clock. Still enough time to dash into town and do a quick restock. The chemist shop carried makeup, and it didn't close until five-thirty. Within five minutes she'd changed into jeans and a shirt and was reversing the ute out of the drive.

Like most regional towns, Strathnairn's main street had more than its share of empty shopfronts. Sometimes pop-up shops took temporary leases for a few days or a week. When she nabbed a parking spot right outside the chemist, she noticed that an empty shop nearby had a rack of clothes hanging out the front. Strath didn't have much in the way of clothes shops – it barely supported two boutiques and a small department store – so someone selling clothes was worth a look. After she'd bought her makeup.

She dithered for all of a minute over nail polish colours, and ended up choosing three – a rich blue, a crimson and a clear top coat. She could decide at home which one went better with the dress. She even remembered to get a fresh bottle of remover. Not a total failure in womanly things. Foundation, eyeliner, mascara and lipstick. Just as well yesterday was payday.

She turned left out of the chemist to check out the pop-up shop. It had about the same amount of stock as a market stall – a rack of clothes out front, a couple more racks inside the open double doors. A decorative timber sign hung in the window. Hand-painted in blues and greens, with a stylised earth in one corner, it read: *Simple Bliss.*

Erin paused to glance over the pamphlets and books on the table beside the rack of clothes out the front. Two piles of books had a twenty-dollar price tag. The cover of one matched the words on the sign – *Simple Bliss: Finding Beauty, Balance and Bliss* – and the other used a similar style and font to proclaim *The Path to Bliss.* The author's name took up a good third of each cover: Joshua Kristos.

Erin's scepticism meter swung straight into the red zone. Joshua, Yeshua, Isaiah, Jesus. Okay, so it was a common enough name, and Kristos wasn't uncommon either, but Joshua Kristos publishing books about bliss? Her father would probably wish he'd thought of it.

An advertising flyer caught her eye and she picked it up. *Discover Bliss*. An invitation to visit a community and enjoy a get-back-to-nature retreat, with the promise that visitors would discover the 'bliss of simplicity' for 'bodily and spiritual renewal'. All for a mere hundred and fifty dollars a day, with three days recommended for spiritual renewal. Erin dropped the flyer back on the pile. She got back to nature every day, and could offer visitors to the park a three-day stay for a whole lot less than four hundred and fifty dollars.

A young woman in a light blue top over loose dark blue trousers came out of the shop with a friendly smile. 'Hello.' She indicated the flyer. 'Are you interested in revitalising your spirit? We'd love to welcome you for a visit.'

'Thanks, but I'm a bit too busy at the moment.' About to turn away, Erin stopped and took a little more notice of the woman. Maybe in her early twenties, her long, light-brown hair was caught back in a plait and she wore no makeup or jewellery, but it was her wrap top that really caught Erin's attention. Similar in construction to the dresses Hayley and Sybilla had worn, it had a narrow decorative woven band on the edge of the bodice where the others had been embroidered.

'Maybe that's all the more reason,' the young woman said gently. 'The stress treadmill damages us so much. My name's Willow, by the way.'

'Hi, Willow. I'm Erin.' She didn't want the young woman to notice her staring, so she browsed through the clothes on the rack as an excuse to linger. Mostly plain colours, cotton or linen or some mix; dresses, tops, jackets and trousers with embroidery and decorative woven bands. Practical, comfortable clothes.

'Everything is made in Australia, from locally grown organic hemp and linen,' Willow said. 'We're a cooperative of artisans. Nothing is factory-made.'

'Locally grown hemp?' Erin put on her best innocent blonde expression. 'I didn't think it was legal.' She knew very well what was legal and illegal. She'd lost count of the number of marijuana crops she'd found in national parks and reported to the police. Industrial hemp required a special permit, and as far as she was aware, not many had been issued in the district.

Willow laughed lightly. 'Don't worry, this is quite legitimate. We have a supplier who is growing experimental crops of low-THC cannabis. Did you know it's a wonderful, ecologically sustainable crop? It uses much less water than cotton, and it's great for fibre, paper and many other uses.'

'Is that so?' Erin lifted a crimson dress from the rack. A lightly fitted A-line style, with a round neck, short sleeves, and buttoned down the front with small polished wooden buttons. But it was the lines of cream embroidery running around the neckline that interested her. Trailing stem-stitch vines with satin-stitch flowers. Not complex, but effective. 'I like this one. The leaves and buds are pretty.'

'We believe in making things that are both practical and beautiful. Would you like to try it on?'

'It's not really my colour.' She flicked through a few more dresses. Yes. There was one. At least one. She held up the mid-blue wrap dress. V-neck, with decorative stitching alongside a narrow band that became the ties around the fitted bodice. She hadn't had time to study Hayley's dress, but Sybilla's dress definitely had the same shape and details. 'This is great. It looks so comfortable and cool. So, do you guys sell over towards the coast? I'm pretty sure a friend of mine had a dress just like this. I think she bought it at a market somewhere.'

'Yes, we mostly sell at markets. We're only new in this area, though, and there aren't a lot of markets here.'

'Yep, Strathnairn is too small for a regular one. But the autumn festival is coming up, and there are always a fair few stalls at that.' Erin didn't have much time to spare, and no clue how to – or even whether she should – ask any questions about Hayley and Sybilla. Gut instinct told her not to mention names or details. Gut instinct and her promise to Nick. She checked the size of the dress, and the price on the recycled cardboard tag. Sixty dollars. 'How long will you be here?' she asked. 'Will you be open tomorrow?'

'No. I'm just waiting for my friend to get back, then we're packing up. We won't be here tomorrow.'

Sixty dollars for a dress she'd never wear but which might provide clues to where Hayley and Sybilla had been? 'Okay,

I'll grab this one now. Do you have a website or contact phone number if I decide I want something else?'

'Yes, we're on the internet,' Willow said as she carried the dress to the table inside. 'But it's so much better to make personal connections, isn't it? I'm sure we'll be back here fairly often. Our new place isn't far away.'

Erin feigned only casual interest. 'Really? Where is it?'

'North of here. Off Millers Road. There's a great set-up for our work, and the main house is beautiful. Very peaceful.'

Off Millers Road. Off Millers Road, which ran to the north of the park, a couple of kilometres from the falls where Sybilla had died.

The table inside had more copies of the retreat flyer and the two books by Joshua Kristos. While Willow carefully folded the dress with unbleached paper to protect it from creases, Erin picked up the flyer again. Three days, four hundred and fifty dollars, and a promise of rediscovering simplicity and finding bliss. When Willow slipped the folded dress into a paper bag, Erin popped the flyer in, too. 'I'm due for some time off. Maybe I'll think about visiting. Things have been a bit tough lately.'

'Oh, I'm sorry.' Willow touched her lightly on the arm. 'Do consider coming. We'd love to have you. There'll be massages and meditation, and when your mind and your body are awakened you'll feel so much better, so much lighter. So blissful.'

We. Always 'we', not 'I'. Just what kind of group of artisans also hosted visitors for awakening retreats? Her gaze fell on the books again. Bliss. Joshua Kristos preached simplicity and bliss. 'This guy – Joshua Kristos – is he some American preacher or something?'

Willow's smile became radiant, her eyes shining. 'Joshua is Australian. He's so wise. So gentle and caring. He changed my life. I would have been lost – probably dead by now – but look at me. I've never been so healthy or so blissful in my life. Oh, please do come to us. Joshua will be there from Sunday. He will show you the way to bliss.'

Alarm bells rang so loudly in Erin's mind that she could hardly summon up an answering smile. Either Willow was a great actress or she believed everything she said. Maybe this Joshua did have all the answers to life's problems. Erin had met a couple of truly wise people in her life. But far more likely his 'answers' related to how to scam money from gullible people. Erin understood too well some of the numerous ways that could be done.

She handed over cash for the dress, murmured something about running late when Willow seemed to want to prolong the conversation, and left the shop with the bag in hand.

Once back in her ute with the door closed, she pulled out her phone. Filling in time last night, she'd entered Steve Fraser's contact details, and she phoned his mobile now.

'I've got something for you,' she said when he answered. 'A dress that's probably made by the same people who made Sybilla's dress and maybe Hayley's. If you'll still be in Goodabri in two hours, I can bring it when I come for the ball.'

'I'm in Strathnairn now,' he said. 'Can you meet me at the police station in five minutes?'

As Erin reversed out of the parking space to drive the two blocks to the station, a woman dressed in loose trousers and a kimono-style top hurried along the footpath with a couple of calico grocery bags. Willow emerged from the shop and greeted her with a beaming smile that faded rapidly to concern. She took the bags from her, placed a hand on her arm as if the woman was unwell, or worried about something.

Erin didn't get much of a look at her but her impression was that the woman was older than Willow, maybe around her own age, mid-thirties. Another one of the 'artisans'? Another follower of Joshua? Maybe both. But certainly not blissful, just now.

Steve was approaching the station on foot when she parked in front of it. He carried a suit bag over one shoulder and a large bag from Dylan's Menswear. Shoving open the door with one shoulder, he waved her through. He shone one of his friendly, not-to-be-trusted grins at Dee at the reception counter. 'Have you got a meeting room we can use, Dee? I need a quick chat with Erin.'

Yet another young female officer he was already on first-name terms with, Erin noted. He probably made a habit of it. Not that there was anything improper in his manner, and Dee – and Tess last night – was well able to handle all types of men. That came with the job, just as it did in the National Parks and Wildlife Service.

Dee buzzed them through to a small room just inside, with a table and four chairs. Steve draped the suit bag over the back of one of the chairs. 'I got the last tuxedo for hire in Strathnairn. It's a tad loose, but if I stick my chest out it will be fine.'

'You're going to the ball tonight?'

'Yeah. Good cause, good opportunity to meet the locals informally. You said you're going, too?'

She nodded. 'And we don't have much time.' So much for doing her nails and pampering herself. She'd be lucky to be ready by seven at this rate. 'Look, there's a pop-up shop just down the road, selling clothes. I think you need to compare this —' she drew the blue dress out of the bag, 'with the dresses the women were wearing. This one's made by some sort of cooperative. See, the tag's got a webside address on it.'

'"Simple Bliss"? My knowledge of women's fashion would fill a pinhead, but that's not a well-known brand, is it?'

'No. But the thing is, the woman at the shop said this group have a place just north of the national park. You know how I mentioned that one of the properties bordering the park changed hands last year? I think that may be where they are.'

Steve whistled. 'You ever considered the police force as a career? You've got further than I have this afternoon.'

Definitely not the police for her. Not with her background. She shrugged off his compliment. 'It was just a piece of luck. The real estate agent should be able to tell you what places have been sold on Millers Road in the past twelve months.'

'I can probably find it online easily enough. I'll go and see this group in the morning. Simon said that Hayley had been involved with some sort of hippy mob up on the north coast.'

Hayley had been into alternative groups? Erin closed her eyes, leaned her forehead on her hands, trying to arrange all the pieces together. A hazy picture emerged, shadowy in places, with plenty of holes but maybe . . .

She reached back into the bag for the flyer. 'Okay. There's something else. There's a guy by the name of Joshua Kristos. I'm not sure of his connection with these "Simple Bliss" people, but I get the impression he's some kind of self-help guru. He's written books all about finding yourself through simplicity and bliss – they had them for sale in the shop. It sounded as though Willow had met him.' She passed the flyer across the table. 'They invite people to visit the community on retreat, and he's supposed to be there this weekend. It might be nothing, but . . . well, if he comes up in your investigation at all, my gut says he could be worth a second look.'

Steve quickly read the flyer before giving it back to her. 'Thanks. Haven't heard of him at all but if the name comes up, I'll remember it.'

As Erin drove home her thoughts gnawed at the issue. There were plenty of communes, communities and other groups around that shared similar alternative philosophies to the Simple Bliss group. Ecological awareness, self-sufficiency, paganism, earth-worshippers, all types of non-mainstream thinking, and most weren't anarchists, rebels or drugged-out dropouts. Hayley could have been connected with any one of those. However, her clothes – and her presence in Goodabri – possibly linked her to this group.

But no matter which way she looked at it, Erin kept coming up against the one question: how could being involved with a group that embraced simplicity and bliss have led to Hayley's death? It didn't make sense. There had to be something else, some other reason why she'd been murdered.

CHAPTER 7

When Erin had described her dress as 'stunning', she'd used exactly the right word. Simon stopped dead in the doorway of the Goodabri ex-servicemen's club function room and stared. He might have been standing there a few seconds before a lady behind him apologised as she squeezed past him. Gathering together a few dazed brain cells, he entered the room, nodding at some people he knew, tugging at the unaccustomed pressure of his shirt collar and bow tie as if it was the cloth that was stifling his breathing and making his chest tight. But instead of banging his head against the wall to knock some sense into it, he stood at the edge of the room near the door and watched Erin.

He found her hard enough to resist at work, in the practical masculine cut of her park ranger uniform. But in that long, rich blue dress that he had a good view of as she chatted with their boss on the other side of the dance floor . . . The style might have been demure, were it not for the fact that the fabric covering her shoulders, throat and arms and dipping low on her back was merely lace. The allure of bare skin behind the strands of blue lace and the panels of lace at the sides of the skirt that every now and then gave him a glimpse of long, naked leg made his brain cells fuse.

It had to be the sexiest, most erotic damn dress he'd ever seen.

It was going to drive him raving mad. All of his efforts these past months to avoid thinking of her in sensual terms shattered. The evening ahead was going to be a slow torture requiring all his strength to avoid making a total fool of himself.

She hadn't seen him yet. He could turn around and walk out and she wouldn't even know he'd arrived. Except what would that achieve, other than to prove him weak and a coward? Besides, others had already seen him. Leaving wouldn't just be cowardly, it would be stupid. Although he'd experienced plenty of heart-stopping fear on the battlefield, he'd always known the gunfire and grenades were aimed at the nameless soldier, not Simon, not him personally. Here, though, reputation, respect and friendships were on the line.

He needed a drink. He needed a dozen drinks, but one would have to do because he had to keep a clear head. There were only a few people at the bar so he joined them, waiting his turn, his back to the room and the mesmerising sight of the woman he'd fallen for months ago, standing with Mal Stewart and laughing as she talked with him. The fact that their boss was happily married and one of the politest, most respectful men he'd ever met did little to assuage his irrational envy.

The dinner-suited guy next to him swivelled on his bar stool, a middy of soft drink in hand, one elbow comfortably on the bar. Steve Fraser. At least with the detective he didn't have to make polite conversation, as if nothing was wrong. Or face awkward conversational silences from people who had heard about Hayley and didn't know what to say.

'Didn't think I'd see you here tonight,' Fraser said.

'It's a good cause. Are you here working or socialising?' The guy must have gone to the trouble of hiring a tuxedo, because he couldn't have made it to Birraga and back for his own suit since this morning. Although he looked as at ease in it as James Bond, Simon doubted he carried formal wear in the back of his car along with his police search and rescue gear.

'Like you said, the rescue helicopter service is a worthwhile cause. Plus this is a good opportunity to meet the locals. Did you get my message?'

'I've been out of phone range. Only heard the beep when I came into town.'

'Order your drink. Then I'll update you outside where it's quieter.'

This early in the evening, people were still greeting friends and no one had yet wandered out onto the small terrace overlooking the rear car park and looking down towards the river behind the club. Simon ignored the tables and chairs and instead leaned on the railing, watching the reflections of the moonlight flicker on the slow flow of the river, drinking the mineral water he'd bought. Whatever it was Fraser had to tell him, he preferred not to be sitting. Or drinking alcohol.

The detective propped himself at the railing beside Simon. He kept his voice low, even though no one was nearby. 'Leah's on her way to Newcastle for the post-mortem examinations. They'll do both women's tomorrow. If you have any objections about Hayley's, for religious or cultural reasons, you'll need to lodge them by first thing in the morning.'

Simon took a sip of his water but it didn't dislodge the hard lump in his throat. Post mortem. The forensic pathologist would go over every inch of Hayley's body, remove her organs, take samples of her blood. Was that the ultimate intrusion? No doubt it would be done with respect, for the sole purpose of finding answers, but he hated, hated the thought of it.

'No objections,' he muttered.

Fraser nodded. Maybe he understood something of the horror. He'd been a policeman long enough.

'Forensics have finished with your place,' he said after a moment. 'You can go back anytime. You may want to get a crime scene cleaner in, though. Insurance might cover that. Assuming there's someone in the region that does it.'

He could go back to his house. Where Hayley had died. The spartan accommodation of the old stockman's hut on one of the trails in the park seemed far preferable. 'Thanks. I'll go over and collect some things in the morning.' And search the place himself to see what he could learn about Hayley's time there. 'Have you found out anything yet? About where Hayley had been living?'

'Not yet. But Erin found a lead that might be promising. I'll check it out first thing in the morning.'

'Somewhere local?'

'Local-ish. It might not amount to anything, but it's all we have so far.'

Fraser wasn't going to tell him where. Not yet, anyway. Understandable, until they'd confirmed it. The police wouldn't want him going there himself until they knew the situation. But he could ask Erin later. Instead of pressing Fraser on the point, he changed the subject. 'You told Erin that you thought she could have killed Hayley.'

Amusement curved the detective's mouth. 'I said I hadn't discounted the possibility.'

Simon felt no amusement at all. 'You should discount it,' he said bluntly. 'Erin isn't stupid. Or vindictive.'

'Oh, she definitely isn't stupid. Very smart woman, your Erin.'

Simon much preferred Haddad's straightforward interrogation to Fraser's matey, good-humoured routine that could trip him up if he wasn't careful. 'She's not "my" Erin,' he said. 'There's nothing between us.'

'Nothing?'

'Friendship. Respect.'

'That's all?'

'Yes.' He wanted to leave it at that but Fraser wasn't stupid either. The cop wasn't the first to assume that something was going on between him and Erin. Before he'd gone away, plenty of people had made teasing comments linking them. Yet no one had teased him about Jo, in the days before Nick's arrival, despite their friendship. Maybe you just couldn't hide the kind of attraction that drew him to Erin. 'She's smart and funny,' he said. 'Gutsy and down to earth and she throws her all into everything. But I was married.'

'Ah. That mattered to you, did it?'

'Yes.'

'That's very honourable of you.'

A car drove into the car park below and swung into a parking space. Tess stepped out, the light catching the satiny, moonlight-coloured gown she wore.

'Don't all decent men try to be honourable, do the right thing? Don't you?' Simon glanced at Fraser, curious about his response, but the man watched Tess as she hurried towards the entrance.

'Me? Honourable?' He gave a short, humourless laugh without taking his gaze off the policewoman. 'No, I can be a right royal bastard sometimes.'

Someone tapped the microphone inside and the MC began her welcome.

'We'd better go in,' Fraser said. 'Which table are you on?'

'Seven, I think it is. Mostly National Parks people.' Including Erin. At least with a table of ten there was a good chance he wouldn't be sitting next to her.

'Someone cancelled so I got a ticket at the last minute. I guess I'm on their table. Let's hope they're interesting people and that the speeches won't be too long or boring. I'd much rather dance with beautiful women. Speaking of which, did you see Erin? That dress – serious wow factor.'

The man was teasing him. Or trying to provoke him. Simon kept his mouth shut and his fists clenched by his side as they went back into the brightly lit function room.

At table seven, Malcolm Stewart had already claimed one of the seats beside Erin. Bruce Lockyer sat on the other side of her, with his wife Mary-Rose beside him. Then there was Rob, one of the field staff, and his wife, Camille; Nick sat between Mal's wife, Susan, and Jo. They'd alternated men and women and, whether by accident or design, the only vacant chair was on the opposite side of the round table from Erin.

Friends, all of them, but none had known he was married until last night. Their greetings were subdued, not the usual cheerful banter, but he didn't read any censure in their faces and the tightness in his chest eased a little. Erin gave him a shadow of her normal smile, her gaze concerned and direct, and he had to tear his eyes away from her as Mary-Rose came around and stood on tiptoe to give him a kiss on the cheek.

'I'm so sorry about Hayley, Simon. Such a tragedy, such difficult circumstances. You know you're very welcome to come and stay with us, if that would make things easier for you.'

'Thank you. And thank you, Bruce. That's very kind of you. But I'm just going to stay out at one of the huts for a day or so. It's beautiful and peaceful in the bush.'

He took his seat between Jo and Camille as the waitstaff – students from the hospitality course at Strathnairn – began serving the first course. He'd scarcely thought about food all day, but the aromas jumpstarted his appetite.

Jo rested her hand lightly on his forearm while they waited to be served. 'If there's anything at all we can do, Simon, just ask any of us. Nick has to be all official and distant because he's acting inspector, but the rest of us don't.'

He wasn't used to seeing his colleague in makeup and a gown, but she was still the Jo he liked, with her practical, no-fuss manner and sharp, logical way of thinking. Her new, shorter hairstyle – a legacy of the surgery after her head injury – suited her. But as much as he liked her and enjoyed working with her, he'd never been at risk of falling for her. Just as well, since Nick had come on the scene and he'd have made formidable competition, for all he seemed civilised and gentlemanly in his tuxedo. Never underestimate Nick: that was the lesson Simon had learned the first time they'd trained together on the dojo mats at the Strathnairn Police Youth Club, when Nick had floored him in seconds despite a leg injury.

'Thanks, Jo. I appreciate it. I understand Nick's position.' And he did, and respected the man all the more for his commitment to his work and to his colleagues.

He let the conversation flow around him as they ate dinner. Light topics. Easy topics. Bruce and Mary-Rose's grandchildren. Nick and Jo's planned trip to Japan. Susan's quilting taking over the house. Erin's dress.

'It is beautiful,' he said in his first contribution to the conversation, after someone else complimented her on it. *You're beautiful*, he didn't say. 'You're very skilled at sewing.'

'You *made* it?' Susan exclaimed. 'I didn't know you sewed. I always imagined you were more into fixing cars and building fences and things.'

A faint blush rose on Erin's cheeks. 'I got the bug when I helped my grandfather restore an old treadle machine. It was a natural progression to learn how to use it. I still have that machine – it's a fantastic piece of engineering and is still going strong, a hundred years after it was made.'

He could imagine her tinkering with the machine, keeping it clean, oiled and rust-free with the same attention to detail she applied to work equipment, the same frown of concentration as when she sharpened a chainsaw. He already loved her for her practicality – she was beautiful to him even in a dusty uniform and with a smear of grease on her cheek and her hair windswept. But after tonight he would always picture her as she sat across the table from him in the sensual elegance of that rich lace, with her long hair twisted loosely into a soft, elegant arrangement at the nape of her neck.

The MC announced the first round of auctions, and all attention turned to the stage as one of the local auctioneers ran through the process and began his spiel about the first of the donated items. Simon watched and listened as the people of Goodabri and the surrounding district rallied to support the vital helicopter service, the bidding lively on item after item. There wasn't a lot of money in Goodabri – employment options were limited and a large proportion of the population were either retired or seasonal workers – but people gave what they could, and many of the items had been donated by locals rather than by big business. Warmth, humour and generosity of spirit flowed, and the dollars raised mounted.

This, *this* was a big part of why he'd stayed in the army and continued to serve. Because less fortunate towns and villages threatened by violence deserved the chance to maintain or rebuild that spirit of community, to be active citizens shaping their own futures. Although he'd confronted terrorists and warlords and people willing to kill and maim for power or money or politics or religion, it hadn't changed his belief, rock solid at the core of him, that most people were good at heart. The bastard who had plunged a knife repeatedly into Hayley was an aberration, a twisted specimen of humanity, not the norm.

When the first round of auctions finished and the music started up again, people began to leave their tables to dance or mingle. Simon made his way to a group of the younger guys from his SES unit, who were carefully avoiding dancing by loitering at the back of the room.

'Jesus, Kennedy, didn't expect to see you here tonight,' one of them said. 'I heard the vic at your place was —' He stopped abruptly when one of the other men jabbed him in the side with an elbow, none too subtly.

'Yeah, she was my wife,' Simon acknowledged. 'But we've been separated for a long time. I can't say I'm really in a party mood, but I came tonight to ask people if they knew anything. We know Hayley arrived in town on Monday. People must have seen her. People may have seen her killer. I'd be grateful if you guys could help spread the word, encourage anyone who may know something to contact the police.'

For the next half-hour, while the band played a range of 1940s and 1950s covers, he moved from group to group, asking for information, pointing out Steve Fraser, urging them to contact him if they'd seen or heard anything. He didn't get to talk to everyone, but he spoke with a fair proportion of the guests, and from the serious expressions and the whispers he heard around him he could tell he'd succeeded in making Hayley's murder a topic of conversation. There'd be plenty of speculation about him and his relationship with Hayley, but between his efforts and those of the police, word would ripple out into the community faster than even the Strathnairn newspaper or radio station could spread it.

He kept his distance from Erin. She danced with a few men – a gentle swing with Bruce, a more laughter-filled attempt to jive with one of the SES guys who seemed to have two left feet, and rather more success dancing to 'Blue Suede Shoes' with Fraser, who apparently didn't step on her strappy blue shoes. Not that Simon was watching her . . . well, he tried not to. There were whole minutes when he didn't look for her at all.

When the bandleader announced the last dance before dessert and the next round of auctions, Erin appeared by his side. 'Come, dance with me,' she said.

He almost refused, but she gave a tiny shake of her head, and although he didn't understand the warning, he took the hand she held out and followed her onto the dance floor.

Slow music – he could manage to move vaguely in time to that. The whole get-close-and-touch-her ballroom hold? He could do that, too. Possibly even without grinding his teeth entirely to dust in frustration. He kept inches between them and didn't dare relax his arms. If he just focused on the top of her head, and not on blue eyes he could drown in, or the texture of lace and the curve of her waist under his right hand, or the fresh, floral smell of her perfume, he might be able to function intelligently.

'Everybody's talking,' Erin said softly. 'There are a few rumours flying, lots of speculation. But no one other than Bruce so far who saw Hayley.'

'What are the rumours?' he asked.

'That you murdered her. That I murdered her. That the guys who ran rampant last year are back and no one in Goodabri is safe in their beds.'

'They're in jail.'

'Yes. I did try to assure Nancy Maguire and the hospital volunteer ladies of that. But hosing down rumours can be harder than fighting bushfires on a windy day.'

'Is that why we're dancing? To hose down rumours?'

'It's not the only reason. But yes, most people think I'm sane enough not to dance with you if I thought you were a murderer. And you'd be unlikely to dance with me if you suspected me. Although that might be more convincing if you weren't scowling so much.'

'Sorry.' Now that she mentioned it, he became aware of his facial muscles aching from the tension. If he tried to smile, it'd likely crack his face. He made a conscious attempt to relax his face, with little success. If only he could hold Erin close, very close, and bury his face in her hair. No. Impossible. That would set the rumours flying at warp speed and place her in a difficult position.

But the longing blazed through all the other discordant, demanding questions in his head and he had to fight his instincts and dig deep for some semblance of control. He needed Erin. He needed her strength, her common sense, her laughter, her friendship, her touch. But Hayley lay dead in the Newcastle morgue and until he had answers, he wasn't free.

The music continued thrumming but he dropped his hands, took a step away from her. 'I can't do this, Erin. I'm sorry. I can't.'

The image of the hurt in her eyes stayed with him as he walked out through the main door, through the foyer of the club, down the steps and into the coolness of the night.

●

He couldn't do what? Dance with her? Bear to be near her? Erin paused in the foyer, uncertain whether to follow him or not.

Among the handful of people chatting in the quieter space away from the music, she spotted Steve deep in conversation with an older woman, someone she didn't know. Despite his focus on the woman, Steve caught sight of her.

'Are you looking for Simon?' he interrupted his conversation to ask. 'He went outside. Tell him not to go far. This could be important.'

She found Simon sitting on a bench in the small war memorial park next to the club. The water jets in the centre of the low, round memorial fountain bubbled gently, the moonlight shimmering on the constantly shifting surface of the pool.

He must have heard the tap of her heels on the paved pathway because he stood up as she approached. 'I owe you an apology,' he said, the tension around his eyes even tighter than before. 'That was appallingly rude of me.'

'There's no need to apologise, Simon. You've got a lot on your mind just now. If you want company, I'm offering it. If you'd prefer to be alone, I'll leave you in peace.'

Despite the shadows, she saw a hint of his normal smile. 'Truth is, I always want your company, Erin. Please, sit with me for a few minutes.' In a quietly gallant gesture, he unfolded a large handkerchief from his pocket and wiped the dust off a section of the bench before she sat down.

She didn't know what to say, what he needed from her at this moment. The camaraderie and light teasing that had characterised their relationship before he went away fell far short of the circumstances now. She'd told him earlier that 'anyone' – that *she* – understood that he needed time to deal with Hayley's death. But the tacit admission of their . . . their what? Interest? Attraction? Affection? She couldn't put a word to that, either, and therefore had no guide to what he wanted from her, now.

He sat near her without touching, leaning forward with his elbows on his knees, hands clasped. He seemed to be staring at the wall of the fountain, where the names of Goodabri's sons and daughters who had served in world wars and other conflicts were inscribed, a small cross carved beside the names of those who had never returned home.

He'd been away, overseas somewhere, in an operation that had taken the best part of two months. She'd tuned in to the morning news on the radio every day of those weeks, dreading hearing of Australian soldiers killed or injured in Afghanistan or Iraq. She hadn't even known for sure if he was overseas, but from the murmured comments of senior Parks staff it had seemed most likely. But he *had* been overseas – he'd confirmed that earlier. And he was still in the army reserve, still a commando, and they could call him up again at any moment.

Every time he went away, there'd be a chance he wouldn't return home. She would have to get used to that. Somehow.

The band had finished playing and the hum of many voices drifted out from the hall. The light breeze brushed her skin through the lace, cool but not cold.

Simon broke the silence. 'My head's so full, I'm not sure where to start. But I want you to know – you're beautiful tonight, Erin. You are anyway, but in that dress you're . . . you look like a goddess. You're breathtaking. Literally. And you have every right to be proud of your skills and accomplishment.'

Of all the compliments she'd received during the evening, his meant the most. He'd said *she* was beautiful and breathtaking. Not the dress. Not that she 'scrubbed up okay' or that he 'almost didn't recognise her' or that the dress 'must have cost a fortune'. And he'd complimented her skills in a way that *did* make her proud.

'Thank you. Dressmaking makes a change from wrangling fencing wire or building walking tracks. Underneath the tomboy me is another side that likes playing with pretty fabrics.'

'I've never thought of you as a tomboy,' Simon said. 'Never. A capable and practical woman, yes. Capable and practical and beautiful and sensual and I wish . . . I wish things had been different tonight.'

Sensual. Every second man tonight had called her pretty or beautiful, and the cheekier ones had called her sexy, but they'd just been light-heartedly flirting. Simon wasn't flirting. He'd spoken aloud what they'd left unspoken, unacknowledged for months. Her libido had started weaving a whole new set of fantasies when she'd first seen him tonight, the black dinner jacket and bow tie a radical change from his work clothes but somehow accentuating his height and muscular power. If she could have taken him somewhere private, stripped off those clothes, let the heat between them build, unconstrained . . .

Her skin flushed, every nerve begging, just imagining the touch of his naked skin. Reality blew a chill wind over the brief flight of fantasy. Not possible. Not now. Not tonight. 'I wish things were different, too,' she said. 'Maybe they will be, sometime in the future.'

'Yes. I hope so.'

She didn't add anything more, because what else was there to say? She'd wait, and see what happened once he'd had time to come to terms with Hayley's death. She closed her eyes against the wave of sorrow. Her determination to be adult, mature and considerate didn't help to fill the ache in her heart, the cold empty place in her bed, or the loneliness in her soul.

The auction restarted inside and the auctioneer's smooth, fast-paced patter created a new rhythm, accompanied outside by the burbling of the fountain.

Simon shifted on the seat to face her, still keeping that small distance between them. 'Fraser said you'd found out something. About where Hayley might have been.'

Glad to have something solid to concentrate on, she told him briefly what she'd learned.

'Simple Bliss? They're called that?'

When she nodded, he said, 'I think you might be on to something. For years, Hayley used to send me Christmas and birthday cards, although they weren't always on time. No letters, but sometimes she included a note – just a couple of sentences. The thing is, she often mentioned bliss, or being blissful. And loving the simple life.'

The instinct that had suggested a connection between Hayley and the woman in the pop-up shop firmed into belief. 'We have to tell Steve. Do you still have the cards?'

'Yes. In a box at the house. If the police haven't taken them already, I'll go look for them.'

'Let's see Steve first. He was talking with a woman, said there might be something relevant.'

Simon's phone buzzed in his jacket pocket and he drew it out, glancing at the number before answering. He paused, listening. 'Yes. We're just outside. Okay, will do.' He stood as he put his phone away. 'Fraser's in the club committee room. He wants us in there.'

The committee room, just off the foyer, was empty save for Steve, Tess, and the woman Steve had been speaking with in the foyer. The woman clutched a handkerchief in her hand, her eyes red, and Tess sat beside her at the table, holding her other hand. Someone had brought in a tray of cups and saucers, as well as coffee and tea pots, and Steve poured out tea.

Erin closed the door behind them, shutting out some of the noise from the ball and the curious onlookers.

'Simon, Erin,' Steve began, passing a cup of tea to the woman, 'this is Catherine. Catherine's the new community nurse at Strathnairn.'

Erin smiled and nodded at the woman as she sat down at the table beside Simon. In her fifties or so, Catherine had silver strands in her hair, a round, kindly face, and a string of mauve glass pearls around her neck that matched the satin of her gown. She wiped another tear from her eye as she said hello to them both. Whatever she'd told Steve, or been told by the police, it had clearly upset her.

'Now, if this was Sydney or Newcastle or even Tamworth,' Steve continued, 'I'd be following procedure and wouldn't be telling you this.' He cast a quick glance at Tess, who met it with her cool, unflinching gaze. 'But it's not. It's a small community in a sparsely populated region and we have to do things differently out here. The thing is, Catherine visited a patient out at Page Hill on Monday morning and picked up a hitchhiker on the way back to Strathnairn.'

Page Hill. Erin knew the locality. About forty kilometres north-east of Goodabri, east of the area of the park where Sybilla had died. And the shortest route between Page Hill and Strathnairn – dirt roads mostly, but reasonable – passed through Goodabri.

'Catherine's description of the woman matches Hayley. Catherine, perhaps you could tell Simon, in your own words, what you told me?'

'I went to Sydney on Tuesday and only got back today. I just heard. About . . . about the murder.' Catherine paused to breathe in, clearly trying to suppress her emotion. 'My condolences, Simon. It must have been a shock to you.'

He acknowledged her sympathy with courtesy. 'Thank you. Please go on. I appreciate your help in this.'

'The woman I gave the lift to,' she began, 'she wasn't actually hitchhiking, but she was a couple of kilometres past where Millers Road meets the Goodabri Road, and she was limping, so I stopped. There's nothing out there. The properties are few and far between, and there's hardly any traffic on the road. She said a friend had given her a ride to the junction and she thought she could walk the rest of the way. But she had some bad blisters and I couldn't leave her there, with such a long way to go She seemed polite and harmless, no sign of drugs, so I offered her a lift.'

Not unusual, out in the bush. You had to be careful, but Erin sometimes offered a ride to hikers or people stranded by a car breakdown.

Catherine took a sip of her tea. 'I didn't quite believe her about getting a ride to the junction – the blisters were bad, like she'd walked a fair way – and it seemed odd her being out there alone, without a car. I tried to get her to talk but she was very reluctant. Nervous, in fact. I thought maybe she was afraid of something or in some kind of trouble, so I pressed her a little. She finally said she had to get to her friend in Goodabri. That she needed his help. She said her daughter was caught up in a cult, and she needed his help to get her out of it.'

Simon started, as though the words had whipped him. His voice harsh, guttural, he repeated, 'Her *daughter*? Hayley has a *daughter*?'

CHAPTER 8

He'd almost shouted the words, when Catherine had told him all she knew. Hayley had a daughter. A dozen more questions joined the hundreds of unanswered ones already drumming in his head, and he had to fight to stop anger overwhelming him. Anger with Hayley. With himself. With this whole damn situation that left him powerless and uncertain.

Ashamed of his outburst, he gritted his teeth and tried to soften his voice for the sake of the woman who had only wanted to help. 'Did she say anything about the girl?'

'No, not much. We were almost at Goodabri, so there wasn't much time. I asked about the cult, what kind it was, and she said she'd never have thought it was a cult, but "he" had changed, she said that he'd lied to them for years, and that he scared her now. I offered to take her to the Strathnairn police station, but she said she wanted to see her friend first. That he'd know what to do.'

He'd know what to do? What bitter irony. He had no clue what to do, where to start, even what to ask next. The question that drummed loudest in his mind, over all the others, was: *Whose daughter?* Who had fathered Hayley's child?

As if she'd read his thoughts, Erin asked, 'Did she give you any indication of the girl's age? Or why she didn't have her daughter with her?'

Catherine shook her head. 'No. I didn't have time to find out. I should have. I shouldn't have just left her in Goodabri. If I'd just done something more . . . But she was so adamant her friend would help her and she said he was a good man. I was already running late for another appointment so I dropped her on the edge of town.'

After everything, Hayley had still believed in him, and again he hadn't been there. The knife in his chest twisted a few more times.

'Did she have anything with her?' Tess asked. 'A bag or a case or anything?'

'Just a little cloth bag. A bag with a drawstring – like a kid's library bag. It was red. I don't think there was much in it – it looked very light.'

A small bag with something light in it that she'd taken the trouble to carry with her when she'd fled. He had no doubt now that she *had* fled – that she'd run away from someone or some situation that frightened her. Why else would she have hidden in his house for days?

He looked at Fraser across the table. 'Was the bag found at the house?'

'Not that I'm aware of. Leah didn't mention it.' Fraser had his phone in his hand, as though he itched to call or send a message immediately. Or perhaps he was only checking the time. He placed the phone back on the table and stood up. 'Catherine, thank you for your time. You've helped us a great deal. Did you come with friends tonight? Or would you like someone to drive you home?'

'No. Thank you. I'm here with friends.' Catherine nervously smoothed the skirt of her gown as she got to her feet. 'I hope you find the person who did this, Detective. That poor woman. And I hope you find the girl, too. She was so worried about her.'

'We'll find her,' Simon assured her, as much a vow to himself as a promise to her. 'I won't stop looking until we find her and make sure she's safe.'

He waited only until Fraser had seen the woman out and closed the door behind her. 'I'm going over to my house to find that bag.'

Fraser didn't object. 'Good. I want to know what was in it. Tess, do you live somewhere nearby? Can you get into uniform quickly?'

'Yes. Just give me ten minutes. But isn't it a bit late to go knocking on doors?'

'We're only knocking on one door. A place out on Millers Road. Your local real estate agent in there,' he waved a hand towards the function room, 'told me he sold it last year. All done through lawyers on behalf of a private company and he didn't meet the new owners. We need to go there and find out if Hayley or Sybilla came from there, and if so, inform whoever lived with them of their deaths.'

'Would you call me afterwards?' Simon asked. 'I don't care what time it is.'

'Will do. I'll also want to know what, if anything, you find.'

If Simon could have gone with them to the property, he would have, but that was a police job. Fraser was already allowing him to return to his place to search for the bag, a concession that Haddad probably wouldn't have permitted. It was a more effective use of his knowledge and time than driving out to Millers Road on what could be a wild goose chase. But if Hayley had been living there . . . Fraser would tell him within the next couple of hours. The detective seemed to be driven by pragmatism rather than procedure, and committed to finding out the truth.

'I'll go find Nick and update him,' Fraser said, already moving towards the door. 'Tess, I'll pick you up at the station in ten minutes. Erin, are you going with Simon?'

'Yes,' she said. 'Two sets of eyes are better than one.'

'There's no need, Erin,' Simon argued. 'You were up all last night. Have a couple more dances to enjoy the ball, and then go home and sleep.'

She gave him the raised eyebrow she usually reserved for the young guys in the SES squad when they were being particularly macho and dense. 'Dance when I could be helping? Sleep without knowing what you and Steve have found out? Not likely, Kennedy.'

He didn't argue any further.

After she'd collected her purse and shawl from the main room, they drove in his hire car the couple of blocks to his house. His LandCruiser was still in the driveway, where he'd pulled up yesterday evening. No one had yet removed the police tape from across the front of the house and the driveway, so he parked the hire car on the road. The houses in the street were darkened. His mostly elderly neighbours usually went to bed early, although a few of the more socially active were still at the ball.

Goodabri didn't run to streetlights anywhere other than the main road, but the moon lit their way as they crossed the front yard and he unlocked the door. The breeze was picking up, blowing a few wisps of cloud across the sky, swaying the branches of the grevilleas under the front windows so that they tapped softly against the glass.

Simon paused in the passageway, just inside the door. He'd liked this old house, the few weeks he'd lived in it. He'd even considered buying it. A crazy idea, investing in real estate in a tiny town like Goodabri, but the place could be done up, and the block of land was large, with plenty of room for a decent shed, a vegetable garden, an outdoor entertainment area. All the things he'd wanted to do for years and never done in any of the places he'd bought.

But as he walked into the house tonight, the memory of Hayley's body lying on the study floor erased that former enthusiasm, and the rooms and passageway seemed small and cramped rather than cosy, as if the very walls were huddling down in despair. If it hadn't been for Erin by his side he might have huddled down against the wall himself.

His phone beeped with a message – Fraser confirming that the forensic officers hadn't found the bag. He showed it to Erin. 'Where would you put a small bag?' he asked.

She drew her light shawl a little tighter around her shoulders, as if she, too, felt the coolness of the house. 'We're assuming it's still here. Whoever killed her and trashed your spare room was looking for something. Maybe they found it and took it. But maybe they didn't. That's what we'll hope for. Do you know which room she slept in? Because if I go and stay in someone's house, I leave my things in the room I sleep in.'

That made sense. Hayley had always been tidy, not left things lying around. A habit belted into her by her abusive father. 'I'm pretty sure she slept in my bedroom. Not in the bed,' he added. 'On a beanbag on the floor.'

'You look in there. I'll start in the living room.'

A reluctance to enter the bedroom made him go to the study door. He flicked the light on. They'd taken Hayley, of course, and only the bloodstains on the polished floorboards remained. He dragged his gaze away from the floor to scan the rest of the room. The drawers in the computer desk had been pulled out and emptied. He couldn't see his flash drives and camera cards in the pile of files and books on the floor. Had the forensic officers taken them? Or the person who'd trashed the place?

His smashed computer was gone, too, and the hard drives. But he'd seen them earlier, so the police must have them now. The fact that the killer had taken so much interest in the computers and drives suggested it was some kind of data they were looking for. Or hoping to destroy. Hayley hadn't carried much in her red bag, but a whole lot of data could fit on a thumb drive or an SD card. Or perhaps they were concerned that she'd left something on his computer – emails? Letters? Images?

The sofa bed in the corner seemed almost undisturbed, although the two small cushions he often propped behind his back when reading had been shifted from their customary spot at one end. He couldn't remember noticing them earlier, but then he'd been too focused on Hayley. No way to know whether they'd been moved before the police went through. No way to know if Hayley had settled down on the sofa with a book, lying on her side, using a cushion to support the book in a comfortable position as she'd often done, or if her killer had searched behind them.

'What did they think you were hiding, Hayley?' he murmured. 'Where did you put it?'

Nothing obvious leapt out at him in this room. Erin's suggestion of the bedroom made sense and he went back into it. First things first before he forgot about them: he needed to get the cards Hayley had sent him. He'd kept all of them, close to thirty of them. A cottage this age didn't come with built-in wardrobes, but the old art-deco one he'd picked up from a clearance sale was a good tall piece with shelf space above the hanging rack. If the police had searched here, they'd left no sign of it, and taken nothing.

He reached up for one of the boxes he stored there. *Paperwork*, according to his own scrawl on the packaging tape that he'd sealed it with when he'd packed up to move to this house. The cards were all in there, along with papers relating to his parents and his own army service.

He didn't open it, just left it on the bed so he wouldn't forget to take it.

Moving around the bed, he picked up the orange blanket and folded it, then stood for a long moment with it over his arm, remembering. He thought they'd been happy, those first few months. Perhaps they had been. Perhaps Hayley had been. But maybe he'd just been happy to have a pretty woman in his home, to have regular sex. He'd only been twenty-one, after all. And part of his contentment might have been his sense of doing the right thing, of being a man and looking after her as a decent man should. His grandfather had certainly thundered at him often enough about responsibility.

All these years later, the only thing Simon was sure of was that he hadn't felt as alive with Hayley as he did with Erin.

He could hear her in the kitchen, opening cupboard doors, her heels clicking lightly on the lino floor. Doing the job that needed doing, thoroughly and without complaint or chatter.

He laid the folded blanket on the bed and lifted the beanbag out of the way. Nothing underneath it. He pictured Hayley curled up there, tucked in between the wall and the bed, hiding, and he got down on his knees and ran his hand along the space under the bed. The police had probably already searched there and he wasn't surprised to find nothing. But as he pushed the beanbag back to search further under the bed, his fingers touched something firm under the faux velvet of its cover. He unzipped the beanbag and thrust his hand between the inner and outer covers, reaching until he felt a twisted cord, a different texture from the other fabrics. He grasped it, pulling it out. The red bag.

Erin came down the hall, stopped in the doorway. 'You found it.'

'Yes. Hidden inside the beanbag.'

'Good.' She frowned, and bit her lip. 'I think there's someone outside.'

He rose to his feet instantly. 'You saw them?'

'No. I heard some noises when I was in the living room. I thought it was just the wind in the bushes outside. But when I was in the kitchen I heard more noises. Footsteps, I'm sure. The blinds are closed so I couldn't see out.'

A sound came from the back of the house – a hiss, a whoosh.

The moment he reached the hallway he saw the reflection of the light flickering against the polished wood of the open kitchen door. Glass shattered, and his single glance into the kitchen before he slammed the door closed showed the back wall of the weatherboard house alight, a window broken and the blinds burning.

Erin, just behind him, had seen it too. Simon thrust the red bag into her hand.

'Go out the front,' he told her. 'I'll grab the box of letters.'

But before she'd made it to the front door, the same fiery whoosh of sound came from that direction, and light danced through the leadlight windows on either side of the door.

Both doors, impassable.

Bastards.

Simon switched into battle mode and moved instinctively. 'Out the study window,' he ordered. He was only three steps from the bed and he grabbed the orange blanket and the box of papers before following Erin. Smoke was creeping out from under the kitchen door and the loud crackling and roar of the flames told him the fire had taken hold. The old timber house wouldn't last long.

He slammed the study door shut behind him for the little extra time it would give them. The window overlooked Snowy's house with the driveway to the old garage at the back. Erin had already tugged at the stiff latch, but he knew it wouldn't allow the window to open wide enough anyway. He nudged her aside and with his arm padded by the blanket, smashed the glass with a few quick blows.

He could see no one outside, nor smell fuel in the immediate vicinity. Only the smoke blown by the wind. He laid the folded blanket over the jagged glass in the window frame.

'Out you go,' he said to Erin, giving her a hand up through the window. She moved quickly, despite the awkwardness of the long dress, the cloth bag slung over her shoulder. His hand held her steady as she balanced for a moment in her heeled sandals on the ledge before gathering up her skirt and jumping nimbly down to the gravel below. He passed the box out to her before he climbed through himself, then grabbed the blanket.

He could hear the fire catching in the roof above the kitchen, the heat hitting the corrugated iron. At the front, the fire hadn't caught so strongly yet, and his LandCruiser in the driveway was still some distance from the flames. He couldn't see anyone in the open front yard, or in the street. But from the lane behind the long backyard he heard the roar of a car engine and tyres spinning in gravel.

'See if you can rouse Snow,' he said to Erin. If she couldn't wake the old man within a minute or two, he'd smash the door down. 'I'll just back the LandCruiser out.'

'And call Nick,' she said. 'At least half the RFS crew are at the ball. He'll alert them quicker than triple-0 will.'

They'd be ten minutes yet, getting their gear and the truck. His cottage would be well alight by then, and there might be a battle to save Snowy's place and the vacant house on the other side of his own – but with the low pressure from his own water tank and no street water, he couldn't fight it, just try to protect people and salvage the little he could. It only took him a few moments to reverse his LandCruiser down the driveway and swing out onto the road, parking behind the hire car in front of Snowy's place to leave space for the fire truck. Erin was still pounding on the front door.

He dialled Nick's number as he jogged across Snowy's lawn, and passed Erin the phone just as Nick answered. While she spoke rapidly to Nick, Simon trod on some of his neighbour's precious flowers to bang on his bedroom window.

He'd never been so pleased to hear the old man's garrulous complaints.

'Fire, Snowy!' he yelled. 'Unlock the door!'

'I'm coming. Hold on, I'm coming.'

Simon could hear him shuffling around in his room, but it took over a minute before the latch on the front door clicked, and Snowy opened it, dragging a dressing gown on over his pyjamas.

Simon stepped inside and took his arm. 'You've got to get out, Snow. My place is on fire. You need to get some distance, to be on the safe side.'

For once Snowy heard okay, and his inherent good sense kicked in. 'Jesus, lad. Have I got time to get my wallet from the bedroom?'

'Super quick, Snow. Super quick.'

The old man moved pretty fast in spite of his gammy leg, grabbing his wallet from the bedside table and a wooden box from beneath it. 'Always dreaded fire,' he said as Simon ushered him out the door. 'Got all the important things in me box.'

'Good on you.' Grateful for the old man's pragmatic cooperation, Simon steered him across the lawn to Erin.

She immediately wrapped the orange blanket around Snowy. 'I'll take him down the road. I don't have my protective gear, dammit. I left it at home tonight.'

She usually carried her SES uniform in case of callouts, just as he did. He shook his head. 'Don't worry. The RFS will be here in minutes. Just keep Snow somewhere safe.'

He unreeled Snowy's garden hose and started damping down the side of the house to protect it, but it wasn't long before the heat from his burning house made him retreat. A siren wailed on the main street, just a few hundred yards away. There was nothing more he could do. The fire truck had powerful hoses, plenty of water, and the crew had all the right protective gear.

For a brief moment he considered going to look for the arsonist, but it had been quite some minutes since he'd heard a car drive away at speed. They'd easily be well out of town by now. Better to wait until the police arrived and they could look for any evidence in the back lane.

So he stood out on the road, in his dinner suit and bow tie, beside Erin in her beautiful dress and Snowy in his grey pyjamas and maroon dressing gown, and watched his house burn. The adrenaline rush of the desperate moments in the house showed little sign of fading; his heart raced, his senses were heightened, and every muscle was tensed, primed to fight.

•

Erin had battled enough fires out in the bush to recognise that the house was already beyond saving. Part of the roof had collapsed, and some internal walls, and flames billowed out the windows. The RFS crew had leapt to work, their strategy to extinguish the flames and prevent them from spreading to the houses on either side. The direction of the breeze reduced the risk to Snowy's house, but the vacant house on the other side remained in danger.

Simon had given her his jacket and she pulled its warmth close around her. When Snowy accepted an invitation from the neighbour across the road to go inside for a rum, he shrugged off the orange blanket and draped it around her, over the jacket, before waving a cheery farewell and wandering off with his friend.

'Are you warm enough?' Simon asked, breaking his silence. 'I can drive you back to the club if you like.'

'I'm perfectly fine. I don't really need the blanket. Didn't want to hurt Snow's feelings, though.' She'd already wished more than once for her practical SES uniform and boots. Somehow, seeing the dress, all the guys forgot she had certificates in firefighting, search and rescue, truck driving and other heavy-duty jobs, and thought she was a delicate flower, needing looking after.

She and Simon hadn't said much with Snowy there, but once he'd gone she quietly voiced the thoughts occupying her mind. 'One of the noises I heard was probably fuel splashing on the back door. Whoever did it knew we were in there.' They'd only just arrived, they'd turned on lights – there was no way the arsonist couldn't have realised they were inside.

'Yes.'

He'd already thought of that, obviously. Not surprising, for a man used to war and fighting.

'But the timing was quick,' she continued, laying out the logic because logic was far preferable to considering what type of person would try to burn them to death. 'Unless someone followed us from the club, they were either waiting for you or they weren't targeting you specifically. Just your house.'

'Fraser only told me tonight that I could come back here. No one could have known that I would. So the primary aim had to be to destroy the place. But when we showed up – well, me, anyway – they must have seen the chance to get rid of me, too.'

She still had Hayley's cloth bag over her shoulder, so she reached under the blanket for it. 'Here. I guess you'd better see what Hayley was hiding.'

He took the bag and then hesitated, fingering the drawstring cord but not opening it straightaway.

The headlights of a car turned into the road and it pulled up behind the LandCruiser. Nick's car, she saw, when he dimmed the lights. Nick and Jo hurried over.

'You're both okay?' Jo asked, giving them the once-over, checking for injuries.

'We're fine. Honestly.' Erin removed the blanket from her shoulders to demonstrate that she wasn't the walking wounded.

Jo never fussed, and now she accepted the assurance as given – one of the things Erin appreciated about her. They'd been friends ever since Jo joined the Strathnairn team, and although Jo had a stack more letters after her name than Erin's Bachelor of Natural Resources, and gave scientific papers at international conferences, she was warm, perceptive, and easy to get along with. In the largely male environment they worked in, Erin valued having someone like Jo around.

'What happened?' Nick asked. 'You said arson on the phone.'

Simon gave a succinct report. No emotions, just facts arranged in precise order.

'A can of fuel and a couple of matches and it's all too easy to torch a place,' Nick said, with the grimness of experience. 'But why didn't the person do it when the murder was committed? That would have slowed down our investigation and destroyed most of the evidence.'

'The murder may have been unplanned,' Simon commented, still with that same emotionless, objective distance. Erin almost envied his military detachment, and yet his abrupt departure from the dance floor earlier this evening, his words to her afterwards and his reluctance to open Hayley's bag all suggested strong emotions that couldn't always be rigidly contained. During the last twenty-eight hours he'd been through hell, on top of whatever horrors he'd experienced in the previous two months. But he wouldn't show any weakness or vulnerability in front of Nick and the RFS crew. Probably not even in front of Jo.

'Do you need us to wait here, Nick?' Erin asked. 'It's going to be a little while before they get the fire out.'

'No. No sense breathing any more smoke than necessary. Steve will want to talk with you, but he won't be back for at least an hour. Can you wait for him? Maybe at the Parks office, if you don't want to go back to the ball?'

'I'll wait in the office,' Simon said. 'Fraser can find me there. Erin, you might as well go home. Fraser can speak with you tomorrow.'

He mustn't be thinking clearly if he thought she'd meekly go home and leave him to deal with this alone. 'I'll wait for Steve with you.'

Jo decided to return to the ball, in a move that Erin suspected was more about leaving her alone with Simon than a desire to socialise. With Steve and Tess still out, Haddad travelling to Newcastle, and the couple of night-duty officers working out of the Strathnairn station on a call elsewhere, Nick had no officers to call on and would be at the scene for a while.

While Simon drove his LandCruiser around to the National Parks office in the main street, Erin gave Jo a lift in his hire car to the ex-servicemen's club, where she planned to pick up her ute and leave the hire car in the relative security of the club's parking area.

'Is everything okay between you and Simon?' Jo asked on the short drive. 'You hardly spoke two words to each other over dinner. And you didn't dance for long.'

He just walked out and left her there, right in the middle of the dance floor . . . Yep, that would be the current hot topic of conversation at the ball. Soon to be replaced with: *Burned to the ground. Heard a rumour it might have been arson . . .* At least with Jo going back in there, she'd put paid to any of the wilder speculation.

Erin turned into the club's driveway and headed for a vacant parking space near her own ute. 'He only arrived back last night, Jo. The wife he never mentioned was murdered, in his house. That's enough complications as it is, without another death, an attempt on our lives, and a bucketload of unanswered questions. So there isn't anything between us, other than our existing friendship.'

'I'm glad that's still intact. I've missed working with you guys. Not much longer now, though – I'm expecting the all-clear on Monday for driving and for resuming full-time work.'

Would it be the same as it had been, the once close-knit team of Jo, Erin, Simon and Mal back together again? It would be good but no, not exactly the same. The events that had led to Jo's injuries, and now Hayley's murder – those shadows would lurk always.

Erin made herself smile. They'd need to keep positive and to celebrate the small victories to get through. 'Yay on the full-time return. Although you might not be so pleased when you see the backlog of paperwork I've left for you.'

Jo snorted indelicately as she got out of the car. 'What do you think I've spent the last two weeks doing while I've been stuck in the office?'

'Avoiding Mal's attempts to cocoon you in bubblewrap?' Erin wasn't entirely joking about their boss's overprotectiveness, and Jo rolled her eyes in agreement. 'Speaking of Mal, can you make sure he knows both Simon and I are unhurt? I don't want him worrying any more than he undoubtedly will.' Or coming straight around to the office tonight to check on them. She could rely on Jo to dissuade him from that.

By now, she thought, Simon would have opened up Hayley's bag. She knew from its weight that it contained more than a toothbrush and a change of underwear. Perhaps she was being overprotective of *him*, but despite his undoubted ability to physically protect himself, she suspected he needed space tonight.

As she got into her own ute and arranged the skirt of her dress so it wouldn't impede her driving, a wave of tiredness and emotion made her want to rest her head on the steering wheel. She resisted the urge. Stay strong, keep moving, keep going – the words became a silent chant.

Steve would be back soon. Simon might have discovered what Hayley was hiding. They might have some answers about who killed her, and why, whether Sybilla's death was connected, and why someone had tried to kill Erin and Simon tonight.

She still wore Simon's jacket over her dress and she pulled it a little closer around her body as she drove. A purely imaginary source of strength, but she needed all the strength she could muster.

•

Simon untied his bow tie, folded it and tucked it in his shirt pocket. He washed the ash and smoke from his face and hands, and made a pot of strong coffee, all the while knowing these were avoidance tactics. He'd put Hayley's bag and the box containing her cards on the desk in the small office behind the main room. The office Erin had been using in his absence. If he looked in the top drawer of the desk there'd be a stash of black jelly beans.

And there he was, thinking of Erin again, instead of confronting whatever it was Hayley had left him.

He carried his coffee mug into the office and sat at the desk. Before he opened the bag, he pulled out the desk drawer. More delaying tactics, but sure enough, the half-full packet of jelly beans sat in the corner. He almost took one, for a form of Dutch courage, but closed the drawer instead, leaving them untouched.

The twisted white cord that loosely knotted the drawstring bag closed came undone easily enough. He opened up the bag and removed the few objects, one by one, placing them on the desk. A small book with an embossed cover. A pencil stub. A pair of folding scissors. A square of cotton with a half-completed embroidery of butterflies, wrapped around a little fabric book with pins and needles neatly lined up in the felt pages. And an envelope with his own handwriting on it – the letter he'd sent her just after he'd moved to Goodabri, ten weeks ago.

He picked up the book. An unlined notebook, like one of the many he'd bought Hayley for her sketches. She'd always carried one, and he encouraged her drawing, because it was one of the few ways she had of expressing herself.

In fact, maybe this was actually one of the blank journal books he'd bought her for her birthday – the Celtic design of the decorative cover seemed familiar. And it was well worn, the gold embossing faded away in places, the page edges thickened through repeated turning.

He opened it to the first page. A pencil sketch of a baby wrapped in a blanket. A tiny baby, all crinkles and frown and yawn.

He turned the page. Another sketch. An older baby, maybe a few months, a beaming smile directed right at him. The next page showed a baby standing, little hands grasping the seat of a wooden chair for support. He kept turning pages. The baby – and it was the same baby – as a toddler, in a simple dress with a bow in her hair. The toddler hugging a small dog. A little girl, maybe three years old, bright-eyed in a short top and baggy trousers. On and on through the pencil sketches he went, page after page, more than fifty drawings, watching the little girl grow up. Some of the sketches were detailed, layered;

others might have been quickly done. But nonetheless it was a loving record of the child's life.

The last drawing showed the girl with her long hair loose around her shoulders, smiling directly at the artist, a small knife in her hand, apparently about to cut a cake decorated with candles. Candles arranged in a semicircle around the number thirteen, iced crookedly on the cake.

Thirteen. The girl had turned thirteen years old.

Hayley had left just on fourteen years ago. He'd last made love to Hayley the night before he'd shipped out, fourteen years ago. They'd been trying – again – to conceive.

Her daughter had already turned thirteen. The daughter she'd come to him to get help for. And she'd brought this little album of drawings, a record of her daughter's life.

He stared at the girl's face, its shape and her features, elfin, dainty and girlish. More like the Hayley he remembered than the lifeless woman on his floor last night. But definitely her child.

Numbness protected him from feeling. A paralysing numbness that radiated out from the large, frozen weight in his chest.

CHAPTER 9

Erin parked at the back of the building, beside Simon's truck. A light burned in the office; other than that, both halves of the building were in darkness. Not enough police in the district to have many people on duty for a second night running – although Steve and Tess should be back soon, and she wouldn't be surprised if Nick was calling Aaron in again. She doubted any of them had slept much since last night.

Her own eyes gritty from lack of sleep and from the smoke, she fumbled with her key at the back door, calling out, 'Just me,' as she managed to unlock it and push the door open.

Simon lifted his head from his hands when she entered the small office. There was no light in the hazel of his eyes. Hadn't been since those first moments yesterday before they'd found Hayley. Only pain, unguarded now, deep and dark.

She pulled out the chair opposite him and asked, 'What is it?'

'She's thirteen.' His voice was rough, hoarse, as though the words hurt him to speak. 'Hayley's daughter is thirteen.'

Thirteen. And Hayley had left him fourteen years ago.

'Did she say if . . . ?'

'She didn't say anything.' He passed across a small notebook.

Drawings. She flicked through the pages. Fifty or more drawings of a girl, from babyhood through childhood and into early adolescence.

Simon stood abruptly and paced to the window, staring out into the night. 'She could be my daughter. Or she could be someone else's.' He set out the statements as facts, as if he'd been repeating them in his head, time and again. 'For all I know, Hayley could have been having an affair before she left. Maybe that's *why* she left.'

If so, she was a fool, Erin thought. No, that was uncharitable and unkind. She hadn't known Hayley. She had no right to make any judgements.

'Did she give any indications of having an affair? Did she have any male friends you knew of?'

'No. She had very few friends. And the last time I saw her she said there was no one else.' He frowned, shaking his head in bewilderment. 'But that would have been after this girl was born. She came back to our place to get some things, but she didn't tell me about the baby.'

'Did you . . .' Hell, she wasn't sure how to ask this. She could almost understand a woman hiding a baby if her husband didn't want children. 'Did you want kids? Was it something you'd talked about?'

'Yes. We wanted a family. Hayley especially, but yes, me too.' He paced the small room, restless, and paused to face her, his back against a filing cabinet. 'I wanted to be a decent man. I thought I'd probably make a good father. But in three years, she only fell pregnant once. And she had a miscarriage. While I was deployed overseas and couldn't be there for her. We didn't have any luck conceiving again. I had to go away again, but when I came back we were going to do all the tests, find out why.'

'But then she left?'

'Yes. She left while I was gone. If she was pregnant again, I never knew.' He gave a long, slow exhalation. 'So there you go. I'm a spectacular failure as a husband.' He gave her a wry smile that attempted to make light of things and only succeeded in making her want to cry for him. 'I hope she found someone who made her happier than I did.'

Words eluded Erin. Words she could speak aloud, anyway. What kind of woman treated a man the way Hayley had treated Simon, who had only wanted to do right by her? A heartless, manipulative bitch? A selfish, self-absorbed one? A woman incapable of caring? Or a woman too damaged or afraid to make the emotional commitment a relationship required?

Whatever kind of woman Hayley had been, she'd done Simon an injustice, and hurt him deeply. Erin wasn't sure she'd be able to forgive her for that. But Hayley was gone and Simon was here, and he'd endured more in the last two days than anyone should ever have to.

'Marriages founder for a lot of reasons,' she said gently. 'It doesn't have to be anyone's fault. You're not a failure.'

He acknowledged her words with another small smile but the sorrow in his face didn't ease. So she went to him, to give him the kind of hug she'd give any good friend in need.

The initial stiffness in his body dissolved after a moment, and his arms closed around her. She'd only meant to give him a quick hug but she didn't step back to end it. Her head barely reached his shoulder, and when he didn't let her go she rested her cheek against his shirt and felt his arms tighten around her, and the light pressure of his face on her hair.

It felt right, holding him, and although she meant to give support, she drew strength from him, too. With one arm around him and her other hand on his chest, she closed her eyes and focused on him, on the warmth of his skin through the cotton shirt, on the rhythmic pulse through her palm, on the intimacy of their bodies close together, touching in trust.

There was heat, too, and desire that could flare in an instant, but neither of them took it anywhere, or said anything. Just that long, motionless embrace, the unspoken need to hold and be held overriding physical desire and all the other concerns and complications. And she was grateful for those moments, for the closeness shared with him.

The sound of a car engine slowing impinged on her awareness, and headlights flashed outside the window. Simon instantly tensed again, letting her go rapidly and striding out of the room, all protective soldier on alert. She followed more slowly, the loss of his warmth leaving her feeling cold and alone.

But it was only Steve's car, and he climbed out wearily, and knocked on the door of their building while Tess opened the police rooms.

'Any news?' Simon asked as he yanked open the door.

'Not much. Come through to our office and I'll update you.'

Tess had the lights on and a kettle boiling in the kitchen of the police incident rooms. Steve collapsed into a chair with his feet up on another one. Erin's feet ached from unaccustomed hours in high heels, and she sat on the edge of a table beside Tess. Simon propped a shoulder against a wall, hands in pockets, his face shuttered. He didn't look at her, as distant now as just a few moments ago he'd been close.

'I heard about the fire,' Steve began, his gaze moving between her and Simon. 'Jeez, sounds like you both had a lucky escape. I'm glad you're okay. Sorry about your place, though, Kennedy. I gather everything's gone.'

Simon shrugged, as if it didn't matter. 'I'm insured. And I lived in a high-bushfire-risk area for a few years, so I scanned important photos and documents. My stepfather has copies. The rest is just stuff. Plenty of people lose far more than I have.' He changed the subject without mentioning Hayley's bag. 'Did you find out anything?'

Steve noted the redirection of the conversation with a slightly raised eyebrow but went along with it without comment. 'I spoke to a woman at the homestead who said she didn't know either woman,' he said. 'She claimed to know nothing about Hayley, or about a child, or about Sybilla. I'm not entirely convinced.'

'Neither am I,' Tess said. 'It was as though she expected us, had rehearsed her response. She didn't show any of the classic signs of lying, but I doubt she was genuine.'

Steve nodded. 'Unfortunately, without something more to go on, we couldn't press her.'

Erin had to concentrate to shift her brain back into analytical mode. 'Did you ask about the dresses?'

'Yes. She just said she and her friends make clothing and sell it at markets from the north coast up into southern Queensland and online. They've apparently sold hundreds – anyone could have bought the dresses.'

All perfectly reasonable, on the surface. But it didn't explain why both Sybilla and Hayley, wearing those dresses, had died in this district. 'Did you see the others?' Erin asked. 'Did you see Willow, the young woman I spoke to?'

'It was close on midnight when we got there. The woman we spoke to – Mary – said her friends were sleeping. I didn't have enough reason to ask her to wake them.' Steve yawned, his eyes screwed tightly shut. He had to be exhausted. They all were. 'I've spoken with Aaron and he's researching a few things. If we can come up with something else, a reason to go back out there and ask more questions, we'll do it in the morning. I don't suppose you found Hayley's bag, by any miraculous chance?'

Erin looked to Simon, letting him answer the question.

'Yes,' he said. 'I found it.' He breathed in, then out, slowly and deliberately before he continued. 'There's a sketchbook with drawings of her daughter. She's turned thirteen already. There's a drawing of her with a birthday cake. I'll go get the book.'

Steve waited until Simon had left the room before he asked Erin, 'Thirteen? Does he know if the girl is his?'

'No. There's nothing in the sketchbook except images. But . . . she could be.'

'Shit. What a way to find out.'

Erin could only agree. He'd wanted children, he'd said. And with his gentleness, his steadiness and his respect for others, he would have made a good father. If this girl was his, then he'd missed out on all those years of her life. That had to be going through his mind. For a man like Simon, it would be hard knowledge to bear. Yet he'd not said one word in anger against Hayley.

•

Simon took a few moments in the silence to reinforce his mental control before he went back into the room with Hayley's things. Too many concerns whirled in his thoughts. He would have to go through them, one after another, when he had time and space to think straight. Right now he would show Fraser the sketches, and then take Erin home to Strathnairn. Tomorrow – no, later today, since it was after midnight – he could do the practical things, like notifying his insurance company and getting the basics he'd need. In the days to come, he'd deal with the rest. Even if the girl wasn't his child, he had to find her, ensure her safety and welfare. He owed that to Hayley. Finding her was the urgent task. Working through all the emotions? He had a lifetime to do that.

But one thing was clear in his mind: if she *was* his daughter, she would have to come first in his life from now on. She'd lost her mother, had no other family. Except him. Wherever she'd been, whatever her personality, her history, her state of mind, if she was his daughter she was his responsibility, now and for the future.

His life would be changed, irrevocably. And because of that, the perfect moment of that soul-soaring hug with Erin would have to stay in the past. Even if he cleared his head about Hayley and dealt with the ramifications of her murder, it wouldn't be fair to Erin to contemplate a future with her if he had a teenage daughter he had to put first.

And he had a lifetime to work through the emotions of that, too.

The bright fluorescent lights in the police rooms stung his tired eyes when he took Hayley's book and the rest of the bag's contents through to Fraser and the others. Someone had made coffee and he accepted a mug from Erin. One brief glance at her and his mental discipline took a hard hit. If not for all of his resilience and emotional endurance training he might have fallen to his knees and howled.

'I've just spoken with Nick,' Fraser said while he flicked through the sketches. 'They've found the fuel can in the back lane. Let's hope Forensics can get some prints off it.'

'Speaking of prints,' Tess interjected, 'shouldn't that book be evidence? Gloves would be a good idea, sarge.'

Simon cursed himself for not considering the bag as material evidence in Hayley's murder. 'Erin and I have already handled it,' he admitted.

'Don't stress over it,' Fraser said, although he took gloves from the box Tess proffered. 'This book is years old. There'll be prints all over it, mostly Hayley's. Listen, the forensic mob won't be back until morning. I'm going to photograph a couple of these images, but if you want to take this tonight, have a bit more time with it, you can.' He shot a conciliatory glance at Tess. 'Take some gloves, though. Just in case we need to dust it later.'

His throat tight, Simon muttered a thank you, grateful for the detective's thoughtfulness. If they had to dust the book, some of those drawings might be ruined. And they might be the only images he'd ever have of the girl – his daughter? – growing up.

Fraser snapped a few photos on his phone from the last pages of the book, and took a quick glance at the other items in the bag. 'I doubt they trashed your office looking for her stitchery,' he said. 'So there has to have been something else. Dammit.'

Something else they'd either found, or which was lying in the rubble of the house.

This time it was Tess who stifled a yawn, and Erin caught it, yawning too. Slumped in a chair with her hands wrapped around a coffee mug, she looked exhausted.

'Right,' Fraser said, pushing himself to his feet. 'Nothing else we can do here tonight. Tess, you're dead on your feet. You're off duty as of now. Nick's ordered a briefing here at eight in the morning so I'll see you then. Simon, if you can drop those things back before lunchtime, I'd appreciate it. Have you got somewhere to stay tonight?'

'You're both welcome to crash at my place if you like,' Tess offered, looking at Erin and Simon. 'There's a spare bedroom and a sofa bed in the living room.'

Simon waited for Erin's answer.

'Thanks, but I'll go home.' Her grin was crooked with fatigue. 'It's about time Cinderella changed out of her dress, and I don't have working clothes with me.'

'I'll drive you,' Simon said, and after only a slight hesitation she nodded.

They took his LandCruiser rather than her ute, since he had to bring Hayley's things back in the morning.

'You can give me a lift back when you come,' Erin said, as they turned onto the road to Strathnairn. 'I'll do the weekend rounds of the camping areas out here tomorrow morning.'

Collecting money, cleaning toilets, taking out rubbish and generally keeping an eye on things. Regular visits that took time because of the distances involved. 'Can't Rob do it?' Simon asked. 'You surely must be due some days off.'

'Rob's doing the three other parks. Besides, I was thinking . . .' In the dim light inside the vehicle he saw her turn to him. 'I was thinking that the fences out near Angel Falls need checking. The fences on the north side of the river that adjoin the private properties up there. We could do that tomorrow afternoon.'

And take a look at the property the Simple Bliss women lived on, if only from the boundary. Simon liked her thinking. 'If the police don't turn up anything new in the morning, you're on.'

'Good,' she said. When she didn't say anything else for a while, he glanced across and saw that she'd fallen asleep. She slept the rest of the way, and he drove through the quiet night with only his thoughts for company. Tiredness dragged at him, too, but his brain was too busy to doze and he kept the vent blowing cool air on his face to stay alert.

She woke as he turned into the dirt track to the farm cottage she rented, the LandCruiser bouncing over the potholes.

'I'm sorry,' she said. 'I meant to help keep you awake.'

'No need,' he told her. He pulled in to park in her driveway, and flicked on the internal light before turning to look at Erin. Strands of her hair drifted around her face, loosened from the soft arrangement, her eyes still heavy-lidded from sleep, his jacket swamping her . . . Desire and need hit him hard.

'You are going to stay, aren't you?' she asked, and then she blushed slightly. 'The bed in the spare room is made up. No sense you driving back out to the park or trying to find a hotel at this hour.'

On long nights in the mountains in northern Iraq he'd allowed himself to imagine driving to Erin's place after SES training or work, going inside with her, closing the door on the world and being with her, just the two of them. With her confidence and self-assurance she'd be no shy lover, and his imagination had revelled in that knowledge. But that was before he'd come home and found Hayley's body. And before he'd heard about her daughter.

He had too many regrets to count, and there'd be no point going over them anyway. And both he and Erin were bone-tired, and sunrise would be here soon enough, with all the demands of the new day.

'Thanks, Erin. I appreciate it.' He'd had plenty of experience at controlling his longing for her. Mental discipline had got him through war and grief and loneliness. Unsatisfied desire wouldn't kill him. It might send him to hell, but a different one than his grandfather had preached about.

However, his resolve and discipline took a nosedive when he followed her into the living room of her cottage and she shrugged out of his jacket and handed it back to him. The warmth of her body lingered in the cloth, and standing close to her he could smell the light floral highlights of her perfume above the smoky undertones. The skin of her shoulders, pale and smooth beneath the blue lace, tempted his fingers, her pulse fluttered at her throat, and her blue eyes, deep and direct, held questions and promises.

He only meant to brush her cheek with his hand, to acknowledge his feelings for her with one small caress, before he stepped away. Instantly, though, she turned her face and kissed his palm, and the bolt of desire speared right through his veins to his heart and his groin and his brain. He might still have been able to resist the craving to pull her to him, but she stepped into his arms and he instinctively drew her in further, body to body. But he just held her, he didn't kiss her, and she understood and cuddled in close, resting her head against his shoulder.

He'd always believed that the notion that a man couldn't control himself was a hideous, deceitful and misogynistic myth. He still believed that, without reserve. But with Erin in his arms he needed all his fortitude to ignore the whispers urging him to put aside his resolve. The devil's whispers, his grandfather would have said. Another one of the old man's beliefs he'd rejected, long ago. He'd seen evil, and it had nothing to do with the relationship between him and Erin.

Erin shifted just enough to lightly touch his cheek with her fingertips. 'I know what we said earlier. So, you tell me.' Her voice sounded calm and sure and husky. 'You tell me what you need. What you want.'

Her understanding and her empathy almost undid him. He couldn't let her think he didn't care. 'I want . . .' He wanted honesty between them. Honesty and openness and trust. His throat gravelly with need, he said, 'I want to kiss your mouth until we're both gasping for breath. I want to taste your mouth and feel your skin, and unzip your dress and slide it off your shoulders. I want to discover every inch of you with my mouth and my hands and my body.' Giving his imagination that much rein fired the heat in his body. Hell was here and now and he was burning in it, and although he could have ended it he didn't. He didn't move his hands. He didn't move them to caress her, he didn't move them away. But he kept hold of her as if he clung to a life raft, and he continued to murmur into her hair, 'I want to make you cry out in pleasure and to bury myself in you and find peace and sleep with you in my arms.'

Her shiver vibrated through his body and her fingers dug into his back. She drew in her breath in a small gasp. 'So tell me why we aren't following through on that, Kennedy. Because I'm aching for you and I want to make love with you here and now, no matter what the future brings.'

He groaned in frustration, hating that it had become about him, rather than her, when she deserved to be cherished and loved and satisfied. 'Because there's so much in my head I can't get straight. When – if – we make love, I want you to be able to believe that it's totally about you and me and *us*, not just some adrenaline reaction or me trying to bury myself in you to forget what's going on.'

She didn't say anything for a long moment. She gradually withdrew from his arms, took a step back, but one hand remained gently touching his shoulder. A last connection she seemed hesitant to break. He didn't want her to break it.

'You have more honour than I have.' Her regretful smile cut straight into his heart. 'As if I didn't know that already. Go to bed, Simon. Get some sleep. Help yourself to anything you need. I'll see you sometime after sunrise.'

She stepped forward again, lifted her head to his and kissed him on the mouth, no fleeting brush of the lips but a promise, brief and hungry and passionate, that almost demolished his resolve. And then she turned and walked into her bedroom, closing the door behind her.

He'd done the right thing. If he told himself that often enough he might begin to believe it. But among all the confusion and unknowns that Hayley's death had brought, the one thing that shone clear and certain was that he cared for Erin more deeply than he'd ever cared for his wife.

And he wished that doing the right thing didn't make him feel so much of a bastard for hurting her.

•

In the quiet of her bedroom, Erin tugged down the zipper of her dress and stepped out of it, her eyes tightly closed, holding back tears.

She wouldn't cry. She wouldn't cry, because who cried when a good man acted with honour and respect? Who cried when they'd been sensible and not complicated matters any more than they already were? But her heart just wasn't listening to all the sensible, rational reasons to hold off from starting anything with Simon.

She draped the dress over a chair and pulled on her yoga pants and a soft, well-worn sweatshirt. Comfort clothes, nothing even slightly sensual about them. She crawled into bed and hugged the spare pillow. Her brain whirred, her feet throbbed from the hours in heels, her body buzzed with unsated need, and her heart ached. Not a good recipe for sleep.

Hayley had been murdered, her friend Sybilla was dead, and her daughter was with a group that might be a cult. And the Simple Bliss group, who'd denied knowing Hayley or Sybilla, invited visitors to experience their life.

Erin rolled onto her back and stared up at the ceiling, still clutching the pillow to her chest. Joshua would be there at the community on Sunday. Surely they'd find the girl before then. But it was already Saturday and tomorrow was Sunday and that didn't give them much time.

Hayley had believed her daughter to be in danger. Whether the girl was Simon's daughter or not, she was just thirteen years old. And someone had murdered her mother.

Erin rolled onto her side again, pulling the pillow close. She had too many accrued days off and needed to use some. She'd do whatever she had to do.

•

Machine-gun fire swept the village square, children and women screamed and died, and old men laughed and laughed . . .

Simon jerked awake, half out of bed before he recognised the raucous cackling of kookaburras outside the window.

He fell back against the pillow, sweat dampening the twisted sheets. He hated waking up like this, the nightmares so fresh and vivid that it took time and conscious effort to disentangle the real from the remembered and from the fears his subconscious tormented him with.

Erin's house. The bed in Erin's spare room. Sunrise, going by the glimpse of light through the gap in the curtains. Daylight, and a mob of kookaburras proclaiming their territory to all and sundry.

And Hayley was dead and Erin could have died last night in the fire and Hayley needed his help to rescue her daughter from . . . from what?

He swung his legs to the floor and reached for Hayley's bag, laying out the contents beside him on the bed. He traced the spiral design on the book cover with his fingers. *What did you want to tell me, Hayley? What do I need to know?*

He leafed through the pages again, looking for something, any clue. Once again, the child's likeness to Hayley struck him. She was clearly Hayley's biological child, not a child she'd adopted. But still he could see nothing of himself in the girl.

His response swung between relief and sadness, back and forth. The relief he understood – a daughter would complicate his life no end. Yet he also discovered that the old, buried grief of Hayley's miscarriage still had the power to hurt, even after all these years. The shattered hopes and dreams they'd shared, for the child, for the family they'd build, still haunted him with questions of what might have been.

But she'd left him and had a child, and excluded him from her life. Except for the birthday and Christmas cards she'd sent each year, he could have believed she'd forgotten him altogether.

So why had she come to him for help? And what threatened her and the girl? Damn, he was going over and over the same ground and getting nowhere.

He dragged on the trousers he'd worn last night but left the shirt draped on a chair, as it reeked of smoke. Trying to be quiet and not wake Erin, he went out the back door and around to his vehicle to get the clothes he'd bought from Dylan's yesterday, and the box with Hayley's cards.

Despite his efforts to make no noise, the water pump kicked in, which meant Erin had to be up. After the dreams he'd had of her last night, he almost lacked the courage to face her, but he went back inside, anyway. The kettle was boiling in the kitchen and the sound of briefly running water came from the bathroom. He found coffee mugs and coffee and had a pot made before she emerged.

'A semi-naked man in my kitchen making coffee? Now I know I'm still asleep and dreaming,' she joked, almost as easily as their usual teasing but for the way she averted her gaze from his bare chest. He should have put the shirt on, smoke and all.

As for her . . . somehow her tousled ponytail, baggy sweatshirt and yoga pants were sexier than her ball gown. And that was a train of thought he needed to derail, fast.

'I'll go wash and put some clothes on, if it's okay to use your shower.'

She took her cup of coffee and waved him towards the bathroom. 'Go. Don't use all the hot water. I may be awake enough to function when you're done.'

He showered, shaved and dressed in army-fast time, and his coffee was still reasonably hot when he carried Hayley's bag into the kitchen. Erin worked at her laptop on the kitchen table, a half-eaten slice of toast on a plate beside her.

'Help yourself to toast,' she said. 'Sorry I don't have anything much else to offer. Grocery shopping is on my to-do list.'

She seemed absorbed in what she was doing, so he put a slice of bread in the toaster and opened the box of cards while he waited. The earliest cards were bought ones: landscape or wildlife photos on the front, blank inside other than Hayley's handwriting wishing him a happy birthday, or a joyful Christmas, in the neat, small letters that had always seemed to him to represent her timidity, her fear of being noticed.

It is beautiful here and I love the simple life, she'd written in one. In another: *It is peaceful being so close to nature*. And in later cards: *I am blissful and happy; My work is joyful and rewarding.*

He'd kept the cards roughly in order of receipt; after the first few years, most of them were home-made, evolving from plain pieces of cardstock decorated with cut-outs of coloured paper to rustic handmade paper illustrated with her own drawings. And still those brief, one-sentence notes assuring him of her contentment, and each one signed from her 'with love'.

He went back through the pile, this time looking closely at the drawings on the cards she'd made, each of them in her simple, naturalistic style. A kangaroo and her joey. A magpie pair and their young one, more fluff than feathers. A possum on a tree branch with her baby on her back. Now he saw it: mothers and babies, time and again. And then there was a drawing of a little girl, hair in short pigtails, hands outstretched, reaching for a butterfly. Another of a little girl bending down, offering something to a pair of ducks. A young girl reading in the fork of a tree, long hair falling forward across her face. The young girl playing a flute, again with her hair concealing her face.

Until now he'd never looked too closely at the pictures. Only enough to notice and be glad that Hayley was still drawing, a positive sign for her. She'd often drawn children, but in the midst of her depression after the miscarriage she'd been unable to pick up a pencil.

His coffee and toast were both cold. He passed the pile of cards across the table to Erin. 'Tell me what you think,' he said.

He'd barely poured another cup of coffee when she said, 'It's the same girl, isn't it? Her daughter.'

Hayley's daughter, who'd chased butterflies, fed ducks, climbed trees and played the flute. A happy childhood. Simple. Peaceful. *Blissful.*

'Hmm,' Erin said, after she'd read the cards. 'I think you need to look at this.' She handed him a sheet of paper she'd had next to her laptop – an advertising flyer, but not a glossy one. Blue and green ink on textured cream paper. The heading read: *Discover Bliss.* 'The woman I spoke to yesterday in the shop gave it to me. She was also selling a couple of books by a Joshua Kristos – apparently he's a "blissful-living guru" who's going to be visiting them tomorrow. So I've been looking him up.'

'And?'

Erin stretched back in her chair and combed her fingers through her sleep-mussed hair. 'There's not a lot. A website, with some extracts from the books, and links to buy them. They're self-published, but available through the major retailers as e-books and as paperbacks. And if the rankings are anything to go by, they're doing fairly well. They're both in the top one hundred in self-help books. I don't know if that means much, money-wise.'

'When were they published?' he asked. 'Because Hayley's been talking about this stuff for years.'

'The first of these books was two years ago, the latest about a year. But there are references to his writings going back longer than that. And you can download some of his earlier stuff from the website. "Letters", he calls them.'

'Letters to?'

'His followers, I guess. He starts most of them with "Dear friends".'

'Does he use a capital for "friends"?'

'No. Not on the ones I've seen. Why?'

'My stepfather is a Quaker – you know, the Religious Society of Friends. My mother became one, too.'

Erin closed her laptop, giving him all her attention. 'Is that why you're so honourable?' she asked, with a wry smile. 'A religious upbringing? You don't talk about your family.'

He hadn't talked about his wife, either. Which probably didn't make him honourable at all. So maybe it was time to let Erin know a little of the background that had shaped him.

'Not exactly religious. My father was a Vietnam vet, and the war turned him into an avowed atheist. Which didn't go down well with my maternal grandfather, who was a strident old-school hellfire-and-brimstone minister.' He could have added 'and hate-filled bastard' but he didn't. 'After my dad died, my mother and I lived with Grandad for seven years or so. It was . . .' He tried to think of an adequate descriptor. 'Volatile, you could say. He and I didn't agree on pretty much anything. But we needed a roof over our heads and he needed a carer after a stroke. So we stayed. He died when I was eighteen. Mum married Ray about the same time I joined the army. Her beliefs were always much closer to his than to her father's.'

Elbow on the table, chin on her hand, Erin asked, 'But aren't Quakers pacifists? How did your mother . . . I mean, did your army career create problems between you?'

'Quakers are very good at respecting differences between people. Ray and I have had some good discussions over the years.' He rubbed his thumb over the geometric pattern on the pottery coffee mug and sought for words to give shape to his thoughts. 'But what it comes down to for me is that it's not an ideal world. There are people out there who torture, burn, maim, bomb and enslave others. Mostly because of religion and territory, and they're not going to be dissuaded from their path. Kids should be able to chase butterflies and feed ducks and go to school without fearing a bomb or a bullet. Or worse. And I guess that's why I do what I do.'

'It's as simple as that?'

'As simple and as difficult as that. I've killed people, Erin. That's the reality of me. And not just because it's my job, or because of orders, and sure as hell not for any god or religion. But because sometimes that's the only way to protect the vunerable.'

Her blue eyes held his gaze. 'Does it worry you that you have?'

Did it worry him? The blood on his hands, the responsibility and accountability he'd taken on? He gave her the answer he'd reached after only a few years in the army. 'Yes. The day it stops worrying you is the day you've ceased to value your own and others' humanity.'

She smiled gently. 'Quite the philosopher, aren't you?'

He carried his coffee mug to the microwave to zap some heat back into it. 'Years of arguing with my grandfather. I read a lot of philosophy and theology in high school to gather ammunition against his arguments. Until I realised that it never worked, anyway. He wouldn't listen.'

'So what did you conclude? About religion?'

'I'm not a believer. And I don't think you have to believe in a deity to have a moral and ethical code. So, what about you? Did you have a religious upbringing?' He wasn't the only one who'd never said much about his childhood or family, but he'd never before asked her directly about hers.

'Me? Hell no.' She gave an uncomfortable little laugh and avoided looking at him by going to rinse her mug out in the sink. 'My upbringing was entirely devoid of ethics and morals.'

She turned away before he could come out with another question, and headed to the door, tossing over her shoulder, 'I hope you left plenty of hot water, because I need to get clean.'

For all that she was one of the most together people he knew, something had obviously hurt her in the past, and he'd just trodden on an unhealed wound.

CHAPTER 10

A few washes with shampoo got the stench of smoke out of her hair. Pity she couldn't get the stain off her soul so easily. Joshua Kristos exhorted his 'friends' to lay down the burden of guilt and other negative emotions and embrace purity, but forgiving oneself wasn't so glibly easy – and the feminist in her had always had a deep mistrust of notions of 'purity' in any context. Besides, the dreams she'd had last night of Simon had definitely not been pure.

And that was as much as she'd let her thoughts dwell on *that*.

She found her last clean uniform shirt in the wardrobe and dressed for work. When she returned to the kitchen, Simon was out in the yard, talking on his phone. From the occasional word she caught, she guessed he was beginning the insurance claim process. She heated water for her thermos, packed fruit and muesli bars into her backpack along with drinking water, and repacked the SES gear ready to go.

With Simon still on the phone, she got out her camera and started photographing each page in Hayley's book of drawings. Scanning would be better, but she didn't have a scanner at home. At least with the photos he would have a record of the drawings before handing the book over to the forensic team. Just in case it was damaged or lost.

As she photographed she looked for anything that might indicate if the girl was Simon's. But each drawing proved only that Hayley loved her child, and gave her no other answers.

The hinges of the screen door squeaked and Simon came back inside as she photographed the last drawing.

'Everything okay?' she asked.

'Yep. The insurance company will send out an assessor on Monday. They'll get the police report and I guess it should be straightforward. Fraser called, too. The crime scene people have a few things from the house and will bring some of them back today. Mostly the kit bag and my rifle that I'd dumped inside the door when we first walked in. My laptop's in the bag, and a few clothes. So that's a help. He wants to see Hayley's cards and things, though, so are you almost ready to go?'

'Yes. But can you drop me at the Strathnairn office? I'll take a work truck from there and check the camping grounds on the way to Goodabri, and meet you there later.'

He hesitated but didn't argue. Maybe he craved a little solitude too, even if it was only for the distance between the two towns. She was coping – barely – with what was and wasn't happening between them, but the continued hyperawareness kept her own doubts and insecurities buzzing constantly, not always below the surface.

Yet she almost changed her mind when he dropped her outside the Strathnairn office. She found it hard to give him a brief wave and turn away, even though she'd see him again in an hour or two.

The drive alone on the country roads with the truck window wound down and the fresh air blowing in her face worked to banish some of the fatigue. But still she couldn't quiet her thoughts, and they jumped around as fast and as crazily as a young joey discovering his hopping potential.

She'd downloaded a couple of podcasts from Joshua Kristos's website onto her phone. After her first stop, at a picnic area, where she emptied rubbish bins, cleaned the toilet bowl and stocked up the loo paper, she connected her phone to the truck's audio system and started one of the podcasts. Twenty minutes or more until her next stop. She might as well do something useful with the time.

Kristos's voice was deep, melodic, pleasant enough to listen to – if you enjoyed listening to people speaking without interaction. Erin didn't. She'd daydreamed and doodled through most of her university lectures and had much preferred the fieldwork and lively debates with a couple of tutors who challenged their students' assumptions.

'Concentrate,' she muttered to herself. This guy could provide a clue to what Hayley had been doing and where she'd been for the past fourteen years.

After ten minutes of Joshua's soothing tones, she thought she could understand why his preaching might have appealed to Hayley. Although could you call it preaching if there was no mention of God, just 'the Unknown' and 'the Unknowable'? But it was all very *nice*, she had to admit. He spoke of love and bliss, simplicity and beauty, self-sufficiency and natural living. He didn't thunder against anything but spoke gently of the disconnection and soullessness of the technology- and consumption-driven world and described the value of retreating and being more connected to nature and one's own creativity.

Erin heard little to argue with, yet she found it dissatisfying, lacking in something she couldn't immediately identify. Substance? Reality? Logic? No. She agreed with pretty much everything he said. The planet was going to hell if consumption didn't radically slow, and she wouldn't be a ranger if she didn't believe in the value of the natural environment and encouraging people to discover it, for their own well-being as well as the land's.

She could almost like Joshua. He might even be a genuine and decent man who sincerely believed what he preached. She doubted it, but she'd met plenty of sane and decent people who believed far more radical things.

A few minutes into the second podcast – one on stilling thoughts and finding peace within oneself – she turned it off. She probably needed the advice, but even in just that short time of Joshua talking about peace and stillness she'd felt her alertness slipping, and driving at eighty kilometres an hour on dirt roads needed focused attention. She knew what happened when a vehicle met a tree head-on, and she had no intention of risking her own life.

At the next campground she did the rounds and then stood in the warm sunshine for a few minutes chatting with a couple with young children, taking a short weekend break. A pleasant couple, interested in and full of questions about the park and the area. They were contemplating moving to Strathnairn, and asked about schools, service clubs and community organisations. They believed in getting involved, in contributing. Their kids, barely school age and full of laughter, ran around the grass of the open area and chased butterflies.

Just like Hayley's daughter.

Erin excused herself and returned to the truck to get on the road to Goodabri. The brief conversation with the couple had highlighted for her what was missing from Joshua's philosophy: it was mostly about self, rather than relationships with others. A view of the world framed by the individual's own desires and wants. Nothing about community and society, or about right and wrong and responsibility. Retreating from the problems of the world, not engaging with them.

Had Hayley retreated from the world? Maybe. From the little she now understood about Simon's wife, Erin had gained the impression of a gentle, possibly fragile woman, not emotionally strong. Perhaps not strong enough to deal with the harsh realities of the world that Simon's army service must have constantly reminded her of.

That didn't answer the question of who had killed her, though, or why. Hayley had wanted to save her daughter from a cult, but even if she had been involved with the Simple Bliss people, there was nothing yet to indicate whether that was the cult, or whether her daughter had run off to join another, more dangerous group.

Erin drove through kilometres of sunlit bushland with questions tripping over one another in her mind. Did Joshua's followers all withdraw from the world? The website had mentioned 'communities', plural, but how many people did that involve? Willow's group north of the park had to be one of them, but to what extent were they under Joshua's influence or control?

Joshua's focus on self, on promises of healing, personal happiness, *bliss*, seemed harmless enough on the surface. It was what might lie underneath it that concerned her. She didn't know much about cults, but she knew about scams, and the easiest way of hooking a person in was to promise them something they wanted.

But the whole purpose of establishing a scam was to make money. A couple of books and some podcasts, hundred-and-fifty-dollar-a-night 'visits', and market stalls with handmade clothing hardly qualified as good earning potential.

She could almost hear her father's voice in her ear asking, *Where's the money in it, honey? Where's the money?*

•

Other than some charring on the eaves of Snowy's garage, the RFS had kept the fire contained last night and the only loss was Simon's house. All of it.

Simon didn't cross the police tape that was once again strung across his driveway, now cordoning off the blackened ruins. Beyond it, Fraser spoke with the arson investigator, but their conversation didn't take long. The detective walked back across the front yard and ducked under the tape.

'Arson investigator confirms your statement,' he said. 'Accelerant on and around back and front doors. He thinks you're both damned lucky. Quick thinking saved your lives. Although I guess that's what you're trained for.'

'Yes. Among other things.' Some of them were skills that he hoped he wouldn't ever have to use again.

'Forensics are working on getting fingerprints from the fuel can found last night. They also found a few boot prints in the dust in your yard leading into the back lane. About a size eight.' Fraser made a point of looking down at Simon's boots. 'Obviously not yours.'

'No. Tess and I had a look around the other night. Around the house, though, not to the end of the yard.'

'They're not Tess's,' Fraser said quickly. 'Besides, they end at tyre tracks in the lane. So they're most likely your arsonist's prints.'

Simon nodded but didn't comment. Not much use having fingerprints or boot prints if there wasn't a suspect to match them to. He'd already spent over an hour with Fraser and Aaron this morning, but none of them had any new leads, and they were still waiting on information from the post office in Lismore and Centrelink social services to track down where Hayley had been living.

And most of the time he'd been meeting with the detectives, the coroner's office in Newcastle would have been conducting a post mortem on Hayley. The fact kept catching him, never far from his thoughts.

'You heading back to Strathnairn?' Fraser asked. 'Or is your boss expecting you to work this weekend?'

'No. He's looking after the Goodabri office.' And worrying excessively. Simon had spent a good half-hour assuring Mal that he was fine, Erin was fine, his belongings were insured, he'd be okay. Mal took his staff management responsibilities very seriously. Too seriously, sometimes. As soon as Mal went to deal with a visitor enquiry, Simon had texted Erin: *Mal in G'bri office. Meet me at Niland campground?* She must have been somewhere in range because she'd replied almost immediately.

'I'm not officially on duty,' he told Fraser, 'but I'll go give Erin a hand with some jobs in the park. I'll probably be out of phone range, but I'll call back in later this arvo.'

Goodabri wasn't large enough to support many shops other than a corner store, but across the road from the Parks office was a bakery that made hearty bread rolls. Simon got there just before their midday Saturday closing time, and picked up rolls, slices and soft drinks to take out to the park for himself and Erin.

He reached the camping area before Erin did, but he'd heard her check in on the radio and knew she wasn't far away. One of the few advantages of Malcolm's obsessive concern for safety was his insistence on radio checks whenever they were out and about alone, because so much of the district had no mobile phone coverage.

The campground that had been a rescue staging ground just two nights before had resumed its usual function. Several families gathered around a barbecue at one of the picnic tables, and an older couple relaxed in folding chairs in front of their camper-trailer, birdwatching with binoculars. Simon spent a few minutes talking with them while he waited for Erin.

'We heard there was a tragic incident at the waterfall the other day,' the husband said. 'Do you get that kind of thing often? Someone jumping?'

Simon had attended two suicides in national parks in his career, but he kept his answer circumspect. 'Not here, before this. The police are investigating.'

'So sad,' the woman said. 'It's a beautiful spot. We went up to the lookout earlier. Is there another campground or parking area near it? We saw a young lad up there – just near the track, not to speak to – but there were no other cars here at the time.'

'Some of the land on the other side of the river is state forest,' Simon told her. 'People sometimes hike through from there.' Although not all that often. There wasn't much in the way of tracks in the state forest for any but keen explorers to access the river from the other side. But people on the private property that also abutted the park boundary in that area could easily access the park, if they wanted to.

A figure seen on the night of Sybilla's death, and a young man this morning . . . Simon definitely wanted to find out more about the people on that property.

Erin's truck was coming down the short stretch of winding road to the campground, so he left the couple and walked over to meet her when she parked beside his LandCruiser.

'Another sighting of someone up near the waterfall,' he told her. 'A young lad, apparently. How about we drive in via Harden's Hut and the fire trail? There's still about the same distance to walk, but we can walk along the river.'

'Good thinking. I'll just finish here first.' She was out of the truck and reaching into the back for the cleaning bucket. 'Did you happen to bring lunch? Because I only have muesli bars.'

'I did. Including brownies.'

Her smile flashed at him. 'Intelligent man,' she said, and it was almost like the old, uncomplicated times between them.

They ate lunch at the rough table outside Harden's Hut, an old stockman's hut on a ridge overlooking the river about six kilometres before it plunged down the waterfall. The trail to the hut was locked, with the basic shack not yet open for use by park visitors. The sun shone in a vivid blue sky and he wished he could relax, enjoy the autumn warmth and Erin's company, but tension twisted along his spine and he kept watch on the scenery around them as though he was in Taliban-controlled Afghanistan or extremist territory in Iraq rather than a quiet corner of north-west New South Wales.

They were both fairly quiet, each caught up in their own thoughts, and they quickly finished eating and dusted off the crumbs. Simon spread a detailed map on the table. 'If we drive the fire trail up to here, it's not far to hike down to the river at this point – which is close to the south-east corner of the property. Then we can walk along the river down to the waterfall.'

Erin's arm brushed against his as she reached to point at a place on the trail a few kilometres from where they were. 'The fire trail is blocked by a washout somewhere around here. The SES crew who searched the other night reported it. And it's pretty overgrown – we'll have to clear it soon. But if we go as far as this high point here, we might have a view down over some of the property.'

As usual, it was a practical suggestion. They'd always worked comfortably together and he'd missed that during his absence. But although he didn't expect any danger this afternoon, he wished she wasn't caught up in this situation, that she was safe at home and uninvolved. Still, he knew better than to try to talk her out of it.

They went together in the service truck. While Erin drove, he compared his GPS data to the survey map to work out the exact location of the property.

'The real estate agent told Fraser that the Harcourt Downs property is two thousand hectares,' he said to Erin, and translated that because he still thought in acres rather than metric. 'That's five thousand acres. Plus the company that bought it is also leasing an adjoining five hundred hectares of Pete Molloy's land.'

Erin whistled. 'That's a hell of a lot more than a hobby farm. That's a working property. Not a big one, for around here, but big enough. And some serious money.'

'Yeah.' He'd thought the same himself. 'Sold for close on two million.'

'Are you sure it's the right place? It doesn't make a lot of sense. A group of women selling handmade dresses for sixty bucks and taking in visitors for a few hundred dollars aren't going to finance a two-million-dollar property deal.'

'Definitely the same place Fraser went to last night. Maybe one of them is independently wealthy.'

Erin frowned as she hauled the steering wheel around for a steep, sharp bend. 'No. There's something screwy somewhere. Remind me to tell Steve to follow the money.'

'Follow the money? I don't think Hayley had much.' She could have asked him for money anytime if she'd needed it.

Or just taken it from their bank account. Maybe he was a fool, but he'd never taken her name off it. He wasn't that much of a fool that he'd left all his savings in it, but there had always been a reasonable sum. Yet after a few withdrawals in the first year or so, she'd never touched it again.

'Not Hayley's,' Erin said. 'Although it would be worth finding out if she has any. The company that bought the land. And Joshua Kristos.'

'Maybe he's a philanthropist.'

'Oh, I doubt that,' she said, with a darkness he rarely saw in her. 'Call it a hunch.'

The few times he'd seen that shadow in Erin's expression was when she made some passing comment about her family. *An upbringing entirely devoid of ethics and morals . . .* She was open about everything but her past, and out of respect for her privacy – and because it wasn't his business – he'd never asked. He was hardly the poster boy for full disclosure about his own. Perhaps some day she'd tell him.

She slowed the truck and changed down to first gear. They'd reached the place where erosion on the hillside had washed a chunk of the fire trail away, the gouge in the track too deep to easily cross. From here they'd get out and walk. Kilometres from anywhere, just the two of them in the wilderness.

He'd had no legitimate reason to bring with him the rifle the police had returned, so he'd left it in the lockbox in his vehicle back at the hut. No reason except the uneasiness prickling his skin. He had a knife in his backpack and one in his boot, that was all. A couple of knives, and his bare hands. Lethal enough, if a threat came close.

He didn't plan on letting any threats come close to Erin.

•

From the top of the hill – a low one, but the highest point in the area – there was a reasonable view to the undulating land beyond the river. Erin could make out parts of Millers Road, and a few buildings among the trees.

'There's a fair bit of timber,' she remarked. A lot, for a working property. From an environmental point of view she appreciated that, but it didn't represent the usual grazing or cropping pattern in the region.

Simon had his binoculars to his eyes. 'Yes. The top half fronting the road is mostly cleared into paddocks but there's a large area of uncleared land along the river. A few hundred acres, at a guess.'

She took her own binoculars out of her backpack and focused in for more detail. She could see the main homestead, a large single-storey house not far off the road, and some outbuildings a short distance from it. One of the paddocks fronting the road wore the green of a late-season crop – perhaps winter feed for stock. Most of the other paddocks were the dry brown of drought, with a glisten here and there of water in a dam. The dark reddish-brown scar of earthworks marked a new dam being built.

As well as the road into the homestead, a few other tracks crossed the land, one straight down from the road to stockyards and a woolshed, one from the homestead to the woolshed, meandering beside a dry creek bed before crossing it, and another leading from the woolshed to the area of scrubby timber. The land wasn't flat, though, and a low rise as well as the trees obscured her view of the area between the river and the woolshed area.

'Is that another building in the scrub?' she asked. 'I think I can see the corner of a roof, to the right of the woolshed.'

Simon shifted his binoculars slightly. 'Could be shearers' quarters. Or workers' cottages. They're often some distance from the homestead on these old properties. Harcourt Downs used to have even more land, a hundred or more years ago. Harden's Hut was part of it.'

'Gone are the days,' Erin commented. A century ago the large properties had employed many people – stockmen, domestic staff, an overseer and manager. Now most of them were run by just a married couple, with maybe one or two casual or seasonal workers during peak times.

She found the top of the waterfall through the lenses and then looked around the area for any sign of a track. Her eye caught a flicker of colour in the scrub. 'Something's moving,' she said.

'Where?'

She tried to focus, find it again. 'East of the falls. There's a rocky outcrop and it's to the right of that. It could be stock, but . . .'

Simon's binoculars were better quality than hers. 'It's not stock. A person. Maybe two.' He lowered the glasses. 'You right to go down to the river now? We might just *happen* to meet up with the neighbours.'

They were less than a kilometre from the river, and made quick time down the slope, hiking in a diagonal line towards the waterfall, the scrub not too thick or rugged. Simon led, choosing the best path, holding branches back so they didn't slap in her face. They were concealed among the edge of the trees but she could hear the waterfall when he stopped abruptly, a hand up in warning. He glanced back, a finger to his lips, and dropped to a crouch.

She hunkered down beside him, where she could see. They were about one hundred metres from the top of the falls. Four people stood on the other side of the river, near where the water flowed in narrow channels between the flat rocks. A woman, holding the hand of a child, a girl of maybe five or six. A youth in a shirt and faded jeans. And another slight figure, a little shorter than the youth, in a long top over blue pants, hair and face hidden by a hat.

Simon had his binoculars out again and had inched forward although she hadn't been aware of him moving. A commando. He'd have done this kind of surveillance for years.

She leaned forward. 'I'll go say hello,' she whispered.

He shook his head, signalled that he'd go.

To meet a woman and a few kids in the wilderness? She vetoed that idea by holding up an emphatic palm. 'I'm in uniform and harmless. You're neither.' In jeans and a dark t-shirt, his face grim, he was all soldier, alert and dangerous, and he would have scared *her* off if she didn't already know how his eyes crinkled when he smiled.

He conceded eventually with a bare nod. 'I'll be watching,' he muttered. 'Signal if you need me.'

She'd brought her small camera, and she took it from her pack before she moved quietly through the trees. She made her way forward a short distance from Simon before she came out into the open, using a rough goat track along the edge of the river.

With the water low, the woman and smaller child easily rock-hopped across the river, following the two teenagers, who slowed to give the child a hand across one of the wider channels. None of them saw Erin approaching.

The route from the lookout to the waterfall had been so well trodden and cleared by the police and SES two nights before that it was no longer overgrown, and the teenagers headed down it, into the trees and out of sight. The woman paused with the child at the falls, trying to see down without going too close to the edge. She gripped the girl's hand. When she turned, about to follow the teenagers, she saw Erin and stopped.

Erin waved a hand and gave her a broad smile. 'Hello! Beautiful day, isn't it?'

The woman gave a slight nod, as if she wasn't certain whether it was a beautiful day or not. Or whether she should be talking to National Parks rangers who strolled up out of the bush.

Erin approached them, maintaining a comfortable, relaxed pace. As she came closer, she thought she recognised the woman as the one she'd seen returning to the pop-up shop yesterday afternoon. Slim, dark-haired, similar age to herself. She certainly recognised the signs of stress and worry in her eyes. If she was one of the Simple Bliss people, she'd missed out on the bliss. So had the child, who chewed her thumb and eyed Erin as though she was an alien with four arms. They had to be part of the group – their clothes were similar to the ones Erin had seen at the shop. Plain fabrics and basic cuts with simple decorative bands.

'I'm Erin,' she said, with her friendliest smile. 'I'm one of the rangers. I've just been upriver checking on some fencing. Are you staying at the campground?'

'No,' the woman said. 'No, we're not. We . . . we live nearby.'

'Oh, you must be from Harcourt Downs, then. Our neighbours.' One of the advantages of being a natural blue-eyed blonde was that when she chose to pretend to be dumber than her actual IQ, people tended to believe it.

'Um . . . yes. But we call the land Serenity Hill now.'

'Serenity Hill? That's a lovely name.' Damn but her facial muscles were going to ache tomorrow from all this smiling. 'Much nicer than Harcourt. Hey, I met this girl, Willow, yesterday. She said she lives up this way. Is she your sister or something?'

'Willow? Willow . . . yes, she's a . . . sister. We live in . . . a small community. At Serenity Hill.'

Although Erin assumed the woman to be in her mid-thirties, apprehension or lack of confidence clearly made her nervous and uncertain.

'Are those your kids that went down the track there?' she persisted. 'We'd better catch up with them because some of the fencing went in a landslide. The boss wants me to keep it closed but people keep ignoring the signs and leaving the gate open.'

Erin kept up the easy chatter as they walked together along the track. 'You said you live in a community? That's great. I'm a big believer in escaping the rat race and getting closer to nature. That's why I do this job. Although the bureaucracy and government red tape drives me mad at times, you know? *So* much reporting and paperwork we have to do. It's mental.'

'That's terrible,' the woman said, and although she sounded genuine her words were hesitant, as if she wasn't sure how to respond. 'It sounds very stressful.'

'Yeah, it is. Sometimes I think about chucking the job in.' And there was a big lie, but she was making up her role as she went along and it was going to have to stray from the truth to be convincing for what she had in mind. 'Money's not everything, is it?'

'No, it isn't. Money doesn't heal the spirit.' The woman spoke quietly, the words heartfelt but without Willow's passion and enthusiasm.

They were getting close to the place where Erin had belayed down the cliff two nights ago, and she could see the teenagers ahead, standing a good distance back from the edge. She needed to mention the idea of visiting the community before they reached the kids.

'Willow gave me a flyer about visiting a community, retreating for a few days. That's your place, is it?'

'Yes.' Despite the opening, the woman didn't move in for the hard sell.

Erin had to push the point. 'Is it worth it? Because I'm due for some days off and, I don't know, I've been so restless lately. I want something, something to be different in my life, but I don't know what. So I was thinking about it all last night.'

The woman stopped walking and told the child to go ahead to join the others. She watched while the teenagers each took one of the girl's hands, keeping her between them as they sat down on the rock, metres away from the edge. Only then did she turn to Erin.

'Forgive me, please, for not being more welcoming. I'm a little distracted. One of my friends was the woman who . . . who . . . fell here two nights ago.'

Interesting that the woman at the house last night had denied knowing either of the women, but Sybilla was this woman's friend.

'I'm so sorry about your friend,' Erin said, glad she could speak with total honesty about that.

But the woman gave a slight shake of her head and tried to smile. 'I shouldn't be sad, as she has found pure bliss. But it was a . . . a shock.'

Breaking one's neck smashing into rocks forty metres down a cliff came nowhere near bliss, in Erin's opinion. But if she was going to visit the community, she didn't want any of them to know she'd seen either Hayley or Sybilla. More lies and half-truths. 'I heard about it, of course. The police have set up just next door to our office in Goodabri. I wasn't working yesterday, but I gather it was an accident? That she maybe slipped on a wet rock?'

'Is that what the police are saying?'

'I don't know. That's what my boss reckoned. He was furious because he thought we'd let people up there. Health and safety nut, he is.' *Forgive me that slight on your character, Mal,* she said silently. Health and safety nut, yes. Furious? Never. Although he might be if he found out what she planned. And he would be wounded if he found out how easily she could lie. 'But you being her friend, you could ask the police. I've met the detective – he seems reasonable enough. For a cop, anyway. Detective Sergeant Fraser. Steve Fraser.'

The woman stilled and all colour drained from her face. 'Steve Fraser?' she repeated, in barely more than a whisper.

Just what the hell had Steve – or his namesake – done to her? Erin couldn't imagine him mistreating anyone. Annoying them, yes. Mistreating? She doubted it. 'It's a common enough name,' she said. 'Maybe not the Steve you're thinking of?'

'Perhaps.' The woman didn't seem convinced but she shook herself out of her dazed state. She glanced over at the kids and called out, 'Tristan! Jasmine! Lily! Time to go!'

The kids scrambled to their feet immediately. The woman held out her hand to Erin with a strained smile. 'It's good to meet you, Erin. I hope we'll meet again.'

No mention of the community, no encouragement to visit, but Erin was grateful for the breakthrough in friendliness. Erin took her hand to shake it and then clasped her other hand over it. 'I hope we will meet again, too,' she said, holding the woman's gaze to emphasise her sincerity. 'And I am sorry about your friend. Be gentle with yourself.'

She wanted to ask her name but the kids reached them then, the youngest one tugging at the woman's top to get her attention. The woman lifted the girl onto her hip, and with a simple 'Goodbye,' began to walk back the way they'd come.

Erin got her first proper look at the two teenagers as they passed her on the track. The lad in jeans gave her a hard stare as he went by. The other one followed him, turning her head to smile shyly at Erin. A girl's face, under the cloth hat. A girl's face with wisps of brown hair framing her cheeks. No longer a child, not yet a woman.

A girl's face that looked just like Hayley's drawings of her daughter.

CHAPTER 11

He waited until the woman and kids were back across the river and out of sight before he joined Erin on the track in the scrub. Watching from out of earshot had strained his patience. Given Erin's animated face and speech, the woman's evident reticence raised questions and he itched to know what had been said. He also wanted to both hug Erin and shake her for standing near a cliff with four strangers, when the lad in particular had been casting unfriendly sideways looks at her; he could easily have rushed her and pushed her over, or struck her with a rock and rolled her over, or tried any one of fifty other ways of harming her.

On an intellectual level he knew she worked in isolated places like this alone most days and was perfectly capable of facing down drunkards, arseholes and illegal shooters. On a gut level, though, he couldn't be entirely complacent about it, when two women had died and someone had torched his house. On an emotional level . . . On an emotional level he was screwed, well and truly.

'The bliss group is definitely at Harcourt, and Sybilla was a friend of the woman's,' Erin summarised as they began the hike back to the truck. 'She's not happy, and I don't think it's just grief for her friend. She was nervous, and even though I asked about visiting, she didn't try to persuade me at all.'

'I saw she was edgy. Frightened, I'd have said. Although not of you.'

'Just how close were you?'

'Twenty metres. If that.' More like ten, some of the time.

She laughed, not quite comfortably. 'Remind me never to play hide and seek with you.'

'You'd lose,' he said, to keep it light. The afternoon was wearing on, they still had a kilometre or more to hike, and his spine prickled between his shoulder blades as though someone had a laser pointing right at him.

'Did you see the girl?' she asked, after they'd walked in silence for several minutes.

'The older one? Yes.' He'd been taking photos of the lad when she'd looked directly his way. With the powerful zoom on his compact camera, he'd looked straight into her eyes. Hayley's eyes.

He took the camera from the pocket on his pack and, slowing his pace, flicked through to one of the photos he'd taken. He passed the camera to Erin. She stopped to look at it properly. 'It is her, isn't it?' she said. 'Hayley's daughter.'

Hayley's child. Pretty and lively and *real*, so much more real now he'd seen her than in the drawings he'd never quite convinced his mind to accept as truth. Real and smiling and showing no evidence of grief despite being at the place where Sybilla had died, someone she must have known. And despite her mother's murder.

'I'm trying to look on the bright side,' Erin said. 'At least we know where she is, and she doesn't look unhappy or as though she's being mistreated.'

'No.' They started walking again. 'Do you think it's possible she doesn't know? About Hayley?'

'That they haven't told her? I don't know. The woman didn't mention Hayley at all, and I couldn't ask. I didn't want her to know that I'd seen either of them.'

'Why?' She didn't answer immediately and there was only one reason he could think of. 'Shit, Erin, you're not thinking about going in there?'

Her shrug answered the question. 'The person Steve spoke to last night denied knowing Hayley or her child. It might be a way to find out more about the girl and her situation. But let's just see what Steve's found, okay? Maybe he's solved the whole thing this afternoon.'

Simon hoped, but didn't believe it. Unless any of the fingerprints matched a known criminal who happened to be walking around free in the district, or a witness who'd seen everything came forward, then the police so far had more dead ends than leads.

Not much point in trying to talk Erin out of her crazy idea right now, though. He wouldn't give her time to come up with arguments and reasons or to talk herself into a corner. And he'd use the time himself to come up with a barrage of logic and facts that didn't involve his own cold fear for her safety.

•

Erin parked the work truck behind the National Parks building in Goodabri and transferred her pack and SES bag into her own ute, left there last night, before she pushed open the unlocked back door of the office. She'd followed Simon back from the park, and heard him make a brief comment to Mal in the office before the front door buzzer signalled his exit.

'He's gone next door,' Mal told her when she walked into the main office. 'Is everything okay?'

'As much as it can be, in the circumstances,' she told him. 'We went for a hike up around Harden's Hut. I figured he needed to get away from things for a few hours.'

'I hope it helped. Must be tough on him. Listen, you should take next week off. You've got heaps of time off in lieu owing and now Jo's back we can cope.'

As if he'd let Jo go out on her own or work anything like a full load. But Jo could fight her own battles. 'I might take a few days, thanks, Mal. How about I give you a call Tuesday afternoon or Wednesday, see how things are going?'

Tuesday should give her plenty of time. If she went to Serenity Hill tomorrow, it surely wouldn't take more than a day or so to suss out the situation. She just needed to find out about Hayley's daughter – Jasmine or Lily – and then the police could do whatever was necessary. Maybe they were worried over nothing. Maybe the girl's father was there and was a perfectly decent man who loved his daughter, and Hayley's murder was a random crime, and Sybilla really had just slipped on rocks . . . and maybe pigs flew north for the winter.

In the police room, Simon straddled a chair beside Steve's makeshift desk, the two of them deep in conversation. Aaron, Tess and Matt all worked at laptops. Aaron leapt to his feet when he saw her and took a chair over to Steve's table for her. Both men acknowledged her with a nod and Simon signalled to Steve to continue talking.

'We've only got preliminary post-mortem results in,' Steve said. 'The official report will take a while, after blood tests and such are done. Likely cause of death – well, we knew that. Not a lot of internal bleeding, so it was fairly quick. A small mercy, I guess.'

Simon nodded, his face carefully expressionless.

'They've also confirmed that she, well, she had at least one vaginal birth. So that confirms a baby. But the thing is, I've had Aaron chasing records and social security. There's nothing under Hayley's name or Medicare number. She's claimed no benefits of any sort under her name for more than thirteen years. No doctor's visits, no baby added to her card, no family benefit supplement, no back-to-school allowance, nothing. And the child's not registered under Hayley's name – or yours.'

Simon swallowed. 'She must have been using another name.'

She had to have, surely. Erin couldn't imagine a woman with a history of miscarriage not consulting a doctor at least once during her pregnancy. And few women did a home birth without at least a midwife. The Medicare benefits applied to all citizens, regardless of income, so there should be a claim somewhere, for something.

'Yeah, that's what we figure. We'll run fingerprints and Leah's going to ask the specialists for facial recognition scanning. We'll also check interstate, but the Medicare and social security stuff is federal, so it doesn't matter which state she was in, activity would still show. If it was there.'

'We saw the girl,' Simon said abruptly. 'We were up at the waterfall this afternoon and a woman and kids came down from Harcourt. Erin spoke with them.'

Erin quickly described the gist of her conversation with the woman. 'I didn't get her name, I'm sorry. But she definitely said that the woman who'd fallen was a friend of hers, although she didn't refer to Sybilla by name, either. She did call the kids, though – Tristan, Jasmine and Lily. I'm not sure which of the girls was which.'

Simon pulled his camera out of his jeans pocket. 'I've got some photographs. A few close-ups with the zoom. They're reasonable.'

'That little thing has a decent zoom?' Steve asked. 'What is it – special military issue?'

A trace of amusement briefly softened the hard lines of Simon's face as he removed the memory card from the camera. 'No. Just top-of-the-range commercially available. And I wasn't all that far away from the subjects. Do you want copies of these?'

Erin hated having people lean over her shoulder when she was working on the computer, so while Steve inserted the card into his laptop and they started going through the images, she stood up from the hard plastic chair and stretched her stiffening muscles.

Hayley's bag and its contents were laid out on a table nearby – the book of drawings, an envelope addressed to Hayley in Simon's handwriting, a half-finished embroidery of butterflies, and a small fabric-covered object about the size of her palm. The book, the letter and the bag itself were in evidence bags, but the embroidery and the fabric-covered object weren't.

Steve saw the direction of her gaze. 'Forensics weren't sure they'd get anything from those and they're swamped so they're prioritising. You're the sewing expert. Is there anything noteworthy or significant about them?'

She picked up the last. A needle book, handmade. Inside the reinforced cloth covers were pockets with a needle threader, lengths of embroidery thread, and a small pair of scissors. The four felt 'pages' of the book held several needles and a dozen or so pins. A practical, pretty sewing accessory.

As she flipped to the back, she noticed a slight, squarish bulge beneath the fabric of the cover. She rubbed her thumb over it to feel the shape. A couple of centimetres in size. What and why? Why insert something inside the cover? She could see no purpose for it. The stiffening inside the cover, whatever it was, was sturdy enough and without any bends or holes.

As she felt over it again, she recognised the size – about the same size as the camera memory card that Steve had just put into his laptop.

She turned the needle book over in her hands, studying the decorative stitching around the edge that disguised the seams. There it was – a three-centimetre section where the thread didn't quite match the rest.

She held the needle book out to Steve. 'I might have found something.'

'Where?'

'In here. There's something under the fabric, and the stitching's been re-done. I think it's a memory card.' She showed him the bulge and he ran a blunt-nailed finger over it.

'Jeez. It is an SD card. Feel the shape of it.' He outlined it with his finger. 'See the cut-off corner?' He passed it to Simon. 'What do you reckon?'

'It has to be. She hid it in there, where no one would think to look.'

'Can you undo it?' Steve asked Erin. 'Can you get it out without ripping the thing apart?'

She took the scissors and snipped the first thread, gently drawing it out. A computer memory card. In a needle book. That had been hidden in a bean bag. And whoever had murdered Hayley had searched and trashed Simon's computers.

It only took a minute to unpick the short section of stitches, and she manoeuvred the card towards the opening without putting her own fingerprints on it. 'You can get it out now,' she told Steve, handing the needle book back to him.

He pulled on a latex glove to remove the card and then paused, holding it in the air in front of his laptop screen, which still displayed an image of Hayley's daughter. 'Dammit. I just want to stick this into the laptop and find out what's on it. But it better go to Forensics so they can take a binary copy of it first and preserve everything on it. Including prints. Shit.'

'How long is that going to take?' Simon asked.

Steve reached across to a nearby table for an evidence bag and dropped the card inside. 'Crime scene officers have gone back to Inverell. I'll get someone to drive it over there now. If we're lucky, we might find out what's on it tomorrow.'

Tomorrow. Erin's spirits sank. But it was already almost six o'clock and Inverell was over an hour away. 'If we're not lucky?'

'They might have to send it to Tamworth or Sydney. I don't know. Aaron, get on to Sandy Cunningham and find out where he wants this. Then get it there, pronto.'

Steve's mobile buzzed and he glanced at the screen before answering. 'Hello, Leah.' He wandered out of the room to take the call, but only paced down the short passage towards the back door, nowhere near out of hearing.

His side of the conversation was mostly monosyllabic at first, punctuated with a few curses. 'We've just found a data card. No, I'll have to send it to be processed. Okay, I'll keep you posted.'

He came back and slumped into his chair. 'She's been called up to another homicide, north of Coffs Harbour. A woman in her thirties. Daughter of a prominent local businessman.'

'Any connection to this case?' Simon asked.

Steve dragged a hand through his hair. 'Who knows? No white dress, but she was stabbed. Leah's on her way there now. We might know more tomorrow, but it's a few hours from here and most likely unconnected. Listen, guys, go. Go to the pub for a meal. Go home or wherever you're staying and get some sleep. I'll let you know if there's any news.'

●

In the process of closing up the office, Malcolm apologised for having to dash off for a family dinner. But he didn't go until he'd reissued an invitation, yet again, for Simon to stay with him and Susan.

'Thanks, but I'll be fine,' Simon said.

'You know you're welcome to stay in my spare room again,' Erin said quietly after Mal had left. She'd been quiet since the phone call from Haddad. And since she'd found the memory card. They'd had a long day and it showed in the strain around her eyes.

He hoped he wasn't about to hurt or offend her now. 'I know that, Erin. You know that I appreciate it. But I'm just going to go bush tonight. There's a lot to think about and perhaps I'll have a clearer head out alone in the starlight.'

'I understand,' she said, and he thought she probably did. She didn't attempt to talk him out of it or insist that he stay with her. 'You've got your sat phone and your radio? Good. Give me a call in the morning.' She smiled, not her full grin but enough to make her eyes shine a little. 'Preferably not to tell me how beautiful the sunrise is. I think I'll be sleeping through it rather than watching it tomorrow.'

He saw her off in her ute without succumbing to the temptation to kiss her soundly. The setting sun cast its last glow and he watched her taillights diminish along the road until she turned a corner. He longed to go with her, to go to her cottage and shut out the world and spend the night, all the nights, with her. His body burned with unsated need and desire but if he gave in . . . He blew out a long, slow breath. Wasn't going to happen. He had work to do tonight and he needed her safely out of the way to do it.

He borrowed some camping equipment from the storeroom and loaded it into his vehicle. Might as well make Harden's Hut a tad more comfortable. Not that he planned to spend much time in it.

Before he left Goodabri and phone reception he dialled a number he hadn't called for a year or more. He thought it might ring out but a gruff voice finally answered.

'Gabe. It's Simon.'

'You okay? Cops called me the other night.'

'Yeah. Thanks.' They'd served alongside each other for more than a decade so he didn't beat around the bush. 'I need a favour. A big one.'

Gabe never bothered with niceties. 'Ask.'

'I need your help for a few days.'

'You still in Strathnairn?'

'Goodabri. East of Strath.'

'Yeah, can do. When?'

'As soon as possible.' Tomorrow, Simon hoped. Tomorrow so Gabe could keep an eye on Harcourt and the girl while he dissuaded Erin from going out there.

Silence for a moment before Gabe said, 'Give me three hours.'

Simon's tension levels shifted down a notch. 'Thanks. Can you bring some gear with you? My place burned down and I don't have much.'

'Tell me what we're doing and what you need and I'll bring it.'

'Surveillance,' Simon answered. 'Large rural property, buildings spread out over hectares. I need to know who's there and what's going on. And I need to ensure protection for a thirteen-year-old girl who's with the group living there.' And for a woman who was likely going to go there tomorrow to infiltrate the group to find Hayley's daughter. He still planned on trying to talk Erin out of going. But if she went,

Gabe's presence would mean they could cover the entire place twenty-four hours a day. Of all the guys he'd served with, he trusted Gabe the most.

'This got something to do with your missus?' Gabe asked.

'Yeah. Someone murdered her. In my house.'

'So that's why the cops asked where you'd been. Who's the kid?'

'Her daughter. Possibly mine.'

When he disconnected the call he mentally corrected the statement. *Probably* his. He'd watched her out there at the falls. There was nothing he could see of himself in her face, but her tall, lean physique bore little resemblance to Hayley's petite, almost fragile figure. It didn't mean Hayley hadn't had a lover, but it narrowed the odds.

In any case, it didn't matter who the girl's father was. Simon had tried to protect Hayley when she was still a teenager. He'd protect her daughter if she needed it, too, whatever the girl's genetic inheritance.

•

Simon had remade the guest bed, neater than it had been before, hung his towel in the bathroom and washed and put away their few dishes from breakfast. He'd left almost no sign that he'd slept under her roof, eaten across the kitchen table from her, held her tightly in his arms for far too brief a time.

And if Erin spent much time remembering that, she'd never get anything done.

She stripped off her uniform in the bathroom and stepped under the low-pressure spluttering of the shower. Hot water to ease her tired body, or cool to energise her? She went for cool and made it quick, washing off the sweat and dust of the day's hike. The energising she'd hoped for didn't happen, but at least it wasn't soporific.

After she'd towel-dried her hair and pulled on jeans and a t-shirt, she returned to the kitchen. She'd made it to Strathnairn's supermarket before it closed for the day, so her fridge and cupboards weren't quite as bare as they'd been. With too much on her mind to cook from scratch, she put a pre-packaged lasagne into the microwave and tore up some lettuce leaves to go with it. Lettuce made it healthy. Almost. But there'd been more salad than chicken in the bread roll Simon had brought her for lunch, and she wouldn't eat the entire block of chocolate she'd picked up at the supermarket this evening.

'Balanced diet,' she muttered to the silent kitchen. 'Something healthy, something unhealthy.' Talking to an empty room probably didn't rank high on the healthy side.

She ate at the kitchen table with her laptop in front of her and the Simple Bliss flyer beside it. The flyer had a web address on it and she typed it into her browser. Saturday night in Strathnairn and it seemed everyone was downloading movies or playing online games, because the browser icon spun for minutes before the page began to load. Rural living meant overloaded network access and no broadband. She'd eaten half the large serve of lasagne before the page appeared fully on the screen.

The site was basic, with a few attractive images of the landscape, the house, vegetable gardens and food. *At Serenity Hill you'll be embraced by the beauty and rhythms of nature, and discover the truths of your spirit . . . In this sanctuary of peace and tranquillity you will find healing for the wounds of the soul and reconnect with your deepest bliss . . .*

'Promises, promises,' Erin murmured. Yet for an instant it truly did appeal. Healing for the wounds of the soul? Oh, she had some great black scars she wished could be healed. If someone could just wave a magic wand, make her past fade to nothing, make her clean and whole and honourable . . . Yep, there went the flying pigs again.

They were serious about encouraging visitors, with online bookings available, and she clicked through to the form. Payment options included credit and debit cards, direct deposit, and – 'for those who prefer' – cash payment on arrival. Nice untraceable cash. That option did little to enhance Erin's faith in the group, but it did mean she didn't have to book and pay now. No, she'd wait until morning, see what news there was, and she could withdraw cash from the ATM in Strathnairn if she decided to go through with it.

After she'd washed her dinner dishes she packed a bag with clothes and toiletries, just in case.

•

While he waited for Gabe, Simon went up to the pub for a meal, running the gauntlet of concerned queries and commiserations as he carried his drink and table number out to the dimly lit far corner of the beer garden. Everyone in Goodabri knew – about Hayley, about the fire. But other than expressing their sympathies and offering support, they left him to himself, exactly the way he wanted it.

He sat with his back to the brick wall of the beer garden, with a clear view through the glass doors back into the dining area. When Fraser arrived, he didn't appear to see him in the shadows, and Simon watched the detective lean on the bar and use that relaxed charm to pump the waitress for information. Fraser was clearly familiar with small towns, understood how they worked and that people who worked in pubs often had the best information. Simon couldn't hear him, but he could imagine: *The hippy mob from up on Millers Road – know anything about them? Do they ever come in here?*

He'd thought Fraser hadn't spotted him, but once he'd paid for his meal order and finished talking with the waitress he came straight outside.

'Carrie says you're not looking for company. Thought I'd ask if you wanted an update.'

Simon pointed at the chair opposite. 'Sit.'

Fraser put his Coke and a packet of crisps on the table and dragged out the chair. 'Nothing linking the vic at Coffs with our case, but her daddy's well connected and demanding a five-star investigation and the media's all over it, so Haddad's there, for who knows how long.'

Simon stayed silent while Fraser took several mouthfuls of his drink.

'The only conclusive thing from Sybilla's post mortem,' he continued, 'is that she fell from a height and died from those injuries. Which we knew already.'

'What about the girl? Can't you just go back out to Harcourt and ask again? We know that she's there.'

'Look, mate, the woman we spoke to last night has already filed a complaint about being disturbed late at night and harassed. And I've got no indisputable evidence that Hayley has a child or was even there, and neither you nor Erin saw any evidence that the girl was abused or in danger. Your unauthorised surveillance photos are of a happy girl in a nice family group. She looks a little like the girl in a sketchbook Hayley had, but it's not proof. So just at the moment my hands are tied.' He tore open the packet of crisps and took one, then pushed the packet towards Simon in invitation.

Simon ignored it. 'You're doing *nothing*?'

'No.' Fraser remained calm, taking no offence. 'Aaron, Tess and I are digging up everything we can find on the company that owns the place, and on Joshua Kristos, and we're combing the records for any trace of Hayley or Sybilla. We've not found much yet. Carrie's given me a name for one of the women up there, though. Mary Saint, she thinks it was. Bought a meal on a credit card a few days ago and Carrie chatted with her. Probably the woman I spoke with. I'll see what I can find on her.'

'How long is it going to take to have enough to go in there?'

Fraser leaned back in his chair and took his time answering. 'Mate, it's more than forty-eight hours since Hayley was found. We don't have a suspect. We don't have a motive. We don't have a witness, and we hardly know anything about the victim. Be prepared for it to take some time.'

'Erin's planning to go there tomorrow.'

'Is she? I did wonder about that.'

Carrie brought over their meals – plates loaded with steak, chunky chips and vegetables. Fraser exchanged some quips with her but she was busy and didn't loiter. Simon waited until she was almost back inside before resuming the discussion as if it hadn't been interrupted.

'Can you stop Erin from going?' he asked.

'Can you stop Erin from doing anything she's decided on?' Fraser countered, and Simon's fist itched to punch the man's grin from his face.

Trouble was, he was right. 'I'm not the law,' Simon pointed out coolly. 'Can't you warn her against interfering in a police investigation or something?'

'I could. Maybe I will. But to be honest, Nick and I have discussed putting someone in there. If things drag out, we'll do it. I can't put anyone local in. They already know Tess is a cop, and they'd spot any other local cops quickly enough. It takes time to get someone in from the undercover squad, brief them, create a persona and get all the backup in place.'

'You're not seriously thinking of encouraging Erin?'

'No, I'm not.' There was no laughter in Fraser's face now. 'But if she's determined to do it, get her to call me first. If I can't dissuade her, I'll ask her to come to a briefing on Monday morning. That way she'll only be there tomorrow night.' He started carving into his steak, but with a telling, sideways glance he added, 'I do want to know how many people are there, how the place is set up, that kind of thing.'

'And if someone else could get that information for you?'

'Well, I couldn't possibly encourage anyone to trespass, let alone invade people's privacy by engaging in unauthorised surveillance, could I?' Fraser said, choirboy innocence positively shining in his face. Until he grinned.

Although he wasn't hungry, Simon tucked into his meal, knowing his body needed the fuel. He'd get that information for Fraser by morning. Erin had said she planned to sleep in, take it easy after the last few days. Simon intended to be back in Goodabri well before she was up and about, and between Fraser's investigation and his own, they should have enough information so that she wouldn't need to go.

CHAPTER 12

Two days past full, the moon still gave good light over the land – and also deep shadows for concealment. On the shadow side of a large machinery shed, Simon checked around both corners, and then signalled Gabe over from the cover of the scrub. He crossed the ten metres of open space, a silent, dark-clothed figure. In the pre-dawn darkness, nothing else moved.

In addition to the machinery shed, Simon counted four other structures on this part of the property. An old timber woolshed; the long shearers' quarters with eight individual rooms opening onto a veranda and a larger room at the end; and two farm workers' cottages. He could see no dogs and no vehicles by the cottages, and the windows were dark. An old truck the size of a removalists' van was parked beside the machinery shed, but the two sets of large double doors on the shed were closed and locked with chains and padlocks.

He signalled Gabe to go to the right, to the two cottages, and watched while he crossed to the first one. With Gabe in place, he used the truck for cover to make his way to the back of the shearers' quarters.

Each room had a casement window in the back wall, three of them propped open a few inches. He flipped down his compact night-vision goggles and risked a glance through one of the closed windows. A double bed took up most of the small room. No heat sources.

A loud rasp broke the silence. And again, gurgling into a snore. Simon hunkered down against the wall as the guttural masculine snore two rooms along settled into a rhythm. But then a drowsy voice mumbled, 'Turn over,' and with a squeak of bedsprings, the snoring stopped.

That made two people in room three. He checked the other rooms. Two more empty ones, but the remaining four each had two people. Ten, total.

He made his way to the woolshed and ducked into the sheep pens beneath it. The earthy smell of dust and old manure filled his nostrils. He remained motionless as small sounds came through the timber floor. Soft footsteps crossed above him. A whimper, winding to a little cry. Whispered, soothing words he couldn't quite make out. The footsteps moved away, barely audible, and quiet settled again.

He moved out of the pens, then stepped out from underneath the shed. The only access to the interior of the shed was up a flight of timber stairs, old, probably full of creaks, and bathed in moonlight. The few corrugated-iron window shutters were a good three metres up, too high to reach. No way to easily see inside.

Grey light seeped into the darkness from the east. Not much time left. He could just see Gabe crouching under one of the cottage windows, and he gestured to him to return to the scrub.

They met at the edge of the tree line and moved fifty metres into their cover, well away from the buildings.

'At least eight in each of the cottages,' Gabe reported.

'Ten in the shearers' quarters. I don't know how many in the woolshed, but there are people in there. Maybe a kid.'

'Dawn's coming. D'you want me to hang around, see what happens?'

'Yeah. I'll go up to the homestead. Meet you back at the river thirty after sunrise.'

Simon moved off, keeping to the tree cover to loop around to the main house without crossing too much open ground. Low in the western sky, the moonlight dimly flickered among a thousand mottled tree shadows. He used the night-vision goggles so he could keep his speed up in the darkness.

On either side of the single-storey homestead were large, open paddocks, but immediately around the house a well-established landscaped garden provided a couple of potential vantage points. If he could get to them, unseen. Two men patrolled around the house, each with his own loop around back, front, and then a figure-of-eight around the garage to one side and the garden sheds on the other. Amateurs, using easily discernible patterns. Foolish amateurs, using patterns that had them meet up on each round, where they stopped for a chat.

Simon used that weak spot in their surveillance to slip past the garden shed to an adjacent cluster of callistemon bushes that provided him with excellent cover, overlooking the garden to the house.

The dawn light was silver now, the darkness receding and stars fading. The two guards did another loop. Not young men, maybe in their late forties or early fifties, but thin and reasonably fit in appearance. Neither of them carried a firearm that he could see. One held a baton, the other balanced a metre-long staff on his shoulder.

Simon wanted to know what they protected, but he could see no easy way to get to the house, and the light increased with every minute.

At the end of their next round, the two men consulted, looking to the east. Neither of them glanced at a watch, or a phone. But one then walked across to the back of the garage to where a large bell hung from a frame jutting off the roof. He pulled the bell rope six slow times, each pull sending a clear sonorous ring across the landscape.

A wake-up bell? It would have been quite audible down
at the woolshed. In the east, a pink-gold glow edged the sky.
Before the sun's rays broke over the horizon, the French doors
facing onto the veranda opened. Six women, all dressed in
sleeveless white dresses like Hayley's and Sybilla's, proceeded
in single file down the veranda steps, followed by two younger
girls, teenagers, in similar dresses, though blue, and two youths
in blue trousers and sleeveless tops. The two guards fell into
step behind the lads.

With minimal movement, Simon drew out his camera and
zoomed in on the faces. The woman who'd spoken with Erin
at the waterfall yesterday was third in the line. The second of
the two girls was Hayley's daughter, with the lad from yesterday
immediately behind her. Simon set the video function on
the camera running, kneeling awkwardly to get a clear view
through the foliage and hold it steady.

The silent procession crossed to the centre of the lawn, then
spiralled around and joined hands to form two circles – an
inner circle of the four males, enclosed by the circle of eight
women. The leading woman, who appeared to be the oldest
– perhaps in her forties – faced due east, and as the first rays
of sunlight beamed across the paddock, she began to sing.
An ethereal, wordless song with a fluid melody that glided
over notes that never seemed expected. When she began the
second repetition, the other women joined in, and the men
began a lower harmony that wove through the women's voices.
On the third repetition, they began a slow dance, the women

moving anticlockwise with graceful dipping and swaying steps, the men clockwise.

It was beautiful. It was unusual. And they sang and moved with such total focus and concentration, such precision, that every nerve in Simon's neck prickled.

It wasn't so much that they chanted and danced to the rising sun that unsettled him. Plenty of cultures performed similar rituals, and although he'd ceased believing in any form of religion or mysticism decades ago, when out in the wilderness alone even he'd been tempted to formally greet the sun and acknowledge the beginning of the day. All faiths and cultures had rituals: the singing of hymns, the rite of communion, farewelling the dead. But in none of those rituals – even the solemn ramp ceremony for a fallen comrade – had he witnessed this total unity of voice and movement. That perfect unison had to be the result of commitment, practice and discipline.

As the sun rose above the horizon, their steps slowed and stilled, the notes died away, and only the birds twittering in the trees impinged on the silence. After several heartbeats, the singers broke into smiles. The men's circle dropped hands first. The two older men approached each woman in turn, and kissed them on both cheeks with some deference before kissing each of the two girls the same way. The young lads did the same before they joined the older men, laughing with them as they all traipsed inside, just a bunch of guys together. The eight women hugged, laughed, chatted, then wandered inside as well.

As the last one went through the door, Simon slipped behind the shed and made a dash across the open ground to the trees, hoping the group was too focused on whatever they did immediately after their ritual to be looking out windows. No one shouted or raised an alarm, and he made quick time working his way back through the scrub towards the river. He was almost there when he saw a change in the foliage ahead – not the muted browns and greens of the bush, but a denser green.

The plants grew taller than him, leafy and healthy. There were a couple of acres under cultivation, and he walked around the plot, mapping the coordinates on his GPS. Two varieties, almost ready for harvest. He snapped a few photos before jogging on to meet Gabe.

'At least fifteen kids plus a couple of women in the woolshed,' Gabe reported when he arrived at the rendezvous point in a rocky overhang by the river. 'Eight men in one cottage, ten women in the other, plus ten people from the shearers' quarters. That's how many I counted coming out and doing a chanting thing at sunrise. They were all still at it when I left. Chanting, dancing in circles. They all knew the ceremony – it seemed automatic.'

Simon whistled low under his breath. 'More than forty there all up?'

'Yeah. Kids ranged from tots to maybe teens. Two girls looking after them, maybe only sixteen, seventeen years old. How many people did you see at the main house?'

From where they hunkered under the overhang Simon could see up and down the river, and he kept scanning for movement while they talked. 'Six women, two men. Four teens – two girls and two youths.'

'Was Hayley's kid one of them?'

His throat rasped with dryness. 'Yeah. I'm pretty sure. The two men were patrolling the house. No firearms that I could see, but batons, maybe knives.'

'Guards?'

'They deferred to the women so protection, not prison guards. Probably sensible since two women have died. They all did the chanting up there too. What kind of clothes did you see? What colours?'

'Mostly browns, different shades. Some blue, some green. Trousers, tops, long caftan things. The young girls with the kids both had light blue dresses. Knee-length.'

'So did the two girls up at the house. The women were in white.'

'Some kind of uniform?'

'Possibly.' Ceremony, symbolism, regulation, hierarchy – this mob had it all. He just had to work out the codes. He took a swig from his water bottle and then slipped it back into its carrier on his pack. 'I have to head into town. I'll be back this afternoon. Look out for a sheltered spot. I want to keep watch tonight, but they're forecasting storms.'

•

Erin groaned and pulled the pillow over her head. Early morning wake-up in the bush – if it wasn't the kookaburras chortling, it was the damn possum tap-dancing on the roof. This morning the rosellas skittered back and forth on the corrugated iron directly above her bedroom, picking up seeds from a nearby tree. They might as well have been wearing hobnail boots.

Squinting one eye open, Erin looked at the window. Gold light angled in through the gap in the curtains. Sunrise. She rolled over to check the time on her phone. Too many dreams and not nearly enough sleep.

The rosellas did another sortie up and down the roof. And then the kookaburras decided to celebrate the new day. When the magpies began their carolling, she gave up, pushed back the blanket and dragged on a robe. Morning had definitely broken. Anyone who reckoned the bush was quiet had never lived in it.

She didn't rush, getting showered and dressing in a summer dress she rarely wore, but she still made it to Goodabri before eight o'clock. The Sunday streets were quiet, with hardly anyone up and about. She waved at Des Holder, out walking his fox terrier. Des Holder, who'd retired from building fences and now drove the school bus.

The school bus that picked up kids from Millers Road.

She parked in front of the bakery – closed on Sundays – and crossed the empty main street to the office building.

Mal wouldn't be in until ten to open the visitor centre for Sunday's short hours.

Movement behind the window blinds of the police rooms showed that someone was already at work. Tess opened the door to Erin's knock. Tess, neat and proper in uniform as always, as if she carried a spray can of starch with her. If she smiled more often they'd probably put her on recruitment posters. Erin hadn't found her unfriendly, just reserved. A woman who regarded her job seriously and who took time to relax her guard to make friends.

'I had a thought,' Erin said as Tess invited her in. 'Has anyone asked Des Holder what kids he picks up in the school bus on Millers Road?'

'I did last night. He doesn't pick up any. Well, not in that part of Millers Road.' Tess had a plunger of coffee on her desk, and she collected mugs from a tray and poured out two cups while she spoke. 'I checked with the Goodabri teachers, too, and showed them the photo of the girls, but they don't know them.'

With less than fifty kids at the school, the teachers would know them all. 'Strathnairn High?' Erin suggested, accepting the offered coffee with gratitude. 'The older girl would go there.'

Resuming her place behind her laptop Tess indicated the opposite chair for Erin. 'I've left a message for the principal. I hope she'll get back to me today. But I spoke with Emily Trasker, who teaches English, and she doesn't know the girl.'

'So they must be home-schooled.'

612

'Or at boarding school. A lot of rural kids board Monday to Friday. If we don't turn up anything today, I'll get on to the boarding schools in Armidale and Tamworth tomorrow.' She gestured to a notepad beside her computer with a long list of tasks, some ticked off. 'I've been on to community services, too. We're working on it, Erin.'

Erin gave her an apologetic smile. 'I should just let you do your job, hey?'

Tess's mouth almost curved into a smile. 'Yes. But if you happen to know anything about holding companies, that could be useful.'

'Can't say I do. Why?'

'From what I can find, the Harcourt Downs property is owned by Serenity Hill Proprietary Limited, which is owned by a holding company that's owned by another holding company registered in the Cayman Islands. Tax minimisation, by the looks of it. But trying to find the actual humans who own the companies is proving impossible. The few names I've found keep drawing blanks.'

'Is Joshua Kristos one of them?'

'No, he's not. But Aaron's been searching for him, and other than his website and books, he doesn't appear to exist either.'

'It's a pen name, then.'

'Yep. But even with pen names, it's not usually hard to find out the real identity. I can tell you the real names of most of my favourite authors. But we've found nothing for Joshua. Not even a photo.'

The mug was warm in Erin's hands and she took a sip of the too-strong black coffee. Tess didn't believe in weak, apparently. Or milk, or sugar.

Erin cautiously broached the topic that had been on her mind since yesterday. 'You know they invite visitors?'

Tess gave her all of her attention. 'Yes.'

'Joshua will be there today. What if I went there for a few days' retreat?'

She expected an instant objection. Tess stilled and said carefully, 'Two women who were probably part of that group have died in recent days.'

'And one of them wanted help to get her daughter out of a cult.'

In a rare sign of vulnerability, Tess briefly closed her eyes before saying, 'Yes.'

Erin had rehearsed her arguments, but she'd expected to use them with Simon or Steve. Not Tess, who wasn't telling her straight out that she shouldn't go. 'I've read some of Joshua's writings. I even downloaded one of the books last night. It all sounds reasonable on the surface, and it won't be hard to pretend to be enthusiastic.'

'Do you know how cults work?' Tess asked, a hard edge to her voice.

'I'm not an expert, but they're scams, right? Suck people in with friendliness, convince them you have what they want, and take their money.'

'And control their lives. Love bombing is just the start of it. Money is only part of it. They separate people from the outside world and use mind-control and brainwashing techniques. Obedience becomes everything. Service to the cult leader and to the cult is required. Deviation is punished by exclusion and loss of the promised love and salvation.' Tess stopped short, gulping in a breath, blowing it out deliberately as if to regain some equilibrium. She clearly had her own demons, possibly more haunting even than Erin's guilt.

'You know about cults.'

'Oh yeah, I know about cults.' Tess let her head fall back for a moment, evidently still trying to regain her composure. 'I've seen what some of them do to kids, too. Girls *and* boys. Believe me, if I could go in there today, find the kids and get them out, I would. But we've got no legal evidence yet, we don't even know for sure if the kids are in danger, and the women at the house have already complained about me, so I can't go in to find out.'

'I can,' Erin said. 'I've already made contact with two of the women, told them how interested I am in visiting the community. I've set the groundwork for running the story that I'm tired and disillusioned and pissed off with the job.'

'It could be dangerous,' Tess stressed. 'At the very least, they'll use all their tactics to convert you.'

'I know about scams. I know those tactics.' Now Erin needed courage to confess. Her heart thumped so loudly she thought Tess could surely hear it. 'My father was a con artist.

A thief, a fraud. Until I was sixteen I helped him run cons. We sold things like fake gemstones and diet pills in shopping centres and online. I sold them to my classmates at school. I know the business, all the tricks, all the manipulations. Tess, I can play roles and lie through my teeth and have people eating out of my hand. If Joshua or his followers are frauds, I'll know it.'

Tess got up and paced back and forth, hands thrust in her pockets. 'I should tell you not to do it,' she said at last, stopping in front of Erin. 'I should remind you that it could be dangerous and that the group is currently subject to a police investigation.'

'You just did. I'll consider myself warned.'

'Listen, I think we'll be in there by tomorrow, if not later today. I know Steve's as suspicious as I am and wants a reason to raid the place to find answers. We're digging as hard as we can, every angle. And we should have the contents of Hayley's memory card by lunchtime today.'

Erin set down her mug on the table and stood to face Tess. 'Then I'll go this morning, start finding out what's going on. I'll phone or come back tonight, or at the latest by tomorrow morning, to let you know what I've discovered. That'll help you plan what you need to do.'

Tess gave her a wan smile that revealed her misgivings. 'Be careful. And get out of here now before I regain my sanity or Steve comes in and talks you out of it.'

Erin had her hand on the door when Tess said her name. She looked back. The young policewoman still stood, hands in pockets, shoulders tense.

'Erin, kids who've been in cults – they won't trust easily. They don't know "normal". They believe that all outsiders are evil and they'll follow the cult leader whatever he says. They're damaged in ways you can't comprehend.'

Apprehension coiled in Erin's stomach and she didn't know whether it was because of the pain in Tess's harsh voice, or fear for the children she'd briefly met.

She swallowed against the tightness in her throat. 'I'll let you know what I find out. You and the specialists can get them out and deal with the issues.'

•

Simon hiked the couple of kilometres through the scrub back to their base camp at Harden's Hut. A fox crossed his path, a young rabbit in its jaws. A few wallabies hopped away from his approach, and an echidna curled into a tree stump, pretending it wasn't there. The sun lit a brilliant blue sky, with only wisps of cloud, but the air hung thicker, the humidity building towards the forecast storms.

Despite being out all night, he didn't stop at the hut to sleep. Sleep could come later. He'd seen no violence at Harcourt, no indication of abuse or fear, but the ceremonial rituals had troubled him. Maybe they only performed the chant and danced slowly in the circle on Sundays. Maybe it was nothing more than greeting the sun and marking the start of the new day. But Hayley had run from them, and someone had murdered her, and her daughter, who was not much more than a child, was under the influence of a group of women who dressed in white and had guards protecting them during the night.

He drove into Goodabri shortly after nine and parked behind the office building. Fraser's car was out the front, beside the local police four-wheel drive and another car.

After shooting a quick text to Erin, he rapped on the back door of the police rooms and Aaron opened it, a slice of toast in his hand. Chewing on a mouthful, he waved Simon through to the kitchen. The scent of burnt toast clogged the air, but underneath it he caught the aroma of ground coffee. He could go months without the stuff if he had to, but that only made him appreciate it more when he had it. Especially after a night out scouting a large property and observing its residents.

In the kitchen, Fraser poured a large mug of coffee from a plunger and handed it to him in greeting. 'That'll get a brain cell functioning,' he said. 'Or blow it to smithereens.'

Simon gripped the mug in his hand and inhaled. Strong, hot, black, and with a caffeine hit that would keep him going for hours.

'American cops get donuts,' Fraser continued in mock complaint as he dropped a couple of slices of bread into an ageing toaster. 'Out here in the bush, we get toast and Vegemite.

Although Tess said there's some yoghurt in the fridge, if you want to, you know, be *healthy*.'

'Toast is good,' Simon responded. Carbs for energy, and he needed energy. Maybe a loaf of it. 'Any news?'

'Not a lot to report. But the good news is I'll have the contents of that memory card within the hour. Assuming I can download it on the prehistoric wires out here. What about you?'

'Good news and bad news.'

'Give me the bad first.'

'There are more than forty people out there. Six women, two men and some teens at the homestead, the rest in the old woolshed and outbuildings at the back of the property. Including fifteen children.'

Fraser whistled. 'What kind of conditions?'

'Pretty good, from what we could see. But they all did a ceremony at sunrise, chanting and stuff. I read signs of a hierarchy – particularly with the separation of the women at the house and the others, but also clothing. Light blue dresses on at least four of the adolescent girls. And the women from the house were all in white.'

Fraser's eyebrows shot up. 'Same as Hayley and Sybilla?'

'As far as I can tell, yes. It's pretty open up there and I couldn't get as close as I wanted. They also had two guards on patrol around the house.'

That made Fraser stop stock still. 'Armed?'

'No guns. Batons. Maybe knives. We didn't see any evidence of weaponry other than that. Certainly no stockpiles of military weapons.'

Fraser visibly relaxed and turned to rescue the toast. 'Good. "We?"' he queried.

Simon grabbed a knife and buttered the slices of toast Fraser passed him while they were hot. 'My old army mate,' he explained. 'Gabe McCallum. I asked him to come up for a few days.'

'So now I've got commandos running around out there, too.' Fraser's tone was only half joking. 'Assure me that neither of you is going to go berserk.'

'He's solid. You needn't be concerned. And he won't touch firearms anymore. So, no guns.'

'I'm relying on your judgement. Make sure he knows not to get in the way.' An order, not a request. Simon respected it, because Fraser had charge of the operation and, despite his frequent levity, shouldered his responsibilities with commitment and professionalism.

'You want the good news now?'

'That wasn't the good news?'

'There's better.' Simon didn't hold back his grin. 'Nice big cannabis crop hidden in the scrub. Two varieties on at least two acres. One's possibly low-THC industrial hemp, but the other certainly isn't.'

Fraser's hoot of delight brought Tess and Aaron to the

kitchen door. 'Oh, you beauty. Best news I've heard all year. You've got the exact location, I presume?'

'Full GPS coordinates of the crop. They've got an irrigation system pumping water from the river. I'm betting they don't have a licence for the industrial hemp crop, the way it's hidden away.'

'That crop's a reason to raid, sarge,' Tess said.

'Yeah, you bet. If we don't find another reason in the computer data, we can use it. Aaron, get on to the drug squad. But tell them not to go rushing in there straightaway. We need to coordinate.'

Simon wolfed down his toast and checked his phone while the three officers discussed possible strategies. No message from Erin. No email, either.

'Anyone heard from Erin?' he asked when there was a break in the discussion.

Aaron looked blank and Fraser shook his head. 'Not yet.'

Tess stood ramrod straight, as if she was on parade. Or facing a firing squad. 'I saw her over an hour ago. She's gone to Harcourt Downs, to visit the community.'

CHAPTER 13

The gates of Serenity Hill stood open. Erin drove past them and pulled up a hundred metres down the road. Bathed in sunlight, the homestead was the image of a dream home – attractive, inviting, surrounded by beautiful gardens and golden paddocks with the bush and low hills for a backdrop.

Her father had 'sold' a property not unlike this in South Australia to an unsuspecting overseas investor. At age twelve, Erin had posed for the happy-family-home photos, taken in the garden while the owners were away, and he'd taken her to Movie World on the Gold Coast with the proceeds. The police never caught up with her father for that one. Perhaps karma did, eventually, when he crossed the wrong mob and ended up in prison.

She blew out a slow breath. Time to go in. Time to become a slightly foolish, disenchanted, thirty-something single girl just looking for love and acceptance and easy answers. She'd spent half the night lying awake, going through ways to alleviate suspicion. If any of the community talked to the locals, they might have heard about her friendship with Simon, perhaps even about her being with him when he found Hayley, although few knew she'd seen the body. The Goodabri locals were also somewhat tight-lipped when it came to strangers, and that might work in her favour. But if not, the incident on the dance floor at the ball now seemed a blessing. So, too, did his silence while watching the fire, and them leaving in separate cars. A rift between her and Simon? Her doubts about his innocence in relation to Hayley's murder? She could make it believable. She'd just have to ensure she didn't choke on every lie.

Act. Perform. Make contact with the girl, Hayley's daughter, find out what she could about the situation, and leave during the night.

Her email to Serenity Hill this morning had been answered within the hour by someone called Mary. Presumably the same Mary who had spoken to Steve Fraser on Friday night. Erin was very welcome to come, any time today.

'Any time' was going to be now, mid-morning, before she lost her nerve.

She did a U-turn and drove through the gates, down the elm-lined drive to the wide turning circle in front of the house. The place had been Harcourt Downs for over a hundred years before it became Serenity Hill, and the well-kept homestead reflected a gracious history.

As she parked, the leadlight front door opened and a woman came down the steps of the wide veranda to greet her. Tall, perhaps in her early forties, she wore her long hair piled in a loose knot at the back of her head. Erin took a moment to switch off the ignition, keeping her face averted to set her expression to reveal no surprise at the woman's white dress.

The moment she stepped out of the ute, the woman greeted her. 'Hello! You must be Erin. I'm Mary. I'm so glad you could come.'

'Thank you. What a beautiful place this is.'

Erin found her hands clasped gently, warm green eyes gazing into hers. 'We're so looking forward to welcoming you. Please, come inside. I believe you've met Willow already? She's just taking some cakes from the oven and will join us in a moment.'

Mary ushered her in, carrying the heavier of her bags for her, inviting her to leave her things in an alcove off the central hallway 'for now'. In an inviting sitting room with wicker furniture and low pine tables overlooking the garden behind the house, Willow joined them, coming straight across to hug her. Willow in a white dress. Maybe it was just a uniform, like women in day spas and hairdressers wore.

'I'm so excited that you came!' Willow exclaimed, her eyes sparkling. 'We're going to have a wonderful time, aren't we, Mary?'

The young woman's pleasure made it easy for Erin to smile in return. 'I'm looking forward to it, I *so* need the break. I told the boss last night that I was too stressed and was taking a week off. You've just got to do that sometimes, you know? You've got to look after yourself, because no one else will.'

'We'll look after you,' Willow assured her, squeezing her hand. 'Now sit down and relax. I've made honey cakes and a pot of peppermint tea. I'll just be a minute.'

'Are there any other visitors at the moment?' Erin asked Mary as she made herself comfortable on the lounge.

'We're only getting established here at Serenity Hill,' Mary explained. 'We're expecting a couple of other visitors, but they aren't arriving until this evening. So you'll be spoilt with attention this afternoon.'

'Sounds great.'

Three more women in the white dresses came into view, walking across the grass towards the house, their steps light and faces animated with laughter. They stepped up onto the long back veranda further down and must have entered the house through the kitchen, as within minutes they came into the sitting room with Willow, bearing trays with glasses, white teacups and a matching white china teapot.

Mary introduced Erin to the three newcomers, Tamara, Callie and Rebecca. Tamara was around Erin's age, but the other two were much younger, perhaps only in their late teens. Young, fresh-faced and pretty, their long hair loosely arranged in fine braids woven together like a peasant girl's crown. Nothing like Erin's own hurried ponytail.

Rebecca placed a small table beside her while Willow knelt at a larger low table and poured herbal tea. 'This is our own organic peppermint,' she said, bringing Erin a china cup. 'Freshly picked just minutes ago. It's refreshing and relaxing for both body and soul. It helps to clear toxins and bring harmony to your body and your mind. And it tastes great,' she added with a smile, before glancing at Mary as if for approval.

Mary nodded at her. Willow then poured for Mary and for Tamara before Callie and Rebecca. If Erin read the dynamics right, Mary was at the head of the hierarchy, like a Mother Superior in a convent, and the younger women at the bottom. Whether intentionally or not, Mary and Tamara sat in two of the three chairs, while the younger ones used the large cushions on the floor, quite relaxed.

Willow brought Erin a small cake on a white plate; a golden-brown cake, smaller than a cupcake, with a sliced strawberry beside it. 'These are honey cakes, made with almond meal and our own organic butter and eggs. We bartered for the honey but we hope to have our own hives soon.'

'Is your community self-sufficient?' Erin directed the question at Mary as Willow was serving cake to the others.

'We aim to be, as much as possible,' Mary answered, her enthusiasm only slightly more tempered than Willow's. 'We grow most of our food, and we make the majority of our clothing, furniture and tools. We practise the principles of reducing and re-using even more than recycling. We also barter with our sister communities and others. But that's enough about us.' Her smile was full of warmth and interest, almost maternal. 'We'd love to get to know you.'

Convincing lies stick to the truth as much as possible. Lesson one in Cam Taylor's school for young scammers. 'There's not much to tell, really. My mum died when I was just a baby. I lived with my dad, and he was a lazy sod, always changing jobs, so we moved around a lot. He got a new girlfriend when I was about sixteen and she hated me, so I had to leave. It was a bit tough for a while but I got by.' All true, in one way or another.

The younger girls in particular oozed sympathy. 'You poor thing,' Callie said, patting her on the hand.

Rebecca seemed awed. 'You're so brave, doing that.'

'But you work in the national park now, don't you?' Willow asked. 'That's awesome, working with the animals. Did you always want to do that?'

Working with the animals . . . Yep, dealing with feral pests, being stung by insects, swooped by magpies, and constantly on the alert for spiders and snakes. Not the kind of cute furry animals Willow – and half the population – had in mind. But the question put her on alert, because she hadn't told Willow on Friday where she worked, and she hadn't been in uniform. The woman she'd spoken to yesterday must have told them. The woman who wasn't here now.

'I love it,' Erin said, truthfully. 'I wanted to do something honest, you know, and good for the planet.' That was also true, although it wasn't the way she'd usually express it. Appearing impressionable mattered here, more than the environmental and ethical reasons she'd chosen her career. 'All the reports and paperwork are a pain, though. All just so the politicians can cherry-pick the figures and pretend they're doing something useful.' Not too much risk in that tactic. Neither Hayley nor Sybilla had left records in the usual databases – social security, tax, licensing or health. All the evidence suggested that the group avoided participation in society, and Joshua's writings prioritised community over society's laws. If they saw the world as 'us' and 'them', she had to align herself with 'us'. 'I really just want to be out there, you know, with nature.'

She took a bite of the little honey cake and the delicately sweet, spicy morsel melted in her mouth. Not hard to let her face light up. 'This is wonderful, Willow! So light and delicious.'

Willow beamed like a child. All three of the younger ones had a kind of youthful innocence that made Erin think of them as girls rather than women. Except . . . the way they reclined on the big cushions. Relaxed, but not with the casual sprawl of teenagers. Not quite provocative, but suggestive. Bare feet and long limbs gracefully curled. A dress artfully slipping off a naked shoulder. The wrap front of a bodice draping just loosely enough to frame the swell of firm, round breasts. Mary and Tamara were more subtle in their manner, but they both had the slightly languid air and elegant sensuality that made Erin imagine courtesans of kings.

Joshua Kristos had written about the beauty of the body, the bliss of sensuality and the gift of ecstasy between two people. Nothing Erin disagreed with, although the ecstasy thing was generally overrated in her experience. Yet other than the young lad yesterday, she'd not seen any men. Maybe they were a happy lesbian ménage. Nothing wrong with that, as far as she was concerned. Perhaps that's why Hayley had left Simon, yet still sent him affectionate cards – she'd discovered she loved a woman more than him. Maybe she and Sybilla had been lovers, partners. Perhaps Sybilla had purposely stepped off the cliff, in grief or guilt.

Erin finished the honey cake, drank some tea and accepted another cake pressed on her by Willow, all the while answering the gently probing questions and talking more about herself than she had for years. She didn't have to resort to many lies, but even still the honey cake sat heavily in her stomach.

When she'd finished her tea and set down her cup, Mary leaned forward. 'Erin, we'd love to help you find the joy and bliss within you. You've chosen to come to our community and we hope that during these few days at least you'll embrace the spirit of simplicity that we believe in.'

'Oh, I do want to. After I met Willow the other day and she told me about Joshua Kristos, I downloaded some of his podcasts, and I bought one of his books last night. I haven't finished it yet, but it all just resonates with me.'

Was that a little sparkle of amusement in Mary's eyes? Perhaps she was overplaying her ready-to-be-converted role.

'Wonderful. It's an important aspect of our lives that we free the body of tensions and toxins so that our energy isn't wasted fighting them. So our suggested program starts with a cleansing, relaxing bath that will begin the process of releasing the built-up tension in your muscles. If you're ready, we'll begin?'

Relieved that there was nothing too mystical to start with, Erin agreed readily, and while Callie and Rebecca went to prepare the bath, Willow showed her to her room, down a passageway to one end of the house. Not a large room, but light and attractive, with simplicity the decorating principle. White walls and a white bedspread contrasted with the warm tones of a small pine table and chair and the colourful view of the garden through the window. Other than the bed, table and chair, there was no other furniture in the room.

Willow clasped her hands loosely in front of her. 'We'll provide everything you need during your stay so that you can disconnect from the toxins and distractions of the outside world. Mary will store your belongings in a locker in the office. She'll give you a key, in case there's anything that you really need. But most people discover they don't need any of the "stuff" that consumerism makes them think they must have.'

Isolation from the world – first step. For all Willow's genuine, considerate eagerness to help her, they were separating her from the familiar.

'My clothes?' Erin queried. She didn't ask about her phone, her wallet, her car keys. Yet. Her phone was no use to her here anyway, and presumably Mary or one of the others would ask for her cash payment sooner or later.

'We'll provide you with clothes made from organic, natural fabrics. You'll love how beautiful they feel on your skin. No poisonous chemicals or plastic fibres. You wouldn't believe what goes into commercial fabrics these days.' Willow stepped out into the passage again. She opened a cupboard they'd passed on the way, and returned with a folded robe. 'Why don't you change into this now, and I'll take you to the bathroom. I'll just be out here, so come out when you're ready.'

Willow pulled the door closed, and Erin stood in the middle of the room for several moments, thinking. She'd made it through, so far – she hoped. The women seemed friendly, interested, compassionate. Their questions had been politely probing but not suspicious.

Love bombing, Tess had said. Separation from the outside world.

Two boxes ticked.

Erin unzipped her dress and stepped out of it, then laid it on the bed. The robe was a standard kimono style, similar to those found in any up-market hotel, except this one was made of a densely woven cotton, or maybe hemp. She unclipped her bra and took it off – stupid to go for a bath in a bra – but after a moment's indecision she left her briefs on.

The robe did feel good against her skin. She tied the belt and went out to meet Willow.

The bathroom was six times the size of her draughty add-on bathroom in the cottage, with a deep sunken bath in the middle, already filled with water. The room had the same simple decorating scheme as the bedroom – white walls, timber finishing and furnishings around a double white vanity and basins. But there were flowers and candles on numerous shelves around the walls, and the timber venetian blinds on the window were partially closed for privacy, dimming the light.

'I'll put on some music and leave you in peace,' Willow said. 'Relax and enjoy.' The door closed behind her, and the soft strains of gentle instrumental music floated around the room.

Erin undressed and stepped into the warm, scented water, letting it envelop her. Her body began relaxing in the warmth. Her brain didn't, despite the soothing music and aromatic oils.

She'd not yet seen Hayley's daughter, or the woman she'd met yesterday. That woman hadn't worn the white uniform either in Strathnairn on Friday, or yesterday at the river. Erin hadn't heard any noises suggesting that there were other people in the house, but it was a large house. Maybe later she could explore. Maybe later there'd be an opportunity to ask about Hayley and Sybilla, or one of the women would mention them.

So far, the five women presented a caring, unthreatening approach. Even if they ticked some of the boxes for a cult, it was a broad term that could include a wide range of groups, not all of them dangerous.

But she'd only been here an hour or two.

She closed her eyes and tried to consciously relax her limbs and muscles. Even if the body-washing was designed to soften her up for the brainwashing, she could still enjoy the first part. They'd find washing a waterproof brain more of a challenge.

•

'How damn long does it take to get a search warrant?' Simon demanded. Two hours since he'd found out that Erin had gone to Harcourt Downs. Two long, dragging hours in which he'd paced through half his boot soles going back and forth between the Parks office and the police rooms next door and come up with fifteen different strategies to extract Erin if the police didn't move soon.

'The magistrate wants more information,' Fraser said, after finishing another phone call. 'We could get a warrant pretty quickly to search for the cannabis crop, but we can't search the rest of the place unless we have more than hearsay and coincidences to go on. Either about the girl or Hayley's murder.'

The edges of Simon's control frayed a little more. 'Have the files from the memory card finished downloading yet?'

'There are over a hundred files on the card so Forensics sent it as a zip file. It's only fifty per cent done and it's been going for twenty minutes. The wireless network link keeps cutting out. Tess has gone up to the station to try downloading on the wired link.'

Simon ground his teeth. Over a hundred files. They'd still have to go through all of them, try to figure out what was significant. More time. More time while Erin was with a group of bizarre people whom Hayley had called a cult and run from.

Fraser slapped him on the back as he headed to the kitchen. 'Chill, Kennedy. Erin's tough and smart. She deals with all kinds when she's working out there alone in the bush. And Tess told us what she said.'

That her father was a con man. That she'd helped him when she was a kid. Close on twenty years ago. Simon didn't care what her father had persuaded her to do when she was a kid. The Erin he knew was decent, straightforward, hard-working and honest.

Simon followed Fraser to the kitchen, and occupied the doorway. 'I looked him up,' he said. In the interminable hours while he'd waited for the police to take action. 'Her father. Campbell Taylor. Convicted of a multi-million-dollar fraud in South Australia fourteen years ago and jailed for ten.'

'And died in a hostel for homeless men six months after getting out on parole,' Fraser added. 'I looked him up, too.' His phone beeped and he checked the message. 'Tess has the files. She's on her way back.'

Three minutes to walk from the police station, two hundred metres down the adjoining street. Simon eschewed a chair and hunkered on the floor while he waited. He checked his phone for a text from Erin. Again. Uselessly, because Harcourt Downs was in an area with no mobile reception. He refrained from sending her a fourth message. Barely.

He heard footsteps, saw a shadow pass the closed blinds, and pulled the door open for Tess. She carried her laptop, and she went straight to the table she'd been using and opened it.

'Right, it's documents. Lots of documents,' she said. 'PDF files, mostly. A couple of image files.'

Simon and Fraser stood shoulder to shoulder behind her to see the screen. 'Don't open anything yet,' Fraser said. 'Let's just look at those file names.'

The files were sorted in alphabetical order, the first group of file names made up of numbers and letters, followed by another group which had a word-number-word format.

'They're dates,' Simon said at the same time as Tess said, 'I think I know —'

Simon shifted slightly to get a better view of the screen. 'This first group. Six digits, year, month, day. Dates and places, maybe? S-Y-D – that could be Sydney. Bris – that'd be Brisbane. And there's N-Y. New York?'

'They're documents, not image files,' Fraser said. 'Probably not holiday snaps. Tess, you were going to say something?'

Tess indicated the second section of the file list, where Simon could make out a few words, and what looked like years – 1988, 1996, 2014. 'These might be academic journal articles, or resources. It's the same way I label readings for my university course. Main author's surname, year of publication, keywords from the title.'

'Was Hayley a student anywhere, I wonder?' Fraser mused.

'She completed her childcare certificate,' Simon answered, 'but she struggled with the study aspect. Maybe she went back.'

Tess pointed at the screen. 'Look at the titles. The words are run together but there's "charismatic", "deviant", and "hypnosis" there, and "psychiatric". I think that these could be articles about cults.'

Not the kinds of topics Simon expected Hayley would research. 'Find the last opened files,' he suggested. 'If these documents aren't hers, the last opened files may be the reason she took the memory card.'

Tess clicked a few menus, found the names of the most recently viewed files. The filename on top of the list had a date about a week prior and the initials 'CHKH', but Simon's gaze stuck on the date and time the file had last been opened.

'Monday morning.' Fraser's voice sounded loud in the still room.

Simon nodded wordlessly. Monday morning. Just after ten o'clock. And Hayley had fled not long afterwards.

Tess pointed at the screen with a pen. 'There are two files viewed that morning.' Before opening them she reached for the notepad beside her and jotted down the names and dates. The second filename included a date ten days ago and the initials NY.

Simon held his breath as she clicked open the first one.

An article from the online edition of the Coffs Harbour newspaper with the headline 'Local Woman's Cult Warning'. She scrolled past the headline and read aloud from the text. '"A local woman has warned against a group that has recently set up on a property in the area. The group promotes healthy, simple living and self-sufficiency, but the woman, who wishes to remain anonymous, says the group is a cult and its leader, who goes by the name Joshua, is a charlatan." There he is. Did Hayley read that and realise? Or suspect it already?'

Simon squinted to continue reading silently over Tess's shoulder. *The woman joined the group more than ten years ago on the north coast hinterland but left when restrictions on members became more severe and sexual services were expected of female members. 'Joshua uses mind-control techniques to persuade his followers to do his bidding,' she said.*

There was more, but Tess hadn't yet scrolled that far.

'Email me that article,' Fraser told her. He had his phone in his hand and dialled a number. 'Copy it to Leah.'

'And to me,' Simon added.

Fraser took a few steps away, phone to his ear. 'What's the name of the Coffs journo?' he asked Tess.

'Jane Cooper.'

'Leah, did your vic in Coffs talk to a journalist by the name of Jane Cooper about a week ago? Yeah. Article about Kristos in the paper with an anonymous informant, on . . .' Tess gave him the date and he repeated it for Haddad.

Fraser waited, listening, and they all waited, the only sounds the buzzing of a fly at the window and Tess's fingers clicking on her laptop keys as she forwarded the article.

Fraser spoke again. 'Yes . . . Right. Shit. Yep, done. . . Okay, keep in touch.' He ended the call. 'Tess, search the rest of those documents for "Joshua Kristos" or for the names of any of our victims. The one at Coffs is Kirsty Hamilton. Leah's been checking her phone records and had them handy. Kirsty made a forty-eight-minute call to the newspaper three days before that article was published.' He dropped his phone on the table, sat down heavily. 'I'd say "bingo", but this is getting way too nasty to be frivolous. Jane Cooper, the journalist, has been missing since Tuesday.'

Aaron swore, and Tess's fingers stopped still on the keyboard.

Simon went to the window and stared out through the blinds. Hayley, Sybilla and Kirsty. All three connected to Joshua. All three of them dead. He breathed slowly in and out, struggling for clear thought and logic instead of anger.

'I'll check the second article Hayley looked at, sarge,' Tess said after a long moment.

Simon glanced over to see the banner of an American newspaper filling the top half of the screen, with a headline below it: *Expert Warns of Cult's Spread.*

"'At an international conference on new-age religion in New York this week, an Australian psychologist has warned about the spread of a quasi-religious cult which promises its adherents bliss and love,'" Tess read aloud. "'Doctor P.J. Hollywell has been researching the group for more than a decade and says that its leader, who calls himself Joshua Kristos, uses advanced techniques in persuasion, hypnosis and mind control to sexually and financially exploit his followers.'"

Simon listened with increasing unease. His training had covered mind-control techniques and how to resist them, but Hayley hadn't had the benefit of that training, or the same level of emotional resilience, and she'd been with this group for years. But she also didn't have much in the way of money. At least as far as he knew. Erin was much stronger than Hayley, physically and emotionally, but despite her background, no way would she be prepared for the kind of mind games a skilled person could subject her to.

They all waited while Tess took a sip of water, her gaze still on the screen. 'I'll skim the rest. He's interviewed people who have left the group. He says there's a hierarchy typical of cults. There's also a sexual hierarchy, who can sleep with who. Sex is equated with bliss but permanent pair bonds are discouraged except for . . . ' Her voice shook. 'Except for the women Joshua chooses as his. Okay, the money. Let's see . . . book sales are a part of it – a million books sold worldwide, he says – but there's stuff here about property and donations of hundreds of thousands of dollars to enter the community. And here he's hinting at drugs.'

Simon gripped the window frame so tightly flakes of old paint speared under his fingernails. Hayley had read those articles. She'd read those articles exposing Joshua as a fraud, and she'd run within hours. She'd been up on the north coast for longer than ten years. If she'd been with Joshua's group then, she'd have known the woman who'd been murdered at Coffs Harbour.

If she'd been with Joshua's group all this time . . . She hadn't had much money, but she was young when she went there. Young, slim, pretty. Young and innocent and sweet and the thought that she might have been manipulated or coerced into a sexual relationship made his gut burn with fury.

Steve's chair creaked as he sat up straighter and leaned his elbows on the desk. 'If there's drugs and fraud involved I'll see if the Feds have got anything on Kristos. But this guy might be a useful source of info – what's his name and where is he?'

639

Tess continued scrolling through screens. 'There's a bio line at the bottom of the article. Doctor P.J. Hollywell. He has a Doctor of Psychology degree from the University of Melbourne, has been researching cults in Australia and Kristos for some years.'

The name tickled something in Simon's memory. Maybe he'd served with a Hollywell.

Aaron typed quickly on his laptop. 'Hollywell, P. . . . Okay, there's a profile here on a professional networking site for a Peter James Hollywell who's a psychologist. Western Sydney . . . Blue Mountains now, by the looks of it.'

'*Peter* Hollywell?' Fraser frowned.

The memory clicked into place. 'I know of that guy. I think. When we were at Holsworthy, those first couple of years, Hayley battled depression. He's the counsellor she saw. I'm pretty sure that was his name. Peter Hollywell.'

'Shit.' Fraser dragged a hand through his hair, more agitated than Simon had seen him before. 'Hayley knew Peter Hollywell?'

'Yes. I think so. You know him?'

'Yeah. Know of him, anyway. My sister —' He swallowed, visibly shaken. 'My sister was a patient of his.'

'What happened?' Simon probed, because clearly something had. 'What did he do?'

'I don't know that he did anything. He certainly didn't do enough. She committed suicide. At fourteen.'

Simon didn't know what to say. Aaron seemed not to, either.

Tess spoke up. 'I'm sorry, sarge. What a tragedy.'

Fraser shrugged, embarrassed, and picked up his phone. 'Let's hope the Feds have something that can help us.'

Simon leaned back against the wall, fists thrust into his pockets, almost oblivious to the police officers while his brain gnawed through the new information. Fraser's sister and Hayley had seen the same psychologist when they lived in the same area. Had to be just coincidence. Must be. Except that the psychologist knew about Joshua's cult. Maybe Hayley had kept in touch with him. But if he'd known she was there, why hadn't he contacted Simon to warn him? Surely patient confidentiality didn't rule out a warning that she was in danger?

The muscles in his spine tensed, urging him to action, to fight. But he couldn't fight an unknown foe. He needed more information. He needed facts to go on, evidence more solid than the nagging, insistent sense that something about the Hayley–Hollywell–Joshua connection didn't add up.

CHAPTER 14

After enough rotations through the same soothing music track that it was beginning to get on her nerves, Erin pulled the plug out of the bath and dried herself with one of the towels on the rack. It wasn't the usual cotton terry cloth but a waffle weave in a natural linen, and surprisingly absorbent. She was tying the belt on the robe when someone knocked at the door.

The woman she'd spoken with yesterday at the falls stood outside, a short distance back from the doorway, now wearing the same white uniform as the others. She immediately gave a tiny shake of her head and raised her eyes towards the bathroom ceiling.

A warning.

Microphone or camera? Erin didn't look up. The thought of either instantly reversed any relaxing effects of the bath.

'Hello, I'm Madeleine,' the woman said brightly. 'I'm sorry I wasn't here earlier to welcome you, Erin. If you'd like to come this way, I'll give you a massage to deepen your body's relaxation and healing.'

It seemed Madeleine hadn't told the others about their meeting, yet they'd known she was a ranger. The muscles woven around Erin's spine tightened. Madeleine trusted her enough to warn her about the surveillance in the bathroom, and to tell her yesterday about Sybilla. Was Madeleine a potential ally? Or was she only protecting herself, not Erin?

The massage room, next door to the bathroom, overlooked the garden through layers of gauzy curtains that shifted and danced with the wind coming through the open casement window. Madeleine pulled the window closed. 'There's a storm coming,' she said. 'I can feel the shift in the air. I think it's going to be a big one.'

Although she'd read the weather forecast that morning, Erin wasn't entirely sure that Madeleine was talking about the effects of low-pressure cells and cold fronts.

If there was surveillance in the bathroom, there might well be here, too. But now wasn't the time to be prudish and give the game away. She shrugged out of her robe and climbed onto the towel-covered massage table, playing it safe with the usual rural weather chat. 'We sure could do with the rain. It was a very dry summer.' She fitted her face into the cushioned hole in the massage table, narrowing her field of vision to a small patch of floor below her. 'I've lived out in the country so long that I like rain.'

Madeleine began to lay warm towels over her back. 'I do too. And it's wonderful how a storm refreshes everything, isn't it? Washes away all the old dust and death and decay and encourages new growth.'

Old dust, death and decay. Erin had never been good at cryptic crosswords. *If* Madeleine spoke metaphorically, she must be signifying a change coming. Encourages new growth – what did she mean by that? Erin hadn't detected in her voice any indication whether she believed that to be good or bad.

The warm oil and Madeleine's firm, steady hands worked on loosening her newly tense muscles. Usually Erin enjoyed a massage, and Madeleine was skilled. But normally she had little more concerning her than an overload of work.

For the benefit of any observers, she'd better continue to play her role. 'I'd love to find out more about the group here. Everyone is so friendly. Have you been part of the community for long?'

The pressure of the hands on her shoulder blades didn't falter. 'Yes, for a long time. Joshua saved my life when I was young. I owe him everything. His wisdom, his love – they transformed me. I found peace, and joy in working with my hands, and bliss in the abundance of a simple life, shared lovingly with others.'

Erin's thoughts bustled with questions, most of which would give her away if she asked them. If not to Madeleine, then to anyone listening. Madeleine said she had known Joshua for 'a long time', Erin noted. Like Willow, he'd 'changed her life'. That seemed a safe topic to explore further.

'I've downloaded Joshua's book – the first one – and some of the letters on his website. He truly is wise, isn't he? And compassionate. Last night when I was reading, I felt as though he was there, that he knew me and was talking to me.' That was a porky. She'd actually felt like throwing the book at the wall, because it continually repeated the same ideas, but tossing hundreds of dollars' worth of electronic tablet at a solid object wouldn't have been so satisfying.

'Joshua has helped many people find joy and bliss,' said Madeleine. 'Although our group began as a small family, his truth and teachings have spread, and our communities are evolving and growing. He is beloved by thousands, and over a hundred of us have devoted ourselves to living simply within his communities.'

Erin hoped there was no camera in the floor, watching her face. Communities, plural. Over a hundred people in them. Bigger than she'd imagined. 'Can anyone join a community?' she asked.

She felt the towels being shifted and then Madeleine began working on her legs. 'Not everyone is suited to the life. Although there is great joy and bliss in living our way, we must all serve the community in a harmonious and constructive manner. So we have a gradual process in which potentials come to know us, and we come to know them. Visits like this are the first step. Those who wish to pursue the path are invited for a longer visit, to learn more of Joshua's teachings. Some then make their first commitment and join the community.'

'Their first commitment? There are those who make more?'

'Yes. There are different ways to serve the community, using different gifts. Some paths require training for the development of specific knowledge, skills and disciplines.'

'You're certainly skilled at massage,' Erin said. Truthfully, because despite her stress and uneasiness, the woman was working wonders.

'Thank you. It is a joy to share the gift with you.'

'Is that what you do here? Provide massages?'

'It is only a small part of my service. I am one of the sisters. We have devoted our lives to supporting Joshua in his work and providing guidance to the community.'

Sisters. Women in white dresses. Hardly a nun's habit, but the symbolism wasn't so different. Although with the sensuality on display earlier, just what kind of 'support' did they give Joshua?

She grappled for an innocent question to ask. 'How many sisters are there?'

'Six in each community. There are also potentials who are selected for training.'

'It must be an honour to serve Joshua so closely.'

Did she imagine the pause? Perhaps Madeleine was simply contemplating the callus on Erin's heel from boots that had never quite fitted properly. Her voice came softly. 'I am blessed by all he has given me.'

Did she mean the child, the little girl? The older girl was Hayley's daughter, but the boy, Tristan, might have been seventeen or so, and if Madeleine was her own age . . . Either Tristan wasn't hers or she'd had a child very young. She said she'd been with Joshua since she was young. Hayley had been with him for years, too, and she'd worn the white dress of the sisters. Erin's gut did an uneasy somersault.

'What about men?' she asked. 'Are there brothers, too?'

'Yes, but not in quite the same way. There are men who have committed their lives to Joshua and to the community. There are brothers who oversee the training of the young boys, and others who accept a particular responsibility for the security of the community.'

The security of the community. Police and soldiers looked after the security of communities. So did spies. The surveillance in the bathroom and here might not only be for lecherous intent.

Madeleine was massaging her toes. 'You are very fortunate,' she began, and for one crazy heartbeat Erin thought she referred to her crooked toes. But she continued, 'Joshua is coming today. He will be here soon. This evening, the whole community will celebrate his presence with us.' She rested a hand on each of Erin's feet for a moment. 'I am finished here. There is a dress for you on the shelf. Rise when you're ready.'

She didn't leave immediately. Through the hole in the massage table Erin saw the hem of her dress swish towards the window, and the movement of the gauze curtains.

Erin rolled over, and reached for her robe. Madeleine had her back to her, looking out between the curtains.

'There is a huge bank of dark clouds,' Madeleine said. 'The storm is almost here. The wind is getting stronger and gusty and I'm afraid that with all these trees and dead wood around, it could be dangerous.' She turned and gave a weak smile, but there was nothing weak in the depth of her eyes. 'Be careful in the storm, Erin.'

•

Simon checked the time on his watch. Five minutes to go. Five minutes before he rejoined Fraser and the others to pool whatever information they'd managed to find in the last forty minutes. Five minutes to the deadline he'd set for himself. If the police didn't turn up something significant or have a plan in place within that time, he was going out to Harcourt Downs or Serenity Hill or whatever they called the place now to find Erin and the girl himself.

On an intellectual level, he understood the wariness of the police – Haddad, Fraser, even Nick – to move too quickly. The fact that there were multiple communities involved and potential fraud and drugs complicated matters and required consultation with other units in the state police, and with the Feds. While the local cops, like him, wanted to raid the place immediately, they all knew they didn't have enough evidence to justify it. Fraser's hands were tied by the rules of due process and police procedure.

Simon didn't have to follow police procedure. His actions were subject only to the law and his own moral and ethical principles. To ensure the safety of Erin and the girl he'd trespass on the grey areas of the law if he had to.

Three minutes to go. He'd had no luck, so far, finding anything of significance in his internet searching. He'd found plenty of fans of Joshua Kristos, people around the world who claimed their lives had been transformed by reading his books, but none of them had met him or lived in a Simple Bliss community. There were a few critiques, too, of the books but not many. In a market saturated with self-help and new-age philosophy, maybe people just moved on to the next one if Joshua's teachings didn't inspire them.

Searching for more criticism of the guru, he typed Peter Hollywell's name into the search box and skimmed the results. A few references to his recent speech at the international conference. A couple of references to an academic journal article about cults. The profile on the website Aaron had accessed earlier. Simon clicked through to it. The brief resumé listed the counselling practice in western Sydney, then one in the Blue Mountains for two years. But according to the dates, that had ended ten years ago. Since then, Hollywell had, according to his own profile, been engaged in 'private consulting'. Very vague, with no current contact details or information about areas of specialty or interest.

Simon went back to the search results and found, down the page, a personal website for Hollywell. It opened on the screen with a few images of coastal scenes, some basic information about Hollywell that repeated mostly what was in the other site, with links to his journal articles and some other resources.

Nothing in the content leapt out at him. But it was the layout and design that struck Simon. Basic, older-style, adequate but not impressive. *Familiar.*

Simon flicked to the Serenity Hill website, still open in another browser tab, and reopened Joshua's website in another tab. Switching between the three in quick succession, he saw similarities in style, in font, in layout. Not identical by any means, but similar enough to raise questions. None of the sites had a designer listed, so he looked at the source code.

He whistled long and low, flicked back and forth between tabs, and scribbled some notes on the writing pad beside him.

The alarm he'd set on his phone beeped a reminder. Time to meet with the others. His thoughts buzzing with unanswered questions, he ripped the page off the writing pad and went back next door.

Fraser was still on the phone but seemed to be finishing up. Tess and Aaron were both back at their laptops, going through the documents on the memory card.

'Hi, Simon,' Aaron said. 'Still working on these. There's a bunch of media reports, mostly boring stuff about Joshua's communities and development applications with local councils, although there's a few about Hollywell and a couple with no mention of either but mention of cults. There are also a dozen or so book reviews. It's basically a press clippings folder. Assuming this is Joshua's, he keeps track of what's being said and what his people are doing. And what Hollywell is doing.'

Tess glanced up from her laptop. 'There's over a hundred academic journal articles. He's gathered a research library about cults, with emphasis on manipulation and hypnosis. There's a couple by Hollywell, one of which refers to Joshua directly, but the others are broader. Nothing that's much help now, though. Did you find anything?'

Simon handed her his notes. 'I don't know. Maybe. It's weird. Peter Hollywell uses the same website designer as Joshua Kristos and Serenity Hill. It could just be a stock template, but I don't think so. There's a reference in the source code of each site to the same company or design business. We need to check that out.'

'Jesus.' Fraser blew out a breath. 'What are the chances of that? Can you get on to that, Tess?'

Tess nodded, and immediately set to work.

'Anything from the Federal police?' Simon asked Fraser.

'They definitely have an interest in Kristos. Nothing firm at this stage though, other than some suspicions. But they're sending me a photo of him. The bloody guy's camera-shy and I couldn't find any online but they've got one.' His phone beeped as he spoke and he picked it up from the table, tapped the screen. And then his expression changed, the way Simon had seen soldiers' faces change sometimes when they faced a living hell. White. No mask of pretence. Just the harsh look of disbelief and dread.

Fraser's chair clattered backwards onto the floor as he stood up. He paced back and forth twice, then leaned his hands up against the wall, his head lowered and his breath coming heavily. 'Oh, Jesus. Oh, fuck.' He slammed his hand against the wall, turned on his heel and walked outside, letting the front door slam closed behind him.

Tess and Aaron were both on their feet, looking uncertain. 'Should we follow him?' Tess asked.

Simon's instinct told him that a man like Fraser didn't need Aaron's innocence right now, or for Tess to see him vulnerable. 'I'll go,' he said.

He caught up with the detective at the end of the block, where Goodabri Primary School's playing fields began and the paddocks stretched beyond, overshadowed by the wide bank of thick, black, angry clouds rolling in from the west. Fraser leaned on the fence, phone in his hand, his head hanging down.

Simon propped beside him. 'You wanna talk about it?'

'Nope. But you want to know.'

'Only if it's relevant to Hayley.'

'Yeah. I guess it is.' A breath shuddered through him. 'My sister was fourteen, having a tough time after our mother died. The sessions with Hollywell seemed to help. She thought he was great, got all starry-eyed about him. But you know alarm bells ring when a teenage girl becomes keen on a guy twenty or more years her senior. I was only seventeen though, didn't know how to raise it with her, and the one time I tried we got into a blazing argument.'

'You were a kid. It's a hard one to deal with even for adults.'

'Yep. But the next afternoon . . . I was supposed to pick her up after school. I was late, and she wasn't there. She'd disappeared. A week later, they found her schoolbag, her clothes and a suicide note near the cliffs at Kurnell. We used to have cousins in Kurnell, used to roam the bush and the cliffs there some weekends. There'd been a wild storm the night she disappeared. The police never found her body.'

'Damn tough on everyone.' Simon couldn't see the relevance yet, but Fraser wasn't the kind of guy to get worked up over nothing.

'Hollywell came to the funeral. Very sympathetic.' Fraser touched the screen of the phone and it lit up with an image of a man. A man in his fifties, with piercing blue eyes, a Hollywood smile, and wavy dark hair brushing his collar. 'That's the photo the Feds sent of Joshua Kristos,' Fraser said. 'But give him glasses, shorter, greyer hair, and he's the image of Peter Hollywell.'

Simon stared at the image, trying to make sense of it all. 'Hollywell *is* Kristos?'

'I'm betting yes.'

'But Hollywell's just spoken at a conference, exposing Joshua.'

'Yeah. I can't work that out.'

Simon's thoughts raced through possibilities. 'They could be twin brothers, I suppose. Or maybe it's one of those multiple personality disorders.'

'Either way, one of them hates the other. If it's that.'

But they still used the same website designer. And the documents on the memory card were just as relevant to Hollywell as to Kristos.

Fraser's phone beeped with a message. 'From Tess,' he said, and read aloud, ' "Same holding company registered all domains and owns company that bought Serenity Hill. Batch of new domains registered last week." Jesus. Hollywell is Kristos, and this week three women connected with him are dead.'

Simon's thoughts raced through all the small pieces of information, linking them, searching for their meaning. 'He's got something planned with those new domains. Has to have. Some kind of mad game he's been playing for years. He outed Kristos as a fraud last week but he can't build on that if anyone knows who he really is.'

Hayley and Sybilla, who'd been with him for years, and the woman in Coffs, who'd known him ten or more years ago. Simon gripped Fraser's arm.

'Hayley knew the truth. That he's both Joshua and Hollywell. Probably Sybilla and the other woman knew, too.'

Fraser had already reached the same conclusion. 'And there may be others who know. He may think Erin knows. Come on.'

They set off at a run back to the incident room as thunder cracked overhead and the first heavy raindrops began to fall.

CHAPTER 15

The weather forecast Erin had read that morning had mentioned scattered storms. The solid black sky to the west appeared to have gathered up every rain cloud in the country and combined them into one enormous, ominous storm front. The wind had turned gusty. A few heavy drops of rain fell, splattering on her skin.

Willow looked up at the cloud again. 'We might have to run for it.'

Halfway between one of the cottages and the woolshed, they quickened their pace. A few metres on, they both started to run.

Her sandals slippery on the still-dusty ground, Erin nonetheless kept pace with Willow, and they ran up the wooden stairs of the woolshed as the intermittent raindrops became a sheet of solid rain. Willow dragged open the door and they dashed inside. The young woman laughed aloud, shaking water from her hair like an exuberant puppy, and Erin couldn't help but join in, the exhilaration of the mad run temporarily overriding her wariness. She liked Willow. In the family she used to imagine as a kid – the family with her mother, as well as a dependable father, and a house they lived in for years – there'd also been a little sister to play with and boss around. That imaginary kid might have grown up to be like Willow.

People milled around inside the woolshed, and a young girl hastened towards them, offering towels, even though they'd escaped the worst of the downpour. The rain pounding on the corrugated-iron roof made conversation almost impossible, but Erin thanked her with a smile. While she wiped her face dry and blotted her hair and shoulders, she surveyed her surroundings.

It was a decent-sized woolshed which might have had twelve or more stands in the days when graziers out here ran sheep. The old stands and pens were now gone, and foldable wooden screens divided the open space into several smaller areas. Some little kids played in a netted-off corner, and around fifteen people were clearing space, stacking fold-up beds and cots behind a screen at one end of the shed.

Willow had already shown Erin the 'women's house', one of the old farm cottages that was now fitted with bunk beds, dormitory-style, and they'd passed the 'men's house', similarly fitted out. The community wasn't entirely segregated: the small rooms of the shearers' quarters were available when a couple wanted privacy. For 'bliss', Willow had said.

Willow handed her towel back to the waiting girl. 'We're going to build another house for the children but at the moment all the children sleep and learn in here,' she explained to Erin. 'The whole community shares responsibility for raising our little ones. But this space is also one of our work rooms and a gathering place.' She clasped Erin's hand. 'Come! I'll show you the looms like I promised.'

Willow had told her about the spinning and weaving workshop before their late-afternoon tour of the community. Erin was particularly interested in the textile production, intrigued by the notion of the self-sufficient lifestyle being taken to such an extreme. The community processed wool all the way through from sheep to garment, and also grew and processed flax into fabric. They bartered for hemp yarn and wove it, then dyed and sewed it. The fact that almost all the garments she'd seen so far, in addition to the ones in the shop on Friday, were entirely handmade astounded her.

Willow showed her to a large enclosed space off to the side of the main shearing floor that would once have been the wool classing and baling area. Behind partitions, weavers sat at five looms of various sizes, the rhythmic wooden clatter of treadles going up and down adding to the rain's percussion on the roof. Two women and two girls sat at spinning wheels and an older man tinkered with a machine, spanner in hand.

'That's the spinning machine,' Willow explained. 'It has ten spindles so it will mean our spinners don't have to spend such long hours at the wheels. We're hoping to get it fully operational soon. We want to be able to have a third shift each day on the looms, but we can't produce enough yarn yet.'

Erin held her tongue and didn't ask how long the long hours were. She already knew no one received pay – everyone had their service to contribute for the good of the community. Willow took evident pride in the community's achievements but seemed oblivious to the issues that might arise. Erin already had the impression that some people's work was valued more highly than others'. Like most ideologies, communism had its strengths as a theory, but given human nature the practice never lived up to the ideals.

One of the young girls at the spinning wheels paused in her treadling and lifted her head to yawn. On catching sight of Willow, she looked horrified and hurriedly restarted her wheel.

Erin turned away and asked another question to draw Willow with her. Those working didn't need one of the sisters watching them. It seemed that in the hierarchy, the sisters ranked only one step lower than Joshua himself.

In the main part of the shed a large space was now clear and a few people, soaked to the skin, carried in bench seats from outside and began to set them up along the sides. The people Erin had seen ranged in age from babies through to men and women in their fifties and sixties. More women than men, but Willow had explained that most of the men were busy with the heavy work of developing the property for the necessary gardens, livestock and cropping.

There was a slight flurry at the door, people getting out of the way as a figure draped in an oilcloth cape entered. A woman rushed to help her take off the dripping cape. Madeleine. Erin followed Willow to greet her.

'Everything's in hand here, Madeleine,' Willow reported. 'We should be finished with the setting up soon.'

Not that 'we' had actually done anything yet, Erin noted to herself.

'Excellent. Joshua has arrived safely. He has asked to see you, Willow, and Rebecca and our new trainees, before the celebration.'

Willow gasped, hand over her mouth, her eyes wide with incredulity. 'Oh, I must go.'

Madeleine's hand on her arm stopped her from running off immediately. 'Christopher has the car outside because of the rain. Go and get the girls and he will drive you back to the house.'

Willow quickly crossed the floor to the netted-off corner and spoke to the two teenage girls in pale blue dresses supervising the children. Erin hadn't had a chance to look at them properly before. The girls instantly rose to their feet and followed her, brushing dust from their dresses, jittery and nervous. They didn't give any attention to Erin as they passed but one paused by Madeleine. Hayley's daughter. Madeleine kissed her forehead, brushed her cheek and watched her go.

BRONWYN PARRY

'Joshua will welcome Willow and Rebecca as our new sisters tonight, and Jasmine and Fleur as trainees. It's a significant day for them.' She smiled as a mourner smiles at a funeral, and standing beside her Erin saw the disquiet in her eyes.

Thankful to know at last the name of Hayley's child, Erin nevertheless was worried by Madeleine's unease. 'What are they being trained as?' she asked quietly.

'Joshua has chosen them to be trained as sisters. If they prove suitable, they will support Joshua in his work and provide leadership to the community.'

'They will serve Joshua?' She didn't succeed entirely in hiding the distaste from her voice. The girls were both slim, attractive – and young. So young.

'Not yet,' Madeleine said, her voice low. 'They must learn how to best be of service to him, and develop their skills and knowledge. But he has chosen them, and they are dedicated to him now.'

A hands-off signal to the other males in the group? Erin suppressed a shudder. The thought of Jasmine learning to be 'of service' to the man made her stomach churn.

They were still standing near the main doorway and people bustled around them, asking pardon when they needed them to step aside so that the long benches could be carried past. Not quite the tugging of forelocks, but they treated Madeleine with an almost formal respect that Erin found uncomfortable. No sign of the usual cheeky, teasing Australian informality that she was used to with SES training activities or other community efforts.

660

'I would like to help,' she said to Madeleine, touching her on the arm and choosing her words with care. 'Is there something I can do? Some way I can help the community prepare for tonight?'

Madeleine clasped her hand and her direct gaze held many questions, although she asked only one, in not much more than a murmur. 'Did you come here to help us?'

'Yes, I did. Just tell me what you need me to do.'

'Come with me.'

Madeleine draped the dripping rain cloak over both of them. Huddled together under it, they went out into the teeming rain and down the woolshed steps. Muddy water ran in rivulets everywhere, the soil washing away under the torrent, huge dark puddles in low ground fast becoming small lakes.

'Don't drink the water tonight.'

Erin could have sworn that was what Madeleine had said, in a low voice right beside her ear, but the wind whipped the oilcloth cloak around them and the heavy rain beat down incessantly, making it hard to distinguish individual sounds.

They splashed through puddles and ankle-deep water, clutching the cloak around them as best they could. Madeleine steered her towards the long building of the shearers' quarters. They ran up onto the veranda, but the winds sheeted the rain almost sideways. Madeleine tugged open a door; when she slammed it shut behind them they were finally out of the wet, save for the water dripping off them and pooling at their feet on the stone floor.

They were in the shearers' kitchen, seemingly scarcely changed since its early days a century ago. At one end was a large stone fireplace with a wood-fired stove and a bread oven inside it, pots and pans hanging on hooks above them. A wooden slab table with bench seats long enough to accommodate a dozen or more occupied the centre of the room. Under a window facing west, water dripped from a leaking tap into a double concrete sink. The south wall, between the kitchen and the sleeping quarters, was floor-to-ceiling storage cupboards.

The wood stove burned, pumping out heat, and the kitchen appeared to have been recently used, with dish towels hanging on the edge of the sink and a stack of plates and cutlery on the end of the table.

Madeleine draped the cloak over a hook on the back of the door. Despite the words they'd just exchanged, she now chatted as if she had no concerns at all. 'This is the community's main kitchen. But today is a fast day, so it's quiet. The children will have a small meal, however. Will you help me prepare it? I can answer some of your questions about our community while we work.'

A fast day explained why Erin had been offered no food since this morning's honey cakes. She'd assumed there'd be food at the celebration. Her stomach rumbled in protest.

Madeleine was taking loaves of bread from a cupboard and must have heard. 'As a guest, you're not expected to fast if you don't want to. We're used to it so it isn't hard for us. Could you pass me that breadboard, please?'

As she sliced bread and Erin spread it with soft butter and honey from the cupboard, Madeleine said, 'You asked about whether people come and go from the community.'

Erin hadn't. She kept buttering bread and focused on Madeleine's words.

'Of course people are free to leave, any time they want.' Madeleine answered the question she hadn't asked with the formality of a teacher explaining something critical to a student. 'But on the very rare occasion that someone who has made a commitment to us chooses to return to the artificiality of the world, they've betrayed their promise and chosen lies over truth. We no longer speak their name and they become nothing to us, as if they never existed, because we are that to them.'

Which explained why, other than Madeleine's oblique reference at the waterfall, not one of the sisters had mentioned Hayley and Sybilla. Two new sisters to make six again, and no one had said why. Hayley had certainly left, of her own volition. But if Sybilla had tried to leave she hadn't made it far.

'What do you believe,' Erin asked carefully, 'about what happens when life ends? I haven't finished all of Joshua's book yet, I'm sorry.'

'When someone passes, we also don't speak their name. Their path on earth has ended. The souls of those who have lived a pure life and found bliss will continue in an even purer form of bliss. But if the soul is not pure, there is no chance of bliss, ever.'

Erin assumed from Madeleine's very careful, formal way of imparting the group's doctrine that the kitchen might also be under surveillance.

'That sounds like a kind of hell,' she said.

Madeleine wrapped the remains of the bread in a cloth. 'Losing the hope of bliss? Knowing that you'll never find it again?' Her fingers tightened on the cloth. 'Yes, it's a form of hell.'

Over the drumming of the rain on the roof they both heard the brisk, heavy footsteps on the veranda. The door swung open and two men in stockmen's oilskin coats barged in. A man well into his fifties, tall and beefy with a face so hard and cold that Erin couldn't imagine it ever softening in bliss. And a boy, maybe eighteen, such confidence in his grin that it bordered on arrogance.

Madeleine greeted them without surprise, as if she hadn't been speaking about hell a moment ago. 'Tom, David, I'm glad you've come. We've just finished making the sandwiches for the children. Fleur and Jasmine are with Joshua so I'm doing this for them. I'll put the sandwiches in boxes, and then if you could take them across, I'd be very grateful.'

'I guess we can.' The older man spoke slowly, twisting defiance through the words.

'Thank you.' Madeleine took two cardboard boxes from a cupboard and arranged the plates of sandwiches in them. 'I still have to knead the loaves for tomorrow but I'll be back across there soon. Have you met Erin yet? She's visiting us for a retreat.'

The man barely nodded at her but the youth gave her a smile that contained more triumph than pleasantness. She acknowledged both men with a smile, then picked up the knives she'd used for the sandwiches and went to the sink to wash them.

'Road's closed because of flooding,' the man said. 'No one can get in now.' He glanced at Erin. 'Or out.'

She should have thought of that already. Millers Road only had a causeway across the river. With such a heavy downpour it would have quickly become impassable. And it turned due north from here, not meeting another road until it joined the highway at the Queensland border, more than a hundred kilometres from Strathnairn. There'd be no police raid tonight, no way for Simon to reach her, and no way for her to leave, other than cross-country in the storm.

In the reflection in the window she watched Madeleine close the lids on the boxes and hand one to the older man. 'I'm sure you'll keep us safe here, Tom. I'll see you across there shortly.'

The men stomped out, Tom throwing a backward glance as though the two women might already be doing something he could catch them out at.

'Tom's the safety coordinator for our community,' Madeleine said evenly when they'd gone. 'He's training David as his deputy. They're very dedicated to protecting Joshua and his people.'

And there was another warning.

Madeleine went to the end cupboard, the largest of them. It was a small walk-in pantry, and Madeleine stepped inside it, out of view. 'Have you ever kneaded bread dough?'

Madeleine asked. 'The dough for tomorrow's loaves has finished the first rise, and we just need to punch them down and knead them again quickly for their second rise.' She emerged holding in both hands a heavy earthenware bowl covered in a cloth. 'Can you grab the other bowl, please? On the shelf on the right.'

In the pantry, Erin saw that the shelf on the right received light from the western window. Beside another earthenware bowl, flour had been spilled – no, dusted – on the shelf. And written in the flour were the words: *Bugs everywhere.*

Erin quickly brushed her hand over the flour to obscure the words, and wrote with her fingertip, *Trust me.* Then she carried the second bowl out to the table and received instructions on how to punch down the risen dough.

'Now we turn it out onto the table to knead it,' Madeleine said. 'I'll just grab some flour to stop it sticking.'

When she returned with the crock of flour, she focused on the dough and scarcely looked at Erin, until they'd finished the five minutes of kneading and she asked Erin to fetch the bread tins from the pantry.

This time the words in the flour read: *Pls save Lily Jas Tris.*

'Oh, I spilled some flour on the shelf, Erin,' Madeleine called. 'Could you wipe it up, please?'

No more messages in spilled flour, then. Maybe that was too risky as well.

I am finished here, Madeleine had said at the end of the massage earlier. Afraid, hounded by the community's watchful security, and begging for help to save her children and Hayley's child.

Erin went to the sink for a damp cloth. 'Of course, Madeleine. Flour's always so sticky but I'll do my best.'

She just had to work out what exactly she would be saving them from, and how to do it.

•

Simon drove as far as possible along the fire trail before he left his vehicle at a washout. The deluge showed no signs of abating, and in his t-shirt and jeans he was soaked to the skin within seconds. Being wet didn't concern him. His disassembled rifle and other gear were secure inside the waterproof liner of his backpack. He jogged where he could, watching the flow of runoff water down the hillside towards the river. He headed towards a place where the riverbed was wide and sandy.

Usually little more than a creek, sometimes dry, the river had already risen by a metre, spreading here across the width of the riverbed. In the narrower channels at the falls downstream it would be roaring through, and the low-level crossing on Millers Road would already be impassable.

In the grey of the rain on the other bank, Gabe moved to the water's edge. 'You're mad,' his voice said in Simon's earpiece.

'It's not that deep,' Simon retorted. It'd be chest deep in the middle, he reckoned. Maximum of twenty metres wide at present. Do-able. Probably.

He threw a line across to Gabe and they secured each end before Simon pulled on gloves and stepped into the water.

The force of the flow pummelled his legs but he kept moving, gripping the rope, one step at a time, hand over hand. Hip deep. Waist deep. Water kept splashing up into his face and a piece of debris hit his thigh, hard. Chest deep. The water dragged at his backpack, dragged at him, powerful and relentless. Sand gave way to rock and he almost lost his footing, but he dragged himself forward, kept dragging forward, hand over hand over hand, to Gabe, to Erin, to Hayley's child.

Waist deep. His legs shaky with the effort, he made it another metre, then another. Hip deep. Gabe waded in and grabbed his arm, hauling him forward. Simon staggered out of the water and collapsed to his knees in the mud.

'Lunatic,' Gabe said, and gave him a hand up.

Simon gasped for breath, his chest burning. 'Road's blocked. No way around it. Dark soon.' As if it wasn't already dark enough with the rain and clouds.

'They're gathering at the woolshed,' Gabe reported. 'Something big's going on. They're scurrying around in the rain and carting benches inside.'

'Have you seen the girl?'

'They took her in a car with some others up to the house. That was a while ago.'

'Did she go willingly?'

'Eagerly.'

'What security is there now?'

'Bit hard to tell. A few guys wandering around looking thuggish and giving orders. No one obviously standing guard though. Not in this rain, anyway.'

Targets split across two different locations made a silent, non-violent extraction one hell of a challenge. Plus they were outnumbered, two to who knew how many? They'd have to come up with a plan and wait for the right opportunity.

Simon resettled his pack on his shoulders. 'Let's move.'

●

The rain slowed and gradually stopped as Erin returned with Madeleine to the woolshed. More people had gathered, the bench seats around the walls filling. She counted forty people, including children, but the other sisters and the trainees hadn't arrived. Nor Joshua.

No one wore dressy clothes, there were no decorations other than strings of white bulbs to light the space, and there was no food, but a palpable sense of excitement and celebration pulsed in the air.

'Perhaps you'd like to sit with the children?' Madeleine suggested. 'I have services to perform so I'll be busy.'

Under the circumstances, Erin would take any suggestion of Madeleine's.

The looms had been pushed back to make room for a few mattresses and cushions, and most of the children sat there, out of the way of the main area but still part of it and able to see. Fifteen children, from toddlers to almost teens, with two older boys with unbroken voices trying to keep the more restless ones entertained with games.

Madeleine introduced her to the group. 'This is Erin. She's our guest, so will you all look after her? Robbie, you might like to explain the ceremony to her.'

Even after the introduction, the children looked at Erin warily. Suspicious of outsiders, as Tess had predicted. Erin sat on a mattress on the edge of the group, near the small girl she'd seen with Madeleine yesterday. Lily. The child gave her a long, grave stare but said nothing, returning her attention to the scrap of blue cloth in her lap that she inexpertly stitched the edge of with thick yellow yarn. Erin considered offering a compliment, or asking what she was making, but a hush fell over the crowd. Robbie scooted over to sit beside her.

The six sisters stood in a circle in the centre of the space, with Jasmine, Fleur and two other young girls in light blue dresses. Mary began to sing, alone, a short wordless floating melody that she repeated once more.

'Focus on the voices,' Robbie whispered to Erin, taking his responsibility seriously. 'Clear your mind and focus on the sound.'

Despite several attempts at meditation at university she'd never got the hang of it. Tonight she didn't even attempt it. Her mind was crowded with concerns and questions and no way would she try to empty it, or reduce her alertness.

The other sisters and the young girls joined in with Mary on the second repetition of the melody, their voices clear and sweet, singing as one. Jasmine kept her gaze on Madeleine, as if she looked to her for guidance, her young face taut with concentration and trepidation.

As the chant progressed, other voices joined in. Men's voices, weaving an alternate harmony through the women's song. Some of the men moved into place, circling the women. Other women formed a circle around the men, contributing another harmony, and the rest of the men around them, so that all the adults were on the floor, singing, swaying with the tranquil, fluid cadence.

Even most of the children stood and sang, and Erin stood, too, glad that their childish voices were never quite in tune with the music, the scratchy edges of their singing holding her back from slipping into the soothing river of sound and floating there languidly.

And then Joshua was there. It had to be Joshua weaving through the circles, touching a shoulder here, kissing a forehead there, embracing a few, clasping hands fleetingly with others, and all the while the singing continued, until he came to the middle of the circle and held out his arms and turned unhurriedly on the spot, there in the centre of them all, rotating slowly again and again as the song wound down and voices became silent and then there was only Mary singing, one pure voice with the last repetition of notes, holding the very last note until it faded into stillness.

Theatrics, the cynic in Erin whispered. Theatrics and stage management and manipulation. And yet the elation infused her body, as if her nerves and muscles and skin had become the music itself, and she wanted to close her eyes, hold on to the perfect pleasure.

It was science, she told herself. Alteration of perception and mood through the manipulation of sensory stimulation, therefore influencing the body's biochemical responses. Whole fields of psychology, psychiatry, neuroscience and marketing studied the intricacies of neurotransmitters and their effects. Musicians and composers and film directors and writers had used an instinctual awareness of these effects for centuries.

Yet none of the rational logic and knowledge changed the fact that a whole lot of endorphins were lighting up her nervous system and her body hummed with a flood of its own natural happy chemicals.

'Beloved friends!' Joshua began, projecting his voice like an accomplished actor on a large stage. 'You cannot imagine how overjoyed I am to be with you once again.'

Erin only caught glimpses of him among the others. Not quite as tall as some of the other men, he nevertheless held a commanding presence.

A hand touched her thigh. Lily, trying to balance on tiptoe to see. The girl was maybe five or six but small for her age. Erin bent down and picked her up, and Lily wrapped her arm around her, settling on her hip with her gaze still focused intently on Joshua, so transfixed that she seemed oblivious to who was holding her.

Erin could have slipped away with Lily now, out the door behind the looms, while everyone was captivated by Joshua.

But even if Lily didn't raise a ruckus, what good would it do? Jasmine was still somewhere in the centre of the group. Tristan was there, too. She could just see him, standing beside David.

And how could she save any of them when she didn't yet know exactly what she was saving them from?

'To be greeted with such love humbles me,' Joshua continued.

Humble? Erin's cynicism punched out a few more of the happy endorphins.

'I am honoured and blessed, so truly blessed to have your love and friendship. You sustain me in the dark places I must walk. You are my lifeline to hope and joy.' He did one slow revolution on the spot, arms held out. 'Each and every one of you is precious to me.' He smiled and clapped his hands lightly. 'Please, please be comfortable. You've all worked too hard serving the community to stand all the time. Rest yourselves.'

The people drifted away, some to the benches, some sitting on the floor. David and Tristan and two other men in dark blue clothes carried benches across for the six sisters and they sat like nuns at the front of a church service, the four young girls in pale blue at their feet. Except nuns didn't wear sleeveless dresses short enough to showcase smooth calves and elegant feet.

Few of the loose-fitting clothes the others wore could be described as a uniform, but as Erin sat down with Lily on her lap she scanned the room and realised that colour was significant. A few people wore a similar drab brown to the dress the sisters had given her. Others wore muted greens or reds. But the six men and youths standing behind the sisters, and the ones on either side of the main doorway, wore dark blue clothing. She recognised Tom standing by the door, without his oilskin coat. His Nehru-style buttoned jacket with a mandarin collar over loose trousers probably didn't conceal much in the way of weapons or communications technology, and she saw no sign of an earpiece, but his solid, alert stance could have belonged beside a US president.

David had a similar stance of controlled power, but he stood right behind Madeleine where she sat with the other sisters, and a smile played around his mouth. Tristan was beside him; although the boy stood straight, worry creased his young face and he stared at Joshua without rapture.

The man himself remained standing in the centre of the floor. He wore white – a natural white like the sisters, not a blinding, commercially bleached white. His clothes might have belonged in Central Asia or the Middle East – a long-sleeved tunic over trousers, and leather shoes that might have been handcrafted.

Joshua's eloquent and passionate message for his beloved friends was about the further deterioration of the world outside. He held them spellbound as he spoke about the spreading of Ebola and other deadly diseases by people flying across the world; the disruption of the jet stream and the warm, ice-melting air blowing across the Arctic; the continuing spread of hatred and violence across the globe; the poisoning of lakes and rivers by industrial processes and chemical spills.

Again, Erin couldn't disagree with most of it. He was fairly right on essential facts if somewhat thin on science and reason.

She'd barely passed some of her science subjects at uni yet she could have made more convincing, research-supported arguments than he did. But his beloved followers weren't interested in science and reason. They wanted to believe, and Joshua gave them something to believe in. They were safe, here, from the terrors of the world beyond.

'My friends, you have chosen the right path. You tread lightly on the earth without demanding more than it can give. You love each other with generosity and loyalty and you abhor violence and greed. You nurture and care for your children and mine with constancy and devotion.'

His children. Lily's dark hair, curls teasing around her temple, rested against Erin's breast. Despite his short haircut, Tristan's dark hair refused to lie flat and tried to curl.

Joshua's wavy black hair framed his head like a halo.

I am blessed by all he has given me, Madeleine had said.

Jasmine had straight brown hair like her mother. Not dark and wavy, like Joshua's. Not dark and straight, like Simon's.

Fervour gripped Joshua and his voice rose, intense and passionate. 'Out there, in the world, greed reigns, but it never satisfies the emptiness. They will eat hamburgers washed in chemicals and never be sated. They buy more and more clothes made by slave labour from cloth coated in poisons so that they don't have to spend a few minutes ironing them. They live in concrete mansions where there is no grass, no earth to connect to, and that will crumble and shatter around

675

them and crush them to dust when the earth, angry with its mistreatment, tries to shrug off the leeches.'

Oh, he was good. A master of the art. Her father had done okay one-on-one, scamming his targets, but Joshua captivated the whole room, kept them mesmerised and spellbound, affirmed and righteous in their choices and beliefs.

'But you, my beloved friends, you have chosen to embrace simplicity, to know yourselves and to give of yourselves. And in choosing that path, you find joy in honest work, in loving others, in the sweet natural tastes of the food that you grow and the water that you drink. You do not gorge yourselves on emptiness and lust for things you do not need and that can never make you happy. You fast to preserve the earth's precious resources and use only what you need.'

There was still nothing *wrong* or evil in what he said. But restraint and fasting were also, Erin's cynicism noted, a pretty handy philosophy if you had dozens of people and wanted to keep costs down.

She still couldn't work out the money angle. There was definitely money. Millions to buy this property, and – if Madeleine was to be believed – install high-tech surveillance. Perhaps making 'a commitment' involved donating to the cause. She studied the people listening so avidly to Joshua. A few couples, some old enough to have accrued reasonable finances, maybe even a home. Perhaps they'd sold everything to join. But four or five couples donating two hundred thousand each barely made a million dollars.

The younger ones couldn't have contributed that much. Tristan and Jasmine must have grown up in the group; David too, perhaps, and Fleur, sitting at Tamara's feet. Erin thought she could see a slight resemblance between the three of them. Fleur gazed at Joshua, rapt, but Tamara and David seemed more fascinated than enthralled.

The three younger sisters – Callie, Willow and Rebecca – where had they come from? Their innocent trust in Joshua and the community suggested they must have been in the group for years. But if they'd been born into it, then it had been going for more than two decades. A long time to run a scam without significant financial return.

Joshua had moved on to praising 'the brothers who keep us safe from those outside who would hurt us, who would deny us the right to live a simple life as we choose'. Then he praised the sisters. 'Like Mother Earth herself they nourish and cherish us, providing succour and tenderness. They support and guide you on your path and are the light we aspire to. They are bliss, and they give bliss, and I love them as they love us all.' The women rose, and he embraced them in turn, holding them close against his body, and kissing each one on the mouth.

Courtesans of kings, she'd thought earlier. Six women in one house with the same lover? That had to be a recipe for trouble.

The eldest, Mary, smiled as she kissed him, as though they shared some intimate joke. Tamara cupped his face in her hands and kissed him with an open mouth, seductive and inviting. Madeleine stepped forward with head bowed, but he curved one hand around the nape of her neck and tipped her chin up with the other and kissed her despite her reserve. And then he rested his forehead against hers and murmured something, and she went so still that time might have ceased to exist around her.

He moved to Callie and said something that made her laugh, and she kissed him joyfully, and Willow gazed at him in awe and accepted his kiss with a blush reddening her cheeks. Rebecca, the last and perhaps youngest, all shining eyes and beatific smile, almost hyperventilated with the caresses of his gentle mouth.

Erin steeled herself to witness him kissing the trainees, the young teenage girls, but he merely enfolded them in his arms and bestowed a chaste kiss on each cheek. Then he faced the group, raised his arms and cried, 'Let's celebrate! Celebrate our joys, our love, our bliss! Music! Singing! Dancing! Joy and love from within us!'

Several drumbeats sounded and a man stepped into the centre of the room with a long drum slung on a leather cord over his body, his hands building the rhythm steadily. Another man pulled across a stool and sat to play a set of African drums, and a young woman with a wooden flute stood near them, inserting intermittent flutters of notes like birdsong into the rhythmic patterns. People clapped hands, began dancing, and a woman ululated, her long, wavering high-pitched tongue-trill darting in and around the bird-calling flute.

Lily had fallen asleep on Erin's lap, and didn't stir despite the shaking of the timber floor under the dancing feet. But some of the dancers came close in their exuberance. Concerned Lily might be trampled or kicked, Erin carefully picked up the sleeping child and carried her to a mattress in the dim light further back where a couple of little ones already slept under a blanket. She laid her down, tucked the end of the blanket over her.

'So sweet, isn't she?' Joshua said behind her. 'And she already works so hard to serve.'

Erin made herself smile before she faced him. His eyes were blue. The bright, intense blue of the ocean on a summer day. No longer young, perhaps fifty, he still looked youthful, and energy and vitality radiated from him.

'Hello, Erin. Welcome to our community. I'm so pleased that you have come to meet us.' He held out his hand to her. 'Please, dance with me.'

A potential disciple refusing his offered hand? She couldn't decline, or all would be over. He closed his hand over hers and drew her into the mass of dancers.

In the centre of the room he crossed hands with her, his grip firm and warm. 'Put your right foot beside mine,' he said.

Hands joined, he began to turn, and she had no choice but to spin with him, her back foot driving the movement, their right feet keeping the centre. He leaned back, hands strongly gripping hers, and the speed and the force made her lean out too.

As the drums beat their rhythm and the flute and voices soared, they whirled, faster and faster, around and around, and she couldn't stop it or miss a step because the centrifugal force would have sent her flying. She couldn't look at anything but him, because otherwise the spinning would make her too dizzy, and those too-blue eyes held hers and he controlled it with his strength and his will and she knew that he toyed with her as confidently as a cat with a mouse.

He eventually slowed, and the drumming slowed, and with several more revolutions they came to a stop. He let go of one hand, but holding the other firmly he twirled her under his raised arm and pulled her in close to him so that her back was against his chest. Her head still spun and she closed her eyes so that the room didn't keep moving around her, and she needed that support behind her lest she fall.

'Oh, you are beautiful, Erin,' he said, and it was no intimate compliment but projected in the voice he used to speak to everyone. 'Friends, this is Erin. She is searching for the truth and has come to us to find it.'

The drumbeat continued, but soft, muted, marking time.

Her head no longer spinning quite as fast, Erin opened her eyes. They were all around her. All of them. Around her and Joshua, and his arms circled her waist holding her tight against him, so tight she couldn't twist her head far enough to see him.

'We have to be careful, Erin. There are forces in the world outside that want to destroy what we have. We have to protect what is ours, don't we, friends?'

The voices of agreement swelled, strong and determined.

'Will you prove your integrity to us, Erin?' he asked.

'Prove it,' someone said. Another picked up the call, and another: 'Yes, prove it.'

They moved in closer, dozens of people, breathless and wired and euphoric from the dancing and the music and Joshua's electrifying presence. If they turned on her, Erin knew there were plenty of places in the bush to hide a body. The constant beating of the drum kicked up a notch, matching her fluttering heartbeat.

'Yes, yes, of course,' she lied. 'I just want to find happiness, to serve the community and be happy.'

'Would you do what I ask of you, Erin?'

'Yes. Yes, I would. I want to love you, Joshua, to serve you.'

'Are you sure, Erin?'

'Yes. Yes.'

His right hand cupped her breast, his left flexed against her abdomen, his fingers dipping suggestively low. She closed her eyes, trying to make her expression ecstatic, and hoped she'd succeed in not throwing up.

He kissed her neck, his breath hot against her ear, and murmured just for her, 'Would you step off a cliff for me, Erin? Would you plunge a knife into your belly for me?'

Her body froze and although her brain screamed at her to fight, run, escape, she could not even think to make a muscle move. Her pulse throbbed in her head louder and harder than the ever-present drumbeat. He knew who she was and why she was there.

He laughed out loud, a rumbling in his chest that reverberated through her body, and although he still held her, his hands no longer caressed her so sexually. 'Oh, Erin, beautiful Erin,' he said loudly, 'I shouldn't tease you so. Later, sweet Erin. Later.'

Later – she couldn't be around for what happened later. She had to get away. But he was strong and she couldn't fight him off and run through a mob of people who'd be only too happy to stop her and punish her for her betrayal.

She tried to step away from him and he released her so suddenly that she staggered on her feet. He caught her hand to steady her and slid his arm around her shoulders. 'You've been dancing too hard. David, some water for Erin.'

She was supposed to want to love him, not wrench herself away from him. 'No. Thank you. I'm just dizzy. I'll be fine.'

'Drink,' he said, holding the cup to her lips.

Don't drink the water tonight.

Panic switched her brain into overdrive. 'I can't. I didn't fast this morning. I didn't know. But I'm fasting now. A total fast.'

'We fast to preserve resources, Erin. But we have an abundance of water today and the tanks are overflowing. You must be thirsty. Please quench your thirst.'

He held her throat and chin tight in one hand, tipped the cup and she could do nothing but take two mouthfuls. She put up her hand to stop him but he tipped a little further and the water rushed her throat so that she spluttered and coughed. He snatched his hand and the cup away, laughing. She'd sprayed water over his hand.

She caught a glimpse of Willow in the group, looking horrified, and she made herself become that, an appalled, ashamed devotee.

'I'm sorry! Oh, I'm so *sorry.*' The tears that welled were genuine. But of dread, not shame. She backed away from him. 'I didn't mean it,' she said. 'I'm so sorry.'

She turned and ran from the woolshed, past Tom, out into the night and down the stairs, around the corner of the building. She fell on her knees in the mud, stuck her fingers down her throat and forced herself to throw up the water he'd made her drink.

CHAPTER 16

Simon watched from sixty metres away as she coughed and retched and sobbed and he couldn't do a damn thing about it because one of the two outside guards was standing near her.

The drumming started up again and through the still-open door he could see them resuming their dancing. The guards had put something into the barrel of water they'd carried up the stairs and it worried the hell out of him, but that had been well over an hour ago. Everyone was still on their feet dancing around like maniacs and no one seemed the worse for wear.

Except Erin.

When he'd seen that door burst open and she came flying out and down the stairs he'd jumped to his feet, ready to run to her. But she'd dropped to her hands and knees and no one had come after her except the burly inside guard who'd casually looked down at her over the railings, and the outside guard who'd leaned over her for a moment as if asking if she was okay and then retreated a few metres away.

She sat back on her heels, wiping her forearm across her mouth, then used her skirt to clean her hands of mud.

The woman from the falls came out the wide door and quickly down the stairs to Erin, the white of her dress a bright flare through his night-vision goggles. Her arm around Erin, she helped her to her feet, and after a brief challenge from the guard – he backed down when the woman in white asserted her authority sharply – they made their way towards the cottages.

The storm had passed, the sky now clear, and moonlight filled the open spaces where the single bulbs on the outside of each cottage didn't reach.

Gabe had gone up to check the house, find out if anyone was still there. That was a while ago. Even with the encrypted radio, Simon and Gabe were on comms silence because they were too close in and he couldn't be sure none of the guards had radios. The encryption only masked the words, not the fact of the signal.

The woman had her arm around Erin as they walked, and Erin's head rested on her shoulder. What the hell had distressed Erin so much? He'd never seen her break down. Even faced with drama and death in their work, she'd sniff back tears and soldier on. But she must trust the woman to show that vulnerability.

The guard patrolling the buildings stopped them but again the woman used her authority and he stepped aside and didn't follow, turning to rejoin his mate by the woolshed. Erin and her companion went up the steps of the first cottage. The women's cottage, Gabe had reported this morning.

Simon checked the location of the guards, planned his route, and set off towards the cottage, looping around behind the machinery shed and using the second cottage as his cover to get to the first. He planned to get Erin out the same way, even if he had to knock out the other woman to do so.

●

For the short walk to the cottage, away from walls that listened and spied, Erin pretended to be distraught, with her head on Madeleine's shoulder so they could talk. The distress was real, but she couldn't afford to be weakened by it. Madeleine seemed closer to breaking point than she was.

'He's planning something. Something big,' Madeleine whispered. 'Tonight. Mary knows, I'm sure. She joined us three years ago, and everything changed.' Her distress almost overwhelmed her. 'In town on Friday – I heard that a woman was murdered. Hayley's dead, isn't she?'

Evidently she hadn't known for certain. Erin squeezed Madeleine's hand. 'Yes. I'm sorry.'

'Was it her husband, Simon Kennedy? Or Joshua?'

Would you plunge a knife into your belly for me? A shudder jarred through her again. Could Hayley have . . . ? No, surely it wasn't physically possible. Once, maybe, but not multiple times. Not cutting your own throat.

'It wasn't Simon,' Erin said quickly. 'Trust him, Madeleine.'

They didn't have much time and Madeleine spoke in a rush. 'She found something, cleaning Mary's office. She wouldn't tell me and Syb but she said it was all a lie. That he'd used us, the whole time, that the children weren't safe. She went to get help. Then Tris saw Joshua at the falls. With Sybilla. He held her hand, and he kissed her, and he stood back and she . . . stepped off.'

The watcher on the cliff top. Had he hoped that Sybilla was still alive? Was that why he'd waited? An inexperienced lad couldn't have easily made his way down to her in the dark.

'I should have left yesterday. That's why we were there. Tris had seen the path on the park side. I thought we could go that way. I didn't tell them I planned it. But then you said – about the detective. I . . . I know him. Steve Fraser. I'm a coward and I couldn't face him. And then David saw us going back.'

They were almost at the cottage. So many questions, not enough time.

'What did Joshua say tonight, when he kissed you?'

'He said, "You're next, Maddie."'

'Why? Why the three of you?'

'We know who he is. Who Joshua really is. And we believed in him.'

•

Simon let himself into the cottage through the unlocked laundry door. The bug scanner Gabe had lent him detected only weak signals here. The bastards had bugged the bathroom and the bedrooms but not the laundry.

The cottage was small and he could hear Erin and the other woman on the veranda, and the creak of the opening front door.

'I'll find some clothes,' the woman said. 'You go and clean up. There are towels in the laundry cupboard. Leave the dress in the sink, and I'll wash it out.'

He breathed a fraction more easily. A piece of luck. He hadn't had much of it up until now. He flipped up the night-vision goggles to let his eyes adjust to the room's darkness.

The corridor light went on, Erin's footsteps approached, and then she was there in the doorway. She started when she saw him move in the shadows.

'Shhh,' he said, a finger to his lips. She didn't say anything. She just walked into his arms and hugged him, hard, and he felt her body shake as if she sobbed silently.

But when he reached with one hand to turn on the tap in the laundry sink, she lifted her head and waited until the water splashed loudly against the metal before she whispered, 'You have to get help. He's mad. He's planning something.'

'It's okay. I'll get you out.' He nodded at the laundry door. 'We can go now.'

'I can't. I have to help Madeleine, and we have to get her kids and Jasmine.'

Jasmine. The girl's name was Jasmine; Lily the little one's name. Jasmine, who might be his daughter.

The woman – Madeleine – came out of one of the bedrooms. 'I've got trousers and a tunic for you . . .'

Erin stood just back from the doorway, signalling her to come in. The water still poured into the sink, making a racket. When Madeleine saw him, fear and hope alternated on her face, but she gathered herself hastily. As she closed the door, she continued her conversation with Erin for the benefit of the bugs. 'Kat's about your size, and she won't mind.'

The door clicked into place, the three of them in the small space together.

'Simon, this is Madeleine,' Erin whispered. 'Please tell us the police are coming.'

'They're not. Not yet. The rivers are up and they can't get through.'

'They have to,' Erin insisted. 'Can you contact Steve? Tell him he has to find a way to come. Joshua's got them all fired up. We don't have much time. I've got to change.' The water still ran into the sink and she pulled her dress over her head and dampened it under the tap, standing in her bra and briefs while she used the cleaner parts of the wet dress to wipe the mud from her legs.

Simon handed her a towel from the cupboard and averted his eyes. 'Joshua is a psychologist. His name's Peter Hollywell. He's been playing some weird game for years, and last week in

New York he outed "Joshua" as a fraud, using mind control, hypnosis and drugs to manipulate his followers.'

Too late, he remembered that Madeleine was one of them. Her face was ashen in pain. 'That's what Hayley discovered?' she whispered. 'That he used us? That it really is all lies?'

'Yes. I'm sorry.'

'We always knew who he was. But we believed him. We believed Joshua was real, and Peter his worldly mask. Then she said she'd discovered it was all lies, and the changes . . . the changes began to seem frightening. Moving here, the secrecy, the spying – he said it was to keep us safe.'

More likely to keep his identity safe, his adherents under control. 'Who else knows he's Hollywell?' Simon asked. He tried to gentle his voice. 'It's important, Madeleine. People who know may not be safe. Whatever he's got planned, he can't do it if people know.'

'Only a few of us, from when it all began. We kept the secret. Me, Hayley, Sybilla, a couple of others who have left. Tamara knows, too, but she – I don't think she believes in him like we did. Maybe she knows it's all lies.'

Her hands shaking, Madeleine tried to rub soap onto the mud on the dress but kept dropping the soap into the tub. Simon closed his hands over hers and took it from her. If they were only meant to be here long enough for Erin to get changed, someone would come looking for them soon.

Erin finished dressing. 'Have you got the sat phone?' she asked. 'Tell Steve there's some kind of drug in the water.

And Joshua as good as told me he murdered Hayley and Sybilla.'

'I'll get on to him.' There had to be a way for the police to come. He and Gabe couldn't deal with the situation alone. Not without risking too many lives. He'd call Steve and Nick and harass them and insist until they found some way to get a show of force in here.

Madeleine touched him on the arm. 'This Steve – Steve Fraser? He's about thirty-six? Brown eyes? His father was also a police officer?'

Simon hadn't really noticed Fraser's eye colour and couldn't see how the hell it mattered, but Erin said, 'Yes. That's him. Why?'

'Then tell him . . . If something happens to me, tell him I beg him to look after my children. They have no one else but him. He's their uncle.'

He stared at her, fitting it all together. 'You're his sister?'

'His *sister*?' Erin echoed.

'Yes.'

He remembered Fraser's face earlier, the pain still raw almost twenty years after the event. 'He thinks you're dead.' He spoke more harshly than he meant to.

Her face as white as her dress, she whispered, 'Yes. Please tell him I'm sorry. More sorry than he can know.'

Boots drummed on the veranda, a hard knock sounded on the front door of the cottage.

Madeleine reached for the laundry door. 'We must go. Or they'll come looking for us.' She'd opened it and was gone before he could object. He could take on a couple of guards, still get them out – but Erin and Madeleine couldn't leave without the children, and their guards were civilians, not enemy combatants, so his hands were ethically and legally tied.

Erin rested her hand on his chest and gave him a crooked smile. 'Watch my back, Kennedy. And if I happen to throw a little girl your way, catch her, okay?' Then she lifted her head and kissed him on the mouth, before she walked out the door, back to Joshua, back into danger, with no weapons but her courage and her heart and her wits.

•

She had no idea what Joshua had planned, but her instincts screamed that he stood on the brink of some dramatic action. His taunting of her, and of Madeleine, the amusement he'd shared with Mary when he'd kissed her, the celebratory gathering of everyone in the woolshed: it was risky, dangerous behaviour, so he had to be confident that he would escape the consequences.

In the woolshed the drumming and the dancing continued unabated and Joshua was in the middle of it all, whipping it up like a ringmaster, encouraging the frenzy. Erin had never been into drugs and didn't know what he'd laced the water with but euphoria and hyper-energy had infected everyone. Even some of the older kids. The woolshed floor vibrated with the pounding of feet and the ceaseless unstoppable drumming. Voices sang and whooped and women ululated while Joshua held a small cask of water under his arm and dispensed it to his beloved followers.

'Water is life! Such beautiful water! Precious gift! Quench your thirst! Tonight we have an abundance!'

They echoed him, celebrating water, cheering and shouting and singing and drinking. The young sisters and the trainees whirled and danced with the others.

'Party drugs,' Madeleine whispered in her ear as they skirted the dancers and made their way towards the dimness of the children's corner. 'He's done it before. He says it's harmless, a path to bliss. But they don't remember, afterwards.'

Three of the littlest ones still slept under the blanket but Lily was stirring, screwing up her eyes in protest at the noise. Madeleine picked her up and held her on her hip and Lily snuggled into her shoulder, her eyes still closed. Tired? Or drugged? Would Joshua have given sedatives to small children?

Erin caught sight of Jasmine on the edge of the dancers, whirling with David, and she had more than one reason to want to drag the young girl away from his groping hands and the lascivious gloating on his face. David had seen Madeleine and the children with her at the waterfall yesterday, and presumably reported it. David couldn't be trusted. She couldn't see Tristan, who could perhaps be trusted, because he'd witnessed Sybilla's death and now doubted Joshua.

She dodged cavorting people and hands reaching out to draw her in, but then a man grabbed her from behind, lifting her bodily and spinning her around, laughing and chanting with the music.

'Water!' Joshua cried, his voice rising above the drums. 'River of water! Come to the river of water!'

'The river! The river!'

'Everyone come to the river! Bring the little ones! All of us to the river's blessings!'

The river. Alarm gave Erin strength to break away from her captor, who spun off obliviously and caught someone else's hands.

The river – swollen by the storm's deluge, it would be a deadly torrent of water and mud and debris.

The first ones were already going, heading out into the night. Joshua called, 'Light! Take the light into the dark! Light the path to the river!' and Mary was there, at the door, with the rushlights they'd made for the outside bonfire before the storm changed the plans and moved the celebration inside. David whisked Jasmine towards the door with him, and before Erin could reach them they were gone.

Soon there were only a few stragglers left. A woman picking up a toddler. An entwined, half-undressed couple making slow progress to the door. Tom, gripping Madeleine's arm as she held Lily. And one more child still sleeping on the mattress on the floor.

Two of them against Tom.

He caught Erin's arm in a vice-like grip before her strike fell. 'Get the child,' he ordered her, and when she didn't move immediately he growled again, 'Get the frigging baby,' and there was a note in his voice that was desperation, not aggression.

She wrapped the blanket quickly around the slumbering toddler, a little boy, and lifted him in her arms.

'Move,' Tom ordered again, and now he had a knife in his hand, held at Madeleine's neck, and he pushed her towards the door.

As they left the woolshed, she caught a strong whiff of smoke. Fire. Its floorboards soaked with a century of lanolin, the woolshed would burn fiercely.

In the night, the ragged line of rushlights twisted and danced past the shearers' quarters and the cottages.

'Keep moving,' Tom ordered, pressing the tip of the knife into Madeleine's neck. 'Erin in front. We're going to the river. All of us are going. I'll kill her if you do anything stupid.'

Her arms full of the dead weight of the sleeping child, Erin's only choice was to follow his orders. Somewhere there would be a chance. And Simon was watching her back.

Away from the shed, she slowed as they passed the women's cottage, but Tom ordered again, 'Keep moving.' Then he dropped his voice. 'She'll still be watching. We have to follow the others. I'm supposed to make sure you don't come back but this isn't right. What he's doing isn't right. We're the only ones who can stop him.'

●

One man and one knife. Just one man, and they were fifty metres behind the rest of the group. No one followed them. The woman in white who'd torched the woolshed was already halfway to the house.

One man and one knife. Easy. Kindergarten easy.

He ended his whispered call to Nick on the sat phone, signalled Gabe and they moved quickly through the trees to intercept the small group. The roar of the river as it surged over the falls and through the gorge made a constant rolling background thunder, and the women and their captor made enough noise on the rough ground to mask his and Gabe's footfalls.

When Gabe stepped out of the trees in front of Erin, Simon fell in behind the man and in one quick move put a throttlehold around his neck and wrenched the knife from his hand.

'Don't!' said Erin. 'Don't hurt him!'

He hadn't been planning to. Much. Not a war zone. Not an enemy combatant.

The man didn't struggle. 'I won't fight you,' he said.

'Tom helped us,' Erin said.

'We have to get to the river,' the man said. 'To the waterfall. He's going to make them go in. He'll make them all go into the water. Madeleine and I might be able to stop them.'

Into the water, where the force of it would suck them under and wash them over the cliff into the seething, churning whirlpools below. Simon dropped his chokehold but kept the knife.

'Please, take Lily to safety,' Madeleine begged him. 'I have to try to save them.'

Upwards of fifty people, men, women and children, standing by that death trap with the twisted man who'd played with their minds for years.

'Gabe, take the kids and Erin somewhere safe. Now.'

Gabe objected but Simon spoke over him. 'Not this time. It's not your fight. Get those kids and Erin off this property and to the police. I need you to do that. I'm trusting you on that.'

In the filtered moonlight among the trees he thought he saw terror on Gabe's face. Giving him kids to save? Exactly what he needed. And Simon had to keep him away from what might happen at the waterfall.

Madeleine thrust her daughter at Gabe. He took the child rather than letting her fall, and shot a pleading look at Simon. Erin stepped forward. 'Take this one, too. You can manage both. You're a strong guy, whoever you are. Use the blanket as a sling, if you like.'

Simon put a hand on her shoulder. 'Erin, go with Gabe. He's a mate of mine.'

She looked him straight in the eye, firm and determined. 'I'm going to the river. We have to hurry.' She grabbed Madeleine's hand and they set off at a run.

Tom began to follow them but then turned and said to Gabe, 'Watch out for Mary. Avoid her. She's in on this. Planned it with Joshua. I believed in him for a long time, but her . . .' He shook his head and followed the others.

'Police should be coming through from the west soon,' Simon told Gabe. 'They crossed the river at the bridge on the main Derringvale road and are borrowing quad bikes from a farmer to cross the paddocks. Meet them and brief them.' He left his friend holding the two sleeping children as awkwardly as if they were live bombs and caught up with Tom, then Erin and Madeleine within fifty paces.

They came out of the trees on a rise overlooking the waterfall. The moonlight shone unimpeded and bright over the open area around the falls. The river powered over the rocks, all the small channels swallowed up into one immensely powerful rush of water, metres deep.

And Joshua stood on a rock overhanging the torrent, arms wide, his followers swaying and chanting on the flat rocks in front of him, their rushlights held high. The gear his goons had carried to the falls earlier this evening had to be a portable speaker system, because the bastard's voice carried even above the thunder of the water.

Madeleine, Erin and Tom scrambled down the slope and Simon almost followed. He stopped, two choices tearing at him. Protecting Erin down there, stopping the carnage . . . but there might be only one way to stop it. Only one way to stop Joshua.

The bastard had no intention of dying out there with his lambs. The road closure had barely put a dent in his plans, and the flooding river was aiding him. He had to be stopped.

Simon slid off his backpack, dropped to the ground, and drew out the waterproof satchel with his disassembled rifle.

'Water is life! Water is bliss!' Joshua proclaimed. 'We are made of water, we crave water! Will you embrace the water?'

Stock. Barrel. Scope.

'Will you embrace bliss? Who will become water?'

Madeleine and Erin had reached the edge of the group.

Ammunition.

'Who will become pure? Who will become one with water?'

'I will!' a woman cried. 'I will!'

'No!' Erin screamed, trying to push her way between the gathered, swaying people. 'No!'

The woman twirled on a rock at the edge of the river, her white dress floating out around her. 'I will!' she cried again, and stepped off the rock into the surging torrent. She disappeared from view in seconds, swept over the edge of the falls.

Unable to do anything to save her, Simon swore aloud but his words were drowned out by cries of joy, of exultation from the group.

'Bliss!' Joshua shouted. 'Such bliss! Who will join us in bliss? Beautiful, beautiful bliss! Eternal bliss!'

They moved closer, all of them, to the water, singing, dancing, captivated by the delusions.

Simon crawled forward, flat on his stomach. Out of the corner of his eye, he saw movement in the trees, between him and the people below.

'Bliss!' a woman cried, and Erin reached her and wrapped her arms around her, struggling to hold her back from the edge. On the far edge of the crowd a young man with his arm around Jasmine pushed through the others, towards the water.

Joshua still stood high on his rock above them, arms held out, his white clothes pale against the sky.

Simon lifted his rifle to his shoulder. They'd go into the water, all of them, within moments, if Joshua wasn't silenced. All of them, willing or not. Madeleine. Jasmine. Erin.

Simon sighted his target through the scope. A civilian. In Australia. A man who was cajoling fifty others to jump to their deaths.

'Bliss!' voices shouted.

Just as the trigger of his rifle fully depressed, Simon heard the double retort of two other shots, blending with the explosion of sound of his own.

Joshua jerked, brought his hands to his chest. For a long moment he stood motionless, before he toppled backwards, falling several metres into the rushing water and then over the edge, out of sight.

His followers shouted, surged forward, perilously close to the water, when a woman's voice cried out, loud and powerfully, 'Stop!'

Madeleine strode between them, a slight figure in white, hair whipping around in the breeze. But when she stood before them on the edge of the rock, hands raised, there was nothing slight about her. She was majestic. Compelling.

'Joshua has ascended to bliss,' she cried, her voice bouncing off rocks and carrying higher than the river's roar. 'But you are not ready. Your work is not done. None of you are ready. None of *us* are ready. Go. Go home and sleep. Tomorrow we will meet to discuss what is next. Go and sleep now. Go and sleep. Take the children with you and sleep.'

She had them. Maybe not in the palm of her hand, but she'd arrested the headlong drive to oblivion.

The youth holding Jasmine pulled her another step forward, and Simon kept the scope on him, trigger finger poised, but someone stepped in – Tom – and with a throttlehold on the lad's neck, dragged him back.

The girl seemed dazed, uncertain, and Erin went to her, took her in her arms, and steered her well away from the water.

And Madeleine kept repeating her message, speaking with love and compassion, and no one challenged her. The urgent, frantic energy of the group dissipated, and they began to drift backwards, away from the water's edge.

Simon took the ammunition from his rifle, slid off the scope, made it secure, and returned it to his backpack. The armour of logic and concentration with which he'd acted began to dissolve and his pulse thudded in his head. More people could have died. Erin could have died. He would play that moment of decision, his hands taking that shot, over and over again. And he'd do it, every time.

At the bottom of the rise he found Steve and Tess, standing back, watching Joshua's disciples from a distance. Steve still held his service pistol loosely clasped by his side. Tess had sheathed hers again, but her hand rested on it.

'Thought it would be you up there,' Steve said, but although he attempted a grin it didn't succeed, and he returned to watching the group, his face pale.

'You both fired,' Simon said, and it wasn't a question.

Tess answered in a flat voice. 'Yes.'

Steve didn't take his eyes off the group and the woman moving slowly through it. 'They'll find his body in a day or two. Then we'll know.'

Which of them had shot him. Perhaps. Depending on bullets and angle and whether they'd lodged or passed through.

In a sense it didn't matter. The other two were serving police officers. Simon wasn't. But on the hill he'd known a murder charge and life in prison was a better alternative to the nightmare of collecting bodies downstream. He slid his backpack off his shoulder and held it out to Steve. 'My rifle's in there. You'll have my statement in the morning. If you want to arrest me now, I understand.'

Steve didn't move. 'We'll talk tomorrow,' he said.

Madeleine continued to move among the group, speaking with them, touching them gently. As a woman who'd spent over half her life under Joshua's influence, her intuition, or her inherent wisdom, recognised what they needed now. It wasn't the truth. If she'd stood in front of them and proclaimed Joshua a fraud, it would have been a disaster.

Steve had to have recognised her, but he made no move to go to her. In the semi-darkness, she wouldn't know he was there.

Erin knew they were there. Simon had watched her, too. She'd taken Jasmine back from the water's edge, far back to safety. And she'd held her while she struggled and cried and eventually quietened. And then they searched together through the group, finding another young woman bereft on her knees, and took her to Madeleine, who embraced them all.

And still neither Simon nor Steve moved.

Smoke drifted over them. The woolshed would have collapsed by now. With everything sodden from the rain, the fire might not have spread to other buildings. If they were lucky. From the things he'd found in the rubbish drums behind the shed, Simon suspected the locked doors concealed a meth lab. That might explain some of the money and the security paranoia, but the highly flammable chemicals made the place potentially explosive. He'd warned Nick on the phone.

'What are we going to do with these people?' Simon asked. The flooded roads wouldn't be reopened until the morning, at least. And they had more than fifty people who would be traumatised and homeless.

Tess had turned away to use the sat phone but she heard his question and broke off her conversation to answer. 'Nick's putting some contingency plans in place. RFS and SES trucks to get them through to the community hall at Derringvale. There'll be paramedics there and he's calling in counsellors. Strathnairn Hospital and the rescue helicopter are on standby.'

It would be a long way around to Strathnairn from here via Derringvale, but accessible. These people would be looked after. But there was a long, rocky road ahead for all of them.

CHAPTER 17

Erin finally found Simon again when she arrived back with Willow and the last of Joshua's people at the cottages. He'd guided others back through the bush ahead of her. The flashing lights of RFS and SES trucks strobed in the pre-dawn light, one more surreal image in an unreal night.

Physical and emotional exhaustion dragged at her but she kept putting one foot in front of the other until the last of her bewildered charges had been reassured by Madeleine and helped aboard a truck.

She could see Simon standing by the shearers' quarters with Steve, and she steered her exhausted body that way and walked the fifteen metres into Simon's arms. He held her tightly, so tightly she could have let him take her weight but she didn't, quite.

'We're on the next truck,' he said. 'Then I'll get you home.'

'Did you see her?' she asked.

He didn't ask who she meant. 'Yes. She doesn't know who I am, of course. She'll be in Derringvale by now. They may take the kids to hospital for assessment.'

Erin lifted her head from the sanctuary of Simon's shoulder. She hadn't seen Steve since the immediate aftermath at the waterfall, and then only from a distance. Now he was there, and Madeleine had put the last of Joshua's people on a truck to safety. 'Go to her,' she told him. 'She thinks you hate her for what she did. For what he made her do.'

Steve hesitated for one long breath. Then he walked across to where his sister waited, watching him, afraid, and he put his arms around her, and the man who pretended to treat life lightly laid his face on her hair and cried.

Erin could hear Simon's heartbeat, feel it under her palm, strong and real and honest. 'Take me home,' she said. 'Take me home and hold me and love me and sleep with me.'

He tensed, his breathing shallow. 'I'll take you home, and I'll always love you. But I . . . They may arrest me for murder tomorrow, Erin.'

She stepped back within the circle of his arms. 'Then I'll fight it and I'll give evidence and keep giving it until they understand that you saved many lives. Callie walked into that water, believing him. Willow would have done it too. And Rebecca. So many others. You saved those lives. All of them.'

'You saved that girl yourself. The one you held back. You saved her.'

'Only because Joshua had gone. If he'd still been there, I couldn't have held her.'

And if Joshua had been there, if he'd asked, Willow would have dragged her into the water as well.

She hoped that when the drugs wore off, Willow wouldn't remember. But Erin would. She'd remember the roar of the water and the smell of mud, and a young girl's dilated eyes and her ecstatic face, desperate to embrace death in her belief of Joshua and his lies.

•

'You are admitting that you fired at an unarmed man?' In the relative privacy of the small area behind the stage of the Derringvale community hall, Leah Haddad shot the question at him.

Simon nodded with more patience than he felt. 'Yes. As I explained to Nick, I considered dozens of lives to be imminently at risk. I'm prepared to give a full statement, and to cooperate with the investigation. You'll want to take the rifle for examination. It's in here.' He handed over his backpack and Haddad took it reluctantly.

'Jesus, what a mess,' she said under her breath, showing some emotion for the first time in Simon's limited experience of her. 'Look, Kennedy, I've already called in Internal Affairs for a full investigation, since two police officers also fired their weapons. They'll be here in a few hours. They'll probably want to talk with you —' she glanced at her watch, 'later today.'

He'd expected to be arrested, but she gave no indication of wanting to. Everything had changed in the few days since she'd arrested him for Hayley's murder.

'I'll be around,' Simon promised. 'I can call down to the Strathnairn station in the afternoon.'

'Good. We'll be in touch.' She handed his pack back to him and dismissed him with a nod.

In the main part of the hall, district services had already swung into action under Nick's direction. The SES squad had brought in camp stretchers and gym mats from the Strathnairn Police Youth Club, but with that done the crew waited at a distance outside, giving Joshua's people privacy.

Dazed, confused, Joshua's followers huddled at one end of the hall, a few asleep, others whispering among themselves, mistrustful of the 'outsiders' and particularly wary of the small group of police officers. The girl, Jasmine, slept on a mat in the corner, her arm protectively around a sleeping child.

Catherine, the community nurse, and one of her colleagues had already spoken with each of the adults and assessed the sleeping ones and the children for responsiveness, while two kindly women from the Country Women's Association moved among the group with sandwiches and cups of tea, gathering names from those prepared to give them. Erin was still in the kitchen at the other end of the hall, briefing Nick and the small team of counsellors and child protection officers he'd assembled.

Simon skirted the group and went outside to wait for her on the veranda of the hall. At a picnic table under a tree nearby, Fraser and his sister, Madeleine, spoke quietly together around the occasional awkward silence. But eventually Madeleine rose and, after a brief hug, left her brother to return inside.

She paused beside Simon, shy but brave. 'I've heard a lot about you over the years,' she said. 'We were only a small group – just a household – when Hayley joined us. She and I became close friends. Steve just asked me about her, and said you need to know. She was already pregnant when she came to us, but she was very frightened of losing the baby. I already had Tristan then, and I helped when Jasmine was born.' Her composure faltering, she sniffed, and wiped damp eyes with her hand. 'Hayley always said you were Jasmine's father, and she felt guilty about not telling you. But she was afraid you'd take Jasmine from her, that she didn't deserve her, because she'd left you.'

The rock-like lump in Simon's throat made words difficult. 'I wouldn't have done that.'

'We were . . . persuaded to believe a lot of things. I don't know anymore what was right, and what was lies.'

'You were very young. And Hayley didn't have a lot of reasons to believe that the world would treat her well.' He said it gently, because the last thing this woman needed was his anger, although the truth was that he wanted to punch a fist through a wall, or into Joshua's face instead of the clean quick kill. But regrets and self-accusation rang even louder in his mind than his anger at Joshua. If he'd looked for Hayley instead of convincing himself she needed to 'fly free', if he'd tried harder to save their marriage, if, if, if . . .

'Steve says you're a good man. Hayley always said that, too. I'll tell Jasmine that she can trust you and believe in you.'

Believe in him? When he'd stuffed up so fatally with Hayley? He swallowed with difficulty. Put his daughter and her needs first. That's what he had to do. 'Does she know? About her mother's death?'

Madeleine shook her head. 'Not yet. After Hayley left, Joshua told her not to worry, that she'd see her mother again soon. Erin said there are counsellors and they will work out the best way to tell her the truth.'

Maybe they'd tell him where to start, too. How to establish a relationship with a daughter he didn't know.

Madeleine put a hand on his arm, looked up earnestly into his face. 'Steve keeps asking me if I was happy. It seems important to him. I *was* happy, Simon. Hayley was happy. Not telling you about Jasmine was the only thing that worried her. Our lives were rich and full of love. It was only when Mary came that it started changing. That Joshua started changing. Mary . . . I think she was like him. That they acted together. And I think they grew tired of us, and wanted something bigger. But all those years before that . . . I did know, then, what bliss meant. And we had it, Hayley and I and the others.'

She left him and went inside, and only then did he see Erin standing in the doorway.

'I heard,' she said, after Madeleine had passed her with a brave smile. She came to him and took his hand and he gripped it, the connection grounding him because she was strong and constant, a rock in his rapidly shifting world.

'Hayley was happy,' she said. 'Maybe it was based on lies and maybe it was because she couldn't cope with the world, but she was happy all that time. Hold on to that. Hold on to me. You're going to make a damn fine father.'

•

From the Derringvale hall they hitched a ride back to Strathnairn on one of the SES trucks. Erin dozed against his shoulder for some of the way but woke when the driver – one of their regular squad – pulled up at her place on the outskirts of town.

The peach-gold light of the rising sun reflected off her front windows as they jumped down from the truck. She found her spare key in its hiding place – her wallet, keys, phone and ute were still back at the main house at Serenity Hill.

He followed her inside but paused in the living room, his backpack still on his shoulder. He hadn't actually been invited to stay. And it was hours since their embrace in the emotion of the scene at Serenity Hill. 'I just assumed,' he began, 'that I could stay in your spare room for a day or two.'

She turned at the kitchen door, and despite everything she'd been through her smile teased him gently. 'You assumed correctly. Except about the spare room. I seem to recall saying something not long ago about holding and loving and sleeping. Consider that an invitation.'

She didn't wait to hear his response. He heard the kettle flick on in the kitchen, the sound of running water in the bathroom.

He had a long list of reasons why he should turn right around and walk back out the door. He had a hunger and a need and a craving that he'd carried for so long that he'd come to believe this half-emptiness was the way it always had been, always had to be.

He'd coped.

Erin coped. No, that wasn't the right word. She tackled challenges, came to grips with problems, found solutions, and if something didn't work and she fell down, she got up, dusted herself off and tackled the problem again.

All the skills and resilience he used to meet the demands of his work, she applied to everything.

His backpack thunked softly to the floor.

She came out of the bathroom wearing an old t-shirt and not much else and kissed him fleetingly and with a taste of peppermint as she passed on her way to the laundry with a bundle of clothes. 'Glad you decided to stay. You can have first shower if you promise not to use all the hot water. Sadly there's not room for two in there. Toss your clothes out to me and I'll put them in the washing machine.'

'Are you sure, Erin?'

She raised an amused eyebrow. 'About the washing machine?'

'About us. I've got a pretty lousy track record in relationships. I failed Hayley.'

She came back the few steps to stand in front of him. 'Don't you dare say that, Simon Kennedy,' she said quietly, and she wasn't teasing now. 'Don't you dare believe that of yourself. You were both young and maybe it was an unequal partnership and a mistake, but you know what? The fact that even after all the time apart she came to you when she needed help – that speaks volumes about the kind of man you are and the type of marriage you had.'

An unequal partnership. With just three words she'd put her finger on the gist of the differences between him and Hayley and the weakness in the foundation of their marriage.

'I guess I married her to protect her.'

'Yep, and you have a caring, compassionate heart under that tough-guy exterior. But I don't need protecting, Simon. I'm not a fragile china doll who needs to be looked after. I won't say no to chocolates or cups of coffee in bed or to having you at my back if there are ever any more homicidal maniacs out there, but I'll be doing the same for you.' She gave him a friendly push. 'Now go. Shower off that mud while I put clean sheets on the bed.'

He showered off mud and sweat and a load of doubts. But he still felt like a teenager on a first date as he wrapped a towel around his hips and emerged from the bathroom. Until she grinned in pure appreciation and slipped past him to the bathroom and he had to wait for her for five long, interminable minutes, during which time he vowed to find a place to live that had a shower big enough for two.

With only a towel around her she walked to him and stopped inches from him, a smile playing on her lips and her blue eyes, so often full of humour and liveliness, shining up at him. He traced the line of her cheek with his finger. Strong, soft, beautiful.

She cupped his face with her hands and the light in her eyes danced in pleasure. 'I've waited a long time for this, Kennedy.'

'Me too,' he murmured. Fourteen years. The physical frustrations he'd dealt with himself, but he'd missed the emotional connection, the intimacy of trusting and sharing, of giving and receiving. Yet he already knew Erin would share more of herself, that he'd share more of himself, than in his past. He trusted her, with his body, with his heart, with all that he was and wanted to be.

Her mouth played against his, teasing and tempting, and her hands slid over the skin of his shoulders, biceps, chest, and he drew her close against his body and returned her kisses, trying to rein in the hunger and need that drove him.

'Don't hold back,' she murmured against his mouth. 'I'm not going to break. We need this now. Affirmation. Catharsis. Love. We both need it.' He felt the vibration of her laughter in her body. 'We can do sweet and tender for dessert, okay?'

Her laughter, her confidence, freed him from his hesitation, from his past. She met his hunger with her own, pulling his head down to hers, tearing away his towel and then her own, setting fire to his body with her touch, skin to skin, exploring him and guiding his hands on her and showing him what she wanted. He carried her to the bedroom with her legs around his waist and they tumbled to the cool sheets together.

He paused then, for a second, to drink in the sight of her, naked, breathless, stunning. Smooth skin over lithe limbs, the curve of abdomen, of breasts, the aroused nipples he planned to tease again, very soon. But her face captured his gaze, and her eyes, and as she drew him down to her, beyond the pleasure and the laughter and the arousal he saw love and trust and peace.

He didn't lose himself in her. He lost his reserve. He lost the concerns that had always held him back. He lost his loneliness. Her beauty and her passion and their trust in each other filled him with joy, and an intimacy of mind and heart he'd never known. And when she cried out in release and gripped his shoulders with strong hands, he let go of thought and found himself in her, together and equal and powerful with it.

•

The sun was setting in a burst of colour as they walked down to the hospital to see Jasmine and her case worker. Tomorrow they'd retrieve their vehicles from the park and Serenity Hill, but this evening Erin was content to walk by Simon's side, savouring the slight chill in the autumn air and the fresh smell of earth still damp from last night's storm. Peaceful. Peace out here in the town, peace in herself, and a new peace between her and Simon, brimming with energy, promise and strength.

There were plenty of challenges ahead – Jasmine, the investigation into Joshua's death, and deciding on and planning the future. They'd both got through worse. They'd deal with it together.

Outside the hospital, Steve sat on one of the bench seats in the small grassed area as though waiting for someone. Sometime during the day he'd shaved and changed but he looked drained and Erin doubted he'd slept at all. They stopped to greet him and to learn any news.

'My father's about to arrive,' he said. 'Aaron picked him up at the airport. I phoned him this morning with the news.'

Erin remembered Steve's comments the first night at the waterfall. Assistant Commissioner Fraser, who had a rocky relationship with his son. And a daughter he'd believed dead for many years.

As if trying to avoid thinking about his father, Steve switched to official mode. 'The critical incident team arrived earlier – they'll conduct an investigation into the two deaths at the falls,' he told them. 'Nick will be in touch because they've asked to interview both of you. But that won't be before tomorrow. They haven't found the bodies yet and I don't know what they'll decide about Joshua's death, but I'm not stressing about it at this point. I know that if the circumstances were repeated, I'd do exactly the same again.'

'So would I,' said Simon. 'If I'd known you were there, I mightn't have. But I didn't know, and people were about to die. I'd make that same decision again.'

And come what may, Erin was glad that he had. If Joshua had lived, she would have battled against impossible odds to save some of his people and might have died doing so. She had way too much to live for, and no intention of dying for at least sixty years.

'I'm off the case now,' Steve said. 'Personal connection and all that. I'll stick around town for a few days though until we sort some things out and Maddie works out what she wants to do. She's helping the police. There's no sign of Mary, or of Tamara. Mary at least knew Joshua's plans and she and Tamara had a long-running dislike of each other.'

Erin thought back to the scene by the river. 'I didn't see either of them at the falls. The last time I saw Mary was at the woolshed.'

Simon nodded agreement. 'Mary's the leader of the women? I saw her leaving the woolshed. But then I had to follow Erin and Madeleine. I'm fairly sure Mary torched the woolshed.'

'Yeah, well, Forensics are still waiting for the ruins to be declared safe, but the bad news is they think there's a body. I haven't told Maddie yet.'

'You think it's Tamara?' Erin probed. 'She knew Joshua was Hollywell. If he was silencing those who knew . . .'

'We'll find out, eventually,' Fraser said. 'There are a few others missing. One or two who went bush before we took the rest to Derringvale. Another couple who scarpered this morning. We've got people out looking for them. They won't get far on foot.'

Erin recognised his frustration. With so much unknown, and a group of wary, scared, distrustful witnesses, it might be days, weeks, maybe even longer before all the truth came out.

Madeleine had said that things had changed when Mary came. But Erin wondered if for Peter Hollywell they had already been changing, if he'd grown bored with the game of his Joshua cult and wanted new games, new power. The notoriety of exposing a cult might have given him that, if there was no one left who could blow his lies. The man could certainly manipulate an audience. The web domains he'd registered suggested he planned new games, maybe new cults that generated more wealth than Joshua's brand of simple bliss could.

'Did you find out anything about his finances?' she asked Steve.

'They're tracking it all down now. But from what he said in that conference speech, many people gave everything they owned to join the communities, and it wasn't just the three here – his followers have established a few communities in the US as well, and elsewhere. People made donations through his website, too – often big ones. And then there's the meth lab. The Feds had been watching him because of that, and suspect his groups have been major suppliers up and down the coast for a while. And Mary Saint . . .' he stopped, became a little cautious. 'Let's just say she is alleged to be a skilled laundress – of the financial variety – and to have *connections* that the Feds are particularly interested in. So if I was a betting man I'd say that what money they made is nicely put away somewhere that she can get to. Oh, and we've also had someone come forward with a description of a woman who could have been her and a youth in a vehicle behind your place on Friday night, Simon.'

'She torched my place?'

Steve shook his head. 'No hard evidence of that. At this stage. And I've probably said way too much already.'

Grateful for his candour, Erin asked, 'You'll keep us informed?'

'Of what I can. But it could all take a while. I'm not officially involved now. Which is a bugger, but I guess we've all got other things to deal with, hey?' He glanced down the road at a police car, heading towards them.

'Simon, just before I go – I'm sure you'll want to do a DNA test and confirm things properly, but you should know that Maddie has told the police and the staff here that you're Jasmine's father.'

Simon's hand gripped Erin's just a little tighter.

Steve was right. The rest was out of their hands, and Jasmine had become their priority now.

They'd talked about her, curled together in bed this afternoon after the hospital called to say that they'd admitted Jasmine for observation and assessment. They both expected there'd be meetings with authorities and health checks, evaluations and ongoing support for Jasmine. There'd also be DNA testing, custody procedures and possibly temporary foster care while it was all sorted out. But at the heart of it was a thirteen-year-old girl who'd need love and support and emotional safety.

Sometime in the last day, seeing Joshua's influence, his control over his followers, Erin had found a new perspective on her father and her own childhood. He hadn't been in the same league, he hadn't been so extreme, but the manipulation, the lies were similar. She'd been only a child who'd wanted to please him, to be loved and appreciated, and he'd used that selfishly. Jasmine bore no responsibility for what had been done to her, how she'd been taught to view the world. And neither did the girl Erin had been, her childhood self.

They farewelled Steve and left him to greet his father.

After a brief meeting with the sympathetic case worker who outlined the issues they expected, she walked them through the wards to Jasmine's room and stopped in front of the closed door.

Erin slipped her hand into Simon's again. 'Are you ready?'

'No.' He stood tall and strong and frowning and serious, and a little scary.

'Relax, soldier,' she told him. 'Different kind of battle. To start with, we're not battling each other and we're all going to win. So smile. Show her your dimples. The ones on your face, anyway.' She kissed one of those dimples lightly. 'You can do this. We can do this. We're in it together, and we make a damn fine team.'

He managed a grin, and then kissed her firmly on the mouth.

'Okay,' he said to the case worker. 'We're ready now.'

ACKNOWLEDGEMENTS

This book is the result of about a year's work, and there are many people who have helped it see the light of day.

I'm fortunate to be part of a close family. My mother, Gladys, my sisters Andrea and Margaret and my niece Lauren have variously critiqued, cajoled, brainstormed, encouraged – and have all believed in me.

My publisher at Hachette, Bernadette Foley, has not only provided her expert guidance on this book, but has supported and encouraged me through all five books with patience, professionalism, good humour and friendship. Likewise my agent, Clare Forster, whose experience, calmness and publishing wisdom I value.

I'm grateful to the editorial team at Hachette, especially editors Karen, Clara and Chris, for all their work and suggestions to make *Storm Clouds* a stronger book.

Once again, police Sergeant Gemma Gallagher has generously provided invaluable advice about police procedure and the realities and challenges of rural policing.

Writing can be a lonely business, because no one can do it for you. I'm deeply appreciative of my circle of writing friends, near and far, who continue to cheer, support and encourage me through all the ups and downs of the writing life.

A special thank you to my readers. Without you, there would be no books. Your emails, Facebook comments, reviews, and your enthusiasm at events always brighten my days and make the long hours of staring at a screen worthwhile.

Finally, as ever, this book would not have been possible without Gordon. His understanding and patience with my distracted writer's brain, my muttering and odd questions when I'm stuck, my late-night writing and my neglect of housework, are legendary. He is truly a hero.

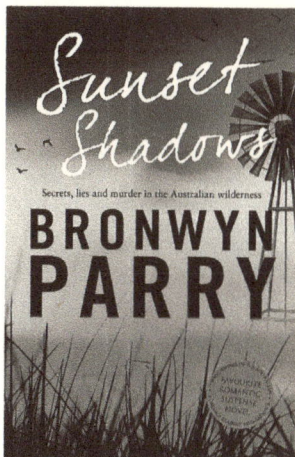

Also by award-winning author Bronwyn Parry

THE DUNGIRRI SUSPENSE NOVELS

Book 1

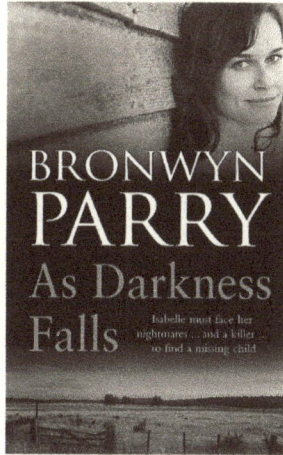

On the edge of the outback the landscape can hide many secrets . . .

Haunted by her past, Detective Isabelle O'Connell is recalled to duty to investigate the abduction of a child from her home town. She and DCI Alec Goddard have only days to find the girl alive, with few clues, a town filled with suspects and a vast wilderness to search. It quickly becomes a game of cat and mouse, with Isabelle directly in the killer's sights.

For Isabelle, this case is already personal. For Alec, his best intentions to keep it purely professional soon dissolve as his anguish over Isabelle's safety moves beyond concern for a colleague.

Their mutual attraction leaves them both vulnerable to their private nightmares – nightmares the killer ruthlessly exploits.

'an impressive debut'
The Australian Women's Weekly

THE DUNGIRRI SUSPENSE NOVELS
Book 2

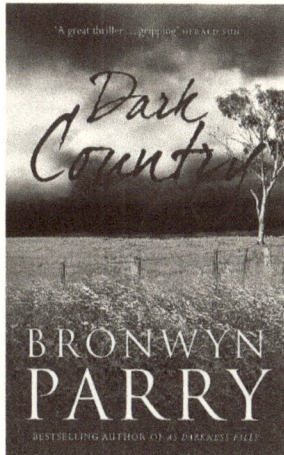

'A great thriller . . . gripping'
Herald Sun

Most people in the small town of Dungirri believe Morgan 'Gil' Gillespie is a murderer, so he's not surprised there's no welcome on his return. What he doesn't expect is the discovery of a woman's tortured body in the boot of his car.

Police sergeant Kris Matthews isn't sure whether Gil is a decent man wronged by life, or a brutal criminal she should lock up. But she does know that he is not guilty of this murder – because she is his alibi.

Between organised crime, police corruption and the hatred of a town, Gil has nowhere to hide. He needs to find the murderer – fast. Kris is determined to help him, but will their search make her the next target?

'Nuanced . . . intriguing'
Weekend Australian

THE DUNGIRRI SUSPENSE NOVELS
Book 3

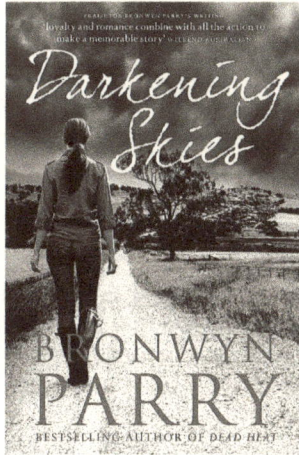

Deadly secrets hidden for years in a small country town are finally revealed . . .

Investigative journalist Jenn Barrett never intended to return to Dungirri, the town she escaped from as a teenager. But startling revelations about local man Mark Strelitz have reopened the investigation into the accident that killed Jenn's cousin, Paula, and she is determined to find out what really happened.

For eighteen years, a gap in Mark's memory caused by the accident has hidden the facts – that he was driving when Paula died and a corrupt police investigation sent an innocent man to prison. He knows he has to set the record straight.

But someone wants the past to remain buried – permanently. Mark and Jenn's discovery will shock the whole town, but only if they live long enough to reveal it.

'There is a strong romantic plotline . . . while the suspense is so well maintained the novels qualify as rattlingly good crime reads.'
Weekend Australian

hachette
AUSTRALIA

If you would like to find out more about Hachette Australia,
our authors, upcoming events and new releases you can visit
our website, Facebook or follow us on Twitter:

hachette.com.au
facebook.com/HachetteAustralia
twitter.com/HachetteAus